For

Your support and friendship are appreciated and cherished!

Squibble's Story

We salute you with great respect sir Knight!

Also by Cutter Hays

✠

The Mouse Knight

SQUIBBLE'S STORY

✠

Written & Illustrated
By
Cutter Hays

To SIR IRV REVKIN -
WITH GREAT AFFECTION,
Cutter Hays

Happy Mouse Publishing
Oceanside, CA

Squibble's Story

Happy Mouse books may be ordered through booksellers or by contacting:

Happy Mouse Publishing
An Imprint Of
Lunaria Press
www.lunariapress.com

ISBN: 978-1-935926-71-9

Printed in the United States of America

For Heide

Beloved Friend
Loving Mouse Mom
Kind Human

And Dedicated To

Liz O'Grady
Without whom you would not
be holding this book

Foreword

✠

I am standing at the grave of my mother. She died of cancer. For those of you without the experience, it is a sad, slow, pathetic death, not worthy of my gentle, noble mother. This is where I come to do all my thinking, and since my years are long now, I think a lot.

I suppose I should start this story at the beginning, but such rules were made by programmed people who want to please a programmed society. You'll find I break most of those rules, and I am certainly happier for it. The rules are stupid. They are made to keep one from thinking for oneself. Such things are for the soulless barbarians of the world, and I do not cast myself among their ranks.

You will see, if you care to look deeply, much more than a mere tale in these pages. They carry my soul, and its profound transformation across the last two years. I wrote it as it happened in my journal, which my beloved master asked me to keep. The artwork is mine, too. Be patient with it please. I've been nothing if not a work in progress. This journal was not intended for publication. It was a personal record of my entire life, and though I addressed the words to some reader (perhaps my master) who I imagined desperately desired to know what I had to say, I hardly believed anybody would ever care. My master published his own story, and I have tried my best to follow in his footsteps, left so long ago across this quiet field.

It was he who told me to dance to the tune of my own music, the music only I can hear, different from all others. He said, "Blessed are they who can single out this wonderful music, and follow it all their lives." Everyone has it. It may be drowned out in all that you do or have done, it may be dim from your pain and experience, but it doesn't stop until you do. It's never too late to be yourself. That was perhaps the only thing I never faltered on: I was always myself.

Thus I am adding these words at the end of my journey, having written it all, drawn it all, and can see it now in hindsight. To me it seems very sad now that it's over, and looking back, I would never have done the things I did or gone the places I went if I had clearly seen what was coming. I don't think any of us would. We'd see the terrors rising to meet us in the future and avoid them. The universe had other plans for me however and cared little for my wounds along the way. Sometimes wounds heal, sometimes they don't, but they define us as much as our happy moments. My master said they give us character. I have been told I have a lot of that.

For all my supposed integrity and honor, I might have avoided the horrors. I did see most of them coming, though I made excuses to convince myself I had not, and I wanted to run. I wanted to hide. Believe me—anyone would have. Yet if I had chosen the path of least resistance, I'd be a different person now, and the fate of many would have been forever altered because of it. My only saving grace was in the fact that I never did buy the whole "great hero seeing the future" thing until the very end. And perhaps that was part of the universe's plan as well. Tricky universe.

I cannot claim normalcy. I cannot say that I didn't see the cost of my choices, and I have no excuses. I saw it all, I was warned several times, and in the end chose to step into the path of destruction. Often along the way I broke down and tried to change it, I really did. But I am not all-powerful. In fact, I am smaller than many think. There are so many dark shades out there, so much ignorance and pain, that someone must step up to the challenge or the world will have nobody to champion it. Evil and tragedy would win by default. So I am the one who stepped forward for my people. Someone had to. Facing demons and slaying dragons is what knights do. I understood the job was dangerous when I took it.

Oh, by the way, I'm a mouse. My name's Squibble.

First Tangent: Magnificent Man

✠

Okay… so sometimes I have these dreams. I see weird things. Things I don't understand usually, until later when it's explained to me by the wise one, who is a chinchilla. But don't let that fool you. He knows everything. Anyway, the dream went like this:

It was a bright sunny day in a city somewhere. It was hot. The pavement swayed side to side in the heatwaves and a magnificent man stood in the parking lot outside a pet store. He was wearing a white suit. He had long, wavy blonde hair. He was striking, charismatic. He looked powerful, not just in body but his face reflected the awesome integrity of his soul. I knew he was good. A good man. He kinda looked familiar, but in dreams you forget all kindsa stuff, so I didn't remember him.

He strode like a king into the pet store and began to look around. It was funny, seeing him be so curious. I got the idea that he wasn't used to being curious, and that he might not have been in a pet store in a long time.

Well, the first thing he saw was the rats in the front window. They were directly in the sun, and they were dying. They had no water, and their food was all gone. Some of them were already still and bloated. The rest looked up at him as if pleading for their lives. They were trapped in that stupid aquarium, and someone had left them there to perish.

The magnificent man got a horrible look on his face, a look of anger that would frighten anyone. His eyes turned dark and some wind from the door blew his hair back. His eyebrows came down, and he was scary. Scary Magnificent Man. He stood up even straighter, and went over to look at the other small animals.

The mice were packed into a tiny aquarium that was way too small for so many. There were easily a hundred in a fifteen-gallon tank. They were swarming over each other, fighting each other for what little food there was and sleeping in their own waste. They had no water. There were dead mice in the tank, lots of them, and the rest were sick. They looked up at him the same way the rats did: "Help us, mister, we're in trouble." Then he looked at the hamsters, the gerbils, the guinea pigs and the rabbits—same story—all neglected, all sick.

This is where the camera would have zoomed in on the magnificent man's terrible face if there had been a camera in the dream. His face grew tight, but he walked as calmly as he could over to a short, fat, balding manager. "Excuse me, your animals are sick and hungry," he said politely. He even smiled.

The manager was busy pricing items to put on the shelves and ignored him. Believe me, that must have been hard to do. Magnificent Man was easily six foot seven. He put his wide hand on the manager's shoulder. When the manager turned and looked up into his face, he paled and I saw terror. Really. Not fear, terror.

"They're waiting for the vet," the manager whimpered. "He was supposed to come earlier this week. And we ran out of food. We get more tomorrow." "Not true," said the blonde man. He was scowling now. "You haven't called the vet at all."

The manager began to shake visibly, but his face became ugly. He tried to raise his pathetic voice, "You don't know any such thing! It's not my fault. The air conditioner is broken. It'll be fixed by tomorrow morning." "The animals will be dead by tomorrow morning," Magnificent Man said. His face was inching closer to the manager's.

The manager was pale enough, but he went bone white. I could feel his thoughts: Why should I put up with this?! I'm the boss here!

I'm in control! "We'll get more animals. Your snake can wait one day," he said.

Now, I got the idea that of all the things the small man could have said, this was the absolute wrong thing. The blonde man's face went all placid and calm, as if he was completely at peace. I knew he wasn't. I could feel it. He smiled softly at the manager, as if he'd done this thousands of times. It was a terrible calmness. "I'd like to buy every animal in the store," he said. "Every animal, living, dead, or halfway in between."

Well, the manager perked up immediately. He was saved from a disaster that might have had his name written all over it! "Why, yes sir!" he said cheerfully. "You're a righteous man for such a kind act, yes sir!" He beamed and ran to the register. He totaled up every animal in the store, looking forward to telling his regional manager that he had sold all their product in one day, and avoided a media incident to boot.

Magnificent Man gathered up every animal in the store and made a phone call. In a short time, a giant air-conditioned moving van with two moving men showed up to take all the creatures someplace better. The good man bought all the cages, aquariums, and all the food and toys the store had as well. He did not comment to the manager that there had been plenty of food on the shelves. He knew that the fat man had lied intentionally.

While the men loaded all the animals and supplies, Magnificent Man took one of the 50-pound bags of rodent food (the good stuff!) and went into a mail-and-shipping shop next door. He came out without the huge bag of feed and went back into the pet store. He went past the manager and straight to an old lady who was mopping the floor. She looked up at him and smiled. "You are the only good person in this place, Ruby," he said. "I try to take care of the poor animals," she said. "I have hundreds of them at home, too many… I can't afford them all, and I can't take any more, but I try."

The man gave the old woman a compassionate look. She was half his size and stooped over, much too old to be working such a poor job. She spent all her income on the animals she took home. They ate before she did. She spent all her free time cleaning cages, only to return to work the next day and clean more cages. And there were always too many to clean. She never got to them as she wanted. No one else helped her. In fact, the other employees laughed at her. Even the manager ridiculed her for actually caring about the animals. "They're just food," he said. "They're product, Ruby, nothing more. It's all about money. You're always going to be poor unless you get that." "Oh, I get it," Ruby said. "The only reason I don't quit this wretched job is because then these poor victims would have nobody at all. I'd rather be poor and kind than rich and cruel."

I saw all of this, and I could see that Magnificent Man had seen it all, too. He wasn't a normal man. I'm not usually that slow—it was the dream. I swear. So he said to Ruby, "Kind lady, your mercy on these poor animals is today rewarded. Go to the nearest store and buy a lottery ticket. Here are the numbers," and he wrote them down. "When you win, please do a thing for me." She laughed, humoring him. "Sure, whatever you want… if I win."

He smiled charmingly at her and said, "When you win, please take this amount (he wrote more stuff down) to this address (more stuff), and hand the person who answers the door this message." He wrote more stuff and gave it to Ruby. She looked it over and smiled back. "No problem, if I win," she said. "You will," he said. "Now get yourself and any others you value out of the store. Go now." She smiled and started to turn to leave, but her smile faded as she looked into his face, and suddenly she seemed to take him very seriously.

I have no doubt that she went right out to the nearest convenience store, used those numbers, and won millions of dollars. But first she went to the store's loudspeaker system and announced so it could be heard thoughout the store, "Excuse me, but there is a fire. Would everyone please exit calmly to the front or rear of the building? This is not a drill. Thank you and have a nice day."

When Ruby left, the animals were all loaded and the other employees were evacuating the building. Except the manager. He was searching for a fire and swearing under his breath about firing Ruby. Magnificent Man stood in the parking lot, a hundred feet from the store front. He paid the men with the van, and gave them an address. He gave them a large envelope, too. They seemed happy and left.

Swaying to and fro in the heatwaves, another man, a beautiful man in a black suit, walked up behind the magnificent man. Despite the heat, he wasn't sweating. Neither of them was. The new man had reddish-blonde hair, yellow eyes, and a way about him that was elegant, but seemed very deceptive. I knew he was a dangerous man. As beautiful as he was, I knew he was to be feared. Yet the magnificent man did not show fear (or smell like fear) at all. He wasn't even surprised.

"Hello, Lou," Magnificent Man said.

"Hello, Mike," Lou said.

They stood in silence a moment and stared at the pet store. Through the window the manager could be seen tearing out what little hair he had left. He was stomping and cursing and screaming at his employees in the parking lot that they were all replaceable, that they were fired, that they were all two-bit idiots.

"Come to watch the show?" Mike said. "They do amuse me so," Lou said. "Plus this hasn't been done on earth in over a millennium. Had to see it for old times' sake." "They know no better," Mike said. "But sometimes they cross the line." "Still doing your job," Lou said, smiling a little. "Will you never learn? They refuse to evolve. They are hopeless." "No, they are not," Mike said.

"I heard you recently incarnated as a rat," said Lou, stifling a giggle. "I haven't been paying attention to rodents lately. Maybe they have more hope for evolution than the apes do." Mike looked right at Lou. "Maybe they do," he said flatly.

"Oh, you've gone over the deep end. Too many ages of working for a megalomaniac, brother. Rodents throughout the Bible, and man's history, have been the scapegoats for evil and plague. They attribute those animals to me and my domain." He smirked in Mike's face. "They call them 'evil.'"

Mike was already past the limit, and I felt he had been in this place many times before. He had a handle on it. He smiled back at Lou. "They are far from evil," he said. "They are, like all animals on this earth, deserving of every chance that humankind has received." "That's not what the book says," Lou feigned surprise. "It says they're food." "At first they were," Mike said. "At first so were humans. Times change. Things evolve. Everyone gets a chance at immortality. Our Father is fair and knows nothing can stay the same. All things grow and evolve."

Lou became irritated. "Are you telling me He's actually going to give rodents a chance at sentient intelligence?" He shifted uncomfortably. Mike smiled. "He already has." Lou sneered and gnashed his teeth. I can't be sure, but I think Lou had fangs. "That's ridiculous. I won't have it." "You cannot prevent it."

"That's what you always think," said Lou. "Well, I'd stay for the fireworks, but I have a sudden appointment with your boss."

"Of course. It was meant to be that way."

"Isn't it always? The game is on. You have chosen a champion then?"

"It isn't a game, Dark One. But yes, Father has chosen a champion, and yes, we are opponents once again, though the innocent stand in the middle, as usual. It is unfortunate."

Lou smiled a frighteningly friendly expression at Mike. "You could always join me," he said. Mike stared back at him with no expression at all. He obviously considered the idea unthinkable. "Go and make your petition to your master," Mike said. That pissed Lou right off. He swore in ancient Hebrew (or something close) and stormed off, shaking his fist over his shoulder on the way out. "He's your master, puppet boy! *Not mine!*" Then the man in the black suit was gone.

Mike went back inside the store and found the manager there, seething in the middle of the empty store, angry as could be. "You did this!" the small man said. "You ruined my day!"

"It's about to get worse, thou selfish, wicked man. Begone from this place. Because you are only stupid and not evil, I will give you thirty seconds. But know this. If you do not receive justice this day, surely it shall visit upon you soon." Then Mike walked out.

The manager spent twenty of his thirty seconds swearing. He knocked stuff off shelves, he stomped up and down. He spent the next five seconds in a cold sweat. Every instinct he had left was screaming at him to run as far away as he could right now. He resisted for another three seconds out of pure self-destructive stubbornness. He made it out the door just as the magnificent man was raising his hands to the sky.

There was a deep, booming thunder, and the air sizzled hot. Sparks flew. A wind rushed down from above, and then a torrent of meteors, fire, and brimstone. The store was consumed in holy fire and burned to the ground in seconds under thousands of tons of thundering wrath of God.

Miraculously, the buildings next to it were not even black with soot. The manager had not gotten far enough away, and his clothes caught on fire from being too close. Although he was put out, he had a fear of fire for the rest of his days. His scorched nametag fell to the ground at Mike's feet. It said "McOrley."

A crowd had started to gather. Mike's stern face raked across them. None could meet his intense gaze. "For its cruelty to helpless animals, this place was found wanting when judgment came," Mike said. He stared hard at the crowd, his eyes blazing blue. "Prepare yourselves, for judgment shall not pass from you soon." He squinted. "It may even rest in the tiny paws of small animals." Then, as the crowd gazed in awe and horror at the crater where the pet store had been, the magnificent man turned his back upon the scene and walked away.

WINTER

Sir Squibble, the Mouse Knight

Great Mouse History

✠

For five thousand years mice and rats have been living with mankind. Hardly ever have they been pets. They've been ignored, trapped, killed, poisoned, and reviled. Most of the time they're "pests," or food for other pets. On top of all that, people sometimes even fear us. They blamed the entire black plague on us when it really wasn't out fault. It was the mites on the fleas on the animals that carried that bacteria, not us. We got a bad rap, man. In those days, humans had mites!

Anyway, mice don't get treated so good, see? But we have feelings every bit as deep and as strong as you do. If you don't get that by the end of this book, I'd have to wonder about your "superior" intelligence. Oh, heck. Truth is, I already do. But I'm not a judgmental mouse. I'm pretty easygoing. So don't sweat it. My point is animals deserve to be treated well, but they haven't been, and we definitely aren't out here for your amusement.

Let's skip five thousand years and go to, like, last year. My wonderful master was just a tiny little mouse who grew up in a happy home for about a day. Then he was returned to the pet store by stupid owners who didn't want "too many mice" and weren't responsible enough to care for their own children, much less some really neat animals. So my master went back to being Snake Food, and lost his momma and papa, and a lot of his family.

By the time he figured out what was going on, he was very sad and depressed over it. His turn came eventually and he got put in with the snake, but he chose not to go down quietly. He got pissed off, fought back, and killed the snake, who turned out to be not such a bad guy. Just another caged animal under human tyranny. The snake happened to be a king, and he knighted my master, making him the very first of the Mouse Knights. I was the second.

My master wrote it all down. He was special, see? Besides having the courage to fight a snake, and the strength and speed to win, he was the first mouse able to read. When the pet store manager would take his breaks or stay late at night, my master would read the books he left open on the table, which was right below the mouse cages in the back room. Those books were the old Arthurian legends and tales of brave knights. My master grew up on the stories and loved them.

When he became a knight, he resolved to find all mice everywhere a safe home. And he refused to believe what everyone said, that all people hated mice. He knew there must be at least one special human, a Kind Human, who would love mice. He made it his holy quest to find that man. Through a very long and dangerous adventure, we finally did. All of this is in his book. He published it, and the money went to the Kind Human to take care of us. It was he that brought the Great Kingdom of Lost Rodents to the safe house. (That's what we call his house.) Lots and lots of mice and rats moved to the Kind Human's domain out in the middle of the Fields of Fate after that. That's where we live now.

For my part in the quest to find the Kind Human, I was made the second ever Mouse Knight. Such an honor! (And from such a great mouse as my beloved master!) I am certain I didn't deserve it, but I'm working on that. Two of our dear friends died on that quest. We lost half our party. Michael Mousefriend, a magnificent rat who turned out to be the Archangel Michael, and a really big mouse named Bigfat, who turned out to be the Mousegod. Without them, my master and I never would have made it at all. They died so that the quest might not fail. I still miss them, even though sometimes I still see them.

I have this... gift. At least that's what Nemo, our chinchilla prophet, calls it. It happens mostly when I'm really in pain, or hungry, or very tired. I can't control it, though Nemo says someday I will be able to. I see the spirit world. I see ghosts or other places (the "astral place," Nemo says), and other things. Angels, stuff like that. All kindsa things. Lotsa cool stuff. Sometimes I have weird dreams, but that's mostly when I eat some of the Kind Human's pizza.

Anyway, I'm not a normal mouse. When I was little I almost starved to death. And all my other brothers and sisters... they did. And since then I've been really scrawny and thin. I look weird. I walk weird. Heck, I'm weird! I don't mind. It makes me really fast and limber, hence the name I picked for myself (and got to keep! Most mice never get a name. It's the greatest honor there is.) On top of that, I have this "gift" that I don't tell anyone about. It's mostly a pain in the rear. It's scary and unpredictable. I don't like it. It makes me wonder whether I'm awake or asleep, or whether I got hit on the head too hard. It started when I pushed myself beyond my limits at the very end of my master's holy quest. I had to carry his wounded, dying body across miles and miles of snow covered wasteland to reach the house of the Kind Human. Everybody says it was amazing. I think it was kinda silly that we had to do that at all, I mean, why couldn't it be easy? But that's what I had to do, and I couldn't let him die, or let him down, so I carried him. He was real heavy. I was weak and tired. We almost didn't make it. We wouldn't have if it hadn't been for the spirit of Bigfat, the Mousegod. He came back and told me to get up and try just a little bit more. I've heard that a lot since then, those words: "just a little bit more." It seems people always want to quit just before they make it.

After the quest was over, the Kind Human drove us back into the city we came from and brought the entire kingdom of rodents back to his house. Then he went out and spent all his money on cages, toys, and medicine for us. My master began writing, and he even got the thing he wanted the most in life—a name. And he married my mom. I just love that part. He's technically my dad, but to me he'll always be my beloved master.

The Kind Human spent hours building my master a huge castle out of cardboard that goes in his equally huge cage. It's got towers an' everything. It's really cool, and many an hour we spend upon it playing pretend battles. Of course, since we're mice it gets chewed up, but when that happens the human builds us another one, better than the last one. He's so cool to us. My master says we're the rarest thing in the world: loved mice.

Then we needed to organize hundreds of rodents from chaos into order. With Nemo's help, we did it. First off, no one was allowed to breed. You should have seen their faces! So many angry mice and rats! Nemo explained to them that if anyone did, they would be working against the safe haven we had been given. They'd be overpopulating the house, and soon we'd all be out of luck. Nemo says it's the same with the humans, but they haven't figured it out yet. I always thought humans were smart, even if a bit on the cruel side. Anyway, the only animals allowed to breed had to have permission of the Kind Human.

Second, the Kind Human needed this thing called money, which I still don't understand, but it would get us food and water and cages and all that. So the smart rodents went to work figuring out how to get it. They're still working on that, and the poor Kind Human barely scrapes by. He gives us everything he has. He even shares his dinners with us. Once my master published his book, we had a little more money… enough to last a little while.

That's where we're at now: kinda well off, but no one knows how long it will last. I told Nemo that's the life of a mouse. You never know when the good or the bad will turn around. And it happens fast. Nemo laughed and said, "That's the life of humans, too, but they don't want to hear that." Nemo is really smart. Master says he's even wise, whatever that is. But he's always right. I haven't seen him be wrong once yet.

It's now a few months after the quest ended. Everything is in order. We have a few rules to follow, and everyone is happy, even the ants and the bees, our allies from the field. My master's brother, BJ, is King, and he sees to the training of the animals personally. He's a real stickler for the rules. Master says he's got an iron fist, but his paws look normal to me. BJ doesn't take any lip. He's king and

he knows it. The only mouse he doesn't boss around is my master. Oh, and he listens to Nemo. But everyone does, so that's nothing special. They call BJ the "Battle Mouse" because he fights so well. One of the rules of the house is "No fighting," but it just says that no rodent may kill another. The males beat each other up plenty trying to see who's boss or where they stand on the totem pole, but no one messes with BJ. No one wants any of that. The Battle Mouse can take anyone (except my master, of course). I've seen him beat up thirty mice at once! I've seen him take on rats. No kidding. They all gave up after a sound thrashing at his teeth. He's really cool.

There have been a few more namings, and a few more knightings, too, for other mice who did great deeds, or risked their lives to help the kingdom. Since Master's book was published, many rodents know how to read now, and some even write. I'm learning, as you can see. My master told me to keep a journal and so I do. He told me to write anything I want, but make it true, and do it all the time. I will obey my master faithfully. I didn't include the first few months of entries because… ummm… Master said it was unlegible. Ineligable. Illegibale. Something where people couldn't read it. Yeah. I argued that I knew exactly what it said, but he said it had to be better. He said Knights were always gentlemice, who knew how to be civilized. That included writing well. Actually, he said gracefully, but I can't see how one would write gracefully. It would look silly. I mean, no one even watches me write, so what does it matter how I move when I do it? But Master is always right, so I tried to improve my writing even though I didn't understand. Come to think of it, I really don't understand much, but I am really good at accepting things. Mice are good at that.

But I do understand some things. Here's what I understand: I wanna be a hero, like my master! More than anything in the world, I wanna be a hero. I want to be loved and respected by everyone, an' when I walk by, I want all the rodents to salute to me like they do him. Or bow like they do to Nemo. Some of them do, but mostly not. Mostly I'm just the master's squire. And even though I'm not really a squire anymore, I kinda still am. That's not something I understand, but I know what I want! I wanna be famous and cool! I wanna be a hero and do something great like my master! More than anything in life I want this. I live for it! I dream of it (when I'm not having one of those weird dreams), and I hunger for it like I hunger for a Cheerio! Mmmmm… Cheerio.

I just went and checked. It's not Cheerio time yet. Sometimes they fall from the sky in the evening. No one's fooling this mouse, though. I know the human drops them. They taste so good! I want one. I would go get one but that's rule number two: "No stealing or destroying the Kind Human's stuff."

My momma, bless her heart, lets me pretty much do anything I want around home. I'm not home much, but that's nice. My momma has always been so nice to me. She kept me alive when all my brothers and sisters died in the cold. We were kicked out by our owners when she had us. See? Stupid. Why wouldn't humans want mice? My momma is such a nice, pretty mouse. She loves people. Her owner named her Tree, because she likes to climb things. Mostly, she said she liked to climb up on her owners' shoulders and lick their ears. They really liked that. Why would anyone abandon her?

So anyway I'm in training. Knight training. BJ teaches all the mice and rats that want to know how to fight and how to behave. Mostly I think it's stupid (anything I don't like is stupid!), but I don't have much say. Master tells me to do it, so I do it. He says I need to learn to do everything that I can. Well, I am pretty sure there's nothing I can't do, so that's gonna take a long time, but okay, I'll do it. I don't sleep much.

The training is fun. I'm one of the fastest mice. And I squish real good. An' I like sword fighting. My master teaches that class. But the philosophy is boring, even though Nemo teaches it. I wanna beat things up an' be brave and knightly! Philosophy is for talking to the air after you've slain your enemy, that kinda thing. Not much use.

BJ works me hard. He says I'm a bit dense but eager and willing. I don't know what dense means. Every time I go to look it up, some other mouse is using the dictionary. I get to use my master's encyclopedias, though, which he lets no one else use. Those are his most prized possessions. He loves them so much. Every day I go to practice, and then I spend time with my master if he has time, and then sometimes I see Nemo who, for some reason, wants me around him all the time. Kinda weird, but he's the prophet, so okay I guess.

After that I play with the guys and the rat twins. The rat twins were made into squires months ago when they came home with us from the city. They're Michael Mousefriend's children. His wife, Baby, had two girls and two boys. My master, in his infinite fairness, offered the squire title to the girls as well, but they didn't want to be knights. (Imagine that! Whoa!) They wanted to make nests and raise kids and all that. So they're on the list of breeding petitions (that list is a mile long, I can tell you! Heck, I put myself on it, too, just so no one else would get ahead of me in line if it ever happens, which my master says probably won't.) The girls were named Artemis and Aphrodite. The boys were named Shiva and Thor.

I went and looked up all those names in the encyclopedia. The girls are kinda cool, but the boys were named after the God of Destruction (Shiva) and some guy who swings a mean hammer called the God of Thunder (Thor). Hmmm… weird. My master chose the names though, and he knows best, so no big. I just shrug and accept it. Life can get weirder than that.

The boys love me and the girls love my mom. My mom is like a sister to them and their own momma, Baby, takes care of all the rats in the house. It's a big job because there's like, a hundred of them. Did you know rats eat mice? Yikes! I didn't know that until they told me. Mike never tried to eat me, but if he had wanted to, I wouldn't have stood a chance. He was huge! Anyway, no one eats anyone else here. The house is neutral ground for all animals. It's another rule: "Don't pee where you sleep," or something like that.

The boys are huge, too, like their dad was, but I can beat 'em. Heh heh heh… I am a fast mouse! I know tricks. Nemo teaches me this thing called Eye-Key-Doh. It means using someone else's stuff against them. It works real good on ignorant little boy rats. I'd never try it in real life. I've seen other mice get hurt doing that, mostly against BJ, who has mice get mad at him on a regular basis and has to put them in their place. He seems to make it work just fine, of course, but he's BJ!

I love the boys. They're cool. We play all the time. I share everything with them, and we go everywhere together. We share bedtime stories from my momma (more Arthurian legends—you coulda guessed, right?) and eat meals together. They are old enough now to come to class with me, but you know what? Even though they outweigh that darn BJ mouse by easily twenty times, he still kicks their behinds all over the field. Shiva says he's "bad ass." I asked what makes someone's rear bad. Shiva said he saw it on TV. So I started watching TV. Wowee. Coool. TV! I watch it every evening now. I learn ALOT. Yeah, I know it's spelled A LOT, but I don't like it that way and nobody says it that way, so get used to it being one word, 'cause this is my journal and I'll write any darn way I wanna, 'kay? Alrighty then! I guess I told you. Don't mess with ol' Squibble! I'll put the hurt on ya. My ass is bad!

Master encourages me to find something to do besides violence in my spare time. That was a hard one. I mean, I really like violence. It's fun. I can even beat up the rats (besides the twins), on account of they're strong but *slooow* compared to mice. And I'm a very fast mouse! No touchum the Squibble!

So… I like doing mock combat (that's what King BJ calls practice). I pretty much rule at it. Except for BJ, or course, and Master. And Nemo. When he wants to he can be pretty scary! He's even bigger than a rat, and four times as fast as a mouse! And there's this girl, one of Bigfat's twenty-five kids that were born in the old kingdom (they're with us now)—she's really big, like he was, and she's really violent. I mean, she's really good at fighting. She goes to the training school. She's a squire. Most of the students are afraid of her. She hits really hard! She doesn't hit me, "out of respect," she says, which I am all happy about. But I saw her hit this one mouse once, and the mouse flew out of his practice armor, right out of it! It blew apart like… like it was hit by a freight train. (See? TV is cool.)

Anyway, he didn't get up, and they had to haul him off to the place where mice go when they're sick. He got better, but it took a long time. They thought he was dead once but it turned out to be a rumor. The next day he showed up for class, and after that, BJ called him Ghost. He's also white, so that helps. After that even BJ always dodged out of the big mouse's way. He says she's not subtle enough, whatever that means. She likes to hit people, knock them down, then jump up and down on them. BJ told her she couldn't do that anymore, and named her Stompy! How funny is that!

Anyway, sorry… that was a tangent. I actually did get to look that word up after my master used it. It means something that sort of goes where it wasn't supposed to. Like a mouse that goes to get a drink and stops by the food dish because there's a pumpkin seed in it, then keeps going to the water after. The pumpkin seed was a tangent. And that was another tangent. Master says I do that alot. (See? ALOT!)

I tried lots of "civilized" stuff. I tried playing chess. I got bored and wanted to break the rules. Pieces only move certain ways. Like the queen. I say if the queen wants to move like a horse, who's gonna tell her she can't? The King? He only moves one square at a time! He'll never catch her! Stupid game.

I tried poetry, because my master said it was romantic and girls liked it. It was boring, too, and what do I need it for? Girls are all over me all the time. They do anything I want. They are my willing slaves. I don't need poetry.

I tried music, and at first that was cool, but it was hard to play what I heard in my head, and I got frustrated. I was never as good as that guy on TV. London Symphony Orchestra. I just couldn't make more than one sound at once. That guy London is a true master.

I tried alot of things and finally gave up. There just wasn't anything I liked. So I went back to wrestling with the boys. Life is about having fun. Doing hard stuff is for the birds.

I do like drawing, but I don't think that's very important, and I never show anyone my drawings. They'd laugh probably, which would hurt my feelings. But I have this journal, and sometimes I do little drawings, like this:

I've been doing that for a few months now, but nobody ever sees 'em. And they probably won't, either. An' you know what? That's cool, because I don't do it for them. I do it for me. I like it.

It's kinda like writing. I like telling stories. I'd love to be a writer and publish a book like my master, but he's a genius and I'm not really, so maybe it ain't happenin'. Besides, who cares what I write? I just ramble on 'cause it's fun. Someday, when I'm a great and powerful hero, then maybe someone will be interested in what this little mouse has to say.

Until then, it's all fun and games.

Tangent: Wrongness and Rightness

✠

So I had this other dream. It was a scary dream, but really sharp and in color, like the first one. Nemo says they're "looseed dreams," whatever that means, which I asked him, an' he said it means, like, prophetic. Cosmic. All that. I was all, "Cool," and went right off to take a nap. This was the dream I had then.

It was dark in a place with lots of mice. At first I thought it was a thrice cursed pet store. (That's my new saying…"thrice cursed." It comes from a medieval story. Cool, huh?) But it wasn't. It wasn't a pet store at all. It had a nasty smell to it, and a really bad feeling. Kinda like… pain. Pain and fear. I don't know how I knew that, but I did, 'kay? I mean, it was a dream. So the place was bad. Really bad. All the mice knew it was bad, but they couldn't get out.

They were stuck in these tiny little cages—really small, like eight inches long by six inches wide! And no toys, no nothin'! Just water and chunks of green stuff for food. It was yucky. It was *stupid!* And they hated it.

Then I realized that all the mice were sick. Alot of them were dying. It was horrible. Alot of them had things sticking out of their bodies, and… every mouse was alone. Not one had any other mouse friend in their cage, and there was no way for one to reach the others. It was very sad. They were all sad mice.

Then I saw in another room, a human in a white coat was doing something to a mouse. Somehow I knew this mouse had been a pet once. It was used to kind treatment, care, and good treats, but now it was tied down and couldn't move. The human was sticking a needle into its stomach and holding it down roughly. The mouse was frightened and in pain. The coat guy sucked out the mouse's stomach through the needle (or something like that) and the mouse squeaked in pain. Then the coat guy turned to put the needle down and knocked over a weird shaped glass of stuff, spilling it onto the mouse. The stuff burned and smoked, and the mouse shrieked in agony. The man swore out loud and ran for something on the wall, but he was too slow. The mouse lit on fire! It writhed and twisted and tried to escape desperately as it burned. Finally, the little straps holding it down burned, and the mouse got loose. It hopped and spasmed around, trying to not be on fire, but it was. It was horrible. I wanted to wake up really bad. Finally the mouse fell over. The man sprayed some weird foamy stuff all over the burned mouse, and the fire went out.

The man talked with another man and suggested they kill the mouse, but the other man said the mouse was "too important to the experiment." All it had to do was live one more day. So they put the charred mouse back into its tiny cage. They did nothing for its pain. It didn't even look like that mouse anymore. Its face was burned off. Its ears were gone. It was bent and folded in half in a fetal position. I couldn't believe how cruel the human was! Anyone could see that the mouse was in terrible pain! But they just put it back and shut the cage door.

The mouse was in more than physical pain. It had trusted humans. In the dream I knew its owner had died—he was old—and the mouse had been given to a family member who didn't want it. They gave it to a friend who didn't want it either, and he put an ad in the paper asking if anyone wanted a mouse. The people who came to get it pretended they wanted a mouse, but they just collected animals for labs. The mouse's fate was sealed when they delivered it to the research program. It was such a heartless thing to do, but the mouse had no protector anymore, no Kind Human of its own to guard it from such things. That mouse, who had never known anything but love and kindness, had now been mutilated and almost fatally burned in a horrible way by a human. The poor mouse felt betrayed. It missed its old human, and it wanted to die.

So the mouse did not give the humans their experiment by living an extra day. It choked on cracked lungs and died convulsing on the cage floor in the dead of night.

Now all of that was bad enough. I'd seen enough horror, thanks. I thought I'd wake up then—I wanted to—but what happened next made that seem like a ride on a friendly rat. It was like this writer I like whose stuff can just make you not like the dark at all!

I watched the dead mouse a long time. It was pretty dead. I mean, I've seen dead before. No moving, no breathing… all dead. The entire place was quiet, just darkness and no noise. It seemed like the mice all sensed something was coming. I didn't, but then Nemo says I'm kinda niy-eev. It's spelled n-a-i-v-e I think.

The burned mouse twitched. I would have jumped three feet, but I wasn't there. Only my mind was really there. My heart jumped though. It scared me pretty bad.

The room got really cold. The temperature dropped until all the mice were all shivering, probably thirty degrees. Most of them were trying to get out of their cages. They were freaking out.

Then a presence filled the place. I knew the feeling: it was the same as the bad man from my first dream… Lou.

Then something invaded the mouse. I heard it crawl down the mouse's charred windpipe and fill its dead lungs with something that was not air, something that was not right. The mouse wheezed backward. The other mice screamed and beat their heads against the cage doors trying to get out. Then the dead mouse turned black.

It was awful, blacker than night. Something like ears grew back on its head, but they were more like horns. Its face came back, but it was twisted and mean-looking. Then its eyes opened, and they were made of fire. Bright fire.

An' that was about it for ol' Squibble, folks! I screamed and hollered and called on the Mousegod to take me right out of there and right now. The Black Mouse was looking right at me!

"AAAAAAAH!" I yelled. "Bigfat, get me out! Get me outta here right now, darn it, I'm tellin' you! Move your fat ass, an' come yank me back now! It's gonna get me!"

The thing from Hell (I knew that it was!) bared a row of shark-like teeth in an evil smile, and said in a voice like gravel, *"Yes, Squibble, I am coming to get you."*

"No way!" I hollered as it got up. *"NOWAYNOWAYNOWAY!"*

But then suddenly I was sitting in a field, at dawn. It was the field outside our house, I recognized it. I could see the back of the house on the hill, but I was probably miles away from it. I was scared. My heart was beating at 1500 beats a minute. (Not joking. Mice normally go at 700 at least.)

The air was cool and a soft breeze told me I was far from the bad place. Dawn felt normal. The house being close by made me feel safe, even if it would take me days and days to get back there, maybe even weeks.

Then I realized I was sitting by the edge of a lake. It would just be a large pond to a human, but I recognized this place, too. It was the place where Michael Mousefriend had fallen with the hawk. He had fallen and saved us all, and he died doing that. But he made himself come back from the grave because we needed him still. *He* organized all the mice of the field, the bees and ants, and removed every obstacle from our path. I never would have made those last few miles to the house of the Kind Human with my master on my aching back without his help. Our quest would have failed without him. He did fall, and he did die, but he came back… because he loved us.

"Oh, Mike," I said. "I miss you."

"I miss you too, little one."

I gasped and snapped my head up to stare at a giant man, illuminated (oooo, big word, huh?) in the golden light of the rising sun. He was huge and robed in white. He had massive wings on his back, and his head had a ring of fire around it. He had golden hair flowing down to his wide shoulders. He was wearing a belt, and on the belt was a beautiful, shiny sword. Even with the wings and different suit, I knew it was Magnificent Man from my first dream. But he looked like an angel.

"Archangel, actually," he said. His voice… he was speaking rodent! It sounded like… like…"Michael Mousefriend," I whispered in awe. He smiled and nodded. His smile was so friendly and genuine. He was so cool.

I ran to him and hugged his big toe. "Mike! Mike!" He reached down and scooped me up. He petted me and scratched gently behind my ears, grooming me. He rubbed my tummy (no mouse will let you do this, so don't try, humans), and we shared a moment of pure happiness. I knew it was Mike. He wasn't wearing a rat body, but I knew it was him. I loved him so.

Then I remembered my recent dream.

"What did it mean, Mike?" I asked him. Mike's face got serious. He set me down by the water's edge. "Squibble," he said as he looked skyward, "Things happen sometimes in other places that decide the fate of things here on earth." I nodded, understanding for some weird reason. "And sometimes, in rare moments, things happen here that decide the fate of other places." He looked down to see if I was getting it. I was. "This is one of those rare times. What is about to happen *must* happen, dear friend. It may seem like God hates you, but he does not."

"Oh, Bigfat doesn't hate me," I chirped. "He can be a jerk sometimes, but that's just his ego. He's really a nice guy. He'd never do anything to hurt me." Mike smiled again, almost laughing. Somehow I got the idea that was rare for him, even though as a rat he had laughed often. "Yes, Squibble, God loves you." I nodded. That was right. Yep. "He loves you so much that he has chosen you for a very special task," he said. "A very difficult, special task. But you must accept it of your own free will."

I opened my mouth. A special task from the Mousegod! That was called a Crusade! A Holy Quest! I was gonna be like my master! YES! I knew it! I knew I'd be a great hero someday!

Michael held up a finger in warning. My mouth wouldn't utter the words I wanted to say! I wanted to agree right away, take the job like a stolen Cheerio and run away with it, but I couldn't speak. Frustrating!

"Squibble, this is not going to be easy. In fact, it is going to cost you alot. Maybe everything. You cannot know how hard this is going to be if you accept. It will make your trek across these fields of fate seem like nothing. I am warning you. If you accept, you can expect the very worst."

I stopped. "This has to do with that wrong mouse back in the dream, doesn't it?"

Mike nodded, his eyes very serious. I thought for about half a second—long for me. For some unexplainable reason I had a flash of something I never experience: caution.

"What if I don't do this?"

"God will find someone else."

"But Bigfat chose me!" I squealed in protest.

Mike nodded again. "Yes. He did."

I looked around. The fields were empty. It was quiet. It was peaceful. I felt no pressure except my own. “Do I get to be a great hero and save everyone?”

“You get to be a great hero, Squibble.”

“Cool!”

“You will change the fate of all rodentkind, and all humankind as well.”

“So cool!”

“And you will suffer for it as well.”

“Eh?”

“The enemy is without mercy, Squibble. He will strike where it hurts the most.”

“Do I get to win?”

Mike chuckled, unable to stop the laugh from escaping.

“That depends on you.”

“On my great strength and my huge courage, huh?!”

“Yes, and your power to persevere.”

“I can be severe.”

“Squibble, take this seriously!” he boomed.

“I do. I will. I accept!”

I caught Mike by surprise by saying that I think, because his eyes got wide. “Are you certain that you desire to carry this burden, tiny mouse?”

I felt afraid for just one second—I think he wanted me to, though I can’t imagine why—but I shook it off. I was going to be a great hero, like my beloved master!

I nodded aggressively. “Yep.”

Mike looked a bit sad then. He lowered his head, as if he knew something I didn’t, which of course he did. Duh… he’s an angel. Er, Archangel. Sorry.

Then he drew his mighty sword. It blazed like the sun. I had to look away. He held up his other hand with his index and middle finger pointing upward, and gently he placed the very tip of the sword on my back. It didn’t hurt at all

“Then Squibble, you are named the Champion of Mice, chosen by God, Protector of the Species. You are given the power to change the history of the world. Rise, Sir Squibble. You are the Prophet-Knight.”

I looked up at him strangely. “Yeah… Of course I’m a knight. My master knighted me. You weren’t there for that. You don’t gotta do it again, Mike, but thanks for thinking of me.”

Then Mike drew back and cast his sword into the lake. It fell like a burning comet, and when it hit the water, it only made a tiny splash. Not the big spray a giant metal thing like that would have made, but a mouse-sized splash. When it subsided, for a moment I thought I saw a mouse paw sticking up out of the water holding a mouse-sized sword, but both vanished into the blue water immediately. The water fizzled for a moment and was still. Tiny ripples reached out for shore in every direction. Mike turned to me.

"Tell your master that he may command me one time in all of this, *one time only*, by this name of God, which is Adonai. Tell him to choose wisely. And also tell him that the lady will grant him his weapon when he is ready."

"Ummm... what lady, Mike?" I looked around for a woman, mouse or human.

Mike picked me up and petted me again. It felt so good.

"I love you, Squibble. Try to remember that in the coming days. I will not abandon you."

"Oh, that's right! Heck no, you won't!" I said. "You're coming back with me to the house! First off, I ain't walkin there by myself—no way! And second, Master will want to see you again. He'll be so happy to see you, Mike! Even if you do look like a human."

"Remember the Black Mouse, Squibble. And the lake. Remember these things."

"Ohhh, I'd rather forget that one, if it's all the same, Mike. That was just a crazy dream."

Mike smiled again. "Squibble."

I perked. "Yeah."

"You're still dreaming."

I looked right into his eyes. "No way!" I said, amazed.

And I woke up.

The Golden Days

✠

In fighter practice BJ makes us learn several basic moves every few weeks. They're all mousey things. There's the nose push, which gets used alot. If a mouse pushes another out of the way with his strong nose, a fight doesn't usually happen. The other mouse figures, "Wow, what a strong nose. I'm not gonna mess with that mouse." Nose pushing is kinda like insisting on having your way.

If that doesn't work, then there's the tail whap. But smacking someone with your tail is pretty insulting, so BJ recommends against it. Then it escalates to biting the tail. That hurts. I've had my tail bitten once or twice. If that doesn't get you your way, then you gotta bite the offender on the rump… hard. And sometimes you hold on, to learn 'em real good. Usually they run away, and you gotta chase them all over the place. Kind of a pain in the ass. Hee hee hee! Get it? Pain in the *ass*? Hee hee!

If a rump bite doesn't work, or the other mouse doesn't give the sign of submission (neck bared, hands folded over the chest, tail tucked), then it's time to get serious. That's when a mouse might kill another mouse. The ladies almost never do this, but the guys do all the time. You just can't put two guys together in the same cage and not expect a fight, and it's usually a bad one. The killing blows are almost all to the head. If a mouse strikes at the head, it means it wants to kill you. Mice go blind, get brained, and have ears torn off like this. It's nasty. One always walks away crippled, at least for a while.

BJ taught us the nicer stuff after that. He taught us other stuff like the fast jump (teleporting he calls it, because if you do it right you move so fast no one can see you), crawling on another mouse (this can be good or bad), the chase ritual, and what various squeaks mean.

For the last several weeks we've been working on hardcore fighting. Teeth are really our only weapon. We graduate to swords and other weapons once we've learned to use everything else first. It makes sense. I kinda wanna practice with my sword, but BJ won't let me have one during his class. I watch my master, BJ and Nemo practice their arts in the basement sometimes. The entire basement is a rodent playground. There's even a climbing wall (a few of them) because the bricks down there are offset and rough. Mice practice climbing to the top and scurrying along the rafters and support beams. The mice that fall land on a cushioned blanket (which gets chewed up on a regular basis). The Kind Human put it there after a few mice hurt themselves falling.

The master swordsmice work out down there in a private room behind the water heater. I get to watch. I try to learn. My master whips that sword around like a pro. It makes swooshing noises and his ass looks bad. He dances and swings, thrusts, parries, reposts... all that fancy stuff. He says he learns it from books. He spends all his other time with his nose in his valuable books. He loves them more than anything, well, except for me and my mom.

The battlemouse BJ practices with anything—teeth, claws, pieces of wood, rocks. He's a brutal fighter. He can use anything that's just lying around. And if he has nothing, then it's worse, because his teeth are deadly. He relies mostly on speed and ferocity, but then you add his skills and he can beat anybody. He can beat my master in hand-to-hand, but not with a sword. No one can beat my master with a sword. No one even comes close. It's like he was born to wield one.

Nemo is weird. He practices this slow, dance-like stuff he calls "Tie Chee." Or "Chee Gong." And of course "Eye-key-doh." All that fancy stuff. He's really good. No one can touch him, not even the Battlemouse—he stopped trying after taking several hundred good falls. If you run at Nemo on the mat, he just twists this way or that a little tiny bit—looks like he's dancing kinda—and next thing you know, wham! You're flat on your back, two feet away!

I love running at Nemo. It's fun. He always tosses me hard on account of he knows I like it. As I'm flying I curl up into a ball like I was taught, roll when I hit, and come up standing. I got it down, see? Then I run at him again. I've seen him take on me, my master, BJ, and even Stompy all at once. No one hit him even a single time. He's amazing.

Someday when I'm really good, it would be neat-o to learn that cool stuff, but it seems more like magic than fighting. I hear that in his private cage, he sometimes floats around while he meditates. I hear his will alone can burn paper. Yikes! He tries to get me to meditate. I can do it... for about half a second. Then I get sick of sitting still. Sitting still is stupid. It's for old, powerful wizards like Nemo, not for fast, zippy mice like me!

So day in and day out, hundreds of mice go down to the basement and have fighter practice in the dusk light and before dawn (bedtime). Everyone gets beat up by BJ, and everyone thanks him for it. We all bow at the beginning and the end. It's cool.

Besides that, I've been drawing and writing some. I really enjoy it, I guess, and I do it every chance I get. Mostly I write in this journal, but I've got some ideas for stories. Master says I should write them in my journal, and no one ever has to see them. I'm okay with writing in my journal, but aren't stories for other mice to enjoy? I mean, what good is a story unless someone hears it and has a reaction to it? Dang. That's too deep. My brain almost fainted.

I like doing art, but it doesn't look right. I see other art that looks much better than mine. I wanna learn to do it really good like that. I wanna have people look at my art and go "Oooo... that's so cool!" I draw alot, and I see some improvements, but mostly I don't really know how to get better. I don't care so much. I just draw because I like to. When I get sick of it, I go do something else. I go play with the rat twins, or hang out with the masters. They talk way over my head, but it's fun being with them. They like me.

I remembered having a weird, gnarly dream at some point. I didn't remember what it was. I told Nemo about it.

"Hey. I had this weird dream," I said.

"What was it about?" said the master prophet. He was chewing on a block of alfalfa. That's what chinchillas eat.

"Oh, it was scary. And kinda nice, too, at the end. I don't remember much else. Something bad and something good. I think Mike was in it."

I musta looked troubled staring at the floor. Nemo sensed it. "It might be nothing," he said, "and if it was important, you'll remember it when the time is right."

"Ummm, what if I don't?" I asked. "Oops!" he said cheerfully. I nodded. Yeah. That made sense.

I told my master about it, too, but he was busy studying his books. He said that all mice had dreams, usually about eating or running. I told him my dreams were weirdo-city. He nodded and smiled at me. "That's 'cause you're not normal, Squib," he said. "It's okay. You wouldn't be happy being normal."

That made sense too, so I dropped it.

Today I drew this picture. I don't know really what it means, but hey, it wanted to be drawn, so I drew it. It's kinda cool.

I wrote a story, too. It was from one of my dreams. It was a weird dream. I'm glad no one reads this stuff. I'd be embarrassed to share it maybe. It's kinda weird.

The Golden Path, the Silver Road

Once upon a time, there was a mouse in a cage of mice that sat in a window by the beach. They were well cared for and their human treated them right. The cage had seven mice in it. One of the mice would always look out over the water at sunset and at night and ask, "What is that?" when he saw the moon or the sun setting on the water.

"That is the path to freedom," one old mouse said. "During the day, it is the Golden Path and takes a mouse to Heaven. During the night, it is the Silver Road and takes a mouse to another life here on earth. But both are fleeting. They vanish quickly. The only mouse who can make it to the end is one who leaves everything behind to do it, because things just slow us down. And once they choose they never come back. Whether they make it, or not."

Well, the mouse was fascinated and horrified at the same time. A golden path to Heaven? A silver road to another life? Wowee, the mouse thought. How cool. The mouse watched the sun go down, and watched the moon set as well. It seemed to take a long time, but it was also clearly a long way. Mice can't see very well, and so the little mouse didn't quite know exactly how far that path was. How long did a mouse have to run to find the end of the road? And which one would he choose if he ever could?

One day the owner accidentally left the lid off their cage. The mouse quickly scurried up and out, and sat on the window ledge. He sat there thinking for a long time. Then a bird came by to eat him, and he had to jump from the window to stay alive. He fell many feet onto the sand. He could not go back to the cage. He could never climb back up to the windowsill. It was too high and steep. From that moment, he knew he had to choose the path or the road now.

The mouse went down to the beach and sat there a long time. He watched the sun set and then the moon set also. By the next day he was tired, hungry and thirsty. He knew that he had to choose before he lost all his strength. He decided Heaven was a nice place, and he wanted to go there. So that day at sunset he ran out onto the water and flew across the Golden Path toward the setting sun.

But as he was running the sun set, leaving him stranded on the water without anything to follow. He knew he was trapped between worlds. He felt afraid. "But if I just sit here long enough," he thought, "the moon will come up, won't it? It wasn't my first choice, but it will set eventually, and the Silver Road will lead me to another life."

The moon did come, and the mouse followed its silvery light on the water until it also set. Frustrated, he waited for the sun. When that came, he followed it until it vanished. Then the moon, then the sun again. Finally, after months, he sat down on the water and cried, "Won't someone help me? I am lost and cannot find heaven or another life!"

Then the sun and moon both came to him. They showed him a path, both gold and silver, back to the beach. There he saw his body washed ashore. It had drowned when he set out upon the Golden Path that first time.

The mouse was sad, seeing his body. He realized that he hadn't been ready to leave, and that was why he never reached the end of his journey. He had carried with him all his love of life, his cares of the world. Now he had nothing to take with him. He knew his life was over.

He set his foot one last time on the golden path, and no one ever saw him again.

The end.

I don't know how good it is or anything. It probably isn't, and it's weird, but hey, it's what came to me, so I wrote it down. I think it's kinda sad, and I don't know why I wrote something sad. My life isn't sad. I'm very happy.

I spent all day today watching TV. Oh, and I played with the rat twins some. We watched TV together. I went to fighter practice in the evening and the morning. I licked my beautiful momma on her cheek. I said hi to my beloved master. I didn't draw anything or write anything of my own, and felt kinda like that was no good. So I stayed up and told the rat twins a story and drew them this picture.

It's from the story that was about this Greek who everyone wanted to kill, even though he was a great hero. So they sent him up against this evil monster with three heads (one of them was a dragon head!), but he killed it with the help of his winged horse. Then they sent him on more missions, and he won them, too. Then they sent many men against him, but he killed them all. And finally, the people who hated him had to give up and say he was great. So cool. In the end he tried to fly up to the gods on his winged horse, an' they didn't think that was cool. He had abused his cool permit and it expired. The main god dude made a fly bite his horse, and the horse tossed him from, like, several miles up. Anyway, the really bad news is that when he hit the ground, he wasn't even dead! He was too strong to die ,but he was crippled and blind the rest of his life, and he wandered all over being crippled and blind—whoa. Bummer.

Shiva and Thor were fascinated for some reason. Neither of them spoke after that and went right to bed. I hope I didn't scare them too much.

I just like the part where he slays the big three-headed monster and proves all those stupid humans wrong. Of course, in the original story the guy wasn't a mouse, but hey, it was my story, right? I was tellin' it, and I say he was a mouse. Humans always hate mice, but mice prevail, see? Mice rock.

For the entire last week just the usual. Mice are getting pretty good at their news skills. Mice learn fast. They learn, like, 50 times faster than humans. Hey, if you only had 700 days to live, you'd learn fast, too.

Lots of mice can read now, and lots of mice are in fighter training to become squires. Thing is, only a King can usually make a knight, and only a knight can make a squire. There aren't that many knights, only a few. Knights can make their squires into knights after they prove themselves, but it takes a long time, and nowadays the King has to give his permission. Of course, my master can knight anybody he wants 'cause he was the very first Mouse Knight, but he hasn't knighted anyone except me. Kinda makes me feel special.

BJ said I'm in the same category as my master and can knight whoever I think is worthy, but no way! First of all, I don't much feel knightly, and second, no one is worthy. Not even me. So I'm never gonna knight anyone. No way.

My master writes letters to other parts of the world and sends them by birds or rats, searching for other mice who can read. He's trying to spread the word that mice everywhere should unite. It sounds like a great idea. He says there are billions and billions of mice in the world. More mice than humans. I told that to Shiva and Thor. They asked why we put up with so much from the humans then, and I thought, good question. I asked my master, and he said that the humans had technology. I said, "Why don't we?" He got a funny look on his face and went to see Nemo. I shrugged and went and told the rats that humans had technology. That, and they can squash us.

"Oh. Yeah, that makes sense," they said. He he hee. They sound like me. They call me "Uncle Squibble," even though I'm not that old. I like it. I like those two. They're nice rats.

My master sends the mice that can read back to the city to teach other mice. They catch a ride with the Kind Human when he goes to work. He goes in the morning and comes home late at night. I kinda feel sorry for him. He works all day and goes to school at night (I don't know what he learns). Then he comes home, cleans cages, feeds us, makes sure everything is right with us. Some nights he takes his favorites, and we get to play on the bed while he watches TV and eats his dinner. Oh, the bed!

He stacks the blankets up, and we run all around inside them—huge mountains of blankets full of caves. It's so cool! They're different every time. He puts out treats and water for us, and we always make a game of sneaking over to his table so we can make off with his food. Sometimes it's pizza—yum! The bed is so much fun. My master loves it. My momma loves it. Even Nemo loves it. It's the playground of the masters where everyone forgets their troubles and just has a good time. I always love the bed.

Anyway, the Kind Human takes some mice with him into the city and drops them off. And there's a specific site that he checks every evening before coming home for picking them up again if they're there. This is how my master and BJ communicate with the other mice. It's slow going because so few mice know how to read yet, but it's picking up. My master says in a few months most of the smart mice in the house will be able to read. Then he can really get things going. They have plans, my master and Nemo. Oh yes, they have brilliant plans. Everything is going to turn out just perfect.

Sometimes people ask me if I will take them as a squire. I've had, um, this many offers: 425. I turn them all down. My master says that before I get a squire, which is kind of a holy thing I think, I have to do a pilgrimage. That means traveling a long way and experiencing a bunch of stuff. He says all knights do it in the old stories. His pilgrimage was the long journey to the safe house in the Fields of Fate where we live. I asked him if that could be mine, too, since I was on it with him, but he says a pilgrimage must be made when you are already a knight. I was just a squire. The Squire Squibble. I like how that sounds. The Mouse Knight Squibble doesn't rhyme. But I'd rather be a knight, I guess. So once the weather gets better, I gotta go do this pilgrimage. I don't really want to… I mean, I have to go alone. I hate being alone, and I'm happy here. Everything is perfect here. I have no complaints.

In fact, life just keeps getting better. It always will.

Dreams and Stories

✠

I'm kinda wondering about these weird dreams. They make me write strange stories. Sometimes they make me think strange things.

Yesterday I saw on TV that in another far away place in the world there are these cool critters called foxes. It was an advertisement for the zoo. (I must go there at once!) Besides the fact that they eat rodents (everything eats rodents, okay? We're used to it...) they live in the desert and can burrow faster than a man can follow with the eye. So cool. And they're really cute. They have huge ears and big bushy tails and kinda look like a really big, lean chinchilla with long legs. Oh, and they're fast. I like that. I like fast. They're called Fennec Foxes. They live in Egypt (which I always thought was just a word meaning "far away," but it's actually a real place), and they're awesome. I wonder if they can read, too.

Then I had this awful dream about the cute foxes. They were in tiny, tiny cages. Cages so small they couldn't lie down or stand up. Just sit there. They were being sold by men in a market as food. People were gonna eat them! The poor foxes were miserable and depressed, and they knew they were going to die. I could tell it was agony being in those cages. Then I saw the most terrible thing: I saw a mother fox with her two kits in the same cage. One of the kits had died because there wasn't enough room in the cage for all of them. Some human had crammed them in, and the kit had been squished against the bars and choked to death. The other one couldn't reach its momma's nipples and was wasting away. It shocked me so bad I couldn't think. It brought back a flash of me when I was tiny: I was starving and clutching my momma's breast desperately to keep warm. We were both dying.

I woke suddenly and my girlfriends ran away because I spooked them. They said I was muttering and tossing in my sleep. (Mice don't really do that.) My eyes were wet so I guess I was crying, too.

I went right away to my master and momma and climbed into their cage. I woke my momma and nuzzled up against her soft fur. She held me while I shook.

"What happened, little one?" she asked, worried.

"I... I had a bad dream," I replied.

"Was it that bad to scare a brave Mouse Knight?" she said calmly. I love my momma. She's always so calm.

"It was bad," I said. "It was about cute things suffering under human cruelty."

My momma grew more concerned and chirped to her husband, my master, who came right away from his books.

"Squibble, what happened?"

"I had an awful dream," I said, and explained it to him.

He was thoughtful a moment and then frowned. "Too much TV," he said.

"What?" I asked, surprised.

"Too much TV. The learning channels can be traumatic for us, Squib. Once I saw a documentary on snakes... There was this mouse..."

"This was a dream!" I chirped, upset.

My momma shook her head sadly.

I looked back and forth between them, horrified.

"You mean… this… this really happens?!" I said.

Master nodded his head. "Yes, Squib. The world is cruel to animals."

I was stunned. I described the dream again in detail. "Are you sure it's that bad?" I asked.

"Worse, often," master said. "Kits are left in the desert to starve because they don't have any meat on them worth eating. More often the animals are just exterminated like vermin. They stand no chance against guns."

I knew what a gun was. I had seen that on TV. What my master and momma didn't know is that nothing bad happened to the critters on the show I saw, and I hadn't seen anything else on any "learning channel." The only thing I usually watched on TV was action flicks and stupid dramas. I never knew there was a Learning Channel.

I was silent a long time. Finally I whispered, "It's like the pet stores."

"There are worse things than the pet stores, Squibble," said my master.

"You're safe here, my sweet son," Momma said. She cradled me gently in her arms. She groomed the top of my head. I was looking at the ground, but I'm pretty sure she made a face at my master.

"Of all the places a mouse might be, Squibble, this is the best. You're as safe here as any mouse gets," my master told me.

But I didn't feel safe. I wasn't sure if I'd ever feel entirely safe again.

Anyway, that dream led me to write this story, which I don't understand either.

<u>The Mouse with 1000 Kisses</u>

> Once upon a time there was a mouse who was given a thousand kisses from his beloved human. He treasured them, as mice don't own much. This was all he had.
>
> But the human got sick and died, and the mouse was given first to a shelter, and then to an evil pet store. In the dirty, sad cage he saw mice that had no kisses at all, and never had had any.

He felt sorry for them, and gave one to a mouse who was his friend. The next day, that mouse was picked to feed a snake, and vanished forever.

There was a momma in the cage with little ones. She kept losing her children to the big hand that came in to grab food for the monster snake even though she fought and fought, trying to pull her babies back into the cage. She always lost and would go back to her corner weeping. So he gave her one kiss for her, and one for each baby she had lost.

He gave kisses to all the scared mice before they died, and at night he escaped the cage to give kisses to every other mouse in the store. He wandered about at night, handing out kisses to any mouse that needed them, and he found there was *always* a need. Everyone needed kisses. He gave them to wild mice, poor mice, rich mice, sick mice and healthy mice. He gave them to pretty mice, ugly mice, and even to mean mice (because it made them nice). He found that everyone who got a kiss was happy. And in the morning he would go back to his cage, having no other place to eat or drink.

He couldn't understand why his turn at being snake food hadn't come. One day when he was old and grey, he found he had only two kisses left. He missed his Kind Human, and wished he could see him again and get more precious kisses. He had been a rich mouse but had given it all away. Now he was poor.

The hand came for him that very afternoon. He gave one of his kisses to the hand as it set him in the snake cage. And, as the snake came for him, he gave his last kiss to it, just before he breathed his last breath.

That was the end of the story. It was kinda sad. After thinking about it, I went back the next day and wrote this ending:

The mouse went to Heaven then, where the Mousegod asked if anyone would speak on his behalf so that he might get into heaven. If no one speaks for you, then you have to wander endlessly until you find another life.

The mouse saw hundreds, even thousands of mice come out of the clouds and speak for him, every mouse he had ever given a kiss to. Then the snake came and said he should be allowed into heaven. And then the pet store clerk who had fed him to the snake, too. She said he was the only mouse who had ever kissed her hand, and she begged his forgiveness for not taking him home like she wanted to. Last of all, his old human came out of the light and picked him up. He was robed in white and had a halo over his head. He was a special human, and he had been all along.

"My sweet friend," the human said, "You spent my kisses exactly as I hoped you would. You gave them to those who needed them most, and the world was a better place for your being there." He kissed the mouse once, and all thousand kisses came back and more. "Now come play in my gardens, and let me give you kisses forever."

That was pretty cool, but I kinda wanted to give it another ending on top of that one. I wanted the mouse to volunteer to come back to earth, to keep helping mice like my master did. I think my master is one of those special souls that will just always be here. He could probably have stayed in heaven, or chosen to go on to become even greater things, but he's passed all his tests. He's a "mouse messiah" now, a truly great being. A legend. You can tell I like him, huh? My greatest wish is to be one tenth as great as he is.

I remember having a dream about that… or something.

But to be great takes all kinds of things. Like a vision. My master had one, right after he was made the first Mouse Knight. I don't have a vision. I just like to tell stories, draw, and be happy. I really wanna be great, but… well, I'm worried that maybe it's just not in me. I don't know. I just can't see myself doing all the amazing things that my master has. People say I have, but I was just doing what anyone would do, you know? Nothing special… just what I had to do.

Today I had a first experience. A mouse died and we had a funeral. Now, a mouse dying happens all the time, everyday really, but this mouse was special. It was my aunt, my momma's sister. She had no name, but she was a nice mouse. When mice die, the other mice take care of them, usually burying them out back in the field. Sometimes the Kind Human collects the bodies, but it's no big deal, just part of the natural way of things. Mice die of accidents, disease, and old age. Mice die like humans do, and when they go, their friends and family take care of it. My aunt was special to the Kind Human. (About forty of us are really special to him.) He cried and put her in a new, mouse-sized wood box with bedding in it. He put some Cheerios and millet in there, too. It was "for her journey" my master said.

Then we all gathered together for the funeral (that was the first for me), and Nemo said kind words that sounded really comforting. My momma cried and my master held her. The Kind Human dug a really deep hole (twelve inches!), put the box with my aunt into the hole, and marked it with a stick. He said it wasn't right that she had no name, so he named her Spot, because she had a white spot on her forehead. So she got a name in death, and everyone thought that was good. Except the whole thing bothered me deeply, and I don't know why. I drew this picture afterward:

And then I had bad dreams. Dreams of the skeleton mouse coming and getting everyone. Everyone was stuck in the ground and couldn't get out. They were clawing and clawing, but they were buried alive. In tiny boxes, without food or water.

I gotta get rid of these dreams. They're driving me crazy! I've been messing up in my classes, and I never do that. It's embarrassing. I have a reputation to hold up, being my master's squire and all. I can't make him look bad.

I told Nemo the dreams. He said I'm afraid of dying. I told him that was ridiculous, knights are brave, not afraid of anything. He insulted my mousey dignity. Prophet or no, I almost gave him a good beating right there for that. Of course I would never have hit him, but that's beside the point! He also said there's more going on than I know about, and that he and my master are looking into it.

I peered at him and rattled my tail a bit. He just laughed and rubbed my head. Grrrrr.

Today something truly rare has happened, something I never thought I'd see. It's amazing… the Kind Human asked my master if he would have kids with my momma.

In the conversation, my master told him how hard it was for the mouse community to not breed and begged that a few select others be granted permission, too, just enough to keep the population stable.

Well, the human said okay! Can you believe it? He gave permission for four mice to have one litter each. My master, BJ, Nemo, and… me! BJ declined, saying there were too many mice in the world already without homes. Nemo has a new girlfriend now.

The human got her from the chinchilla ranch. She's kinda uppity, but Nemo likes her. My master and momma have promised me brothers and sisters. Wow! What will it be like? I never knew my other siblings. I often wonder what it would be like if they had lived.

As for me, well, I don't know. I don't really want kids. They're a pain, always crawlin' all over you, chasing each other around and gnawing on everything. (Okay, I still do that, but... whatever.) They eat all the good food. They use all the toys. Master said I wouldn't have to do anything, just "hook up" with a girl (that's what they call it these days on TV). The girl, whoever I wanted, would raise the kids with the help of the rest of the mouse community. My kids would get special treatment. They'd be cherished and loved, always have warmth and water and food. Everyone would want to take a turn caring for them. Everyone wants these kids but me, it seems. The human really likes me, and I appreciate it, but I don't think I'll be making little Squibbles anytime soon. I'm much too busy trying to be a great hero! No time for kids. Nope. Momma and Nemo really think this is a good idea, but they don't run my life!

My master does.

The Runt

✠

Today at fighter practice there was this new mouse. He was really small. Tiny. He looked kinda ragged, like he hadn't washed up. And the weird thing was everyone was whispering about him. They said he was crippled. I couldn't see anything wrong with him just sitting there, but when he moved he couldn't walk in a straight line. He would always turn in circles to the left. He got around that way, but it was bizarre. BJ was teaching him a special "mouse fu" that used only turning and spinning moves. The little guy was eager to learn and very determined, but he just couldn't fight. He didn't have any balance. Then someone said this little mouse was nobility. That meant he was one of my master's brothers!

I crawled closer to watch him. He kinda did look like my master. The pointed nose, the fur quality, the muscular build. But he looked disheveled (means messy), and he was half the size of a small normal mouse. I asked Ghost why he was the way he was, and Ghost said his hearing and balance were destroyed by a disease when he was just a baby. He had wanted more than anything to be a knight. My master let him join the program.

Now I've never disagreed with my master on anything, but that little runt shouldn't even have the chance to be a squire. He just can't fight. He'll never hold his own against a real opponent. He just should give up and live what decent life he can until he dies. He'd die quick as a knight anyway and would probably get other people killed with him. I thought it was arrogant of the crippled mouse to assume he could cut it as a knight. More likely he'd need watching after. As determined as he was, he wasn't getting anything except a good beating in class. The others were going easy on him, so I didn't. I smacked him around good, even bit him a few times, to discourage him from throwing his life away on something he could never achieve. As I was doing it, I said to him, "Don't quit the day job, kid." The mouse didn't say anything back to me at all. The entire day, he didn't say anything. Weird mouse. He was the first one there that evening and the last one there that morning before we all went to bed.

I really don't know why he bothered me so much, so I went to talk with Nemo about it. Nemo said that the mouse was deaf and dumb, on top of having his balance destroyed.

"Well, that's just stupid!" I chirped. "Why would anyone let him become a squire?!"

"He's not a squire," Nemo said. "He's trying to *become* one. It's all he wants in life. Surely you understand that."

"But he's *crippled*," I said. "No one will take him. No one even wants him. He should go away."

"You don't know any of that," Nemo said. "Why do you feel so hostile to the little guy, Squibble? He's aspiring to be like you. He adores you."

I looked up at the sapphire chinchilla, shocked. "No way. Don't tell me you saw that garbage with your powers?"

Nemo looked a little miffed. "No," he said. "Everyone knows it. Scratchy told us himself. He can read and write."

"How can he even hear BJ during lessons if he's deaf?" I asked.

"Your master taught him to read lips," Nemo said.

"That's just lame," I said, flustered. "How can a mouse that can't even walk straight read and write and read lips?!"

"Perseverance."

"Bah."

"Why do you hate him so?" asked Nemo. "What does he make you afraid of?"

"Nothin'!" I said.

"He threatens you somehow. What is it? I've never seen you like this. You like everyone. And everyone likes you."

"He's stupid!"

"He's one of the smartest mice in the house. He's never behaved in any manner short of perfect integrity and courtly manners. He learns faster than almost anyone in the science classes."

"Who needs that stuff anyway…"

"You should be nice to him, Squibble. He really admires you."

"All I'm gonna do is beat it outta him," I growled.

Nemo loomed over me, looking down at me from five times my height. "You won't do that," he said.

"An' whynot?" I quipped.

He rattled his bushy tail like a mouse sending a challenge. "Because if you do, I'll come beat it out of *you*. No knight would ever beat on a crippled mouse doing his best."

My eyes got big. Nemo had never threatened anyone that I had ever heard of. He had the reputation of being very peaceful and Zen-like, but right then he looked pissed. I suddenly had to be elsewhere.

"Ummm… okay," I said. And I left.

After that, I left the little runt alone in class. He'd fail on his own anyway. I went and talked to my master about it, but my master obviously liked the half-grown pawn. So I let it go and changed the subject.

"Master, why did the human put food into Aunt Spot's coffin?" I asked.

"For her journey," he answered as he was reading.

"Yeah, but… she's dead. It's not like she's gonna eat it. Or go anywhere, for that matter."

My master turned to me, took off his glasses, and smiled. "It's an Egyptian thing, Squibble. They believe the soul makes a journey after death to whatever lies beyond."

"Oh," I said. "So the food goes with her?"

"Yeah."

"Oh. Okay. It wasn't very much..."

"She'd find more on her own," he said. "Between here and wherever she believes she's going."

"Where is she going?" I asked. I thought it was a really smart question. I suddenly wanted to be very smart. "I think mice go wherever they believe they'll go," my master said. "I think all beings do. I could be wrong."

"Oh..." I paused. "Where do you think I'll go, Master?"

He chuckled. I loved that. "Wherever you want to, Squibble."

"I'll go wherever you want me to go, Master!" I said eagerly. Then he looked a bit troubled.

"Squibble, you're a grown mouse—and a knight in your own right—but you act like the squire you once were. Are you okay?"

I looked myself over. "Yeah, I think so," I said.

"I mean upstairs," he said. "I worry about you sometimes."

Puzzled, I looked at him. "You think I'm a loon?" I asked.

"No, no," he laughed. "I just wonder why you aren't out creating this greatness for yourself that you want so badly. Doing great things, accomplishing great missions, all that. Pretty soon all your friends are going to be adopted out to good homes, and you're still here."

"But Master," I said, inching toward him, feeling kinda sick, "I don't want to leave you. I like it here."

He put his arm around me, and I felt better instantly. "Kiddo," he smiled, "you never have to leave. No one is going to kick you out. I love having you here. You're my best friend."

"Really?!" I beamed. I was on top of the world.

"Yes, squirt," he said, and scratched my head. "I love you dearly. But I figured you'd want to be on your own and make a name for yourself someday. You could help so many mice. You could be greater than I am."

"Nah..." I said.

"As long as you think like that, you'll never ever try for it, Squib. Have some faith in yourself. Many other mice are trying harder than you are. You're naturally good, and your status here puts you way up on the pecking order. You don't really have to try. But you want to, don't you?"

"Yes," I said truthfully.

"Well, to do that, you have to leave the nest sooner or later."

"You mean my pilgrimage," I said, feeling afraid. I didn't know why.

“Like that,” he said. “Many other mice have already gone on their pilgrimages and some have even returned already. They’re the envy of every mouse. But besides that, don’t you have anything you really like to do, or want to accomplish? I mean, you have very unique and powerful gifts.”

“Ummm…” I decided I could tell him. He *was* my beloved master. “I like to write. And I like to draw.”

“Why, that’s great, Squib! Can I see?”

I was suddenly very ashamed and scared. I couldn’t say no to my master, but what if he laughed at me? I might never write or draw again. I felt trapped.

“Maybe later? I don’t have them right now…” I squibbed.

“Oh, yeah, okay. Sure, Squibble. Anytime at all. You can interrupt whatever I’m doing. Just come by my cage and bring your awesome stuff. I’d love to see it! I’m sure it’s really good!”

“Ummm… okay,” I muttered.

“That’s a very worthy goal, Squibble. Better than taking huge risks and rescuing a few mice at a time. The pen is mightier than the sword.”

“No way.”

“Way. Believe me.”

“I do, Master.” Then as I was going to leave, I turned around at the edge of his cage. “Master?”

“Yes, Sir Squibble?” he said cheerfully.

“Where do you plan on going when you die?” I paused, shuffling about a little. “You know, so I can go there, too.”

He thought about it.

“Well, when King Arthur died, the fates came in their ship to take him away to paradise for all his hard work,” he said. “I guess I’d make my way to the shore—that place I came to on the beach when I was little—and wait for them at dusk. Either that or maybe I’d like to come back as a mouse and live a normal, responsibility-free rodent life.”

“Ha ha!” I giggled. “Like you’d ever get away with that, great Master!”

“Oooo, don’t curse it, Squib!” he winced. “I really would like to go to paradise, check it out, then maybe come back here and just hang out. No big destiny, no giant task to do.”

“But you’re… the Mouse Knight. The Mousegod appointed you.”

“Well, maybe he’ll consider it a job well done when I die and give me a vacation. Could you ask him for me, Squib?”

"I will!" I chirped, "And I'll be waiting there for you when you die, to greet you an' all that, with Bigfat an' Mike!"

My master looked seriously at me. "Squibble, you have to outlive me. My work is done. Yours has yet to begin."

"Noway." I stated it as fact.

"Yes," he said. "It is most likely I'm going to be waiting for you when you cross the Rainbow Bridge, Squibble. I'm older than you—"

"By like two months!"

"My health isn't what it was. That bad cold I got on the last part of the quest? That was Mycoplasma pulmonis."

I felt a tinge of fear, a stab of adrenaline to my gut that told me something bad was in the air. That name had an awful ring to it that I could not explain. I just hated it. I cocked my head to let my master know that I didn't understand.

"It's a disease," he said. "A bad one. There is no cure."

"But I didn't get it," I whined, suddenly very afraid.

He smiled. "You were stronger than me."

"I didn't get picked up and smashed by a hawk several times either!" I protested.

"Okay," he gave in. "But I have this cough that won't go away now, and I can't run like I used to. I'm weaker than I was, my faithful friend. That disease took something out of me. You'll probably outlive me."

"But... you got over it, Master."

"One never gets over mycoplasma, Squib. It stays there forever, waiting to come back."

"But if there's no cure, then..." I swallowed, eyes bugging out.

He looked back at his books. "It's fatal," he said softly, "eventually."

I threw myself into his fur. "Oh! Oh Master!" I choked on my words and felt a huge lump of something really heavy in my tummy. "Don't leave me!"

He held me tight. "I won't, Squibble, not yet. The Kind Human has medicine. He takes us to a vet if we're really sick. I'm not kicking off anytime soon. All I'm saying is that you're probably going to live a long time, my young, strong, brave mouse. If you don't die doing something amazingly courageous and stupid, that is. Someday you're going to have to deal with it. Someday we all do."

"Noway!" I chirped. "No way no chance no way!" And I trotted off, pretending to be very happy.

"Love you, Squib," he called after me, sounding amused.

It was only afterward that I thought about our talk and realized a few things. By "unique and powerful gifts" he had probably meant my weird ability to see the spirit world when I'm whacked out. He probably wasn't talking about my art or writing. He hadn't seen it yet. Nobody had.

Knowing my master was sick and would someday die was the beginning of a long road, the rest of this story really. It was the beginning of my childhood's end. I hated it. I felt unsafe, like a mouse out during the day without cover.

I realized some other things, too.

He liked that little crippled mouse because the runt was trying to do something great with his life, against all odds. Just like my master. Then a horrible thought hit me: what if my master took him as a squire? He's the only one that might. I'd be a laughingstock. He might, too. Oh, I hoped that wouldn't happen.

Nemo's words really stuck with me. They always did. Why did that little mouse worry me so? It wasn't like he could hurt me. Even if some idiot did take him as a squire, what did it really matter? The midget would get killed in the first real fight he came across. What was it to me? Nothing, I thought. So I tried to forget about it.

But it bugged me really bad. Why *wasn't* I accomplishing great things? Why wasn't I living up to my potential? I knew I could be great. I knew I was *meant* to be great, I just knew it. It was all I wanted in the whole world. I mean, I love drawing and writing, but… that was meant to tell stories. Maybe stories of being great. Yeah…

Meanwhile I was treading water like a loser. "If I'm gonna do something great, stupid," I said to myself, "it's gotta change." I knew it was true, but… I was a happy loser. I liked my life as it was. Why did it have to change?

I would have to get over my fears. The idea scared me, isn't that funny? I would be done with fighter practice in a few weeks. I was going to graduate. Right after that, I'd be expected to go on my pilgrimage. That's when the other knights went. Every month at least one or two went off in some direction, searching for their true path. That's what a pilgrimage is for, to find your true destiny.

I wondered as I was falling asleep what mine would be. As I drifted off, the last thing that came to me was that my master really did love me. He truly did.

And that made me sleep like a baby.

Ceremonies and Celebration

✠

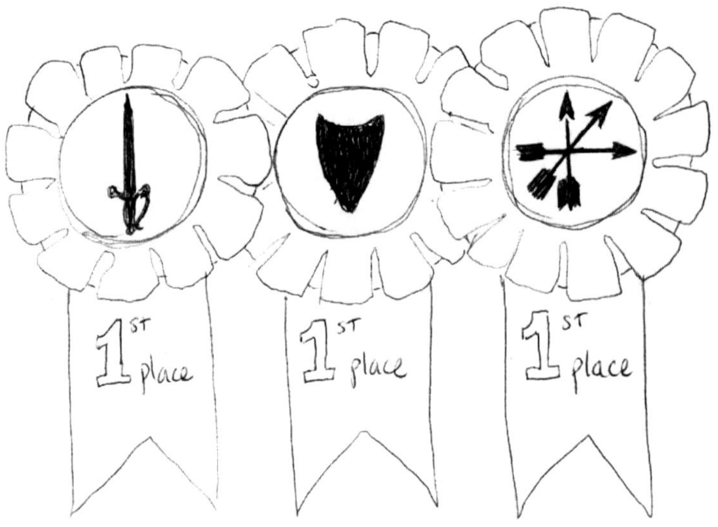

Well, alot has happened in the last week. My class graduated from fighter school. I was at the top of the class of course. The experience was slightly ruined by the fact that runt boy came in second. He wasn't even supposed to graduate in my class—he started late—but BJ said he had earned it. Boy, I've never been so insulted. Anyway, I resisted the urge to kick him off the podium at the ceremony where I got a ribbon for beating all the other mice in sword fighting. I won shield, spear, and missile weapons, of course, with my trusty ol' slingshot. Never leave home without it. Stompy won hand-to-hand. She floored 60 mice by knockout to win. Yow.

Then I got my first taste of ice cream when we were celebrating! Woweee! Ice cream! It was so neat. The Kind Human put a bowl down for us and we lapped it up until our snouts were frozen. It tastes so great. You know, five thousand years mice have been living with humans and I bet that's the first time a mouse has gotten ice cream! What's up with that, huh? We've gotten a raw deal.

Well, suddenly, right in the middle of the celebration (and according to tradition), one of the Mouse Knights stood up and took Ghost as his squire. Then another knight stood up and took Stompy as a squire! Then another took someone else, and so it went—the finest were chosen. That little flea, Scratchy, wasn't though, and he had the nerve to look at me the whole time. Ha! He was so disappointed. His head was downcast, and he was crying. That'll teach him. He'll quit now for sure. I was afraid my master would take him, but he was only at the ceremony for a short time, and then he was called away by a messenger mouse over something important. It must have been real important, too. He wouldn't have left my graduation for anything stupid.

Nemo announced the rodents who had recently been adopted to good homes in the city. Shiva and Thor were among them! My boys, my playmates… they'd be leaving soon to have great lives as loved pets in a good home. I was happy for them but kinda sad over losing them, too.

Then the three knights who had just graduated stood up, and each one announced their pilgrimage. One was going to the mountains far away. He would return when it began to get cold again. Another would go visit the ants and bees and spread word of our alliance to all the hives and nests that didn't know about it yet. The third one was going to go see the ocean. After they finished, Nemo looked at me. I swallowed hard and stood up.

"I'm… going, too," I said. Cheers and hoots greeted me from the audience. One mouse I couldn't spot yelled, "About time!" I'd find him later and bite his rump.

"Yeah," I continued, "I'm going to go to… ummm… the city!" More applause. I was making this up as I went along. The city was dangerous. I couldn't think of a more daring quest. "To free mice from pet stores, spread the word of our existence, and to search out great evil and… and destroy it!" Mice stood up, hopped around, chirped and squeaked. Everyone loved it. I did, too. It sounded grand. A worthy pilgrimage!

After the celebration I went to my master's cage to find out what was such a big deal that he'd had to leave, and it was being guarded by ten armored mice! They let me in (lest I put the hurt on em'), and Master came out of my momma's nest. His face was flushed, he was breathing funny, and he looked stunned but happy. Very happy.

"Come inside, Squibble. Be very quiet!" He dragged me into the nest box.

It was dark inside, but I could see and smell the babies. My momma had had her litter. She had five children. Tiny, wee things, the little pinkies. They squirmed and squibbed under her for milk. She smiled at me. It was a dream come true. I gaped. Those were my brothers and sisters. I had a family!

They were so small and fragile. Was I ever that small and fragile? My momma licked me. She looked tired. I got to sniff one of the babies who was white. Of all of them, only one was white. I asked my master why.

"Well, we don't know, Squib," he said. "It shouldn't be white. Your momma is a cinnamon colored mouse, and I'm an albino. By all rights, having a white child is impossible."

"Then he's a miracle," I said. I looked at the little white thing. He was cute. And special somehow. I knew it.

My master smiled broadly. "Yes, I guess he is. They all are."

I touched all of the little mice, and my master said I should bless them. I asked what that meant, and he said, "Say something good about them so they have fine lives. You're a knight. It's proper."

I thought about it a moment. It sounded like a job for Nemo, but I was sure the Prophet would get to it soon enough. My blessing was just for fun. My master was indulging me, letting me feel important. So I did it.

"May all your children live worthy, healthy and righteous lives, from their first day to their last, my master."

He hugged me. I beamed. "That was a great blessing, Squibble. Thank you, Sir Knight!"

I trembled with glee. "Oh, thank you, Master!"

Eventually I had to leave to let my momma rest, but I would come back. I would always come back. I couldn't forget the faces of those teeny little mice, my family.

As I was leaving to go home, there was Nemo outside the cage. Beside him was Scratchy! The little twerp. He must have done something to get me in trouble. Well, it wasn't gonna work. I hadn't done nothin'!

I zipped up to them both, making it clear I could run in a straight line. "Help you?" I said to Nemo. What if he was here to beat me up? But I hadn't done anything!

Nemo smiled and looked at me kindly. "Squibble, little Scratchy was heartbroken that he wasn't chosen as a squire. He was second in his class and worked harder than anyone to achieve it. Nobody chose him because they all thought you would take him. He didn't want to come, but I dragged him here to ask you if you might consider—"

"Hell no," I said sternly.

Scratchy turned to go. He looked ashamed. As he should be.

Nemo caught him with his tail. He looked angry at me now.

"Squibble, you're jealous," he said.

"Of that little runt? No way!" I said. Scratchy looked mad then, and even had the nerve to rattle his tail at me! Why I'd...

Nemo held me back with his paw. It was like a cartoon where a big guy holds a little kid away by the top of his head. I was pushing hard, but I just couldn't go forward to teach that little punk a lesson! My feet spun under me, and I fell down.

I was so humiliated. "I hate that little cripple!" I chirped. "He'll never be a knight! *Never!* I'll challenge him myself if I have to!"

Nemo took Scratchy up in his arms. The little mouse was in tears. The prophet stared harshly at me. "You have some hard lessons to learn, Squibble, knightly lessons. Humility and compassion, for starters. Your honor wouldn't be worth one piece of grain if you challenged a crippled mouse. Especially after he beat you."

Oh! Oh, the nerve! How dare he say that to me! I got up to kick his sapphire ass, but he was already hopping off. I was furious! I went down to the basement and beat up a bunch of big mice. Then I beat up some more. I jumped into the sparring ring and didn't leave until dawn. Boy! I might even have been able to hit BJ, I was so mad.

Afterward, when I was worn out and trembling with my rushing thoughts, I wondered, "Why was I so mad?" It sure didn't feel good.

What bothered me the most was that Nemo had never been wrong before. Well, there's a first time for everything. Yessir.

Tangent: Something Slithery This Way Comes

✠

I had another dream that night. I was very disturbed before I went to sleep, and I am sure that made it much worse.

I was in the city. It was my pilgrimage, but I couldn't find anybody. No people, no mice, no rats, no animals… The whole place was empty. I wandered a long time with no food or water. It was very cold even though I thought it was supposed to be summer.

Then I came to a huge hole in the ground. I mean, it was human-scale huge, like, a mile across. And inside, piled on top of each other, were humans and animals. All dead, all burning.

I gasped out loud, and out of the shadows came ragged mice, starving, dirty, and beaten. One of them was my master! He looked ancient… bent over and ragged—

"Squib! Come quickly! You'll catch the plague standing there!"

I rushed into the alleyway where there were many other mice, all looking worse than the first group. It was dark. The sky wasn't as bright as it should be. The air smelled awful, I suddenly realized. Burning flesh and fur… yuck!

"Master, what… what happened?!" I exclaimed.

"The Black Mouse," he wheezed. He was gravely sick. I felt a pang of terror stab me in the heart. "It brought a plague down on us, then a famine. Finally, a war…"

"The four horsemen of the apocalypse," said Shiva. He was missing an eye and an ear. He wore nightmarish armor made of red metal. He looked burned. And old. "It was conquest at first—raids, attacks, terrorist stuff—then the rest. He had them out of order, but the idea was the same."

"Where's… where's momma? Thor? The children?" I asked, frightened.

"All dead, Squibble," my master coughed. Blood sprayed out of his nose and mouth. I recoiled in horror. "They died."

"Oh… Oh NO!" I squeaked. "No! How? Why? Why did this happen?!"

Shiva looked up at me with his one eye. He looked hardened by pain, like polished steel hard. He looked like the god of destruction.

"Because you forgot to warn us, Uncle. It was your job to champion us, remember? Your job!"

I was in utter shock. I remembered my dream with Mike. I started backing away, but their eyes followed. A strange, psycho mouse in camouflage clothing was cleaning up my master's face as he sank to his knees.

"But… that… that was just a dream," I whispered.

Shiva shook his head side to side.

I nodded vigorously, as if insisting on my point might make it true. But the other mice all gazed at me with contempt. Shiva was right. I had accepted the task.

"It's been two and a half years since you said you'd be our champion, mouse," Shiva hissed. "Humanity found out about us. They tried to kill every last rodent on the earth out of pure panic."

"They… they wouldn't do that," I said, knowing otherwise.

"They did. Apes. Fear of the unknown. Rather than face their brutality and ugliness, they tried to wipe out the witnesses. Over ten billion of them."

"What happened?" I choked.

Shiva smiled then, a wicked, evil grin I'd never seen on a rat before.

"We fought back."

I turned to look out across the cityscape. The buildings were torn down. The horizon was burning. The sky was blood red. The ground was brown with dried blood. It was a nightmare.

"How?" I screamed. "How did rodents do all this?!"

My master coughed and crawled to me with his blood-caked face. "Technology," he croaked. "We had to fight back. We had to."

Then, all at once I remembered the dream before Mike, and my master saying this was all caused by…

"The Black Mouse! It's evil! It's coming to get us!" I shrieked.

At that very moment, as if I had summoned it, the shade of that dead mouse stood in the back of the alley, covered by darkness, its fiery eyes burning like hot coals.

The mice reacted immediately, but it wasn't fast enough. BJ, first to attack, was cast aside like garbage. Twenty mice went down fighting, all of them Mouse Knights. Nemo squared off with the demon mouse in a sorcerous duel of wills and faded away to nothingness. Finally, there was no one left. My master flung himself against me to shield my body with his own. From behind, the horrible mouse ran him through. A cold black sword, burning like it was just taken out of the forge, pierced my master's body and went through my chest, stopping just a millimeter from my own heart. I was stabbed. My master was dying. I felt such pain. My master looked up into my eyes.

"You can't let this happen, Squib. You're our only hope."

Then he died and collapsed on me in a bloody mess. The Black Mouse pulled back for the blow that would end my life and swung.

Clang! The arcing black weapon was parried by a shining, blazing sword of golden fire! Holding that holy sword I saw a mouse in the most magnificent armor. It was made of lobster shell and snake scales like most knightly armor mice wear, but also made of steel. The mouse had a flowing green cloak and a magnificent helm on his white head.

The new mouse beat the shade back with blow after mighty blow. He fought as though possessed. He fought like a warrior god. I had never seen such skill, not even from my master or BJ. The Black

Mouse stood no chance. Fury showed on this new mouse's face, glaring from the slit in his crusader's helm. It was intense. This holy warrior would never give up. The Black Mouse turned and fled.

The warrior mouse ripped the helm off his head and lowered his sword for a moment to gaze at me. He looked familiar. He looked beautiful and strong.

"Get up, Squibble! Wake up and save us!"

"Who are you?" I gasped. He smiled. I knew that face! "I am your own blood," he replied. "You named me, brother. Surely you know me now."

I did! I did know. "You're… *Percival!*" I said. "You're the… the Lord of the Mouse Knights!"

He nodded, yanked his helmet back on, and turned to pursue the Black Mouse.

"Prevail, Squibble, mighty prophet and champion of us all!" he yelled as he ran off. He was so fast! "Prevail!"

Then two tiny paws were grabbing me, pulling me away from the alley and into a single beam of sunlight reaching down out of the sky. The mouse pulling me was taking me to that light in wide, rotating circles. I looked up into the face of Scratchy, wearing armor and bearing a sword at his side.

Just as I hit the light, I heard Percival's voice echoing, "Prevail…"

Then I woke up in a cold sweat.

And I forgot the dream immediately.

Surely I'm Forgetting Something

✠

All I knew was that morning I was troubled. I wanted to go see Nemo, but that big dummy had insulted me. I went instead to my master. He was really busy bringing my momma food and drink.

"Hi, Squib! Help me carry this stuff..."

I did. We went into the nest. My mom was really tired and thin looking. Some other girl mice had come over and offered to help care for the babies—lay across them, keep them warm, all that. I was shocked by how tired my momma looked. My master fed her and groomed her. She went to sleep under his tender care.

Later we snuck out into the main section of the cage by the big blue wheel my master loved to run on. He looked at me as if he knew something was wrong.

"Yeah," I said. "I… I'm having really bad dreams."

"Why do you think that is?" he said. "Worried about the pilgrimage? You don't leave for another month, until spring gets warm enough."

"Nah, not that," I said quietly. "I'm confused, Master. I don't feel like myself lately. I hate that little runt, Scratchy, and I never hate anyone. I don't want to leave here, but I do want to be a great hero, like you, with all my heart."

He smiled that reassuring, confident smile that always made me feel better. "Maybe you're just nervous? Or is this serious?"

"Serious," I said without hesitation.

He nodded. "Okay. We have to take this to Nemo then."

I shook my head. "Nah."

He cocked his head and looked the "Why?" look at me.

"Because he's stupid," I said.

Master laughed. He knew "stupid" was my catchall word for anything I didn't like. "Not getting along with the Prophet?" he said. "I don't always either."

"Really?" I asked. It was more understanding than I had dared hope for.

"Oh, yeah," he said. "Being a prophet is no fun. You always tell people what they don't want to hear. They don't listen, and then the future you saw comes true, despite your best efforts…"

"OW!" I chirped, and bent over.

"Squibble, what's wrong?" He held me up.

"My head hurts!" I said. "It was what you said! It made me scared!"

My master has only looked seriously worried a few times in his life, but this was one of them.

"Like him or not, we're going," he said.

"Yes, Master," I whimpered. My head felt like someone had hit it with a baseball bat. In moments we were at Nemo's cage.

"We'd like to see Nemo," my master said to Nemo's girlfriend. She stood blocking the entrance. "He's sleeping, mouse." Her tone was stuffy and disrespectful. If I hadn't felt so awful I'd have bit her rump. My master was patient and kind.

"It's very important. Please wake him. He'll want to see us."

She snaffed (blew air out her nose—it's a chinchilla insult) and went to get Nemo.

"You should have beat her up, Master!" I said.

"Life isn't about who you can beat up, Squibble."

Nemo appeared at the cage door. His girlfriend looked chastised. "I'm sorry," he said. "Come in."

We explained everything to him. I told him I couldn't remember my dreams, but they were driving me crazy.

"You have them every night?" he said.

"Yeah. Some are worse than others," I said.

"Do you remember any of them?" he asked.

"No, not since a few months ago. Pretty much when I got to this house, or a little bit after, I don't remember them anymore."

He and my master looked at each other, as if communicating on some level I couldn't hear or see.

"Squibble, do you know what hypnosis is?" Nemo asked.

I shook my furry head.

"It's kind of like magic," my master said to me. "Nemo can put you in a trance—it's like sleeping—to get you to remember your dreams. You won't even remember it all unless you want to."

"Wow! Cool!" I said. "Can you teach me to do that?"

"Maybe someday," Nemo smiled. "It has many other uses. It can be used to delve into the deep unconscious mind, where no one goes themselves. It's possible to convince someone they can lift huge masses of weight or not feel cold in the snow, and believing it, they then possess these new powers."

"I gotta have it," I said. "I'll be careful. Promise!"

Nemo went on smiling. "I'll consider it. Meanwhile, may I hypnotize you?"

"Sure," I said. Then I paused. "It won't hurt, will it?"

"Not a bit."

"Okay. Can you make me not cold in the snow?"

"Of course," the prophet said. "Come over here and look into my eyes."

I did.

"Well, what are you waiting for?" I asked.

"We're done, Squibble." My master was sitting next to Nemo. He hadn't been there a moment before. They both wore expressions of serious worry. I suddenly felt weird.

"Way?" I said, amazed.

"Way," my master said, trying to smile.

"How long was I out for?" I giggled.

“Three hours,” they said together.

I gasped. That was a *long* time! It must be almost dawn. Soft orange light was filtering in through the windows. They were right.

“What did you find out?” I asked.

“You asked us not to tell you,” my master said.

“What?!” I exclaimed. “That’s *stupid*! Tell me!”

Nemo shook his head. “Squibble, we heard some pretty intense things while you were under. We spoke to Bigfat, and to you. But not you right now, you from the future.”

“No waaaay!” I gaped.

“Yes,” Nemo said. “And they told us some very disturbing things, and they would not even reveal everything to us, which is even more disturbing.”

“No way did you talk to a future me,” I said. “That’s from South Park. I’ll behave, I promise. Now tell me what happened.” I smiled.

They looked at me in silence. They were serious! My mouth hung open. There was long silence. “We cannot tell you yet what we heard,” my master said. “Please trust us, Squibble. You told us it would change everything and upset you deeply.”

“*I* told you? Oh, this is confusing! You guys are weirdos.”

Nemo nodded at me, then looked at my master. They nodded at each other. We all laughed. “Yep,” Nemo said. “That’s for sure.”

“Will I stop having these dreams?” I asked.

“No,” Nemo said, “but I think I can teach you to control them. And maybe much more on top of that.”

“Cool! Hey, what was my future self like?” I asked.

They stopped laughing. My master looked at Nemo, and Nemo didn’t know what to say. My master looked at me and smiled carefully.

“He was a great hero,” he said.

“Oh, YAAAAY!” I shouted. “COOL!”

I grinned, cocking my head. “Yeeeaaah… I know you guys are putting me on. The hypnosis didn’t work. It’s okay, you can admit it. Squibble isn’t that lame. I catch on to some things.” My master came over and put his arm around me. “Yeah,” he said. “That could be.”

“He he he! I knew it,” I said. “You guys are a riot.” I went hopping off toward my cage. “But I’ll still learn it, Nemo, ‘cause it sounds way cool.”

Nemo nodded.

I waved to them. They waved back.

Then they vanished from sight as I descended the ladder from the table.

Those guys… what jokers.

When I got to the play area it was empty. I went to the back yard and saw that the new class of fighters had just finished their practice. It was dawn. Everyone was going to sleep. Where had those three hours gone?

Suspicious, I went outside and sat in some snow.

I sat there for half an hour.

I felt warm and comfortable.

My heart gave an uncomfortable lurch in my chest. Stunned, I went back into the house. Everything seemed somehow… not real. I knew this was how I felt when my powers happened. I looked around. Ahead I saw many mice around my master's cage. They were all pearly and glowing.

Bigfat was there and glowing, too. I kinda looked at him like he had three eyes. I didn't mean to, but I was wigged out. I nodded to him as I approached the cage. He nodded back and smiled at me. I looked up and saw Mike (in his angel form) standing over us. He smiled, too.

I went inside and saw Nemo sitting there with my master and a few other mice, mostly my master's family. BJ had just arrived.

"What's going on?" I said, breaking the silence.

"Oh, Squibble," Master said. "We couldn't find you. We're naming the children. This is Leaf, and this is Branch," he pointed to a girl and a boy. I nodded. "This is Muadib," he pointed to another tan boy. I smiled. Good name. He pointed to another tan girl. "And this is Gaia." I stepped closer. The last child, the tiny white baby, was squirming in my mother's grasp. "We can't seem to figure out this one," he said, looking at me.

I stepped forward with all eyes on me. Feeling like I was watching myself in a movie, I knelt down and put my hand on the little albino's head.

"His name is Percival," I said, "Lord of the Mouse Knights."

Preparing to Leave Paradise

✠

It's nearly spring. The air is warmer. The bees and ants know it already, and mice can sense it, too. Every once in a while a field mouse will pop out of the grass and stare at us training out in back of the house, but for the most part they are invisible. The field is full of them. There may be millions. We'd never know it. They're stealthy as ghosts and ten times as fast. For some reason they revere us, often leaving gifts of grain or fluffy cotton. I guess it's touching. Without their help we would never have made it to the house. I wish they were friendlier, but their lives are hard, and it makes them skittish.

Soon I will be leaving for my pilgrimage. I'm kinda scared. I took on too much maybe. Nobody else wanted to go to the city. It's very dangerous. A mouse can so easily get run over by a car, or eat poison (set out by humans to kill mice), or any number of other things. I remember the city from my youth, but back then there was a mouse kingdom underground. Everyone stuck together. Nowadays the city is an abyss of dangers for a lone mouse. Cats, rats… even other mice. But mostly people. People are scary. I hope I don't meet any people.

Now that's kinda silly, eh? Hoping I don't meet people in a human city, where I'm going to free mice from their tyranny. Yeah. Okay, Squibble.

Well, today a gnarly thing happened. (Gnarly means intense.) Fighter practice was finishing just before dawn in the early light when out of the bushes jumped a feral cat! That's a cat that's gone wild. It was starving, and it devoured three mice before anyone could act. BJ grabbed several javelins and hurled them at the beast, but that just made it mad. It came for BJ but couldn't catch him. He yelled "Retreat! Run for the house!" as he kept the cat busy, but it was sure to spell the end for him. The king was going to die protecting his people, which I suppose would be glorious and all, but there were some there who wouldn't have it. Two of the knights who had announced their pilgrimage ran from the house, in full armor, and drew their swords. They engaged the cat to defend BJ, against his orders. One lost hard—he died. The other struck a mighty blow against the cat's leg by sticking the plastic cocktail sword right into its ankle. Boy did that cat howl! Then it struck out with its claws. The second knight lived, thanks to his armor, but he won't be fighting anytime soon. Or going on his pilgrimage.

BJ hit the monster in the face with five lances, but it kept coming. The king was tiring, and the reinforcements from the house were going to be too slow. I was one of them. I was loading my slingshot and yelling for my master when I saw what happened.

Two streaks of gold and white shot past us. Shiva and Thor jumped upon the cat without hesitating for even a tenth of a second. The cat was surprised by the attack, but even more so by its ferocity. The rats fought like insane psychopaths. They tore that cat several new holes and took its eye. They wouldn't let go or let down. They would certainly have died eventually, but for BJ. The king ran under the cat, and while the twins were in mortal combat, he struck it a deadly blow to the side with a javelin. It screeched and ran away into the field with the rats still on it. They dealt it a few last blows, then dashed back to the house, snatching up BJ on the way without missing a step. The king was exhausted. Everyone was.

That evening, for their heroism in combat against a mighty foe, and for saving the king's life, the rat twins got what they had wanted all their lives. They were knighted.

My master himself made them knights with the blessing of the king, to the cheers and homage of the entire household. Those two boys blushed so hard their golden hoods turned red. They were the heroes of the day and instant legends. They had not suffered one scratch from the cat. We all celebrated that night, and everyone had to call them "Sir"—"Sir Thor... Sir Shiva." They loved it. Their momma immediately set to work on their armor suits, because in a week they were to be adopted out to a loving home in the city. The Kind Human had found them a good place to live, happy and carefree, for the rest of their days. No rodent could ask for more. It would be paradise.

We were all going to miss them, especially me. They were like my own sons I never had. But who could deny them a good life as a loved pet? Every rodent wants that, and so few of us get it. People request rodents from the Kind Human all the time, but he says 99% of them are liars just looking for snake food. He screens people very carefully these days, and he'd never give any of us to anyone without being absolutely sure it was a safe, loving home we would go to.

It's funny how fragile he thinks we are. Mice are pretty tough, but he handles us like we're made of glass. And he's tough as nails. I mean, nothing can take out a human, but especially *this* human. He's young, healthy, and big. He wears the black hides of other huge animals he's killed on his back and legs. He rides a gigantic thing called a Harley Davidson when he's not using his truck. Taming that Harley must have taken some work, I tell you. It's really loud.

I had a few lessons with Nemo over the last few days, learning some tricks with my breath, and how to do hypnosis. I practice it on the girls sometimes, but it doesn't work. I think it's a bunch of hogwash maybe. Nemo tells me about other things—deep, wise things—but I don't really get it. I have a hard time sitting still and listening. It was the same in philosophy class.

I have lots of girlfriends. About... ummm... maybe a hundred. Most of them are just fun to be with for a little while, maybe chase them around… They squeak alot. It's fun. I don't really take 'em too seriously, but there's this one. She won't give up. She hangs around all the time, and she's really persistent. I have to tell her to go away in the morning, because she actually follows me to my cage! I'm like, "What do you want?" an' she says, "I want to have your children." An' then I laugh. Nemo or Master must have sent her to try to seduce me. He he he. Won't work on ol' Squibble. I make her go home each night. She's really pretty, and she likes me alot, but I've got better things to do with my life than be crawled on by little furballs. No thanks.

She is really cute though… and really nice to me. She even brings me cheese that she begs off the human. She doesn't eat it herself. She brings it to me. I don't know any mice that would do that. Kinda makes me wonder. I've taken to calling her Favorite, because she's my favorite of the giant horde of girls who are after me. But no one's gonna get me!

Well, today it was time to say goodbye to Shiva and Thor. Everyone who was anyone was there to say goodbye. They were given their armor, weapons, and shields. The shields were blank. I told them they needed a crest—a symbol to represent their knighthood and what they believed in. They said they'd think about it, maybe a picture of the house… Then they were gone, taken by the Kind Human in his truck to the city and their new home. I'm happy for them. They're getting what everyone dreams about. The Kind Human has only so much time, and he's real busy (like a mouse) all the time. He hardly has time to hold us every day, even his favorites. He often feels bad about it, but he's given us this perfect place, this paradise of our own. That's enough. Shiva and Thor, they'll get personal attention now, every day until they're old and ready to die. It sure can't get any better than that, no sir.

Afterward, the masters and high-ups held a secret meeting about something important. I snuck to the door (such a mousey thing to do!) and listened, but all I could hear was arguing and even heated words! They were coming from my master! Ohhh boy, I'd never heard or seen him mad before, an' it scared me to think of it, so I decided not to stay. Besides, I'd catch it for sure if I were caught. When I turned around to go, there was Scratchy behind me, watching me.

Darned pest! He'd turn me in for sure. I got mad. I went up to him and stared down at him. I'm a small mouse, but he barely came up to my chest with both of us sitting up.

"You better not tell on me, twerp," I said threateningly, and rattled my tail.

He shook his head no and held up his practice shield. He was either asking me to spar or challenging me to a fight, I couldn't tell which. I felt red-hot rage boil up in my chest. I kicked him hard in the face. He squeaked and fell back, stunned. I jumped over him and shook my paw in his face.

"You little runt! You ever challenge me again an' I'll bite you so hard you'll feel it for a whole month!"

He started crying. I knew he couldn't take it. "You'll never be a knight!" I yelled as I turned my back on him and left. "Knights don't cry!"

Later that night I was hanging out with my master and his kids. They were crawling all over me. (See? Told you!) But it was kinda fun. They were really cute. Little Branch and Percival really liked me. I figured Scratchy would tell for sure now, an' it bugged me so much that I couldn't help but let it out.

"So I was listening to the meeting, and... then I kicked Scratchy!" I blurted suddenly.

My master stopped his reading and looked up sharply.

"What?" he said.

The kids scrabbled off me in a heartbeat. They sensed the tension coming. They ran and hid in the nest.

"I was a sneaky mouse an' listened to your meeting a little bit... an' then Scratchy challenged me to a fight so I kicked the little turd," I said.

My master first looked angry, then concerned. "What did you hear, Squibble?" he asked. He took off his reading glasses. It was always serious when he did that. I felt scared in my gut. I knew it. I was in trouble.

"Nothing," I said.

"Really?" he asked, and leaned forward to put his squinty voodoo eye on me, the look that I couldn't lie to even if I wanted to.

"Swear!" I said, and took the submission posture. "Just heard you yellin' 'bout somethin'. Couldn't tell words..."

"Okay," he said. He seemed to relax a little. "Squib... I'm sorry we're keeping things from you. I can't explain why, but you must trust me that it's important. I wouldn't keep anything from you if it wasn't very, very important."

I smiled. I wasn't busted after all. "Oh, I know, Master. I trust you totally!"

He smiled back. "Thank you, Squibble. Are you preparing for your pilgrimage? You have to pack yet. Your mom and I have some things for you… Hey, did you say Scratchy challenged you?"

"Oh, yeah," I said, "but I kicked him for his insolence. He's not even a squire! Challenging a knight to a fight! The pleeb!"

"What was he doing when he challenged you, Squib?"

"He brought me his shield. A practice shield from fighter school. All he's got since he didn't make it to squire, he he he."

My master lowered his head and shook it sadly.

"Squibble, he wasn't challenging you. He was asking you to teach him. A challenge would have been a sword."

I felt a pang of guilt. "Oh."

My master put his paw on me. "I know you feel jealous of him…"

"Do not!" I blurted.

"Squibble!" he said sharply.

"Sorry, Master…"

"I know you have strong feelings about Scratchy, but understand he idolizes you. You can break his heart without even trying. He grew up wanting to *be* you, Squibble."

"Well, that's stupid," I said. Only I can be me…

"No, it's not," Master said. "Many, many mice want to be you, only he had the courage to actually try. He's crippled for life, and he had the guts to actually enter fighter school, and try for squirehood. He was offered the title before he even graduated, you know."

"No way!" I said, shocked.

"Way," master said. "Four different knights offered him squirehood. All of them asked to take him as soon as he graduated. He was very good at the techniques BJ taught him. You should see him fight."

"Why didn't he take the title?" I said, perplexed.

My master smiled. "He told us, not in so many words, that he would take no one as a master except you, Squibble."

"No way…"

"Way."

I lowered my head. That was intense. I'd never seen a mouse so determined. Maybe I had been a butthead. Nah.

"I don't want him!" I said.

"Your loss," my master said. "And sadly, his, too."

"Yeah!" I said vehemently.

"You're going to have to deal with those issues someday, Squib," he said.

“Or what, Master?” I asked, genuinely curious.

“Or they’ll come get you. Like demons,” he said, smiling. I knew he meant it, but he was funny. He leapt upon me playfully and gently bit my neck. “Demons!” he chirped. “Get ‘em before they get you, Squib! Always take the first blow against demons! Ha ha ha!” He wrestled me around, and we had a great time of it. I squeaked and laughed and cried when he tickled me. Oh, how I love him! And I feel so loved because of him. What would I ever do without my master?

I woke up the next evening and couldn’t find Shiva and Thor. I’d had a disturbing dream about them, but I couldn’t remember what it was. I was really bothered about that for a moment, that I couldn’t remember my dreams, but then I remembered that my two favorite rats were gone, and I’d probably never see them again. I was sad.

Oh, it’s nonsense, though. I could go see them anytime I want… just get a ride into the city from the Kind Human, and ask him to take me to see Shiva and Thor… He’d probably do it. I know he goes to school in the city somewhere, after work and on weekends. He could drop me off, I’d play with the boys, and he could pick me up after. Yeah. I worry alot for nothing.

So I was walking around, going to check out the field and the battle practice. It’s hard not going anymore… Now I’m supposed to go to the masters’ classes, but I don’t really feel like a master, so I sometimes don’t go. I came down into the basement by one of the many mousey backways (holes chewed in the walls and floors) and heard some mice talking in hushed tones.

“Shiva and Thor would tear us to pieces,” a mouse said. His voice sounded familiar.

“But they aren’t here anymore to protect him.”

“Nemo is, and so is ‘the master’, himself.”

“But someone needs to teach that arrogant little jerk that he isn’t all that special. I hate it how he parades around!”

“He doesn’t contribute anything.”

“He throws attitude around like it’s three-week-old bedding.”

“If anyone can teach him a lesson it’s you, Stompy.”

“Yeah. If any of us challenged him, it’d be just a bunch of peasants challenging the ‘mighty knight.’ But you could floor him with one punch, the skinny stick mouse.”

I figured they were talking about Scratchy. I’m kinda dense sometimes. I was about to step out and lecture them on it, despite how much I resented the little twerp, but as I stuck my head around the corner I saw how many there were—maybe forty mice! Mostly familiar faces, mice I had trained with, even mice I had taught. I pulled myself back. My heart was beating fast.

"He's not a poor fighter, you know," Stompy's voice said. "I wouldn't want to be on the receiving end of that sword or slingshot!"

"We'll take his sword and slingshot away, then you nail him! It'll be funny." I knew the voice of that mouse. I had called him a friend. I had taught him to use a bow.

I felt a pang of something bitter in my mouth. It felt awful.

"Squibble's just a lazy mouse, full of talk and hot air. He rattles his tail everywhere and thinks he knows everything. He's just a useless runt."

"I don't know…" Stompy said.

"Oh, come on," another mouse said. "Everybody hates him. He thinks he's loved and adored. What a joke. Everyone knows what an immature waste of food he is. He'd be dead by now if it weren't for his 'precious Master' and Nemo."

They were talking about *me!*

I felt my stomach sink into the floor. I felt sick.

"I've had a hundred mice ready to take out that weakling before, but no one wants to for fear of the masters."

"Squibble is a master," Stompy said.

The other mice laughed. There were alot of them! Way too many. "That'll be the day! He's a momma's boy at five months old! He's a joke!"

"His very presence humiliates the masters," said another mouse that I knew… another one I had thought was my friend. He always bowed when I went by and called me "master." Now I knew he had been mocking me the entire time.

I hung my head down and tears welled up in my eyes. I wanted to go kill them, tear them apart, but I felt weak and sick. I felt a heavy blow had been dealt to my spirit by this stab in the back. I had no idea everyone hated me. I really thought everyone liked me. That's how they acted to my face. Even the instigating mouse. I had recognized his voice. He was a fighter in my graduating class. He had lost an ear to a fight with one of my master's brothers. He was a stupid, mischief-making, gossiping freak, and it shouldn't have bothered me that he started all this trouble.

But it did. I thought I had friends, and the ugly truth was too much to bear. I turned and ran away. "If you do it, we'll give you all our treats for a week!" was the last thing I heard.

I ran and ran, back to my cage. I threw myself into my bedding and cried bitterly. I felt wounded so deeply that nothing would fix it. I hated those mice. Hated them! I imagined terrible things happening to them for their black betrayal. I thrashed around. I bit things. I tore things up. I whipped out my plastic cocktail sword and slammed it into the wooden toy I always played on until the blade snapped (that takes alot of effort!). Then I turned around to get another and noticed Favorite was behind me in the shadows. My favorite girlfriend… My face was caked with tears. I was panting and sobbing at the same time. I expected her to be terrified, but no. She just looked at me with… compassion.

I went over to her, and she held me. She groomed my fur as I cried. She made me feel better. She was kind and gentle to me, and it felt good. It eased my pain somewhat. She really was a cool mouse. Pretty, strong, confident… not afraid. I liked her lots.

I was so appreciative that I wanted to give her something in return, and I only knew of one thing she really wanted. So I did that. Maybe it would give her what she wanted, maybe not. Anyway, it felt good, and I didn't care much anymore. She'd make a good momma if that happened. I'd never know either way. Afterward I left while she slept in my nest. I guess she could keep it.

I guess I should have gone to my master, or my momma. Or Nemo. But I didn't. I wandered far outside the house into the hills, into the Fields of Fate. It was a dangerous, reckless thing to do. Owls and snakes and other nameless horrors lurked out there, waiting for their chance to catch and eat a field mouse. I was twenty times slower, and my coat was so light it practically glowed by comparison. I was just a sitting duck. But I didn't care. Right then I didn't care if I died.

I hated that one-eared mouse for what he had said. And all behind my back! He was nothing but a coward and a troublemaker. A proper knight would go and soundly thrash him in front of everyone, maybe even kill him for insulting his honor.

Except… what honor? My entire reputation was built on something no one had ever seen, not even my own master—he was out cold the entire time. I really hadn't done anything for the mouse community. The stupid gossipmonger was right. I was worthless. I was five months old and still a momma's boy. (For a human, that was 25 or 30.) Time to leave the nest.

I felt terror grip my heart. I didn't want to leave! And I didn't want to grow up. It meant being unhappy and depressed. It meant fighting (for real!) and growing old. In the end, it meant dying. I was petrified. In that moment, for one second, I realized I was going to die. Someday. And what then? Nobody knew. Nobody really knew. Maybe all my visions had been delirious hallucinations. Maybe I was wrong. Maybe Bigfat didn't exist anymore, and my messed up brain that can't accept loss just made me see him because I couldn't handle stuff. Maybe I'm a loon.

Then the moment passed. I was very glad for it. That all sounded so wacko! Those dreams I can't remember must be driving me totally crazy.

I gotta do something. I gotta leave. I gotta take my pilgrimage, show these mice what I'm made of… show them I can contribute… Heck, I'll show them! I'll make the biggest contribution to mousekind ever! I'll even beat what my master did! Well… that just can't be done. But I'll come close!

Like it or not, it was time. I had to go do this unpleasant, lonely thing that I'd been putting off and dreading. I hated it. I hated One-Ear for it. I hated all the mice who didn't have the common decency to tell me they were upset at me so I might apologize or fix it. No, they just chattered away behind my back like a bunch of shrews, a bunch of cowards. There's no worse word in the knightly language. Cowards deserve to die.

I hated Scratchy. I hated myself. In that moment, I'm not sure I didn't hate the whole stinking world for being so cruel and unfair to mice. We never did one thing to deserve it! Not one thing. Someone oughta do something about that.

I had known even back with Favorite. I had known I was going to leave. Sometimes... you ever just know something? Like, with no rational explanation? You just know something is going to be a certain way, or happen just like this or that? Well, I do. Often. It usually doesn't suck. This time it did. Yeah...

So the next day, at dawn, when the human was waking up to go to work, I was waiting at the front door. With my armor, my slingshot, my sword (and a few extras), my backpack full of cool stuff, my cloak, my shield, and my helmet. Everyone else was asleep. I had written a note for the human asking him to take me to the farthest part of the city he could find. No one would be the wiser.

Except that they were. My master and my momma were not only up, they were waiting for me. They came out from behind the curtains. They each had a small bag of stuff.

"Sir Squibble," my master said. He smiled sadly, knowingly.

"That's Squire Squibble to you, Master," I said.

"Oh," he said, pretending to ponder, "I recall making you a knight. But if you don't want the title, I guess that's okay..."

I shifted my feet, deeply disturbed.

"You're going on your pilgrimage then?" my momma said, sounding as disturbed as I was.

"Yeah," I said, "an' I might not come back."

My momma gasped.

"That would be a great loss to all mousekind," Master said.

"Not really," I said.

"You may do what you wish, Sir Squibble," Master said, "but you're always welcome here."

"You so sure about that?" I said.

"Yes," he said. "It would break your mother's heart and mine to never see you again, Squib. I'd spend the rest of my life wondering what had happened to you."

I felt myself aching to cry. I couldn't do it. Knights don't cry. Squires shouldn't either, for that matter.

"Well, I'm goin'! An' until I do something great, I'm not even thinking of coming back. So don't wait up for me."

My momma started crying then, and my master was clearly upset. I wanted to comfort her, to stop my pilgrimage, to not go. I didn't want to grow up! No no no! But if I caved in now, it would be the end of my self-respect. It would be the end of everything.

The human came striding down the hall in his motorcycle boots and saved me from breaking. He picked me up and looked at the note. Then he looked at me. My master and momma scrabbled up his leg and onto his arm with me.

"You sure you want to go this far away from our normal drop-off point, little one? That's more than eight miles!" the human said.

I nodded vehemently.

"Squibble, what are you doing?!" my master hissed. He read the note. "That's the worst side of town! It's not even a little safe for mice!"

I ignored him. I looked right at the human.

"Well, okay, I guess the Knights know best," he said. "Any pickup time?"

I shook my head no. My momma cried out, ran to me, and put her arms around me. I almost broke right then. It was so close.

"Squibble, come to your senses!" my master ordered. I was pretty sure I already had, but he saw it in my eyes when I looked at him. I think he saw alot of things then.

"This… this is some stuff for you, dear son," my momma said. She put the two bags she and my master had been carrying into my backpack. They were heavy. "For your journey." She kissed me on the top of my head tenderly. "You're a grown mouse, and you make your own way now as all mice do. I pray you know what you're doing. I will think of you everyday."

"You've got the new kids to worry about, Momma," I said, almost in tears. "You don't need me anymore."

"I love you," she said.

"As do I," my master said. "A very old, wise mouse once told me, 'Do right and fear not.' I have always lived by that."

The saying struck me as deeply profound, even as upset as I was. I was immediately curious to know who said it to him, because we didn't know any wise old mice. Maybe it had been King Arnold back in the Old Kingdom? Well, it didn't matter now.

The human set my master and momma down on the edge of their cage, then turned around and opened the giant front door. Chilly morning wind blew in from the mountains. My master and momma looked up at me with forlorn eyes and faces painted with sadness. I felt sudden panic. I was seeing them for the last time maybe. Very possibly the last time…

I wanted to tell them I loved them, too, I really did. But if I had, I would never have managed to stay in the human's hand as he closed the door behind us.

Spring

The Pilgrimage of One Mouse Knight

The Fall of Sir Squibble

✠

All of the following chapters involving my pilgrimage I wrote later, after it was over. You'll see why. I recalled everything perfectly, though, so nothing was left out. What you are about to read are the specific events that forged me into the mouse I am now. Other events followed, and more are yet to come, but my pilgrimage set in motion everything that came afterward, I am certain. It was not in the least what I had been expecting. If I had stayed back at home none of it would have happened. It was required of me that I wake up, grow up, and remember my dreams. I just had no idea how hard that would be. I would not have undertaken it if I had known.

The street in the early morning was dark, and the air was frigidly cold this close to the ocean. I sat there watching the Kind Human drive away. Like the others, he had asked me not to go. He told me he'd miss me and worry about me, but in the end he had to do as I asked. He had promised to give us what we wanted, to recognize us as sentient beings, and I wanted my freedom. He always gave any rodent its freedom if it wanted it, provided it knew what a dangerous thing it was asking for. To date, no mice had asked. Oh, mice went on journeys, knights went on pilgrimages, and messengers went everywhere, but they all came back. Everyone knew they came back if they could.

The outside is very dangerous to domestic mice. We aren't equipped to handle it. That's why the journey my master set out on from the city to find the Kind Human was so amazing. No one thought he'd make it twenty feet, much less fifty miles! Everyone wanted him to make it, though. They believed in him, against all odds. I've heard of domestic mice being abandoned in the wilderness—or even in someone's back yard—and not living one hour. I've heard of mice dying of fright and anxiety. It's really scary to us. We've lived with humans for 5000 years. Nature considers us a free lunch. We haven't the speed or the camouflage any longer to protect ourselves. What we have now is intelligence. But I knew the moment I saw the car drive away that I had thrown away that one great advantage.

I had been terribly stupid. My heart lunged in my chest and I panicked. I ran after the car waving my arms and chirping at the top of my lungs, but there was no way he could hear me or see me. It was too late. I'd doomed myself as sure as if I'd put the noose around my own neck. I watched the car disappear over the horizon in the direction of the rising sun.

My eyes welled up with tears as I looked around me at the empty, bleak landscape of asphalt and dirt. Trash filled the gutters. Alleyways were full of lurking shadows. The salty air made everything damp and miserably cold. I didn't even know which direction the normal drop-off and pickup point was. I did know it was miles away. Much too far.

So that was it. I had killed myself. I would never see my master again, or Nemo, BJ, or anyone. I'd never sleep in my nest again, never eat millet or ice cream again... I was going to die a cold, lonely death, and probably a violent one. I was scared and shaking. I thoroughly regretted my decision. I would have given anything to be back home right then. I'd go kick the snot out of those back-talking, low-down, no-good, miserable vermin mice and be happy about it. I'd make everyone proud of me somehow, but not this. Not this! I couldn't hack it here! I was scared out of my wits!

I ran for a tiny crack in the brick wall and hid there. My heart was humming like a mini turbine, moving too fast, making too much noise. My scent wasn't even covered. Oh, what a stupid, stupid mouse I was! In the real world without Kind Humans, stupid mice die. I was a dead mouse. So dead!

I was suddenly hungry, even though I had eaten before we left. I was thirsty, too. I hadn't brought anything to drink, but I had brought some food. I began munching on some corn I pulled out of my backpack when I noticed the two sacks my master and momma had given me. I opened them right away while I ate. My hands shook.

My master had given me some Cheerios, some millet, and a sharpening stone for my swords. He also gave me ten metal balls, the most deadly ammunition for a slingshot. They were BB's, and they were very rare. Sometimes mice found them in the field and brought them home. My master had polished them and given them to me. To our kind, trying to learn technology, these were worth their weight in gold. They had so many uses for mice, but master had given them to me. I took three of them and put them in my pockets for easy access.

But what my momma left me made my master's gift look cheap. She had given me a honeycomb, full of honey, and sealed with beeswax. No wonder it was so heavy! It had come straight from the bees, and they gave it freely to no one except my master. Honey could revitalize a mouse no matter what was wrong. It was magic elixir, the nectar of the gods. With that, I might make it to the pickup point.

Honeycomb was precious beyond measure to a mouse in my position. My master and momma had known it would be. I shuddered to think of what they would have to do to repay the favor from the bees. Something hard. Bees always made you do something hard. Or, just maybe, they were grateful to my master for finding them a warm place to stay through the harsh winters. Either way, they *never* gave out honey or honeycomb. They guarded it with their lives.

I was a little happier now. I was a Mouse Knight, after all. I could make it to the pickup point, wherever that was, and go home. That would be my pilgrimage: survive, make it home. I could do it. My master had done far more.

Inside me, it didn't sit right. I knew I had more to do, but it sounded like a good start, and I was still petrified. I had to do something, so I set out in the direction the Kind Human had gone, which would be to work and school in the city.

I walked for hours, hiding in the corners and gutters, until the city came awake. Then I was almost noticed by a few people. If I got caught, that would be the end of me. I'd be fed to a snake or—much worse—they'd wonder why a mouse was wearing armor and carrying a backpack. I'd expose the entire community of smart mice and then… Well, according to TV, they send those FBI agents out to get you! The guy who looks for flying saucers and the girl who doesn't believe in them, they'd come get the safe house, and it would all be over. All the mice, everything my master had worked so hard for would be gone. Because of me, stupid Squibble.

A child finally saw me when I got clumsy and tired. I had wandered out from the gutter a few inches, and the stupid kid yelled, "Look! A mouse!" and ran toward me. I was horrified. Never in my life had I been that alarmed. I wasted a desperately-needed second standing there, then turned to dive back into the trash that lined the gutters. As I dashed for cover, I was almost run over by a car. It missed me by several inches and sent me sprawling. I recovered and lost myself in the garbage. The child and his friends didn't give up, though. They pawed through the waste mercilessly, not caring how dirty they got, and pounded the trash with their feet and hands. I had to keep moving or they were going to kill me. They were kicking the trash out of the gutter where I'd been, trying to find me. I guessed they didn't want a pet mouse, because if I had actually stayed where they were flailing I'd be dead now. What wretched creatures! They didn't want to catch me, just kill me. Kill the mouse. Kill the vermin.

Then one spotted me and yelled to his buddies. They came stomping and smashing toward me again as I took in as much road as I could and as fast as I could do it. Three kids on their way to school—not bad for a first encounter. I'd rather have met a snake.

The kids were going to reach me. They were too fast, and I was wearing too much gear. I couldn't jump up to the sidewalk with all the weight on me, and if I ran out into the street, either the cars would get me or I'd be out in the open for them to stomp my furry head in. I was gonna die. "Oh, I'm sorry, Momma!" I thought, "I should have told you I loved you!"

Suddenly there was a sewer grate, and I leapt down it carelessly with glee. The kids cursed and stomped on the grate, spitting and seething. They poked sticks into it and poured their lunch drinks down it. They were really disappointed at not getting to maul me to death with vicious cruelty. What monsters.

Now I was in the sewer. It was nothing new to me. I'd been here before. The entire old mouse kingdom had been real close to the sewers. Of course, human sewers ran for miles and miles. I didn't know the way through them, but I knew some basics. One, don't jump off anything steep. Two, avoid going down too far. Three, rats owned the sewers, and rats ate mice. I must avoid the rats, as badly as I needed their help. They might not care that I was a Mouse Knight. I was alone.

I wandered the sewer for days. I ate all my millet and Cheerios. They went fast, and I was hungry. I couldn't tell day or night down there, so I walked as fast as I could until I was tired, then slept, then walked again. I tried to stay to the clear ways, but I got real dirty. It stank down there. There was no way to avoid the grime. I got wet, I got filthy… I hated it. I stopped to wash several times an hour, but it didn't matter make any difference. I was very thirsty, and there was no clean water to drink.

I must have been insane to think this was going to be easy. Before I'd left the house, my idea of a pilgrimage had been this nice, kinda lonely walk in the park. Maybe literally. Chat with a few fellow mice ("Hello, why yes, I am a Mouse Knight. Would you like my autograph?"), eat junk food from the leftover carnivals or parties (yum), and maybe free a few animals from pet stores (real easy if there isn't a guard dog). But… no. Here, at the beginning of my pilgrimage, I had already been terrified, cold, sad, chased by stupid kids, and soaked in sewage. Whee. We're having fun now.

After a day and a half I was so thirsty I had to risk drinking the sewer water. I found the cleanest stuff I could by smell, and it still upset my tummy. I got lucky—it didn't kill me. It just made my trek miserable. While I was at it, I chanced eating some rotting food that was down there as well. I had to, or I'd starve to death. It was nasty and foul. I had to fight off maggots and bugs to even get at it. Oh, my dignity had fallen far. I wasn't far behind, I feared. With each passing hour I wondered more and more how I was going to live through this. Reality had reared its ugly head, and I doubted it would go quietly back into the mists again. This was my dragon.

Maybe a week went by. I lost track. I was tired and sore, and much too weary to think. I started seeing things in the darkness that might or might not have been there. It was scary, and I was totally vulnerable. Four times I slipped and fell down into water, once onto hard concrete. If I hadn't had my armor, that fall would have crippled me, or worse. It was only five feet, but that's about a hundred to a human. It took me an hour to get up again after that fall, and everything hurt. Stuck in that place I felt damned, as if the world above had moved on and forgotten me. I was wandering without direction, lost underground in an abyss of stink and despair.

Sometime near the end of the week, I came across rats. I was lucky to be downwind of them, otherwise that blind error would have cost me my hide. They were eating the dead corpse of a dog. They were big, black rats, not like Mike or the others that I had known. These were mean rats. They would tear me apart instantly. I crept and crept, wary of any noise or movement that might tell me I was being stalked. It took hours to creep around them. My legs ached and cramped several times. I had to be patient. I forced myself to move slow. It was sheer agony. After I had escaped them, I ran for an hour to make up for moving so slow. It had really bothered me. I hate being slow.

A day after that, I ate something that gave me gas and almost killed me. I lay on the cold cement rolling around for hours, moaning. It felt as though my belly was ten times its normal size. The pain was all I could feel. I couldn't die down here, I just couldn't! With all my remaining energy, I crept out of the sewers and into the world of men again. I came out in the middle of the night and collapsed behind some stairs and trash cans. It was very cold.

It was night when I woke up. Same night or another, I don't know. I was very hungry and cold. I needed water. My tummy was normal again, though, so I got up to look around.

I was somewhere in the middle of the city. Probably called Egypt… The streets were empty, the lights all out. I peered out of the poor hiding place I had and sat still for a long time. My mouth watered just thinking of the honey in my pack. But I wasn't that bad off yet. I'd save it for a real emergency.

My patience paid off. Across the street I saw a mouse dart from one building to another. I was just about to run over to that building and shout hello when a cat sprang from a dark doorway and landed on the mouse. I heard it squeak. The cat had it pinned. The beast would play with the poor rodent for hours before allowing it to die, if it didn't die by accident first. The mouse might have been fated to perish, except that it had the good fortune to fall right in front of a very famous Mouse Knight.

As scared as I was, as alone as I felt, and as weak as my body had become, I ceased to notice in that moment. I suddenly had a purpose that made sense in the midst of all this stupid chaos and despair. My fear went dim. I simply didn't care enough to be afraid any longer. Any knight would know what needed to be done now.

I stepped out into the light of a street lamp, high overhead. I loaded my slingshot with a stone from the pavement and whistled at the cat. It looked at me. So did the mouse. The mouse had an expression of horror and disbelief on its face. The cat ignored me and went back to tormenting the mouse.

So I let fly. My aim is better than anyone's. That includes BJ. No one can even come close to my skill. I've lived with that dear slingshot my master made for me on our first journey for four months. I practice every single day and I never go anywhere without it. I sleep with it. You get the idea. The cat got beaned at a distance of forty feet. Right in the head.

"Hee heeee!" I thought. Nice shot. Oops!

The cat abandoned the pinned mouse to lunge after me. The mouse got up, shook its head in disbelief, and ran, limping, to the safety of a crack in the wall. As it took one look back, I nodded to it. There you go, my good man, be sure to tell them who saved you.

The cat charged as I calmly reloaded. My master said you must never panic. Even faced with a charging dragon, the old knights did not lose it. They and their steeds did not falter. Neither did I. I let fly with another rock and pegged the cat in the ankle. It stumbled and fell. I reloaded.

The beast rose, mad as a hornet (yeah, hornets are always mad—it's true). It resumed its charge, screeching for my blood. I let fly again. Its ear suddenly had a hole in it. The cat yowled but did not turn aside. I began to worry, maybe a little late. It was only fifteen feet from me now, and coming on flaming paws, claws extended. Hold it together, Squibble! I reached into my pocket and brought out one of the BB's.

"Don't make me use this!" I shouted as I aimed. "Turn aside and take quarter, sir!"

But I could see it was not going to happen. So I let the deadly bullet go. It struck the cat right on target, straight in the forehead. My pressure on the slingshot cord had been just right too—it didn't go through to his brain, it just stuck there in his skull. The cat now had a copper third eye for the rest of its life. He fell, tumbled, and thrashed in pain. He looked at me with horror on his face. Yeah, cat, that's right. A mouse just beaned you with a BB. Now run.

I reloaded another BB. The cat spun on its heels and ran yowling back up the street.

My legs were shaking. I hadn't realized how scared I'd been. In the moment, it had seemed the perfect thing to do, what I'd done. And it went smoothly. I call that flowing. Flowing with the universe. Flowing with your heart. If you're doing what your heart wants you to, everything works. The heart knows best. Always knows better than the mind. Nemo taught me that, and I saw it all right then in action with the cat. I hadn't felt afraid. I didn't give myself time to feel afraid. Everything worked. It was rightness. Sometimes everything just works. When things that should work don't, that's wrongness. Wrongness sucks.

I put the BB back in my pocket. I pulled another out of the backpack and carefully put it in with the remaining two. Always three BB's in the pocket. Three is a good number for everything. I had brought two extra swords. Too bad I couldn't carry two extra shields. Of course, that's what squires are for. Maybe I should have brought Scratchy. Make him carry all my stuff. Nah. He'd have gotten us killed with his spinning bit. Can't run straight. No good at all. I was still mad at the little twerp for some reason.

My legs were trembling something fierce. Maybe I had been afraid but just hadn't felt it. Oh, who cares? Maybe alot of things, huh? Maybe I should stop saying maybe.

I put the slingshot back around my neck, under my armor, where I always kept it (close to my heart). It had been modified several times by my master to make it hardier and sturdier. It had been practically rebuilt from the ground up. It was a perfect weapon in my book. I loved it.

I decided that it was time for a treat after such a glorious victory, and since my limbs felt like Jello, I trotted over to the alleyway the mouse had darted out of and broke out my precious honeycomb. I was gingerly taking the wax off one off the capsules when I heard something scuff the pavement behind me. I quickly sealed the capsule again, put the honeycomb back in my backpack, and turned around.

I was facing a huge mouse. Not as big as Bigfat but close, and he wasn't fat. He was just big—a lot of weight, a lot of muscle, and a lot of bad attitude right in my face. He had almost twenty mice behind him. He looked mean and rough, like he'd been through the wringer several times… the wringer of life. He had scars like BJ did, and several notches taken out of his ears. His fur was dirty and splotched with old stains. He was standing too close to me for me to draw my sword, and too close for me to get at my slingshot. I was caught holding my backpack with both hands, staring like a frightened child. I'd say that was pretty accurate. I was frightened, and that huge mouse made me feel like a frightened little boy again. He was ugly and nasty. He radiated meanness.

"Ummm… hi," I said.

"Gimme your sniffy," the mouse croaked. He meant my honeycomb.

I was instantly terrified. I felt adrenaline shoot through my system again. These were not domestic mice. They were the same species and not field mice, but they had never lived in a house or a pet store. They survived on the streets like the rats in the sewer. They had an edge about them that made them dangerous and unpredictable. Their very smell told me they hated me. I was in real danger.

"I… I'm a Mouse Knight," I said too quietly.

"What?" the mouse barked. He stepped closer. I stepped back.

"I'm a… Mouse Knight," I said. "I think you should leave me alone." My fear was all over the place. They could smell it for certain. And my voice carried it if my scent didn't.

The mice chattered and chittered insanely. They hopped around like a bunch of loons. They pretended to lunge at me and then backed off. But the leader just eyeballed me without flinching.

"What's that?" he said. "What's a 'mouse night'?"

I risked stepping back once more and this time he didn't follow. Now I had room to draw my sword, but I didn't. I was scared silly, paralyzed with fear.

"I am a defender of all mousekind," I said, holding my hand to my breastplate made of lobster shell. "I am a hero. I saved one of you from that cat." I didn't sound convincing.

They all laughed then, maniacal, screw-loose laughter. I hated it. The leader turned to his gang and said, "A hero! The pet-mouse thinks he's a hero!" They laughed some more. I should have drawn my sword then. On reflection, it might have worked. It certainly would have worked better than what I did do.

I grew a little angry, trying not to be so afraid, and said, "See here, sir…"

Then the big mouse bit me. Hard. I felt a stabbing pain in my hip and fell down, saying, "Ow," for some stupid reason as though making a simple comment at a social gathering. He had gone right through my armor where two pieces met. I wasn't surprised. Mice can exert over 24,000 pounds per inch of pressure on a single spot. The human mouth, by comparison, can do about 400. The armor had been designed to protect against teeth, and it would have worked, but the big mouse was too strong and too good at biting. He got me right where the belt, chestplate, and backplate came together—the chink in my armor. It hurt terribly, and I was stunned by the blow. I didn't know what to do. It was the first real mouse fight I'd ever been in. And I did the worst thing possible. I froze up. I panicked.

"Take off that stoopid suit," he commanded. "Do it NOW!"

I shuddered, got up, and obeyed. Full of humiliation and shame and fear, I took off my armor, took off my helmet, unbuckled my sword belt, and let my shield fall to the ground. I couldn't believe what I was doing, but I felt weak. I felt I had no strength to fight back. The fear took it all out of me. Oh, my master would have been so ashamed. I had given in to a bully. I had always been told bullies were cowards at heart, but this one didn't look it. He looked like he ate rats for breakfast. I watched myself remove the last of my protection and let it fall to my feet.

I stood there naked except for my slingshot around my neck and my tunic, shaking like a leaf. I saw in the crowd the mouse I had saved from the cat. He was playing along with the rest of them. He had probably been the one to go get the rest of them when he got free of the cat. Some gratitude. He didn't even look happy to be alive. He looked like the rest of them—evil and vicious.

I was in tears, I was so scared. "Please, let me keep my things," I said. "I need them. I'm on a journey…"

"I don't care!" yelled the big bully mouse, and he bit me again, this time in the shoulder. I fell down again, more out of fear than pain. The other mice moved to close in to tear me apart, but the bully mouse motioned them away. I cried. I was bleeding, and my bladder had let go. I was lying in a pool of my own urine…

"I'm a Mouse Knight!" I whimpered. "You can't do this to me!"

He laughed and mimicked me. "I'm a mouse night," he said, trying to sound stupid and doing a good job. "You can't do this to meeeee!" He danced around like a stupid idiot. The other mice all laughed. They jeered and lunged at me, stopping just short of landing blows. "Look—he's peed on himself! HAW HAW HAW!!"

As I struggled to get up, he shoved me and said, "Gimme that thing," meaning my slingshot. Other mice were ripping my backpack apart, destroying my things, devouring my honeycomb. Oh, no… not my momma's priceless gift! It broke my heart to see it lost like that, taken by monsters and criminals.

Then I realized he was threatening something even more dear to me.

I clutched the slingshot to my chest. "No! I can't give you this! Please, let me go!"

Then the mouse lunged for my head. I barely dodged in time, and I only moved because some other force, perhaps many days of training, seemed to move me. I felt myself ducking, and then felt the blow land. It had been aimed for my eye! It fell instead on my skull, shook my brains, and I saw stars. Blood ran freely down my face.

That had been a killing bite! He was trying to *murder* me. I knew the blow from BJ's school. That hadn't been a dominance attack. My heart leapt in my chest. He meant to end my life!

Eyes full of tears, screaming like a girl mouse, I felt his second blow break my leg. It snapped like a twig, and blood sprayed all over him, which he seemed to like. He sat back a moment and guffawed to his gang about my pain… and my oncoming death.

Pain and agony filled my body. Terror filled my mind. The smell of my own blood and pee filled my nose. I couldn't think. I was petrified. I knew in that moment I didn't want to die. I knew then I truly did have a fear of death. I had seen too much of it, and I didn't want to go there. Not yet! Not like this. Anything but a coward's death!

I heard a distant whining sound, as if a wind were whipping through the buildings and their broken, dark windows. When the sound came close, I heard a voice. It sounded like someone I knew, but I was too far gone to recognize it.

"Run, Squibble!" it said.

The bully had at me then with some of the other mice, as the rest tore into my things and finished off my honeycomb, scarfing it down instead of savoring it. I felt more bites, all numbed for some reason. I knew I was being killed.

Then a real wind hit all of us, a strong gust from the sea. It pulled up the dust and trash on the ground and tossed it into everyone's eyes. It was strong enough that it threw some of the mice from their feet. It gave me a moment and some space.

"I said *run*, you little punk!" said the wind. It was Bigfat's voice.

I was up and gone. I couldn't feel anything, much less my broken leg. I knew I was running funny, kinda to the left, but I didn't care. The ground made weird motions and sometimes I fell on my face. Blood was everywhere. My slingshot came up and hit me in the face several times. I looked back and saw the big mouse and several of his cronies right on my heels. I would normally have left them in the dust, but my condition was crippling my speed.

I dodged around every piece of trash on the street. I took a few more bites from mice behind me—they were weak compared to their bully boss. I took the bites on my ass, which is probably the best place to take them. Not like I had a choice. I kept running, hopeless and scared to death, and they kept chasing me. The only advantage I had was BJ's training. He always made us run and dodge in our armor. Now I was without it, and that made me a lot faster. Still, I was barely holding my own. They were going to catch me. I was tiring out.

I ran across the street and jumped successfully (for having a broken leg) onto the curb of the sidewalk. I skittered over the sidewalk and ran for a building that had the lights on. Some of the mice couldn't make the jump to the sidewalk, but most off them did. I couldn't slow down for a second. I was still taking bites from behind. I smelled blood. A lot of it. My hindquarters must be a bloody mess, I thought. I felt sick to my stomach thinking about all the stuff I had lost. Or maybe I felt sick because of all the blood I had lost. My leg hurt now all the way up to my neck. I was on the edge. I couldn't go much farther.

Up ahead I saw a door opening, and light poured out. To most mice this was a dead end—no sane mouse would go near people. But I had been raised as a pet, and although I knew better, I also knew that not all people would immediately kill a mouse. We scared them initially, and that might give me some time. I headed for the door. Just ahead of me the cat I had beaned with the BB came out of the door. He turned, looked right at me, and bolted back inside. I heard a human's voice saying, "What's into you? First you wanna go out, then you don't..."

I flew through the cracked door. The other mice stopped. The bully mouse was cursing me. "I'll get you, stupid mouse!" he yelled. "I'll get you!" The human never even saw me. It was paying attention to the cat, which was huddled in a corner staring at me with horror. I hissed at it, which had the exact effect I wanted—it fled from the room at top speed, and the human followed. I ran the other direction.

I searched the kitchen first. Sure enough, I found an opening into the walls through a cabinet. Once inside the walls, I was relatively safe. I skittered down and into darkness. I fell a few times, once landing on the three BB's in my pocket—ouch. Everything was ouch. I crawled pathetically around on cold cement beneath the house, bleeding everywhere, lamenting my losses. I was doomed now. To make matters worse, I smelled other mice. I wasn't alone.

And with that thought, I passed out cold.

Tangent: Something Wicked This Way Comes

✠

I knew I was dreaming.

I was out in the dark city. I had been abandoned by the Kind Human, but not by choice. Apologizing and crying, he had left me and the rest of us from the safe house out in the middle of the street. Something was terribly wrong. We had no armor, no equipment, no food or water… Then he drove off, even driving over several of us. Eight hundred mice, left in the middle of the street… Something in my head screamed that this was wrongness, but I was too scared to figure it out. So there we were, alone and terrified.

I took all the mice the way I had gone before, and we ran into the bully mouse and his gang. They brutally killed my master and my momma. At that moment I forgot I was dreaming. I thought it was real. It became real in my mind. The terror set in.

After they had mauled all the leaders, including BJ, no one would stand up to the bullies. They held up my armor and laughed at me, showing everyone else how I had caved in before. They said it was my fault. The bully mouse told everyone it was my fault they were abandoned. The human didn't want any coward mice. Then BJ, dying slowly, all his limbs gnawed off, turned on me and called me a coward. The rest of them began to bite me. I fled for my life again, but this time from my family and friends. And this time, as I was getting away, I ran around a corner and right smack into the Black Mouse.

It stank like it was a week dead. It felt warm, like burned coal. I smelled smells I had never smelled before, which I later learned were sulfur and brimstone. Its eyes burned through me like fire. I was on fire. Flames burst into life on my fur.

I turned around, burning, and went back around the corner to face the hateful mob.

"It's here!" I cried. "You have to run!"

They laughed and bit me. They broke all my limbs. They tore out my fur. They kept right at it as the Black Mouse came around the corner and ran BJ through with a dark sword. They would not relent from killing me even as the evil mouse lay into them, slaying animal after animal. They fell even as they refused to look at what was happening.

"Oh, you fools!" I cried. "Look at what is happening! Wake up! Wake up!"

But they would not listen, and by the time the demon was done with them, I was a ruined pile of torn flesh. I could not move any part of me. My bones were crushed, my muscles torn apart. My guts lay all over the street and only one eye still worked. Through it, I saw the Black Mouse drinking my blood and laughing. I tried to scream but I had no more mouth. Then it gestured, spreading my red life liquid all over the bodies of the mice. To my horror, the bodies stirred. Then all the dead mice got up. They got up even though they were still dead, and they came to bite me again, to eat me. The Black Mouse had raised the dead. Turned my friends and family into zombies.

Then a white, armored paw was on me. I was standing somewhere else… a battlefield. Everyone was dead. The bodies of mice and men speckled the landscape. Too many mice. Percival was standing before me, covered in blood, clutching a shining sword made of metal in his other paw. It danced with white fire. His face was grim stone.

"We should have listened to you," he said. "Now it's too late."

Then I was sitting in the hand of Michael the archangel. It was dawn in the Fields of Fate.

"A very hard, special task. But you must accept it of your own free will," he was saying. I could not speak. "Squibble, this is not going to be easy. In fact, it is going to cost you a lot. Maybe everything. You cannot know how hard this is going to be if you accept. It will make your trek across these Fields of Fate seem like nothing. I am warning you. If you accept, you can expect the worst."

Suddenly I remembered everything. Absolutely everything.

"I'm dreaming!" I said.

Mike nodded.

"Oh, Mike—I've made an awful mess of it all!" I cried.

Mike shook his head. "No," he said softly. "Outside these dreams, it is happening how it's supposed to happen."

"I'm having these messed up dreams every day!" I shouted. "Every day for the last several weeks!"

"They are powerful," Mike said. "Your gifts are manifesting themselves. The enemy sees this and seeks to curse you, to break you… frighten you away."

"But it's terrible!"

He nodded again. "Do you want out now, Squibble?" he asked. "God will not trick you, or let you choose something that you do not know the price of."

"Can this get any worse?" I asked incredulously.

He nodded again. "Many times."

My eyes got wide. "What will happen if I quit?"

"You lead a normal life. God will choose another champion. You are not being forced to do this."

"Why me, then?" I asked.

"You were found worthy," he said.

"Oh, no *way*!" I said. "I'm not even close."

Mike scowled a bit. "Who knows better than God?"

"Bigfat never seemed that smart…"

He kept scowling.

"Yeah," I gave in. "Who knows better than the Mousegod… nobody. I guess if he says I'm worthy then I might be."

"Why you, Squibble?" he said. "Truly?"

"Yeah…"

"Because no one else will do as good a job. No one else will take it so seriously." He looked into the dawn light. "No one else is you. The Prophet Squibble. A mighty hero."

"Oh," I said. *Prophet?*

Long silence followed. I finally looked into the blazing eyes of Michael. "You know I have to do it. The Mousegod knew I would, too."

"You have free will."

"And with it, I chose this a long time ago, didn't I?"

He nodded. "You did."

"We all did."

"Yes."

"Thank you, Michael."

"Thank you, Squibble."

"Can I remember my dreams now?"

"Yes."

"Okay."

As I felt myself waking up into the land of pain and suffering, I remembered every single one of my dreams, so many I couldn't count them. Dreams of everything, and every sort. And all of them signs, signs of what was to come, combined with dark nightmares trying to twist the signs out of reality and into scary-ville. I was overcome by awe and a deep feeling of anxiety as I went over every dream I had had since my first dream with Michael, the vision of the pet store. None of them were good. They all had darkness laced throughout them. They were nightmarish fantasies, full of death and pain. Each one was horribly traumatic. No wonder I had forgotten them!

But one thing I couldn't understand. They contradicted each other. Like normal dreams, they made little sense. They told of many futures, not just one. In most every single one, the mice of the safe house fell upon hard times. In all of them, I went through my own private hell. They blended together in a huge mass of fear and pain. I knew that, with time, they would fade as dreams do. Though I remembered them now, I had to choose carefully what I would consciously remember because I had to get back to the safe house as soon as mousely possible to warn everyone of what was coming. By then I might remember very little. My journal had been destroyed by the mouse gang along with my things, and I had no way of writing any of it down. It would have taken too long to do that anyway.

Now you know why I had to rewrite all this later. My entire pilgrimage was made without the means to record it.

And it turned out to be a very, very long pilgrimage.

Heide and Fred

✠

I woke to a mouse grooming me. At first I thought it was my momma. Then I remembered what had happened. I sat bolt upright and scared the female mouse who was tending to my wounds.

"I have to warn them!" I shrieked.

Babies began to cry and squeak in alarm. I was in a nest made of old couch stuffing and newspapers. We were below the house I had run into. This mouse was a new mother. Ten babies were curled up near her. She had been licking the dried blood from my fur. She was frightened, but ready to defend her children from me if I was dangerous.

“I’m sorry,” I said. Pain shot through my body. Instead of squeaking in agony, I said, “Ow,” like it didn’t matter, like I was just sipping tea. My body burned with fever. I was getting sick.

She cowered a little less.

“I won’t hurt you or your family,” I said. “I need help.”

“I know,” she said. “Duh.”

Oh. Smart mouse.

“How long have I been here?” I asked.

“Many days,” she said. “I feed you. I bring you water.”

I looked at myself and tried to laugh. Laughing hurt, and I looked terrible. Of course I looked like I needed help. I tried to get up and couldn’t put any weight on the broken leg. It felt cold. Well, that was probably it for me as a mouse. Best bet, even if I could reach a vet, they’d amputate the leg. I’d be a cripple from now on. I immediately thought of Scratchy. I felt guilty pangs of conscience. I’d be like him.

There was one chance. I had attended all the boring classes on medicine that my master had taught. Mouse medicine. I’d gone because it was my master teaching, not because I wanted to know anything about medicine. But it had been him speaking, so I had listened.

“You have to set my leg,” I said to the mouse. “But you might have to break it again first.”

“Do what?” she said.

“You have to set the bone,” I said. “It’s broken. You have to pull it apart and set one broken half into the other so it fits perfectly. To pull it apart you’re going to have to use your teeth. It’s not set right. If it heals this way I’ll never be whole.”

“I can’t do that,” she said.

“You have to,” I said with desperation, “or I’ll never walk again. And I really need to walk again. Soon!”

She timidly crawled over to me. It seemed that she had strength in her. She wasn’t a weak mouse. “I’ll try,” she said.

I showed her just what to do, and we went over it several times. She asked all the right questions. I was impressed with her confidence. She was a good mouse. I hadn’t fallen into enemy territory. She was a stroke of good luck.

When the time came, I said, “Okay. Do it.” And she did. My leg immediately shot unbearable pain through my entire body. I gritted my teeth against it, unwilling to cry out. I’d been enough of a coward lately. Enough to last the rest of my miserable life! My teeth gnashed as she pulled, then tenderly turned the bone this way and that, feeling for the right position to put it back where it belonged, together with its other half. It took more than half of forever, and I was in a cold, deep sweat before it was over, shaking uncontrollably. But she did it. It looked right. The bone felt straight. I winced in agony and relief. I felt as weak as one of her babies.

"Okay, now we have to bind it," I said. She immediately set out to find things to bind it with. We used parts from her nest, sticks from the house wood, and whatever else we could find. We made a cast and bound the leg. She was amazingly efficient and smart. She didn't get grossed out or shy away from the gruesome task. I never had to tell her anything twice. I liked her.

Once it was over, I said, "Okay, now I need antibiotics. I'm going to get very sick."

She shrugged. "I don't know what that is, or where to get it," she said. "The human might know—"

"HA! You're joking, right?" I grimaced through pain. "I'll just walk in there and ask him."

"Her," she said.

"Hmmm?" If the human was a she, I had a better chance. They usually were afraid of mice, but my master had said that in general, the female humans were more compassionate.

"Her name is Heide," she told me. "She likes mice."

"*What?!*" I chirped. Despite the pain, I sat up.

"She likes mice. She used to have one. I would talk to it at night. I learned a lot. Like where the cookies were…"

"Another Kind Human?" I said, unbelieving. I thought we had the only Kind Human. My master thought there weren't any others. Could this be true?

"You're a smart mouse," I said.

"Takes brains to survive around here," she said. "How did you get so beat up?"

"Lack of brains," I said. "I need to know if that human will listen to me. Do you think she will?"

"Can you talk human?" she asked.

"No, but I can write."

Her eyes got big. "I've heard a story about a mouse that could read and write! Months ago, the story went all around the city. A mouse that found a haven for a bunch of outcast domestic mice. They called him—"

"The Mouse Knight," I finished for her.

"You? You're… the Mouse Knight?" she asked, awe in her voice and eyes.

I hung my head down. "No," I said. "He is my master, and if I'd been him, I wouldn't be in this stupid situation now."

"Then he's real?!" she exclaimed.

"Yes," I said. "He's real."

"And there's really a haven? A safe place for mice?"

I nodded. "Yes. It's called the safe house. It's in the Fields of Fate."

"That's so far..." she said, squinting.

"Tell me about it," I said. "I walked there."

She just looked at me with respect. It was a new thing. This was not feigned respect, or old respect, or respect because I was my master's squire. It was mine. It was just for me. It felt good.

"You are an amazing mouse," she said.

"Nah," I said. But she never quite lost that awed look in her eyes. I can't say I didn't like it. She thought I was cool.

She cared for me for a week or so until I had some of my strength back. But, as I predicted, I began to feel sick, and my leg was swelling up and turned purple and sickly yellow. She brought me food and water. She had her kids to take care of, too. It was a lot of work. She never once complained. She was so tired that her short naps consumed her with fatigue. She'd be out the moment she lay down. Her kids would always wake her, mewling for milk. Hassles though they be, she seemed absolutely dedicated to them. The kitchen was quite a journey from her nest, yet she made the trip a thousand times those nights, trying to find me scraps from the floor, trying to feed herself and her kids.

Then on a slightly warmer day, I woke. My leg was swollen and purple, a giant bloated thing. I felt ill. She had piled up a bunch of cereal she had found in the cabinet. It wasn't Cheerios, but it was good.

"The human will trap you and kill you if she finds that you chewed a hole in her cereal," I said in the dark. "It was worth the risk," she said. "But I don't think she will. Heide likes us. She leaves the cookies out for us now, once she found that we had snuck into the pantry to nibble on them."

I thought about that... a human that gives mice cookies. It didn't seem possible, but the mother mouse wouldn't lie to me about it. There was no use in it. I had to go speak to this human. It was against the laws of the safe house, revealing our intelligence, but I was in dire straits, and it was time to bend the rules. My master always said that when you couldn't win any other way, start bending rules. If that didn't work, break them.

“I need to get up to the human,” I said. “I need to ask for her help.”

“I’ll help you.”

No ‘that’s crazy’ or ‘you’re stupid,’ or even, ‘you’ll endanger my babies.’ Just ‘I’ll help you.’

I’m not amazing.

“You’re amazing,” I said.

She let her babies feed until they went to sleep, then put her shoulder under mine. “I do what I’ve gotta do,” she said. And she helped me all the way up to the house. She pointed out the kitchen, the living room, and told me where the human was. She also told me where the cat would be. She said she’d be back in an hour or so, and every hour after, to look for me. I nodded, and she vanished.

Well, it didn’t take long to find the human. She was in the living room watching TV. She was watching my favorite show, the one with the brave captain and the first officer with the pointed ears. So cool. I was going to settle down to watch, but the cat found me first.

He sure looked funny with that BB stuck in his forehead. The human hadn’t noticed it yet, obviously. He caught me sitting down on the top of the couch, and I couldn’t get up with my broken leg very quickly, if at all. He had me.

So I turned around deliberately and went back to watching TV.

“I am your death, mouse,” he hissed.

“You’ll be my irritation if you don’t shut up,” I said. “I like this show.”

I could smell the fear from the cat. It was working. Good thing, because it was all I had. He was uncertain.

“I will eat you… tear you…” the cat said.

“Blah, blah blah,” I said. “Already been tried. You, the mice, the snake, the hawk, the whole stinkin’ world. Now take a number and shut up.”

I had my back to the cat. I couldn’t see it, but I could feel its hesitation. I also felt its desire to kill me in one blow, which it could certainly do. But it hesitated because it was afraid. Why was the mouse so brave? What secret weapon did it have? Would it hurt as much as the last one did?

“Why are you in my house?” it said.

“I’m here to speak to your human,” I said. “Fetch, boy.”

The cat growled in anger. I turned around with my best irritated face, the one I used to use when Shiva and Thor messed up my cage. "Do not make me come up there and finish what I started, cat."

The cat's eyes widened, and it turned from me, jumping off the couch. It went over to the human, complaining about the mean mouse with the dangerous magic. Of course all the human heard was meow. But she got up, and came over to where the cat led her. Her eyes widened, too. She squatted down so her head was level with mine. Since I couldn't move without pain, I sat there trying to look calm.

"A mouse!" she said. Oh, very good, human. You're clearly the detective, Batman.

"It's got a hurt leg," she said. She slowly reached to pick me up. I let her. Pain.

"What happened to you, little one?" she said. It was the same tone of voice the Kind Human used. She did like mice. My gamble had come through.

"Piss off," I told the cat. It did, swearing at being ordered about by a scary mouse.

I smiled at the human and licked her finger.

"Oh, you're so friendly," she said. "Would you like something to eat? I have some mouse treats…" She took me into the kitchen. There was an old mouse cage there, still full of toys and a nest box. And there was a wheel. Oh, how I longed to run on a wheel again, but I might never get to do that now. There was a computer on the same table, along with some papers and pencils. She set me down by the computer keyboard and went to get the cookies. That's when I had an idea that changed mousekind forever. I knew how a keyboard worked.

When she came back she set the cookie down and sat at the table. "There you go, cute mousey. I know mice like cookies." Then she looked at the computer screen, and a puzzled look came over her face. It said, "Need your help. Wounded in battle. Need antibiotics."

She shook her head and cleared the screen. She tried to feed me the cookie again. I swatted it away. "Now, don't bite me," she said warningly. Her jaw dropped as I jumped onto the keyboard and typed "No cookie. Antibiotics."

She just stared for a good long time. Her look was worth the trouble. I grinned.

"Did… Did you just type that?" she asked.

I went over to a cup of pencils and pulled one out. I chewed off the graphite end and took it to a piece of paper. "Yes," I wrote.

"Oh… Oh my god," she said.

“Hello,” I wrote. Hmmm… Keyboard was easier. I went back there.

“This… This is amazing…” She looked pale, like she was going to pass out.

“Don’t pass out,” I wrote on the computer. “I need your help.”

I waited a good five minutes while she composed herself. She looked at the screen, at the tiny note I had written. She struggled with it. Finally, it seemed like she was going to be okay.

“I always knew mice were smart,” she said. Then she shook her head to clear it. “Antibiotics… I don’t have any. I did once. I had a mouse once.”

“Pet?” On the paper I wrote an arrow toward the cage.

“Oh, yes,” she smiled. “Tiny was his name. He was so sweet. I had to take him to the vet once, but those meds are long gone now.”

“What happened to Tiny?” I wrote.

“Oh, that’s a terrible story.” She looked distressed. “You don’t want to hear that.”

I nodded. Sure.

“I had him for a year and a half. My family went on vacation, and I had to go, so I took him to this pet hotel. It was called “Paradise Place Pet Hotel.” They assured me everything would be okay, but when I came back…” Her eyes welled up. I put my paw on her hand, and she petted me. She knew how to pet a mouse. “When I came back, they gave me this… mouse… in the cage I had brought Tiny in. And it wasn’t Tiny. It was white, just a feeder, like Tiny had been, but I could tell right away it wasn’t Tiny. It ran from my hand, and Tiny always came out to greet me. It didn’t even look like Tiny. I told them they had the wrong mouse, but they said that was the only mouse they had. I looked around the place, and they had a lot of other animals, but no mice. They had a snake though, and it had a lump in it. So I lost it. I got really mad, and I screamed for the manager. The owner came out and explained very apologetically that an employee—who had been fired—had ran out of food for several animals, and so he fed my mouse to the snake.”

I gasped in horror. Heide was crying now. Oh, how terrible.

“He apologized and said he told someone to go get me a new mouse “to make up for it.” But that wasn’t what was going on. They had thought it would fool me, replacing Tiny. They thought I didn’t care enough for my little friend to know his face, his behavior, his… his soul. I guess the cruel trick would have worked on most people… I don’t know. But I was destroyed by it. I tried to sue them, to take legal action, but I couldn’t prove that the mouse they replaced my baby with wasn't Tiny. So they got away with that awful crime. They fed my darling, priceless baby to a snake for no reason, except that they ran out of food for it."

I sat there a long time looking at her. It was an open wound, and she was still suffering from it. She was a Kind Human. Her grief at the loss, the terrible story she told—that was proof. She knew her mouse from a thousand others. She could have picked Tiny out of a huge crowd of mice. Tiny had met an undeserved end at the hands of uncaring humans who valued a mouse at no more than 99 cents. I think my opinion of humans at that moment hit rock bottom.

"What happened to the other mouse?" I typed.

She shook her head. "I tried to keep it, but I couldn't. It reminded me of Tiny's premature end in the mouth of a snake. I couldn't bear it," she sobbed. "I tried…"

I looked at her. She hadn't answered the question.

"I gave it to a friend," she said. "One who had other mice."

Other Kind Humans? What a discovery.

And what a horrid story. "I'm very, very sorry," I typed.

"I told you you didn't want to hear it…"

"But I did," I wrote.

She nodded. "I must be going crazy," she said. "I miss Tiny so much. He trusted me, and I left him with those butchers. I keep imagining his end, wondering why I wasn't coming to save him. I haven't even been able to clean out his cage. Now I'm talking to a mouse. It even looks like you have a cast on your leg. I'm insane."

"No," I wrote. "Many mice know how to read. And write."

"You're… you're kidding?" she asked.

I shook my head no.

"Could Tiny read and write?" she asked.

"Maybe, if he'd been taught."

Her face showed her shock at all the new information.

"You can't tell anyone about me," I wrote.

"I promise," she said. "But I have to get you to a vet."

I shook my head no again. "Vet won't help me."

"Why?" she asked.

"Don't know about mice. Don't care. Will try to put me to sleep because of my leg."

I hopped around lamely thinking of it, then went back to the keyboard: "No one must know that I can write! And I hate vets! They poke you and prod you."

She seemed ready to argue but then stopped, probably thinking about Tiny. She had seen first hand what humans were capable of. "What do I do then?" she asked.

"Do you know where I can get antibiotics?" I wrote.

"I'd try a pet store," she said.

"Can you take me to one?" I typed.

She nodded her head.

"At night, when they're closed," I wrote.

She nodded again. "Isn't it dangerous?" she said.

"What isn't for a mouse?" I wrote.

She laughed sadly. "Yeah, no kidding…"

But first I wrote, "Do you want to make Tiny proud of you?"

She nodded.

"Wait here for me," I typed, and hobbled to my feet. I crawled to the curtains, lowered myself painfully to the floor, and vanished under the sink.

When I came back with the mother mouse, Heide had set up the cage already. The mother looked at me questioningly. Heide was smiling. She had guessed what I was going to ask of her.

"For everything you've done for me," I said to the mother mouse, "you deserve this. I think this human will take good care of you."

"And my babies?" she asked.

"I don't know," I said. "Go get one, and we'll see."

When she returned, holding a tiny pinky gently in her mouth, Heide was deeply moved.

"Ohhh, the tiny little thing," she breathed. "Is she asking me to take care of her and her family?"

I nodded. "Will you?" I wrote.

"Yes, I would be honored," she said. "Is this the cookie stealer?"

I nodded and smiled. She smiled back. She reached out gently to pet the mother mouse. The female mouse tensed, but held still. Brave mouse. "You won't ever have to steal another cookie again, sweetie," she said.

The mother looked at me with infinite gratitude and vanished to go get her babies, one by one.

"These are probably Tiny's children," I typed. "She was his friend."

Heide looked even more surprised and gazed down with new affection at the tiny pink baby. I could see she knew it was true. Her eyes watered up again.

"I'll give them everything I ever gave Tiny," she whispered. Then she looked at me.

"Thank you."

Boy, did that feel good.

The cat jumped up on the counter. "No way!" he said.

I looked him straight in the eye. He wasn't used to that. Not many mice could do it.

"Way, cat," I said. "Furthermore, if any harm whatsoever comes to this mouse or her family, I will be back to deal with you! And less mercifully than last time!"

The cat shrank back, fearing for its life. I stalked forward until I was inches from its face. "Am I perfectly clear?" I said, growling the words.

The cat nodded.

"Oh, Kitty!" Heide said. "Are you going to be the guardian of the nice mice?" She eyeballed him hard. She knew what was up. "Don't hurt these mice, Kitty, understand?!"

The cat meowed at her, avoided my eyes, and ran from the room.

"Don't worry," she said. "The cage has a lid he can't get through, and I'll make sure they're safe."

I wrote "Thank you."

When all the babies were in the new nest (with fresh, soft bedding), the mother licked me. "We owe you everything," she said.

"I owe you more," I said. "And I will do more one day, I promise. But now I am in a race against time to find medicine, or I am going to get very sick and die."

"I understand," she said. "They have medicine in the lab."

I peered at her hard. "What?"

"At the lab, they have medicine," she repeated. "Sometimes pet mice escape from their owners. I met one once. It knew about the lab."

"What is… the lab?" I asked, fearing the way she said it. It brought back bad visions of my dreams.

"It's a place where humans keep mice," she said. "That's all I know. I think it's bad, because it was mentioned with great fear."

"Great evil," I whispered.

"What?"

"Nothing. Just something I promised a… a while ago." I looked at her. "You need a name for helping me. You risked everything to do that. If you'd stayed in that basement those other mice would have come and found us. They'd have killed you and your babies."

"Not without a nasty fight," she said. I smiled. She was so brave.

"We need a name for you," Heide said to the mother, as if reading my mind. I looked at the mouse.

"How about Fred?" the mother mouse said. I looked at her like she had three heads.

"Don't joke," I said. "Those things can stick!"

"I like Fred," she said. I looked at her silently. "I do," she said. "Can that be my name?"

I shrugged. Whatever.

"Her name is Fred," I typed. "Mine is Squibble."

"Hmmm… strange name for a female mouse," Heide said. I nodded. "But okay, Fred it is. And nice to meet you, Squibble. That sounds familiar. A friend of mine has this book—"

"No resemblance," I typed quickly.

She shrugged. "Okay."

I smiled at Fred. Fred smiled back. "You're named now," I said. "A loved pet."

She hugged me. Her babies squirmed around my feet. One of them clung to me. I felt my chest warm and my face blush.

I went to the edge of the table. Heide bathed me with warm water and soap, careful not to get the cast wet. Then we rested until that night. I said goodbye to Fred and wished her well. Heide wrote down her address and phone number for me, on a tiny piece of paper, which I stuck in my tunic over my chest hoping it would act as armor. I don't know why she wrote that stuff down for me. It's not as if I could come back, or use a phone, but okay… whatever.

I took a toothpick and made a walking stick/crutch. I bound my leg further with tape and toothpicks. It hurt a lot, but to face what I was about to attempt, I was going to have to ignore it. I didn't think there were going to be any antibiotics at the pet store. They just let mice die when they got sick.

I knew what was coming. My dreams made it plain as day. I just didn't want to admit it.

I realized I had been doing that for a long time.

Great Evil

✠

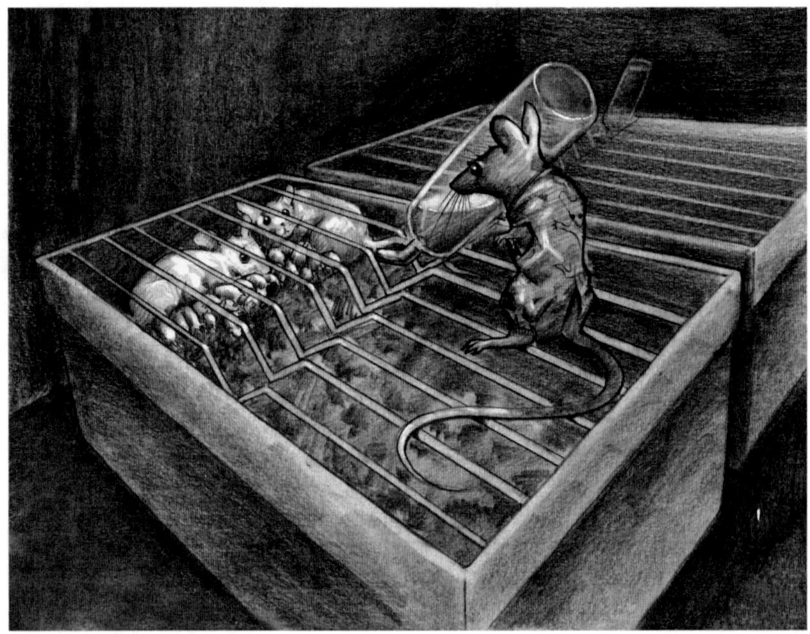

Heide talked to me on the way to the pet store. She seemed happy to have someone to talk to. She told me she belonged to a rat and mouse club. They had a web site and fairly regular meetings she used to go to with Tiny. She said now that Fred was around she might go back. Without a pencil lead or computer I could only listen, sitting on the dashboard watching the city go by at speeds I couldn't begin to hope for on my own. It made me wish I had a mouse-sized car.

She told me about the members of the club, and that the club was worldwide. She was talking about thousands of Kind Humans—amazing! I couldn't wait to get home and tell my master what I'd found. I'd be famous in my own right. My pilgrimage wasn't turning out so bad. I figured I'd already been gone three weeks or so… hard to tell how much time had passed. I wondered what was happening back home. I missed everyone.

Then we stopped.

"Pet store," she said. "None of the pet stores around here are very good. I try to avoid shopping at them. I hate how they treat their mice." She opened the door and carried me to the sidewalk. "I'll wait here," she said.

I nodded and hobbled to the door. I could have squirmed under it with ease, but the cast was problematic. I had to squish it down, which hurt like crazy. I felt sticky, hot liquid squirt out of my leg and soak the cast. It smelled bad. That odor would attract predators from everywhere. It screamed, "Sick mouse! Free food!" I would have to take care of that, and keep my nose alert for trouble.

It took me hours to search the store and find the mice. Once I did, I had to climb up to some bookshelves. It took me another two hours to do it. My leg felt like it was on fire the entire time. The pain ran from my toes to my back. My belly felt weird. It felt much worse when I got to the mice.

There was a ten-gallon aquarium crammed full of mice. There must have been fifty of them in there. Their food was soiled. Their water was dirty. The males were fighting and many of them were wounded. Some were dead, half buried in the moldy bedding. But that wasn't what held my attention; it was the two ridiculously small cages next to the ten-gallon tank.

They must have been no bigger than eight inches long, by four high and five wide—not even enough space for a mouse to stand up! Within each were not one, but two mothers… with children! Two in each cage, with over twenty babies. The bedding was filthy. The water was a tube crammed into the bars of the lid, and the food was strewn everywhere. It was a nightmare. My master had told me things were worse than I knew, but to see it was heartbreaking. Those mice had nowhere to go! They didn't even have room to stretch. My eyes welled up with tears.

"How long have you been here?" I asked one of the mothers.

"Where?" she asked, looking fatigued, her fur messy, her energy spent.

"In… in that cage…" I said.

"As long as I can remember," she said. "I was born in it. They brought me here in it."

I put my hands over my mouth. Wrongness!

I leapt up on the thick wires and struggled with all my might. I could not bend them. There was no release mechanism. No loose lid, no way to rescue them. The cage was sealed tight. The metal top had to come off somehow, but I saw that it was clamped solidly onto the cage sides. It was going nowhere. I was powerless to help these poor mothers. Frustrated, I hopped about, squeaking.

"You'd better get back in the cage," the mother mouse said wearily. "They punish the ones they find escaped."

"I didn't come from that other cage," I said. "I came from outside."

"What's 'outside'?" she said. I gritted my teeth—this was so hard!

"Freedom. Space to move around. Clean food. Fresh water."

She sighed and squinted. "Oh, I'd give anything to be in that big cage over there," she nodded toward the ten-gallon aquarium next to her with the fifty mice in it. I gaped. "They have so much room. And so many friends… Maybe someone would help me take care of my babies."

She hadn't even heard me. She was lost in her enslaved world. To her, the hell next door was heaven. I shook my head. "What happens here?" I said.

She looked at me. I saw she was old. Or maybe the captivity had aged her. "Humans come. They take my babies. At first I tried to take them back. I tried to bite. I tried to pull my precious children back into the cage, but the human hand was too strong. Too strong… They took all my babies. Then they put a mouse in with me for a few days. The only company I get, though it's always a different mouse. Then I have more babies. Then they come to take them away again. I always fight the hand, but it is too strong… I hope my babies have good lives. I hope they aren't put in tiny cages."

Her babies were fed to snakes. I couldn't tell her.

"How many times has this happened?" I asked.

"I can't count that many," she said.

"Can you count?" I asked. She nodded. "How high?"

"I can count to twenty, because I once had that many babies."

I felt something in my stomach heave. How could humans be so cruel?! They act like they're the only animals on the whole damn planet!

"Does every pet store do this?" I said to myself, horrified.

"Where I come from there are thousands of mice, and all of them in cages like this one," she said. "I never saw such a huge cage like that one until I came here."

My cage, back at the safe house, was 25 gallons. Full of toys, good food and fresh water always available… I had it all to myself. And I could leave anytime I wanted to…

"I want to help you," I said, eyes blurry from tears, "but I can't. I'm not strong enough."

She smiled at me slowly, as if drugged. "I don't need help."

I leapt off the cage. I couldn't take it anymore. I searched madly for drugs. I sniffed for them, I looked in every nook and cranny. There was nothing. I finally went back to the mother mouse and described the smell of antibiotics. It was near dawn. I was taking far too long. The human was probably gone by now.

"I knew that smell," she said to my surprise. "Back where I came from, where all the tiny cages were."

I swallowed. "Was it called a… a lab?"

She nodded. "That's what the humans called it."

Oh, I did not want to go there! I wanted to go home. I wanted my mommy more than I ever had! The evil and horrors of the world were beating my soul down. At every turn was some new terror, some shocking, sick surprise. *Why?* Why was everything so wrong?

My first instinct was to blame humans. They had made the world what it was. But then something told me to hold off on my judgment. There was much I didn't know. I might be wrong. BJ always said assumptions were stupid, for stupid mice.

Weary with pain, frustrated, disappointed, and terribly saddened by the mothers' predicament (all the more for having to leave them there), I went back out toward the street. I had seen great evil; there was no doubt about it. Despite that, I felt that I had not yet met my true enemy. The thought was daunting.

Flashing red and blue lights assailed my eyes. I ran forward to the glass door of the pet shop and saw a car had pulled up behind Heide's. It had different colors, and the flashy lights were coming from the top of it. It also had a powerful beam of light that lit up Heide inside her car. There was a man in some sort of uniform talking to Heide through her window. Heide seemed to be arguing. The man got angry and said something loudly, handing Heide a piece of paper. Heide looked frantically at me, or actually at the door because she couldn't see me, and then started her car. She drove away very slowly, looking back the whole time. Oh, no!

The man got back into his car and stayed there, writing inside. He stayed for a long time, eating a donut.

I had lost my new Kind Human. I was growing sick. I had a broken leg. My only option seemed to be to go to this horrible place called a lab, which I feared with all my soul because of the things I had seen in my dreams. The Black Mouse was born there in the lab. I did not know where it was or have even a general direction. I had no equipment, no food, no water, and I smelled like lunch to every animal within miles.

To quote TV, I was up the creek without a paddle.

Survival Instincts (And Then Some)

✠

You ever have one of those days that was so totally messed up—absolutely nothing would go right—that you wanted to go back to bed and hide? I was having that day. Only I had no bed.

From the beginning of time, mice have been in my situation. Rain comes, washes a poor mouse right out of his den and into strange territory where he must immediately scour the place and search for food and shelter, the whole time keeping an eye out and avoiding predators. Until about 3000 years ago or so, humans had been in this predicament, too. It's like that saying: "The best laid plans of mice and men…" No one promises you anything in life. It's a huge gamble. You do the best you can to tilt the odds in your favor, but no one really knows what's going to happen, and random events can kill you. Then you're dead—bam—just like that. Ride over, please exit to the left.

Only I had this gift. I didn't need it in order to know that I was a step away from death, but my mind was starting to lose it. I was going into that fuzzy, weird place where my body stops mattering so much and I see the spirit world. For the first time, it didn't scare me so badly. It didn't really matter very much. I mean, what could it hurt? There was *something* to all this spirit stuff. Nemo had made me immune to the cold of the snow. Maybe I could give it a chance.

I limped into an alleyway and plopped down near some trash. I ate part of an apple that had been discarded for days. Oh, if only my family could see me now. How ashamed I was. How humiliated and low I felt. A Mouse Knight, grubbing for trash to eat—what a sight. I had truly made a mess of things.

I decided to try meditating. I took "mouse lotus position" (well, kinda, because I couldn't bend my broken leg) and focused on nothing—just like Nemo had taught us. I let all thoughts pass through me on their way to infinity and let my mind go into the darkness. I forgot that I was in pain, and I forgot how scared I was. I imagined a river, with a dock reaching out over it. It was an old wood dock, like the kind a family might build on their land. It looked like a small river, maybe 70 feet across. It flowed leisurely, and the water was soft and bright. The sun was setting, and the colors in the sky were tranquil. The clouds traveled along like the river, heedless of their destination, unconcerned about their destiny. The temperature was wonderful, and the scene was one of total peace. There was only the light on the river, and the sweet sound of it slowly passing by. I heard a beautiful, distant voice:

"This is a powerful place you've built, Squibble."

I had a memory of my master saying something about this very scene once, and suddenly there he was next to me, saying it, and we were sitting together at the end of the dock.

"Squibble, life is like a beautiful river, passing us by under a bridge, or a pier. We see all kinds of things from that place where we watch. We see things on the water, in the water, in the air... Sometimes we can pick up a few treasures as they float by, but mostly we watch as everything passes, on its way to someone else's pier. We get to watch everything in life; the experience is all we have. It's all we take with us in the end, because once things float on by, Squib, they're gone."

He shifted and looked meaningfully at me with his deep red eyes. "Our lives float by with the river, and then they're gone, Squib.

They're gone." Then he faded away, and I felt him float on by, down the river, happy and carefree.

I was sad to see him go. I so wanted to hold onto him, but it had been a miracle in itself that he had come to sit with me on my dock. Just being so close to him for that short time had been a precious gift. I knew I could not keep anything here in life. It was useless to try. For some reason this made me unbearably sad. I saw such beautiful things floating by on the river—friends and family, treats and toys, fun and laughter... I also saw sadness and despair, broken hearts, and disappointment. Every bit of it drifted on by, at exactly the same speed. I could do nothing to stop any of it.

I knew I could pick something out of the river, if it drifted close enough, but even then, how long could I hold it? And that would mean looking away from the majesty of the river to focus on something else. Not that that would be wrong... I felt there was no wrong here, none at all, just experiences. No good or bad, no judgment at all. Just the river, the sky, the sounds of it all. How long had my master been gone? A moment? A week? A month? Maybe a year? Time had stopped. It had no meaning.

Sitting on the dock, I remembered my master saying to me, "Death is like life, Squibble. It's just another journey." He was not smiling as he always did. It was raining. "Souls travel to the sea, and wait there for the dawn, or the sunset, depending on which sea..."

"How long does it take?" I asked, picturing myself at the edge of some sea, a shining and noble soul, ready to be rewarded for a life of faithful service. "What happens then?"

My master looked to the horizon, a longing in his eye. "Well, it takes a while to get to the sea, little mouse, and on the way a soul has time to think on its life, and what it meant."

"And then?!" I asked, eager and excited.

My master looked at me and forced a smile. He looked tired. "Then the ship comes, Squib. The shining ship of the fates, to take that soul to paradise."

"Cool!" I exclaimed. "And then?!"

"Anything you want then," my master said.

"Anything?!" I gasped. "Even ice cream?"

He laughed, coughed, then laughed again. "Yes, precious friend. Even ice cream." He petted me. It was heaven, so nice... A raindrop hit the side of his face, and it looked like he was crying even though he was smiling.

Then I was back on the dock, sitting there over the middle of the river, watching it pass me by. It was sunset. I was old. I had come to this dock many, many times. I knew it well. The water had not changed. This place never did. Only I had changed. I was alone.

I woke in the late evening sometime in the dark. The ground was shaking. A trash truck was coming to collect the trash, and I would be collected with it. I tried to get up and run, but had forgotten I had a broken, swollen leg. I fell and squeaked in pain. I wanted my mommy. I wanted to be back on that pretty dock where nothing mattered. But I wasn't. I was struggling to survive in a cold, harsh world, and I'd better get used to it or perish. So I limped as fast as I could with my crutch away from the trash cans. The ground trembled, and I fell repeatedly, but I just got up and kept going.

It was certain death I was trying to outrun. I didn't look back once. As the trashcans were lifted into the sky, bits of refuse fell all about me like a crumbling building. Any number of them could have smashed me to death, but I got lucky. Some liquid spilled out onto the pavement and made puddles. I made it to shelter next to a fallen brick. I waited until the trash truck rumbled on, then crawled out and lowered myself to the shiny pool, quivering and weak. I drank, remembering how pathetic I must look. Look, hell, I *was* pathetic.

I painfully crawled several blocks, stopping to rest at each one. I was lost. I had no idea where I was going. My only hope was to find that dreaded lab and somehow steal antibiotics. That place sounded like a dragon's lair, designed to keep mice trapped inside. I wouldn't stand a chance there. Maybe there was an alternative.

I found a phone booth. I climbed up onto the shelf where the phonebook sat—it was closed of course—and nosed until I found the "P" section. I was pretty sure "pharmacy" was how it was spelled. (Not with an "F" like it sounded—weird language.) Then I chewed. I chewed into the phonebook. Mice are good at this, and it wasn't wood. More like loose wood, all those compressed pages. It went well, and it was fun, but by dawn I still wasn't through to a part of the page I wanted. I didn't even notice it was day until a human flipped the phonebook open.

Busted! I snapped my head up and gazed into the face of a fat old lady. Seeing a mouse burrowed into her phonebook, she screamed and threw the book back onto the shelf. Only my little gnawed-out cave saved me for being squished to death. She ran screaming from the booth, cursing about mice. Stupid human. You're much scarier than I am.

I recovered from the shock and scurried as best I could down from the shelf and into the nearby alleyway. All day I slept and ate trash, drank icky water and watched the phone booth. Lots of people were mad about the chewed pages, but no one tried to throw the book away. It was on a chain anyhow.

That night, many hours after the sun went down and the street was deserted, I crept back into the booth and continued my excavation of the pharmaceutical section. Finally, I found phone numbers and addresses. Hee hee! What a smart mouse I was! I tore out several sections with addresses on them and folded them carefully, lining my tunic with them, front and back, like armor.

I was amassing quite a collection of paper. It made me wish I had one of my favorite books to read. The mice back home all took great pride in reading, and the house was full of books with mice reading them. My master had personally read over a hundred books, including every single treasured encyclopedia he owned that the human bought for him. Mice competed to see how many books they could read, and how much they remembered. I was different. I only liked a few books. They were by this guy, Stephen King. He was really cool. He wrote stories, and one was about a dangerous guy searching for the tower. I can't die before I know how that ends! No way. I gotta live to read that. Another one of them was about a mouse! That mouse was so cool, and everyone liked the mouse except this stupid guy. Anyway, I figured Steve liked mice. My master says he's a great writer, so I learned a lot from his writing. Or at least I tried to. I'd always get lost in the stories and just keep reading. I missed out on a lot of "important" books like medical journals and math an' all that, but who cares? I loved Steve's stories. They were important to me. When we put in requests for new books from the Kind Human, I'd always write his name on the list. Everybody would look at me like I was a loon, but they were obviously a bunch of stiffs who couldn't appreciate a good yarn unless they were chewing on it. So sometimes I got the books. And what I wouldn't have given right then, in that stupid city, to find a King book!

So I spent another three days looking for a gas station. I knew from my trips with the human that gas stations had maps. When I found one, I snuck in and robbed them of a map. (If I were a human, I'd leave money or something, but I'm not, I'm a mouse, and mice steal stuff, okay?)

I couldn't carry the whole map at all, so I tugged it open on the floor and managed to find where I was on it. I located the pharmacy addresses, too. Using where I was at for the center, I chewed out a circle of the map that included all of them. Now I had a smaller piece with everything I needed. I folded up this partial map and tried to stuff it in my tunic, too, but it wouldn't fit. So I made a cloak out of it. Fine with me—wear the map. While I was there I ate a bit of candy bar and beef jerky. I got a drink of some fresh water below the refrigerator—mmm, good! Then I washed off my leg, found some soap and cleaned it. Puss and nasty stuff oozed out of the tear in my skin where the bone had come through. It burned and hurt, but it looked like it was still set correctly, a miracle considering what I'd put it through. I made a new splint out of more toothpicks and clean toilet paper. I wrapped it good and tight.

I stuffed my tunic with all the goodies I could carry and started on my way toward the nearest pharmacy. It was hard. I was sick and weak, but mice have an advantage in this department: when we get sick, the last thing to go is our ability to move and act normal. That's because if we acted sick out in the wild, we'd instantly be obvious as a target for predators. They look for that kind of thing. Mice have learned to act normal until they are on death's door, and then they leave the nest and die. Maybe some predator spares them some pain by eating them and making it quick. This behavior always bothers the Kind Human, because he can never tell which of the mice are sick until it's almost too late. He keeps antibiotics on hand. Smart human.

Anyway, because of this gift to mice by the Mousegod (thank you, Bigfat), we can be sick and travel for some time and act fairly normal before we suddenly drop dead. My master almost did that on our first quest. He was hurt really bad, much worse than I was now. I still couldn't feel my rear end. It would bleed when I sat down on it, so I spent most of my time laying down or standing on one leg when I was still.

I was getting better at using the crutch, and I shortened it so it worked better. I was making about a quarter of the time I would without the break, but at least I was moving. I found things to eat and drink most everywhere. Always trash, but humans throw away some pretty good stuff. I even had pizza. I guess they've forgotten what it's like to starve.

I steadily grew sicker. It took me a week or more to reach the first pharmacy, and every step was agony. I would have fainting spells and dizzy moments, and I sometimes felt like my guts were swelling.

Finally I made it. I sat and waited for the pharmacy to close, but it didn't seem to be happening. At midnight, they were still open! I thought, "What's up with that?" and went to read the door behind the shopping carts. It said "24-hour pharmacy" on it. Grrrrrr!

Well, that meant either a search for another one or just braving this one. It would be very foolish to try to rob humans while they were there, but I was really sick. I was losing my appetite, and that was the beginning of the end.

I decided I had to risk it. My master told me never to do that, and going in while the humans were awake was a big risk. Sorry, Master. I have no choice.

I said a word to Bigfat, asking him to make me invisible to the humans, and snuck in the back.

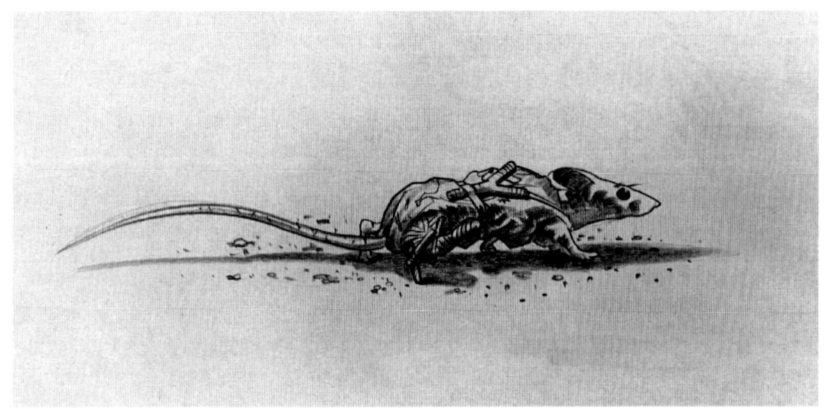

Drugs!

✠

Inside it was dark, but not as dark as I wanted. In the movies, they'd cut the power an' all that, but I hadn't read all those technical manuals, see? I didn't know how to even find the power cables, much less cut them. I could, however, quickdraw a gun real good if I had one. Yessir, that I could. Oh well.

I snuck up into the ceiling and moved along until I could see down through the cracks into the pharmacy itself. There were drugs everywhere, but all on shelves… really hard to climb shelves. Grrrrr. They couldn't make anything easy on mice. Somebody probably invented shelves so mice couldn't get anything good.

I clambered down a corner on a pipe to get onto the counter and began to search for antibiotics. I knew what they smelled like. There were a few loose pills under things, but no antibiotics. They smell kinda… sour. I found a package that said it had an alcohol pad in it. I needed that, too, so I khybed it ("khybe" is slang for steal… TV is good… TV is friend…). Then I scuttled down to the floor.

I found all kinds of drugs on the floor! I filched some of them for later, stuffing them into my tunic. I had no idea what they were, but maybe they were cool. I took four pills—'cause they were small—but still no antibiotics. I was going to have to get up onto those shelves.

There was one human working there. She was a mousey-looking girl with big round glasses, and she looked bored. She was reading a book and sitting in front of a computer. Hmmm… a book. No, Squibble, focus. Focus.

The girl was clearly absorbed in her book, so I had time to work. I found some string in a drawer, I found a paperclip. You know what's comin'… I saw this on TV. Except that I couldn't budge that paperclip to turn it into a grappling hook—it was too strong. Grrrr. I bit it and chewed on it to no effect. How frustrating! Now I had to come up with another ingenious plan. I climbed back up the pipe, and about halfway up I leapt helter-skelter toward the medicine shelves. Hey, nobody said I was all wise, okay?

I fell about two feet and landed roughly—and very painfully—among some gauze pads. That was real lucky, because if I'd landed on the bottles it would have made a loud noise, and the human certainly would have freaked out. As it was, it wasn't totally silent, and she looked up. I remained totally still (just like a mouse) and waited until she went back to her book. I want a book…

Then I lurked hard, inspecting every bottle and trying to decipher what was in it. I only knew the names of a few antibiotics, but I had another problem, too. At the safe house I had been given oral syrup. If I found it, how would I carry it? If I found capsules instead, how would I know how much to take? I decided "first things first": gotta find the stuff.

There was nothing I could use on that first shelf. I did see a medicine I recognized—Furosemide. It was for heart trouble. The Kind Human had some of that in his fridge. I hadn't thought about it before, but now I wondered why.

There was no way to get to the lower shelf but to hang over the ledge and try to swing my way into the next level. If I missed, I'd fall seven feet to my death on the tile floor. I couldn't think of that, though, or I'd never have the courage to try. So I blanked my mind and gave it my best shot. The ledge was very slippery, and I almost fell while lowering myself over on my belly. I gnawed the edge of the shelf to give me pawholds, and finally I was hanging by my arms over potential doom. I swung… Once… twice… thrice… I almost slipped and fell the wrong way! On the return swing I let go, and this time I crashed into the bottles. I was right—it made a loud noise.

The girl was up and over to the shelf in a heartbeat! Trying not to moan in pain, I limped quickly away and hid behind the boxes in the farthest, darkest corner of the shelf, hopefully out of her reach. I was trembling.

She picked up the bottles, rearranged the shelf some, and peered into the dark corner I sat in. Obviously her eyesight was as bad as a mouse's because I was in plain sight and she didn't appear to see me. She did look perturbed, though.

"Ummm… hello?" she said.

Hello, human. You'll forgive me if I don't come out and shake your hand.

"Listen… if it's spirits or something… just… don't get all nasty, okay?"

He he heee. Yeah, spirits. Mouse spirits, lady. Beware.

She cautiously went back to her seat and began typing something on the computer. She might be sounding the alarm. I had to hurry. I looked at the rest of the bottles on the shelf. No luck. Then I looked out across the rest of the pharmacy. It was ridiculous. There were at least ten racks, each with nine or ten shelves in each. Gahhh! How was I going to do all of them?

I repeated my flip trick and continued to explore. I started to get better at it—especially with chewing just the right pawholds in the wood first—and got in the habit of looking for landing spots in or on quiet things. I tried for soft things, too, 'cause each time I landed it felt like someone had hacked my leg off.

Twice I made noises and the girl looked around, but I was already gone a-hiding. She was growing increasingly concerned though, I could tell. Secretly it delighted me to scare a human. They deserved it for all the frights they've given us. I wished she was the big stupid fat lady from the phone booth. I kinda liked this girl for some reason. I couldn't say why.

Finally, I worked my way to the bottom of the rack. I had grabbed drugs that I knew the names of, or that looked or smelled familiar, and stuffed them into my tunic. When the tunic was full, I made a small side-pouch out of a tiny plastic baggie I found that was obviously supposed to hold small pills. I used my string to sling that around my back, and I was ready to collect more. Squibble, the

Medicine Collector. That's Doctor Squibble to you, sir, I thought happily.

I went up another rack and found that by climbing up the side, I could step off onto any shelf I wanted. I had been risking my life for nothing! Oh well.

On the sixth shelf, I found that I could only step off the side onto the top of a bottle, so I did. Unfortunately the bottle tilted into others, and they all fell off the shelf, taking me with them to the floor. I fell on my back, and heard a sickening crack. I saw stars. I saw my river and my dock for a brief flash. I lay there stunned as the human got up and came over to the scene, almost stepping on me. She stopped just short of killing me and stared down at me and the mess I created. To top it off, I saw the bottle I had fallen with said "Baytril" on the side—my antibiotic!

With all my strength I tried to reach the bottle. My leg was shooting horrible pain all the way into my bruised head. My limbs were slow and sluggish. I had taken a very bad fall, but at least I wasn't paralyzed. That was almost certainly because I had padded my body with folded up papers. Everything hurt like crazy, and I was in no shape to run. I pawed at the bottle, desperately trying to get at the pills inside to save my life.

I tried to dodge as a glass cup went over me. It almost pinched my tail off and barely missed my head. The human had me! I felt great disappointment and dread. So this was my fate. It sucked. I deserved better.

"Got you, little spirit!" she said.

Yeah, got me. Whee ha.

Thinking that I had very little air in that glass and might never wake up, I went limp. Then I passed out from the pain.

The Lab

✠

MY PET
MOUSE NEDZ
MEDIKAL ATENSHON
PLEEZE TREAT
HIM AN LET HIM
GO.

THANKZ.
-DArel

When I woke there were voices. I expected to hear Bigfat telling me off for being so stupid, but they were human voices. It was the girl, and she was arguing with a security guard. I was still under the glass, and the damn Baytril was still within arm's reach… if I could have reached through solid matter.

The glass was frosted, hard to see through and blurry. I could see the figures of the two humans and hear them, but I couldn't see details. That's normal, though. Mice can't see lots of details anyway.

"You can't take him there. He'll get experimented on and die," the girl said. Oh boy. That didn't sound good.

"But it's a mouse from next door," the man said. "They've specifically asked us to return their stock when we find it, and my boss—your boss too, missy—has given strict orders. I'm gonna do what I gotta do."

"Darrel, you psycho, this isn't a mouse from next door—it's brown, not white!"

"Ma'am, I'm obeying orders, like a good soldier."

"You're not in the army anymore, Darrel, jeeze!"

"I still have my integrity, though," the man said, and he came over to the glass. He slid a piece of cardboard under me—I had to jump to avoid getting my toes cut off, thankyouverymuch!—and took me up to eye level. "Sure is a little guy," he said.

"He's going to be tortured and killed in that insane place," the girl said. "Just give him a break. Let me take him. I won't tell anybody."

"No can do, ma'am. I have my orders."

"Damn your orders! I'm sick of your weird psychosis. This isn't the green berets—it's Pharmart!"

"Yes, ma'am," he said, as he carried me out of the room.

"And my name's Kristin, not 'ma'am,' moron!" she yelled after him. He ignored it. He marched (no kidding) out the back door and to a neighboring door in the row of buildings next to the pharmacy. He took out a big ring of keys and unlocked it. I immediately smelled mice—lots of mice. I also smelled sickness, fear, and pain.

I knew without thinking that this was the lab. I was going to be put in hell. My stomach sank. I *had* to be brave now. If I panicked here, I would be doomed for certain. My heart was racing, and my mind was flying through a hundred thoughts, most of them bad. I forced myself to reason through the panic and pain of my swollen leg. "Reason, Squibble," my master had said, "is what the humans say separates them from the animals. But we have it, too. It's our greatest weapon. Reason. The ability to respond instead of react." *I had to reason!*

Ok. Well, there was good and bad in this. The bad: I would probably be experimented on, it would be found that I could read, and the safe house would be found and taken by the government or something stupid like that. It would be the end of everybody I loved. They'd be subjected to heinous experiments because of me. We'd be at mankind's mercy. HA! What a joke! Mankind's "mercy"... As if there was any. The bad sounded pretty bad.

The good side was not nearly as good as the bad side was bad. It was simply this: they'd have drugs here. They'd have Baytril. I held my mind on that one thought. I was a Mouse Knight. I had a duty to escape and warn the safe house of the coming danger. I had to live.

I was put roughly into a cage half the size of a small shoebox. It was dark. All around me I smelled blood and urine. The guard shut the steel-barred door rapidly after taking the glass away. He had not even noticed that the mouse he had just deposited was wearing clothes and sporting a sidebag. Hastily he scrawled a note on a piece of paper and attached it to the cage's door hinge with the pencil. And that was where he messed up.

I waited for him to be gone, which he was in no time. I crawled to the bars on shaking legs and reached for the pencil. I had to be very cautious, or it would fall to the floor far below and my chances of escape would be shot. My limbs felt like spaghetti. I now had a fever. I felt as though I was back in front of the bully mouse, robbed of my strength. I used my tail to wrap around the writing tool just in case. Then I gnawed off the tip, and it was mine.

After stowing the pencil tip, I worked at the paper for an hour to get it all inside the cage without ripping it. The rest of the pencil was loose then, and I struggled with that, suffering greatly because of my illness and the weight of the pencil, until I got that inside too. Things were looking up, even though I felt like I couldn't breathe and I was dying. I now had a pencil, a paper, and the door latch was loose.

"Hey," a voice from the cell above me said.

"What?" I said impatiently. "I'm working here."

"You're not white."

"You're Batman."

"No, I'm not. I'm a mouse."

"Yeah. I figured that," I said.

"Get us out."

"Working on that myself, thanks. Can't worry about everyone."

"But they do terrible things to us here," he whined. He sounded like Scratchy. I was about to get mad, but I remembered how that little twerp had turned down so many offers of squirehood just to be my squire. As much as I hated admitting it, that took guts. I wish I hadn't kicked him. Or maybe just kicked him softer. I almost missed him along with the others. Compassion finally kicked in.

"If I can get out, I'll see what I can do." It was the last thing I wanted—more responsibility. But I *was* a Mouse Knight. If I could get out, why couldn't I get them out, too?

"Thanks!" said the other mouse. "You're the *mouse*!"

I perked my ears up. "Hey—that line is from TV," I said. "Where'd you learn that? And how'd you know who Batman was?"

"They have a TV here," the mouse said. "It's over there on the counter with all the pokey things and the rats."

Pokey things? I shuddered.

"Rats?" I said.

"Yeah. Rats."

"Not good enough that they abuse mice? They gotta abuse rats, too?"

My work was going well. I had erased most of the guard's message and was adding my own. He he heee!

"They also experiment on guinea pigs, hamsters, and other animals."

"Jerks," I said.

"Yeah," the mouse said. "We oughtta blow 'em up!"

I giggled. "Yeah, maybe we oughtta do that."

"I have two brothers in here," the mouse said.

"Good for you," I replied. My note was finished. I carefully replaced it, and the pencil, on the cage door. I kept the pencil tip though.

"You gotta get us out," the mouse said. "I'll be your best friend…"

"I already have a best friend," I said.

"I'll do anything. We all will!" Many voices chirped their agreement. There were a lot of mice here, maybe a thousand. None of them were doing very well. Egads… I felt so sorry for them, but I had to escape first.

"I'll see what I can do," I said, not knowing what else to say. I sat back and ate some of the bland food in the cage. I drank some of the water. I was hot, burning with fever. I wasn't going to last much longer. My leg felt like it was huge. My stomach felt awful from not being able to pee or poo. I had to get medicine fast.

I was asleep in the morning when the humans came. There were two of them in white coats. I listened to them going through their routine for the first half of the day. As I listened, I became aware of three things. First, they knew how smart we are. They just don't know we can read yet.

Second—and this hit me in a sudden flash—I realized it was only a matter of time before they *did* know. I even sat straight up as the thought came to me. It couldn't help but happen someday. The more mice we taught to read and write, and the more mice that went to foster homes, the higher the chance that someday, someone would figure all of this out. In fact, it was eventually inevitable! No matter what, it was going to happen. And what then? We'd *all* be in labs!

Third, they were doing terrible things to these mice! Things that hurt and things that were horrifying just to listen to. Mice screamed in agony, screamed in terror, and then sometimes the screams just stopped. The smell of fresh blood and urine would fill the air, and the rest of the mice would all fall silent for a moment. I guess they were probably cringing in horror like I was. The experiments—whatever they were for—could not be justified in my eyes. They had no way of knowing exactly how much pain and terror they were inflicting, but they did know it hurt. Oh yes, they did! They were guilty. They just didn't care!

I *had* to do something about it! About all of it! The mothers in the pet stores, the labs abusing the animals, and the scary fact that, unless… unless mice made peace with humans somehow, it was all over. We couldn't fight them. They were too big and too strong. They had technology. Oh, what a mess! What a mess.

"Look here," one human said, reaching for my cage. He had snuck up on me. I quickly lost my outfit and stashed my tunic, bag, and all the paper and drugs in the back corner of my cage. I was burying it with what they called bedding when the door opened. The human reached in quickly and grabbed me like an expert. I resisted the urge to bite him. He held the scruff of my neck with one hand and my tail with the other. Then I realized I had forgotten to remove my cast! Oh no!

He was reading the note. He read it to his friend out loud.

"My pet mouse neds medikal atenshon. Pleeze treat him an let him go. Thanks. -Darel"

"That Darrel sure is a character," the man said. "Can't spell worth beans."

Best I could do on short notice, human, I thought.

"Well, what do we do? We can't let him go," the other one said.

"Yeah, but we can treat him. Darrel will come get him. It looks like the army boy tried to make a cast for the leg here. Huh… Looks pretty good. I wonder how he got the mouse to stay still for that?" he said.

The other guy came over to look. "Wow. Yeah, really nice work. Well, we'd normally euthanize it, but the cast may actually work. Here, let me see him."

I acted like a stupid, normal mouse as I was transferred to the other hand.

"Yeah, looks very sick. Respiratory, runny eyes and nose... Swollen leg—it's bad. We'd better get on it if Darrel's going to keep his pet."

They took me over to the cold steel table and gave me a few shots under the skin. It hurt, but I didn't move. Shots were great, just exactly what I needed. I'd still have to find medicine, but those shots would hold out for a while.

"This mouse is really friendly, Dave. Look, he doesn't even move..."

"Probably sick as a dog."

"Yeah. Poor fella."

They were partially right. My appetite was all gone, and I probably would have been dead within days without that medicine. I was having a hard time thinking straight, or seeing straight for that matter. For example, the rats I saw in their cages on the counter... Two of them looked exactly like Shiva and Thor.

And they were looking at me, too, like they'd seen a ghost.

"Squibble!" one said. "No way!"

I perked my head up. "*Shiva?!*"

The man grabbed me by the scruff of my neck again. I was really sick of that.

"Oops, he got some energy back," the man said. He lifted me off the table to put me back in the cage.

"Thor! Shiva!" I cried.

"Uncle Squibble!" they yelled to me.

Then I was back in my cage. The man fastened the latch tightly this time. There was no way out.

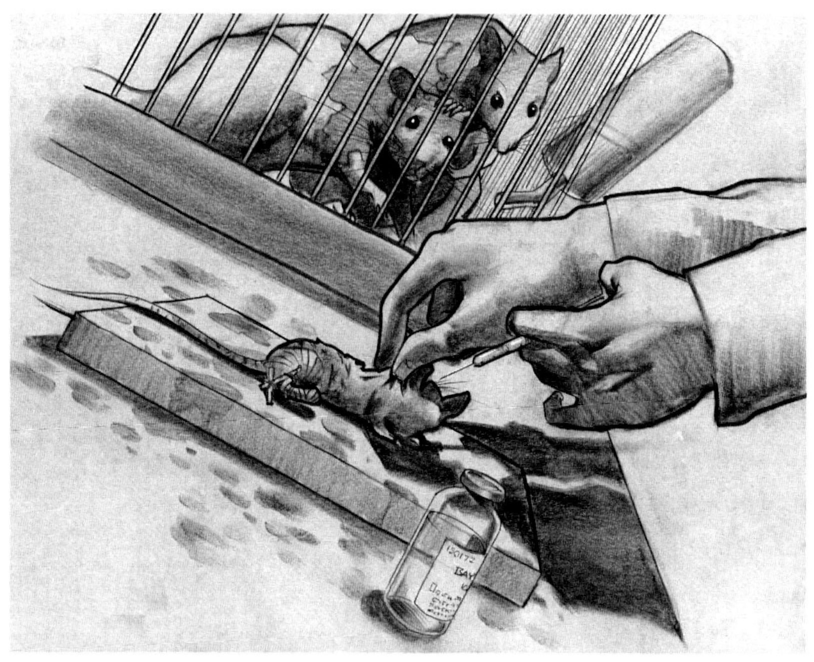

The First Rodent Army

✠

The drugs began working almost immediately. I felt much better. I could relieve myself, and wanted eat and drink again. My body felt as though it had been through a mouse grinder, but I was alive.

I had to know how Shiva and Thor got here. I had to get out of this stupid place. The cage latches were mouse-proof, much too difficult for one of us to unlock if it was fastened tight. One of us maybe not, but a rat, especially a big one (or two)…

The next day the white coat guy came again and gave me more injections. I had my speech all prepared to the boys.

"Okay boys, answer quick. I won't be here long. Are you okay?"

"Hell, no," Thor said. "They feed us weird stuff and stick needles in us! Of course we're not 'okay'!"

Shiva slapped Thor. "Respect Uncle Squibble!" he barked.

Thor lowered his head. "Sorry, Uncle."

"'S okay," I said rapidly. "Can you get out?"

"No," Shiva said.

Thor snaffed. "That was a stupid question! Don't you think we'd be out of here if we could?!" Shiva shot him a look and he said, "Sorry, Uncle."

"It's the drugs," Shiva said.

"What are they trying to do?" I said as a needle penetrated my tented skin and I felt cold liquid ooze down my spine.

"They're running an experiment," Shiva said, "trying to make rodents smarter."

I scoffed. "Too late," I said.

"Yeah, we mess with 'em!" Thor snickered. "We run the maze really good sometimes and really bad other times. Sometimes we just sit there on our butts. We've got all the other rats doing the same thing. He he heee!"

"We have to escape!" I said. "I have to deliver a warning to the safe house! It's life or death!"

Shiva looked at Thor. "We'll work on it," they said together.

Then I was taken back to my cage.

Another day passed. I kept feeling better, but I had a long way to go. I began scarfing the stupid food they provided like it was yummy, trying to build strength. The man took me out for my shot at the same time as the day before.

"I've got a plan," I told the rats.

"It'd better be good," Shiva said. "The rats in the cage next to us died last night after their injection. The ones down the line from them, the day before. We're next."

"Then it has to be tonight," I said as the needle went into my skin. "And we have to take everyone with us."

They looked at each other. "Heck, yeah!" Thor said, and pounded his fist against the metal bars.

The man looked up, puzzled. Shiva and Thor made ridiculous faces at the man, but of course, he couldn't tell. They just looked like rats to him.

"You know, sometimes I'd swear these rats know what we're doing," the man said to his colleague.

"Well, we've seen a lot of weird stuff," his friend said. "Maybe they do. After all, that's what we're trying to do, isn't it? Make them smart."

"What if they're smart already?"

"Well, then they wouldn't need our help," the man at the computer said. "And why would they stay here? It's not exactly the Ritz."

He finished with me and went to put me back in my cage. I'd have to be fast now. Broken leg or no.

The moment I touched ground, I raced to the back of my cage and dug up my crutch. I raced back to the front of the cage just as quick and, after making sure he wasn't looking, stuck my crutch in the latch as he closed it. It stuck halfway open as I had hoped, and he was none the wiser. He must have closed millions of latches in his lifetime. He never checked them anymore. He he he. He went back to work and I smiled.

That night, in the dark, I opened my cage. I put on all my gear, loaded up all my paper and drugs, and my side pouch. Then I scrabbled up to the mouse above me.

"Hey," I called to him through the bars.

He had a bruised head and his eyes were bugged out. His nose was bleeding. He looked at me like he was stunned, eyes not quite focusing.

"What are you doing?" I asked.

"Running into things," he said sadly.

I cocked my head at him. "Why?"

"Nothing else to do. Lack of stimulation. Boredom. Insanity. I hate being in this tiny, empty cage. All the mice do this. We go stir crazy."

"And hurt yourselves?"

"Sometimes. Some mice do backflips all night long, one long repetitious, mind-numbing wait for death. Some spin in circles. Some gnaw their fur off. Some even come to look forward to the painful experiments the humans perform on them. At least it's an end to the monotony."

My heart went out to these poor victims. "That's sad," I said.

"Yeah."

"Well, no more. If you can all handle it, we're getting out of here."

The mouse perked up immediately. His ears went stiff and he looked excited for the first time in his miserable life. *"Really!?"* he chirped. "It is true? Oh, Sir, we are so at your service!"

"That's good," I said, "because I am going to collect. Now get everyone ready."

I scrabbled down to the cold floor. Once there, I stopped without knowing why. Just a bad feeling or something. Suddenly a chill crept through my bones. The place was all dark. Sterile. Dead. The only noises were those of deranged, sick animals. This place was wrongness. Then I remembered.

This was where the Black Mouse had been born.

My flesh crawled instantly, like when you realize that the monster is in the same house with you… that the terrifying phone call came from your own number, or you hear the harsh snap of a twig right behind you in a dark forest at night. I suddenly felt terror. What if it was still here?!

I rushed as fast as I could with a broken limb up the computer table to the top and then over to the metal shelf where the rats were, trying really hard to forget my last horrifying thought.

"Uncle! You got out!" Shiva exclaimed.

"You're the shit!" Thor said.

"What?" I chirped as I studied the latch. "Don't offend my mousey dignity, boys!"

"It's TV slang," Shiva said. "It means you're way cool!"

"Oh," I said. "Okay then."

Their latch was different. It was made against smart rats. I wouldn't be able to open it with the crutch. But the lab men didn't count on a mouse who had some small knowledge of physics, nosirreebob. So I went and got one of the long pokey metal things they use to probe rodents with (ewww) and levered the latch open with the help of the twins. Shiva and Thor bounded out, covering me with licks and hugs. It felt good. I handed the sharp pointy probe thing to Shiva.

"Here. Take this, and Thor, you get one, too, and go open every cage there is!"

The boys were covered in bruises, scabs, and abuse. I gawked at them for a second before whispering, "How did this happen to you?"

Thor, frowning, growled, "Humans."

I turned to Shiva, who had always been the more intelligent of the two, though both were geniuses. He was scowling as well.

"The humans who adopted us moved," he said. "They gave us up to another set of humans, who, in turn, decided they didn't like how playful and friendly we were. They didn't really want to play with their pets. They just wanted us to amuse them with antics from our cage. They never let us out. They often forgot to feed us. We got sick of it, and started escaping to get food and water. Hey, it was that or die. They didn't like that, and they gave us up to a shelter. Things were *much* worse there. I won't go into it, but the horrors were… terrible." He had a haunted look in his eye. So did his brother.

"We were abused on a regular basis. Tortured. Made to do awful things," Thor continued. "They teased us by putting us in the cat cage for minutes at a time. They tried it with every animal in the kennel. Even a snake. It was made very clear that our end was to be soon—they were going to 'put us to sleep' if no one came to adopt us. What a joke. No one was going to adopt rats, and they were going to execute us for existing."

I was mortified. It had never happened that the Kind Human had misjudged an adopting family. There must have been a mistake. My heart was heavy for my boys. They had been through too much. It showed on their faces. They were no longer kids. They had been forced to grow up.

"What did you do?" I asked, stunned.

"We tried to do what we thought you'd do," Shiva said. "We kept trying to be friendly, to be loved, to be accepted. We tried to believe in the best of everyone, hoping we might get adopted. We talked our way out of most fights with the animals, even the cats, and we did tricks for the humans who ran the place, even though we hated them. We thought if we tried long enough, *someone* would love us and take us home."

"We tried, Uncle," said Thor. He fixed a scary gaze on me. It had fire in it. "We really did."

"I believe you," I said. "What happened then?"

"We came up against an animal we couldn't reason with. He was an insane killer, straight from the street. We couldn't talk our way out of it. He hurt us both badly. We would have died."

I swallowed. "So…?"

"We killed him," Thor said. There was no emotion in his face at all. Shiva showed a similar coldness. My gut felt like it was sinking. My boys had been hurt. On the inside.

"It was a dog," Shiva said. "A big one."

"We blinded him first, then took him apart at the neck."

"We used every nasty trick BJ ever taught us, and then invented some of our own."

They both looked at me as if standing before their judge. "We had no choice, Uncle," said Shiva. "The fight took hours."

A moment passed before I could answer. "Boys…" I choked on my words and recovered. "You did what you had to do. Like knights."

I saw a hint of a smile in Thor's eye.

"After that we had to take out others," Shiva said. "The entire place went apeshit on us. Everyone thought we would murder them. They thought we were monsters. The cats came to take us out."

"But we took them out," Thor said menacingly. "Other animals hid and some fled, but all the cages came open. As if something just let everybody out. It was freaky. Half the animals there acted suddenly possessed, like the dog. Insane. Gone mad."

I immediately thought of the Black Mouse.

"We fought all night," Shiva went on. "We fought all over that place, we busted it up good. We fought to our rodent limits, and well beyond. We went into a fighting trace, a berserker rage. Some of those animals didn't quit even when they looked dead. No normal creatures would have kept fighting with the punishment we dealt out. Nothing would have. Then a fire started out of nowhere. It was surreal, Uncle." He looked away, into the grim past. "Like fighting in Hell."

"Yeah," I said, thinking about my dreams. Fires. There had been fires in my dreams.

"The humans came… they took everybody away. We ended up here."

"It's been a month," Shiva said.

Had I really been gone that long? Probably twice that, at least.

I remembered something my master once told me.

"Be careful when you fight monsters," he had said. "Lest a monster you become."

But his favorite quote of all time, the one he infused into my very soul, the one he lived by…

"Boys," I said, "my master said, '**Do right, and fear not.**' And that is what I intend to do here. Are you with me?"

"Oh, *hell* yeah!" they said together.

Thor got a pointy probe spear and looked admiringly at it. It was all metal, with wicked twin forked ends, each bladed on the inside.

"This has potential," he said.

Shiva nodded. "I've had it with plastic weapons. We need the real thing."

"We need guns," Thor said.

"We need to free all the animals," I said. "Let's get busy."

We freed the other rats first, after they agreed to not eat any mice and to obey the sons of Michael Mousefriend. Everyone knew who Michael was, apparently. His name went far in that place. Good ol' Mike.

The rats, armed with tools, freed the mice, starting with my upstairs neighbor and his two brothers. Over a thousand mice and a hundred rats lined up on the floor. I addressed them from atop Shiva.

"You have all said you would be in debt to me for freeing you. If you still feel that way, say so now."

The mice and rats cheered and chirped. They were gladly in my debt.

"Very good," I said. I felt like a hero. It was the high moment of my entire pilgrimage. "Me and my friends need to get home. We need two things from you, one now, one later."

"Name it!" cried the mouse who'd had the cage above mine.

"First, we need you to all spread out, all over the city, and look for a corner street with an art school on it." I described the pickup point that the Kind Human visited every night after work and school. "We need to know where it is, and how to get there. We need a network of mice and rats working to this goal, because we need to achieve it quickly."

The rodents all cried their support.

"Then, once that is done, I need something else. Something that may seem strange to you, but I have a plan. It's a grand plan, and it's just begun in my head, but if it works, we might—I say *might*—just never have to worry about humans again. We might have our chance at freedom once and for all time. Are you with me?"

Cheers went up loud enough to wake the dead. I hoped they wouldn't, and I hoped the humans couldn't see this. What would they think? Well, I knew what they'd think.

"I need all of you—your friends, your family, and every rodent you can pass this holy charge on to—to collect *money*."

The room went silent. Puzzled faces looked back at me from the crowd.

"Green, paper money of the humans, coins, gems, jewels, sparkly things. Any kind of money you can get. Any way you can get it," I said with authority. "I will tell you where to send it, what to do with it."

After a long pause, the mouse I had befriended said, "Why?"

I puffed my chest out as much as I could. "Because it's needed," I said. "Humans value it, and it can lend us power."

"But… you need a human to spend money," a rat said. Shiva chuckled. So did Thor.

"What you're suggesting is huge," a mouse said. "Use money to aid our cause? Get the help of humans? Only one mouse has ever tried anything like that, and he never came back!" Murmurs of agreement came from the crowd.

I lifted my chin. "Indeed? And do you know why?" I asked them.

Silence.

"Because he made it!" I exclaimed. "He achieved his holy crusade, and found the Kind Human. I know, for I was his squire!"

The crowd gasped and recoiled in awe. Like one huge wave, they fell backward and let their mouths hang open.

Shiva stepped forward, stood up to his impressive rat-height, and held a hand out. In a deep voice, he loudly announced, "Ladies and gentlemen, I give you… Sir Squibble, *the Mouse Knight!"*

The group stayed perfectly still one moment longer wearing faces of awe, then went crazy. They hopped, chirped, and spun around. They leapt upon each other and did little dances. The mice hugged rats, the rats groomed mice. After a time, they were before me, all standing up straight, all at attention like soldiers. They had heard the legend. They knew who my master was.

"Will you follow me?" I said.

They cheered. The floor shook with their stamping feet.

"I name you the first rodent army," I yelled across the room. "I name you… the Legion of Miracles!"

More cheering. More stamping. More hope.

I turned to the mouse who had been trapped above me all his life. He was standing with two other mice, his brothers.

"I need a Captain and two lieutenants," I said. The three mice stood at attention and saluted. I nodded. "Very well. Your names will be Sneaky," I pointed at the thin, dexterous looking one, "Squeaky," I pointed at him because he had been squeaking non stop since he got out of his cage, "And… Clyde," I put my paw on my friend. "Do you accept your names and titles?"

They vigorously nodded. All the rodents cheered the naming. It was my second time. Fred had been the first.

"Let's get out of here and stir up the city," I said.

They charged the door immediately, and it did not stand up to the determined teeth of so many rodents. The first rodent army, the Legion of Miracles, was free.

Riding on the back of Shiva in front of a gigantic horde of loyal followers, I felt like a real knight for the first time in my life.

Good Deeds Done With Honor

✠

The Hordes of Squibble, as they later came to be known (I like that title even better than the Legion of Miracles), dispersed into the city in every direction, spreading themselves thin over a range much too large for even a thousand mice. I didn't know if they would actually find the pickup point. But I knew our chances were now better than they had ever been before. I sent them with wisdom and knowledge I had gained from experience: how to survive in the city, how to avoid cats and wild mice, how to find food and water, how to camouflage so they wouldn't be glowing neon "eat me" signs. Their chances were better now than they had been in the lab, and soon they'd get better still, for I had plans.

Shiva, Thor and I snuck back into the lab and found antibiotics. Finding them was easy. Figuring out the right dose was the problem. We found the good stuff—Baytril and Doxycycline. They had a liquid form, but we had no way of getting into it without breaking the glass. So we took pills, and decided that a small nibble twice a day would probably do the trick. We made the backpacks for rat twins out of small medicine bags and string, and filled them with goodies from the lab—medicine, gauze, medical tape… all kinds of things. Pieces of this and that and anything else we thought we might need, including the bland food they had fed all the captive rodents.

It was almost dawn by the time we were done. I would have loved to stay and see the look on the humans' faces when they came back to an empty lab, but nope. Gotta go! Mice don't stick around when they gotta go. We went.

The three of us holed up in a brick wall. It was about three blocks from the lab. Some of our travel was during daylight, which none of us liked, so we had finally had to make do, but it turned out to be better than we had hoped. The hole went way back into the wall, and it was kinda warm back there. Some of the heating from the building made it pleasant. It was spacious and near a water leak from a clean source. (Oh, praise the Mousegod!)

We were exhausted, but before we went to bed I told the boys how I got to the lab, and what I'd gone through to get there. I really wanted to leave the part about the bully mouse out, but I didn't. They had confided in me their shame, so I returned the favor. They just looked at me and nodded. That gaze of affection and respect never changed. Such good boys.

We slept all through the day and into the night. It was deep sleep of tired rodents who had done a righteous night's work.

At least it started that way.

I had dreams of Shiva and Thor in bright red armor, made of steel, using guns and flamethrowers against an unseen enemy. I saw burning fields and screaming mice. I saw mice killing each other and bees in battle over their heads fighting other flying terrors. I saw ants marching to war by the millions. I saw the Kind Human, dead on a burning field of battle. And, finally, I saw the Black Mouse again, standing in front of me with an army of insane animals that were driven by the power of the undead evil thing in its dark rodent body. I was standing on an opposite hill, my army behind me. An army of Mouse Knights. Just as the horn sounded and we were about to charge, it began to rain.

I woke up to rain, the sound of it, the smell of it, outside. Our shelter was untouched, and still warm. Thor was asleep, curled protectively around his fragile mouse-uncle. He was warm and snugly. Shiva was awake and grooming himself, unaware my eyes had opened. Then he was practicing slow moves with his new metal spear. He looked strong and defiant, majestic and dangerous, like his father had been. He was really a large rat. He must weigh in at more than a pound and a half, and he wasn't yet done growing. Moving with fluid grace and perfect form, I saw him then for the first time as an adult rat—and a fine warrior. I would not wish to be caught at the business end of that iron point. Heavy as it was, he moved it with great speed and control. These boys had absorbed everything BJ had sent in their direction, and then some. I thought I had done well, but they had it down. I knew I couldn't take them anymore. I knew our playing days were over. Now they were dangerous rats, and they were done with childish playing. It was a moment of sad nostalgia for me, knowing that those times were gone. Much was lost now, and more was yet to come. I felt this was just the beginning, and I felt the first pangs of regret at so eagerly accepting my title as champion of the Mousegod. I was afraid of what it was going to cost me, and I knew not the price.

I tried to remember my dreams, but they swam away from me on the river, and became ghosts in the back of my mind. I kept the general feelings and thoughts in the front of my mind, holding them against the day I returned to the safe house when I could warn everyone. But those dreams and thoughts, day by day, seemed less important, and farther away. They were just dreams. Here and now, I was struggling for my survival.

Since coming so close to death, and looking my own fear of it (so obvious now) in the face, I knew that nothing lasts. Nothing at all. My playtimes with Shiva and Thor, beloved as they were, were only the very tip of the iceberg. In the end, entropy swallows everything. Death comes to all, and nothing can stop it. It was the heaviest thought I had ever had in my short little life. I was eager to be rid of it, at once!

"We're gonna need to find more food an' all that," I whispered.

Shiva stopped his pole on a dime and turned to look at me. "Pet stores."

"Yeah," I said. "Pet stores." Click. "I know one, and... we need to do something else there as well."

"Something?" Shiva asked.

"Something right," I said, "And fear not."

He grinned.

It was a journey to the pet store. I still had my map, and it led me back on a reverse route directly to the place where the trapped mother mice were. The journey was long. I rode on Shiva's back because of my leg. Oh, how thankful I was for him! The idea of going all that way again on foot terrified me. My leg was slowly shrinking to the right size again, but the smell of infection and sickness was not gone by half. It still hurt to stand on, or even move. Mice normally heal quickly, but I had pushed this about as far as I could have. Stupid Squibble.

The journey, which had taken me about two weeks, took only two days—wow! Two healthy rats travel seven times faster (at leisure) than a sick mouse. It made sense. I told the rat twins how grateful I was for their presence.

"We love you, Uncle," Thor told me as we hunkered down below some cardboard boxes in a wet alleyway across the street from our target. "Without you, we'd be dead now."

"Same here," I said. "You guys are worthy knights."

"You make us look like chicken feed," Shiva said. "You're the greatest knight there is!" He toasted Thor with a piece of crusty bread. They didn't mind eating trash, it seemed.

My head sunk down. "I don't think so," I mumbled. They looked at me funny, but I think they understood. Despite the scene at the lab, I would always know that I had surrendered to a bully. I had given him my precious things, and I had let his cronies destroy what was mine. The humiliation would follow me the rest of my life. No knight would have let that happen.

It was dark and quiet except for the noises of nocturnal animals like us. We found another hole in the wall (okay, okay… we *made* a hole in the wall, but don't set out the rodent traps just yet, okay?) and inside it was even nicer than the last place: warm, heated, and some modicum of fresh water available. This place would do nicely. We hastily made a nest and went outside, armed to the teeth with whatever we could find. Shiva and Thor made slings for their sleek metal weapons so they could climb unhindered, yet draw the spears quickly if need be. Quite the genius architects, my boys. We slinked (slunk… I like slunk better, even if it isn't a word. Well, it is now!) across the street and hopped the curb. I could go under the door but they couldn't, so we found a way in the back (more vandalism—did you know two big rats can go through a cheap wooden door in under ten minutes?) and it was game time.

Pet store rescues. Mouse Knights had gotten a reputation for it. Anytime all the pets mysteriously vanished from a pet store, the rodent world knew it was one of us. We just couldn't stand to see our kin sold as snake food, and knights would never sit still for such blatant cruelty. Other Mouse Knights had gotten it down to an art, and even kept notch marks on the back of their shields to record how many stores they had liberated. I think the record so far was thirty-three by a single knight.

Of course, by now, the humans were more than a little upset about it and blamed animal rights activists, though they could never quite find the group… nor any evidence of the group. It had made the news. I remember watching it with glee from the safe house. Anytime we saw news attributed to our rodents, we knew it, and we all laughed. The humans just couldn't figure out what was going on. Probably because we were beneath their notice, so they'd never catch us. Who would ever guess that intelligent rodents were breaking other rodents and critters out of captivity? Science fiction that was. An' they could go right on thinkin' it.

So we got up to the mothers with their babies. It had been a little while and there was a new batch of babies under both mommas. I didn't want to think what happened to the others. It was a miracle I had even gotten back here. I was doing my best.

I told them their days of suffering were over. They were keeping these babies. They couldn't comprehend what was about to happen, since their entire lives had been spent in the tiny cages no longer than nine inches, but they were full of joy. The rat twins chewed the plastic off in moments and the metal lids sprang free. We put all the little ones in a blanket and made a carry-hammock for them and the moms. Shiva and Thor did all the carrying. We had to take the kids one by one down off the shelf, though, and the moms got to help. Once they understood what was happening, they shook with excitement.

"You mean we're really free? Forever?" one of them asked.

"I can't promise it's going to be easy or safe," I said, "but yeah. You're free."

She just stared at me in wonder. It was a weird moment.

No domestic mouse can survive in the wild, not for long in the street without some sort of edge. We had no place to put these mother mice with their babies except that hole we had prepared across the street in the wall. It went back quite a ways, and it was heated. We took them there, then went back several times to the pet store to filch the food and supplies they would need. Once that was done, we freed all the other animals with the understanding that the mice would guard the mommas and babies, and hunt for food for them.

I left further instructions that if any other mice came, the ones we just freed would ask if they were from the Miracle Legion. If they were, they would tell the new mice that orders from Squibble were to find a safe, underground environment for a new mouse city. It had to have heating, food, and water readily available. I told them to look in the basements of restaurants and hotels.

Sooner or later one of my faithful would come by, and the fifty-some mice I rescued that evening would join the legion if they wanted to. Most of them expressed desire to join. Within a week, I guessed, the mommas and babies would be safe. Until then, I would scout with Shiva for other members of the legion and news of the drop-off/pickup point. Thor would guard the mice. They couldn't have a more fearsome guardian. Thor eagerly agreed and was treated as divine by those mice.

Shiva and I scoured the city for a week, each night traveling in a new direction from the "nest" and coming back to it at daylight. We were able to travel many city blocks In every direction, sometimes twenty or more. Shiva was a fast rat, and he knew we had a mission. Still, the city was so gigantic. I couldn't even begin to comprehend it. It was like a human trying to fathom the depths of space. Twenty blocks was nothing.

In that week, we found many more pet stores, and many more miserable animals. Shiva and I looked at each other upon finding the first one, and he said "Why not?" I agreed wholeheartedly. We freed them all, and told them where our nest was.

I gave them the same orders I gave the others. Mice are good at gossip. Surely now the word would spread rapidly. I could issue orders to any mouse, and within a week it would be all over the city. During that week we also found an art school for humans that was open at night. It was called an *atelier* (which later I learned meant "studio" in French). There were people there drawing and painting, and a few teachers telling people how to do it. I was instantly fascinated, and Shiva had to drag me bodily from the peephole we were spying through. I marked the location of the school, though, and it was just a few hours travel from our mouse hideout. I wondered if this was the school that the Kind Human went to, but what were the odds? There must be hundreds of art schools in the city, and this one wasn't quite on a corner. I knew I'd come back to this one, just as often as I could. Who wouldn't want to draw and paint?

Weeks passed.

Some of the mice wanted to come with us on our scoutings, and some wanted to scout in other directions. We had scouts, guards, and gatherers. It was a well-organized outfit. They started calling me Lord Squibble. I can't say I minded. My nest was over three hundred strong now, not including the mommas and babies (well over 100 there alone). We tried to outfit the guards with weapons, and Thor taught them how to use them all day long. He was at least as tasking as BJ, maybe more. All I heard was complaints when I got back. To which I'd say, "Well, nobody's making you do this. You can always quit." And they'd say, "Oh, no my lord, I'd never quit! I wanna be a Mouse Knight someday!"

They all wanted to be Mouse Knights. I wondered, was there room enough in the world for that many knights? I wasn't about to make that decision. I handed out military-type ranks, but I didn't so much as even *think* about making one squire. I thought of home alot. I dreamed alot. Disturbing, deeply emotional dreams from which I often woke crying. The rat twins never said a word.

As soon as I got a break, I went back to the art school for an entire day and just listened and learned. It was wonderful. The things they said made so much sense. It was like someone opening a magic box of answers to me. I could just reach in and use it immediately. Within the first room, as the students went on break, I risked exposure to sneak down to the floor level. (The peek-a-boo hole was up high in the ceiling, which was great, because I could see everyone draw.) I took me some paper, and if the students even noticed that the ends of their charcoal pencils were chewed off, they made no noise about it.

So I began to draw along with the students and learn. Mice learn very quickly, and I made it a point one day a week to make Shiva take me there and pick me up when I was done, so I could study at the Atelier for six hours straight. My teachers were this guy named Jeff who ran the whole place—he was really cool and I liked him alot—and this guy named Ron who was so fast I couldn't believe it! And good. Fast and good, just what I want to be. He could whip out a drawing in ten minutes and it would be perfect. He was a genius. And almost, *almost* as fast as a mouse!

Between the two of them they showed everyone what to do, drew in front of everyone, and gave their secrets away to the students. No one does that, especially artists. I was touched by their nobility. They really wanted to share this powerful knowledge with everyone who wanted it. Then they'd go around and draw on people's drawings, showing each how to make it better, and the student got to keep the drawing! I wished I could go down there and say, "Excuse me, sir, but what's wrong with this drawing? It looks off, and I can't tell how to fix it." I imagined they'd sharpen their pencil up real good, and draw right on my drawing, and show a little mouse how to get better at art. Maybe they'd even sign it for me. It was a dream, of course; more likely they'd scream and slap me or run away. But somehow, Ron and Jeff didn't seem the type to do that. They seemed cool to me. So cool I almost went down there several times just to see what they'd do. Who knows? Stranger things have happened. Maybe they *would* let a mouse sit in on class. But of course, then our secret would be out. I couldn't do that, no matter how much I wanted to.

So I stayed out of sight, and learned by absorbing everything I saw and heard. It worked well enough. I drew many live models and desperately wanted to paint, but I couldn't figure out how to steal oil paint and all the stinky stuff that goes with it, so I just watched and learned. I promised myself that at some future time I would figure out how a mouse could paint in oils. It looked so fun. I took tons of notes, and studied them on my rare spare time back at the base.

Whenever I had a spare few minutes, I would draw something. It was usually Shiva, Thor, or a mouse (big surprise there—hey, I was surrounded by them), but on occasion I snuck outside to draw a human sitting on a bench or something. Humans are hard to draw.

On occasion I had a nagging thought. I only went to the Atelier once a week. What if the Kind Human was going to *this* school? Maybe just not on the day I went. What if this was the one, and that corner was *the* corner? Ah, what were the odds? I dismissed the thoughts when they came and took care of business back at the base.

More weeks passed and turned into months. By April, we had over five hundred mice and had moved to a new location under a hotel building. The new mice called it the "New Kingdom," after the first mouse kingdom where I had grown up. Everyone had heard of the old kingdom in the stories and fables, just like they had heard of my master. The new place was actually an *old* kingdom, but I think "new kingdom" sounds more cool, so I let them call it that.

Soon the entire city knew about "Overlord Squibble." (It got better and better, and I did absolutely nothing to stop it!) The best part was that while technically these mice were all members of Miracle Legion, they heard me calling them the Hordes of Squibble. My name for them spread like wildfire across the city, and I never heard the term Miracle Legion again. He he he hee!

I had made some new makeshift armor from lobster shells down by the beach brought to me by mice wanting to join. A mouse who had lived in a toy store brought me a plastic helmet from a toy knight, just like the one my master wore on his first journey, and the female mice made me leather tunics and belts, sheaths for our weapons and even a blue cape for my back with a hood. Other mice raided bars after hours and brought back plastic spears and swords. I gave the mice who had gotten to level five in Thor's training program permission to use them. Thor had ten levels to his class. No one had made it past five yet. I told them if they made it to six they could begin wearing armor. Not full lobster plate, but cloth and leather maybe, like the men-at-arms of old.

I missed my master. I always felt that I was flying by the seat of my pants, making everything up as we went along. I never knew if I was doing it "right" or not, but everyone seemed to have great faith in me. So I didn't give it too much thought. I was so busy keeping it all going that I didn't have the time to let my mind wander. I came to relish with all my heart the one evening I spent at the Atelier, drawing until my soul sang. I loved it. It was pure and free of grief.

Getting better at drawing was something to strive for that I loved to do. Without that, I might have suffered from the constant demand on me by my horde.

I had been in that city for two months at that point. Time, to mice, is much different from humans. One day to a human is like a week or two to a mouse. We only get one hundred weeks to our lives on average. That's it. One day is a long time to us. So a week to us is like a year to a human. A human year is half our lives. So many mice never make it even that far. Disease or accidents catch them first. Two months is *nine human years*. Do you understand? A big chunk of my life. A long, long time.

I constantly missed home. In my few spare moments, I wondered what was happening there. My leg had healed, and I was quite glad for it. I didn't know if it would or not, but I was a young, strong mouse, and it worked fine. Fred had set it correctly. It pleased me to think of her and her children being cared for tenderly by Heide. I missed Heide. My own first Kind Human.

I began to walk to the Atelier by myself at nights once a week, even in my armor with all my art stuff, and it didn't bother me much.

I had quite an army by now. I had over four hundred warriors, three hundred gatherers, and so many scouts I couldn't count them. The original mouse kingdom I had come from had been about this big. If a mouse showed up wanting to join, which happened about thirty times a day, I'd tell them "You're a scout," show them a map, and tell them "Go here and stay one day and one night, then come back. Report all you see." We gave them supplies, but the distances were long and hard. We would lose half the mice who came to apply, but hey, that separated the mice from the men.

Through this amazing network of mice, I "saw" the entire city. I heard almost everything that went on and had to sift through it for signs of important things. Shiva and Thor were flabbergasted by the efficiency of the system. They suggested making it global. I told them I might just do that if we needed to.

I refused to be called "king" or anything like that. BJ was King, and I told everyone so. Their loyalty was to him first. I told them all about the safe house and our brothers and sisters far away. I told them about the old kingdom, and about all the brave deeds of my master. I spoke so often and so intensely about my master and the other legendary rodents that they became like gods to those mice, beings completely magnificent and yet completely unseen—the heroes of mythology. They worshipped my master from afar, and I wondered if he knew it.

My dreams never stopped, and several times I would wake to see the Black Mouse staring at me from some shadow… only to wake again and realize I hadn't been really awake. I dreamed of back home and talking to Nemo. I had those dreams alot. I dreamed of taking walks with my master. And I dreamed of the kids—Percival and the others, growing and learning at ridiculous speeds, even for mice. I dreamed that happiness reigned in the safe house, and that I was missing it. That was okay. As long as they were happy. I dearly wanted to see my momma, and thought of her many times each day. I wrote her many letters while I was the commander of my hordes over a hundred, and many with drawings of what was going on in my life. I piled them up in a corner and would add to it daily.

I joined in the classes and taught the mice how to fight. I taught them how to read. I taught them how to write. I even taught some how to draw, using the very words my unknowing teachers had used while I was watching. Mice would bring back anything that had words or pictures on it. We were very poor, but mice are exceptional at making something from nothing. The smartest mice excelled and were given rank.

Missions were planned and executed. Sneaky, Squeaky and Clyde came back and found our new nest, as did many of the original Miracle Legion. They were trained. They always volunteered for missions, and because they were officers in my army, I let them go all the time. They were amazingly efficient and smart. Clyde would go upstairs in the hotel and watch TV. I would join him sometimes when I could, which was almost never. One of those times, he saw a huge explosion on the screen, and his eyes lit up.

"Oooooo, my lord, we have to learn to do that!" he exclaimed.

"Mmm… why for?" I said.

"'Cause it's big and pretty and goes *boom*!" he gleefully chirped.

Yeah, Clyde was a little off his rocker. That's okay. He and his brothers were as loyal as they come.

He immediately set about to collect books and notes and whatever else he needed to make explosives. I let him do it, because I knew what mice were capable of, though I was a bit concerned about the possible consequences. When Shiva and Thor joined in eagerly, I became worried. Together, they set a hundred mice on the task. Within the week, they blew something up, and took out part of our nest. No mice were hurt, but several were deaf after that. I told them to blow things up far away from then on. Clyde became a colonel, in charge of demolitions. Shiva and Thor were my generals.

I had about 50 officers, all told. All good mice. All willing to die for the nest.

True to my commands, the mice brought money. You cannot imagine how much. People drop coins all the time. They lose paper money just as easily. They lose jewels, rings, necklaces, and bracelets. And what they lost, my mice collected. Sometimes it took many mice, sometimes even rats, to do it, but they brought it all home, and we buried it deep within the cellar of that hotel, with one exception. Once every week I took some of it and left it in Jeff's office at the Atelier art school. His classes weren't free for humans, and I shouldn't get them for free either. They were worth every cent of that money and more. I thought he didn't charge enough, but I left him sixty dollars every week, which added up to the cost of his classes. I was a Mouse Knight. It was the right thing to do, and it didn't even put a small dent in our treasury (which grew at an exponential rate as more mice joined us). I imagine it drove him a bit crazy wondering where that money came from. He he he.

I practiced my meditation whenever I could, which was almost never. And I never did get back to that dock. I was not to visit my dock again for a very long time. I could see it when I tried, but I was never quite *there* as I had been that one time. I guess my powers require some sort of injury, pain, suffering, starvation, or other stupid thing to work. Fine with me. I don't make the rules. If Bigfat wants the gig to work only with suffering, who am I to argue? But I wasn't about to tweak myself in order to get all spiritual. I could do without.

Interesting reports came back to us through the network of scout mice. The rats in the city had organized into a huge gang to come take out my mouse nest. There were over seventy rats in this gang, calling themselves Heaven's Vermin. They were tough rats, and said that rats being friends with mice was preposterous. (Well actually they used a much nastier word than that, but hey, fill in the blanks.) I was worried and pondering what to do when Shiva and Thor went out without my knowledge, met the gang in the street, and trashed them within an inch of their lives. They slew the leader of the gang, and assumed command. Now I had seventy hard case rats under my control. They obeyed Shiva and Thor without question. They reminded me of the samurai I had seen on TV, and my twins were the Shoguns. Such good boys, those two.

Other reports included things such as the humans had put guards in the pet stores, making our jobs more difficult. We had to be quiet now. Oh, no! How difficult! (Snicker.) Mice had to be quiet. Imagine that. The missions did not even slow down.

There were some reports that mice were observed wearing things, reading, writing, or even operating technology. The newspaper published an article about the "vanishing rodents" from pet stores all over the city. Nothing I could do about that (except be amused), but many reports were clearly things where mice just got sloppy. I reprimanded mice harshly each time if I found out who was responsible. Sometimes I even kicked mice out if they did it repeatedly. There was no room for mercy in that department. The humans must not know.

Meanwhile, I took to studying chemistry. I was fascinated by the drugs I had from the pharmacy and the lab. They could do so much. They could mean the difference between life and death. I sought to understand. Before I could do that, however, I had to go back and relearn math, physics and a bunch of other things I didn't pay attention to as a young mouse. I set to the task, using books we found in the trash, and shared all I found with my boys.

It was during this time that the rat twins discovered the internet. Nothing was ever the same after that. They would sneak up to hotel rooms at night, turn on people's computers, and surf for hours. Learning, learning, learning! I went up with them several times. You could literally just type in a word and thousands of books or articles would come up that you could read on the subject. It was a free, unlimited source of information. (Did you know the humans use a thing called a mouse to push the little pointy thingy around the screen? That chunk of plastic does not even *slightly* resemble the beauty and artistic grace of a mouse! The rats and I learned to use the keyboard. There's this button called "help" on the screen—and it does! We read everything—*everything*—that "help" had to offer us. We learned a *ton*.)

Other mice learned of our new pastime, and soon rodents all over the city knew about the internet. I had created a monster. As long as that monster was on our side, that was fine with me. Some mice sat in front of the stupid screen all night. I would get bored with it eventually and go back to my duties, or go draw. And nothing, not all the millet in China, would stop me from going to art class on Saturday nights.

The labs in the area had all been raided several times. We took drugs, science info, and tools. They tried to get smart and made their facilities "mouse proof." They installed doors we couldn't squib under, walls we couldn't chew through, and electronic door codes. Thanks for those door codes, humans. Thank you very much.

We even got on the news. The show "funniest animals" had a clip of several mice talking and when one realized the camera was on them, he alerted the others and they started acting like stupid mice again, eating, running on their wheels and grooming themselves. This scene happened three times. They'd go back to talking, realize the camera was on them again, and suddenly they were acting like normal mice. The clip made the news. The humans laughed about it. So did I and my officers, after demoting every single one of those stupid mice for almost letting the cat out of the bag. In the end, it was laughed right away into nothing but a funny video someone had made. No one took it seriously.

I wondered if the safe house saw that clip. I wondered how all my friends were.

One mission of those long days stands out in my mind, and for good reason.

We had just liberated a colony of mice from a pet store—we had gotten about fifty from there—and we were also loaded up with medication from raiding a lab. (I had learned more about medicine and drugs in the last two months than ever!) We were taking a side street back to the nest. It was always our habit to take a new route (this is alien to mice, who usually fall into ruts), and we came across a building that smelled of animals. It wasn't a lab, or a pet store, or even someone's house. Then I saw the sign. It said "Paradise Place Pet Hotel." My heart froze in my chest. This was where Tiny, Heide's beloved pet, had met his dark fate.

I had told Shiva and Thor absolutely everything by now, and they knew instantly why I was gaping. We were overloaded with stuff, and past quota, but we went in anyway. They had no mice, but they did have many other animals. None of them were happy to be there, and many had clearly been abused and tormented.

"What do we do?" I said to my generals. "These are pets, they have homes."

"We send 'em home," Shiva said. "Show 'em maps, send 'em home."

"Then we burn the place," Thor growled.

"What?" I chirped in shock.

"We burn it," he repeated. "They'll keep abusing animals if we don't."

I looked to Shiva and saw that he clearly agreed with his brother. His face was stone fury.

I thought it over. My brows came together thinking of Tiny and what they did to that poor mouse, who was used to nothing but tender care and love.

The brothers were right. Everyone was looking to me for a decision. A leader must never hesitate. My master never did.

"Burn it," I commanded.

Shiva and Thor grinned from ear to ear.

So we let out every animal in the place. We told them if they waited their owners would come get them in the morning, most likely, or they could use our maps and head home. It wasn't going to be easy, but they unanimously preferred it to the abuse they were suffering in that stupid place.

And you know what? As I watched it burn to the ground, I felt better.

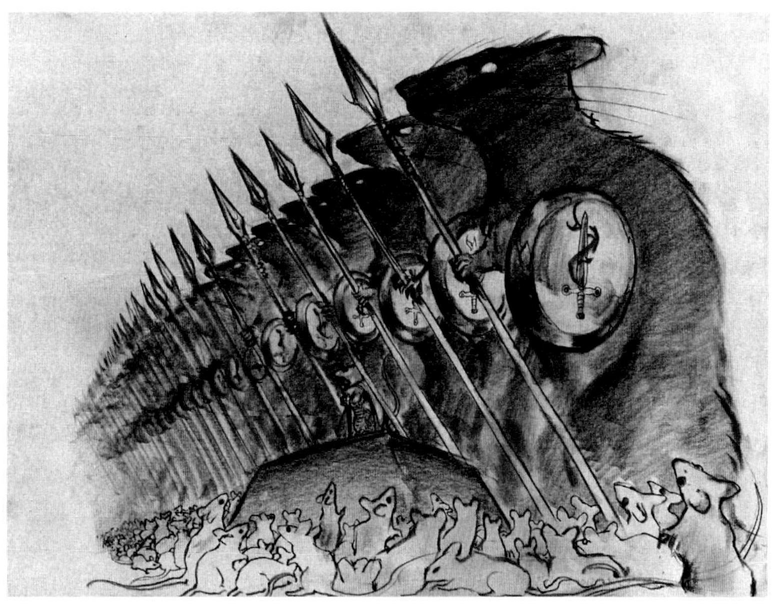

"That's for you, Tiny," I said.

By May I had a kingdom that topped a thousand, not including the scouts. Once scouts had done three scoutings, they were promoted and could join the kingdom. The sick, old, mothers and young were exempt from this initiation.

The rats got their own unit title, because nobody liked the word "vermin." It was a rodent insult. Because they wanted to be feared and respected, Shiva named them "The Swords of Michael." They loved that, and the name became known on the street overnight. Once trained, they were truly the Roman centurions of my army.

By the middle of May, there had *still* been no word of the Kind Human or the pickup point. I had not seen him in the art classes, at least on Saturday evenings. I began to despair. Then a report came in from a scout. He brought a piece of paper and said pieces just like it had been strewn all over the city near the first pet store the rat knights and I had liberated. The paper said:

> Squibble. Looking for you forever.
> Please come home.
> - Heide

My human had not given up on me!

I asked the scout what happened at the pet store. They and several other scouts who had been to that area said that every night a car drove up, waited there for fifteen minutes, and then drove away.

Every single day for almost three months. She had not abandoned me after all. What a wonderful, dedicated human.

I dug out my old supplies. I had stashed them in my quarters, a very private place where no one but my generals were allowed in. I found my old drugs, my old paper I had used as armor. One of them had Heide's address on it. Wearing my new armor, bearing my new shield and sword and all my old stuff as well, I put my slingshot around my neck, gathered up a squad of my finest men, and went, not knowing I wouldn't be coming back.

IF I'M
ASLEEP...
NO
DISTURBUM!
The Grotto of The OverLorde

Reunion and Return

✠

It was not hard to find Heide's house, and it turned out to be quite close. It took me and my squad of soldiers a few hours to get there. Shiva came with me as my friend and mount while Thor commanded the nest. I passed well clear of the place where I had encountered the mouse gang. I had no reason to, not now, but I did. Some wounds never close, maybe. And to tell the truth, I was still afraid of that big bully mouse. I hated his stupidity and his reckless violence, but I feared him. I knew what I should have done, but for some subconscious reason I didn't, and I felt ashamed for it.

We sent a mouse up to the doorbell, and he rang it.

Heide answered and looked around in puzzlement, at human eye level, of course.

We all went inside while she stared out at the night, and took up formation behind her on the open carpet. I saw the cat peer around the corner and grimace. It was quite amusing.

Heide turned around and gasped, clutching her chest.

"Oh, my god!" she exclaimed.

I took off my helmet and bowed. My men followed my gesture.

Her eyes went wide and she sucked in breath. "Squibble? *My* Squibble?" She asked. I bowed again.

She squatted down to see me and smiled. "My, my... You've come far in the world, little mouse." She put her hand down, and I stepped gladly into it. "You better watch it, looking like that, or your secret's gonna be out."

I motioned to the kitchen. She giggled and walked us over there. My men followed on the floor. Shiva gave the cat a death stare, and it vanished like wind.

There on the counter were two large glass aquariums with open tops. In one were Fred and her daughters, and in the other were her sons, all of them grown up. I felt a pang of shock. How long it had been! These mice had so recently been pinkies we held gently in our mouths while carrying them. Now they were full grown mice, all staring at me as if I had landed in a ship from outer space. Heide placed me in the cage with Fred, and there she was, as beautiful as I remembered her, and just as smart.

"Is... is that... Squibble?" one of her daughters asked in awe. Fred nodded, beaming with pride. She ran over and licked me, groomed me and stroked my fur.

"It's so good to see you again," she said. "I was so worried."

She wouldn't have gotten the news, being a pet mouse now. I smiled back. "I have come far."

She nodded and offered me a Cheerio. I gasped in surprise and took it immediately. Then I thought twice. My men and Shiva should eat before me. There was a ramp leading out of the cage to the kitchen counter, which was all set up for mice to roam about on. Heide let these mice do what they wished, just like back home. Such a kind human. She knew the mice understood her.

I crawled out and onto the edge of the counter. My men were all down there, happily munching Cheerios Heide had tossed them. I sighed. I should have guessed. I savored my treat. Soon it was gone, replaced with memories of home.

"Does the cat bother you at all?" I asked Fred.

"Oh, no," she said. "Quite the opposite. When the other mice come in to harass us or steal our treats, he chases them off. I think he's taken kindly to us. I even chat with him sometimes. He's not so bad."

"Other mice?" I asked, feeling a chill go up my spine.

"Yeah… mice from outside. Sometimes they find their way in here."

"One at a time or in numbers?"

"One at a time."

I cringed at the thought of the bully mouse coming in here and hurting or killing Fred and her family. She needed protectors. Not that I didn't trust the cat. Well, okay, I didn't.

I went over to the cage of the boys. They had no ramp. It looked as though they had been fighting each other. Heide had never had multiple mice before. She didn't know males fought to the death, even siblings sometimes. It was just mousey testosterone. At the safe house we all had an understanding, and plenty of brawling pits, exercise and other ways for the males to get out their aggressions. It had been the first order of business to avoid fighting and unwanted pregnancies. Mice breed way too fast, and before a month is up, an unsuspecting human can have twenty mice from one single litter, and twenty more coming next month. Multiply that by hundreds of mice and you have a serious problem. Many mice had gone to their fates, unwanted and rejected, because foolish humans let their pets breed, or couldn't tell what sex a mouse was. Then, ending up with twenty mice, they freak out and abandon them all. Way to go, huh?

"Better let me in there," I said to Fred.

"Ummm… They know who you are, but…" she said, "well, they might try to test their dominance anyway."

"Yeah, I know," I said. "That's why you should let me in there."

Fred was used to my ways, and knew I would do what I wanted, so she got Heide to put me in the cage. Apparently they had worked out a simple but effective way of communicating by Heide watching Fred's gestures and body language. Most impressive.

So there I was, surrounded by young, strong mice eager to test my mettle. They stalked around me and rattled their tails, but they were cautious. Fred had told them about me.

I took off my sword belt and let it fall to the ground. I grinned, remaining perfectly relaxed.

"Someone wants a piece of this mouse?" I said.

They came at me. I feigned and dodged, sending them sprawling into the glass wall of the aquarium. I sent some spinning into the wheels, sent them falling over each other, and threw them into their toys. I worked them. Hard. I even used a little aikido. It felt fluid. Smooth. They never knew what hit them.

Less than half a minute later, lying in a bruised pile, they eyed me as if they weren't sure if I were the Devil or God.

"Give?" I said.

They all showed the signs of submission except one mouse. He and I fought for another three minutes. That's a very long fight for mice. He was big and strong, and fast. He had no moves whatsoever, but he made up for it in sheer ferocity. If he had been trained, he would have beat me, I think. But in the end, I put him down, bit him hard on the shoulder, and held him down. He surrendered. A hard thing for him to do in front of the mice he had been dominant over. This mouse had humility as well. I liked him.

He prostrated himself before me. "Oh, you are worthy, Lord Squibble," he said, "just as we have heard!" He looked back at the others. "My brothers and I beg you to teach us."

I laughed. He had no idea that's *all* I had been doing these last months.

"Behave, do as I say, and then maybe. Someday. You're in charge here. Enforce the rules I'm about to speak." He bowed low and nodded his head.

They all nodded. So I told them. No breeding with the female mice. Boy, they didn't like that, but they agreed. No fighting with each other, and they had to respect their momma and protect her no matter what, especially from other mice. They all agreed. I told them it would be more punishment from me if they faltered, and then they'd never get training. They understood.

Coming out of the cage, I told Fred, "You can put a ramp on that cage now, as well." The look on her face was sheer respect. It made me feel good. Her sons could now enjoy the life of free-range mice.

You know, that big mouse became a Mouse Knight, much later, under some other knight. He did make it.

Then it was down to business. I had Heide take Shiva and I over to the computer. Shiva was glaring up at Heide, and Heide was nervous in the path of such hatred. We could smell her hesitation, but she still picked him up. I held onto my friend/steed, making sure he would not harm this Kind Human. He shrugged me off, as a gesture that he was not about to disobey me, but neither did he forgive the human race for his trauma. I couldn't blame him.

"My," Heide said nervously. "What a big rat… and what a large… spear… he has…"

As I went over to the keyboard, Shiva mumbled, "All the better to remove your eyes with, my dear."

"Shiva, be nice!" I said.

"Sire," he growled and put the spear down. He let Heide pet him, on the armor, of course. I could smell how it infuriated him. I worried about his future.

Once at the computer, I typed away at the keyboard.

Need to get home, I typed.

Heide sat down at the table as my men clambered up the drapes and achieved the tabletop. They resumed formation and stayed there.

"A rodent army," Heide said. "It's kinda of scary. Someday, someone is going to notice, Squibble."

It's inenveeble, I typed.

"You mean inevitable," Heide corrected.

Whatever! I need to get home. You're my only way. Please. It's important.

"Well," she said, "I knew I couldn't keep you, but after losing you at that pet store I felt like I had let you down. I worried about you day and night. I came right back after the cop was gone, but you were gone too. I looked until dawn. I couldn't find you anywhere. They all know me at that pet store now. I go around calling your name. I even tried talking to the mice. Didn't work."

I know you tried to find me, but I didn't know it then. I'm not used to humans who care. I should have waited. (Story of my life.)

"What are you used to?" Heide asked.

My momma was abandoned outside by her owners when they found out she had babies, I typed. *All my siblings died of cold and starvation and I only barely survived. That's why I'm so skinny.*

She made a compassionate face and petted me softly. "I'm sorry, little mouse. Sounds like your life hasn't been easy."

Some yes, some no. I desperately need a ride out to the country. I need to go home. Please.

"I'll take you," she said. "Do you want to go right away?"

Shiva looked at me with doubt in his eyes. He really didn't trust humans anymore. I wondered how he'd feel about our own Kind Human.

We need to go in the day, I wrote. *So you can find the house I describe to you. I don't know the way, exactly. Just descriptions of the way and what the house looks like. We start by going away from the ocean.*

"That's not much to go on," she said. "But come morning, we'll set out and give it a try."

I typed out a long description of everything I knew about the countryside and the safe house. It was from a mousey point of view, but I thought it was pretty good for an amateur writer.

"We'll find it," she said. "We'll get you home at last."

Thanks, Heide, I typed.

She petted me in response. It felt nice.

That night we all stayed in Fred's cage, though it was a bit cramped. Her aquarium was easily two feet and some long, but Shiva made it seem small. My men behaved themselves quite nicely with all the women; they were perfect gentlemen. Heide dumped a whole pile of Cheerios into the cage and we had a feast. Then we held counsel.

"I can't take anyone with me," I told my men. "The safe house is full enough already. It's against the rules of the King—our King—to increase the number."

"What are we going to do?" Clyde said. "What will we do without you, my lord?"

"You have enough mice, you're trained, you're smart. You'll do okay without me."

"Thor and I are staying," Shiva said.

I did a double take and stared at him.

He nodded. "We talked it over before, knowing this day would come. We thought it would be when we found the pickup point, but we knew it would happen either way. We'd love to go back to the safe house, but really, our experiences here in the city have made us realize that safety is an illusion. There really is no such thing. We talked about it, and we both want to stay here. We'll guard the nest, see its numbers grow, and train everyone who wants to learn. My brother and I feel we have a holy quest to perform, and it's just starting to come clear to us what that is."

My heart sank a little. I understood, though. All great heroes have a holy quest, a vision that comes to them for them alone. It wasn't surprising that Shiva and Thor had one, and that it would be the same for both of them. Heck, the only person who was missing one was me, although that was slowly changing in my head.

I nodded, still surprised. "Are you sure? I mean… anything could happen to you in the city, Shiva. Anything. Run over by a car…"

"Stuff *has* happened to me in the city," he said. "I've survived so far. I just feel this is where I need to be."

"Yeah," I said, looking down. "Yeah."

I looked up again and forced myself to be strong in front of my men. I was likely seeing my dear boy for the last time, but I had to be strong. I had not said goodbye to Thor. I hadn't known I wouldn't be back. Kinda stupid thinking. I had thought all along that Heide might be able to take me to the safe house. I'd even taken my things. Why had I thought I'd be back? It was the same "asleep" thinking that caused me not to check the art school on the other days of the week. Boy, it got me in alot of trouble. My master always said, "Think smarter, not harder." I needed practice.

"Okay, Shiva and Thor are in charge," I said. "In the event that they aren't there, then it will be someone they name, one of the high ranking officers. Not you though, Clyde. Nothing personal."

"What!" he protested.

I turned to him. "Let's say humans come into our nest below the basement and find our little kingdom. What would your orders be?"

"Blow 'em up!" he gleefully chirped.

"Exactly," I said, and turned back to Shiva, who was spinning his finger around his ear looking at Clyde. (Clyde took this as a compliment, nodding his head up and down wearing a psycho smile that looked just like Jack Nicholson.)

"Keep everything running. Let the numbers grow as big as they need to. Keep the standards strict and keep the discipline tough."

"Don't worry about that, boss," Shiva said.

There was a pause. I smiled. "I won't." I took the piece of paper with Heide's number and address on it and gave it to Shiva. "This might help. If you ever need anything, come here or call and squeak, I guess." They laughed.

Shiva said, "Shouldn't you keep this, Sir?"

I shrugged. "What for? I'm going home."

He nodded hesitantly. "I guess so." He took the paper.

The men all snapped to attention and saluted me.

"It's been an honor to serve with you, Sir," Sneaky said.

"We owe you our very lives, and we won't forget," Squeaky said.

"Thanks for the demolitions," Clyde said. "Thanks for everything."

I saluted in return. "You are the finest soldiers in all the mousey world," I told them. Some eyes got a little damp. "I will miss you."

"Will you ever be back, sir?" one asked.

Another pause. "I don't think so, men. I don't think so. You will carry on without me, and remember that you all belong to the same kingdom as I, the same one as the heroes I've told you about."

"Yes, sir!" They all said.

"Remain ready," I said. "Train for the worst. One day, mousekind may need you."

They all nodded vehemently.

I had no idea how true my words were until much later.

In the morning, Heide was ready and woke me up from my slumber. I was sleeping against Shiva, who almost took Heide's fingers off when she reached down to rub my head. He stopped when he smelled who it was, but it was a close thing.

"He's scary," she said.

"You have no idea," Shiva said in an icy tone. I gathered my things. As I did, I felt a pang of regret in leaving. I wouldn't get to take another art class. I wasn't going to see the twins again. My time of knighthood glory was over.

As she picked me up, Heide said, "Squibble, I have too many mice in my house now. All over the place, not pets—mice from outside. They're into everything because I won't set traps or put out poison. Sometimes they harass Fred and the others. What should I do?"

I'd already handled most of it, but…

I hopped down onto the computer table and wrote out a little song. When it was finished, I did a little dance. I made it up. It's called the "No Mouse" dance. I shared it with Heide. It goes like this:

No mouse, no mouse…
Mouse leave my house!
Don't wanna hurt ya
Can't afford ta feed ya
Will ya…
Please go, please go
An' no one need ever know
Cause there's…
No mouse, no mouse
Left in my house… *My* house!

Shiva looked at me in wonder, and my men thought I was insane, but I was fairly sure it would work. I mean, what mouse would stay after seeing a human sing that and do the jig? No mouse.

She slowly nodded her head and said, "Ooookkayyy, Squibble. I'll… I'll do that thing there when I see a mouse."

I nodded happily and got back in her hand. For no rational reason, I was sure it would work. Like magic.

"Ready?" she said.

I nodded.

I waved goodbye to Fred, Shiva and my men. They waved back. I felt sad to go. I had spent three months here in the city. Such a long time for a mouse—twelve human years. Some mice only live three months. I was sure I would never *want* to come back. Not after my experiences there. I wanted to see my master and momma again, to write and draw again, to see Favorite and play on my wheel again. I longed for home. I longed for security, even though what Shiva said haunted me. *Safety is an illusion…*

But at the same time, this had defined part of me. I was going to miss them. I hated the city, but I was going to miss my new horde. Not miss being a leader, just miss being that liked and depended upon. They didn't *really* need me, but they felt they did. And they treated me with great respect. I knew now that aside from a very few rodents, that had been a first for me, being so respected.

I'd be lying if I told you the whole experience had changed me. I was still the same ol' Squibble that came to the city stupidly and stubbornly. I was still afraid of that stupid bully and his maniac mice. I was still a child at heart. I had done what I did because it seemed the right thing to do, and it was what I had been trained to do. Children are very good at doing what they are taught to do, and when one is out of options, I have found that most mice (and humans) will go back to what they were used to, even if it was uncomfortable or painful. In other words, we go back to our cage. When we're scared, we go back to the place we were raised. I was raised by a Mouse Knight. That's what I know.

And now I was leaving that behind to go back to what was comfortable. It seemed tragic, somehow. I wondered if I had made a bad choice. And from that day on, I was to wonder that an awful lot.

Once in the car, I got up on the dashboard and tried to navigate Heide around. The sun baked me in under five minutes, and I almost passed out. My armor made it worse, so I had to get out from under that brutal glass. I climbed up on Heide's shoulder and asked her to roll down the window a bit. I stayed on the opposite shoulder so a strong breeze wouldn't blow me out of the car and end my trip real quick.

Mice are really good at sounds and smells. Not so good at seeing. Brown mice with brown eyes, like me, see better than albino mice, but we still see mostly large shapes and movement. I couldn't direct her to the safe house by sight, so I had to do it by smell. And by what she described to me.

What she described for the first ten miles of our trip was construction. Torn up earth and destroyed landscapes to make room for human dwellings. Great sections of land torn up and ripped to pieces. Bushes and trees smashed under the giant tires of tractors and the tank-like treads of human machines. She didn't know it, but she was describing a holocaust to a mouse. In that field there had been thousands of mice, and now they were buried in their nests, dead of suffocation or crushed by the weight of the human technology. Dead in either case. Entire families. Babies. Whole tribes. All wiped out without a single thought by the humans.

And worse, this was the dreaded future. Every bit of land could go this way as the humans breed out of control like uneducated mice. So far, Mother Nature has not put them in their place for it. They've expanded like a bad bacteria, covering everything and destroying as they go, clearly heedless of the damage they're causing, long or short term. Unless something drastic happens to change it, the wild places of the earth are endangered. Within a few human lifetimes, it could all be gone. And the mice might go with it, at least the wild ones. They would never be able to be pets. They were not meant to be domesticated.

I recognize that tree you described—right here.

As the wind blew my fur and I directed Heide (one tap for right, two for left, three for straight, four for stop-I-gotta-think), I knew there were only a few possible solutions. Most of them were flat out impossible. Heck, the humans themselves had given up on it. Every one of them thought, "It's too big a job for me, one person can't fight against this," and they went right on consuming and destroying. Kinda like burying their heads in the sand. "If I can't see it maybe it will go away" thinking. All that kind of thinking ever got a rodent was death. It wouldn't change for humans. By the time they realized how bad they'd messed up, it would be too late. For them *and* us.

I realized in that moment of clarity that domestic mice would not survive without the humans. Five thousand years, maybe more, was too long. If they went, we went. And they were going pretty fast.

Yeah, that smells familiar—left here.

If mice ruled the world it would be different. I mean, humans solve everything by violence, no matter what they claim. In the end, it all comes down to that, if people aren't willing to surrender or talk. With humans, might makes right. Mice think that way, too, but they bite each other on the rump and call it a day. Well, except for Clyde, but he's a product of human intervention. And TV. Maybe TV isn't so good after all.

Go straight here. This road is long and has green grass on one side, and yellow on the other, just as you said.

Humans had the means to end their existence for the first time in history. They had giant weapons that would kill millions of them at once... and millions of mice with them.

Keep going straight.

Someone had to do something. Mousekind and humankind were both in mortal danger!

Straight.

But the hugeness of it! The enormity of such a task. Good Mousegod, it was overwhelming. How would *anyone* do such a thing? You'd have to... I don't know... convince them that hostile aliens were coming or something. Nah, that wouldn't work. They'd still be mean to mice. Maybe aliens were coming, and the aliens were giant mice! Yeah. And they wanted to see how humans had treated their little cousins they left behind. Yeah, that had potential. But... nah. It was science fiction. Humans would never buy it. And the idiot who was going to attempt this would have to have proof. Solid, serious, indisputable evidence. The kind that would make the whole world stop and listen. Otherwise it wouldn't fly.

Stop! Go back. (Sniff) Go left here.

"But it's a dirt road, Squib."

Perfect!

I was glad that wasn't *my* job. Whoever had that job was out of luck. Someone was gonna have to make humans—all of them—stop and think.

The stop part was easy. The think part had me worried. Humans really hated to think, and if you forced them, they crucified you an' stuff. And whatever you do, don't prove they're wrong, because they'll just deliberately keep on doing wrongness just to spite you, even if it means their own destruction. What a wonderful animal, the human. (That was sarcasm. I learned that from Shiva.)

Stop!

"That's the house you described, Squibble."

Yes, it is!

I hopped out of the car and down to the ground as Heide opened the door. "You want me to come in with you?" she said.

I panicked. Everyone would know I had leaked our secret. Even though I had discovered other Kind Humans, it might not be okay with everyone. It was a cardinal sin to expose our intelligence. I would hate to come back home just to be kicked out again and have no place to go. I shook my head, even though a nagging feeling told me not to.

"Are you sure?" she asked. "I don't want to leave you behind again."

I looked at the old house, smelled the smells. So simple, the smells of the country. So few and clean compared to the overwhelming city. From two hundred feet outside the front door I could smell other mice, the bees and the ants. This was home. It was strange that I couldn't smell many mice, but it was early yet.

I looked up at Heide and motioned for her to go.

She reluctantly got back in her car. "Okay, little mouse," she said, "But if you ever need me, you have my phone number."

I nodded. I wrote "thank you" in the dirt with my sword.

She smiled. "It was an honor and a pleasure meeting you, brave Sir Squibble," she said. "May all mice be so lucky." I blushed. Then she drove away, very slowly, making sure she stayed on the dirt road and didn't hit any mice that might be foolish enough to be out in the day. Like me.

In a short time, she was lost to sight. I had a vision of the Kind Human driving away, leaving me in the city, and how doomed I had felt. But now I was safe.

I turned around and faced the house.

I was home. I thought of my TV and my wheel and my treats, forgetting all about holy quests and imminent doom. Surely now, everything would be okay.

Oh, please let everything be okay.

SUMMER

The Tribulations Begin
The First Horseman: Conquest

Safety Is An Illusion

✠

I strode up to the front steps with pride, the setting sun at my back, coming back from my long pilgrimage a master and commander of an entire army of mice and rats. My chin was high, my cape was flowing behind me. My shield bore my crest (a happy dancing mouse) and my tail was pointed straight up in victory.

Upon reaching the top step, I was alarmed that there were not scads of mice playing on the porch. Of course, there was still some sunlight left. Maybe they weren't awake yet, but that was unlikely. In fact, there were no rodents anywhere except one.

He was big and muscular looking, an amazingly healthy mouse. He was standing by the side of the door like a guard. He had a bow and a spear. He wore the armor of a knight (and fine armor it was), and himself wore a cape of dark green. His chin was up and his sword was sheathed in his belt. I had never seen so handsome and fine looking a mouse. He seemed familiar somehow, but my master's family ran throughout this place. He had brought at least 20 of his brothers and sisters to the safe house when he came. This mouse was wearing his colors—dark forest green. Surely many more mice had become knights in my absence.

He snapped to attention perfectly and said in a charismatic voice, "Halt! Who goes there? Friend or foe?"

I removed my helm and answered his stance of attention.

"It is I, Squibble, second of the Mouse Knights and master of the slingshot, squire to the first Mouse Knight and Lord of the Hordes—um, Lord of some other mice. Somewhere. Kinda."

He eyed me warily. He never shifted his stance, nor did his scent betray any fear.

"*The* Squibble?" he asked slowly.

I nodded. "Mmm hmm," I said. "And eager to have a fine meal and a warm bed, if you please," and I tried to step by him to the little mouse door the Kind Human had built at the bottom of his own big door.

But... he stepped in front of me!

"I'm sorry, sire, but times are hard, and you're going to have to prove you are who you say."

"What?!" I chirped. "Are you blind? I am Squibble! Any mouse will confirm it, pleeb! Now out of my way."

He actually grinned. "I'm afraid I cannot, Sir. I have been charged with guarding the house, and that is what I shall do. Prove your title and entrance shall be yours."

I was stunned. My very integrity was impugned! I drew my blade and stepped back.

"You shall have your proof, you arrogant rodent! And then some!" I said, challenging him to chivalric combat.

Casually he leaned his spear against the wall and took his bow from his back, setting it on the porch. He took his time with the quiver and arrows, as if I'd reconsider.

He smiled (something so familiar about that smile!) and drew his blade. It was also green. "So be it, good Sir. A duel for proof it is."

I attacked in a fury, moving with fine footwork, throwing several perfect shots at his chestplate in rapid succession, only to have each and every blow parried with ease. He paused when I did, instead of countering me. He was not even trying. I gaped, but only for one tenth of a second, then doubled my attack in earnest.

The challenge was brutal, but only to me. He parried every blow, sometimes just leaning to one side and letting my sword miss him by a millimeter. He playfully danced around me, reaching out and tapping my blade when I would slow down. He even dropped his shield. So I did the same, out of noble courtesy. Sword to sword and tail to tail we sparred, and I could not come near him. I tried kicks, twists, and lunges. I tried thrusts, sneak shots, and speed blows. I tried leaping over him, going under him, and to my failure, disarming him. Nothing worked. It didn't even come close to working. He worked me for minutes along the porch, back and forth, back and forth. I was heaving and gasping for air. He wasn't even breathing hard. I had never seen such amazing footwork in my life. This mouse was better than any swordsman I had ever met. He was faster than BJ, stronger than Stompy, and his moves… they were poetry in motion. They were unbelievable.

But he was still making me mad! By this time a few other mice had come outside and were watching the fight. They looked bad, malnourished or something. I couldn't tell, as my attention was entirely upon the upstart I was facing.

"Come on then!" I shouted. "Don't go easy! You insult me, Sir!"

He appeared taken aback, and then shrugged.

I regretted my words instantly. He took off the kid gloves and let me have it with a barrage of the finest, most precise attacks I had ever beheld in my life. They rained upon me. I was not quick enough to stop even one. My armor took the blows, but it was clear that I would have been dead several times over without it. He ended the magnificent series by slapping both ears with the flat of his blade to disorient me, disarming me, and then placing the swordtip against my exposed throat. Only one other mouse knew that move, and he had never taught anyone but me.

Recognition dawned on me in a flash. My eyes were as wide as could be.

"Percival!" I whispered, holding perfectly still at the end of his blade.

He withdrew his sword and bowed low. "At your service, my brother."

The last time I had seen him he was a squirming little pinky. His eyes hadn't opened, and his only words had been squeaks. This godlike mouse before me was he. I could see it in his face, his body shape and his stance. He was my master's son, and a sword master beyond compare at the age of three months.

"No one has ever come close to beating me like that," I said. "That was amazing!"

He bowed deep. "I thank you, Sir. Coming from you, that is a serious compliment. Our teacher was one and the same."

I continued to marvel at him (he was twice the size of his father) as the other mice gathered around. "Is it really Squibble?" they said. "Has he come to save us?"

I looked around. It had not been my imagination. These mice looked scared. They were jittery and hesitant. Not the peaceful, happy mice I had known when I left. These mice were afraid of something. They were not fat or content. They had an edge about them, and all of them were armed. It reminded me of the city.

I returned my gaze to Percival. "What's going on here?" I asked. "You said something about hard times…"

He nodded. "Yes, but it is better explained by my father or Nemo." He moved to the mouse door, and all the mice reverently parted before him. He made an "after you" gesture with his arm, picking up his spear, bow and arrows, and handing them to another Mouse Knight (also wearing armor). Going through the door, I heard him tell the other knight that he had the early evening watch, and to keep a sharp nose to the wind.

Once inside, I could smell fear. It was crowded inside, with all the cages and mice as I remembered, but there was a pall of anxiety over the house. Everyone heard something happening outside the front door, but no one knew what had happened. Now, as I came through with Percival, the crowds sighed relief. One in every three mice I could see bore weapons. One in four had weapons and some sort of armor. I saw many Mouse Knights. More than five times the number the house had when I left. I peered around in wonder. No cages lay on the ground anymore. They were all propped up on wood or cement blocks. Many were on strong shelves made of steel. Most of the mice seemed to be in their cages. On all the windowsills were guardian mice, bearing missile weapons, gazing out at the field. Some of them were gazing at me, too. They looked angry, though not at me.

As we walked, I had to know.

"What's happened to paradise, Percival? What happened to my home?"

A crowd had gathered behind us, but they stayed well back. Whispers of my name and Percival's reached my radar-dish ears. They spoke as if they were seeing a ghost. I had one of those trippy moments where I wondered if I wasn't in one of my weirdo dreams. It sure seemed like it.

Percival said, "We have been attacked." He looked at me. "Several times."

I stopped. "What?!" I clenched my fists. "Who would dare?" Then a paralyzing thought embraced me against my will. "Not humans?!"

"No," he said. "Mice."

I stared. "Eh?" as if I hadn't heard him.

"Mice, snakes, other field creatures, hawks, coyotes, feral cats… all coming from the field, and every one of them insane. Driven mad by some invisible force." He looked back over his shoulder as if he could see through the wall. "We fear a virus, but if so, no one here has caught it yet."

I shuddered. I was too late. "It's not a virus," I said.

His eyebrows went up. He was too well bred to ask, assuming I would go on. And I would have, but at that moment my master came running to greet me. He, too, was wearing armor and a sword. With him was BJ, and a very thin, stringy female mouse. She and BJ were armed and armored as well. A female knight?

"Master!" I cried, and threw myself into his arms. He accepted my affection whole-heartedly, returning the gesture as our armor made a clank noise against each other. My heart lifted a little, only to sink when I heard him wheezing.

I pulled away and looked at him, worried. "Are you okay, Master?" He looked tired, thin, and... stressed out. He was worn and weary from something. Not the bright, healthy mouse I had left behind.

He smiled. "Yes, Squib. Just asthma. From the mycoplasma I had when we came here."

Everyone sat still a moment. There was so much to say, but in true Squibble form, I got the important stuff out right away. It had only been waiting at the tip of my tongue for four months.

"The evil Black Mouse is coming to get us!" I blurted. "I have to warn everyone!"

"We know," my master said.

"Fire and brimstone! Horsemen! Death and suffering! It's horrible... I'm doing my job! See, Mike?" I stared up at the ceiling, raising my arms. "See?! I'm doing my job! Helloooo!"

BJ looked at me and then at my master as if to say, "Has he gone mad?" My master coughed (it sounded like a squeak) and put a hand on my shoulder. He gripped my armor tightly. "Squibble. We know."

"War on the humans... mice in labs... mice in pet stores!" I blathered on. "It's the end of the world unless we—huh? You know?" The other mice were looking at me as if I had grown a tail out of my head, except for Percival.

Master nodded. "Yes, we know. You told Nemo and I before you left."

I cocked my head sideways. "But that was a bunch of hogwash."

"Nah," he said.

"They're just dreams...?" I asked hesitantly.

He shook his head. "No."

I was confused. Seeing it, he led me off to the side, away from everyone else. Quite a crowd had gathered, and they all looked as though they thought maybe Squibble had baked his brains on his pilgrimage. I felt stupid. But I had to do my job…

I was looking down at the floor, a stupid, foolish mouse again, feeling small and unimportant (just like when I had left) as my master spoke to me.

"You warned us of this, Squibble," he said. "Nemo and I took you seriously. You spoke of this and more. Much more. This is just the beginning. But we can't tell everyone. It would only work against us."

I looked up. "How?" I said. "Don't they have a right to know?"

"That a demon is trying to kill them all?" he said, raising his eyebrows. "That powers beyond their control have targeted them for doom? They'd panic, my friend. And they have nowhere to go."

I nodded. That made sense.

"You didn't tell us everything," he went on, "but you told us enough. Since you left we have been training every willing mouse to fight, and blocking all the open holes from outside. These attacks against us have been largely unsuccessful. Though it seems the enemy does know something of tactical warfare. It's very, very good and tricky, whatever it is." He patted me on the shoulder. "We can get you caught up later. I'm so glad to see you back, Squib. I'm so glad you made it."

I was reeling from sensory overload. It was alot to take in all at once, and I had the feeling it was going to get alot worse. Still, I was glad to be back. This was my master here, standing right in front of me, as I had wished these last three months to see. I was home. I could hear the TV. I could smell food and treats. I breathed slowly and recovered my calm. It took a few minutes. My master casually groomed me while I got myself under control.

"Percival is big," I finally said. "And he's amazing."

"Yes," he said with pride. "He was a perfect student. Always eager to learn, and he learned so fast. I've never seen a smarter, faster mouse."

"You, Master."

"Oh, I'm afraid not. He beat me, BJ, and Nemo by the time he was two months old. We had to knight him then."

I snapped up, mouth open.

"Yeah," my master said, smiling, "He beat us, and then asked us to keep teaching him. He wouldn't accept the title of King. So we kept teaching him. We're teaching him still, though he's fast coming to the end of our knowledge. Well, me and BJ. Maybe not Nemo. But Branch studies with Nemo more than Percival does."

Branch… Oh, yes, Percival's brother. "What's he like?" I asked.

"He wants more than anything to be like that sapphire chinchilla," my master said. "He wants to do magic—real magic, mind you, the kind that left the world with Camelot—and be a wizard. He's a wonderful mouse. You'll meet him." He seemed to be holding back something. I could feel it.

"What—" I began to ask.

"How was your pilgrimage?" he interrupted. "Did you do what you set out to do?"

I had set out to destroy great evil. I remembered.

"No," I said. "Leaving was stupid. I shouldn't have gone like that. I left because…"

"Because you thought everyone hated you," he said.

"What?!" I chirped. "Is everyone psychic but me?!"

"No," he grinned. "We figured it out when Scratchy went on a beating rampage and started kicking the hell out of a whole bunch of mice. He made them confess to their plot, pathetic as it was, and beg our forgiveness." I was speechless again. It was getting annoying. "You should have seen them," he said. "They didn't stand a chance. That little whirlwind went through them like melted cheese."

I turned then to look back at the crowd, all of them clearly talking about me. There, ten feet away and among them, was Scratchy. He was holding my backpack and my shield that I had left on the porch. He smiled timidly at me. The backpack was bigger than he was. He hadn't grown.

"How… how many mice were in on that… plot against me?" I asked carefully, not really wanting to hear the answer.

My master leaned in close and whispered, "One."

"No way," I said. "I heard a whole bunch of mice…"

"All bullied and manipulated by One-Ear," my master said. "As it turned out, he'd been working on it for weeks. They just went along with him out of sheer peer pressure." I shook my head, disbelieving, and he put an arm around me. "Squibble, it's easy to hate a mouse in a high place. Or one who's so good at things, or so smart," he rubbed my head. It felt great. "They envied you. It's a short step from respect to fear. He turned their respect to fear with his words. That did the rest. When the others saw how stupid it all was, they repented. They didn't know you, after all."

I was still looking at Scratchy. He would smile at me every ten seconds or so. He was obviously nervous, and put my things down carefully, especially the shield.

"What happened to One-Ear?" I asked.

"Nothing," my master said. "We sent him to the bottom of the totem pole by exposing his childish attempt at drama. Nobody listens to him anymore."

"Oh," I said.

"I knew you'd come back okay," he said, smiling. "I believed in you. Can't say I wasn't worried though. Letting you go was the hardest thing I've ever done."

"You knew how dangerous it would be," I said.

"Yes, I did." He was serious now.

"Why did you let me go?" I asked. "I nearly died several times!"

"Squib…" his mind was working overtime. I could see it. "I didn't want to. Nemo told me I had to. For the good of the future, he claimed. Still, I very nearly fought him on it. I almost challenged him for the right to make you stay."

"You would have challenged Nemo?!" I exclaimed. "He's a hundred times your weight!"

"Ah, been there done that," he said, and waved a paw. "Besides, this was my best friend, son, and squire we're talking about. I knew what hell you had set yourself up for. I myself was lost in the city once, remember?"

"Not for very long," I grumbled.

"In the end Nemo convinced me that he was right," my master pleaded his case. "He always is. He can see the future."

"That meeting I was listening to," I said, "it was about me. The heated argument." He nodded. "But you let me go."

"Squibble. Don't be stubborn. I didn't want to. Aren't you listening? I had to, or you wouldn't…" he stopped himself.

I peered at my master. "What? Wouldn't what? Become my future self? The all-powerful hero Squibble?" I was upset now, the stress of my months in the city finally caught up with me. Plus, I was on a roll. "I'm not so sure being a hero is all that great," I said bitterly.

"Oh, you don't mean that," he said. "It's all you've ever wanted."

"The price is pretty stupid," I complained.

"The greater the hero, the higher the price," he said. "In all the stories..."

"I don't care about the stories!" I yelled. "You let me go and didn't come rescue me! You let me go!"

He looked at me hard for a few seconds.

"Squibble, you were a grown mouse. Maybe not inside, but you were a knight." His stare, as usual, went right through me. "If you hadn't gone, you'd have stayed that way the rest of your life. And we would have no champion. You know this. And so did we."

I sat in silence for a long time. He was right. I hated it, but he was. My feeling of abandonment was my own head trip.

"My pilgrimage was hard," I whined. "I didn't know life could get so hard."

My master looked back at the other mice, then back into the house. When his face turned back to me, it had that stressed out, tired look to it again. He took a deep breath.

"It's about to get harder, Squib."

I stared at him aghast. "What could *possibly* be harder than..."

He interrupted me again, which is unlike his noble, mannered self, and he seemed in a hurry to say something to me because it was difficult.

"It's your mom, Squibble. She's sick."

Tree

✠

I sat there, unmoving, looking pathetic. My head sank and I stared at the floor.

"What kinda sick?" I asked softly.

"The kind that she won't recover from," he said. "Cancer."

Something hurt me inside then. It shot out from my chest in lightning bolts down to my toes and fingers. It left a black, empty, burned place in my soul that got worse from then on, and I have carried it as a scar ever since. It started then, in that moment I was told my mom was going to die.

"Cancer?" I asked.

"It's a disease," my master said.

"Yeah," I said. I sounded sheepish. Stupid. Sad.

"She's almost gone." He came carefully and put a hand on my cheek. "She was waiting for you to return. She's held on an awful long time."

I shuffled slowly at his feet. "Master, you have to save her," I begged. "She's my momma. You have to save her."

My master's gaze fell to the floor, then slowly rose back to meet mine. His eyes were full of willpower and tears.

"I'm sorry, Squibble," he said, choking out the words. "This time I'm gonna let you down."

I ran from him, past the other mice. From the looks on their faces they knew already. Of course they did. That was why they hadn't said anything at first. They were relying on my master to break it to me. I ran past them and up the shelves to my mother's cage. It was still there. Nemo was sitting outside it, looking sick himself. He said nothing as I whipped past him and into my mom's nest house.

Inside, I sucked in air at the sight of my mother. She was rail thin, just skin and bones. Her eyes looked tired, and she looked like she was two years old, when she was actually less than half that, still in her prime. I could hear her shallow breathing and smell the sickness in her lungs with every breath. Her mouth was moving a little each time she breathed, and I heard a pitiful whistling sound coming from her throat. She didn't smell me. Her face looked depressed, her once bright eyes dim. I wouldn't have recognized her by sight. That failing shell… she was barely in it.

"Momma," I said, gentle and soft.

She turned her head and stared at me. It took a moment for her to register me there in her dark nestbox, then she smiled. "Hello, kitten," she said.

I began to cry at the sight of her, the sounds of her choked voice. "Momma," I repeated, and came over to her. I went to embrace her, and when the armor got in my way, I tore it off my body like some parasite I loathed. I hugged my momma. She squeaked in pain though, so I backed off and instead licked her lightly around her sad eyes. She licked me back. It felt so good. But then the feeling was interrupted by the horror that this might be the last time I'd ever feel that. Reality had finally come to me. It did not come in the city, when I was beat up, or in my search for drugs to save my life, not in the lab, nor in the nest when I was commander of a thousand mice. It came then, in that nest, holding my dying momma who was more precious to me than anything on the earth. Nothing could ever replace her, and nothing could save her. I was utterly powerless. I begged Bigfat to help her, I begged Mike to intervene. I whispered to her sweet things and told her about all the high points of my pilgrimage, making it sound like a grand adventure instead of a lesson in fear and pain. She was so weak. She could barely talk. It was all the energy she had to stay awake, and finally, as the night grew very dark, she couldn't. I held her anyway.

Sometime in the night, hours later, my master came into the nest box. I smelled Nemo still outside, sitting there meditating. I smelled other mice just outside the cage, nervous and not knowing what to do. My master sat with me a long time. An hour or more, without saying anything. He put a hand on her back and groomed her a little. She moaned in her sleep.

My head hung low, my eyes had changed. Inside, I felt as though I was the one dying. I know that's so terribly selfish, and believe me, it got much worse in days to come, but at that moment, I felt I had come home to hell. The thought crossed my mind that I had been better off not coming home, but no. Then I would never have seen my momma again. At all.

"Do you want to be here when she goes?" my master asked.

I just looked at him, not able to shake off my shock.

"It won't be pretty," he said grimly. "Nemo thought to spare you the ugliness of it. I said it was your choice. She's your mom."

I just stared. My eyes were full. It was as though I were seeing him through a glass of water.

"It's up to you, Squib," he said. "It's up to you. You're grown up now."

He turned and left the nest. I heard Nemo stir, and they both left. Shortly after, the other mice below left also. I could smell that the last two to leave were Scratchy and that strange, lanky female mouse that had been with BJ when I came into the house. I was alone with my dying momma, and soon I would just be... alone.

"I'm so glad you're alright," she croaked. She petted me once before she hadn't the strength anymore. "I was so worried."

"I'm sorry, Momma. I'm so sorry," I said. It hit me then how selfish and stupid I had really been. Every day she must have looked out the window into the fields and wondered how I was. How could I have done that to her? I had literally worried her sick. This was my fault.

If you want to remember her beautiful and free of trauma as I wish I could, then skip ahead. Because I did stay for her death, and as my master had promised, it was not pretty. It was only me and my master there in the end. The human had put her on anti-pain drugs, but hadn't the heart to euthanize her. It was the first time he had lost one of those mice closest to him. Out of several hundred, I guess you could only choose a few to be really close to. My mom was one of them. He used to take her out for hours at a time, with my master, and let them play on the bed together, crawling endlessly over the mountains and in the tunnels made from the blankets. My mom, she was always more interested in crawling on the human, spending time with him, same as my master, and that endeared them both to his heart. She was his most affectionate mouse, he always said.

In the end, she suffocated. The cancer in her lungs cut off her air, and she choked. I would like to have not seen it, and would probably be better off if I hadn't, but then I would have wondered the rest of my life. It began with a clicking noise, and then she began to gasp for breath, opening and shutting her mouth as wide as it could go. Her eyes were bulging from their sockets in terror and pain. I couldn't bear to watch it, but something wouldn't let me turn my head. My master and I were both crying. Neither of us had imagined it would be so terrible. In retrospect, a violent death at the hands of a snake or animal would have been more merciful.

She twitched once, then again. She panicked. She sprung up onto her legs, on strength she did not have, and ran outside the nest. We followed her out. Mice know they're dying, and will use their last strength to get as far from the nest as possible so their body doesn't attract predators to the living mice. Almost no mouse dies in bed.

Outside, she spasmed and convulsed so violently that her head hit several of the toys hard. She jerked and leapt almost a foot into the air, only to land painfully and spring up, trying to run away again. Trying to run away from her death. Sheer animal terror, with no conscious thought attached. I prayed that she was somewhere else already, and that her body was all we were seeing, in its last throes of struggling to survive, a futile struggle it had already lost and didn't know it.

My master and I couldn't hold her down. Her body was flopping around like a fish out of water. Desperate and full of horror, she flung herself blindly all over the cage. Finally, mercifully, she landed and was still, eyes bulging grotesquely, legs still twitching. Still trying to run from the Reaper.

But she was dead. Her mouth opened and shut a few more times. Her chest heaved a few more times, then she trembled all over, her eyes squinted in agony, and she was still forever.

For the first time in his life, my master broke down. It had been too terrible. He heaved deep, mournful sobs and doubled over my mother's corpse. In one of his exhalations blood sprayed out of his nose and all over his face, my mother's back, and onto the floor. Too horrified to do anything at all, we both ignored it, but I knew it was his lungs. My dreams had shown me this ahead of time, his scarred lungs where blood would clot and finally burst in times of stress, spraying out of him like a fountain. He had not achieved his dream without a dear price. His safe house, his Kind Human, and his holy quest had crippled him. Seeing him there, wrecked and dispirited, crying on my dead mother was all I could take. Something snapped in me then, broke outright, and I knew I would not be the same after that. I could feel it in me like broken glass grinding into an open wound. I stared like a retarded child, not comprehending what I was seeing. It was as if something finally gave in me that had been waiting six months to do so. All at once, the dam broke.

I saw golden light. White, blazing, golden light shining into the house from the window. It was the light of dawn, but it was more than that. This light was too pure. And all around us, there were softly glowing mice. Many mice. Little mice, too young to be away from their mother, all standing around Tree and her broken mate. Then I saw my mother, glowing and lit by radiance not of this world, step out of her body and take her dead children to her. They had waited all that time. Waited for her.

Above us, I saw Michael standing, holding open the gates of the sky. He was looking at *me*. Not at my mother, but at me. I looked back, bright as he was. I had nothing to say at that moment. His face was full of compassion and strength. His power was beyond anything I had ever beheld, as he guided the tiny little mice to the first step in their journey. I watched all the spirits go, walking into the sky on their way to the shoreline, slowly, reluctant to leave this place. Reluctant to leave…

My mother turned when Michael pointed and looked down at me. She smiled sweetly. Her face, now full again and not sick or sad, was more spectacular than it had ever been.

"I will be back when it's his turn," she said and looked down upon my master. "I love you, my dear son." Then they were gone. Mike went last, sorrow for me and what I had ahead of me, I guess, showing on his chiseled face.

At last it was dark. My mother's body and the sounds of my master's racking sobs were the only things in my world.

Some time later I remembered mice coming and bearing away my mom's body. Nemo was looking at me like Mike had. A knowing look, full of sympathy and concern. I didn't care. BJ and the children came and put their paws on my master. Percival, Branch, Leaf, Muadib and Gaia all surrounded their father. They were all grown now, every one of them. All beautiful, healthy mice, all mirrors of their parents. None of them looked like me. Branch turned and gave me a knowing look also, like Nemo had. He was only three months old. If his genetics were anything like Percival's, they were both *Ubermice*—destined for great things and blessed with many amazing gifts. Maybe he could indeed see whatever it was Mike and Nemo saw. I didn't care. My senses were stunned from the blow of my mother's poor death. The vision afterward, which stayed with me (I saw many mouse spirits all over the house, many of them walking with us, but clearly not living) did not change things. My heart was broken. It would not heal anytime soon.

It was the beginning of my descent into the underworld. It was the start of my spiritual pilgrimage. I felt my happy-go-lucky self leave me, and depression took its first cold grip on my soul. I walked in tiny shuffles, my eyes downcast, and heard not one word anyone spoke to me. I almost felt my spirit falling. Falling into darkness and despair.

All that bright sunny day, it never hit bottom.

Summer Rain

✠

I hadn't slept in two days. To a mouse that's a ridiculously long time, and my senses weren't all working. I couldn't think clearly, and everywhere I looked I saw the spirit world meshed with the "normal" one. Nemo had come to talk to me, as well as my master and some others—BJ, the lanky female mouse, and Percival. I ignored them all, absorbed in myself and trying to banish the sight of my mother's awful death. But nothing worked.

I hadn't eaten, I hadn't rested. I went back to my old cage, which the Kind Human left open and unchanged for me, except to clean it. Favorite was there. She was listless and unresponsive, just laying there in the corner by the food and water, though she was clearly happy to see me. She moved her head all around and tried to smile. I asked her if she was sick, and she said no. I asked her why she was weird, and she said, "The others didn't tell you yet?"

"About my mother, yeah. She died."

"No, not that…" she trailed off. She looked at the ground, as if guilty of something.

"You mean there's *more* bad news!" I exclaimed. I was very angry, but my body wouldn't pay for it, so I sounded just… tired. I had imagined a happy reunion with Favorite so many times, and now this. It ruined everything, and I stormed off. I didn't go back to my cage. I avoided everyone. I didn't want to hear any more bad news. Ever.

So the beginning of summer found me standing on the porch alone in the middle of the day. It was raining, and in the distance there was a rainbow. It was one of those early summer rains, warm and soft. The sound of it was all about me. The smell of it was fresh in my nose. The sky was only partially clouded, and beams of sunlight fell through to the wet fields below. It was a scene of lonely serenity and profound beauty.

There was a stout knight on guard by the front door, but he ignored me. I think it was Ghost. His armor was all bleached white, and I remembered him from fighting school. He made knighthood. Amazing. They were coming out of the frikkin' woodwork in an age when knighthood was supposed to be near impossible to achieve. Stupid. I walked to the edge of the deck and sat there, dangling my legs off the side and lost in delusional thought. Occasionally a raindrop fell near me. In no time I was wet.

"Sire," Ghost said cautiously.

I turned my head and rattled my tail.

"Beg your pardon, my liege," he said, "but without your armor or arms, you might not want to be out here during the day… or night, for that matter."

"Why not?" I said.

"The house has been having raids by insane animals. Many mice, even some rats, have died."

"Yes, I can see them all."

Ghost was taken aback by this, looked around, then probably decided that I was a loon. "You aren't safe out here, Sire."

"No one is safe *anywhere*, knight," I snapped. I sounded bitter to myself. I slowly realized I was bitter. Bitter that nowhere was safe. Didn't my master suffer and sacrifice his health so that mice might be safe? That damn Black Mouse was going to take that from us now? Nothing was sacred.

"I was just trying to…" Ghost began

"Bother me to death," I finished. "Leave me alone. Percival might be able to beat *me*, but I bet I can beat *you*. Even without a sword."

He saw that I meant it. It gave me some dark glee to see his face change to an expression of worry for his own hide. Without a word he went back and stood by the door again.

The land was glazed in golden light, green light, yellow light, red light at the horizon. I didn't know what any of it meant, but it certainly was pretty. The spirit world was sure awash in color. I had lost track of time and sat there, hungry and thirsty, for hours. I saw big lights pass overhead in the sky that weren't the sun or moon, and little lights dance in the fields. I somehow knew the little lights were the spirits of field mice. I saw the wind moving over the land, and the clouds high over us full of the footprints of angels who had passed that way. I saw the earth alight in a deep tan and green light. I saw the beams going up and down from the earth to the high places. I saw other mice begin their journey to the sea, and I saw many others stay, confused and lost. Like watching a movie with too many special effects, the story was lost on me. I couldn't guess what made the world go. I marveled at it. I stared and stared. I saw doors, pyramids, egg shaped things laced with millions of strands of glistening cords. I saw stars rise and stars fall. And through all of it, I wondered what force had decided that my gentle mother deserved to die so horribly. I wondered what it would decide about me. Was there any reason and rhyme to the universe? Was it all some terrible roll of the cosmic dice?

Before I knew it, night was falling. The sunset was a hundred times more spectacular than the day, seen through spirit-vision. It was like watching the chariots of the gods come to collect all the souls of the dead, waiting out yonder, by the waves. The setting sun had a million arms, spanning out across the solar system, reaching into eternity and beyond. Too much to think of for a little mouse. Too much. I was paralyzed with overload.

But one thing stood out. Over the horizon, between the shoreline with its setting sun and the tiny, old wooden deck I sat on, was the city. And the city was a black hole.

There were lights in it. Light of souls, many of them. But beyond that, no earth light, no heaven light, no sky light. It was one giant black dome with a million smaller lights inside it, struggling to shine and survive in the vast emptiness. It made me shiver. I wondered if all cities were like that or just ours. But you know, that's how it had felt while I was there—black and empty. I had been afraid to die there. I was afraid to die anywhere, especially now, but of all places, not there. My soul might never find its way to the sea. The city was one big spiritual maze. I thought of Shiva and Thor. Somehow, they belonged there now. There was something dark about them now, too. I felt a sadness set into me that had been waiting for its moment to pounce. Our lives were tragedies. I saw it then, clear as day.

"What you're missing is that they are also comedies, dramas, and masterful works of art," Nemo said. He had been sitting next to me for some time, staring out at it all.

"Is this what you see all the time?" I asked. I knew he could see what I did. I just knew.

"When I wish to," he said.

"You can turn it off?"

"And on. At will. So can you."

The offer was very tempting. The clever rodent. But I wasn't going to give in that easy.

"You already have an apprentice," I said. "Branch."

"Yes, he'd love to talk to you. Everyone would. They all have questions, things to tell you, and help to offer."

"Yeah, well pee on that."

"Don't," he said with meaning. "Don't ever pee on help, Squibble."

I grumbled something even I didn't understand.

"Your bad attitude is only making things worse," he said. "It's understandable, but someday you will have to get up and keep going."

"Is that right?" I said.

"Yes," he said. "And the sooner, the better. We all need you more than you know."

"Oh, my future-self me, right? Not the Squibble-is-sad-so-leave-me-alone me."

"You, period."

"Well, maybe I don't wanna do this no more," I ground my words together like an angry human crushing a hated thing into the dirt. "Maybe this is for the birds."

"Maybe it is," Nemo said, "but you chose it."

To that, I could say nothing, but I did anyway. "You're annoying, Mr. Know-it-all."

Nemo laughed. It was a genuine laugh, not cynical or angry.

"Yes, I know. I'm sorry. Will you let me teach you to use your new powers? Please?"

I looked up at him for the first time. He had said please? To me? I was still mad. I was going to be a difficult mouse.

"Why should I?" I said, lifting my nose to the master whom hundreds begged to be taught one tiny thing by.

"Well, if you do, you'll be able to vanish into thin air," he said.

My eyes got wide. I couldn't help it. My child inside wasn't dead yet, and it loved that idea. "No way!"

"Way," he said, giggling. "And maybe levitate, or even read minds."

I started. "You were reading mine back there, while I was sitting on the porch!"

He nodded. "How very mousey of me, eh?"

I rattled my tail. "Don't do that again, stupid!"

He didn't appear even slightly flustered by being called stupid. No one else would have ever dreamed of doing that to him. Afterward, I couldn't believe *I* had done it.

"As you wish," he simply replied.

Silence held a moment.

"Could you teach me to cure cancer?" I said.

He considered it hard, looking through me with spirit-vision.

"Maybe," he said. "If you wanted to."

"I do," I said.

"Come to me in the evenings," he said, meaning just before dawn, "And I will share with you what I know."

"No tricks, sorcerer," I said and shook a finger at him. "No manipulation, no magic-language poo. Plain mousey English."

"Okay," he smiled. I saw he was missing some teeth. Then I noticed that his ear was notched in several places. And his fur was unkempt. He was skinny, like some of the others. I could see his ribs. And his complexion was pale.

"What's going on around here—" I began to ask, but then I smelled an old but familiar smell behind me.

A rattlesnake!

I spun not fast enough. The creature did not even pause to consider its prey, nor to parley. It was coming on at full speed and leaping for the deck (and me) without thought. Its eyes were glazed over, as if possessed. Snakes do not leap as it did, nor strike past their body length—we knights have all learned that. But this one was doing both. I was too tired and weak from not eating. It was going to land its fangs in me. I saw all this, and didn't much care.

But then there was a sapphire flash. Nemo was moving faster than I had ever seen him move. He was faster than a mouse. Faster than the snake. And faster even than my eyes. In the next tenth of a second, he had intercepted the snake in mid strike, and had it behind the head, was breaking its neck, twisting in midair with all his body weight behind his teeth. The snake dropped to the deck dead before it knew what death had claimed it, and I was still turning around.

Down at the door, Branch and Percival had come barreling out of the mouse hatch. Percival had a drawn blade and Branch was chanting some kind of word in a weird hum. He had his hands extended forward like he was going to cast a spell or something.

The snake stopped twitching as Nemo severed the head and spat it back over the edge of the porch.

"Master!" Branch exclaimed. "Are you alright?!"

Nemo wiped his mouth off with his paw and then wiped his nose at the snake. "Yes," he said. "I'm not that sick yet."

I did a double take as my slow mind caught up with all that had happened. I saw Nemo shining in brilliant sapphire blue hues, and the snake's body was a black, empty shell. It had no soul.

When I looked up at Branch I saw that he had a golden radiance around him, full of lights like I had once seen around the spirit of Bigfat. There were trails moving through the air following the movements of his eyes and hands, like slow lightning in multiple colors. Maybe he was going to cast a spell. Normal mice didn't look like that on the spirit plane.

Normal mice didn't look like Percival either. He was blazing white. Pure white. His armor looked like mirrored steel, his sword, made of rainbow colored metal. His eyes were pouring forth light, and above his head sat a ring of the sun.

A halo.

They must have noticed me staring dumbly, for Branch came forward, tucking his glowing paws into his robes and explaining, "Nemo is ill, Squibble. Like your master, but he was born ill."

I continued to stare like a loon, squinting against the glory of the Mousegod's energy, for surely that was what I was seeing. The energy of creation, the power of life and then some. My eyes got wide, narrowed to slits, then got wide again. I wiped them with my paws and looked again.

"Oh..." I whispered. "You're not normal mousey beans at all..."

Branch laughed. Percival looked concerned for me.

"Of course, we're normal beings," Branch said. "You should see *yourself* with the second sight!" He gestured toward the window. "We just have more power than others, brother. We're closer to the source."

I climbed up the drainpipe and onto the windowsill. In the reflection I saw my own dancing lights. My own blazing glory. It was muted and dimmer, and somehow screamed of agony. I saw in my aura deep sadness and loss. Powerful, amazing potential... and... and...

I couldn't look anymore. I closed my eyes and fell off the ledge, to be caught by Nemo.

"You're exhausted, little one," he said. I looked around and saw my master, the lanky female mouse, and BJ. They all looked very concerned. They took me inside, weapons drawn, surrounding Nemo as he carried me. I saw the big chinchilla's sallow face as he smiled down at me like he was looking at a child.

"When you wake, your sight will be normal again," he said.

And with that thought, I lost consciousness.

Weird Mouse

✠

I woke two days later. I felt better. The past several days were a blur in my frazzled mind. I don't remember what was real and what was not. I had many strange dreams, all fading away like the twilight colors at sunset as soon as I opened my eyes.

I was lying in my nextbox in my cage. It smelled mostly like Favorite. I thought of her and remembered she had been sitting there, listless and depressed when I had come home. Then, like a ton of bricks, it hit me that my mother was dead. I remembered everything, and my heart sank into my stomach. I felt sick, and my eyes began crying without my permission.

Slowly I crawled out of my nest box, lethargic and sad. It was almost dawn of some day or other. Favorite was *still* sitting in that spot I had left her in days ago. It didn't even occur to me to ask what was wrong. I just got disgusted and left my cage immediately. On the way out I saw someone had left all my things at the foot of the ramp that led into and out of my cage. My armor, sword, helm, shield, backpack, side pouch and all the pills I had collected. Someone had also left a brand new, empty journal book and several tiny pencils—humans have some use for them, I suppose, but they're so small we can use them kind of like a large stick, so we do. There were also a few stacks of carefully cut drawing paper set on a thin board with homemade clips on it, just like the students at the Atelier used. Small sprigs of bamboo had been cut to mouse-pen size and the ends sharpened and split in the middle, making me crowquill pens—a new medium I hadn't tried yet—and with them was a bottle of black ink small enough for me to carry around. Someone had gone through alot of trouble to do all this. I was used to pencil tips and makeshift ballpoint pen ends.

I looked back at the food dish. Favorite looked up at me imploringly, maybe hoping for a grooming or a kind word. I saw the dish had millet and Cheerios in it—very special goodies—and the cage had been cleaned.

Favorite had a pathetic look on her face, like someone begging for a treat. But she didn't move, and the treats were right next to her, so I climbed out off the cage and went on my way across the house. I didn't know why it bothered me so much. No mouse likes a lazy mouse. Maybe that was it.

The house was quite empty. And quiet. It wasn't yet time for mice to be going to bed, and I wondered where everyone was. I scurried down the hall and into the back room, the human's bedroom. Nemo's cage was there, and so was his nasty girlfriend. She was busy stuffing her face with pellets and ignored me. I didn't like her, but hey, Nemo hadn't gotten to choose his girlfriend. The human chose for everyone when he went to the ranch or the shelters. Rarely could we come along. If he took Nemo to the ranch and Nemo picked out his own girlfriend, it might kinda give our secret away, and it was a good way to pick up diseases. So I guess she was the Kind Human's best try at picking for a chinchilla. I wondered if Nemo liked her.

I climbed down a mousehole and into the basement. There were many mice there, almost everyone. Hundreds of mice, all standing in formation or busy doing fighting drills. Almost twenty of them were in armor. Several were in lesser armor, carrying spears or other weapons, and wearing colored sashes with stripes on them (to denote who their teacher was and their rank in the class, I guess. I used military ranks, they used colored sashes.) The more stripes, the higher the rank I guessed from the looks of it. The floor was alive with movement and the yelling of sergeant mice training recruits. In the middle of it all was BJ, teaching his famous fighting class. There was so much happening it was hard to look at. I wondered what the human thought of all that stuff.

Scratchy was down there teaching with BJ, and his sash was purple—the color of royalty! It had seven stripes on it. No one else had even five. BJ had made him an assistant teacher. If anyone had taken the runt as a squire he'd have to wear those colors, the colors of his knight. But no one had, unless BJ... nahhh... no way.

When I was seen at last all the activity around me stopped. Like when the gnarly guy walks into the saloon in an old Western and all the music stops—everyone turns to look at him. It was so comical I almost squinted my eyes and said, "Dyin' ain't much of a livin', boy," but I knew no one would get it.

So there I was, being stared at by all kindsa mice, most of whom knew me already, or should have anyway. It was a strange moment. Finally, I broke the tension by smiling and waving stupidly. Everyone went back to what they were doing. I left the way I'd come. That was just too weird.

Out back, more mice were training. My master was teaching swordfighting with Percival at his side. High up on a hill, overlooking the training camp was Nemo, and next to him a tiny, sitting, robed figure that could have been Branch. I was going to head up there when I was accosted by mice.

"Hey—it's Squibble!" one said.

"Hey, Squibble—tell us about your pilgrimage!"

"Yeah, they say you went insane!"

"Did you have to kill lots of things?"

"Someone said you died and came back to life."

I stopped and held up my paws.

"What?" I tilted my head at them and demanded.

"Yeah... They say you're a prophet now, like Nemo."

"Ummm... no." I said.

"They say you got your butt handed to you by Percival!"

"Yep," I confirmed.

"They say you can see the spirit world," one chirped.

"Sometimes," I said.

They all fell silent.

"Really?" one asked after a while.

I nodded. "Yeah."

"What does it look like right now?" one asked.

I looked around. My vision *had* returned to normal, thank the Mousegod.

"I can't do it all the time," I said.

"Oh yeah, I *bet*," said one smarmy mouse in back. If it was One-Ear, I'd bite his rump clean off.

They all laughed. It made me mad. It reminded me of the bully mouse and his lunatic Gestapo.

"Don't laugh at me!" I yelled. They kept on laughing. They were used to good ol' pushover Squibble, who always laughed with everyone, ignorantly unaware that they were laughing at him. Well, those times were over.

"I *can* see things," I said. "I'm not lying!"

More laughter. The more serious I got, the harder they laughed. It was absurd. They were insulting my dignity.

"Hey, predict the future like Nemo does!" one of them said, clearly not believing in supernatural powers at all.

"Okay," I said. They all fell silent. I looked right at the mouse who had just spoken and stepped up next to him. "You're going to be in pain for days."

What I said just registered when I bit him right on the face. Hard. Something crunched under my teeth and I followed it up by hitting him twice and kicking him in the throat. Gasping for breath and horrified, the mouse leapt a foot in the air and vanished toward the house. I laid into them all, snorting and stomping and calling them idiots and disrespectful cretins. I bit, kicked, flung them and hit them. They had practice weapons, I had nothing, but none of them fought back. They were too busy trying to get away. They screamed and yelled, dropped their weapons and fled.

"Aiiiieee! He's gone insane!"

"He's trying to keel us!"

"He's a loon!"

"With really strong teeth!"

Then I was alone in the back yard, at least for a radius of about ten feet. Huffing and puffing, I spat on the ground and rattled my tail. My eyes were bloodshot and my jaw ached. But I had shown them!

"NEVER make fun of me!" I screamed after their running butts.

Then I sat down hard. I felt like crying. Some of those mice had been my friends. Of course, I didn't know who were my friends anymore. They were plotting to hurt me—maybe even kill me—a few months ago. Now they all thought I was insane. That would explain the looks I got in the basement. Squibble, the first great Mouse Knight's faithful squire, goes on pilgrimage, and comes back loony. They'd all shake their heads and make "tsk tsk" noises and look at me funny when I passed by. Insane mice were tolerated about as well as lazy mice.

This was not the reunion I had in mind when I came back. This sucked.

I saw a glow approaching me and looked up to see my master and Percival coming toward me. But I was seeing them in spirit-vision. Their halos and auras were bright white and white-gold. Around my master's nose though I saw red mist, like something trickling out of him when he breathed. His hurt lungs, I thought. The combined radiance of both mice made me squint my eyes. The hundred or so students they had been teaching were going back inside for the day. Lessons were over. Dawn was almost upon us. My spirit vision faded away.

"What was all that, Squib?" my master said. He was wearing his armor and holding his sword. So was Percival.

"Nothin'," I stated.

He looked at me sideways. It used to make me laugh.

"Nothin'?" he imitated me, trying to get a chuckle out of me as it used to, but again it reminded me of the bully mouse doing his Squibble-is-so-stupid dance, and it made me angry. I knew he was trying to be nice and gentle with me, but fury took hold in my damaged soul.

"Nothin!" I yelled suddenly, popping to my feet. They both jumped back in alarm. "Nothin! *Nothinnothinnothin!*" And I ran off.

Well, so much for a nice reunion with my beloved master.

Frustrated and confused, I went and scrabbled up onto the bed of the human, and ran all over his blankets for a while. Until he felt me and woke up, of course.

"Squibble!" he said, grabbing me roughly. "You know no one is allowed on the bed when I'm sleeping!" He took me back to my cage, petting me, and put me next to Favorite. She hadn't moved.

"I'm really sorry about your momma," he said to me. "And I am *very* happy to see you back home after leaving you in the city. That scared me pretty bad, little mouse. It was like Nemo all over again. Let's not do that again, okay?"

I thumbed my nose at him for ruining my good time, but I doubt he noticed. When I turned around Favorite was giving me that pathetic look again.

"What!" I chirped at her. She looked sadly away. I grabbed a Cheerio and vacated the premises one more time. By this time I was pretty livid, and sure enough, here came runt boy Scratchy and his perfect timing, climbing up to see me. He was still wearing his purple sash and had something in his mouth. I didn't want to know what it was, for surely it was something that was going to anger me further. I knew I'd kick him or worse, so I lit out the other direction and made a foot long jump between shelves to avoid him. Then I flew down the ramps to the floor and ran back across the living room and down the hall again, determined to climb on the bed now that the human was taking a shower.

If you tell a mouse they can't go somewhere, or can't do something, it's a sure way to make that mouse determined to do that very thing. Mice are like that. And I was a very stubborn mouse. So—to the bed it was. I'd show that human!

But when I got up there, Nemo was perched at the top of the great cliff-of-blanket waiting for me.

"Gonna run on the bed!" I said.

He stepped aside. "Okay," he said, "but I thought we had an appointment."

I stopped and got that startled look on my face mice get when they hear something funny.

I peered at him. "Reeelly?"

"Yes, you said you'd let me teach you some powers."

I kinda remembered that. "Did I now?"

"Yep."

"Well, it better not be boring, 'cause I'm all into not being a bored mouse."

"It won't be," he promised and vanished into thin air.

My eyes got all round. I sniffed and sniffed, but that chinchilla was *gone!*

"Whoa!" I said. I looked around for him cautiously. "Whoa," I kept saying when I found no trace of him. I skulked low to the blanket surface all over the place. No Nemo.

Then I saw him over by his cage. I ran over there, down off the bed, and up onto his little table.

"How'd you do that?!" I chirped.

"Do what?" he said innocently.

"Be all gone an' stuff!"

"Oh," he said casually. "Was I gone?"

I rattled my tail. "Don't work me over, mister chinchilla! Tell me how you did that!"

"Why?" he asked.

I perked up and looked as though I'd heard something again. "Umm…" *'Cause I wanna do it*, I thought. Hmmm… "It was kinda cool," I said. "Not extremely impressive, mind you, but amusing."

"Oh, indeed," he said.

"Yeah. Like that. Indeed."

Suddenly, Branch was sitting next to me. I jumped half a foot straight up. "EEEEE!" I squeaked.

When I landed, I tried to swat him and succeeded. "No do that!" I quipped. He snickered. They both looked at me. Nemo raised his eyebrows.

"Yeah, okay," I said.

"Okay what?" Nemo asked.

"It might be… kinda cool if… maybe you could, um, sorta, possibly… teach me a thing or two."

"Please," Nemo said.

"Well, since you insist," I said.

"*You* say please," he said.

Branch folded his arms.

I sat still. I was considering grumbling when Branch put his arm around me. "Bro'," he said, "Nemo is sought after all the world over. In some places they consider him a god."

"Reeelly?" I said.

“Yes,” he said. “The sapphire gene is almost extinct now. There will soon be no more sapphire chinchillas left.” I began to pay attention. “Of course, it’s not the gene that makes him wise. He’s special, like our father is.” By that he meant my master, of course. Yeah. Special. “Nemo doesn’t teach just anyone. Last month we had a delegation from China here asking him to teach them.”

“*China*! “ I blurted. “*Mice* from China?”

Nemo nodded. Branch said, “Yes. He taught them all for as many days as they could go without food. It turned out to be seven days, and he had to *make* them eat then because they were willing to starve to death to learn his lessons. Then they returned. They invited me to come study at their monastery in Tibet. I think I want to go.”

“Wait,” I said. “Mice came here from China, and you starved them?” I said to Nemo. The chinchilla frowned.

“No,” Branch said. “You don’t understand. It’s part of their practice to meditate and do away with worldly things that interfere with enlightenment. Nemo was honoring that.”

“Kinda against the point, don’tcha think, if they keel over from hunger?”

“No, it sharpened their senses, and they remembered everything to the very word that Nemo taught them. They were grateful.”

“They were hungry!”

“Squibble, other mice think differently. Field mice have a whole different set of beliefs than us. Are they wrong?”

“No, they’re just weird.”

“According to rumor, you’re the weird one around here,” Nemo said. “Supposedly you’ve gone off the deep end.”

“Stupid gossip,” Branch said, defending me.

“Mice love to gossip,” Nemo commented.

“Yeah, well, I think I know whose fault that is,” I said, gritting my teeth, “and when I find him, he’s gonna pay.”

“My point was,” Branch went on, “that you must open your mind to new and different things if you want to study with Nemo, which is an honor and a privilege beyond measure.”

“Yeah, well, he asked me to study. I didn’t go to him.”

“All the more honor!” Branch exclaimed.

“Okay. Yeah.”

“Squibble, what do say you give me a week to impress you,” Nemo said. Branch let his jaw hang open at that. Nemo had probably never said that to anyone in his life. “If by the end of the week you aren’t impressed, you can do whatever you want to do.”

"I can always do whatever I wanna do," I said.

"Great wisdom," Nemo said. "You are teachable."

"I have a teacher!" I said.

"Your master?" Nemo said. I nodded vehemently. "Why don't you go see what he says about it?"

"Okay," I said. I looked at Branch. "Are you really going to China?!"

He nodded slowly. "Mom's death affected us all, brother. It was very sad. I have nothing more holding me here anymore. I'd love to keep studying with Nemo, but he says I've learned all I can from him for what I want to do—now I must go learn from the Chinese mice."

"What is it you wanna do? Kung Fu like Kychwang Kain?" I said, excited.

"No. I want to do magic."

I paused. Looked around. "*Mmmm.* Rabbit from a hat?"

He shook his head, a bit upset. "No, no. That's prestidigitation. Parlor tricks. Easy stuff." He pulled a piece of millet from my ear.

"Whoa!" I said, and ate it. "Can I have another?"

He did it again. I macked that one, too.

"What, you got a pocket full of millet or something?" I asked. He chuckled.

"Something like that. But the point is, no matter how good it looks, it's fake."

"Reeelly? I couldn't tell."

"No one can, except the trained eye. But it's still fake. I wanna do *real* magic! Really real. Change the weather, throw lightning and fireballs—all that cool stuff!"

"Yeah!" I chirped. "You're my brother all right. Cool stuff!"

He nodded and put his hands back into his sleeves.

"Hey," I whispered. "Meanwhile, can you teach me about prestidation? Especially with millet?"

He smiled at me. I liked him. "Okay," he said.

And so we stayed up all day, and he taught me magic tricks. I got the hang of them right away. They were cool. Somewhere in there, Nemo went to bed. Pretty soon, everyone was in bed but us, and we were pulling Cheerios out of hats.

The Prestidigitators

Ashes to Ashes

✠

I've never been a very tactful mouse. I know alot about tactics, but that's different. Those I studied with my master. Tact is when you could say something smoother or better and get more of what you want, or avoid a conflict. Being tactless is like just saying it how it is and damn the polish. I like telling it how it is, but more than that, it just never occurs to me to not tell the truth. This ended up costing me, because when mice would ask me if I was really out of my mind, I'd say no, but if they asked me if I see things, I'd say yes. I'd even describe the things to them and read their auras for them. I was trying to be my friendly old happy self and not the bitter, depressed self I was fighting, but it backfired on me, and within a few days the entire kingdom thought I was a nutcase. Mice would avoid me like the plague. (Hey, the plague wasn't our fault anyway.) I felt alone and lonely most of the time.

After Branch went home, I fell asleep in front of Nemo's cage as night came, then woke up just an hour later to Nemo's girlfriend screeching at me like a harpy to begone from her porch. I told her it wasn't her porch but Nemo's, and she tried to pee on me. Female chinchillas can aim their pee and hit targets up to twenty feet away with it! I didn't know that. She missed me, but I took off running, that's for sure. Rude woman!

I went somewhere, I can't remember where—under the refrigerator, I think, because no one ever looks there—and fell asleep. By the time I woke up it was almost dawn again.

This time when I went outside to the training area, everyone got out of my way. Fine. I noticed that I was the only knight without armor or a weapon. I saw the skinny female knight teaching a class on missile weapons. She wore a blue sash. All her students had blue sashes with stripes on them. Scratchy was there again, next to BJ, demonstrating Aikido.

My master looked tired from a hard day of training soldiers. It looked as though the nest was getting ready for some serious trouble.

"Hello, Squibble," he said. "I apologize for offending you the other day. I meant no harm."

"Yeah."

"What can I do for you?" he said, ignoring the class, which stood at attention.

"BJ didn't take the little half-chewed twit as a squire, did he?" I asked.

My master ignored the insult to Scratchy, which I knew he didn't like. "No," he said.

"Oh, good."

"But he offered."

"What!" I exclaimed. "The *King* offered to take a squire? A… a midget squire?"

"He sees the value in Scratchy that you clearly don't," my master said.

"What happened? Why isn't Punky Stupid in armor by now?" I asked.

"*Scratchy*," he intoned the name over my mockery, "refused."

"What a moron!"

"He wants to be *your* squire, Squibble. He turned down the *King* for it."

"Utter idiot, since he ain't gettin' it."

He was thinking of biting me. I could tell. I made the submissive gesture and cut him off. He smirked at my smartness. Then he giggled. I giggled too. Then I remembered my reason for coming.

"Nemo wants to train me in my powers," I said too loudly. Some mice in the lineup chuckled.

"Hey!" my master bellowed. "That's a *Mouse Knight* you're scoffing at, maggots! Now get down and give me three hundred!"

"HEY! THAT'S A MOUSE KNIGHT YOU'RE SCOFFING AT, MAGGOTS!"

The lineup of recruits gasped and fell down, doing push-ups. Good thing mice have short arms, I thought. I felt warm all over at my master's display of defending my honor. BJ looked at us from all the way across the back yard, as shocked as the troops were to hear my master yell. He never yells.

"That oughtta keep 'em busy for a while," he said, and turned back to me. "I think that's a great idea, Squib."

"You do?" I said.

"Yes."

"Howcome?" I asked.

He put a hand on me and groomed me a bit between the ears. Although he was putting on a cheerful face, I could see the weariness in him. It showed in his eyes. He missed my momma, and until now I had selfishly thought I was the only one affected so. My mom had been his true love. I felt sorry for him. How could I have been so blind?

"Nemo knows alot," he said. "Much more than I do. He's older than any mouse. He's read a ton of books. And he's connected to the spirit world on a level I can't even begin to comprehend." He played with my whiskers affectionately. "But you can, Squib. You've got the touch."

"I'm insane, you mean."

He scowled. "Don't you believe that gossip nonsense," he said. "Mice gossip. They just do. No stopping it. They're gonna be mice, so don't let it bother you."

"But it does, Master."

He thought a moment, his nose in his hand. "Yeah. You're very sensitive, Squibble. You have fragile feelings. The problem is, heroes have to toughen up some."

"Or alot," I said, thinking of the city.

"Yeah. Alot."

"Master?"

"Mmm…"

"Shiva and Thor were let down by their human," I said. "Our Kind Human sent them to a bad home. They were put in a shelter and abused."

My master's face sank, and I saw his fatigue clearly now. He was thin and pale. He didn't look good. The shield of bravado fell from his face, and I saw the sadness there. There was more than I had thought. Way more.

He turned and looked back at his troops. It didn't take long for speedy mice to do 300 push-ups. It was almost dawn anyway.

"Class dismissed!" he yelled. A mouse somewhere rang a chime. Mice everywhere began to pack up and go in for the day. To sleep.

He turned back to me. "I'll share that with the human. Are they all right?"

"Yeah. Kinda," I said. Not really, I thought to myself.

"You haven't told anyone about your pilgrimage, Squibble," he said. "I gather it wasn't all you hoped it might be."

"It was really hard," I said. I showed him the scar on my leg underneath the fur. "I didn't like most of it." I pondered what it was safe to tell, and then, "Master, I think I found great evil."

"The Black Mouse?"

"No... different. But..." I described to him the pet stores, the poor mothers in their tiny, tiny cages, and the laboratories with all the horrors they inflicted on mousekind. I described things in detail, but I left out anything having to do with me or what I did there. I thought he'd be mad if he found out how much I had risked (or completely blown) the Kingdom's secret.

He thought about it as we walked back to the house. Apparently it wasn't safe to stay outside anymore, day or night.

"That *is* great evil, Squib. That is."

"Someone's gotta do something about it!" I said, ignoring the fact that I pretty much had, but only in part of one tiny city. The world was a big place. My master's power could reach that far. Not mine though.

"Well, I'd say that's so," he said. Then he smiled at me. It was a wide grin. "Squib, I'd say you found your holy quest!" He turned to me and put both paws on my shoulders, looking me right in the eye.

I knew he was right, but I hadn't expected that. Such straightforward confirmation of what I had to do in this life. I didn't *want* it to be my job. It was too big. But worse, I felt that this part of it was just the tip of the iceberg.

"No, Master! You could go abroad—get all the mice to change it—get everyone to cooperate! If anyone could get the humans to change, it would be you! I can't do it!"

He laughed. "Squibble. We'd need a *talking* mouse in order to reach humans the way they need to be reached. Writing it down for them ain't gonna cut it. Their own prophets have already done that. It didn't work. And we don't have any talking mice."

"There *has* to be a way, Master!" I said with clear desperation in my voice. I was remembering all those poor mothers who were constantly losing their children.

He looked me over seriously. "You'll find a way, Squib." I opened my mouth to protest, but he put a finger over it. "It will be you, Sir Squibble. It feels right. My holy quest is over. This one is yours."

"Oh, but Master... it's so huge... I can't do it alone."

"I doubt you'll be alone, kiddo."

"Will you help me?" I brightened up.

He smiled sadly at me and kissed my face. "If I can, my dear friend, I always will. Always."

"Oh, thank you, Master."

"No problem, Squib. Want some dinner before bed?"

"I'm… kinda not hungry anymore."

"Yeah. We've all lost weight. It's stressful, losing our security. These attacks are crazy. They come out of nowhere."

Of course, the attacks weren't what I had meant, but I nodded.

"What are we going to do, Master? Why is everyone training?"

"We can't let them take our house," he said. "We're well defended here. In the beginning they killed alot of mice. Almost a hundred in the first wave…" He stopped short, looking at me. I didn't know why, but it made me feel bad. I returned his look with one that said *what?!*

"We're… we're ready for them now, Squibble. They can't get inside again," he said.

"But what then?" I said. "We can't hold them off forever. Aren't we going to fight back?"

He looked astonished. "Against mice, Squibble? Kill our own kind? We can't do that. No, never. We'd be no better than humans then. No… no, we can't do that."

He sounded severely set on that. I worried suddenly. From my perspective, we were very close to being "human" as it was.

"But these mice are insane, Master," I explained. "The Black Mouse has driven them mad."

"They're still mice," he said, and looked at me as if to say, "The issue is decided. We can't kill other mice, Squibble."

I sighed and nodded. He always knew best. Every time I ever thought I was right and he wasn't, it was never true.

"Yeah," I said. "Okay."

As we were going in, many mice were coming out. The Kind Human was leading them. It looked like a parade, all formal and dressed up. In the Kind Human's hands it looked like he had a cloth or something wrapped around a box. My master looked up and then down.

"What's that, Master?" I asked as the human went past us and the mice around us.

He looked at me. "Your mother's funeral," he said. "The Kind Human is going to bury her."

The Kind Human dug a deep hole in the vast back yard that stretched into the Fields of Fate. As he did so, all the mice of the Kingdom stood still. As he finished, it began to rain.

I didn't know what to feel. I certainly didn't know what to think. My head went numb and my chest just ached. I wanted more than anything to feel my momma's sweet kiss on my head one more time.

The human was reading something out of a book. It had to do with ashes and dust. I thought it was strange, but what in my life wasn't strange now? I thought I should be crying. Many mice were, but I couldn't. I was beyond it. The feelings growing in me were not content to be expressed by tears.

"My poor Momma," I said. "I'm going to miss her every day of my life."

My master sighed. I regretted my words instantly.

I looked at him. We were in the front row of course, and we both saw the little coffin as the human opened it and placed millet and Cheerios in—to help my momma on her journey. Then the human showed my momma's body the light at the edge of the horizon and told her to go there, to find it and to go home. He was crying, and he wished her peace on her journey. The box was closed and covered in a plastic bag. (I didn't know why until later. It was so that wild animals (or insane ones) wouldn't dig her body up.)

Then the human put her in the ground.

"Master… I know you loved her," I said carefully.

"With all my heart," he whispered. "We had such a short time together, but far better than none."

"What will happen to her now?" I asked, sounding worried.

He kept staring at that dark hole, my mother's grave, as he spoke. He wasn't happy anymore. He wasn't smiling.

"Death is like life, Squibble. It's just another journey." The rain picked up as the human began to scoop dirt back into the grave, sealing my momma in forever. "Souls travel to the sea, and wait there for the dawn, or the sunset, depending on which sea…"

"How long does it take?" I asked. I saw my poor momma, walking through the Fields of Fate all alone, maybe lost. "What happens then?!"

A forlorn look spread across on my master's face, as if he was trying to see the soul of my mother in the spirit world. He was looking out over the horizon. "Well, it takes a while to get to the sea, little mouse, and on the way the soul has time to think on their life, and what it meant to them," he said.

I had to know if my mother was going to make it.

"And then?!" I asked.

My master smiled at me, even though he was so obviously tired. Tired to his bones and further.

"Then the ship comes, Squib. The Shining Ship of the Fates, to take that soul to Paradise."

I breathed a sigh of relief. I could see my momma on a boat. Not lost in the fields. On a happy boat.

"Cool!" I said. "And then?"

"Anything you want then," he told me.

"Anything?!" I gasped. "Even ice cream?"

He laughed, coughed, then continued laughing. "Yes, precious friend, even ice cream." He reached out and petted me, even though he was so sad. I smiled back at him, hoping it would cheer him up, when a raindrop grazed his cheek, and fell down his face, making it look like he was crying.

But he was smiling.

My poor master.

Surprise Number Two

✠

The next day after dawn, I woke to a silent house. Amber sunlight filtered in through the windows. Everyone was asleep. I cursed at myself for oversleeping—I had forgotten my appointment with Nemo!

I raced down the empty hall (boy, it was weird being up in the day) and into the human's room. He had already left for work. Nemo was waiting for me in a blanket by his cage. Sitting next to him was that lanky, female mouse I had seen around. She was wearing armor and a sword. She had a cape on, like Percival had. It was blue. I was going to have to speak to her about that. She didn't know it 'cause I was gone. *That's my color, dearie. You can't have it.*

"Sorry I'm late," I said.

"When you're late it shows disrespect for the waiting party," Nemo said. "And damages your honor."

I grumbled something under my breath, which he definitely heard with those enormous radar-dish ears.

"Do you disagree?" he said.

"Nah. My master says the same thing."

"Okay then." He preened his whiskers. The female mouse was unnaturally still. She seemed nervous. "Shall we start?"

"Okay. Impress me," I said.

"You know that training is not easy," he said. "And first you must face some things, do some homework."

"What's that mean?" I said, not liking it.

"Get things out in the open, face facts, deal with stuff."

"Yeah, I do that all right."

Nemo scoffed at me—out loud! I was setting myself up to be offended when he waved his hand. "Don't bother," he said. "You're as wrong as a mouse out in daylight."

I was trying to figure out whether he'd insulted me again when he got serious and stared me in the eye. "Squibble, this is going to be hard to hear. But you need to hear it, and we can't start until you do. I'm sorry to add to your troubles, but it must be done. It can't wait any longer."

"Oh, that's just great—," I began.

"Will you hear it willingly?" he asked. "If not, you may go and hear it from someone else."

I grimaced. I could see Scratchy holding up a darn sign with something horrible scrawled on it. "I'll hear it… I guess."

"Okay." He shifted his weight. "You want it nice and easy or short and fast?"

"Short and fast," I said, not meaning it.

"Very well," he said. "You know that the first several raids that hit the house took us completely by surprise. We lost about a hundred lives to the enemy."

"Yeah, and we're gonna lose hundreds more unless we hunt them down and kill that stupid Black Mouse. We're trapped in this house like sitting ducks," I said.

Both Nemo and the girl looked at each other in surprise.

"I am very impressed that you know that," Nemo said. "That is great wisdom." I smiled. "But it's not the point," he said. I stopped smiling. *Get it over with, furface.*

The female mouse said, "The enemy soldiers came into the house on the first attack, after killing many on the porch, and no one was ready." She looked ashamed of it. Maybe she had been a knight on duty… Nah… she was way too young. "Of those hundred, the enemy selectively killed mice who were not albino. They ignored the albino mice."

I cocked my head. "What does that—"

"They were looking for brown mice," she continued. "And they went right to the correct cages. They knew the layout of our house already."

I started to get that sick feeling again. I wanted her to shut up now, but she didn't.

"They went straight to your cage, Squibble. It was surrounded only by a few mice. Nobody guessed they'd head straight for it. Only four mice stood in the way of sixty insane lab mice. They *were* lab mice. What they were doing out in the middle of the Fields of Fate was anyone's guess."

"My cage?" I hissed. *"Mine?"*

She nodded. "Of the four mice that defended your cage in those desperate first seconds, only one barely survived. But he couldn't stop them from getting to your family."

"My… you mean Favorite… but she's…"

"You had a family, Squibble." Her eyes were tearing up. This was as hard for her to say as it was for me to hear. Nemo put his paw on her. It seemed to give her strength. My eyes were saucers. My darned heart went through my stomach again. I hated the feeling by now.

"Favorite had ten kittens after you left," she said. "Eight boys and two girls. She herself fought with the ferocity of a mother mouse," she lowered her head. "She killed half their number with the last surviving defender mouse, but it wasn't enough. She was crippled. Paralyzed by a spinal bite, and when the last defender was bashed unconscious, the enemy began killing the babies as she watched. All of this happened before most of the Kingdom even knew we had been invaded at all. The attackers went straight for your cage."

I heard it all. I heard everything she said, but it was as if it wasn't happening to me. There was a high-pitched buzzing in my ears. I felt lightheaded.

"My… my master…," I whined.

"He came as quick as he could—with BJ and Nemo, and the others, but he was too late to save most of them."

"He… he wouldn't let that happen…," I said.

"He had no choice," she said. "It all took only sixteen seconds!"

Sixteen seconds… Favorite and some poor fighter had lasted sixteen seconds against sixty insane mice. That in itself was amazing. But not amazing enough.

"How many… how many…" I couldn't finish. It was just beginning to sink in that Favorite had given birth once I'd left. I had missed it. I had missed it all.

"All of the babies died," she said. "Except one. Your master and the cavalry saved one baby, and Favorite's life, though she regrets it now, and the last defender."

"Why… why isn't … why didn't… why didn't my master tell me all this?" I whispered.

"I wanted to do it," she said.

"Why?" I asked. "Why do you know so much of it?"

"Because I was there," she said.

I stared like an idiot.

Nemo leaned forward and gently said, "This is your daughter, Squibble."

She stood there before me. My daughter. My only child. The blue… her lanky shape… her big eyes…

We stood there a long time.

At last, I said, "What's your—"

"Squibette," she said. "Your master named me after you, Father."

We rushed toward each other at the same time and almost knocked ourselves out meeting in the middle. I held her close. She smelled just like me. She looked just like me. Oh, how had I not noticed? My only daughter.

In that moment, she was the most precious thing to me in existence. Overwhelming sadness filled me from top to bottom. I felt my soul fall farther, held up only by the thin cord that was Squibette. It was all too much to bear, too much to take in. Nemo, knowing this, left us to our grim reunion and went back into his cage.

I held onto my daughter for hours there in human's room, soft golden sunlight drifting down in beams around us. Neither of us spoke. I just held onto her. She was so skinny. Under the armor, she was too skinny. Of course, I had been, too.

Favorite hadn't been playing games with me. She couldn't move from her spot without dragging her body by her front arms. Oh, how sad. And how poorly I'd treated her.

It all made sense now, how people had looked at me funny. How no one knew what to say to me. I had thought they saw me as a lunatic, and in that presumption had created that reality. But I had been partly wrong. It was pity. They were all staring at me with pity. I don't know which was worse.

But above all the turmoil, chaos, and dark thoughts, above all the regret and remorse, I remembered that here, in my hands, I had my daughter. The one who saw it all, and lived to tell about it. Here… in my hands, living and breathing. My daughter.

It was my anchor to sanity, I tell you.

Eventually she fell asleep in my arms. I lay back against Nemo's cage and cradled her in my lap. As she slept sweetly, I gazed down at her with wonder and awe in my soul. She was the most beautiful thing I had ever beheld. I stared and stared. I had missed her growing up. I would never see her as a baby. I didn't get to teach her to read, or to fight. I didn't get to hear her first words or watch her crawl for the first time.

I stared until dusk. I stared until I fell asleep from exhaustion and overload.

Stupid Lessons of Wisdom

✠

I woke sometime around three in the morning. My daughter was being pried from my arms. Without knowing what I was doing, I lunged forward to bite whoever or whatever was taking my treasure from me. I had lost enough already.

My teeth hit steel. Steel attached to lobster hide armor around the biggest mouse I had ever seen. Even bigger than Bigfat. Without moving my teeth, I looked up into the face of Stompy. She wasn't small to begin with, and she had grown.

"Wha ah oo doooih?" I asked. My teeth were clamped onto a quarter, one of two, somehow merged with the shoulder pieces of her armor. Great idea, that. I would have had to use dimes.

She smiled. "I am taking my tired friend to fighter practice," she said. "Squibette teaches the slingshot class."

Squibette looked back down at me and winked pridefully. I let go of Stompy's immense mountain of a shoulder and smiled back.

"Slingshot?" I said.

"Mmm hmmm," Stompy said.

My gaze of affection and pride in my daughter-knight said it all, I guess, because she kissed me on the cheek and said, "You weren't here to teach it, Father. I had to step in."

"But who taught *you*?" I asked, getting up.

"I asked the first of the Mouse Knights to, but he said he sucked at it," she said. "He told me to do what you did: live with it, practice every waking moment, and never let it out of my sight."

"And you did?" I asked.

"No," she grinned. "I actually prefer aikido and swordfighting. But I practiced alot. Enough to teach class."

"He he hehe," I laughed.

They giggled with me, and I walked them to the practice fields. I did not speak the entire time, just looked at them. They were clearly fast friends, like Bigfat and I had been at the end. Stompy was his daughter, and besides her weight, which she seemed to relish, I could see him in her. I remembered when she was small and first came to fighter practice alot of mice called her fatso and gave her trouble. At first she withdrew from mouse society. It seemed she would quit. She was worried no one liked her. I told her that it didn't matter, and that her father wouldn't have cared. She idolized me at that point, and asked me to tell her all about her dad, which I did. I taught her his favorite move, the mouse bounce. She learned it in no time. The next night when she showed up for class and someone called her fatso, she walked calmly back several feet as if she were leaving, then turned around suddenly, and charged. In all that space, the offending mouse didn't have time to dodge. I think everyone was stunned at how fast she could run with all that bulk. What they didn't think about was how much power that mass had on impact at high speed. The heckler mouse must have flown three feet. No one made any comments after that. After that and the beating she gave Ghost, no one ever said anything ever again except compliments. After a while, she stopped caring what others thought. She grew past her father.

You'd think she would have been grateful, but my wounded soul remembered her being with the group that was going to waylay me on One-Ear's advice. She just didn't seem to fit in. Of all those mice who I thought were my friends, I couldn't see Stompy doing such a stupid thing. My instinct told me I was wrong to be angry at her. I decided to test it.

"Master tells me One-Ear got put at the bottom of the totem pole for his stupid scheme to get me beat up," I said.

Stompy didn't miss the clue. She stopped, turned around, and said, "All the mice there felt real bad, Squibble. They were just spineless suckers. One-Ear had a sly tongue on him, he did."

"How did anyone even figure it out?" I asked.

"Your master figured it out," Stompy said, "after Scratchy beat everyone up."

"That was after Stompy beat the hell out of One-Ear," Squibette said.

"Eh?" I said, looking at Stompy.

She looked down. "I know why you left," she said. "Someone told you or you overheard us. I'm sorry for ever even being there. I went out of curiosity mostly. I wondered why so many mice were listening to that lame brain."

I stared dumbly.

"One-Ear said something that made Stompy mad," Squibette said, "so she put the hurt on him."

“What was it?” I asked, gleeful that One-Ear had been stomped.

“He offended your honor,” Stompy said. “I told him he had to go after you and bring you back to the safe house if he wanted to clear his name.”

“He refused, of course,” I said.

“Yeah, he’s a coward, but that’s what he called you for leaving,” she said. I ground my teeth. Oh, how I hated One-Ear right then. “So I let him have it. No one insults one of the First.”

I felt rage building in me for that pathetic troublemaker. Stompy saw it and put a hand on me. It was really big.

“No one calls a great hero a coward,” she said, looking into my eyes with a serious face.

I felt a lifting of my spirit. At least some believed in me. It was enough to keep me going for a while. I felt refreshed and a little better. Then I thought of Favorite. I had to go to her. I had some apologies to make.

As I said goodbye to them, I went past Nemo’s cage again. He was curled up on one of his big logs, asleep. He looked thin. His breath looked shallow. The Fields of Fate had cursed him, I could feel it. It had claimed my master’s health and Nemo’s as well. Somehow, I just knew. He didn’t look well.

When I reached my cage, I snuck in and went to the corner. Favorite was there, trying to hold herself over the edge of the food bowl with one paw while eating with the other. It was sad. She wasn’t doing a very good job. She couldn’t stand up to take a piece of food, or bend over to hold it while eating. I came up, sifted through the food dish for a pumpkin seed, and handed it to her. She dropped it. Trying to eat the tasty morsel without her hands, she just pushed it into the bedding. I snatched it back up and held it for her while she ate it. No words passed between us as I held every piece of food she wanted to take in. I held her head for her over the water dish the Kind Human had placed in the cage while she drank. She couldn’t reach the water bottle.

“I’m sorry,” I said. “I didn’t know.” She nodded, silent. I saw deep depression and apathy in her. She had given up somewhere along the way. She was just waiting to die. I guess any mouse that had lost the use of half their body might expect the same. It wasn’t supposed to happen. Mice wounded like that are eaten. Or they starve to death. No one lets them linger. But Favorite was lingering, and she hated it.

I sat with her for a while. She was still and quiet. I tried to make conversation, but it was like talking to a rock. I groomed her, and moved her to a better place inside the nest. I spent another hour gathering food for her and wrote a note to the Kind Human asking him to put the water dish right outside of the nest opening for her. I wondered if he was going to euthanize her. No one in the safe house had ever been euthanized, but mice spoke of it. No one even knew how it might happen, but everyone knew that it meant your life was over when it happened to you.

It looked like Favorite was waiting for that.

I couldn't take that for long, so finally I had to leave. Near dawn I went back to Nemo's cage. I saw the mice coming in from fighter practice through the window. The sky was a dark azure blue with deep space above it. So clear and bright. Not like in the city. I sat and admired it. I watched my master and BJ conversing with several other knights near a concrete block put there for the teachers to stand on. Stompy and my daughter were with them. She was a fine knight. A fine mouse. So pretty and so strong. I felt a pang of deep regret at missing her growing up. I missed everyone growing up.

When I shifted my stance lightly, Branch was standing in my peripheral vision. I spun.

"Don't *do* that!" I hissed. "Scary scary!"

"Sorry," he said. He had bags packed. Just two—a backpack and a side bag, like mine. He was wearing grey robes.

I felt another pang. "You're leaving?" I said.

"Yeah," he said. He looked around. "The Kind Human will take me to the airport on his way to work. I'll sneak aboard a plane to China. Once there, it's many hundreds of miles to the temple, but I'll have the help of other mice who know the way."

I marveled at it. So dangerous. If anyone caught him on the plane, he'd be toast. He'd be done for a hundred times over if he got caught anywhere. No mouse that anyone knew had ever crossed the ocean. Or ever been on a plane.

"Your own pilgrimage," I said.

He smiled. "Yeah, though I'm not a knight, I guess so."

"You're going because you miss mom here too much," I said without knowing why.

He looked down. He put a hand on my shoulder, and I could feel the emotion in him. Heavy. Like a weight one has to carry for the rest of their lives. We shared that particular weight.

"You have great talent," he said. "Nemo will teach you how to use it, older brother."

"Yeah, maybe," I said. "Be careful, okay? That's such a gnarly journey."

"Father is worried sick," he said, "but he knows better than to tell me there's anything a mouse can't do." He took a last look around the house. "This is what I want."

"It's the path of your heart," I said. I had seen this moment before. In my dreams. Like the funeral.

"Yes," he said.

"Learn real magic," I said, and hugged him. I had known him too little, and now, like my mother, he was going beyond my reach.

"Fireballs and lightning bolts!" he exclaimed, raising a fist and shaking it. "Or bust!"

"Weather control!" I said, raising a fist also. "Prestidigitation is for the pleebs!"

"The pleebs!" he agreed.

A moment of silence fell between us.

"Take care of father," he said.

"I will," I said.

"His health is beginning to fail him. He wheezes during the day when he sleeps."

"I will always be there for him," I promised.

"I'll curse you if you aren't," he smiled.

"Yeah. Okay."

"I know you will be," he said. "You always have been."

I nodded. He turned, hopped off the table, and skittered across the carpet toward the door. The human's alarm clock blared, and he groggily turned over and slapped it. Rising, he saw me staring after Branch.

"Hello, Squib," he said. "Keeping strange hours, you are, little mouse."

You don't know the half of it, I thought. He gently scratched me behind the ears, which I tolerated, and then went to take a shower. When I finally looked back from the hallway where Branch had gone (it was the last I'd ever see of him, I was sure), Nemo was beside me. Those wizards… Always appearing all mysterious-like. Can't just walk in like normal, noooooo…

"Glad to see you," he said.

"Yeah."

"Ready for your lesson?" he asked. "I seem to have lost my previous apprentice."

"Is he ready?" I said. "Ready to go all that way?"

"Oh, yes," Nemo smiled toward the dark hallway. "Branch learned the ways of enlightenment as fast as his brother Percival learned the ways of the warrior."

"Yeah. Well, okay, I'm ready… I guess, unless you have more shocking news, or maybe you're going to tell me I grew a fifth leg while I wasn't looking or something. Are we done with the nasty shocks?"

"You didn't like meeting your daughter?" he asked.

"Yes!" I answered immediately. "But learning that the rest of my family died horribly and knowing I wasn't here to prevent it sucked!"

"You would rather have remained oblivious?" he said.

"Nah," I confessed.

"Okay, then. The answer is yes."

"What answer?"

"To your question. Do I have more shocking news, more unpleasant surprises. Most definitely. And the universe has a thousand times more than I do for you."

I just stared at the big chinchilla, aghast.

"Well, why are you looking at me like that?" he said. "Did you expect life to be a smooth, easy ride? Did you expect the trouble demons to leave you when you came here to this place?"

I pretended to think about it, looking down and then up, with a paw to my chin. "Ummm… yeah."

"Yes, I know you did," he said, sounding deep. "That's why this all hits you harder than it hits others, Squibble. You were a very optimistic mouse. And you're very sensitive."

"Nah," I said.

"Oh, you were doing so good there for a minute," he said.

"Wheee," I said.

"Difficult mouse?" he said.

"Yeah," I folded my arms. "Now impress me."

"Okey dokey," he said and slapped me right off the table. I thudded down on the carpet below and snapped upright, gazing at him in shock.

I rushed up there to beat his sapphire ass, but he wasn't there.

"How was that supposed to impress me?!" I shouted. "Anyone can do that!"

"Well, that's the problem," he said from above me. "Anyone can make you mad." He was sitting on the top of his cage. A good four foot leap from his previous place. Great act of dexterity, but I was not so easily impressed.

“So what!” I chirped. “If they do, they’ll suffer my wrath!”

“Ooooooo,” he said. “Mouse wrath!”

“Yeah! That’s right!”

He stepped off the edge and vanished.

I blinked. Prestidigitation again. But a second later he came hopping around the corner of the hallway into the bedroom. The Kind Human stepped over him coming out of the shower and walked into the living room.

No way could he have made it so quick. Not even him.

“Hmmmm…,” I mused, as he hopped back up onto the table beside me. “What was that?” I said.

“Teleportation,” he said. “Are you impressed?”

“Uhhh… nope. Nuh-uh.” I was, though. Way impressed. I fought actually believing it, but I was impressed.

“Good,” he said. “Because I want you to be impressed by everyday, normal things from now on,” he said.

“Like?” I said, tilting my head smarmily.

“Like your daughter,” he said.

I snapped my head back and my ears went straight up (as if I’d suddenly heard something!), and I froze like that. For a few seconds he let it sink in. It did. I had been very impressed with my daughter. More than I had ever been by anything. Maybe even… my master.

Without moving his lips, I heard his voice in my head.

So can we get over the idea of being impressed by powers and flash? he said. No sound did my ears hear. It was telepathy.

I didn’t really wanna get over the cool stuff, and he knew it.

“Powers and flash are only symptoms of the real power,” he said, “of wisdom and spirituality. They come and go, kind of like colors as fire gets hotter or cooler.”

“Fire gets hot or cool?” I asked, amazed.

“Yes,” he said and raised his paw. It caught fire. I yelped and shrank back. Mice no like fire.

As I watched, the fire became orange, then red, then dark red, then went out. I had almost breathed a sigh of relief when it suddenly returned with a bright flash, blue and sharp. I could feel the heat from seven inches away, but his hand wasn’t burning! The fire became a brilliant light, a blazing ball of sun. Then I couldn’t see anything anymore. When my sight returned, he was sitting there like nothing had happened, grinning.

“Witch!” I cried.

"That would be warlock," he said. "I'm male. But anyway, how would you prove it? What if I just did those things… in your head?"

"No way!"

"Maybe way," he said. "Maybe I did them on the spirit plane and made you see it there with your gift. Maybe it didn't happen at all."

"I felt the heat!" I said.

"You thought you did," he said, and touched me with the paw that had been on fire. It was cool. Almost too cool.

"Aaah… Was it there or not?!" I squeaked, desperately wanting to know.

"When *you* can tell *me*," he said, "then maybe you can begin doing it yourself. Until then, let's start with wisdom, shall we?"

I nodded, feeling out of my league. Which I'm sure was the point. It had worked.

"Okay, but don't mess with my head, okay?" I said.

"Sure. Haven't yet," he said, and hopped over by the side of his cage to get a book.

We studied all that day. We studied poetry. It was the beginning of my lessons in power with Nemo, and I remember it well. I remember hating it with all my heart. It was the most boring thing I had ever tolerated. I wanted to be anywhere but there. Watching TV, playing, sparring, writing, drawing… even chewing my own leg off. He even threw in English lessons for me on how to write better. The proper do's and don't's of writing, or at least the basics. I asked him if he'd ever seen my writing, and he said no. I then asked him how he knew I had any problems with my English, and he said because he'd seen my writing. Oooooo! I was ready to flatten someone by the time I was through. The lesson only lasted an hour, but that's a long time to a mouse, okay? If I were human, that would have been two days!

Stalking away in frustration, I decided I had learned nothing at all and told him so. He said that didn't matter, that I'd remember it anyway. He had a way about him of making me angry.

Of course, everyone did.

On the way back to my cage I passed by my master's cage. I had been staying up all day of late, and I saw little of him. He was sleeping in his nest-house alone. He looked sad. I could hear him wheezing, just like Branch had said. In all the time we had lived here, I had never seen him alone. My momma had always been with him, sleeping on him or curled up with him, or under him. Like happy mice.

It seemed the happiness of our magical palace was fleeting. I wondered what he was dreaming of now, but I knew. He was dreaming of my mother, like I did. When they were good dreams, waking was agony, realizing she was dead. When they were bad dreams, waking was still agony. I had both kinds. I hoped he did better.

I wrote a little note, and snuck in to put it beside his nest-house porch. It said "I love you, Master." I didn't sign it. I didn't need to.

I wanted to go back to my nest, but Favorite was there. I should have gone back and gone to sleep, but the thought of her depression and despair frightened me. I knew I should have been there to comfort her. Her waiting for death terrified me. I didn't know why. I couldn't make myself go. Instead, I went to the Kind Human's desk, loaded up on drawing equipment, and drew. I drew and wrote the rest of the day, in a dark corner of the house, all alone. I got lost in it, I loved it so. Time passed quickly in that trance state, and before I knew it, it was dusk. I was tired. I went back to my cage. Maybe I'd sleep in one of the tower toys.

Squibette was in the nest, sleeping with her momma. I was relieved, but still felt shame at avoiding her just because she was crippled. It was an ugly emotion, and something within myself I didn't want to admit, much less face. It was cowardly.

I dug some treats out of the food bowl and put them at the entrance to the nest box. Squibette woke up, saw me. She took a Cheerio in her mouth and smiled at me around it. Then she offered it to her momma, who woke up groggily only to turn it down.

How had things come to this, I wondered.

I turned to see Scratchy staring at me from the other side of the glass of my cage. I stared back, and he vanished.

Squibette came out of the house finally. We made our way to one of the tower toys. There was room for two in there.

"I'll go back and sleep with mom," she said. "After a bit."

"Yeah," I said.

"She's really depressed."

"I know. Does that little runt come around here looking for me often?"

She looked confused. "Runt?"

"Scratchy."

Now she looked shocked. "He had a bad ear infection at birth," she said. "He almost died. It's not his fault..."

"He's a pest," I remarked.

Now she looked mad. And disappointed. It hit me in the gut like a hammer.

"That 'runt' was coming to see my momma," she said.

"Whatever for?" I said, worried about saying something wrong now.

"He visits her, brings her his treats, makes sure she's as happy as she can be…"

I made a motion with my hand to go on.

She sighed. "Scratchy was the one who saved my life," she said. "He took many mortal blows to carry me to safety and almost died from them. When he finally collapsed, he fell over me, that I might be missed by the enemy. Or at least they'd have to go through him to get me. It took everything Nemo had to save him, he was so badly hurt."

I was speechless. My stomach shrank. My heart was trying to sink through me while beating against my insides like a fist.

"He was the one who saved her, too," she gestured with her nose back to the nest. "He was the last warrior. The few friends he had all died in the fight. They were only there when the attack came because he spent every day guarding your home while you were gone. He told his friends it was the most noble job in the whole world."

My eyes were huge. I didn't know what to say. I imagined Nemo towering over me saying "See? You stupid, petty mouse. I told you so."

"He almost died… saving both of you…," I said. I swallowed. "Why wasn't he knighted for that?" That was something my master or BJ definitely would have knighted a mouse for. No doubt about it.

"He refused it," she said, and left the tower toy. I followed, pressing the subject.

"Why?!" I said. "Why would he do that? It's all he ever wanted."

She turned to look at me before going into the nest box to comfort her poor mother.

"Because he wants to be knighted by *you*."

With that, she left me in my shame, alone.

Conquered

✠

The next day, I was awake (of course) when the attack came. The front door guard squeaked loudly, waking the many named mice who slept in the front room, my master among them. He shouted "To arms! To arms!" and ran down from his cage, buckling on his sword and armor.

The door guard perished before he could get inside, and we heard creatures flooding over the floorboards of the deck. Myself, Stompy, Squibette, BJ, Ghost, and several other knights and squires were the first to arrive at the mouse door as it was struck by something large. Always bolted from the inside, they couldn't freely come in, but it sure sounded like they meant to one way or another. I was the only one really ready, but I wasn't wearing any armor. That'll teach me. Hey, it was my first attack.

"Archers to the roof!" my master shouted.

"Mice forward with the shield wall," BJ yelled.

"Someone wake Nemo!"

"I am already here," Nemo said. He was squinting in that chinchilla death stare he had when he slew the rattlesnake and saved my life. It was really going down. A battle, a real battle. My first. Mice were flooding in from everywhere as a horn sounded. I realized suddenly—and now with a real fear of death—I was completely unprepared.

I turned around to dash back to my cage and don my equipment, and there he was. Scratchy was lumbering toward me bearing all of my things! He looked ridiculous under the mass of armor and equipment. He had even brought my slingshot and bag of ammo. He was moving in slow circles toward me, though clearly breaking his back to move as fast as he could.

I ran to him and yanked the breastplate off him. He dropped the other things and helped me to buckle it on. I didn't argue—I didn't have time!

The heavy thing against the door began to get louder—and there were more of them. My master was setting soldiers in formation. Shield wall, then swordsmice, then pikes. Archers behind.

Scratchy put the stuff on me in a third the time it would have taken me alone. It was as if he practiced day and night (maybe he did), and knew just what to do. I was ready to go in no time, and he handed me my shield. Then, bowing low on one knee with his head down, my sword.

When I ran for the front line, he stayed behind.

"What!" I yelled. "Aren't you coming?"

His head perked up and his eyes got wide. He frantically pointed to my cage—where Favorite was. There were thirty other armed mice up there already.

"No!" I yelled over the battle din, and motioned him to come to me. "A squire belongs with his knight! Get a sword, stupid!"

His face beamed. His eyes welled up with tears, but he snatched up a bag of swords, his own practice shield, and raced after me—in circles, of course. The little runt actually managed to keep up with me.

At the front line my master stood, ready for the fight. The mice there at the front had left me a space next to him, which I took right away. Scratchy nosed his way into the line next to me. My master saw and smiled at me as I unslung my slingshot, loading a copper BB. I made a face back at him.

"Enemy at the rear gate!" A mouse shouted from the basement.

"Rear guard—go!" BJ shouted. One hundred armed mice took off running in that direction. The back was already guarded, but if they called for help, reinforcements were needed.

"This is a big attack," BJ said casually.

"Biggest yet," my master declared.

They both looked at me.

"What!" I chirped. But I knew what they were thinking. The Black Mouse was after *me*. It was me he wanted. Why?! No fair!

We heard the thunks of arrows pelting the enemy from the rooftop. We heard creatures scream and fall. Something growled at the front door. That was no mouse.

"Cat," BJ said. "They have a cat."

"Squibble, ready?" My master said.

I nodded briskly. I pulled back my legendary slingshot and aimed.

"Open the door!"

The mouse door swung open when a guard released the latch, revealing two giant paws.

SPUNG! I let a BB fly right between the toes. The cat howled in pain. I was reloaded before he could even hit the ground. I let another BB fly at whatever was behind the cat. And another and another. There was no measurable space of time between my shots, just one constant motion and a repeating thrumming sound of the rubber band. I heard later that everyone had been watching the volley I let loose in awe. Even BJ.

Everything behind the door perished or moved.

"Now—charge!" my master screamed, and barreled forward, sword thrust out in front of him.

The mice made a funnel formation, and two by two, left the safety of the house to take the fight to the attackers. I was out right behind my master and BJ, moving aside immediately to let others out.

A rock clanged off my shield. I swung my sword at a rabid white mouse to my right and dropped him with the flat of my blade to his head. It was utter chaos. There were so many mice—at least two hundred. It was a huge assault. I saw the cat, its eyes blazing with possessed fury. There was a hawk circling overhead, diving at our archers.

"They have a hawk!" I shrieked.

"And five snakes!" Ghost yelled.

"Four!" Stompy yelled as she and Squibette dispatched one using the Rikki Tikki technique—jump behind the head, bite, and hold on!

"Archers on the roof, retreat!" BJ yelled.

"We can't take out that hawk," BJ said to us.

My master smiled. "Squibble?"

I slapped one more mouse aside, sheathed my sword, and readied my slingshot. "Make room for me!" I cried out.

"Vanguard—make way for Sir Squibble!" BJ commanded. Mice attacked straight forward to the edge of the porch. Thirty mice hurled themselves at the cat to keep it busy, but it was charging me anyway. I had enough time for one shot. I ran forward, sliding to a halt at the very edge of the deck, holding my slingshot raised and ready for when the hawk came into sight.

Stompy threw herself under the cat's feet and it stumbled, buying me time. Mice tried to yank a tightrope across its path, but it just pulled them all along for the ride. Sometimes being small sucks. That cat had it in for me. And now, the entire field could see me in plain view.

The hawk showed and banked, diving for the fleeing archers. I let fly and heard a satisfying *whack!* against its skull. It dropped from the sky, thudding on the rooftop.

"Hawkslayer!" a mouse cried.

I turned just in time to yank my shield up against the force of the cat's charge. It still hit me full speed, knocked the wind from me, and blew me back off the deck, down the stairs, and right into the enemy. My slingshot flew from my hands and landed two feet from me.

The entire enemy army stopped then. They all looked right at me, as if they all shared one mind, one thought: KILL SQUIBBLE.

Scratchy flew off the deck, heedless of damage from the long fall between steps. The enemy came at me. ALL of them! Every single one. Snakes, the cat spinning on its heels, and well over a hundred mice. I was going to be surrounded and buried if I didn't retreat immediately.

But my slingshot! I couldn't lose it! I desperately looked at it, lying vulnerable twenty-four inches away.

"Squibble!" my master commanded. "Fall back!"

Scratchy was charging in. He was the only one.

"Fall back, I say!" my master yelled.

I hesitated. I should have either gone for the slingshot right away, and stood a tiny chance at reaching it, or run for the porch, but I did neither. I hesitated! In front of everyone.

"In the name of the Kind Human, Squibble!" my master screamed, and leapt off the top step. BJ, Stompy, and the others followed him faithfully. The enemy was closing in. The blank-eyed zombies were one inch from my slingshot when Scratchy, a white, circular blur, snatched it from the ground and spun his way to me.

The cat was pouncing over the enemy lines for me when a spear lodged itself in its nose. Deep.

It howled, landed among the enemy, and thrashed in pain. I looked to the porch and saw Sir Percival there in bright armor, four other spears in his left hand and another ready in his right. He cut a mighty figure against the background, head lifted, eyes confident. He nodded to me.

The front line reached me and my master smacked my helmet with a resounding clang.

"What are you doing?!" he yelled. "They're after *you*, Squibble!" He grabbed me and launched me toward the other mice in the direction of the porch. "It's *you* they want!" The other mice all grabbed me and handed me off backward like a moving runway. Scratchy threw me my slingshot. I caught it and clutched it to my chest. Mine. My precious.

I was back on the porch in several heartbeats. Archers from the roof had come down through the lower door and were covering our retreat. The front line took a bad beating backing toward the door. Three knights fell in combat, and many soldiers. Scratchy took many blows from teeth and claws, having to run in circles to get back. Finally Squibette grabbed him and carried him. They made it back, and we fought until our backs were against the wall. I had used all my ammunition. When my sword snapped against a snake's head, Scratchy faithfully replaced it instantly.

"Full retreat!" Nemo's voice bellowed over the fighting. "Back into the house!"

A stiff wind rose at our backs, driving the enemy backward. Some of the possessed mice climbing the stairs fell off. We began filtering through the mouse door two by two, as we had come. My master and I were last.

"I'm sorry," I said.

He turned to me and I could see his eyes alight through his crusader's helm. The eyes said it all: *I could have lost you!*

Then we were through the door, throwing the bolt just as the cat recovered enough to ram his head against it.

BJ wasted not a second. He ordered reinforcements and medical attention to the wounded.

"The fight is over," Nemo said. Matter of fact.

BJ turned. "Prophet, how is that? They have us boxed in, and I saw more coming.

"It's going to rain," the chinchilla said, eyes closed.

Outside, thunder rippled across the sky. All the mice looked upward, outside and in.

As the first few drops hit the roof, the safe house army cheered. No mouse, possessed or not, will stay out in the rain. And it turned out to be true. The enemy dissipated, the cat ran away, and the battle was over. All that was left were the wounded and our heavy breathing.

My master was wheezing fiercely. He pulled his helmet off as if it were choking him. His nose was covered in blood. He spat it out until he could breathe again.

"High Council convenes at once," BJ stated, and began crawling toward his cage. Other knights began following—Percival, Stompy, Squibette, my master.

"Coming?" my master said.

"Me?" I put a paw on my breastplate. He nodded. I came.

The High Council consisted of me, my master, Nemo, BJ, Stompy, Squibette, and Percival. Though many others waited outside, this was it. The mice who made the decisions. I felt intimidated to be one of them. No one had let me know I was High Council.

"We were beaten," BJ said.

"Yes," my master agreed.

"What?" I piped up. "We kicked their—"

"They would have broken in eventually," my master said, wiping his nose. "They had heavy infantry"—he meant snakes and cats—"and serious air power"—the hawk. "We have nothing like that."

"Maybe," Nemo said. Everyone looked at him. I wondered if he had made it rain, or if he just knew it was going to. "Raven helped me once, when I was desperate. Raven might help us."

"If this Black Mouse can call on any numbers it wishes, then we're going to be outnumbered eventually," Percival said. "Does it have no limit?"

"None that we have seen yet," Squibette said.

You don't know anything, I thought. *Wait 'til it starts raising the dead.*

"These attacks were foolish until now," my master said. "Now that Squibble is back, he will throw everything he has at us."

"What do we do?" I said. "We can't leave our home…"

He shook his head. A pang of terror hit me in the tummy. I suddenly knew the only thing that would stop the attacks, or thought I did.

"I have to go," I said.

"Oh, that's absurd," my master said. "You're not going anywhere."

I expected someone to debate him, to see my logic, but no one did. In fact, they agreed.

"Yes, you must stay. We aren't giving up our secret weapon," Nemo said.

I shook my head. "You're all a bunch of loons. I'm no secret weapon. I'm a little mouse that freezes up when I need to move!"

"Happens to the best of us," BJ said.

I stared at him. "Nuh-UHH!" I said.

"Uh-huh," he replied. "When I was little, I was bought as a pet. My owner stuck me outside on her deck, six feet above an asphalt driveway in summer. I had no food or water except when she remembered I existed, which wasn't often. Cats hunted me at night, cruel children tried to poke me with sticks during the day. I lived in a planter, fighting my way over every inch of that eight-foot deck for two months of my life. I was grateful it was cluttered with so much junk. So many times I came so close to death, and each time I swore I couldn't go on. I wouldn't last another day. I wanted to give up. I was thirsty, starving, and had no rest. I hated humans, and often… often I froze up in the beginning, terrified and not knowing what to do."

I was shocked at his confession. So was everyone else except Nemo and my master.

"But… how did you live?" I asked. "I thought you were in the cage with my master when they all got taken to the snake…"

"I was," he said. "I was. But in truth, I am probably your master's uncle, not his brother." At this my master's eyes got round, and he looked at BJ in shock. BJ chuckled. "Could very well be," he remarked, and continued, "One day a human came in the night and picked me up, kidnapped me off the deck. I had heard that I was the third mouse on that deck. Two others before me had bit the dust up there. Or they fell off and were too wounded from the fall to ever get back up there again. I heard the kids with their sticks chased my predecessor into a crack in a brick wall that was too small and stuck sticks into him until he died there. I thought my fate was upon me, but the human was halfway kind. He took me back to a pet store, asking them to put me up for adoption. He couldn't take me because he had cats. They swore they'd take good care of me, but as soon as he was gone, they plunked me right in with the feeder mice again. It was the same cage I'd originally come from. Funny how things work. That was all before your master was born."

There was a moment's silence in reverence to the King's story. What a life he'd had. No wonder he was such a fighter. A mouse would have to be to survive that.

"What does BJ stand for?" I asked, while he was revealing all.

"Billy Jack," he said. "It was a movie I saw once, through the screen separating me on the deck from the human's living room. I was always trying to get through that screen, or at least get the human's attention—to remind her I was dying. I could smell food and water inside. It was torture…" He got a far away look in his eye, but came back. "Anyway, it was this character in the movie. I liked him. He had to survive alot of crap, too."

I resolved to ask the Kind Human to rent this movie. He rented *Mouse Hunt* for us once. We all watched it together, him and several hundred mice. It was a good time.

"Back to business," BJ said. "We've been effectively conquered. We cannot fight from this position, defending our women and children. What do we do?"

"We cannot take the fight outside to him," Stompy said. "It's his ground, and we have no help."

"We could ask the field mice for help," I said.

BJ nodded. “That’s a good idea, Squibble. They don’t often interfere, but they might come if we asked them. We’ve never asked their help.”

“They are a shut lot,” Percival said. “They keep to themselves. I have never seen them in my wanderings as a young mouse.”

“Nor will you,” my master said. “They are twenty times faster than we are and can vanish in the blink of an eye into the wild. But as fighters they have no equal. They fight every day of their lives just to survive. They would be very helpful indeed.”

“We have to get a messenger to them,” Stompy said.

“Better send many,” Squibette said. “Because most of them won’t make it.”

“She’s right,” BJ said. “We have to assume our enemy is smarter than us.”

Yeah, he probably is, I thought. *Stupid Black Mouse. You killed my family. I’m gonna see your head roll if it’s the last thing I ever do. I swear it on my name.*

“Okay, we send messengers to Raven and the field mice,” BJ said. “We defend until then and see what happens.”

“We cannot go to war,” my master said quietly.

All eyes turned to him.

“Why not?” Percival said respectfully.

He looked up at us. “We can’t hurt other mice like this. This is what the enemy wants. He’s demonic in his tactics. We’re so busy fighting ourselves, possessed or not, that we aren’t doing what we’re really supposed to be doing.” He looked right at me.

“Yes, I agree,” BJ said. “Our quest is to save mice, not fight them. It’s a huge diversion tactic. A very good one at that. If we end up fighting ourselves, we’re no better than humans. “

“We aren’t,” I said. Now it was my turn to get stared at. Clearly I had offended everyone’s mousey dignity. I snaffed. “It’s true,” I said. “They got themselves into the mess they’re in by thinking that they were better than all the other animals. Now we’re doing the same thing. We’ll inherit their problems the more we become like them.”

Nemo smiled and gazed at me, nodding. I had impressed him. The others thought it over, and one by one, nodded also.

“This enemy we fight was the enemy of humanity first,” Nemo said. “He has only recently turned his attention to rodents. He knows how to fight men. He does not know how to fight mice. We must avoid war at all costs, but if it comes to that, there is our strength.”

Everyone nodded again. It was ominous, what Nemo had said. How old *was* the Black Mouse? What was Nemo talking about? It gave me goosebumps.

"We will hold here," BJ said. "We will speak to the Kind Human, tell him of our trouble. We will send requests for aid. We will test the limits of our adversary."

Everyone agreed. The council disbanded. In the end, my master and I were walking along the living room floor as dusk was falling. Following ten steps behind me was Scratchy, holding my extra swords, a bag of BBs, and my shield.

"You've made him very happy," my master smiled, glancing back.

"Yeah, whatever," I said.

"He will serve you as faithfully as you served me," he said. "Maybe even more so."

"Impossible!" I blurted. He laughed. I was being serious.

"Anyway, you've done the right thing," he said. "You may freeze up once in a while, but you always do the right thing, Squib. I have faith in you." He put a gloved hand on my shoulder and looked me in the eye. "I am proud of you, Sir Squibble."

I blushed. Scratchy looked away from the tender moment. "Thank you, Master," I said. I smiled like a little kid. "Master?"

"Yes, Sir?" he asked.

"What are you going to ask Michael?" I said.

He looked puzzled. "What do you mean, Squib? Mike's dead."

"I mean the archangel Michael."

He shook his head as if trying to hear me correctly. "Ummm... haven't seen him lately," he said, chuckling.

"No, really. For your favor. What are you going to ask him? Maybe you could ask him to squash the Black Mouse," I grinned, picturing it. "That's what I'd do."

"Squibble... I am not understanding you, I'm afraid."

"Mike said you could have one favor. From him personally. Don't you remember?"

"No," he said.

I shook my head. "But... I told you everything when I was hypnotized, didn't I? My dreams...?"

He looked concerned. "No, Squib. You didn't tell us any dreams. You told us many things, alot of them very disturbing. But you told us none of it might come true. Or some of it, or maybe all of it. You said the future was a road with a million forks in it, like a tree, ever reaching upward with smaller and smaller branches. You told us you were speaking to us from some two years in the future. But you mentioned no dreams."

Oh my Mousegod.

"Oh… Oh, Master, I thought I had told you *everything!* I've messed up real bad! Really, really bad!"

"Slow down, Squib," he said as I was turning in circles. Anxiety gripped my heart. Scratchy was looking at me puzzled, obviously wondering why I was imitating him. *Because I'm a moron*, I thought.

"Master, Mike said you could call on him one time in all of this… all this… this… junk. He asked me to be a champion of the Mousegod, and I said yes… stupidly… and… and this is all my fault. My fault!"

"Slow… Squibble," he said.

"Okay… Okay…" I fought to breathe. "He said you could call on him one time."

"For what?" he asked.

"Anything!" I squeaked.

"Uh huh…," he said. "And what else?"

"Ummm…" I fought to remember. My mind went blank for my efforts, of course, but then I remembered talking to Michael. ("Can I remember my dreams now?" I had said. "Yes, Squibble," he said. "You can.") I looked up into my master's eyes. "He said your sword would be waiting for you at the lake. He said the lady would hold it for you."

He looked confused. "My sword? The lady?"

"Yeah. By the lake," I said.

His face went ash white. His eyes grew into circles. *"The Lady of the Lake?!"* he chirped.

"Yeah," I said. "A lady by a lake. Yeah. Mike tossed his sword into the lake… his glowing—"

"Excalibur!" he exclaimed. He was way out of it. He looked as if he were seeing Mike right then, staring into space.

"Ummm… Are you okay?" I asked, waving a hand in front of him.

"Squibble, are you *certain* of what you just said?" he stared at me with frightening intensity.

"Yeah," I said. "Yeah, pretty sure."

He slapped himself in the face. He looked back at me. "This is *huge*, Squibble," he whispered. "Bigger than I had ever imagined. I have to go see Nemo!" And he ran off, lightning quick.

Funny Master. As if he were surprised he had a sword sitting in a lake.

Way Too Much to Write!

✠

Well, it's been three weeks since I wrote in my journal. I've been so busy. Alot has happened. I'll try not to write a novel here.

Nemo never did really impress me, but what he said about my daughter did, so I am studying under him. Well, alright. He *did* impress me, but I didn't admit it, okay? Anyway, I frustrate him with constant questions. I kinda enjoy that. He hasn't taught me anything gnarly yet, no fireballs... Psychology. Just a bunch of self-help "know yourself" stuff that totally bores this mouse! He asks me how I feel about things, what I think about things. He wants me to get in touch with my soul an' all that. I said, "Look, I'm in touch with it. It's mine, okay? It ain't goin' anywhere." He said, "Are you sure?" and freaked me out. Hate it when he does that.

Sometimes he makes sense. He tells me dreams are important, and that he thinks I have a powerful gift (same gift that lets me see the spirit world). He says that, taken far enough, that gift could allow me to see the future. Actually he said "all the futures," whatever that meant. If there are gonna be lots of them, I'll take the cool one where I win and the Black Mouse bites it. I asked him how I use it, and he said I might not want to. He said it carries heavy responsibility and power. Yeah, he made it sound intimidating, but I know he's just messing with Squibble's mind. Yep. Nobody wants Squib to have power. Maybe they're afraid of what I'd do with it. I'd make myself really big. Like, a thousand feet tall. And I'd go to all the humans and say, "See? How do *you* like it, eh? EH?!" Mmmm... Oh, maybe I see what he means. Yeah.

In this last week he has started teaching me how to turn my spirit vision on and off. We begin each lesson with a few minutes of still, silent meditation. Boy, that stuff is hard! How long have you ever seen a mouse sit still that wasn't asleep? Huh? Huh? You haven't. Doesn't happen. But he makes me sit still—and *not think*—for minutes! GAH! By the end of that I'm ready to do two thousand laps on the wheel. He catches me if I think, too. He says he can see it in my face. That chinchilla is sneaky, I tell you. It's hard, but if I could control my spirit vision that would be cool, so I keep going.

The house has been raided every single day for three weeks. They're wearing us down. My master won't let me go outside and fight. He says they can't risk losing me, or giving the enemy more motivation. I *hate* it! What's up with *that*? "I'm supposed to be a warrior," I said, and he said, "No, you're supposed to be a hero." Whatever that meant. I can't *stand* sitting back inside while everyone fights to defend our home. It's driving me crazy. As if I didn't have enough problems already. Now I have nothing to do while everyone else risks their lives being honorable. So I've taken to writing and drawing alot.

My master talked to the Kind Human, informed him of the situation. The human has a pretty open mind. He took it well, though he liked the idea of mice picking on other mice even less than my master did. He set up fences, walls of stone, and closed up all the random mousey ways into the house. Now there are only two: the front and the back. One way in, one way out. Old mouse rule. Despite this, the attacks continue. The Kind Human sometimes gets upset, goes outside and collects all the crazy animals. He gets bit several times, even though he wears heavy armor. The mice swarm him, the nutso birds peck him, the snakes try to bite him. (He wraps his boots in thick leather and cloth so they can't get through—ha.) He rounds them all up in a huge net or blanket, and takes them far away in his truck. He told my master that he dumps them off somewhere across a river where they can't get back here easily. He said that, once they've gone a couple of miles, they return to sanity. They all scatter, going their separate ways once he lets them go. But it's alot of work. He only does it when he's fed up. Still, he's our giant. Our guardian angel. What would we do without him?

The Kind Human plays with my master (and sometimes me) every night. It's wonderful to have playtime again. My master has long conversations with him about many things. My master has to write alot to talk to him. The conversations involve my master writing with the help of a few assistants (like me) on paper with pencil leads an' the Kind Human talks in response. It takes a while. I usually watch TV in the long waiting periods if I'm not writing.

One-Ear came from nowhere and apologized to me. Can you believe it? At first I was gonna beat him up, and I had to hold Scratchy off him. He seemed really afraid of the little runt, and genuinely sorry for what he'd done. He was thin, hungry, and dirty. No one lets him eat. He's nobody now. He has no friends. He sleeps in the lower levels of the basement with the ants. Ants don't use bedding. He's lucky it's summer. Anyway, I told him to go away. He asked me if I would be his friend. I said I'd think about it. He gave me a whole bag full of millet he's been collecting from treat time, which was amazing. Amazing he had that much, considering he has to wait until all the other mice are done to feed at all. It genuinely seems like he wants to be my friend. He grovels well, anyway.

Messengers were sent out to the field mice. None returned. After twenty mice went—probably to their deaths—we stopped sending them and never heard anything from the field mice. Maybe they were all already possessed, but something told me that wasn't possible. The field mice were too pure. We hadn't had one field mouse come attack us all possessed an' stuff. Not one. The enemy was all lab mice. Mostly severely abused, sick, or—just recently—dead already. No healthy mice ever came to attack. It made things easier. It was the same with the other animals. All of them were sick or injured, or in some way compromised. Every one of them had some weakness that allowed the Black Mouse to get hold of them.

I tried taking care of Favorite, but she's depressed to the point of deep withdrawal. Squibette cares for her, and Favorite will take food from her, so that's how things have been. It's sad to go home and see her suffering. I know the human is going to euthanize her soon. I told Nemo this and he said, "No one is this house has *ever* been euthanized." I said I was afraid of it. I dread it. He said that my fears were controlling me, and as my power grew, they might control reality as well. Nothing he's ever said scared me more. My dreams are all nightmares. If they start controlling reality, we're done.

I had one dream… I can't forget it. It's one of those that stays with you until you die. It was very simple, but terrible.

I was standing on wet, grey earth. It was raining. The world was a depressing shade of blue. I was standing alone in a graveyard of thousands of sticks, the sticks the human uses to mark the graves of mice. I couldnt believe there were so many. Thousands and thousands.

It was lonely. I was alone.

Then my vision went below ground, like a special camera effect on TV. I saw the inside of my mother's coffin.

It was dark but still dimly illuminated by something from everywhere, just enough that I could dimly see her corpse, resting on the soft bedding, surrounded by cheerios and millet, soaked in water. Water was dripping down through the wood of the coffin, onto her head, and running down her face, across her eyes, to the damp floor. It was all happening in a total silence. Only the tiny drip of water could barely be heard. She was still. Dead. But in the dream, I kept expecting her to move, to wipe the water off her face… something. It was lonely and horrible that she was trapped there underground, in that tiny box, and that it was leaking… like tears. It was cold and lonely in that awful coffin. And she would be there forever.

That's all the dream was, that silent, dark scene. It lasted a long time. A really, really long time.

I don't know if you can feel the same sadness through these words, but the vision was one of utter despair. Complete hopelessness with no light at the end of the tunnel—ever. It was so awful I woke crying and could not function that day. I just lay around, doing nothing. I did not go see Nemo. I did nothing. I couldn't get it out of my head. I still can't. And because of that dream, I stopped going to her grave every night. I just can't take it, thinking of her that way. Or the thought that this is where we all go, into the earth like that. I told Nemo about the dream later, and he said I didn't have to picture my mother in that way. I could choose how I wanted to remember her. I told him that the dream was so traumatic my mind kept going back to it for some stupid reason. He contemplated that for a while, and then finally said only, "There are great powers at work here, Squibble." Yeah, no kidding. This just in.

I had other dreams. Dreams of wars. Dreams of fire, which I thought was Hell. I was visiting Hell in my dreams. It looked like a black field of scorched earth. The smell was terrible, and smoke covered everything so I could barely see. My eyes were watering, and my lungs burned. Dead bodies were everywhere, charred into husks. I called out and called out but no one answered my cries. In most of these dreams I'm either alone, or something bad happens to the people I'm with pretty quick. I'm so sick of these dreams. I can't take much more of this. No one could. They're much worse during the day, so I sleep at night, and stay up all day long. I never see anyone anymore. When I'm awake, they're asleep, and when I'm asleep, they're awake. My master and daughter are worried about me. Rightly so. I feel my hold on reality slipping. I act like nothing matters, when in truth I am thinking endlessly about sad things. My poor momma, and how she didn't deserve to die like she did…

Favorite and how she doesn't deserve what she got… the bully mouse back in the city… the lab and all those suffering animals… Bad things. None of these good mice did anything to deserve all this. It's as if no good deed goes unpunished. It's dragging me down, but I can't seem to stop it. I'm becoming depressed, and that's not like me at all. I was such a happy mouse. I want to be happy again.

I had another dream around this time that confirmed that the first dream I had with the flames wasn't Hell. Or maybe Hell has many levels, I don't know, but the dream was awful. It was frigidly cold. More cold than anything I had ever known. Lost souls were wandering around, crying and hurting themselves. It was dark like night. I knew there was no way out. The lost souls knew it, too, and their wails reached me on that cutting wind. My feet hurt, then froze. My tail broke clean off. Eventually, I died, but it took a long time. And just before I did, I had another dream, except this one had once been real.

I was a tiny baby. My momma and I were outside for the first time in our lives, abandoned by our human. It was cold, like Hell. It was beginning to rain, and my momma was trying to keep us warm, my sisters, brothers and me. One by one, my helpless family stopped mewling. Then they stopped breathing. I watched as they went silently into death one at a time, my momma clutching each one and trying to warm them back to life, only to lose another to the weather and the cold ground. We were in the front yard of my momma's owner's house. They had kicked her out for having babies. They had abandoned her—just put her outside and left her (and us) to die. And we *were* dying. I remember wicked hunger stabbing my teeny stomach. I no longer had the strength to cry. I didn't know what was happening, but I knew that in a little while, I would be like the others—blue and cold and still.

My momma clutched me to her, and I was latched onto her nipple, feeling it run dry, as she begged the Mousegod with all her heart to spare her last child. I felt her tears hitting me on the top of my head.

Then I woke up, desperate for any way out of the hell I fell into when I slept. I thought I was at the end of my wits. I couldn't take it.

I watched more and more TV to escape. I ignored Scratchy when he wanted to play or train, which was all the time. He was a pest. I didn't know why I made him my squire. It seemed the right thing to do, but he annoyed me so! Sometimes I lost my temper and told him to go away in a harsh tone. I didn't know why he made me so angry. When I did this, he would go and run circles all night, at blurring speeds. Just run in circles all night, nothing else. Later it reminded me sharply of the disturbed mice in the lab, the mice that had nothing to do and went insane because of it. At the time, I didn't give any thought to Scratchy's plight. He couldn't run on a wheel—he couldn't go in a straight line. He couldn't really play on toys or balance on ropes. He couldn't enjoy most of the things we other mice take for granted. But in that time of dark depression, I was only thinking of myself. I think that's how it works. If one could get outside themselves and gain perspective, they might free themselves of depression. But the very nature of depression keeps the victim focused on the pain, on themselves. I don't know. It's just a theory, one of many I thought about later during the long hours of the day.

I wrote stories. I'd written several. I wrote one about a mouse who never had fresh water in his life, had never even seen it except once, as a tiny baby. All his life he wanted only to have fresh water, to taste water that wasn't spoiled or old or contaminated. He never got it, and in the end, died of old age having lived a life of abuse and neglect. When he passed to the other side, a nice mouse met him by a beautiful, flowing river, and told him, "Don't worry, little mouse. Now you'll have fresh water always."

My stories were all tragic like that. Sad, depressing, kinda beautiful… And kinda profound, maybe, but they seemed sad to me. I didn't think them up, they just came to me. From where, I didn't know. My drawings were the same. I couldn't draw my momma anymore, even though I felt I ought to draw her in Heaven, happy and peaceful, or something like that. I really wanted to. Instead, I drew sad, dark things. Too often. So I decided to use my willpower and draw better things. I tried to compromise. I created a comic book character called Amazing Mouse. Amazing Mouse could do anything he *thought* he could. The catch was that he had low self esteem. So the book was about his adventures in trying to think he's okay. In the process, he based his self esteem on how his public treated him, which, in turn, was based on how many good deeds he did. But… he needed the self esteem to do the good deeds! Cool, huh? He was trapped in this never-ending loop—a Catch-22. I wrote and drew the first issue. It was so much fun I thought I'd keep doing it, maybe even send it off to get published! Nemo said he'd help me with that. He had envelopes, stamps, and all that… addresses of publishers, and the human said he'd help me, too. Everyone liked the book. I thought, Maybe I'll be famous and rich.

I did another story I really like called "Angry Mouse." Here it is:

<u>Angry Mouse</u>

by Squibble

Once upon a time there was born a little mouse who wanted only to find a loving human who would treat it nice as a pet. Instead, he was sold as snake food. But the snake wouldn't eat the terrified little mouse for some reason, so he was flushed down the toilet.

The little mouse survived almost drowning and wandered in the wilderness until it was almost dead from thirst and exposure. Finally, some kids happened across the mouse and took it home. The mouse was overjoyed. Finally, the kind humans would treat it right—pet it, love it, give it treats! But the kids abused the mouse, flinging it across the room, letting their cat play with it, and making it swim around in the bathtub until it had no strength left to swim.

They would always save the poor creature just before it died so they could have more fun the next day. At night it was frigidly cold and the mouse had no nest.

In the day it was unbearably hot, and he was placed near the window in the sun, with only a tiny, ever changing strip of shadow to protect him. The mouse tried to be good, to lick their fingers and smile and be cute, but all he ever got was cruelty in return. He tried hard not to hate them. He said to himself over and over, "Not all humans are bad… I'll find the ones that are good. I will."

The kids finally gave the mouse to another child, who was going to feed it to another snake. All the kids wanted to watch the mouse die horribly, but just before the sad mouse was flung into the cage with the snake, the sister of the snake owner screamed and batted the mouse out the window. Hurt and frightened, the mouse fled back to the pet store, hoping to get a better owner. He climbed back into his old, familiar cage in that dirty, hostile place and competed for food and water against the other mice until new hands took him home.

This time, he thought he had made it. They played with him and gave him popcorn and some toys. He was happy for a few weeks. But soon they began to ignore him except to throw popcorn into his cage on occasion. He longed for their touch, to play on their shoulders, to hear them talk to him sweetly as they had once done, but they had forgotten him. He began to starve. They stopped feeding him and gave him no fresh water. He had only popcorn, which wouldn't keep him alive. Finally, they let him go (kicked him out) into the cold.

It was snowing by then. Still, he said to himself, "All humans cannot be bad! I will find the few that are good."

He sat out there in the cold, freezing to death, until finally some humans came and took him home. He was full of hope and gazed into their faces lovingly, promising them he'd be the best mouse they ever had if only they'd show him any kindness at all. But these humans turned out to be the worst of the bunch. They experimented on him, poking him and prodding him with needles and blades, cutting him open and sewing him back up again. They put him in a tiny, seven-inch cage with nothing at all but food and water. No toys, no other mice, and never a kind word. Never.

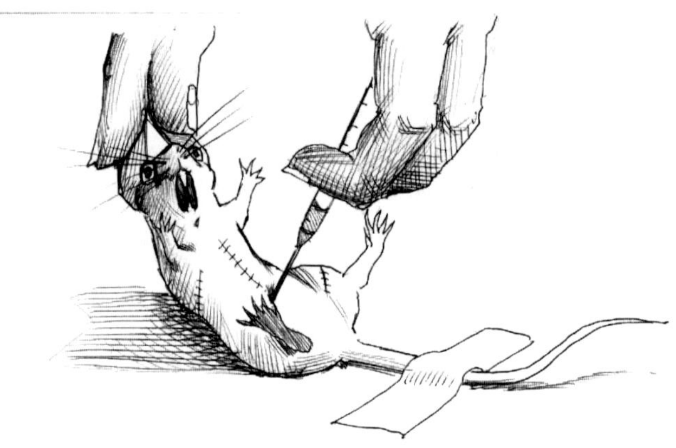

After many months of this, the mouse was worn and sad. He wanted to give up and die. Still, he said to himself, "There must be *one*. One kind human. And I will find him. I will."

So, when the time came for him to be euthanized, because he was too old to be any use in the experiment any more, he squirmed out of the human's grasp and ran away. The humans tried to catch him, but he was too fast. He made it away, and returned to his cage at the pet store, because he knew no other home.

A new set of hands took him, and though he tried not to get his hopes up, he couldn't help it. He desperately wanted this to be the kind human. He sang to the human and wrapped his tail affectionately around the human's fingers, and made no attempt to escape at all. The human smiled at him and seemed amused. Could this be the one? He's smiling at me, the mouse thought. His little heart raced at the though of finally eating a treat, or sleeping in a nest box lined with soft cotton.

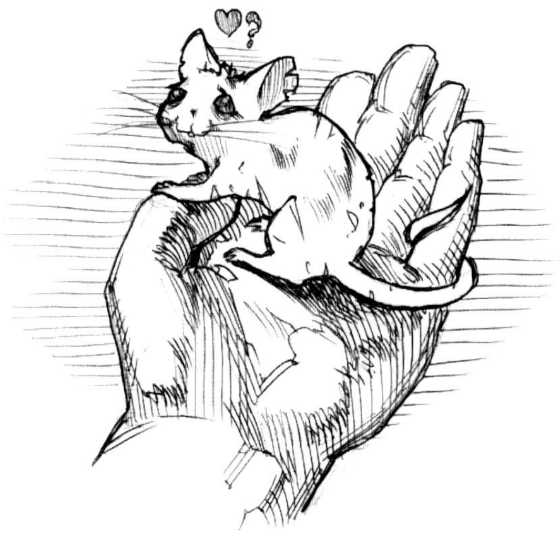

But he was put in a gravel-bottom cage to be a snake's dinner.

Oh, how the mouse cried. He cried and cried. His whole life was spent on hopeless fantasies. There were no kind humans! He snapped when the snake came for him, and let all his fury out at once. He killed the snake, bit the human viciously when it reached in for him, and ran off.

Then he went insane and embarked on a mad spree of long-repressed rage. He went to snake holes and beat up the snakes. He went back to the pet store and beat those snakes up, too. He kicked owls and hawks out of their nests with their babies. He frightened cats and dogs. He bit small children as well as adults. He lurked in the shadows at shopping malls and leapt upon unwary passersby. He especially liked the big, fat, screaming women. Them he terrorized muchly.

!
ANGRY MOUSE!

He lived like this, barely eating, barely surviving, and caring nothing at all for his life, for many months. Because he had nothing to lose, he was a fearsome creature, throwing himself at his enemies boldly. In time, the entire city lived in mortal terror of this psycho mouse.

But the mouse was crippled inside and couldn't die. He was sad. He had given up all hope, and now he was old. He had come almost to the end of his time, and he grew sick. He could not keep fighting, taking wounds, and bearing scars as he had when he was young. His life had been wasted chasing dreams only to find torment and pain.

So, sitting on a windowsill at the mall, he waited for some cruel human to crush him to death and end his miserable, joke of a life. He sat there, sick and hungry, all day. No one would come near him, even to kill him. Finally, he fell off the ledge to the hard concrete below, and lay there waiting to die.

A pair of hands picked him up, but he had no strength to bite them. He did not want to be food for a snake. He hated snakes. But now the choice was no longer his. He was too sick to fight back.

The human took him home and gave him medicine. He put the mouse in a big, clean cage with lots of toys and a nest box lined with soft cotton. Each day, the human would come and speak kindly to the sick mouse, who could only lie on his side and watch.

When the mouse was recovered enough to bite, he did. He bit the human a good one. He made that human bleed!

But the human just petted the sick mouse and said, "Poor little mouse. I know you've been through awful times. I'm sorry." Then he gave the little mouse a Cheerio.

The little mouse couldn't believe it. He refused to believe it. It had to be a trick. It just had to.

But as the days passed by and the mouse got better, the human always had kind words to say to the mouse, and always came bearing treats. He faithfully gave the mouse his medicine, on time, every day, and petted the mouse even if it bit him. By the end of the week, the human had band-aids all over his hands, but he still spoke softly and still picked the mouse up.

It slowly dawned on the damaged mouse that he had finally met his kind human.

And, knowing this, he knew he was loved. He could feel it in every corner of his sad heart. He licked the kind human that night for the first time. The human kissed the mouse in return. The only kiss the mouse had ever had.

It was the next morning that the kind human came and found the mouse, curled up in its next box, with a smile on its little face. The mouse had passed away of old age.

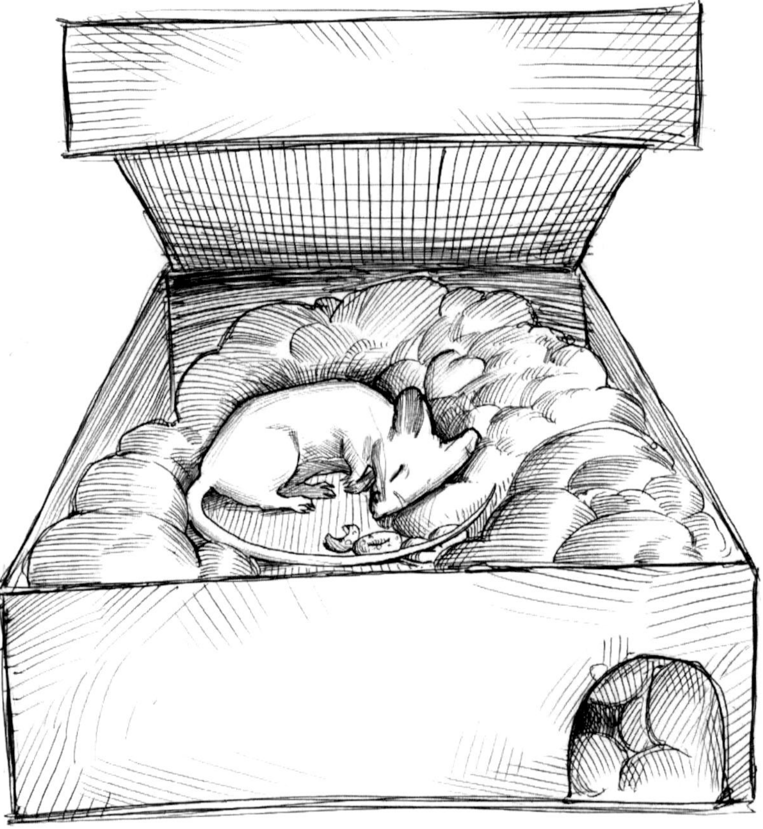

THE END

Impressed

✠

Never in all this time of my writing, drawing, and being depressed did I ever not think of my mother. I thought of Shiva and Thor. I thought of Branch. I thought of Squibette, and frequently left treats for her at her nest box. I let her and Favorite have my cage, pretty much—I had no use for it anymore. I didn't see them often, or even sleep there. I slept in a corner of the living room under the drawing table, in a small forgotten box the human had lost. I moved all my stuff in there, and that was where I worked during the day. A full month and then some had passed since my return. I was far removed from the world of normal mice by now.

One morning I went to my lessons with Nemo and he was smiling, holding a letter in his paws. A real letter, with a stamp and postage an' everything. You could see the question mark pop up over my head. He handed it to me. It was addressed to "Lord Squibble" and had the safe house's address on it. The return postmark was from Tibet!

"Branch made it!" I cried. Nemo grinned widely and nodded.

He said, "Open it. It's to you."

Here is what Branch's letter said:

Dear Squibble,

The plane flight was hairy. Sneaking past everyone at four in the morning was easy, but to get aboard I had to sneak into luggage, which they promptly closed on me. Once aboard, I had to chew my way out, only to find that it was freezing cold in the luggage compartment! I thought that was it for this mouse. I searched and searched and found a way into the pet area (they have a pet area on planes—I didn't know this!) where it was warm, but there was a human who checked on things every once in a while. The flight was long. Really long for a mouse. There was a pair of guinea pigs that let me share their food and water. They were a nice couple. I hid with them when we disembarked and snuck out before they were put with their humans.

Once in the airport I snuck my way around to find maps—only to find that everything was in Chinese! Did you know there's, like, 47 dialects or something just in Hong Kong?? Wow. So again I thought my trip was for nothing. I was supposed to meet monk mice here somewhere, and I didn't even know where. I started to panic, but remembered Nemo's empty mind trick. (Thank you, Master, since I know you already know what this letter says, don't you?) It worked like a charm, and I sat there and meditated for a long time. Eventually, the monk mice found me. Cool, huh? They said they homed in on my vibrations—much higher than other mice. They said I have potential.

When I first arrived, I sat meditating on a balcony. They gave me a bowl—a Tibetan spirit bowl, they called it—and a gong to play it with. (It hums!) I watched everyone picking rice and working in the fields. What a spoiled, arrogant American I was! I assumed they'd treat me special and teach me cool things, but no. They ignored me for days except to fill my bowl and show me where water was. When I finally asked one of the masters why, he simply pointed to the field. Duh! I slapped myself and went down to do my share of work. A few days after that, I was admitted into the temple and my training truly began.

It has been magnificent. I do "chi gung" (energy cultivation) every morning and evening, meditate four times a day, and learn mantras (chants that set your mind to a particular frequency, like wisdom or peace). I have included very detailed drawings and instructions for you, brother, on how to do these things. I am not sure Nemo even knows (forgive me if it is not so, Master). You would do well to practice every day. The chi gung makes you very healthy and powerful, and some say that if it gets strong enough, you can even levitate or heal people with it!

(At this point I looked at the rest of the envelope and there were, indeed, about 40 pages of mousey drawings with notes—I was so excited!)

I am enjoying my time here. It is where I was meant to be. I have already learned to speak Chinese Mouse very well. They tell me no one has ever mastered it so fast. I asked them when it might be that I got to throw fireballs and control the weather. They laughed and said I had a funny sense of humor. No one has ever accomplished those feats, they said, except in ancient legends. I was reminded of father's stories of knights and dragons. Maybe it's all just a myth. Probably. Kinda disappointing, but they tell me that all disappointment comes from expectation. I think they're right. Well, I won't expect *to attain great magics, but I sure ain't givin' up! (He he he!)*

Please take care of father. He's not the same since mom died. Share this letter with him and the rest of the family. I miss you, Squibble. I hardly got to know you, but I know there's good reason for that. Nemo said

you're going to be the mightiest of us all someday. That must be a heavy burden, and not many will understand.
Be strong.
Love,
Branch

There were drawings of the temple, of some of the monks he knew. The art wasn't great, but the point got across well, and his heart was in each pencil stroke. It warmed my heart that he had made it. I thought he was going to become just one more lost tragedy in this whole stupid mess. I didn't realize it, but tears were flowing down my face.

"You miss your mother."

I looked up at the chinchilla and nodded.

"You feel that you're wasting your time with me, and by sitting around, doing nothing."

I nodded again.

"Tell me how you feel, Squibble," he said gently.

I hesitated. He nodded as if to let me know that there would be no consequences for this action. I felt calm and somewhat safe even though I didn't really believe in safety anymore.

"Okay," I said. "I feel this is all stupid." I hopped to emphasize my point. "Stupid. We're sitting around, trying to hide me, when the enemy is just picking us off. This is a horror movie where no one can hear the music! He has limitless numbers, and ours go down a little every day. And I can't *stand* doing nothing! I hate it. It's making me crazy."

He nodded. "And?"

"And you haven't taught me nothin' worth diddly!" I blurted.

He nodded again. "And?"

"And Scratchy is all around me all the stupid time like a leech! And Favorite is crippled and it's not fair! And my master is sick and he's not supposed to be sick! He's supposed to be strong and majestic!"

Nemo nodded. "And?"

I frowned. I was on a roll now. "And I forgot to tell my master the most important thing! An' now it's too late 'cause we're stupidly surrounded by stupid zombies! An' that's just *stupid!* I bet no one sleeps well at night! I mean… in the day… an' I don't even get to see my own daughter 'cause I can't sleep! An' I watch… I watch too much stupid TV! It's doing something to my head!"

Nemo nodded. That was all.

I huffed and puffed. "Well?" I said.

"Well what?" he asked.

"What do I *do* about it!" I chirped.

He cocked his head. "I don't know."

"Oh, mister brilliant master! Why are you so powerless anyway? I saw you do presti-digaform or whatever, but you can't do any *real* magic. Can't *really* help anyone, can you? Maybe you're a scam artist. Yeah… just tryin' to *pretend* you're a great wizard or prophet or whatever. Maybe my master's… maybe he's…"

"Wrong?" he said.

"Yeah! That! An' there is no such thing as magic! An' maybe there's no hope neither, an' maybe *everything sucks!* Everything's STUPID! *STUUUUUPIIID*!" I snorted and stomped and hopped and leaped. I ran my head a couple of times into the cage to see what Clyde felt (it hurt). I squeaked in helpless frustration and thrashed about mindlessly. Finally, I was worn out.

"Feel better?" he said.

"No!" I lied.

"'Please take care of father. He's not the same since mom died. Share this letter with him, and the rest of the family. I miss you, Squibble. I hardly got to know you, but I know there's good reason for that. Nemo said you're going to be the mightiest of us all someday. That must be a heavy burden, and not many will understand. Be strong,'" Nemo said.

I gaped. I checked the letter. It was still in my hand.

He had it exactly. Word for word.

He couldn't have read it. It was sealed. Too many pages to hold up to candlelight… no… he couldn't have read it.

"How did you do that?!" I demanded.

"Branch knew I could do it," he said.

"How did you do that!" I repeated.

He smiled. "Prescience."

My ears went up stiff. (Heard something!) "Whassat!"

"The ability to see all the futures," he said.

I was suspicious mouse. "No way."

"Way."

"What am I going to do next?" I said.

"You're going to go talk to your daughter, then your master, then come back and talk to me," he said.

"Nuh-UH!" I said. "What if I just don't, huh? What if I just… go back to my stupid box an' draw the day away?"

He was silent with that I-know-it-all-and-you-do-not grin on his furry face. Grrrrrr.

"Okay, how does it work, Einstein?" I said, putting the letter behind my back and the other hand on my hip.

"I'm glad you asked," he said. "Would you like to learn? Because our time grows short."

I was suddenly concerned. "Howcome?"

"The enemy is very shrewd, Squibble. These attacks are just a diversion. He is preparing for the real attack shortly, and when it comes, there will be nothing we can do against it but survive."

"That *sucks*!" I squeaked. "This is a two-bit horror flick! We need to go gank his sorry butt right *now*!"

"Gank?" he said.

"Mess him up good! We bad!" I exclaimed.

He gave an "okay, whatever" look and said, "Not a bad idea."

"Thassright!" I said. "I'll learn your magic trick another time. I gotta go tell everyone what the deal is!"

"Okay," he said.

"You can teach me prestiwhatsit tomorrow."

"Okay, Master," he said, still smiling.

"Yeah. Das' right." I lifted my chin and zoomed off, carrying the letter from Branch.

A moment later I was at my cage. I dropped off the letter. Though it was late, Squibette was up talking to Favorite. She was speaking in soothing tones, saying kind words. Her head came up, and she saw me. I smiled like a fool. She groomed her momma some, then came over to me.

"I never see you anymore, Dad," she said.

"Yeah," I said, shifting my feet. "Sorry."

"No one sees you anymore. Mice are beginning to say you've lost your mind, or want to leave again."

"They don't say I'm a cowardly, worthless cretin who's afraid to fight?" I asked.

"Oh, no!" she snapped back. "The Lord of the Mouse Knights, the King, myself, none of the honorable would ever let them say that about you! They know better!"

"I thought they'd just make stuff up about me."

"No—your master beat them to it," she smiled.

"Reeelly?" I asked. I skinched closer. "What does he tell them?"

She skinched, too—just like me! "He told them you're preparing to save us all, in a manner that no other mouse could. He said you're learning great power."

(Heard something!) My head popped up and my ears went aperk. Mice do that alot.

"Great power called channel nine," I mocked. "Sometimes channel thirteen."

"He seemed very convinced," she said. "He doesn't lie often."

"He never lies!" I insisted. Then I saw she had tricked me. Tricky mouse! She smiled. I laughed. Chip off the old block. "I have to go tell him that enough is enough. We have to go gank the Black Mouse."

She nodded. "I agree."

"You do?" I said. "I thought no one around here wanted a war."

"No one does," she said. "But it's not as if we have any choice."

"Let's go together."

"Okay, Father."

So we went. Strangely, we found my master awake in the middle of the day. He was poring over his precious encyclopedias. He was looking in "D."

"Hi, Master!" I said.

He took off his spectacles and peered down at me from his special research table. He smiled. He looked tired, and hadn't removed his armor. I noticed it was well used—dinged, bent in places, dirty and marked with many teeth scars.

"Oh, hello, Squib. And Squibette." He smiled wider. "How are the both of you this fine day?"

"How goes the battles, my lord?" I said.

He climbed down from the book and took rest with us. He ate an oat laying there. He wiped his brow, cleaned himself, and picked up his tail to observe a bandaged wound on it (one of many). "Not so good, Squib. We can hold out for almost ever, but we lose a few mice every day. They lose tens, hundreds, it doesn't matter. We drive them back every time, but they keep coming. It's crazy." He shook his head. "The other day we finally took the time to observe one of the fallen mice. It was in *rigor mortis*."

"What's that?" I said. It didn't sound good.

"That's when a body has been dead a long time, it stiffens and grows cold," he said. "The mouse we 'killed' had already been dead. Dead when it attacked us."

"I knew mice couldn't survive the journey to the safe house," Squibette hissed. "That's the answer—they don't!"

My master nodded his head. "Yes. At least, most of them. It seems we are up against a diabolical foe with no reservation, and no morals of any kind. He is sending these mice from the city at us, in huge waves. Some die somewhere along the way. And get up. And keep coming."

"That's horrible!" Squibette said in horror.

You ain't seen nothin' yet, I thought, thinking of my dreams. Why, in fact…

"I had this dream last night," I said.

"Yes, I hear you're sleeping at night?" he said in a concerned tone. As if a human had said to another human "You're sleeping all day?"

I nodded. "Yeah."

Silence.

Finally he thrust his head at me. "The dream?"

"Oh yeah," I said. "I had this dream that the Black Mouse was eating our children."

"Father!" Squibette shrieked.

My master winced and made a face. "That's pretty bad, Squibble."

"That's one of the nice dreams!" I chirped. "I can't stand it anymore, Master! We're sitting ducks! We have to go kill this stupid mouse now!"

He lowered his head.

"What!" I said.

"Squibble…" he looked up. "You don't know what war is like. No one does. It's terrible. No one wins. It's the very last resort. War is what this mouse wants."

"With all due respect, Sir," Squibette said, "How do you know what war is like?"

He nodded and motioned for us to come over. He had another volume of the encyclopedias open, and next to it, one of his favorite books of all time—one he read over and over—*Le Morte d'Arthur*. He showed us pictures in both. They were pictures of war. Squibette squinted her eyes and shied away, but my master grabbed her and made her look. To me, these were illustrations of my dreams—detailed drawings of bloody horror.

"This is what happens in war," he said. "It is not glorious. It is not valiant. It's… stupid," he said, imitating me (quite well).

I got busy looking at the drawings, studying them, trying to learn from them how to draw like that (they were by Gustav Dore), when I came back to reality. My master looked at me as if to say "Were you listening, Squibble?" and I looked back as if to say "I'm jaded, Master… these dreams are killing me." Both of us got the messages loud and clear. Like telepathy. Like magic.

But Squibette was deeply affected. "Those… those are men," she said. "Not mice."

"Mice die like men," my master said. "And men die like mice, though they refuse to admit it."

"Yeah," I said.

There was a long silence.

"We can't go to war, Squibble," he said. "But we can find this Black Mouse… and kill it." He went back to the "D" encyclopedia. "I have been studying our foe."

"Reeelly??" I said, and hopped up with my daughter to sit next to him on the page.

"Yes," he said. I looked at the top of the page and it said Demons. I shuddered.

He nodded. "It's not just *any* demon, either," he said. He pointed to a picture on the page. It was a man… kinda. It had wings and horns. Kinda like the Black Mouse without the wings. The caption said, "Lucifer, Prince of Darkness. By Gustav Dore"

My eyes got wide. I had kinda known this, though I didn't know how, but I had known.

"The Black Mouse is… is… the Devil, Master?" I asked.

"If not the Devil himself, some part of him, or one of his high ranking agents," he said.

“I guessed this from your descriptions of the Black Mouse after you told me Michael had offered to help. Before that, I just thought we might be dealing with some small, pestering demon. A lower rank, a nuisance. But a mighty angel like Mike wouldn’t be allowed to help if this enemy was not his own equal.”

“There are really demons?” Squibette said in shock.

“Oh, yes,” my master said. “Though they aren’t allowed to walk the earth for very long, or for any light reason. Squibble, your mission, your holy quest... it must be very important if the high ranks of Hell wish to stop it.”

“Master?” I said, swallowing hard and looking at the picture. “Why is it important that Mike said he’d help you once?”

He signaled to a series of helper mice, who flew up the table at his request, grabbed a bunch of ropes, and waited. My master set a long place holder into yet another encyclopedia (the table was full of them, he loved them so much). He drove it in all the way, and at the end of it was a ring attached to the ropes, which, in turn, were attached to pulleys, which led to the helper mice. They heaved, and the book came open. A few shoving pages later, he had the right entry before us. It showed a mighty, shining angel with a blazing sword standing on two continents at once, one foot on one and one foot on the other… really big. It was Michael, as I had seen him. He was pointing his burning sword down at… Hell, I guess—this burning place below the earth, where another angel writhed in anger and wrath, wrapped in flames, lying among the ruins in defeat. It was Lucifer.

"Michael and Lucifer are brothers," my master explained. "And as the rules of engagement for cosmic forces declare, one isn't allowed to act without the other also having the power to do the same."

I perked up. "Well, that fixes it!" I said. "Ask Mike to smite the Black Mouse but good, an' we can all go back to our Cheerios!"

My master grinned at the joke, but said, "It doesn't work like that, Squib. They don't directly smite each other often. Mike allowed me to decide what he would do. It has to be something very, very smart. Smarter than the Devil."

Squibette whistled softly and said, "Wow."

"An' Mike gave you the sword," I said. "Don't forget."

"How can I?" he said almost to himself. He seemed deeply disturbed. "That is the sword of kings. Excalibur. The Holy Avenger."

"Cool. Let's go get it, and smite the—"

"It's not so simple, Squibble!" he exclaimed, startling me. He held up his paw, and said, "I'm sorry. I'm sorry. It's just… that sword comes to one person—man or mouse—only once every thousand years, if that. It's a huge, ungodly responsibility. I don't know if I'm up to it."

"Of course you are," I whispered, as if someone had told me the sky was not blue.

He shook his head. "That sword is a weapon of immense power," he said, the awe clear in his voice. "If I take hold of that sword, my fate is decided. Everyone's is. That sword is meant for wars. It is meant to bring peace the hard way. Its original purpose was to unite the land. In the old days, that couldn't happen without battle."

"Okay, so we can kill the Black Mouse without it," I said. "I'll bean him with a BB." My daughter laughed, trying to stifle it.

My master smiled. "Oh, I love you, Squib." He hugged me. Daylight entered my soul. "I wish this enormous task had not been put on you, dear one." He held me close so I couldn't see the tears on his face, but I smelled them. “I wish you had been allowed to live a carefree, happy mouse life.”

“Yeah…,” I said. “Me, too. I wish that, too.”

He held me at arms length. “So do all who live in such times, eh?” I nodded. “We need to go talk to Nemo.”

“What?” I said. “Why?”

“He can tell us how this is going to turn out. What the best choices might be. This is no decision to be made lightly.”

“But… but…,” I said. No way. Ears went aperk again. My eyes got round. Oh, my Mousegod. “He… He said… He said…”

“Squib?” my master said, passing a hand over my face. “Seeing ghosts again?”

“No…,” I said. “But I bet I soon will be.”

When we returned to the master prophet, he had not moved one inch from where I left him.

And he was still wearing that grin.

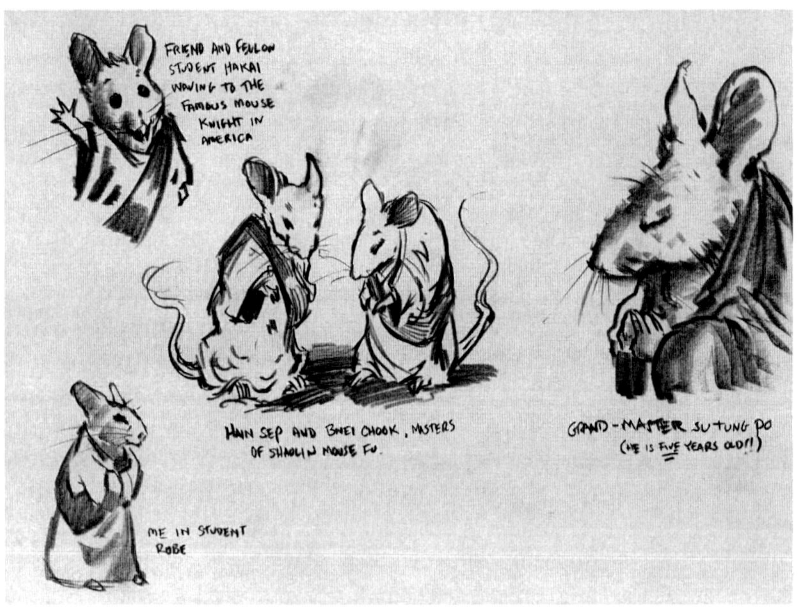

Nemo's Story

✠

"I think it's a trap," Nemo said.

My master nodded. So did Squibette. And, y'know, I could see it, but no.

"Ummmm… no," I said. My master's head snapped up so fast you'd think his neck hurt. No one ever said no to the 'almighty prophet.'

I had their attention anyway.

"It's a trap," Nemo repeated. "You know, Squibble. 'A horror movie where no one can hear the music'?"

"Even if it is a trap, we gotta go," I said. "We can't just sit here an' let him abuse our people. King Arthur wouldn't have."

That got him. My master pursed his lips and his eyes frowned, but I could tell he knew I was right. "And I suppose you have to go along," he said.

"Dasright," I said. "Maybe he'll ignore the house altogether if we go fight him head on."

"Except that he won't fight fair," Nemo said. "He's a *demon*."

"I know this cool movie where this guy kept saying that an' he got all busted up by a golfing club," I remarked. "You can bless our weapons," I told the chinchilla.

"I can," he said, "But I am no match for the Dark One."

"You told me all of us could do anything we believed we could do," I said.

"This creature is millions of years old, Squibble. Maybe billions."

"Well, can you do great magics or what?!" I said.

"I have my limits," he said. "Everyone does."

"Shyster!" I accused, and shortly thereafter received a sharp nip from my master right on the rump. "Ow!"

"Squibble!" he cried. "Respect!"

"Sorry, Master…," I sulked, "but he's got great magic an' he's not using it for us."

"Nemo will use what he's got when the time is *right*," my master said. "Just as we all will. Only a fool fires all his guns at the beginning of the fight."

I struggled with myself, but I lost. "Who says that's bad, huh? Huh? What if you smite 'em real good in the very beginning, an' then there isn't a fight 'cause… um… cause they're smitten!"

"Worthy tactic," Nemo said. "The Germans used it in World War Two—it's called a *blitzkrieg*. But it requires the element of surprise, which we have lost."

My master turned to the prophet. "What are we to do, Master? We cannot wait and be pecked to death."

Nemo shook his head. "No. I think you're going to go anyway. But knowing it is a trap might help. And something else may as well. I never told you my tale, of my time in the fields."

Everyone was silent, especially me. We all knew the field mice called themselves the Tribes of Nemo, but no one knew why.

"Would you hear it now?" he asked. We all nodded our mousey heads.

"Very well…"

It was a spring of three years past. I was a young, healthy chinchilla then, come from the ranch where I had escaped by leaping into the long, comforting hair of the Kind Human who shelters us even to this day. I leapt into his hair and refused to come out, hiding behind his neck. He fell in love with me, and I with him, and he took me home. I was one of only a few sapphire chinchillas at the ranch, and I was very expensive. The human was poor, but he worked out a deal with the owner to paint a banner for them to hang at the fairs. The ranch was not cruel. They did not sell animals for fur coats, but it was lonely, and I knew I was destined for better things—much as your master knew it as well.

So I came home with the human. He made me a huge house and held me every day. I spent my evenings with him, and in the morning I was the first thing he would come see. But my cage was by the window. I could see outside. I could see the melting snows, the waving grass, the animals and the sun. I could see the stars and the moon. I could see the hills, the mountains, and the horizon. It was too much, and one day I asked the human if he would let me go. He did not know animals could write then, and he was shocked. It took him a few days and several sessions of communicating to believe that his new pet was sentient, but he finally accepted it. He asked me if freedom was what I truly wanted. He warned me about the predators, the temperatures, the dangers. I was young and foolish then...

(Nemo pointed right at me!)

...and I insisted that I had to go. I had to know what being free was all about. Mice have been domestic for over five thousand years, and such things matter little to them if they are being treated well, but chinchillas have been with men as pets for only a hundred years or so! Really only in the last forty. I felt the call of the wild.

The human was heartbroken. And by this, I know how much he truly loves us: he let me go. He felt as if he was sending me to my death, and that was almost the case, but he respected my urgent wishes and released me onto his deck one fine spring day. He told me that he would leave water and food on the deck every day for me, and look for me at dawn and at dusk. He asked me to be careful, and come back if I ever wanted to. He would leave his door open.

So freedom was mine. I frolicked and played, and ran far. Very far. I ate all manner of things, and drank from streams. I hid in the day and came out at night. I shuddered at the cries of owls, and I watched the moon rise and set without glass in the way. Oh, I was cold, and often hot, but it was small price to pay. And even though I missed the human, I loved my freedom.

I knew I was the only chinchilla loose in the fields. The field mice knew it, too. They would stare at me as if I were an alien from another planet. They knew not what to make of me. I would race them, and catch them sometimes, then let them go. Nothing is as fast as a healthy chinchilla. Not even a field mouse. In time, the field mice would play with me. They would show up to race or chase, or they would jump upon me unawares. Especially the young ones. They were my friends.

One day I met my first rattlesnake. He was about to strike a terrified baby field mouse. I leapt upon the back of the serpent without thinking, and rode it with my teeth until it stopped moving. The mouse raced away, home to tell its people of my deed. Within a few days I woke to the smells of many field mice surrounding me, though of course I could not see them.

"We need your help," they said.

I was willing to help my new friends, but their problem was a complex one. Their life was a sort of hellish existence. Gather food, be chased, be hunted, run away, build nests, frantically try to produce children, then die in the mouth of some animal, or have it all destroyed by a rainfall or other natural event. I felt for them, these tiny animals. They had been doing this for thousands and thousands of years, and now they pined for something different.

Though I had read very few books at that time, I used only common sense to solve the problem. I told them that if they banded together into tribes—large groups—the predators of the field would not know what to do and might shy away from them. That way, they could also combine their knowledge of water, food locations, and dangers. They could build nests in places where rain would not destroy them and break the rules. They could become less like mice and more like humans. Just by acting a tiny bit differently. Dig where field mice would not, build where they normally would not, do things that would confuse their enemies. Defend one another. Unite!

Well, I had no idea how big the very first mouse fad would become. In short order, the entire field was united, building huge nest villages, and calling themselves the Tribes of Nemo. It was not just the mice—the bees, the birds, and the ants all wanted in on this new life of success. I had become their leader. They came to me with every problem, the small and the large. I quickly realized that if I was to really help these poor, simple folks, I needed wisdom. I set out to find the masters of such lore—the owl, the frog, and the raven. Owl I found easily enough, in a great tree at the edge of a small, serene lake. He asked me why he should talk to me when I was really just a huge meal to him, and especially when I was helping his prey. I had no answer, so he asked me to return when I had one. I left to find the frog, who also asked me why he should talk to me, since warm blooded mammals were none of his affair at all. He told me to come back when I had something to offer him.

I searched and searched for Raven, but could not find him. Then the mice came to me on my journeys and said, "Great prophet, we have found a black bird who was wounded in a battle with the hawk. The bird is asking for your help." I ran there as fast as I could, and the mice came behind me.

Sure enough, there was Raven, almost dead, barely fending off a giant hawk that had it in mind to devour him for supper. The hawk cursed me, saying, "Damn you, strange mouse! This is all your fault! I was eating mice left and right, but now they have scouts, and now they hide from me everywhere. Now they have order, and some small measure of power—because of you! Because of you I am reduced to eating this pathetic trash-digger!" And with that he rose from the ground to end my life.

Now, time stood still for me for the first time in my life. It was as if it was frozen, and I was the only one that could move. I could think as clearly as a sharp blue sky. I was calm and at peace. Fear did not touch me. Like you, Squibble, it took great terror and desperation to bring it forward. This beast had the power to destroy me, and he was enraged. But I saw, in that moment of his rising, that he had been wounded by Raven. He had a flaw in his tail. He was hurt there.

More than that, I saw the possible futures spreading out before me like a crack growing in ice. I saw the most likely future—my death, if no one did anything to change it—and I saw all the branches of that future and what caused them. I saw years into the future. I saw your master fighting the very same hawk. I saw the very horizon of futures. It was a great and mighty moment of revelation, and changed forever who I was. In that tiny fraction of a second, I saw years and years of possibilities, and I saw one end that satisfied me. Only one.

But the way to that end was fraught with pain and suffering for many! It was the least easy of all the roads I could have chosen. And worse, I would be choosing it not only for myself, but for countless others. They could not see the road ahead, and only I had the power to turn off of it and make another, better road. Only I had the power of foresight. All of this did I realize in a single heartbeat.

Then time began to speed up again, and I realized my decision was upon me. I chose the best way I knew how—for the end result instead of my own safety.

As the hawk grabbed into my flesh with his mighty claws—

(I saw my master shiver at the tone in Nemo's voice, and surely at the memory of those very same talons.)

—I screamed above my pain and horror, "Mice! To me! He can be beaten! He can be defeated and you shall know that you are not just food!"

But I already knew what would happen, and most of the rodents ran, giving in to their primal fears—slaves to their instinct. They fled as any mouse would do before a hawk. But I did not say this to save myself. I said it because it had to be said so that other things might happen.

As they fled and the hawk rose, I yelled after them—"Remember! You are not food! You are living, breathing creatures of God! You deserve your chance to become mighty! But you must take it! TAKE IT!"

One single mouse, a mighty warrior and chief of his tribe, defeated his instinct and pounced upon the hawk. It ignored him as I knew he would. But as the mouse prepared to bite into the hawk's flesh, I told him, "Nay—hold your vorpal teeth, friend."

"But, Master," he said, "You are dying! The hawk will eat you!"

"That may be so," I said, "But you must carry the message to your people that you faced the monster and lived. *You must endure, and go back." I stared him right in the eye and said, "You must carry your courage back and infect them all."*

So the mouse and I rode the hawk, he on top and I underneath, until we came to a small lake. You know the one, I believe. It was there that I kicked the hawk in his injured tail, causing him to fall from the sky to a low altitude. He panicked, fearing the water greatly, and ever thereafter was deeply afraid of that lake.

"My lord!" my master exclaimed. "Even then you were setting us up to succeed in the far future!"

Yes. Every move was on purpose. Every decision, crucial. Just before we hit the water, I told the young mouse to jump—jump and swim to shore. As he did, I cried to him, "You are my messenger! Fly with all speed!"

He did so. I saw him hit the water, swim to shore, and make away with amazing swiftness, even for a field mouse.

"What happened to him?!" I squeaked, breathless at the amazing tale. "Did he make it?!" Nemo looked at me and smiled broadly.

Oh yes. Oh yes, Squibble. He made it. And you shall meet his great-great grandson someday. You shall name him a defender of someone most dear, and his name shall be appropriate to his swiftness.

But that mouse thought me dead, for the hawk carried me off. And I thought I was dead, too, for perhaps I had pushed things too far. The chances of my escape were slim, and they all depended on a very uncommon role of the dice.

But fate went my way on that day. When we landed, the hawk was about to tear into me with his sharp beak when not one, but three ravens landed on him and attacked him in savage fury for wounding their king. The hawk retreated, cursing me and swearing revenge (which he took out on you, most noble knight) and was gone. The ravens carried me back to their king, who lay crippled on the ground. He taught me to heal him, and thus use the first of my newfound powers. Then he said that he owed me a lifelong boon, one that he could never repay. I told him of the frog and the owl. He told me that it would not begin to cover his debt, but that he could answer those riddles for me. And so he did, for it turned out that while the owl had wisdom and the frog knowledge, the raven was the lord of cunning.

So I remained with the raven and his flock for some time, learning from him. When I was healed, it was summer. My young grey coat had turned sapphire, as all of my rare breed do. My belly and ears had turned white. I suppose the few mice that may have seen me thought me a ghost.

I departed for the frog in the heat of August, found him buried in the dry earth, and brought much water to revive him. I told him that if he helped me, he could count on a place that was always wet, even in summertime's most wretched heat. He agreed, and I told him about the lake. I took him and his family there. So it was that I studied with the frog by the lake for another month and learned much.

When my time was done there, I went to the owl (who had been watching most of my actions all along, for he lived by the lake) and told him that if he taught me wisdom, it would be a long time coming to the field mice at this point. I had already helped them, and nothing could reverse that, but since I had done this thing, there would be ten times as many field mice soon, and surely a creature as great and wise as he would know this meant more to eat for him. Not all field mice could avoid being food. The natural order of things had not changed.

Owl laughed and said I had been talking well to Frog and Raven. "That was all I wanted," he told me. "To be your last teacher."

And so he was. I stayed with him in his tree (the tree above the lake) for the entire remaining summer and fall. As the first snows fell, I returned to the Kind Human, who saw me coming from the bench he had built on the deck for that very purpose. He had sat there every night for hours, looking for some sign of my survival, thinking that he had sent me to my death. I had been so selfish, and foolish, but see what came of it. Had I not acted thus, you would not be here now. The human embraced me and took me in again. My health had suffered greatly from my journeys, and I had wounds. And I have never again left this house in search of freedom.

Silence held us in a death grip after such a magnificent tale. I had not imagined it had been so hard for Nemo, as it had for us. I could begin—just begin—to see now how it was all intertwined. The delicate, tiny threads of destiny that held everything together and decided what happened next. It amazed me. I was speechless. Nemo was the greatest, wisest master anyone could ever have. He had lived it. He had done all that, suffered all that… for us. He was no shyster. I was embarrassed and humiliated that I had said such things to his face. And he had tolerated it with infinite patience. With love.

"Thank you," I whispered in awe.

"You're welcome, mighty hero," he replied.

Mouse Hunt

✠

I was ecstatic. For the first time since we came to the safe house, my master and I were going on a real, live adventure! We were gonna go kick the Black Mouse's butt!

All our stuff was laid out before us. It was alot (a *lot*, okay?!) of stuff. We had swords, armor, shields, helms, backpacks and side packs. We had water bags (two each) because it was summer and water was getting scarce. We had millet, BBs for my slingshot, tools to repair our armor, and capes made fresh for us by Gaia and Leaf. Gaia was a genius at making things, and Leaf was a miracle worker with clothes and sewing. They could make anything. They informed us of how they'd improved our armor design, and they were right. We could move much better in those suits now. They had closed weak points, improved strengths, and they knew how to treat the lobster hides that the Kind Human brought home—they knew how to make them just soft enough to flex under a blow, but hard enough to protect against damage. The new armor was twice as good as it used to be. I was sad that I had lost my very first suit in the city (damn that bully mouse!)—my momma had made it for me (sniff). I eagerly accepted the new stuff though, since we might need it. It would be too hot in the summer, even at night, to wear it while traveling, but most of it folded up and we could carry it in our backpacks.

We had rope, little grapnel hooks, even mini surgical kits. I knew a bit about mouse medicine from studying it in the city, and my master knew *everything*, so we were okay. We took antibiotics (one pill each, and one pill would last ten mice for weeks) and antibiotic cream for wounds. We took a tiny compass the Kind Human had given my master, telling him, "Here you go, buddy—in case you ever get lost and want to come back here." It was really neato. The adventure was going to be splendid! (My master uses that word. *Splendid!*)

Scratchy came wheeling up toward me, spinning to the left with all his heavy gear. When he got to me, I looked down at him with a frown. (Hey, I can't explain it, okay? I just can't stand the little runt!)

"Where do you think *you're* going?" I asked.

He put on a frantic face, hopeful and desperate at the same time, and gestured wildly outside and to me.

"Ummm… no," I said.

He whined.

"Squires do *not* whine," I said.

His ears went back. He was suddenly miserable.

"Begone, varmint," I said and waved him off.

Dejected and covered in a black cloud of rejection, he shuffled off (to the left).

My master was watching the whole thing. He clearly disapproved.

"Squibble," he said, "what if I had treated *you* like that?"

I looked at him for a moment and then at the broken figure of Scratchy, retreating in his crippled way back to his cage to sulk or run in endless circles for hours. I had no idea why I was such a butthead to the little guy. But it was too late now. He was gone. I had the strong feeling I had made a mistake.

I looked guilty and avoided the subject.

"Where we goin' first, boss?" I asked.

My master frowned. Shaking his head, he checked his swords for cracks or flaws.

"Well, we're kinda hoping he'll find us, Squib. I know it's a trap, like Nemo said, and we're the bait."

"OOOOoooo... *Mission Impossible* stuff!" I chirped.

He looked at me. "You're really excited about this, aren't you?"

I rolled my eyes. "Let me think about that—*yes!* A chance to get away from Squibble-can't-do-this and Squibble can't-do-that an' having to either study chemistry all the time or watch TV or write or draw... Yeah. I want out. I wanna be an escaped mouse!"

"I thought you hated those things, Squib..." He got a confused look on his face as he was loading his backpack. "You study chemistry? And *like* it?" He grinned.

I shrugged. "I got into it at the lab and while I was in the city. I don't know why I like it. I feel as if it has great power. Somehow I'll need it, I think." I didn't tell him that chemistry had taught Clyde to blow things up, or the rat twins to melt steel with acid. I really wanted to tell him everything. I was scared. I was gonna do it anyway when suddenly there was the tromp of many feet. Twelve soldiers lined up on either side of us, armed and armored in plated leather. They had swords and spears. Four had bows.

"Whassis?" I asked.

"Our platoon," my master said.

I shook my head. "No way. No platoon."

"BJ's orders," he said. "It's a good idea, Squib. You don't actually think we can take the Black Mouse by ourselves, do you?"

"I sure do!" I quipped, rattling my tail. "This trip is for old times, Master! Just me and you! No... platoon!" I looked at the men, but they were oblivious, honored to be chosen, and more honored to be in the presence of my master. Gah!

"We need them," my master said matter-of-factly. "They come."

I reduced myself to begging instantly. "Oh, Master, please no. Let this be our secret little quest... like Frodo and Sam. We can sneak up on the bad guy... sneak... sneak up an'... an'... an' *GANK him!"* I made a throat twisting gesture with my paws, gritted my teeth. "GRRRrrr!"

"Heh heh heh… Squib, you're very cute, but this is serious. We're hunting for a *demon!* It's a grand idea, because he won't expect it, but we have to be ready for him."

"NooooOOO!" I whined.

"YeeeEESS," he said. "Men, you all know the legendary Sir Squibble." He waved a hand at me. The men snapped to attention, drew their weapons, and bowed as one unit.

"SIR!" They saluted me.

Yeah, yeah, take a number. My master didn't know I'd had tons of that back in the stupid city. I grinned back at them and waved. "As you were," I said. They relaxed.

"Oh, good at this already," my master said. "Catch on fast, Squib. Fast mouse."

"Yeah. Fast and disappointed."

"Awwww…" He ruffled my fur. "It'll be an adventure, Squib, just like you want, but we're gonna cover our backs, okay?"

"…Okaaayy."

"You get to order them around," he said.

"Reeelly?"

"Yeah. Men, Squibble is the commander of this expedition. You'll take orders from him, understand?"

"SIR! YES, SIR!" They bowed to me again, and as one, said, "My Lord Squibble, we are yours to command." They looked like a cyborg army.

I hummed the theme to *The Twilight Zone*. No one got it.

Nemo and the others bade us farewell at the door. The Kind Human was there, too. Everyone wished us luck and safe travel.

"Should you not look in the city?" Nemo said.

I shook my head vehemently. "Nah. City's stupid."

"He's kinda right, Squibble," my master said. "Maybe we should start there."

I shook my head twice as hard. "Noway."

"Why are you so against it?" my master said, getting interested. Drat. I made too big a show of it.

"He's traumatized from his experience there before," One-Ear said. He had snuck up behind everyone. "Don't make him go back."

Everyone looked at the rankless mouse with surprise. Me included. He had saved my bacon. He winked at me and smiled when everyone looked back at me.

"Um… yeah. Right," I said. "Besides, the rats have everything under control there."

"Are you certain?" Nemo said. "They were such gentle boys."

"Ummm… yeah. Yeah. I'm sure." *Boy, if you can read my mind, you sly chinchilla, you better keep your mouth shut.*

Don't worry, Squibble, came the reply in my head. *Your secrets are your own.*

(Heard something!) My ears shot up like rockets, as if someone had bit my ass.

"Squib?" my master asked, worried.

"Nothin'!" I chirped, too quickly. "Let's go! Gotta go! Go now!" I picked up my backpack and gear (way heavy!) and bolted for the door.

Behind me, I heard the Kind Human say, "My little buddy, if you need anything, you just ask. I'm worried for you. Please come back to me, okay?"

I'm sure my master nodded or whatever. The human worries about us too much. The platoon of soldiers and my master came marching down the wooden plank the human had put over the stairs. They met me in the red light of the sunset, and we waved goodbye to everyone. Nemo was smiling at me. Behind him, Scratchy poked his scruffy head out and looked at me with wet, sad eyes.

I stopped and stared.

What if I had treated you like that, Squib?

I would have been broken hearted if he'd done that. I would never have had the spirit to endure as Scratchy had. Maybe that was why…

A hand suddenly came around Scratchy's face and yanked him backward out of sight.

"Get out of here, you little punk!" One-Ear yelled. "He doesn't *like* you, see?" He stood tall and proud in Scratchy's old spot next to Nemo, sure I would approve. Part of me did.

But Nemo did not. He twitched his great tail hard, sending the mouse flying much farther than Scratchy had gone, as the huge crowd looked on. His face twisted into a scowl that actually looked like disgust. He wiped his nose, a chinchilla gesture of distaste.

Scratchy came back, crawling slowly, upset by what the one-eared mouse had said and looking to me to see if it was true. His body shook. His eyes looked so sad. *Oh, why me?* I thought. *What did I do to deserve a midget cripple that would graft his entire existence onto how I treated him?*

I gestured "come here" while looking aside and upset.

Gleefully the tiny mouse bounced right down the stairs, ignoring the plank. In seconds he was by my side, hopping and shivering in excitement.

My master was smiling.

"Happy now?" I said.

Scratchy grinned ear to ear and licked my feet. My master nodded slowly.

So we left the safe house in the middle of summer, traveling at night, and going in the direction of the city on foot. We tried to be discreet, but 26.5 mice wearing armor and bearing swords made that something of a joke. I was miserably tired. Within the first hour it was past my bedtime. Through the night I just got more weary, but managed to stay on my feet, even with all that stuff. I don't know how… I wasn't used to marching, much less with so much equipment. It was really difficult. My bad leg started to bother me some.

But the night was warm and the field quiet. Whenever our scouts would see movement in the air they signaled and we dropped. Our capes made us look like the ground. They were all dark green, signifying my master's colors, but it was a very grayed out green, and hid us perfectly. By dawn everyone was bushed. We dug a giant cave (because we hadn't found any natural shelter) and slept, leaving mice on watch by shifts through the day at the entrance of our cave.

As tired as I was, I had resolved to begin practicing the chi-gung moves Branch had given me in his letter (which I had brought), so I wearily busted them out and followed the instructions for fifteen minutes or so. It was really easy, kind of like a slow dance, with deep, low breathing. Next to me, Scratchy imitated my every move. By the end of it, I was still tired, but my body did not ache one bit. Maybe Branch was onto something. It gave me great pleasure that Nemo had *not* taught me this. This was mine! I set my willpower to do this practice each and every night before bed, not missing one. And always Scratchy was there, matching my every move like a strange, stunted, white version of me.

Within four days our water had run out, but my master had planned for this. He had spoken to the bees, and the flying allies knew we were going to need guidance. We followed the flight path of bees to water and dense flowerbeds. We flagged them down if we wanted to send messages back to the safe house. Worker bees are kinda stupid, but they can remember things really well.

Scratchy kept up with everyone, even racing ahead to act as a scout at times, with his weird circular movements. As crippled as he was, he had compensated for it in amazing ways. He wasn't slow.

I was in heaven, on an adventure with my beloved master, but he and the men were concerned. There wasn't anywhere near as much water as had been here in the spring. This was our first summer in the safe house, and we knew nothing of the wilds. We also didn't know a drought was coming. We had no clue and no way of getting one. We had stepped out into what would become the harshest summer the Fields of Fate had ever known. And before we knew it, we had gone much too far.

Mouse Trap

✠

We had been trekking through the fields for two weeks and five days. We were a haggard bunch. Water was so hard to find we spent most of our time seeking it, instead of the Black Mouse. Wherever he was, surely he was laughing at us. We were pathetic.

We took off our armor in the first two days. Simply too hot. Then the real heat came, leaving no dew on the grass in the early morning, and no moisture anywhere. The heat wave was awful—easily ninety-five at night, and well over a hundred in the day—dry, cracking heat. If we were to find ourselves stuck outside in it even one time, none of us were ever returning to the safe house. It was brutal. Waves of mouse-cooking temperature marched across the fields all day long, only slightly retreating at dusk. And wind had fled from the land the first day of our journey. We had not felt one breeze. Doing my chi-gung in the evening before bed was agony. It must have been for the runt too, but he was there every night without fail.

My happy adventure had turned out to be another stinking disappointment. I could enjoy nothing. We were too parched to speak to each other. We spent all our time running bee lines after water, and every step was stupidly difficult. And, finally, at the three week mark (three years in human time), we were farther from the house than anyone had ever been since our journey to it. That's when the bees stopped.

No more bees. Just one night, we woke and there were no bee lines. None in sight at all.

I swallowed, wishing I had some saliva, and looked at my master. He looked worried, and his breath was ragged in his throat. His breathing could be heard from far away.

"What do we do now?" I croaked.

"Now we're in trouble," he said. Scratchy looked alarmed that my master would say such a thing, for he wouldn't unless it was absolutely true. I was alarmed as well.

"This sucks," I answered. He nodded without hesitation.

"This was the trap," he said. "If the Black Mouse has powers like Nemo, he knew this would happen."

"If Nemo knew, why did he let us go?" I said.

"He warned us, but Nemo makes decisions for no one, Squibble."

"But he can see the stupid future!" I complained. "'Hey, guys, don't go yet—a drought and a heat wave are coming and you'll cook your brains.' That would have been easy, huh?"

"Yeah…" my master looked at his backpack, resting against a rock. "But he can see what would happen if we didn't go, too. He knows so much, it's impossible for us to know why he says or does what he does. It must be complicated and hard being him."

Scratchy shook his head rapidly as if clearing his ears.

"The least he can do is send us water," I said.

"We're out of his range of power," my master said. "He cannot help us now."

I got an idea (heard something!) in my hot head. "Are you *sure*?" I said.

"No," he answered, "but I think so."

"How do the field mice survive?" I asked.

"I wish they were around to ask one," he said. "I haven't seen hide nor hair."

"They see us," I quoted. "They always see us." Scratchy peered about, wary and concerned.

"I wish," he replied. "But I have felt no eyes on us this whole way. Can't you feel it? We have been strangely alone so far."

I did feel it. It was eerie. Like the fields were dead. "I don't like it," I said.

"Me neither."

"What do we do now?" I asked. He always knew.

"I don't know," he said.

No wayyy!

"Master?" I whined, afraid.

"What would you do, Squib?" he asked me.

"Turn back, or make for water," I answered. Another option was growing in my mind, but I didn't know how to make it happen. Yet. So I kept my mouth shut.

"Yeah," he said. "This was a mistake. We're never going to find that evil mouse. He's not chivalric or honorable. He's hiding from us."

"How mousey!" I fumed.

We both laughed until it hurt our throats too much. Then we turned around and headed back in the direction we came.

And that was when it happened. The real trap was sprung.

On a far hill, one we had come over the previous morning, we saw them. Zombie mice. Zombie snakes. Zombie cat. They had been following us. No wind. Couldn't smell them.

Our way back was barred. They were far away enough that it would take them time to reach us, but we were had. Too tired and thirsty to outrun them. They didn't have to worry about thirst—they were dead already. If there'd been the *slightest* breeze, we would have smelled them!

My master didn't hesitate one second.

"To arms!" he cried, though we didn't stand a chance.

Hurrying to put on my armor with Scratchy's help in the fading light, I scoured the skies for any chance of putting my plan into action. I no longer had time to refine it. Now it was the only thing standing between us and death.

The enemy charged.

"We have a few minutes!" my master told the men. "Drink the last drops from the water bags. Then draw polearms. Archers, prepare to fire!" Spears came forward, bows behind. The swordsmice (us and ten others) stood in front. "Sell your lives at a dear price!" my master bellowed.

The enemy covered the distance, the cat out front, running awkwardly with a wounded paw. Funny… like he could feel it.

I helped Scratchy put on his armor.

The men held their ground. Every one of them would die without running. They were chosen because they were elite. BJ himself had chosen them for this mission. They were *ubermice*.

My master used the last of his water to mix into a bit of tea leaves. It was what the human gave him for his asthma. Tea with honey. He swigged it down without the sweet and shook his head at the bitter taste. Then he drew his sword and waited. Scratchy offered me his water. I told him to drink it.

The enemy had covered half the distance when my prayers were answered. In the dim light of dusk, an owl flew overhead.

I yanked my slingshot back with great speed and plinged off a shot. I missed. Within a second I had another stone set and sent that one up after the first.

El smacko! Right in the chest.

It bounced off at that height, of course, but it did the job. The owl looked down and saw us. I hid the slingshot immediately.

"Squibble!" my master shrieked. "Have you gone *mad*?!"

I nodded. "Yep!"

The owl spread its wings and fell on us, silent as death. I was betting it all on my intuitive idea. Putting all our eggs in one basket. It *was* crazy. The enemy was almost on us.

The mice saw what was coming and reacted as true warriors, drawing their arrows and spears back to deal with the first and more certain death before facing the second.

"Do not fire!" I shouted.

My master looked at me as if I'd truly lost it. So did the men. Only Scratchy maintained his confidence.

"Am I not in command?" I said to him. "Didn't you tell me I was in command?!"

He nodded, and jumped for cover. The mice scattered as the owl fell the last fifty feet in a wicked stoop.

I jumped aside with my squire at the last second as he thundered to the ground.

The owl was grand and frightening. There's something in mice that forces us to be petrified of such predators. This was a true dragon. Much worse than a snake would ever be, though at that point on the scale it didn't make much difference. The owl turned to face me, wings spread in attack stance. Scratchy hid behind me. I thought of my poor mother, and it gave me the strength to face it.

"**Draw your weapon, mouse**," it boomed.

I shook my head. "I plead for your help in the name of Nemo, mighty owl!"

The owl drew back. His wings folded some. I could feel the eyes of my master and the men on me like laser beams.

The owl cocked its head almost upside down, looking me over. I pictured my mom, proud of me, believing in me. I did not flinch. I could feel Scratchy trembling behind me, clutching my leg.

"***What do you know of Nemo?!***" it asked me.

Now the gamble part.

"I know you are the owl that taught him," I said, my voice steady but dry. "I know you taught him to help others, because it is wise to do so. And I know him because I am his student, Sir Squibble, the Mouse Knight! And we need help from you this very minute, Sir, and I know Nemo would have asked in my place! You have little time to decide!" I pointed behind him.

The enemy was upon us. They were covering the last twenty feet.

Owls are wise indeed. And I had been right. This was the same owl that had taught Nemo. That was why the chinchilla had told us his story. He knew I would have to know. I had to know or we would all have died then in that field. And some of us did, but not all.

The owl swung a mighty wing and batted the cat aside, showing us his decision. As a snake struck for the great bird, he caught it by the head in his beak. His other wing swept across the ranks of the zombie mice and scattered half their forces.

Then they were on us. I drew my blade and dispatched one foe and another on the return swing. Scratchy launched into his bizarre fighting style that BJ had created just for him, based on rapid circles to the left. He took two enemies down before I had my sword back from my first swing. I slammed a zombie down with my shield and kicked out against another. I dodged and swung, dodged and swung. My master was at my side in a heartbeat, fighting at my back. Scratchy was doing circles around us faster than my eye could follow, taking enemies down like a rotor blade. The soldiers were fighting around us in formation, spears backing up swords, backed up by bows.

"Genius, Squibble. Genius!" My master said.

Nothing could have given me more strength in that moment than his praise. I redoubled my efforts and more enemies fell.

The soldiers were not unworthy. Hand picked by BJ, they did not even slow down from thirst or hunger or fatigue. They each brought down ten mice, and then the snakes came upon them.

As powerful as the owl was, he had his talons full. Two soldiers died to the bites of vipers and one was crushed to death by a constricting gopher snake. That snake fell as the other mice took advantage of their brother's sacrifice. Two more died to the vipers before the archers could fire, but the arrows bounced off. The cat and the owl were sparring above us, yowling and hissing as the snakes struck and struck against us, knocking mice everywhere. Even those who got shields up in time were bashed to the ground and lay still. A snake struck at us. I pushed my master aside and Scratchy pushed me aside at the same time. As we landed I sprang to my feet and spun to defend Scratchy, who I was ready to see being devoured by a serpent, but the mouse had spun around the snake's head at the last moment, and blinded it with two strikes of his own. Then zombie mice piled on the little mouse, and finally they had him down. We were being annihilated, and then the *really* bad news came.

The dead mice were rising. They were getting up and coming at us again.

"The Black Mouse is near!" I shouted. "The dead rise against us!" I leapt into the pile on my squire and my master joined me. I flung them all about. I struck them from his body. I bit and tossed. His armor had held, though it was in bad shape. He lay surrounded by the dead, still rising. We yanked him from the pile and ran back toward the owl.

"Do not lose heart, men!" My master yelled, and threw his sword into the eye of a serpent. "Fall back! Fall back to me!"

I picked up a charging zombie mouse and threw him with aikido into a striking snake. I felled another and used him as a shield against a zombie mouse's bite. I slammed my metal shield into the face of another. The soldiers rallied around my master, gathering the fallen comrades who still breathed and dragging them along. There were ten standing mice, including us. I handed my master my sword and Scratchy handed me an extra.

A rattlesnake rose up before us, then another and another. The owl was overwhelmed by the cat, who had him against the ground, though two soldiers had buried their spears in his brain. Several more snakes were about to strike against him. I could see death looming over us. Everything looked like it was happening in slow motion. Blades and spears flashing everywhere, arrows flying like crazy. Mice falling, armor cracking, the ring of claws and teeth as the soldiers broke their last weapons. My vision went spirit-world on me and I suddenly existed in both worlds at once. I did my best to ignore the spirit side and fight to my last, for surely this was it.

Then, in a howling cry of attack, the ravens descended on our enemies. Black talons rained down on the snakes, driving their heads into the ground.

Field mice sprang from all around us—a *ton* of them—to engage our zombie enemy. They were howling the name of Nemo as their battlecry.

What effect the name of that chinchilla had! We were not outside the range of his power at all. Not even a little!

Within moments the enemy was destroyed. The zombies torn apart, the snakes beheaded. The cat was finished. There were six of our original party standing, back to back, panting heavily, shaking with adrenaline. My fist was frozen around my sword. I would have to pry it off.

My master fell to bandaging the wounds of those still alive. It turned out to be four. Ten of us survived the enemy's trap. I sprang to the top of a rock and shouted at the top of my parched lungs, "You see, black devil?! You shall not have us, demon! You will fall! Do you hear me?! You will pay for the lives you have taken! I swear it on my name!"

The ravens and the owl raised eyebrows at my outburst. I jumped down to bandage Scratchy, who was covered in wounds. I didn't realize it, but I was as well.

My master conversed with the owl for a long time, relating to him the circumstances of our plight, telling him about the Black Mouse and the attacks on the safe house. The ravens sat in listening, as did many of the field mice. He told them the whole story, from the time we arrived at the safe house until now. It seemed to me that a million years had passed.

When he was done, they told him that the entire field had gone into hiding. There was a malicious presence, like that of a very frightening predator, but somehow twisted and wrong (dead mice that walk), and no animal in its right mind would have anything to do with it. So the field had all but shut down. Normal predators still fed, animals still foraged for food, but nothing wanted to go near the dread smells, the bad things, the strangeness everyone sensed. All agreed that our enemy was their enemy.

Now, I was seeing things two ways while I was trying to fix Scratchy, who was in really bad shape. First off, I thought my mission was a failure. No Black Mouse appeared, and I had led us right into a trap. The thought was depressing. (It would become more so in the next months ahead.) I fell for the oldest trick in the book, really. In my enthusiasm to kick ass and my desire to go on one more mission with my master, I had messed everything up.

On the other hand, I couldn't help but feel as if… as if things were *meant* to turn out like they were. As stupid as that sounds, I felt in my gut that things were supposed to be that way. Of course, this led to a whole new series of thoughts kinda like, well, *why* is everything *supposed* to be so stupid then? But that wouldn't go anywhere, and I knew it. No matter how much I wanted answers, all I got was more questions.

Scratchy was in pain, and had lost alot of blood. His small size had almost killed him when he was piled on and couldn't dodge or spin. His armor had saved his life, but barely. I didn't know if he'd make it back to the safe house—assuming any of us were going to.

My master was still talking to the owl a ways off, and I couldn't hear him (even with my big ears). After a time, he came over to me and said, "How is he?"

I replied, "Bad. Got bitten several times, head injury, tail is limp."

He looked down at Scratchy. The squire looked back up at him through a bloody face and gave him a right finger up. It's the equivalent of thumbs up, since mice don't have thumbs. My master smiled at the hurt mouse.

"The ravens are going to help us bury our dead," he said, "and then they're going to fly to the lake and bring us water in our bags."

"What if they fly off and leave us without our bags?" I said.

"Then we're dead mice," he said. "But we can't go paranoid on ourselves now. They're the only allies we've got, and they're good ones. The field mice know the way back to the house. They're willing to send warriors with us to help us out. With the ravens bringing us water and the field mice guiding, we oughtta make it."

"Yeah," I said. "I'm sorry."

"Sorry for what, Squibble?"

"For leading us on this stupid mouse hunt."

He pursed his lips and contemplated me for a while. Then he put a hand on my shoulder and said, "It was the right thing to do. It's what I would have done." He always knew the right thing to say. I felt better right away. I smiled at him. He smiled back.

The ravens took off with all our waterbags, including those of the dead, since we needed them more. My master and I, and the surviving mice who could work, dug graves for the dead and buried them as deep as we could. The other five wounded, including Scratchy, just watched.

As I dug I looked up at the owl, who was just watching us with that gnarly gaze of his. None of the field mice would meet his stare, and I understood why. His eyes glowed. His face was formidable, and his soul was full of strength. My second sight had vanished after the battle, but I could still see his power. This was Nemo's teacher. Just the willpower to watch us bury several days' worth of meals when he was clearly famished made a deep impression on me. I wondered if there were Owl Knights. He saw me staring and swiveled his head and his luminescent eyes straight toward me. When I didn't look away, he squinted a bit and gave me the tiniest of nods. Nemo's teacher. Even *I* was impressed by that.

When we were done the ravens returned with many bags full of water. They told us the lake, for some reason, was free of the wrongness feeling, but all around it the feeling was immeasurably strong. So the enemy had the lake surrounded, and in great numbers.

Yet the birds had not been jumped at the lake. Maybe the enemy couldn't approach it?

We rested until the following night, through the unbearably hot next day and into the dusk. I sat under a jutting rock, looking into the sunset that slid to and fro in the heat waves. I performed my chi gung with Scratchy watching longingly, and then we were set to depart that cursed place.

One raven would remain with us the entire way, watching and circling, scouting for enemies. That one could easily reach the owl or the others quickly if needed, and would also refill our water when it got low. If we really hurt for food, he could bring us talons full of grain grasses. It was clear that everyone in the field revered Nemo, that they would go so far and hard out of their way for us. The field mice clearly did *not* want to be there, but they were with us always, skulking along like Indian guides—never seen unless they suddenly popped out of the grass, often scaring us and enjoying it.

The journey back was longer than the journey had been to the trap. We were cautious, wounded, and many times I had to carry Scratchy on my back. Normally I would have been angry, irritated, and ungrateful for him, but he had fought hard in the battle, and I felt sorry for him being in such pain. My master said he saw Scratchy save my life in the fight. Not being one to ever lie, I had to believe him, and it would have been easy to miss something happening behind my back I guess. If I hadn't brought him, that might have been me being buried back there. In that lonely field. I didn't want to think about it. Or maybe I was just too tired and hot to care. Who knows?

Several times the enemy tried to attack us. We always had word of their coming, and we hid. It was a shameful thing to do in my mind, but I knew it was wise. The Black Mouse was sending huge groups after us, sometimes as large as hundreds. Like ghosts, we skittered back toward the safe house under cover. Twice we had to engage the enemy, because we had no choice. We lost two more of the soldiers—two of the wounded ones who insisted on fighting anyway (they *all* did). Eight of us left, we skulked and hid and lurked our way back to the house, and summer passed us right on by. I lost track of time out there in the hinterlands, but it was at least four weeks.

By the end of it, I'd had my adventure with my master, though it was quite shy of a happy story, and Scratchy had healed enough to walk and practice Chi Gung with me again. By the second week on the return, I could feel energy moving within me when I did the chi gung. It felt like… heat, or tingly electricity. I could feel it in my hands, feet, tail, and stomach. It kept me strong, even when I was hungry or tired. Branch had been right—it *was* great power. My master even started joining me in the mornings before we made camp and in the evenings before we left. His illness all but left him. His wheezing stopped. I never did know if that was the tea he made, or the Chi Gung, but he started acting healthy again, and walked with some spring in his step. He was only one year old, after all—still fairly young for a mouse. If he had been human, he'd have been about forty.

Still young. Yeah.

On the eve of the last day, the field mice pointed over a hill that I recognized. Somewhere right near where I was standing had been the spot of my final collapse during our original quest. I had fallen and could not rise. That was when the spirit of Bigfat came to me in a hallucination (or was it?) and told me to keep going. The house had been over the very next hill, and a line of bees had led us to it. I had been ready to quit just before I won the final mile. I never forgot that. Almost everyone quits just before they make it. That's when things are the hardest.

"Thank you," my master said to me, standing there in the stillness and fading light.

"For what?" I asked, looking over the horizon and lost in memory.

"I never thanked you," he said.

"Ummm… for what?"

"Saving my life. Carrying me all that way. Finishing my holy quest. Not giving up."

"Oh… that," I said. "No big."

"It was," he said, turning to me. "It *was* big." His face was serious, staring right at me while my eyes soaked in the landscape.

"Well, maybe," I said.

He licked me. "It was as big as it gets."

I blushed and came out of my trance. He had gotten my attention. I giggled and smiled.

"I realized just now that I had never thanked you. Sorry," he said.

"Nobody's perfect," I joked, grinning.

"I thought you always said I was!" he accused, and ran after me when I fled, laughing. "My entire reputation was built out of your mousey gossip about me!"

The raven tipped its wing to us and flew off. The field mice had vanished back into hiding. The other soldiers followed close behind, one carrying Scratchy. We raced all the way to the house, in good spirits to be home.

That was, until we got to the door.

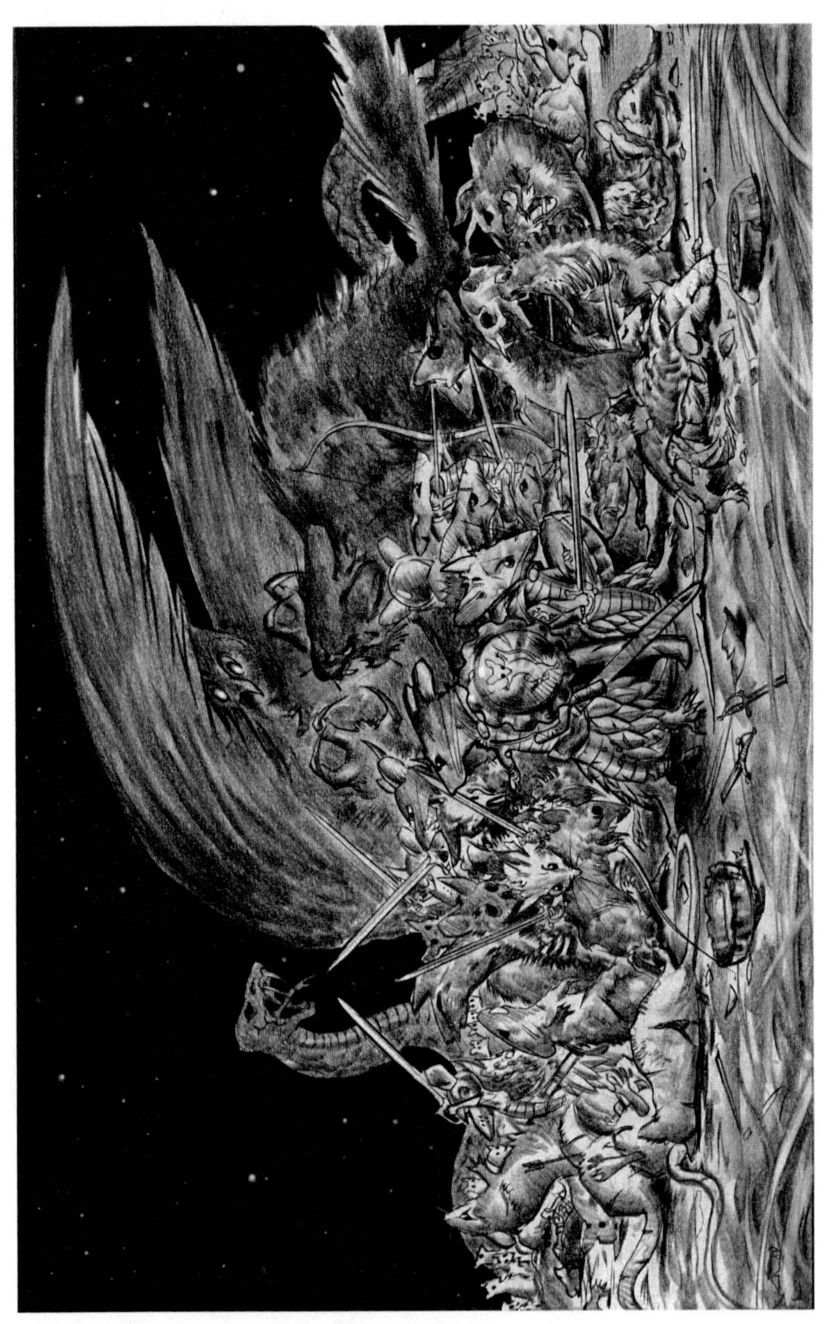

Fall

Entropy

The Second Horseman: Famine

✠

It was the first night of fall when we finally came home. We came home to chaos.

There was no door guard at all. Alarmed, we drew weapons and rushed in.

There were mice scrapping in the dining room, the first room past the door. They were skeletons of mice, actually—not literally, but they were that thin. Starving. When they saw us enter, they gawked and scattered to the dark corners.

My master went over to where they had been and picked up a corn kernel.

"Food," he said. "They were fighting over food!" He dropped the kernel and looked about. "What's happened here?" he demanded. No one answered him. Instead, mice fled to every corner of the house, mostly into the garage.

The house was stuffy and much too hot—only one window was open. The garage, where most of the mice were set up anyway, was cooler. But there was a stench there, unmistakable in its flavor—the smell of death. Everything was out of whack. Nothing felt right.

The garage was quiet, and none of the usual sounds filled the place—no wheels, no climbing, squeaks or chewing noises. We saw mice everywhere, but they were mostly sitting still. I felt depression, hopelessness, despair… These things flowed through the air as though I could reach out to touch them.

We gawked like silly youngsters.

"What happened?!" My master said.

Percival answered from behind us. "The Kind Human is gone," he said.

My master swung around to face his son, once so healthy and strong, now rail thin. My master's face fell. "No…"

"There is more to the tale," Percival said. "You must hear it, but first come back to Nemo's cage, quickly. Bring your weapons."

We went through a dark house, and all the mice avoided us. Many faces looked out of dark holes, hiding places and cages. They were gaunt and drawn mice.

At Nemo's cage everything was a mess. The human's bed was not made, as it usually was. Nemo's cage was splattered in dried blood, and a group of thirty armored mice stood guard outside it. The relief was clear on their faces when they saw my master coming across the floor. Once inside the cage, all I could smell was damage. Damage to the cage itself, and to Nemo. He was lying on his side, hissing his breath into damaged lungs through a swollen face. He was out cold, frighteningly thin, and looked dead.

"Explain now," said my master to his son.

Percival obeyed immediately. "The Kind Human went missing two weeks ago. Just before that, Nemo's girlfriend went insane, and attacked him. He always was small and fragile for a chinchilla, and he didn't stand a chance. There was no warning. Chinchillas strike at the head to kill, and Nemo took several such blows. We got there too late, but in time to stave off the final death stroke. Holding off that female chin was the worst battle this house has ever seen, Father—she killed fifty of us. Several knights, and many of the remaining rats. No one could stop her. She was possessed."

"Is that a fact?" my master said.

"Yes. Nemo yelled it just before he was knocked out."

"Go on."

"We had been assaulted not once since you left," Percival said, "and we figured they were coming after you as you intended. We were discussing sending out rescue parties…"

"Stick to the subject," my master said.

"Yes sir," Percival answered. "The female would have finished us all off—none of us could touch her. She was ten times faster and a hundred times our weight. Another hundred mice fell, wounded—most of our good fighters—and finally the human came home and heard the racket. He grabbed that girl fiercely. 'You don't *do* that to *my friends*!' he shouted and stuffed her into a box. Then he cleaned up the mess, tended to the wounded, and wept over Nemo. The prophet really and truly appeared dead, but Leaf said she could feel his breath from his nose. Sure enough, he was not dead, but in deep torpor."

"What's that?" I blurted.

"Comatose. Sleep without dreams, damaged," Percival said. "The human was going to bury Nemo—he was very, very upset—when we pointed out that he wasn't dead. So the human called the vet to come over at once and he did. Doctor Bausone looked Nemo over, tended to his wounds, but couldn't wake him. He said it would be left to fate now, whether he would recover or not. He told the human—and us because we were listening—how to drip fluids and liquid food into Nemo's mouth so that his throat would reflexively swallow to keep him alive. The female chin was still going crazy in the box and finally chewed her way out of it. She came at us, but the human caught her in midair, and left to take her straight away to the ranch. The doctor left at the same time. We never saw either of them again.

We don't know what happened. It's been two weeks. Nemo is barely alive, the house is sealed except for a small window. The heat is unbearable during the day, a drought is going on, and the food is running out rapidly. Three days ago, all hell broke loose and mice reverted to their animal instincts—fighting over everything, hurting or killing each other, and not responding to authority or reason. It was all we could do to retreat to Nemo's cage and use it as a base camp."

My master looked very disturbed and angry. "Where is BJ?" he demanded.

"Wounded in the fight—he rushed the female chinchilla first."

"So you are in command here," my master said.

"Yes," Percival answered. "I know I've done poorly," he choked on the words, "but it was the best I could manage. I can't beat sense into our own people. It's as if *they* are possessed." He looked down at the floor, ashamed of his failure. I knew how he felt, and my heart went out to him.

"I know you did your best," my master told him. "The trap wasn't for us, it seems. It was for Nemo. And we fell straight into it—all of us. We've been very stupid."

Yeah. I felt stupid all right. Looking there at Nemo, I saw our enemy's thinking—treacherous, no rules, dirty, below-the-belt fighting. We needed wisdom now more than ever, and our one source of it was gone, unreachable by any earthly means.

We were pretty well done for now, starving, overheated, trapped, and most of our best fighters wounded. But I had an idea—and it was crazy—so I said nothing. Just remember that I had a crazy idea then, sitting there looking at Nemo. I'll get to it later.

"Who else perished?" I asked, worried. Scratchy nodded emphatically.

"Your daughter," Percival said as I felt my heart skip a beat, "is fine. Stompy is, too, and Ghost. BJ is bad off. It's a miracle he's still alive. We lost many others without names, but, my lord," he bowed his head, "Gaia died in the attack."

My master's daughter. I heard his chest make a horrible grating sound that might have been a choking sob. His eyes, full of tears, were hard. His face never changed. He nodded.

"She was one of the first on the scene. Was even headed right toward Nemo's cage when the treacherous attack occurred. It was she who warned Nemo of the first blow, else he would not have survived at all. She claims she heard a voice in her head tell her to go to the cage from her sleep. She told me this moments before she went."

"Who's voice?" my master asked, struggling to push the words out. His nose was bleeding.

Percival looked at me hesitantly.

"Oh nooo," I said. "I was all gone an' everything!"

But everyone looked at me.

"Are you sure she said it was Squibble's voice?" my master said.

Percival nodded and sealed my condemnation. Now I was labeled for something I didn't even do—or at least, not yet.

"I'm… I'm sorry," I said. "I would never have… I didn't… I wouldn't…"

My master steeled himself and put his bleeding nose in his paws. He looked up, eyes showing the strain of the news, and said, "Yes, Squibble, anyone would have done it. It saved Nemo's life… And maybe it was the only way." He looked at me. There was no condemnation there, but the others smelled differently. "Gaia was always sensitive that way," he said. "She would have been able to hear you. No one else would have."

"Nemo would have," I cried.

"Nemo wasn't asleep," Percival said in my defense.

"It shouldn't matter!" I said. "He was the all powerful Nemo! If my future self or… or whatever… tried to warn him, it shouldn't have cost Gaia her… it shouldn't have done that! That was stupid!"

There was silence for a full minute as everyone sat around. Below us, a horde of starving mice had gathered from all around the house, garage, and basement. My master looked down at them with fury.

If they were possessed, the demons left them under the intensity of that dread gaze.

"SO!" he yelled in his most powerful voice, standing up straight and drawing his well-worn blade. "We leave and you all turn into *animals*!" He pointed at them. "You know better! *You obey the leaders here or you don't stay!"* He was furious. I had never seen him so angry!

"There will be no more fighting—no more killing each other over food, no more doing our enemy's work for him! I am ashamed of you! Things go bad and you fall apart... like... like *vermin* instead of the courageous, smart mice you all are! You will shape up this very second or I will personally kick every one of you out the door, into the burning fields, and you can fend for yourselves! I have returned, and you have let us all down. Now you will do penance for it! You shall obey me—and my knights—or get out! Now, who wants to leave? Go!"

No mouse moved. Everyone was stock still in shock. Even Percival. Even me!

"Fine! Then you will endure this tribulation with integrity, by the Mousegod!" he thundered. "And you will **not** break, do you hear!? You *will not!* We are against a terrible foe, and every... last... one of you will summon the courage, and strength, and honor to do what is required of you, just as Nemo would. Now begone from my sight—until you earn back my respect!" The last was almost supernatural in its echo—and the mice vanished into the dark.

Once every mouse was gone but the base camp group and its knights, my master sagged and choked. More blood came out his nose. He snaffed and wiped it away violently, as if greatly annoyed that he was not well. He looked tired. Not an ounce of that had shown a moment ago, though. Not one ounce.

"We are under siege," he whispered. "We must not fold."

So my master told Percival and the others everything we had encountered on our mission, the horrible failure. We saw BJ. He had been slammed into a wall by that stupid chinchilla, and then stomped on several times. He looked as bad as Nemo, maybe worse. At least he woke up sometimes, to eat and drink. Though he could not move except to crawl on his front legs (I was reminded sharply of Favorite), he insisted on reaching the food and water himself, and wouldn't let anyone help him. Tough mouse. Very tough mouse. No one spoke of replacing him as King. No one dared challenge him, even in his crippled state.

Stompy, Squibette and Ghost had taken bad wounds. Stompy had been bitten by the rabid chin, but it had only pierced fat and muscle. Squibette was been thrown ten feet, and her armor had broken her fall. It also destroyed the armor, but that's what it was for. Ghost's shield had splintered, he'd gone through ten swords, and finally took a tail bash that sent him to the floor.

The rats had come from their spot on the porch, and the female chin had taken them seriously, being more her size. Not knowing what was going on, they were reluctant to attack her—that was, until Percival yelled "Kill her! Do it *now*!" and they all rushed in. But too late. If they'd had surprise, they might have won, but once she was aware, nothing could stop her.

"It's as if a dark spirit powered her," Percival said. "And after that, the spirit went into the entire house and caused mayhem and chaos in all our people."

"That's *exactly* what happened," my master said. "But we have returned, and the angels Nemo sent with us have also. That evil spirit has no more power here."

"All along it was a trap for Nemo…," I murmured. Master nodded.

"Why didn't he tell us? He had to be all mysterious an' everything! Couldn't just say, 'Hey, everyone, look—if you leave, the Black stupid Mouse is gonna gank me an' the human, and drive the house insane, so pretend to leave an' we'll get him when he shows up!' But noooo… he had to be all prophet-like an' sacrificial an' stuff. You know, the villains always tell James Bond what they're gonna do instead of just killing him, and then they wonder why they lose."

Everyone was looking at me. I was getting sick of that. "What!" I chirped.

"What makes you think the Black Mouse ganked the Kind Human?" Percival said, stumbling over the word ganked with his proper English tongue.

"Isn't that obvious?" I said. "The Kind Human would never abandon us! He's toast!"

"No! Don't say that, Squibble!" my master cried. He loved the Kind Human dearly, more than any of us.

"It's the only explanation," I said. "He's gone! We're on our own!"

"No! Not true!" he claimed.

"Wakey wakey, Master!" I pointed around. "He would *never* have left us like this."

He got mad then. You can't push anyone, even a saint, as hard as my master had been pushed.

"He's not dead, Squibble, by the Mousegod! Not dead, do you hear?! You're scaring everyone and discouraging *me*!" he yelled.

I shrank back, alarmed. His tail actually rattled at me. He stopped immediately, but the damage was done. I ran away.

I went and hid in my corner nest box, which had been demolished by rioting mice. My drawings and writings were strewn all about, chewed on, peed on. My stuff was in ruins. I spent the rest of the night putting it back together with Scratchy's help, crying the entire time. I knew why he'd yelled, but it still hurt. I yelled just as loud at Scratchy while he pestered me, trying to make me feel better, and finally I banished the little runt. I told him to go to the base camp and guard Nemo, or listen to the plans they were making, or something—just go away. Finally, I was alone.

The mission was a stupid, wretched failure. Within hours every mouse would know. It was my fault Gaia was dead along with fifty other mice, and a hundred others wounded. My master was upset, the house was suffering a drought and a famine, and that was my fault, too. I wanted to die. I crawled into my busted house and curled up in the dark, sobbing. When dawn came, I could not go to sleep.

And sure enough, my prediction came true. The next night, every mouse knew I was responsible for the miserable failure of the mission that left the safe house unguarded, and might also have been the cause of the king being crippled, Nemo being almost dead, and the Kind Human going away. And us being doomed.

It didn't take a genius to figure it out. We came back empty-handed, having been beaten within an inch of our mousey lives, struggling just to walk. Everyone knew the mission was my bright idea, because I had gleefully told them all before we left, filled with visions of glory and victory, parading back through the door with the Black Mouse's head on a pike, the hero Squibble. Everyone already thought I was crazy. Now I was stupid as well. No one would listen to me now. My days of honor were over.

I spent some time with Favorite, grooming her and fetching what tiny bits of food were available for her (and giving her mine), but she was depressed beyond all reason. She had grown rail thin, more so than any of the others, even with her daughter caring for her constantly. I tried to cheer her up, but there was little cheer in me, and I could not fake it for long. Finally, I retreated back into solitude. I could not take being near her, and unless you've been in the very same situation, you might not be quick to judge me. It was horrible. All joy and play had left this mouse who had, only months before, been jubilant and full of energy, happy to be alive. It was unbearable because it was so sad, but also because I was quickly following the same path.

My master organized the mice as only he could. They all obeyed him without question. Rations were given out each night, a tiny amount to each mouse, and every cupboard and pantry was raided in the entire house, even some we had to chew our way into. The human would have understood. With the rats help we pried our way into the refrigerator. We gathered everything in the entire house that we could reach, and I actually came in handy. My trick of navigating high shelves was of some use when we had to loot the high levels of the kitchen. I taught other mice to do it, all of whom looked at me with the thoughts visible that I was leading them to their dooms. But none of them died, or were even injured. So *there*, heathen unbelievers.

All the food we could gather was not much. Everyone went hungry. I went to the High Council meetings, now much smaller than before, because I felt I had to. Not out of duty, but sanity. I could not give up, though I really wanted to. I could not. If I did, the Black Mouse won. I went because if I didn't, I'd sit in my crumbling house and do nothing. At these meetings, the mice discussed strategies for survival and for beating the demonic enemy (which everyone now had a very healthy respect for). BJ insisted on being present and awake for each one. An agonizingly long week passed, and no one had any solutions. The best idea seemed to be to send a courier back to the city to find help, but no one would make it, and everyone knew it. Not one of us was at full strength, and even if we were, that journey was deadly even without tons of zombies lurking the tall grass.

I spent the rest of that time in the week doing only mindless, robotic things. Drawing really bad art, meditating, and doing my chi gung. I did tons of chi gung, hours on end. I went over and over Branch's notes and religiously corrected every mistake I made. I made up new moves which felt right. I did it all because it was the only escape available to me—by myself I could not turn on the TV—and because it was the only thing in my life that felt good anymore, the only thing I felt I had control over. That and my art.

My master sent squads of brave mice out into the fields to gather what little wheat grass remained, and sometimes they didn't come back. All of the ones that survived reported that the house was surrounded by the enemy, and they could not sneak with large amounts of food. Maybe sixty grains of wheat went into the stockpile of food each night, and several hundred came out. By the end of the week, we were all starving.

Water was scarce also, and many mice had drowned in the toilet bowl trying to get to the only obvious water source in the house. Now that water was bad, and none of us could use it for fear of disease. No one had the strength to turn on the faucets, even with ropes and levers, the stupid slippery things. We found leaks in the pipes down in the basement, and other small sources, but it was not enough, and the heat began to kill mice. A few each day passed on, and all our dead were put in a hole down in the basement, for we could not abandon them outside to be raised by our enemy. None of us would damn our friends so.

I was finally ready to listen to Nemo. He finally had my respect, and he was lost to us. The irony was terrible, and seemed to follow me like Scratchy did. Now, when I needed him the most, and would finally listen, he was gone. But I knew what he might suggest, so I set to work on it. I asked my master to teach me hypnosis. He had learned it from Nemo, and I had had a few lessons. I learned it well enough right away, and used it on myself immediately. I told myself I felt no hunger. I gave all my food to Favorite and Squibette, though for my daughter I had to sneak it into her rations one grain at a time. She would not have accepted if she knew. My chi gung seemed to sustain me, and while I knew that wouldn't last forever, it was a kind illusion for now, so I entertained it. I could see that Percival was doing the same thing with his food, and he winked at me knowingly. He did not have the benefit of hypnosis to defy hunger. His sheer willpower was awesome. I taught him chi gung, and he practiced every night.

The heat in the day was awful, the house stuffy and oppressive, upwards of a hundred degrees. The council said that normally we'd all be dead in such temperatures, especially Nemo, because his thick, fine coat made it all the hotter for him. No one could explain why we weren't dropping by the hundreds, but we weren't. Many thought living through it was worse. At night, the house was quiet and lonely. Nobody wanted to run around, play, or use their wheels. It was a house of darkness, and my heart was at the center of it.

Very few pet mice who are really loved have ever experienced real hunger. I had known it only as a tiny baby, but that memory was enough. By the second week into fall, every mouse was gaunt and weak. By the third week our numbers had dropped off by several a day.

BJ suggested eating our own dead.

Seriously, it was a good idea. We thought about it, but my master vetoed the idea. He said the enemy would be delighted at the damage it would cause our souls to do such a thing. Had it been pure survival without demonic intervention, he might have said yes, but this had been done to us. It was not just bad luck. If our integrity was all we had left, he said, then we would have to eat that and not each other.

My chi gung was growing powerful. I could feel energy coursing through my body with each delicate movement, and the sitting meditation had my mind off in la-la-land while my body charged its internal power with deep breathing and relaxation. I tried to reach my dock out there on the water. Sometimes I got close, but it always eluded me. That was okay. I went other cool places. But in the mortal realm I had dropped forty percent of my body weight, though I felt it not at all. I had more strength than anyone, and no one noticed. Perhaps no one cared.

Then, one day, I was resting my hand on my daughter while I sat there meditating, and she was talking to me. It was a rarity that anyone came to visit me in my hovel, but she made a point of it almost every evening, even if just to touch noses. She said I was becoming deeply depressed, and needed company. This just in.

Anyway, my hand rested on her for about fifteen minutes one evening while I was meditating, and afterward she went away, to return at dawn. I had gone back to my anti-nocturnal schedule and was just rising for the daylight hours of peace and quiet from a long sleep of disturbing dreams. She told me she felt great, energized. Not hungry or weary. She asked for more, so I shared my morning meditations with her as well, and showed her the chi gung. She told me, "Be careful, father—you have a secret weapon there."

Ding. The light bulb went on over my head. Finally.

From then on, I did all my chi gung in Nemo's cage, right next to him. And in my seated meditations, I used his big body as a backrest. No one said anything, and not many people ever came into the cage except to trickle powdered food and water down the poor guy's throat. I would do both moving and seated chi gung in his cage for six hours a day. And that was when I started using my bright idea—the one I told you about earlier.

No one could reach Nemo by conventional means, and I still didn't have enough control over my spirit sight to click it on at will, but I might have more power in my dreams, and Nemo had told me dreams were the crossroads between this life and the next.

So I set out each night in my sleep to find master Nemo.

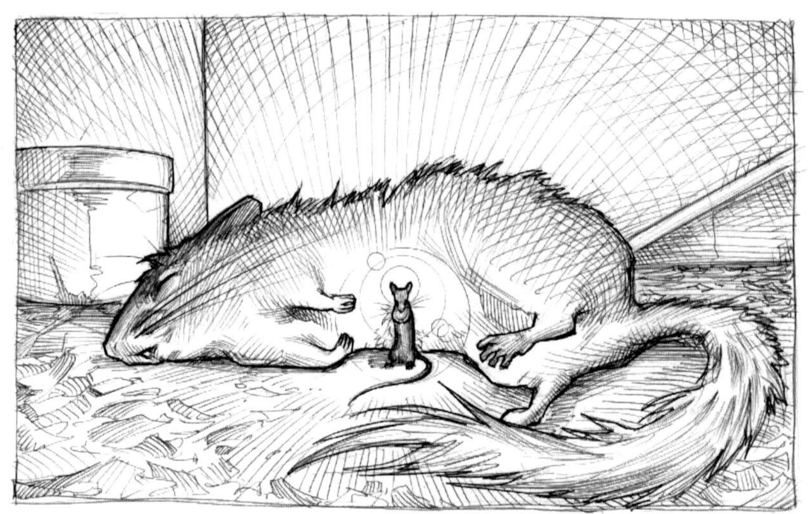

Squibble's Journey Into the Underworld

✠

At first I could not even remind myself I was dreaming. I kept having those weird, stupid dreams about death and suffering and all the awful things I kept seeing in our future (everyone dying of starvation, for example). But my chi gung seemed to stabilize me, and I would drift off to sleep with my mind focused on only one thing: to remember I was dreaming. Nemo said that was the beginning of lucid dreams, which were the beginning of the power to leave one's body for real.

I got it on my fourth try. I was dreaming of my poor mother when all of a sudden I realized she was dead. Then I realized I was dreaming. (Ears perked—heard something!) My momma in the dream then smiled sweetly at me, told me she was proud of me, and faded away. All around me was mist and darkness. I counted my fingers. I looked at my body. I was here, and still asleep. Groovy.

I knew that before my bad dreams had come, I could fly, levitate, move things with my mind in dreams. Nemo had told me all such powers were the mark of an advanced soul in the astral plane (dream world). Well, as stupid as I had been, I counted myself pretty advanced, yessir, and so I set out to fly over all this mist.

And I did!

It fell away below me, and I could feel wind in my fur. Stars appeared above me, and they were spectacular. I saw the moon and the city below me in the mists. I saw the ocean, and the moon's silver path across it. I banked and went the other direction, not wanting to die just yet, and headed for the mountains. It had always been much too far for any mouse to travel, though some knights had tried on their pilgrimages, and I had always wanted to see them. Now, I reached them in minutes. The snows were gone, leaving the forests bare and the high rock's peaks exposed. I landed on the very top of the highest peak, and looked out over the world. Normally, I knew, it would be cold up here, even in late summer, but in the dream I wanted it to be pleasantly cool, and so it was.

I spent a few minutes gawking at the glory of it all, forgetting everything my waking life had piled on me. It was beautiful. I felt free and happy. Then I remembered I was dreaming again, and snapped out of it (almost woke up in fact, but forced myself back into the dream). I wasn't here to sightsee.

"Mike, Bigfat," I called out to the heavens, "We need your help! The safe house is starving, the human is missing, and I'm a dummy. Please help me find Nemo. We need him now more than ever!"

Without a pause, a cave formed in the cliff side of the gray rock. It was an ominous cave. It *felt* ominous. And furthermore, I knew Nemo was down there. I don't have any rationale or reason to explain it, but I'd learned to trust my gut instincts the hard way. I just knew.

"You're kidding," I said out loud.

"Nah," came a voice behind me.

I turned and saw Bigfat! Glowing, sparkling, radiant-with-his-golden-aura Bigfat! I was so happy. I was only that happy once before—when my master had gotten his beloved name.

"Bigfat!" I cried. "Oh, everything's gonna be okay now! You gotta help us!"

"Help is on the way, kid. And it's you," he said, grinning.

"What!" I exclaimed. "No... no nonono. Not me. You and Mike gotta help everyone in the safe house!"

"You, kid," he insisted. "You wanna help Nemo? He's down there. Go get him."

I looked into the evil cave.

"Ummm... Nah, I'll pass," I said. "You bring him here, 'k?"

"Not how it works," he shook his huge head. "You gotta go get him."

I snaffed, displeased. "Where is that anyway?"

"The Underworld!" he said ominously. Lots of ominous 'round here.

"Oh. Okay. Definitely not going in there. You go."

"Not my job, kid."

"Oh, yes it is!" I claimed. "You're the Mousegod!"

He sighed and put his face in his paws. Then he straightened up, thrust his big chest (belly!) out at me, and boomed in an echoing, thunderous voice, **"Then I command you to go, mouse! Go and find your friend, I say unto thee! Thus speaks the Mousegod!"** And he pointed down the tunnel. He seemed a thousand feet tall. I was agape in awe and fear. I ran lickety-split down the tunnel, mouse instinct taking over and fleeing to the one dark place with cover. Only once inside did I realize I had been duped. Darn that Bigfat! The Mousegod has a weird sense of humor.

And, of course, once inside, there was no way out.

So let me tell you this story. It isn't original. It's about this guy, Orpheus. The humans named a reeelly expensive pair or headphones after the guy, but besides that he was a Greek hero, kinda. My master told me about the Greek myths 'cause he really loved reading them. This one isn't happy. (What a surprise, huh?) It goes like this:

This Orpheus guy loves this chick. Real love an' all that. They get married, and I think at their wedding this other guy named Pan (not Peter), tries to get the chick to sleep with him. Well, she says no, of course, and so he curses her, and she gets bit by a snake (snakes… why did it have to be snakes?) and dies.

Bummer for Orpheus on his wedding day, so he freaks out and goes into the underworld to get her back, even though everyone tells him not to. The rules are, only heroes can enter the underworld, but only great heroes come out again! Basically, no one ever comes back. But in he went, on account of he wasn't thinking straight probably.

So down he goes, until he comes face to face with Hades, the lord of the underworld (kinda like Greek Satan), and he goes, "Hey dude, gimme back my wife." And Hades goes, "Oh yeah? How bad you want her?" And Orpheus says, "Bad. Gimme." So Hades says, "Okay, but here's how it works. You turn around right now, and walk out of here—all ten thousand miles of it (uphill), and never once look back. She'll be behind you after you exit my domain, but if you look back even once to check, she's mine forever."

Well, it's not like the guy had a choice, but he agrees. So he turns around, and marches all the way back up to the surface world. The whole way back, he doesn't hear even one sound behind him. He begins to freak out, thinking, *What if Hades lied to me? What if she's not back there at all?* (Hades was known to do this to people… he wasn't a nice man.) So, just before the exit, as it's *right in front of him* and he's about to make it, he looks back! (At that point when my master was telling the tale I let out with "NO WAYY!") And sure enough, there her spirit is, right behind him, but the Underworld swallows her up instantly and she disappears forever.

So the guy totally blows it, and if that wasn't bad enough, when he comes back into the light of the real world without his wife, a bunch of people get pissed and chop his head off! But wait, this gets better—his head doesn't die, and he lives his entire life unable to die, as just this head! (Shoulda quit while he was "ahead"… Sorry, couldn't resist!) So he's totally veed (slang for "vetoed"), and on top of it, he loses his whole body.

Greek myths are kinda like that.

And now, thanks to lazy-ass Bigfat, here I was. Right in the Underworld. Whee ha. I wished he was here so I could bite his ear like I used to. It always kept him in line. Now that he's the Mousegod, he's gotten full of himself… and that's alot of full, let me tell you.

The entrance was gone. The only way was down. I could see the stairs appear before me like phantoms. That's all the underworld is—a place of scary phantoms, illusions, and shadows. Everything tries to trick you. You're never sure of what's real. The darkness has horrible faces and makes weird noises. I remember my master saying that Orpheus had to stay on the path. If you leave the path, you're done. *Veed!*

So, cautiously descending the staircase, I did not stray one inch. On one side of the stairs it was a sheer dropoff into an endless (I was positive) chasm, and on the other side it was a cliff face, but that ended after the first oh, hundred miles or so.

There's no way to tell time or distance in a dream. There's no need to eat, and of course you're already asleep. In the underworld there's no sun, so I had only gut instinct to go by, and it told me I had traveled a *very long way*. And it had taken a very long time. Except there was no time. But if there was… Well, you get the picture.

My master had greatly under-exaggerated the scariness of the stupid place. The faces in the dark were monsters—grotesque snakes and mutated lizards, bleeding zombies of mice I knew and screaming bodies without skin. Those were the nice ones I saw. The dark noises coming from things that I couldn't see were so bad they couldn't have belonged to anything better than something straight out of H.P. Lovecraft's stories of horror. (I read one of those once… the human had it sitting around. I didn't sleep for three days.) Now those gibbering terrors were just out of reach, waiting for me to miss one step and fall from the path. I knew if that happened, that was it for ol' Squibble, asleep or not.

The shadows shifted and changed, and there was never any one reliable light source, just the dark reds and blues of that nightmare place and the dim illumination of the path.

The path went on forever. I walked ten thousand miles. I was sure of it. Then another ten thousand, and another. I passed through dark forest, and black mountains, though frigidly cold desert and empty haunted mesas. I passed by dark waters with no waves on a dead ocean, and through graveyards covered in mist. (That might have fooled a human, but the path had a very faint smell that kept me on it, even if I couldn't see it.) I was always, always going down. I descended thousands of staircases, passed under hundreds of archways into caves. Most of the time my senses told me there was no ceiling above me—that this place had no roof. I was in another dimension… a cursed dimension of damnation.

My travels in that place could fill books, but eventually I came to a flat plane that went on for many long miles. All around me the light was steady, although the shadows still flickered, and I could smell brimstone (How did I know what brimstone smelled like? I just did, O-KAY?). No faces or noises accosted me, and after becoming so used to my grim companions, I felt lonely and small. I walked in that silence forever, and my feet became heavy. Fatigue descended upon me, and I felt then as though I'd been walking the forever that I had. By the time I reached the gateway I was on the verge of collapse.

The twin mountains rose like horns, up, up and into the dark sky, to points bending over ground below. They looked as if they were a million miles tall, and maybe they were. At the very tips a huge, ancient chain stretched across the gap from one to the other. It swung back and forth ever so slowly in some dark wind that I could not feel so far beneath. Before me, between the mountains, was a giant throne. And on the throne was a giant.

Now, I'm used to things seeming big to me, okay? I'm a mouse. But this guy would have been a mountain himself to the tallest human, hundreds and hundreds of feet tall. And he was in armor—dark, engraven, ornate armor that was wrought with decay and a feeling of being older than the earth. On his head he had a great helm, through which deep, burning red eyes gazed at me. At one side he had a mighty sword that could have cleaved the safe house itself in half just by falling, and on the other side was a magnificent shield made of rusting metal that still somehow looked unbreakable. His chainmail glittered all about him under his black surcoat, though it, too, also looked rusty and decrepit at the same time.

The lord of the underworld gazed down at a tiny mouse. Hades looked down on me.

"Ummm… Hi?" I could think of nothing else to say. And I was kinda scared.

The ground shook and his armor made thundering noises as he leaned forward to peer. His burning eye slits narrowed. He removed his helm. I saw this cartoon once about Hercules where Hades had blue flaming hair, and he was kinda funny. Well, this guy had hair on fire, all right, but it wasn't funny. It was scary! Scary big giant guy on fire. I wanted out, but I knew why I had come.

"Mouse," he boomed. **"Why do you dare to disturb me?"**

"Oh…," I said meekly, "I'm sorry. Wrong address?"

He glared. I summoned spine immediately.

"I need Nemo back," I said.

"Indeed?" He said, growing by a few hundred feet. **"And how much do you desire this soul?"**

Oh… Oh, no way. But what was a mouse to do? I had come this far…

"Bad," I sighed. "Gimme."

He laughed then, the ceiling (there was one!) raining stones down from the earthquake his booming caused. He leaned down to me, looming over me, and the glow of his eyes lit me all around. The great, empty sockets of those fiery caverns burned with cold light and, like the fire on his head, shed no heat. Overwhelmed but unable to look away, I shivered in the slithering mist.

"You know what you must do," he said.

I nodded. "Yep."

"Then go, little mouse. Do not look back even one time."

So I turned, and I went.

The way back was ten times as long as the way there. All the way back the weight I had felt there at the bottom of the underworld grew on me, like this favorite story of my master's about a short guy and a ring. The weight stayed, and grew… and grew. It was all uphill. I felt hunger, then pain, then fatigue. I kept going. I'd gotten my knighthood by going on when no one else could. Hades didn't know who he was talking to back there! I wasn't any ordinary mouse… I had made it across the Fields of Fate. I was good at suffering over long miles. Good ol' Bigfat… he knew that. I was a fool to doubt him.

And, sure enough, the entire way the only thing I ever heard was my own footsteps. Not one hint that anything—or anyone—was behind me. No faces in the dark, no noises in the shadows. Nothin'. Not one scrape of a foot or sound of breathing. Not one peep.

I began to wonder if Hades had tricked me. I yearned to look back. Was Nemo really there? Was my entire epic journey for nothing? I had to look!

Ahead of me I saw the light of the night sky. I saw the real world, the exit. And more than anything I'd ever wanted, I wanted to look back!

Well, *almost* more than anything. What I really wanted most was to be a great hero.

Remembering this, I caught my head in mid-swing as it was turning to look behind me, and snapped it back forward with every ounce of my will.

"Orpheus," I said. "Thanks, man."

I stepped out into the starlight.

"HADES, LORD OF THE UNDERWORLD"

Heaven Sent

✠

"Well, that's it. The food's all gone," my master said. "Within the week, we'll be dead mice. The few remaining here will probably resort to cannibalism. It's a pathetic, sorry fate. We deserved better."

The High Council sat around him. Everyone looked sad. No one liked what he had said, mostly because it was true. I was there to speak to him. The meeting was over with another scheduled in eight hours to see if anyone had any bright ideas, and everyone shuffled away. Knights carried the king away on a platform. I could tell BJ hated that, but he couldn't walk. He might never walk again. Then my master would have to be king, and he didn't want to.

"Master?" I said.

His head hung down, depressed. “Yes, Squib?”

“Master, I had a dream,” I said quietly.

“You have them all the time,” he said. He sounded tired.

“I had a good one.”

He perked up. “Really?” He scooted in close to me. “Do tell.”

I told him about the dream with the underworld.

“Your idea of good is kinda strange, Squib, but okay, if you say that’s good, then it probably is.”

“But it means Nemo’s soul isn’t trapped anymore,” I said.

“You think it was trapped?” he asked. “By the Black Mouse?”

I nodded rapidly. “Yeah.”

“Well, if that was so, and you freed him, that’s very good. How sure are you that this wasn’t just a… a dream?”

I shook my head vehemently. “No, no… it was all real-like and I saw everything in perfect focus. I knew I was dreaming the entire time. In the other dreams—the bad ones—I never know I’m dreaming. That’s what makes them so scary.”

“But Nemo’s still in a coma,” my master said.

“Yeah,” I said, looking back at the room. “I don’t know why. He shoulda woke up.”

He put his paw on me reassuringly. “Keep up the good work, Squib. I knew you’d come up with something to help. You’re gonna have to be my muse now that your momma’s gone.”

“Muse?” I asked, cocking my head.

“Yeah, my inspiration. Every genius has a muse, an angel that inspires them to do their holy work. It’s Greek,” he said, smiling.

“Like Orpheus!” I chirped.

“Yes, you remember. Like Orpheus.”

“Poor guy,” I said. “I owe that dude.”

My master made a confused face, but he was used to my weirdness. He chuckled.

“I can’t be your muse, Master. You’re mine!” I exclaimed.

“We can be each other’s, okay?” he said. “I need one now.”

“I’m not a very good one,” I said, looking down. He grabbed my hairy chin and snapped my head back up to look at him. His tail rattled.

“You don’t think like that!” he said. “You’re a knight, Squibble, a Mouse Knight. You’re worth a billion dollars, a thousand lives, ten tons of millet. You’re unique, and there isn’t another Squibble in the whole world. I cannot replace you. You’re my best friend.”

My eyes watered. Love for my wonderful master welled up inside me, covering all the pain, confusion, and garbage that stopped me from remembering what he said was true.

"Thank you, Master," I whispered.

He let go of my chin. "Don't you forget it, Sir," he said, and snaffed for emphasis. I grinned. "Besides, the word "muse"—notice how mouselike it is. In Greek it's *mousa*."

"No way!" I said, perking my ears in the "heard something" fashion.

"Way," he went on, "And the word "mouse" itself came from *mus*, which is "muse" without the "e" at the end. So there. You've got the job, buddy."

"He he he… Buddy!" I echoed. We giggled together.

And the doorbell rang.

Suddenly my master was all business.

"DOOR!" he bellowed. Mice erupted from everywhere, running for the door. We had practiced for this. Our chance to get help, even if it meant exposing us.

Everyone ran for the front door. Barreling out the mouse entrance, we found the door guard squashed flat, armor and all, squished like a grape. It was disgusting. The next thing we saw was the delivery guy from the post office walking back toward his car. He probably didn't ever know he had killed the door guard, who was supposed to perform crazy antics to hold his attention long enough for us to get there and give him a message asking for help. The door guard had been a faithful knight. Now he was gone, and his death had been a horrible one under the shoe of an unsuspecting human.

For some reason, One-Ear was in our group. He had a weapon in hand. He smiled at me and waved. I guess he was trying to redeem himself by participating in a dangerous mission. Good way to do it.

Mice riding on rats jumped the stairs and pursued the postman, but he was already getting in his car. From all around us the enemy popped up—hundreds of them. We were too far from the stairs and not far enough to the postman. His car started.

"Retreat!" my master yelled. "To arms!"

I spun to see a gopher snake coiling to strike at me. Insane zombie mice were everywhere. I was pulling my slingshot but wasn't going to get a chance to use it. My master had his back to me. There were about fifty of us, surrounded by hundreds of them—and they had snakes.

The gopher snake struck as I was reaching for a BB in my pocket to load my trusty slingshot. I wasn't going to make it. I wasn't wearing armor. It was my end, and as it happened, I thought to myself, *This kinda sucks.*

Then something spinning in left circles caught me and whisked me out of the snake's path. At the same time, Artemis and Aphrodite, the rat daughters of Michael, zoomed by and grabbed my master and several other mice. The snake hit no one, and we beat a hasty retreat back to the door, fighting every step of the way.

The fight was bitter. We lost ten mice and twenty more were wounded. The enemy had been waiting for us to come out just like that. When we got to the door, we saw something that made our adrenaline shoot through our systems like lightning.

Against the door was a huge package—a fifty pound bag of mouse food—the good stuff. It was leaning against the door with our address on it. My dream flashed into my head—the first one I had written down, with Magnificent Man and the dark man. Mike had sent this food to us. He had known we'd need it!

The enemy knew it, too!

I turned to look at my master, desperate. He was already looking at me with the same expression on his face.

"Stand your ground!" he cried. "Hail the house!" he shrieked through the door. "Send everything we've got! Send it all! We have to hold the porch! Send *everyone*!"

From inside I head BJ bellow commands. Archers from the roof began pelting the enemy with arrows and stones. Soldiers blasted out the mouse entrance while the rats ran back inside to get the door open.

The enemy assaulted us with fearless fury. They threw themselves upon our blades, hoping to overwhelm us by sheer numbers and weight. It would have worked, but for my master's genius. He ordered shield mice to the front, pikes behind those, and swords to the flanks. Archers behind us all, over the enemy beyond the porch, and to each side as well. The enemy fell in huge numbers. As I fired and fired my slingshot I looked for the Black Mouse. I was saving my last BB for him.

He didn't show, and soon I was out of ammo. Scratchy handed me a sword (if it hadn't been for that little midget, I'd have had no weapon at all then, plus I'd be dead), and took my side for the fight. We advanced when my master said forward, and stepped back when he said fall back. We held the line for minutes while the amazing rats worked the door and finally got it open.

The giant bag of food fell into the house, narrowly missing rodents as it crashed to the ground. The enemy, seeing the great portal open at last, redoubled their efforts and began to die in great numbers. Unfortunately, so were we, and starved as we were, we were no match for them. Our side was tiring quickly for lack of sustenance, while they needed none. We were losing mice right and left. The front line of Knights were taking terrible beatings. I heard the constant snap of plastic swords and the cracking of armor. Fur and teeth were everywhere. I slapped a rabid mouse off Scratchy's hide and lunged, running another one through. Moving as fast as I possibly could, I would only hold out another minute. My master was visibly slowing. We'd never get that bag of food into the house, and now it was blocking the door. Hundreds of rodents pushed and shoved at it, but there was no way. Laying flat like it was, no amount of rodents would ever be able to budge it. Game over.

Use the force, Squibble, came a voice in my head. My ears went straight up as if a huge exclamation point just appeared over my head.

I slashed at another zombie. "Whozzat!" I demanded. My master spared me a confused glance before returning to his dirty work.

Squibble, do you trust me now? the voice said. It sounded familiar. It sounded like Nemo.

"Yeah. Okay," I said, cutting over and over.

Relax, the voice instructed.

"Umm… no thanks," I said. "Busy killing horrible zombies."

You have to if you want that food, Squibble.

"Oh, pee on that!" I exclaimed.

"Are you hit?" my master yelled over the battle din.

"No, Master, just insane," I cried back.

"Okay," he said, and cut the legs out from under a zombie chewing on his armor.

Do it, Squibble. Relax completely, the voice said.

"Even relaxed I don't have enough power to move that bag," I told it.

I do, came the reply.

I looked down at Scratchy. He looked up.

"Boy, can you defend us both for a short time?" I asked.

He nodded his head so fast it was a blur.

I handed him my sword and went limp.

And the next thing I remember, we were inside, and the door was closed. Everyone was looking at me as if I'd grown a second head.

"Eh?" I mumbled.

"Squibble," my master said. "That was *amazing…*" The look on his face was strange. Other mice were hauling bodies and wounded to the back of the house. But the knights—the vanguard of our defense—sat there staring at me as if I were on fire. Not one of them blinked.

I felt fuzzy. (In the head, not the fur, okay?) I sat up, not realizing I had been lying down, and rubbed my head. "Wha… happened?" I said.

"You mean you don't know? You don't remember?" my master asked.

I shook my head. I saw mice carrying Scratchy's body off on a palette of cardboard. Right next to him on another palette was the crushed body of the door guard. Panicking, I leapt up and raced over. His eyes were open, though he was covered in blood. His armor was in tatters. Shards of broken swords lay all about him. And he still had the presence of mind to wink at me and hold a finger up like a thumb. He grinned. I smiled back.

"Well done, Squire!" I chirped.

He squiggled in delight and then chirped in pain. I put my paw on his head as they took him away.

"He'll live," said a medic mouse. Yeah. We have medic mice. "He's going to be a long time healing though."

I waved goodbye to my faithful squire, and turned finally to see everyone still staring at me as if I had ten tails.

"What!" I yelled, holding up my arms. (That was a mistake—they were as sore as could be.)

My master limped up to me. He was pretty bad off, too. He'd taken a beating out there. Everyone had.

He squinted at me for a time, laying a hand on me like he always did. Finally, he said, "Squib, *you floated the bag inside*. And then you shut the door."

(Heard something!)

"Nah," I said, not believing it. I had kinda thought the voice in my head really was insanity.

My master pointed toward the bag. It lay five feet inside the doorway. No rodents could have moved it so far. And the door was indeed shut. The rats were locking it while staring down at me in awe.

"It was Nemo," I said. "He did it."

My master smiled. "Whatever."

"Really! It was Nemo!"

"Okay, Squib," he said, smiling.

I leaned close. "Master, you have to tell them it was Nemo! They already think I'm a loon!"

He shrugged, turned around and held up his sword. "It was Nemo that performed the miracle!" he shouted.

The mice cheered and hopped about. The rats bruxed their teeth. But BJ and the vanguard Knights just stared at me with the hard eye.

"Doesn't matter," my master said, grinning. "They saw you point your paw at the bag all Jedi-like, and it moved. Not a little bit, Squib. It rose three feet off the ground and floated inside as the door slammed behind us. No one is going to forget that."

"Yeah," I said, "but look how happy they are that it was Nemo and not crazy Squibble."

"Pay it no mind," he said. "You *and* Nemo saved us."

"Yeah," I said, but I was unhappy about it.

That unhappiness faded minutes later when the bag was opened. My master and BJ had all the mice organized into ranks and rows. Even so, there was almost a mad dash for the food when the smell of it hit everyone. Fresh food pellets, millions of them—fifty pounds worth. It spilled out in a small pile onto the floor next to where the rat girls Artemis and Aphrodite had chewed a small hole. The remaining Mouse Knights, who numbered twelve, guarded the food pile without even looking at it, faithful to the kingdom.

"This won't last us forever," my master said to the crowd. "A much shorter time that you think," he went on. "We will still ration it out." Sighs of disappointment and snaffs of anger rose from the crowd. "But our deaths have been put off for now, so be grateful for this chance to think… and eat!"

Mice were handed four pellets each, and soon, everyone was eating. My master made me eat one of mine, but the rest I gave to Favorite and my daughter. My daughter tried not to take the one I gave her, but I commanded her to and she had to do it. He he he. Rank is good for something.

There was no return address on the bag. It had come with an apology by the post office for being lost in the mail so long. So. The Black Mouse had tried even against this sneaky move to foil us. My master and I exchanged telepathic glances. Our enemy was uber-nasty. Really, really bad. Smart, devious, and probably had powers like Nemo. We were in deep trouble.

Over the next hour the sun came up all the way and all the mice went to sleep, fed and happier. But that single feeding had put a noticeable dent in our new food supply. My master was right. We wouldn't last long even with Michael's amazing gift. It was just giving us a small respite. Maybe that was all we needed.

I went back to my hovel in the corner, underneath the human's desk, and did my moving chi gung. Then I went to Nemo's cage and stared at him for a moment. His body was withering away. I could see every rib he had through his fur. Gingerly I sat down against him and did my sitting chi gung for hours until the sun went down and the house came awake, and I fell asleep.

Lessons from the Astral Plane

✠

There on the other side of sleep, Nemo was waiting for me. It was a wide, open field at night, full of glorious golden wheat and plants everywhere that a mouse could eat with delight. He sat among some strawberries, looking fit and healthy as he had before he'd been attacked. He had some Cheerios.

I hopped up beside him and looked at the Cheerios with great desire. Looking up, I saw him smile.

"Have some, they're the next best thing to real ones," he said.

I ate one. It tasted real enough. Fine by me!

"This is the astral plane," Nemo said. "This is where I live now while my body heals… *if* it heals."

I stopped in mid munch and glanced at him.

"I might not," he said to me. "I was born with an immune deficiency problem, Squibble. All sapphire chinchillas have it."

"What's that mean?" I asked around chewing.

"It means my body is weaker than most," he said. "It cannot fight off germs or disease as well as others. Like the poison the Black Mouse used against me through my girlfriend."

"You were poisoned?" I gasped.

"As well as mortally wounded… in the head," he said.

"We have to tell my master!" I exclaimed. "He'll quest for the cure—he'll… he'll know how to fix it."

"It cannot be fixed," Nemo told me. He munched a Cheerio, as if nothing was wrong. "It will have to heal on its own, or not."

"Howcome you never told us you have eyemoon fissency?" I asked.

"Heh heh heh," he chuckled. "I don't know it… on the other side. Not yet. By the time they find out, it will be too late."

My jaw hung slack. "But… but why don't you know it? Couldn't you know it if you wanted to?" I said.

"Yes, if I chose to," he said.

"What's up with that!" I chirped. "And just like… just like what was up with sending us out into the heat and the stupid field when you knew it was a trap! All you had to say was, 'Hey, guys, do this or that, and let's avoid the trap'! For that matter, why don't you just tell us where the Black Mouse is and zot him with an eyebeam or something?!"

Nemo chuckled again, like Buddha (kinda like Bigfat, too, come to think of it).

"Because then things would have happened differently, Squibble. And as it is, things happened just perfectly."

"What?!" I exclaimed, furious. I threw my Cheerio to the ground. "Not even! My momma had to suffocate? My master has to wheeze all the time? All those mice had to die—and starve! No *way*!"

"Yeah," he said. "Way."

"NO!" I yelled. It echoed across the sunset sky of the dream field.

"Yep," he said, calm as could be.

How infuriated I was. Infuriated mouse! I stomped around.

"You wanna see?" he said.

"What!" I zipped over to him. "Yeah, lemme see!"

"You have to learn how, Squibble."

"Okayteachmenow!"

"It carries a huge weight, small mouse," he looked serious at me. He put the power on me. I could feel the weight of his warning. It slid right off my naivete shields.

"Yeah, okay already. Let's do it." I said.

He sighed. "Didn't Mike's warnings make an impression on you?"

(Heard something!)

"What? How'd you know about that?" I said.

"There are massive powers at work, here, Squibble. Listen to me. If you want my training, we have to skip all the small stuff now. We don't have time any longer. We have to dive right into the big stuff, the real power. And right away. I don't even have time to burrow through your thick skull to really make you believe my warning. What I am offering to teach you is how to use your prescience."

"Whazzat!" I said.

"The power to see all the futures," Nemo said. "And choose one. Many times."

"Cooool!" I said.

"No!" he snapped. I jumped back. "Not cool. *Hard.* Hard, dangerous, and heavy on your soul more than anything you could ever imagine." He softened and leaned toward me, tilting his head and making a compassionate face. "You will wish I hadn't taught it to you, my dear mouse."

In a hard-earned flicker of wisdom, I asked, "Then why do you want to teach it to me?"

He pursed his lips and said, "Because you must know it to bring about the great plan."

"Ohhh," I pretended to know what he was talking about, then turned to him and frowned. "What great plan is that?"

"The one you haven't come up with yet. The one to save all rodentkind."

"Ohhh… that one. Yeah, I had kinda thought I already did that by warning the safe house."

"That wasn't even the tip of the iceberg, mouse," he said.

"And… you can see all this?" I said.

"Yes."

"In… the future."

"Yep."

"And you're sure this is what I gotta do?"

He nodded. "Uh-huh."

I sat down and pushed the Cheerio pile aside. "That kinda sounds sucky."

"Parts of it will be," he said. "But what have you wanted more than anything in the whole world, Squibble?"

"Well," I looked at my tail. "I used to want to be a great hero, but now I'm not so sure."

"Don't give up your dream. It is noble and good."

"It costs too much, seems to me," I said.

"Is that so?" he asked. "Did you expect it to be free and easy?"

"Well… yeah." I admitted.

"Why?" he asked.

"Because it always is in the stories. The heroes always seem to get everything in the end," I said.

"What stories are these?" he asked, genuinely puzzled.

"Teevee," I said.

He frowned, nodding. "Squibble, TV is programming made for stupid people. It brainwashes you. It makes you dumb."

"Hey… don't hack on my TV!" I argued.

"But I shall!" he proclaimed. He stood up and gestured at the air around him. "Real stories, Squibble, are full of conflict and strife, like life. TV would have you believe that if you just lie down and don't think, that everything will be well for you. All will be provided by others, it claims, and all the while you grow lazy… and stupid."

"Who makes TV that way?" I asked. "It sounds like a giant plot."

"It sort of is," Nemo said. "A plot to get humans to spend money, be content with their lot, and sleep in their souls so they cannot see what is really happening around them. It is a plot by evil in the world. Not one being, but many, affecting many. On such a huge scale that no one can really see it."

"And they call me crazy," I said. "There are good shows on TV! Like… like… *Star Trek*!"

"Yes, you are right, Squibble. Nothing is black and white. There are some good uses for TV, like education, and that show you mentioned is pretty cool. But 99% of TV is not good for you, not good for anyone. It is a way the masters of the world use to control the masses."

"This FBI guy on TV would agree with you," I said. "He's all about conspiracy theory, too."

"I know the show," he said. "But I am telling you the truth. The sooner you give up TV, the better. Read real stories instead. Like your master does."

Ouch. Touché. I turned away, sulking.

"Do you wish to begin learning what I have to teach you, Squib? It won't be easy. We'll have to go very, very fast," he said.

Boy, that crafty chinchilla knows just what to say to this mouse. He said fast. I like fast.

"Yeah, okay. Sounds like there's no way around it, anyway."

"Oh, but there is."

"Yeah?"

"Everyone dies," he said. "Not some. All."

"Oh…" I made a stupid face, sticking my already huge two front teeth out. "Okay, duhhh, I guess I'll just let that happen then… huhhhh…"

"The training will be hard," he said. "I have never had so little time to train someone in so much."

"Yeah, bring it on, fuzzball."

"You will have to practice all the time."

"I ain't givin' up my chi gung," I said, whirling around face him.

"You won't have to—that's a very integral part to all of it, in fact."

"Good! More good news, please."

He grinned. "You'll be a mighty, powerful, and respected hero by the end."

"I better!" I chirped, pointing at him. "'Cause so far, things look pretty bad. Bad deal so far."

His face fell into seriousness once more.

"They're going to get worse, Squibble." His eyebrows fell over his blue eyes until he looked sad. "Much worse."

The Hermit Squibble

✠

I took to spending all my time in my box, doing chi gung, recording my thoughts and drawing my ideas, or sleeping. Mostly sleeping.

It would be impossible to share everything Nemo began to teach me. He went too fast for me to even comprehend most of what he said. His words were way over my head. The concepts and theories he was spouting out in the dream realm were intense. He would show me they worked, and I was impressed all to heck, but I couldn't remember much of it once I'd woken up. He said I didn't have to. He told me that the astral self and the physical self were different beings. In a waking, lucid dream we are who we were meant to be, he said. We had much more power than we ever could while awake. In dreams, we could do anything we believed we could do, with few limitations.

He had me believing it by the time I could float on nothing. He told me that in real life he might have been able to move the bag of food, but it would have cost him everything to do it. Through me, with my youth and strong chi, it was easy. I was just a channel for his astral power. Just as I barely got that idea. He got alot deeper, really quick.

The short of it was, my astral self would understand and remember the lessons, and my waking self didn't have to. Which was fine, because my waking self was having trouble with that.

I would stop him and ask many questions, which never annoyed him. His answers didn't always jive with me very well, but he always answered.

I asked him if I could use my powers to see where the Black Mouse was. He said yes, but then what would I do? I said, "Gank him, of course!" And he nodded. Of course, he said. And that would get me killed. The Black Mouse, he said, already knew how to use his powers. Far better even than Nemo himself did.

Okay. *That* was scary to hear.

"Howcome then he doesn't just smite us?" I asked.

"Who's to say he won't?" Nemo replied.

Every darn time I think he can't get any scarier…

He gave me things to practice while I was awake. Every day, I had homework. Sometimes they were strange things. Draw this feeling or that thought. Write down what I thought about this or that. Those were easy ones. Once a day I had hard work, too. New and difficult chi gung moves, or intense concentration exercises that made my head hurt. And he always encouraged me to try to produce powers (like super powers!)—moving objects with my mind, reading the thoughts of other rodents, seeing the futures, or being able to make things hot and cold… all kinds of weird stuff. He gave me a list of these powers a mile long. He said they were called Siddhas or something like that. He said they were proof of progress, but I didn't see any powers pop out of my head or hands. I had no real proof in the waking world that my dreams were real. Not since the bag incident, which *I* didn't even see.

Scratchy recovered slowly. I spent a few minutes each day doing chi gung near him, which delighted the runt. He would watch me in glee while I went through my advanced movements (he was learning them, too, as I later found out—the freak has a darn good memory!). Afterwards, I would go put some chi into him, like I did with Nemo during the sitting part. He always gave me an adoring look after that, which bothered me for some reason, and I would go away. He seemed to heal in no time. Maybe it was the chi. Maybe not.

I practiced this waking and sleeping routine of Nemo's for weeks. I dreamed during the night, and was awake in the day, and saw almost no one. It was a different world in the day. The house was empty and quiet. It was peaceful. My master told me rodents talked about me behind my back, saying all kinds of weird things. Nothing like what One-Ear had said, but they were pretty spooked about me. I was just the weirdest thing that ever hit the earth to them. Well, then I didn't mind not seeing them often, I told my master. I was getting used to being alone, which I found kinda sad and ironic.

It occurred to me that as long as Nemo didn't die while his body was in a coma, our arrangement was quite sneaky. Sneaky like a mouse. The enemy might have no clue I was learning so much, being able to see only that Nemo was still unmoving and I slept often. My master agreed. Nemo was tricky, because he had to be.

During that time, Branch wrote again. I took the letter into my dreams (just thought of it, and there it was) and showed it to Nemo. He asked me to write back to Branch, and when I was done, he had a note to add to it. So I wrote back a long letter, explaining everything that was happening around the safe house. I told him his chi gung rocked. I drew a picture of him and me beating the snot out of the Black Mouse. Then I told Nemo I was going to mail it out. He asked me to add this:

> *Branch: From Nemo:*
> *The time has come but we need it more than you do. Do it when you get this, and let it rip. –Nemo*

"It will be months before that letter reaches him," Nemo said.

"*If* it ever reaches him, you mean," I said.

"The monks will deliver it to him," Nemo told me.

"What, the monks like mice? The monks can read English? The monks know Branch's *name*? You're dreaming!" I exclaimed.

"All true," Nemo said with a straight face.

"Oh, no way," I moaned.

"All true," he insisted. "Furthermore, do you think you're the only one I'm training? I see Branch at least once a week."

I was amazed once again. "But… but you said the range of astral spirits was very limited—"

"To those who are inexperienced, yes," he smirked. I snaffed.

"So this monk is gonna deliver this letter to Branch, an' he knows where Branch's… hole in the wall, or nest or whatever is?" I asked.

"They treat animals very well over there," Nemo said. "They especially like mice and rats. I wouldn't be surprised if Branch lives better than the monks do." He paused. "Although the mail system there is much worse than here, and our adversary has already proven he can delay mail."

"Branch gave away our… our secret?" I said, amazed.

"It's no secret to those monks," said Nemo. "They would know at first glance anyway, and they aren't about to share their knowledge with a world who would kill their little friends for it."

That stopped me and made me think. That's what the world would do. The scared apes would kill all the smart mice. They'd never own up to their mistakes, never be able to admit their crimes and apologize. They'd just do what they've always done and try to eliminate the evidence of their disgusting behavior. Ugly. I decided to change the subject.

"Your body ain't doing too well, dude," I told him. "You comin' back or what?"

"That is not up to me," he said.

"Oh yeah? Who's it up to? Bigfat?"

"Sort of," he mused. "It's more up to fate… and you."

"Me?" I started.

"Yeah," he said, imitating my voice when I say 'yeah,' which is often. Yeah.

I frowned. "Hmmmm." I wasn't going to dignify his cryptic mystery further. He loved being mysterious an' all that. He liked it even more when people didn't understand him right then, but got it later, like I often did.

So he trained me that evening in telepathy, which was super easy in the dream world, and super hard in the waking one. I kept trying to project "You bother me" into Scratchy's head, but he never gets it. When I told Nemo that I had managed to clean up my act with the runt, he said, "Yes, on the outside, but he still bothers you."

"Of course he does!" I said.

"Why?" he asked.

"Ummm… umm… Because."

"That, and 'I don't know,' 'maybe,' and 'but' aren't acceptable answers here anymore," he told me for the twentieth time.

"So what do I do if I really *don't* know then?" I said, exasperated.

"You *find out*," he said.

"Oh, yeah."

"So, why does he bother you?" Nemo said.

"What, like… find out *right now*?" I asked, amazed.

"No better time. Time is like food right now, Squibble."

"You mean running out."

"Ah, you aren't as stupid as you pretend."

"Of course not…" but then I realized he had gotten me to admit I acted stupid. GRRRR!! That chinchilla was wayyy too smart.

"So now you owe me two answers," he said.

"Yeah, yeah yeah," I grumbled. "Okay, Scratchy bothers me because he's clingy and stubborn, an'… an'…"

"And just like you," Nemo said.

"Well, if you knew the stupid answer, why did you ask me?!"

"You have to find stuff out for yourself, being set to do things the hard way as you are," he said.

"Oh yeah?"

"Yeah."

"Hard way, huh?"

"Yeah."

"So why do I act stupid then, smarty?" I asked.

"So you'll seem so cool when you act normal."

"Oh! Ohhh… you… why you… GrrrrRR… Why I oughtta…"

"If you think you can take me on this plane you've got some astral bruises coming," Nemo told me. "I'm a hundred times faster here than I was back there." He smirked.

Stupid chinchilla. I imitated him with a twisted face and danced around all smug, hopping to make it known that I was unhappy about it. He laughed. All I'd done was amuse him. I couldn't win.

When the evening came to an end, I woke up to the light of dawn, a strange, pariah mouse in his own house. I put Nemo's note at the end of my letter to Branch, wrote his name and address on the front, put our return address, and put a whole bunch of stamps on the envelope with the help of Artemis and Aphrodite, who gingerly took the letter all the way to the mailbox outside, at the end of the driveway, with a score of guards. They were not accosted at all. Maybe the enemy had gone away. Yeah. And maybe pigs fly. But the next day, the letter was picked up by the mousesquasher postman guy, or at least the rats said the little red flag was down instead of up. So the letter was on its way.

Many council meetings later, all the sharp minds of the safe house, including mine, had come up with only a few ideas.

One, we could get to the city and get help. I knew Heide would help us, but telling them about Heide would mean telling people how badly I'd compromised our secret and almost exposed everyone by being caught in a lab. No thanks. Still, if we could get to the city, we might find out what happened to the Kind Human. Maybe. However, reaching the city was almost an impossibility. Many knights would volunteer, but they'd die. It would be a waste of life.

The second idea—much more plausible—was to enlist help from the field mice. That would mean going out to find them (good luck) and surviving the expedition, for certainly the enemy would be on us then. I guess maybe the enemy didn't consider mail a threat, and, of course, it wasn't (until later). I thought about whether or not it could be used that way, but couldn't come up with anything. Anyone who got a letter saying, "Help us... Starving, trapped by demons... —The mice" would just laugh. I only knew of one address that would work, and I had left that back with Shiva. Oh, I had blown it bad. I should have asked Heide to stay when she dropped me off. I should have kept her address.

Another idea that was posed was to gather what forces we had and take the offensive, but even if my master and the High Council went for that idea (and they most certainly would not), that would mean leaving the women and children unprotected. Not to mention the house itself. Now that the human was gone, this house was all we had. It was ours, and we had to defend it. Leaving our only defense to traipse out into a world where the weather itself would likely kill us, much less the enemy or predators, was just plain stupid. Of course, that was just what I'd done recently. *Sigh.*

So in the end, we decided our best course of action was to hold out for the end of the drought, cooler weather, and see if anything good came our way. Hold out until the dice fell in our favor, which Nemo seemed to think would eventually happen. I carried his messages to the High Council and back each day. I was a messenger boy. That was okay. Each night I took a list to Nemo and used my mind powers to memorize what he told me to tell the council. On waking, I wrote it all down and went straight to the meeting.

BJ and my master estimated we could hold out another few weeks with the food Mike had sent us. It was really wholesome food, and while everyone was hungry, no one was dying anymore. By the middle of fall we had lost a third of our number. Almost 300 mice. BJ and my master set all able bodied mice, including females, to training. It wasn't intense training that would use up alot of calories, but they trained anyway. We tried to find weapons for everyone, and in the end had to improvise. We were out of plastic cocktail swords. We started using toothpicks, popsicle sticks shaved down, and if it came to it, the good old standard was what we'd fall back on—teeth.

I spent some time each day with Favorite. She'd try to groom me sometimes, but mostly she despaired of life. It was heartbreaking to see it. Her body was wasting away, sitting there in the corner. She had to drag herself by her front legs (not a mouse's strong part) just to go to the bathroom. Sometimes she couldn't make it. Squibette and I cleaned up her messes, but with no human to clean our cages, things were getting bad quick. By the time we had gone through half our food, mice were no longer living in their cages. The ammonia smell from so much urine in the house was choking us and making many mice sick. My master was faring very poorly through it, because of his scarred lungs. He had a handicap right off the bat. We ran out of his tea rapidly, and couldn't find any more in the cupboards. His breath was ragged and rasping throughout the day and night, even with the chi gung. I felt so sorry for him.

We forced the kitchen window open all the way, but none of us had the strength to undo the locks on the others. And the enemy would find their way in through the screen of the open window, so my master asked the bees to guard it at first, but zombies don't much care about bee stings, and the bees die after using their stingers. After a few rounds of that it was the rats guarding the window ledge, and they'd just kick the zombies off the ledge with polearms if they showed their faces.

So, to be grossly blunt, there we were, in the unending heat, without enough water, living in piss and dung, surrounded by a near-invincible enemy, and dying slowly but surely. I was alone and lonely most of the time, and didn't even have time to pursue my writing or art outside of Nemo's lessons. I was miserable and depressed. Everything looked bleak and doomed. Not exactly the glorious life I had expected as a Mouse Knight.

No Escape for the Mouse

✠

"I'm getting depressed," I told Nemo in the astral plane.

"I'm not surprised," he said.

"Of course you aren't," I said cynically.

"You miss your mom."

"I used to dream of her every night, before coming here to be with you," I said.

"Now that you're doing this training, Squibble, your mind gets no rest. You never really dealt with your tragic losses, the trauma of your pilgrimage, and other things… your fear of your master dying, for example," he explained. "You need something to rest with—something to take your mind off all this, or you'll wear out."

"Take my mind off the dying house, the abomination of an enemy that won't let us alone, and my master's constant wheezing? What could *possibly* do that?!" I whined, wearing a bitter face.

"A girlfriend perhaps?" Nemo said.

"Oh, *wrong* answer, wise guy. My girlfriend is crippled and despairs of life. She wants to die. She sits there waiting for someone to put her out of her misery. It's unbearable to watch, and I'm powerless to help her."

Nemo bore a sad face. "I'm sorry, Squibble. I know this is hard on you. Harder than on anyone, perhaps."

"Yeah," I said. "Not as hard as it is on Favorite."

"Matter of perspective."

"Matter of I can use my stupid legs!" I chirped. "I'm making great progress here in the dream world, big guy. None whatsoever in the world where it matters. I can do anything here in dreams, and nothing out there. Nothing at all. This is stupid. What good is it?"

"Are you sure you can't do anything out there?" he asked.

"Ummm… pretty sure," I snapped. "Last time I tried to incinerate the Black Mouse with my eyebeams nothing happened."

"You're trying big things too soon, like Branch always did. Try small things."

"I do. I try all the things you say to—levitating small objects, reading people's thoughts, all that. I can't even get to my 'special place.' Nothing's working for me at all."

"Chi gung? Spirit vision?" he asked.

"Well, my chi gung feels really good, and keeps my hunger away, and I feel… all energized-like, but I still can't turn on the damn spirit vision whenever I want to. Not at all. Maybe I'm just a reject mouse, an' no one wants to admit it."

"No," he said. "That's not the case." He floated up for mantra chants, and I floated up with him. He brought up his halo and I brought up mine. Crackling energies that flowed as golden nectar, glowing pure power, fell from the sky and filled us. We assumed our stances there in the air and the sky around us changed to rubies. "I would pursue the chi gung if it works for you, and lay aside the pressure of having to perform."

"But… the pressure is *real*," I said. "If I don't perform, we're all gonna die, or I won't do what the Mousegod wants, or something bad. It's too much pressure! I hate it!"

"Yes," Nemo said. "The pressure is real, but if you focus on that, you'll never make any progress at all. The greatest warriors of all time, like the God Shiva, went into battle like it was no big deal. Focused on winning, worrying about nothing, smiling like they were walking in the park on a nice day. Don't give your fears any power, Squibble. Until you learn to make your power obey your conscious mind, it will obey your subconscious. That can be bad. Don't help the enemy. Relax."

"Easy for you to say."

"Yes, but true nonetheless. You must not worry at all. You must treat this like a huge game, and set your mind to win it."

"I don't even know what to *do*," I complained.

"You will when it is time," he said. I coulda guessed that part, being that it was cryptic and mysterious an' all that.

"If I could see spirits, I might be able to go find Mike to get us out of this mess," I said.

"Yes, maybe, but it might very well be that this gift only functions in times of pain or trauma, Squibble. Some spiritual gifts work like that."

"That's lame," I said.

"Everything must be paid for," he said. "Never forget that. Nothing is free."

"That's not true. What about love?" I said.

"What I mean, Squibble, is that everything has a balancer. For love there is apathy (not hate), and for the Black Mouse, there is you."

"We're doomed," I said, and went into chanting.

The large bag of food lasted the three weeks that my master predicted. Then it was gone. The house was too hot. We had mice taking all the sewage out back under heavy guard and everyone was told to go to the bathroom outside or in a corner in the garage. We began starving again, this time rapidly, as we had exhausted all our alternatives.

My chi gung hit its all time high at that point. I think it had something to do with starving, I'm not sure. It felt stronger on an empty stomach. I was sitting against Nemo's body doing my sitting meditation chi gung when he suddenly woke up. Everyone made a big fuss over it, and we had to give him the rest of the food in order for him to recover. He was almost gone—just skin and bones—and he told me that my chi gung had brought him back. He also told us that he was as near to death as he could possibly get, and it had shortened his lifespan considerably. He knew now that even if he had food and clean water, he might never be as strong as he was once. He was a terrible sight. He looked like one of the zombies. But he was awake, and it improved the abysmally low morale of the house to see his return.

I guess if I had a day of fame, it might have been that day. It was not in battle, or at the head of troops, or anything glorious at all. It began with bringing Nemo back, and he told everyone I had done it with my internal power. All of a sudden mice weren't making fun of my "weird movements" anymore. All of a sudden everyone wanted to do it, but they were too weak from lack of food.

In the same very hour, BJ was brought before Nemo, who told him that he couldn't heal his leg. Nemo said he was too weak, and the leg too badly injured. BJ would never walk, or fight, again. The King's face fell into deep sadness, which I sympathized with all too closely, and he asked my master to name a new king.

That's when I stepped in. I'd had it with all this sadness and bitter disappointment crap. Just *had* it. I was sick to death of poor endings and doomed stuff. No way was BJ gonna be doomed. He'd fought through too much crap to be doomed. I asked him to delay the new king announcement an hour or so, which he agreed to, though he was wondering what I was up to. I went to Percival and Scratchy and asked them to go through a series of very advanced moves with me, and we did chi gung together. At the end of it, I asked them if they would give me their energy and showed them how. They did not hesitate at all, suspecting what I was about to do, and Percival even smiled through the whole thing. They both had more chi than most mice, having practiced for some time, and I wasn't about to ask my poor master. He needed his.

When it was done, I was glowing like a light bulb inside. I felt as though I could have run all the way to the city and back without rest. I went immediately to BJ, still breathing in the chi gung fashion, and laid my hands on his leg.

There was a sickening pop, and the King almost bit me in reflex, but I kept pouring the golden nectar of life into his leg. Nemo watched with wide eyes—as wide as everyone else's. I didn't know if I could do this… I didn't know if chi gung could actually work miracles and heal bones, but I was sick of watching everyone I loved suffer and rot away. I focused my anger into pure energy, and refused to believe that anything was impossible for one determined enough.

BJ's eyes got widest of all, and his body trembled. When I was finally finished, I didn't even feel tired. It was as if while I was doing it, more power was flowing into me from the heavens. I wasn't out of energy—I had more than I started with. I felt as if I was going to explode, and it was wonderful.

BJ got up and stood on his leg. The crowd gasped. My master came up to the table by Nemo's cage and saw what had happened. I saw him smile in pure admiration for me. BJ hopped, spun, kicked, and danced. He laughed uncontrollably.

"Sir Squibble!" he yelled. "The miracle mouse!" The crowd took it up. I was in my fifteen minutes of fame. The entire house came around Nemo's cage, saw the chinchilla awake, BJ dancing, and me smiling. Nemo grinned at me hugely.

"That's an awful lot of nothing you did there, Squibble," he said.

I was astonished. Chi gung could *do* things! It kept Nemo alive long enough for him to find his body again. It fixed BJ's leg.

Favorite.

I jumped off the table, three feet up, without using the ramp or the bed, and raced off in the direction of the dining room and my old cage. The crowd made awed noises at my supermousey leap, and went back to congratulating the King and Nemo.

But my fame, and my brief moment of light, was to end there.

When I got to the cage, it was empty. Favorite wasn't there anymore. I looked everywhere. When I came out, my master and Squibette were standing outside the cage, watching me.

"Where is she!" I demanded. "I can fix her!"

Their faces told me before their voices did. I felt a sick sinking in my center. Almost immediately, my chi began to ebb away, escaping through the hole in my heart.

"She died this morning," Squibette said, her face long and dark.

I slumped. How could this be happening? Not now. Not when I was able to heal her.

"She was trying to run on her wheel," my master said, "like she used to love doing. I think she was trying to pick up her life again. She had decided to go on living, and not give up."

"What happened?" I said. My voice sounded hollow and robotic—completely empty of emotion. Just one more stupid thing happening to us here in Hell. Apathy broke into my soul and began carrying away the little joy I had.

"She got her rear legs caught in the spokes of the wheel," he said, "and she tried to fight her way free... It fell over on her. She was stuck in the water dish the Kind Human provided for her. She drowned."

I laughed almost maniacally. She drowned. In a house with no water. It was insane. Stupid and insane. Everyone had gone through great trouble to keep her water bowl full, to provide her with food, love, and attention... and the first time she tries to come back to the world of the living... she dies in water?! Oh, that took the cake. That was just too much. Too much for ol' Squibble. Yessir.

No fair.

I slowly crawled out of the cage, knowing I would never again set foot in there. Kind of like my mother's grave which I couldn't visit. Every step up the ramp on my way was like the way out of the underworld. My steps were too heavy. My heart was beating too slowly. The world took on a dark cast all about me, and somewhere far off I heard evil laughter. But this time, as I got to the top of the ramp, there was no way out. No escape to the world of light. Instead, I walked down the other side of the ramp, and with each step, my soul fell back into the underworld. My mind shut down, all my chi but the barest spark left me. My soul collapsed. I hated everything and everyone then. I would have bitten Bigfat if he'd shown himself. Of all the unfair, stupid, cockamamie, crazy ironies. Favorite was innocent. She had done nothing wrong, and her life had been mostly hellish, ending in a gruesome death of pain and fear. I couldn't take it anymore. I just couldn't.

As I went by my master, it looked like he was going to be silent for the first time ever in a moment of my suffering, but as I was already past and descending toward the floor (and my own rock bottom), he said, "Don't give up, Squibble."

I looked back up at them. Squibette looked horrified. My master looked gravely worried.

"Her body…," I said, praying they hadn't put it with the others in the basement.

"No," he said. "Not with the others. We cannot bury her yet, but we put her in the freezer."

The freezer. Hell.

"I can't take any more," I said. "No more."

Then, bereft of my wonderful chi, my body gave out from hunger, and I fell off the ramp. I don't remember hitting bottom.

"There is more to come, Squibble," Nemo's voice said. "You must not give up yet."

I opened my eyes to the astral plane, but this time I was unaware I was dreaming. It just seemed kind of familiar. We were in the house, but it was completely empty. Golden light filtered through the windows. The house was clean. No cages, no furniture. Empty. Barren. I could feel it was cold as well. Despite the warm light flowing into the house in beautiful beams, the house was lost.

"What's happening?" I asked, unable to remember what had come before.

"You're dreaming," Nemo told me. It didn't sink in. I could not wake within the dream, and all my powers on the astral plane were useless.

"Where am I?" I said, suddenly afraid. "Where's my momma?"

Nemo looked deeply troubled and said nothing, probably realizing what was going on.

"How did you get here?" I asked him.

"Now that I have returned to my body, Squibble, I have some small access to my powers. I wanted to see these bad dreams of yours for myself."

"What are you talking about?" I said, confused and frightened. "I want my momma!" I ran all about the house, panicked like any ordinary mouse. I leapt at walls and scraped at doors, but nothing would open. It was getting very cold. The light was fading from the windows, and as the last of that saving light vanished, I felt black damnation set upon the house. I was sure I was back in Hell. And Hell was cold.

I leapt up to the counter, scraping and bruising myself to reach it, trying to follow the light over the horizon like a dear and departing friend I could not let go of. But the window prevented me, and I saw the bodies outside.

Bodies of mice and rats. Left there to rot. Human footprints littered the ground. Yellow tape plastered the outside of the house, reading "Condemned." Smashed bodies of mice lay in the deep trenches of tire tracks. There was my master, his eyes bugged out of his skull from suffocating. Stompy and Squibette, my daughter, lay side by side, run through with pencils. What was left of Shiva and Thor was scattered about the porch, detailed by burn marks from the explosion that had killed them. There were mice in mousetraps, their necks and backs crushed. There were mouse bodies that were still foaming green at the mouth from the rodent poison they had eaten, desperate for any food at all to fill their starving bellies. The bodies of my babies I had never met were being swallowed by zombie snakes—a twisted wrongness, since they had no need for food. Hundreds of mice lay flat where humans had stomped them to death. Pools of water were full of corpses from the humans washing the house out with fire hoses. My jaw hung open in horror. I clawed viscously at my eyes, never wanting to see again, knowing this vision would never leave me. I was screaming.

Nemo was beside me, gazing out over the scene with an equally terrified reaction, when I ran blindly over the counter and broke my back against the kitchen floor. Crawling on my front legs, helpless and in terrible pain, I found the way to the back of the house. And my mother's grave.

"Ooohhhhhh," I moaned, inching toward it, "Mommmmaaa... nooooo!"

I wept and moaned at her grave, realizing she was dead for the first time. The shock was too deep. I would never see her beautiful face again. Never hear her tell me I was wonderful. Never feel her gentle teeth grooming me behind the ears. Ever again.

"Nooo... No... no... nooo...," I crooned. I heard something scrape behind me, and when it didn't smell like Nemo, I turned.

The Black Mouse impaled me with its dark sword, just above the part of my guts where I couldn't feel anything. My mouth opened in gasping agony as I died. The Black Mouse laughed and laughed.

When I woke, I was gasping for air and cold. It was dark. At first I panicked, thinking I was in Hell again and there was no escape.

Percival put both hands on me, steadying my frail form. I was very thin. I weighed half of what I once did, and I had no strength. I knew that I was awake. I also knew I had had many other dreams like the one I just described, some worse. Many of them I could not remember.

"What is it!" I screamed.

"Calm!" Percival said. "Calm, Squibble. He's awake!" he yelled to others. Other mice came running. BJ, Stompy, Squibette, and my master surrounded me. Not dead. My eyes were bugged out in terror.

"Go get Nemo," my master ordered. He looked like he was on death's doorstep. They all did. Even Stompy was rail thin. She had gone from 120 grams to something no more than 30. It was freakish.

How long had I been asleep? Every bone ached. Every muscle felt as if it were frozen. Then I remembered Favorite, and my soul rolled over in its grave. I began weeping.

Nemo hopped up next to everyone. We were in his cage, and I was in a makeshift nest in a corner of it. From the look of it, I had been there some time. The heat was gone. It was cold.

Nemo's paw went to my head and the other to my chest. I felt warmth and energy trying to enter my body.

"Accept the chi," he said.

"You… you don't have any!" I argued, remembering.

"Squibble, much time has passed. I have some small amount to spend as I wish. Take it," he said.

I let myself relax, and my body drank the precious energy in. At once I was more alert and aware. My master was not in armor. It was night. I trembled with weakness.

They let me recover for a time. They gave me water to drink and food to eat. I didn't question the gifts until I remembered our predicament. I stopped eating.

"It's okay," my master said. "We found old food in the trash outside. Even some Cheerios." He didn't tell me how many died getting it. I'm not sure I wanted to know. Back to eating trash. And the horrible thing was that it tasted good. Very good.

They let me recover for a few hours before telling me what had happened. It was Nemo who explained it to me, looking haggard and exhausted from giving me too much of his badly needed energy.

I had been in a deep coma for two weeks—two years for a human.

In that time, mice were dying of starvation. No one had the strength to wear armor anymore, nor the strength to practice with weapons. Without letting up on the drought, the weather had turned to a cold bitterness. My master hoped it would slow the zombies, and it had, not having moving blood in their veins to keep them mobile. But their number had quadrupled from what everyone could tell, and now the house was utterly surrounded.

In those two weeks, I had been given the treatment Nemo had gotten to keep him alive, and now I understood with great compassion how the poor fellow had felt upon waking. It felt like I had been dead. Nothing worked right.

Scratchy had not left my side in all the time. He alone wore armor still, and bore a sword. Two, in fact, in case I should need one. He smiled at me gratefully. I was too tired to smile back.

Nemo told me that he had been with me those two weeks, riding along in my dreams. From the faces of everyone around me, he had told them the gory details of how horrible my nightmares truly were. Pity filled their faces. The last thing I desired. I wondered if life could get any worse, and stifled the thought before it could come true. Tremors shook me all the way through. I felt violated by Nemo and a stranger to the real world. I knew why he had done what he did, and I probably owed him my life, but it made me no less angry. Reality was stark and grim, and my other option was a terrifying world of pain and suffering. I was trapped, and no mouse likes that. No animal… no one can deal with that for long. Even here in reality, there was no escape.

"We had no idea," my master said. "I'm so sorry, Squibble. I'm so sorry, my friend."

I looked away, unable to bear the shame of his knowing my dreams. I wished I could vanish.

"Please, everyone, go away," I said. "Just… leave me alone."

Scratchy shook his head, but I said, "Yes, you, too. Go."

Not really knowing what else to do, everyone left. Since it was Nemo's cage, he stayed, but went over to the corner and nibbled on something rancid and disgusting.

I was alone in the dark. I wished I could summon Mike. I had some words for him right about now. I wished I could demand

Bigfat's presence, and chew him out. How could he let it come to this? Then I remembered that this was only the second horseman. There were supposed to be four. I forgot what they were.

"Plague and War," Nemo said, eating quietly.

"Get out of my head you stupid… chinchilla…," I breathed. It took some effort. "I'll… kill you."

"When you're better maybe. 'Til then, I am your only psychic defense." He looked up at me. "Your dreams are a confusing mixture of prescience, and visions from both high and low. The good is trying to help you, and the bad, trying to drive you insane."

"Hard to tell who's winning," I panted. "So this stupid crap is going to get worse then? I hardly had any *good* dreams."

Nemo came over to squat beside me. His face was grim. "I have looked into the future, Squibble. I cannot tell you all of it, but now that I know you have the same gift as me, I can tell you some. You can no longer change certain things."

"Why not!" I squeaked, and fell into a coughing fit.

He waited until I was done and said, "Because once you can see the future, you are bound by it."

"That's stupid!" I gasped. "I can do what I want!"

"And what, pray tell, will that be?" he asked.

NO hesitation: "The right thing!" I said.

He nodded. "Exactly." My eyes got wide as I understood. "You will do exactly what Squibble would do, and anything else would be unacceptable to you. You will see this through no matter the cost to yourself." Shock invaded my belly, making me feel unstable and queasy. He went on, "Now that you can see the end results of your actions, you will do… the right thing. The future is set." He went back to his eating. "And you wonder why they chose you."

I sat there in the dark, in a diabolic trap of time and my own morals. If I wished everything to turn out well in the end, I saw just a tiny fraction of the suffering we would have to endure now. I understood, in that moment, why Nemo had done some of the crazy things he had done. I understood his story much better now. And above all, I understood that my understanding had just begun.

"Tell me," I whispered.

"I will be short and simple," he said. "War is coming."

"My master will never go to war," I said. "Not against other mice. Not even dead ones. It's wrong."

"You will be the one to convince him," Nemo said, looking at me from across the dark cage. "War is wrong among humans when it's fought for petty reasons—greed, wealth, luxuries. But this war is against true evil, Squibble. Your own oath before your pilgrimage was to fight true evil, was it not?"

It had been, indeed. I remembered it well. I remembered how eager I had been. How full of life and happiness. A whole different mouse. Tears came to my eyes again, and all I could think was of how much water I was wasting. Sadness had me in an iron grip and was not about to let go. I felt I would never be happy ever again, and remembering my naive cheer of youth only made it worse.

It was almost winter. I had slept through my first birthday. Most mice never saw their second birthday. I had always looked forward to a grand, wonderful birthday party with all my friends and family. I had imagined all sorts of treats, fun, and attention. Of course, none of that was to be, and instead I had spent my "party" writhing in nightmares and pain. How very sad.

Half of my life was over. Half of my life was over.

"Before the war, the enemy will hammer us down. We will suffer, and many will die. We are only halfway through this tribulation," Nemo said with a matter-of-fact voice, like a scientist telling someone what happened when a nuclear bomb exploded. Removed and detached. I stared at him in the dark, unable to say anything. My throat felt tight. I was choking on my stupid, wasteful tears.

"Your greatest moment of hardship has yet to come," he turned to look at me. His eyes reflected eerily in the moonlight coming through the window. He looked haunted. "Your holy quest has barely begun." He turned back to his 'food." "More than that, I cannot see," he said.

"Cannot see," I said, "or won't tell?"

In response, he simply remained silent.

I knew he was right.

There was no escape.

Captain Kirk

✠

I was watching TV. The rats had managed to figure out how to turn it on, and it was welcome company. It was during the day, estranged mouse that I was, and I was the only one weird enough to be awake. I was watching a wonderful show, one of my favorites. The characters were in a terrible situation—certain doom. There was absolutely no way out, but the captain wouldn't give up. He simply refused, and he broke the rules. They all made it out of the situation by doing gnarly, unheard of stuff that no one had thought of. They won in the end, because the captain had thought outside of the box. I thought of my master.

Then my head came up and my ears went straight. (Heard something!)

I scrabbled off the bed. Nemo watched me go with one sleepy eye as I crawled across the floor into the living room. I found Stompy's hideout and woke her and my daughter up.

"What's this then?" Stompy moaned. "Bit early, Sir Squibble?"

"Hit me!" I ordered.

Her eyes opened all the way. Squibette was up in a flash. Scratchy had seen me running across the floor and came zipping up next to me, doing his little circles to the left.

"Don't do it!" Squibette told her friend. "He's sick."

"Oh, with all respect, daughter, shut up," I said. "Stompy, hit me as hard as you can."

Her face was confused and a bit frightened. "Umm… Why for?" she asked.

"I need to break the rules! Now do it!" I yelled.

Nemo came up behind me along with my master, summoned by the commotion. Stompy looked at my master, begging him to help her out of this.

He looked at Nemo. Nemo knew. He was smiling.

"Do it," Nemo said.

Stompy looked at Squibette. Squibette shrugged. Stompy's face twisted uncomfortably.

"Sir… I mean no disrespect by this—"

"I know! Now let fly. Hard," I said.

"Ummm… Where exactly…?"

"In the head!" I chirped.

Everyone winced in anticipation, and she wound up her fist. Even without all of her massive weight, this was going to hurt.

POW! I saw stars, then the floor. I staggered up, looked around, and said, "Again!"

"Oh, for crying out loud!" Stompy complained, but Nemo interrupted her.

"Do it."

POW! Floor. Stars. Gahhh. Pain.

I looked around. Fuzzy… tilting kinda, but normal.

"Again!" I commanded.

"Squibble—," my master began.

POW!

Floor. I moaned. I couldn't feel my body. I flipped myself over onto my back and saw…

Angels!

YES!

I broke out into a grin. Stompy drew back for another blow.

"Whhooa!" I said, holding up my hands. "Good enough!"

"Well, thank Mousegod for that!" She breathed.

I jumped up, tilted crazily, and my master held me up. I picked the nearest angel with wings. "You!"

He turned, surprised to be seen, much less addressed. He put a hand on his white tunic as if you say, *Me?*

"Oh yeah," I said. "You! I've got something for you to do!"

"Mortals do not command us," he said to me. "Nor do mice."

I growled and balled my fists. Time to do the Captain Kirk on his sorry ass. I stepped forward, but Nemo got in my way.

"Tell him this…," he whispered to me, and he told me glorious words of power, words so ancient that a million generations of mice would not begin to cover it. Words from ancient history, from the days of King Solomon. More powerful words he never taught me since that day.

I spoke the words to the angel. The reaction was stunning. Every angel in the room turned to me, their haloes rising around their heads. Some of them drew their swords, those that had them.

"Those words are for kings and great priests only, mouse," the angel threatened. "You may not use them."

"Yeah?" I said, all Kirk-like. "Well I just did! Now you gotta do what I say! And how do you know I'm not a king or a priest? Huh? Huh?"

The angel was silent. He looked at his comrades, always there in our house. They had nothing to say. I remembered it from the beginning. The first time I had used my gift in the safe house, there had always been angels. Playing with the animals, who could sometimes sense them. Ever since Mike died in the human's bed, there had been angels. Every time my second sight came on. Angels.

My angels now.

"What is your bidding?" the angel said.

Whooo HOO!

"Get us some food, pronto!" I said. Now mind you, the other mice could only see and hear one side of this. I looked insane.

"I knocked his marbles loose," Stompy whined.

My master shook his head. He knew what was happening. He was grinning, looking upward at what he couldn't see.

"We cannot affect the material plane like that," the angel said.

"Well, go kill the Black Mouse!" I commanded.

"We cannot. He is greater than any of us here."

"Heal the sick!" I said.

"We have been," he said. "To the best of our ability, including *you*." His tone was icy. "Why do you think the entire house did not perish in the heat?"

"Grrrr! Well then, smite the godless hordes around the house and give us a break!"

The angel smiled. He had been waiting for someone to ask him for that. "Consider it done!" He waved his hand, and the angels with swords walked through the walls, going outside to kick holy ass. They looked ready for a fight. The angel I was talking to prepared to leave.

"Not you!" I said. He stopped, bowed slightly, and looked down at me. "Bring back my momma!" I said.

"I cannot."

I hopped with fury. "*GRRR!* Why does it feel like I'm in a Chinese restaurant and nothing on the menu is available?!" I yelled. "What can you do then?!"

He grinned. "I can go get you help."

I stopped. Cocked my head. "Reeelly?" He nodded. "What kinda help? Nothing tricky now…"

He gave me a look that said, I'm an angel, stupid. I'm not going to trick you. "The Kind Human," he said.

My eyes went wide. "Go!" I ordered. And he went.

I jumped for joy. Outside, we heard the enemy squeaking like crazy and retreating as if they were normal mice running from fire. Everyone went to the windows and doors to behold the spectacle. In every direction, zombie animals fled. Some dropped dead as they should be, and the living ones, free of mind control, shook their heads and vanished in white light. The safe house was being freed, at least for some distance around it.

My master turned his amazed head to me and gaped. "Squibble! What have you done?!"

"Broken the rules, Master!" I said.

He nodded, proud. "Good boy." He hugged me. I could feel his ribs against mine. "Good boy."

Return to Disaster

✠

The Kind Human returned. He was driven up the long driveway the very next day in a car that looked familiar to no one but me. My heart leaped in my chest. The car was Heide's.

Our Kind Human dashed out of the car before it was even stopped. He was wearing a strange robe, lots of bandages, and that was about it. He got to the door, panicked, and as he turned around, Heide threw the keys at him from a bundle of his stuff.

Mice flocked out to the front of the house to greet the one human they loved so and thought they'd never again see. I remained behind, trying to sort out what had happened. How in the world did Heide know the Kind Human? What had gone on?

My master was the first to be picked up by the human, tears running down his furless face. Upon seeing the condition of his animal kingdom, the tears flowed heavier. He unlocked the door and came limping inside, with Heide behind him. He covered his mouth and squinted at the smell of death and urine. He unlocked every window and opened the place up, my master riding on his shoulder.

Heide saw me sitting on the end of the dining table and came right to me.

"Hello, Squibble," she said. Her smile was genuine, but laced with worry. "You look kinda thin."

I nodded slowly.

The animals all followed their human around and around the house. He wasn't walking right. The Kind Human had been badly hurt. The next place he went was Nemo's cage, where his moans of horror could be heard all the way in the kitchen. He came out, cradling his first pet, his son, who was now rail thin and barely alive—as we all were.

"You want to know what happened?" Heide asked me. I was looking at her as if she were a spirit. I wasn't sure she wasn't. All around me I knew angels stood guard, though I could no longer see them. I nodded slowly again. Spaced out mouse…

She sat down in a chair after checking it for rodents, and leaned on the table.

"I got this very strange package," she said. "It was a note with a request, but no explanation. There was also a check for one quarter of a million dollars." (Heard something!) I looked at her, now interested. "It was made out to me, by someone named Ruby. She gave me very explicit instructions that the money was for me, to help rodents, and that there was this man I was supposed to find. His name and address was on the note, and I remembered dropping you off here, to your Kind Human." I scooted up to her. Pausing on her arm, I crawled onto it. I was the first mouse having all this explained. By the look of our Kind Human, he was consumed in grief and guilt. He wasn't going to be talking for a while. He kept apologizing to the animals. Over and over.

"I looked for your Kind Human," she said, "but no one answered the phone, and I couldn't remember the way back here, though I tried. I looked up his work phone and they said he hadn't been in in a week. I finally tried the hospitals, and there I found him. He had been in a car accident, caused by a rabid animal he was transporting. He was in a coma."

A coma. Nemo's girlfriend. That possessed psycho. It all made sense.

"There was a huge, strange man in the room with him," she said. "Really handsome and powerful." I perked up again, seeing it coming. "His eyes were so blue, and he had long blonde, wavy hair. He told me it was my job to guard the man now. He asked me if I'd gotten the package from Ruby. I was so shocked I didn't know what to say, and that was when your Kind Human woke up."

That Mike. He's still looking out for us. There's hope.

"The first thing he did on waking and finding out how long he'd been asleep was to leave the hospital against doctor's orders. He made me drive him out here right away. The rest you know. He's got some very bad injuries. They might not heal at all."

I stared at her.

"Give me a sign, Squibble, that I'm not crazy, okay? Sometimes I still don't believe that mice can read, or understand me."

I shook my head.

"Thanks."

I nodded.

"I bought your book."

Not my *book, human.*

She showed me a copy of *The Mouse Knight* she had put in her back pocket. It was out in paperback now, eh?

"I have much more respect for you now, Sir Squibble," she said with a smile. "And it wasn't hurting to begin with."

That book was going to cause us trouble, it was.

I smiled back. One more on the very small list of people that didn't think I was a lunatic.

Heide was sent back to the city to get food immediately, and the Kind Human sat down, still apologizing, and had a "talk" with the mice he loved. He had seen the basement. He had seen the garage. I could tell it ate him up inside. He felt responsible, and although he wasn't, he kinda was. Guilt sat on him like a big, fat, black mouse, chewing on his heart strings.

I wasn't in on that conversation they had then. When the advanced mice communicate with the human it isn't fast. We had no computer at the house. The mice have to point to words in a book, or write words out on paper to get their side of it across. The human is always patient, and it takes a long time. They told him about everything he'd missed, and what we were up against. My master decided to confide in him completely, and no mouse was going to stop him apparently. I saw his forceful gestures and wild hops as he conveyed his messages to the human. He had said we needed the human on our side. From the beginning, we needed a human. Now that we had almost lost that human, I saw for the first time that he was absolutely right. Without the human, our intelligence meant almost nothing. We couldn't buy things, couldn't use cars, couldn't even pick the phone up to call for help without several of us in on it (or Stompy at full weight). We were as dependent as they come, but looking up at the human's face, I saw that he needed us, too. Without us, he was alone. We were his children. It showed on his face—his shiny, tear-streaked face. He felt he had failed us.

I guess he took all the news well, even though he looked a bit bewildered and not a little confused over some points. He never let go of Nemo, and the chinchilla who looked so mighty and wise to us now looked like a sleeping baby cradled in the arms of his loving father. The human asked alot of questions. The meeting lasted several hours.

By the time it was over it was well into the middle of the night, and Heide had returned hours ago with so much food it took her and our human many trips to bring it inside. She brought hundreds of pounds of food. She had bought trashcans to put it in—the really big ones—and the human carved a small hole in the bottom of each with his pocket knife so we would always have access to nourishment. Then he filled two more trashcans with 60 gallons of water and sealed the tops but for long plastic tubes coming out, which rested on a two by four that any mouse could reach. He made sure we would never suffer like that again to the best of his ability, even if he were gone. The entire time he apologized to any mouse who came to see him, taking time to bend over (though it was so obviously agony to him), pick up the mouse and kiss it. His face never untwisted from that knot of worry and guilt. The strange thing was, he'd been in a coma, too. Like me. Like Nemo. And he looked every bit as thin as we did. His body reflected the state of the safe house in general—wounded badly, in great pain. The synchronicity was eerie. As a young mouse I would not have seen it, but as I sat there, unmoving (like I never would have before), I saw things. Deep, meaningful things that Nemo would have been proud to hear of. I saw how much the human loved us. I saw how much we loved him. I saw how fragile and easily broken we are, and for the first time I saw that he was no different.

He always said we were his little angels. I had always wondered if he knew how fragile his little angels really were, and now he surely knows. But for the first time I knew how fragile he was. Our big angel. One of three.

Finally my master came to me, holding a Cheerio is his mouth for me. I looked at it like it was from Mars.

"Eat it, Squib," he said, sounding happy.

"You go ahead," I said, still watching the human trying to fix the house while in pain.

"I already had several. This one is for you."

In that same moment, Scratchy came up on the other side of me, also with a Cheerio in his mouth. He looked miffed that the idea wasn't original.

"Not hungry," I said.

My master put the Cheerio down, worried. "That's ridiculous," he said. "You haven't eaten in days. You're nothing but skin and bones, Squibble. I know you were giving your portions to Favorite and Squibette."

"Now you know about the other Kind Human, too," I said.

"Yes!" he exclaimed. I looked at him, cringing. "It's wonderful!" he said. "Why didn't you *tell* us, Squibble? That deed is every bit as mighty and as magnificent as my own holy quest was! Why didn't you tell anyone?"

I sat there, stunned. At last, I said, "I… I thought you'd be angry."

He shook his head. "No way! You are a knight. Knights have to do what they think is right, and sometimes…," he looked at the Kind Human in the distance, cleaning up dirty carpet, "that means breaking the rules."

"BJ will crucify me," I said.

"BJ is going to give you a medal," he said cheerfully.

"What's that?" I asked.

"It's something they used to give great warriors, to show that they were great. Humans still do it. We're going to take up this tradition, and you are the first mouse to ever get one!" He beamed at me.

"What is it?" I said.

"Well, humans wear them, and we made some, too, but to mice metal is heavy, so we figured we're gonna do it a couple of ways. One is reputation. Once everyone is told what you got, no one will forget, that's for sure! Second, on top of an actual mouse-sized medal and ribbon, you'll have the right to paint a symbol of some kind on your shield and armor. The symbol we've decided upon for great thinking is a mouse hopping out of a box. Cool, huh?"

“That’s what I get? A medal for great thinking?” I said, liking the sound of it. I started to perk up.

“Yes, Squibble. No mouse has ever gotten a medal. It was BJ’s idea, and Nemo seconded it. You are the very first. Someone will put the real one around your neck, and pin the little bar on you.”

I cocked my head and straightened my ears. “Cooool.” I looked around. “So cool.”

“Yeah,” he said, and picked up his Cheerio very slowly. He took a slow, savoring bite. “MMMmmm MMMM! Sooo good, this Cheerio—”

“Mine!” I snatched the Cheerio and held it close before going to work on it. I hunched over it, expecting it to vanish, or some other mouse to fight me for it. My master laughed and smiled. Scratchy gingerly put his at my feet, and I started on that one next. It pleased the midget greatly.

It was long, hard work for both humans to clean the house. Every minute of labor was torture to his broken body, but he would not allow Heide to do it all, and he would not rest. In the mornings it took an hour for him to be able to move, and in the evenings he could not lie down without moaning in agony. Our Kind Human began weeping again when he had to dispose of all the rotted bodies in the basement. He dug a mass grave for them and buried them outside in the back yard. We all attended the funeral, and in the same ceremony, Favorite was buried near my mother. My heart felt like it weighed an entire pound as I watched her coffin lowered into the ground. I thought of my momma’s funeral, and looked up. It had not rained since that time, and everything was bone dry, except our faces. It was unnatural that this late in the season rain had not come. More black magic, no doubt.

The ceremony to decorate me with that medal came right after that, which I felt was weird, but I liked everyone clapping and chirping for me. Everyone seemed to like me again. I had gotten back my honor to some degree, bestowed upon me by King BJ, Nemo, and my beloved master. It was a high point in my life, and they called me smart in front of everyone. BJ even said “Not crazy. Smart! Smarter than any of us have been,” as he put the medal around my neck and pinned the smaller representation onto my tunic. I loved what he said, the pride in his face and the look of delight in my master’s eyes. I painted a mouse hopping out of a box on the inside of my shield and armor. Scratchy watched me do it with great interest. I could tell he wanted a medal very badly.

Then the human erected a wall of bricks around the house. It stood fifty feet from the house and was three feet high. He built it to the drawings Nemo and my master drew, which depicted battlements, and dug a deep trench on the other side of it, a foot across and three deep. Deep enough to trap snakes. He put wire mesh up inside that, and set up humane mousetraps all over the field. Our side (the good guys) had instructions to avoid the outside period, and no one wanted to go out there in winter anyway, but we were warned about the traps.

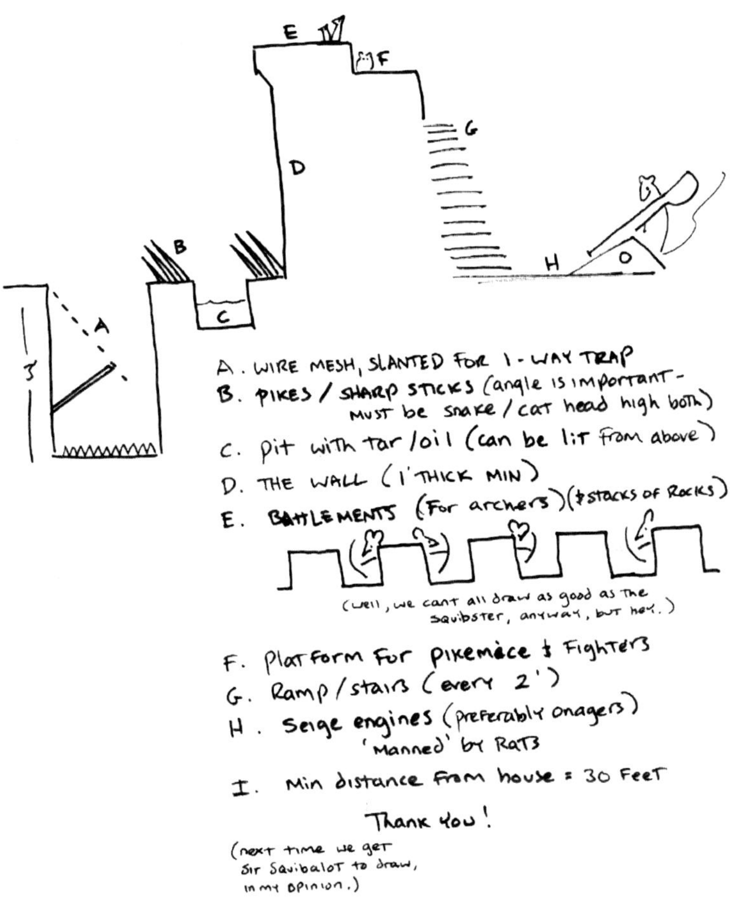

My master told the human about the zombies. They probably didn't need to eat, and probably didn't care about traps, either, but the human was overcompensating for everything out of guilt. He bought us new cages (I think Heide paid for everything, because our human was always poor), threw his old junk out of the house to make more room for us, and bought a stereo that played calm, peaceful music during the day for us to sleep by (or not, in my case). He and Heide brought many, many toys home (they must have cleaned out every pet store in the city… I wondered what Shiva and Thor might make of that) and set up intricate webs of ropes for us to climb. They built wooden play houses and castles for us in every room, and set tape on the floor to designate where humans could and could not walk in the house, leaving us free to roam about at will.

Finally, one day, it was just he and I. Everyone else was asleep, and Heide had gone home. I was sitting on the edge of his bed, looking at the blank TV. He came home with his arms full of something and found me there like that.

He put his mountain of stuff on the bed with a pained hiss and sat down next to me. "Want it on, Squib?" he asked.

I nodded without looking up. He clicked it on. He flipped through the channels until I squeaked at one. He stopped there.

"I'm sorry, Squibble," he said. I turned to look at him. His face read as sorry. He smelled sorry. I wondered why. It wasn't like he tried to crash his car. He had almost died. Damn that stupid Black Mouse. Damn all psycho girlfriends, too.

I nodded, not having pencil or paper nearby.

"You've been through hell here, and I wasn't here to protect you," he said, lowering his head. "I deeply regret it. I won't let it happen again. Not ever."

I nodded.

"My favorite little guy tells me you all are trying to avoid a war."

I nodded.

He was silent a time. I could see his mind trying to work itself around the concept. I went back to watching TV. Finally he said, "I guess I should have expected it, since you can read. I should have seen it coming. All this talk of demons and angels, and powers, and gnarly stuff… It's a bit much to swallow…"

You said it, brother. I mean… nod.

"I wish there was something I could do, but this seems like your evolution… your test as a race." He petted me and scritched me behind the ears. I liked it. I looked up at him questioningly.

"Humans were tested like this, too," he said. "Still are, in fact. If we fail, we have no place on the earth." He looked out the window toward the mountains. "It seems to me we're failing. I'd hate to see mice fail, too. You deserve more than we do, and yet humans do nothing but hurt and abuse you poor guys. It's not fair."

Yeah. No kidding. Preach it, dude.

"I wish we could all get along," he said, and got up to continue his work around the house. My head tilted some, realizing he'd said something heavy there that I should have gotten. It was as if a clue had fallen into my lap, but I couldn't figure it out. There was something in his words… some special feeling it gave me… like *deja vu*. Oh well. I'd talk to Nemo about it… after *Babylon 5*.

The next day I was sitting in my hovel when the human came to the desk. I got ready to run, thinking he didn't even know I was down there and might step on me by accident (since mice weren't supposed to build nests outside of their cages), but he squatted down and smiled at me. He had another armload of stuff. Books.

"Hi, Squibble," he said. I lifted my nose at him. He put the books down beside my nest and set them apart from each other, opening the heavy covers so I might turn the pages myself with some effort. I came out, curious mouse that I am, and looked them over.

"Nemo and your master told me you aren't doing too well," he said. "Depressed and sad over losing your momma and Favorite. I understand. I went out and got you these to cheer you up, little friend."

There were several books on art. Leonardo da Vinci, Michael Whelan, some art god named Moebius that I really liked, George Bridgeman, and Andrew Loomis. That last one was old smelling. There were other books as well: physics, chemistry, biology, and a book on pharmacology. He also put a brand new box next to my ruined one, with fresh cotton bedding in it. There were Cheerios in the bedding already. He knows alot about mice. He knows too much. I smiled and my eyes watered up. My master must have told him which books to get. These were the very books they had at the art school in the city. But he wasn't done.

He set down a watercolor set, and a ton of tiny colored pencils, brushes, and a bunch of little cups. He went back and came back with tiny pads of paper he must have gotten cut just for me, and a sandpaper-like block of stone with a water well in it, and inside that he put water. He pulled out a black block of ink and rubbed it in the water. Taking it out, he dipped one of the brushes into the water while I looked on, transfixed. He painted some lines on the paper.

"You can make your own ink this way," he told me, "and when it dries up, which is fine, you can just add more water to make it work again. I'll come by every day and fill up your water containers so you can paint or ink as you like."

Oh, I was so happy! I hadn't known anyone knew how much I liked art. I looked at the science books. No one knew I liked that either. No one. I looked up questioningly at the Kind Human.

"Oh, Nemo told me you might like those," he said. "I told him you'd be dangerous knowing that stuff," he laughed, "but I got them for you anyway. If you're gonna be a smart mouse, you might as well be really smart, huh?" He grinned. I got that weird *deja vu* feeling again, like he was trying to tell me something important without knowing it. I ran up and jumped onto his chest. He giggled at my fearless leap as I ran up him to his face and licked his lip. It seemed the best thank you I could manage.

"Oh, you're welcome, Squib," he said. "I love you, too, little guy. I just want you to be happy. Maybe this stuff will help." He set me down gently and carefully backed out from underneath the desk, which was mine now, I guessed.

I spent hours poring over my new stuff. I had never had *stuff*. My master had his dear encyclopedias, but I never had anything. Now I had lots. Lots and lots.

My master visited me later that evening.

"Wow, that was fast," he said. "I told him what you liked only this morning. Your collection looks bigger than mine almost."

I was to and fro, hopping from one book to the other. "This is so cool, Master! Look at what it says about drawing people so simply… mannequins… and… and it has drawings of skeletons, and muscles! This one over here says that the best thing in art is to love what you do! And this book over here has answers to questions I always had about the chemical makeup of that stuff they used on us in the lab—"

"Lab? They used stuff on you in the lab, Squibble?" he asked, suddenly concerned.

I stopped, frozen. Oops.

"There's alot you didn't tell us about your pilgrimage, my little knight," he said.

"Yeah," I said, sounding guilty.

"It's yours to tell or not," he said, "but I'd love to hear it. You had a great adventure, and I wasn't with you for it. I feel left out, kinda."

I looked at him. How I wish he'd been there! I thought about everything I had been through in the city. I wanted to tell him all of it, but some part of me still feared someone getting mad at me for it.

It just hadn't sunk in that they knew about Heide and they weren't angry. There was some block to spilling the beans that I couldn't put my finger on, and so I didn't. I didn't like it, but I stayed quiet. So unlike the old me.

My master picked up on it and ruffled my head fur playfully.

"Do what you want, Squib. You're okay with me, pal."

I smiled.

"Are we gonna be okay now, Master?" I asked. "Things are looking up, yeah?"

He grew a serious look. "Maybe," he sounded unconvincing. "Somehow I doubt our adversary will be satisfied, or that walls and trenches will keep him out." He saw my look of concern, and groomed me a bit. "But don't worry, Squib. Things are okay for now, and we have room to plan. We have some time."

"I hope he's slow," I said. "I hope he gives us as much time as we need."

"The Black Mouse?" he asked.

"No," I replied. "The third horseman."

We both sat in silence for a long time.

WINTER

The Great War

The Third Horseman: Plague

✠

The third horseman gave us no time at all. He was, in fact, waiting right outside the door the very next day. It was one of our own knights, come back from a long pilgrimage. We had thought he was dead, for no mouse had ever lived that long out in the wilderness. He looked half dead, and at first we thought him a zombie, but the protections of the angels still held, and he had used the last of his strength fighting the zombies to get back to his dear home.

He was covered in bites, and his armor was decrepit and in tatters. He had no sword, and no squire. He said he had lost both long ago—the sword to enemies and the squire to the heat. He was bedraggled worse than we had been in the last five months. I've never seen a mouse so bad off. Many mice were holding his wounds shut, including One-Ear, their paws on deep, ugly gashes and festering sores. His face was burnt by something. His rear leg was broken badly, and had been for weeks. It had gangrene and was useless. His front legs were both torn up, and his left shoulder looked broken. He had a giant lump encasing his left side and shoulder, immobilizing it. It looked as if mice had tried to chew around his arm to remove it. He was covered in massive scab tissue, and he had lost too much blood. One of his teeth was broken and his tail was missing entirely. He had no ears. One eye was out. The sheer courage it took this crippled mouse to reach us, over the wall, past the trench, through the hordes that must be out there somewhere, was staggering. We had no words for it. We tried to help him, but he died shortly after reaching us. He was only half aware of anything, and his last words were, "Thousands… too many…"

We didn't need to guess what that meant. It meant the enemy was massing an army, somewhere near enough to the house that this knight had seen them, and it cost him his already hard-won life. Maybe he had been captured and tortured. Later, we did not blame him for anything. He had not known what evil they had planted in his dying body. He just wanted to come home. See his friends. Have a nice meal and be warm in his old bed. Animals in pain or trauma always return to what they know, and this mouse was lucky enough to know something other than an existence run by cruelty. He died in his bed. That much, at least, he had earned.

We were planning hard what we might do against this army and the Black Mouse when, a few weeks later, the first few mice became ill. Their breath was labored, and they grew weak in a very short span. Normally, mice will cover up symptoms of illness, for in the wild, if they did not, they would be lunch. By the time one can tell a mouse is sick, it is often near too late to help. The Kind Human did not know this, and knowing no better, took the four sick mice to the vet. I shuddered to think of his vet bill, but he was a responsible guardian. He knew the job was going to be expensive when he took it.

He came back with three bodies. The mice had not lived long enough to be saved. By the time he got back (in just under three hours), more mice were sick. He had left one mouse body with the vet for a necropsy—that's where they take the mouse apart to find what caused them to die. It was a good idea, but the results would be slow. No one cared much for mice.

Nemo, me, and the High Council were not blind to what was coming. In a house where normally everything was pristine and clean for the animals, this was not normal. Within two days there were thirty sick mice. We knew something was up. This was not the result of the refuse we had lived in when the human was gone. This stank of evil. This was foul.

We asked the human to buy Echinacea and goldenseal and put them in the water supply. The vet told our human that antivirals might help and had given him some, but he simply had not enough time in a day—even if he hadn't had to work—to treat all the sick mice. At first he tried, but the numbers grew overwhelming. BJ told everyone to avoid contact, rest alot, and eat plenty—all the things that might increase immune systems, but the bug, whatever it was, continued to grow. By October near Halloween, half of everyone was sick, and 75 mice had died. The human was running himself ragged trying to figure out what to do, and was clearly almost powerless.

I asked for a copy of the county vet reports, the necropsy, that came a week after the first incidents, and the human gave them to me. Reading them, I realized that I understood some of it. My chemistry and biology studies had paid off, and now I had access to even more books. I began immediately spending most of my waking hours learning as fast as I could. I still did my chi gung, and still trained with Nemo in my sleep, where I was learning to send my soul far from my body and see what was going on in other places. My goal was to reach Branch in China, but so far I couldn't see it happening. Wasn't even close.

Heide would stop by once a week and say hello to everyone, but on hearing of the plague, she stopped coming over. She could not risk her own animals, and everyone understood. The last we heard, she and a friend named Mary Ann were using the money to create a rat and mouse club that would have the power to shelter and rescue rodents. We had their phone number now, and the human replaced his phone with one light enough that if we had to, with the help of the rats, we could use it. Heide told me if the safe house was ever in need, to call and chirp three times loudly into the phone. Help would come.

But no one could help us against the disease. With my chi I was able to temporarily stave off its effects from one or two mice, giving them a chance to fight it and live. I did this with my daughter and Stompy, who fell ill near Halloween and remained that way for some time. Stompy, having not regained her former weight yet by far, was doing quite poorly. She did not want to die by illness, but in combat. I had to agree with her. The death our people suffered from the plague was a horrible one—it amounted to choking and suffocating because of fluid in the lungs, but only after losing their minds. Apparently the virus (or whatever it was), melted lung tissue into mush and the brain couldn't get enough oxygen. Mice would convulse and spasm like my poor momma did, but it wasn't as quick. It took a long time, and they died in pain and terror.

I hated the Black Mouse more than anything in the entire world, and I studied without rest trying to beat his stupid third horseman. And, of course, from doing that, I expected to get sick, but my chi gung carried me through. What a coward this evil was, to attack us through such diabolic, insidious means! Why could he not face us? I desired to duel with him more than anything. Before, I had been afraid, but now I didn't care. I wanted to have just one chance to pay him back for all the damage he'd brought to us, to this house and our families. It was a merciless lesson in the nature of evil, which is not, as most would guess, the evil one sees on TV. Real evil either acts good (and we believe it), or will not show itself until it's too late.

That would be very soon.

As the world outside our contaminated house grew cold, we knew fear. What if it killed us all? It very well looked like it would, and the safe house would be no more. Why was evil winning? Why was this happening to us? I fell into bitterness and most were ahead of me in despair. Only the highest among us held out—my master, BJ, Nemo… those mice. Percival had not succumbed yet, but my master's other daughter and my sister, Leaf, died of the deadly illness. She died in her sleep in peace, thank the Mousegod. Now he had only two sons left to him. And me.

Percival took to pacing and his chi gung grew extreme in the moves. He hated the Black Mouse also, for he respected the same things I did: courage, valor, honor. He had lost both dear, gentle sisters to the enemy now, and seen many of his friends pass away. He could not fight back. He had no way of venting his rage upon a visible enemy. His wrath, when it fell, was going to be terrible. By the time his temper burned past his unbelievable willpower, it was much worse than BJ's. In this alone, he differed from his father. My master was gentle and soft spoken unless roused to great ire. Percival was the same, but once his anger was unleashed, he had no upper limit. Over the weeks that the plague fell upon us, his eyes grew redder and brighter, and if anyone would mention the Black Mouse, he would spit and leave. I began to worry, and Nemo confirmed it, that as much as our bodies were being assaulted, our minds and souls were under attack as well.

Despite the quarantine, some mice fled the safe house to certain doom outside, though they knew they would never be let back in. The safe house was closed now, to all. We free mice, who had all been rescued from cruel cages, were again caged. The vicious irony ran deep. I imagined the enemy laughing at us. He had to be. I squinted, rattled my tail, and studied harder.

I had no other scientist mice to bounce my ideas off of, except Nemo. I wish I had the owl to talk to, who would certainly be able to help, but now the outside was off limits more than ever. I found the twisted truth quite cold, in that, as soon as the human had built walls to keep our enemy out, we had been shut in.

Nemo helped me with my studies, but before long, I had gone beyond his knowledge of medicine and chemistry. I asked the human for more books, specific books that were listed at the ends of the ones I had for more study. He brought them. When I desperately needed a break, I would paint or draw, which never failed to refresh me. How I loved being lost in the world of creation. It was pure. I could fashion any reality I wanted, or explore my own deepest feelings and thoughts. The latter was often disturbing, so most of the time I drew pictures of the Black Mouse getting his squidgy face kicked in, which Percival loved. He had several hanging all over his cage, and he let no one chew on them at all.

On Halloween Eve, we heard coyotes howling outside the house. They sounded wrong. Their voices were thick, as if strangled, or filled with fluid. Their noise, normally beautiful and enchanting, was now haunted and broken. We all felt chilled to our bones. The demon was growing stronger with each passing day. Now he had taken the wild dogs. He had giant monsters.

We all knew we had to do something, but we were barely managing to stay alive. We were losing this fight. Good was losing. It wasn't like the stories, not at all. It wasn't fair. I spent many a minute gazing upward at Bigfat, scowling and showing him my teeth. Boy, when I got up there, I was gonna bite his ear so hard!

The human quit his job and, supported by Heide's money, stayed at home constantly to help as many mice as he could. The vet came over several times and took samples from dead mice. He said he'd never seen anything like it. The disease tried to change normal tissue into something else, and the result was catastrophe. He said he couldn't even locate an actual virus. Doctor Bausone was ultimately cool, though, and did not condemn our house or report us to the human authorities as he was obliged to. He liked mice, and he was on our team. Besides, he claimed it had not spread outside the house that he knew of, and for that we were grateful. He knew what horrors we would endure if the government or the normal people found out what was going on. Perhaps that had been the Black Mouse's plan all along, for our vet to report us, and we would all be taken away, to die lonely and alone in test cages, sick and dying for science. I gave the Black Mouse, wherever he was, the bad finger.

Doctor Bausone is one of our angels, demon. You can't have him.

The doctor turned over all the reports from their research to the human, who would in turn hand them over to me. I had the human ask specific questions of the doctor that had him replying with some strange looks indeed.

"Becoming a vet, dude?" He would say, half joking.

"Rocket scientist," the Kind Human would answer, and they would laugh.

Don't laugh too hard, humans. I'll start on rocket science next.

Over the weeks I got slow results. It was not a virus. It was something else. Some kind of thing that passed from one mouse to another, somehow, but it wasn't a natural virus, that I was sure of. Nothing in nature was this cruel or this thorough. Nemo agreed, but what to do about it?

By November half of us were dead. Squibette and Stompy had recovered with my help, but they would be a long time in healing fully. Through the direct intervention of the human's drugs and Nemo's powers, none of the inner circle had fallen ill yet besides those two, but Artemis and Aphrodite were now sick. The backyard was nothing but a giant graveyard. The Kind Human was a frazzled wreck, running himself ragged, ignoring his pain. And finally, the inevitable happened.

One day I left my tiny lab (yeah, I had one now, thanks to the human) to speak with my master, but he wasn't in his cage. Thinking nothing of it, I walked down his ramp to go see if Nemo had seen him, and saw him lying prone on the floor, three feet under the ramp. He had fallen!

I raced down to find him gasping for breath.

He was sick.

Staving Off the Reaper

✠

from the house to get an oxygen tent for my dying master. His lungs were already in bad shape. It didn't look good for him at all. He had been trying to leave his house in the middle of the day. He had been trying to get to help… or maybe… maybe he was doing the "mouse can't die in the nest" thing and was trying to get out of the house. It was a strong mouse instinct. My stomach clenched at the thought of my poor master, fighting for air, scrabbling outside to die and falling off that high ramp.

My heart wouldn't stop racing. Panic and anxiety had my soul in a vise grip. Nemo laid his hands on my master's tiny, struggling body, and kept them there, as I did, until the human returned with the oxygen. My master received several shots under the scruff of his neck, which he reacted to not at all. (This frightened me greatly, since no mouse likes shots, and all of us thrash about and squeak at them.) Then he was put in the tent, limp and apparently lifeless. The human went to his knees and prayed. We all joined him, the entire household.

When I looked up, I could see spirits. I saw all the dead spirits of the house. I looked for my mother, but did not see her. I could see the confusion in their empty eye sockets. Many of them did not know where to go. They were lost.

I looked around for the angels, but there were only small lights over some of us, mostly the inner council. Nowhere could I see an angel, and that was a first. It worried me deeply. But there was a soft light over my master, and it looked kinda like the light of Michael's sword. It gave me a touch of hope.

I told BJ and Nemo about the visions I was seeing.

"Prepare yourself to lose him," BJ told me. "He was not strong to begin with after being through so much."

Others looked at me in sympathy.

"No!" I screamed. "No, he's not going! This would be a stupid, stupid death for someone like him! He's not dying here!" I stomped my feet. My mind rebelled against the very idea. It could not happen! Could *not*!

When I gazed up, eyes full of tears, Nemo was staring at me. I could not read his face at all.

I ran back to my lab and house, ignoring transparent spirits in my way, who were all crowding around my master's tent as if they were still alive. When I got to my place under the desk, I saw how my abode had transformed. My house was completely concealed by study books and lab equipment, everything from tiny vials to bowls and stacks of notes, liquids and powders. I even had the power to make fire with a candle the human trusted me with. My mind went back to the lab I had been trapped in. It even smelled similar.

The lab.

Suddenly, I knew. I turned around to go back at top speed and get Nemo, but he was right behind me, and I slammed into his soft fur, falling over.

"The lab!" I chirped.

"What then?" He asked.

"The thing… the bug… it isn't a virus! It's a… a *thing* concocted by the Black Mouse… *in a lab*!" I exclaimed. I knew it was true. I felt it.

“Amazing,” Nemo said, sounding unsurprised. “You might be right.” He frowned. “Chemical warfare.”

I stopped and looked at the chinchilla with the supernatural powers.

“He’s not going to die, is he?” I asked him.

“Why don’t you look and see for yourself?” He said.

I stood there a long time. I wanted to look. I was afraid, plain and simple. I knew I could not handle it if my master died. Ever. I just had to die before him, and that was that. I could not look, even if I knew precisely how, which I didn’t. I finally shook my head.

“Can you counter the disease?” Nemo asked me.

“I don’t know,” I said. “I’m going to need help. The Kind Human, Doctor Bausone… even you.”

“I am at your service, Sir Knight,” he said. “As I am sure they are as well.”

“What will happen if I cannot find a cure?” I said.

“We all perish.”

No fancy answer, no “see for yourself,” no mysterious question-answer. *We all die.* I swallowed hard.

“Then let’s get started.”

He nodded.

“One more thing,” I said, while I had him answering things straight for once. His ears perked, listening.

“My holy quest, my real calling… Is this it? To save everyone?” I asked.

“Everyone here, no,” he said.

“Is it to defeat the Black Mouse?” I asked.

“Part of it, but… no,” he said.

“What is it then?! I still do not know!” I exclaimed.

Nemo shook his head. “That you absolutely must discover for yourself.”

I growled and stomped a foot. I didn’t have time to get angry, or throw a fit. I really, *reeelly* wanted to though. Stupid! Why wouldn’t he just tell me what it was and spare us all a lot of effort?!

I went back to my lab and gathered a bunch of notes. I scribbled on them for a minute, and handed them to Nemo.

“Take these to the Kind Human and have him get them to the doctor,” I said while still writing with my other hand.

“Yes sir,” he said.

“And be quick about it, Squire,” I said, while I had him as my servant, “or you’ll be doing something horrible involving cage corners and a toothbrush for days!”

He snickered and went, lightning in motion. Gone in a flash.

Now I had real reason to work, and a lead I could work with. I prayed the Mousegod, if he had any mercy left in his fat hide, grant me great speed and wisdom now. I needed it more than ever.

I would work for hours on end, remember that there was actually food to eat, and then work some more until I was starving again. I had gotten used to not eating. The guilt-ridden human put scads of treats all about the house, trying to atone for his absence and all the lives it cost. Nemo told me our guardian was having a hard time forgiving himself. Finally I would break down and stuff something in my face, then go back to work.

Only one thing really interfered with my work, and that was the dread fear that I would find my master dead in the oxygen tent next time I visited him. Because of this I would go every couple of hours and check up on him. I'd take him treats and try to get him to eat. His face was haggard and drawn. His backbone stood out and I could see his ribs through his messy fur. He made sickening clicking sounds when he drew breath, and his eyes seemed to never close. His suffering was deep.

"Don't give up, Master," I said. "You told me not to, so you can't either."

"Not… going to, …Squib," He managed. His face was covered in dried blood from his coughing, and I cleaned it off for him. My master. The mighty hero… now reduced to this by our tribulations. I felt burning rage in my chest that I could not aim at anything. Certainly not fate. Not the Mousegod, as much as I wanted to. I always aimed it at the Black Mouse, but it never struck the target. That coward would not face us.

My master's dream was perishing before his eyes. His true love was dead, and his people were reduced to a fraction of their former number. More died every day, despite everyone's best efforts. We all felt helpless, and more than a little hopeless. Trapped, beaten, and doomed. But there was one of us, in this tent, that must not think that way. He was the light for all of us, and if he died, that light would certainly vanish forever. I could not carry it; it was far too heavy.

"You have to fight, Master, like you fought the snake," I said.

He looked at me through strained eyes. "I hate fighting, Squib."

My ears perked up. “What?! The mighty Mouse Knight? Nahhh…”

He nodded. “I… I do. I love peaceful things… reading… friends… writing…” He stopped to breathe for several seconds, “I hate fighting and hurting things… It… it should not be necessary… ever.”

“I could have your encyclopedias brought over, Master,” I told him, hoping it might cheer his downtrodden spirit.

He tried to smile and failed. “I’m too tired to read, Squibble… I can’t focus my… eyes.”

My heart felt heavy for him. “Oh, Master,” I said. “I’m so sorry. Please don’t die.”

“I’m so tired,” he said.

“You can’t give up!” I said. “Can’t. No way.”

Fearing his answer, I went back to my work. He looked so sick.

I ordered more books, studied more, studied harder, and most of all, tried to think smarter. Every time I thought I had it figured out, there was some new piece of medicine or science I did not know that sprang up to oppose me. The human was giving my master antivirals, bronchodilators (they make it easier to breathe), antibiotics, and fluids twice every day. He was getting alot of shots. Just the stress from that alone was enough to do in many mice. I spent my dreaming hours with Nemo searching for a cure as well, but in a very different way than my usual method. We ventured deep into the astral plane, and asked creatures of legend questions about what was going on. We visited spirits, unicorns, sphinxes and dragons. Real dragons, not snakes. It wasn't so bad in dreams because I could make myself bigger if I wanted, and not feel so small. They all told us the same thing. The Black Mouse had blended black magic with science. In the recent years of history, spirits had figured out technology, and were beginning to control it. The frequencies of devices like computers, televisions, and cell phones… the spirits were learning to use these things. It only took them 50 years. That was pretty fast for beings used to slow evolution. In order to find the cure, we would have to do the same thing—blend magic with science. Many of them had suggestions. Nemo and I memorized them, and he began working with me both awake and asleep, twenty-four hours a day.

Then, one evening when everyone else in the house was awake and I was asleep, I came back from a deep astral expedition and bade good day to Nemo. He departed to wake, and I decided to check on my master from the astral plane. It could be done—Nemo had taught me to do it, though it required great concentration—but when I got there and brought the real world into focus, there was a strange mouse in a white robe sitting next to my master's tent.

I knew immediately this was no normal mouse. I could not tell if it was on the physical plane or just the astral, but it seemed real enough to me. It had a soft, waving glow about it, like the sparkle souls give off, but dim and with many tiny stars in it. I was afraid of it for some reason, my instinct telling me to run away. Well, that's the advantage of being an *advanced* mouse (*Mus musculus superior*)—you can be stupid if you want and ignore instinct.

When I approached, it turned to me, and my heart skipped a beat. Beneath its ragged cowl, there was nothing but a mouse skull! The robed figure was Death.

"Shoo!" I waved my hands at the apparition. "Go way!"

I felt rather than heard a chuckle. It scoffed at me.

"You can't have him!" I cried. "Begone from this place!"

It turned back to gaze at my gasping master and ignored me.

Frightened beyond reason, I lunged at it to bite its head clean off. It turned and struck me with what looked like a scythe. I woke up instantly, and knew that I'd been "killed" in the dream. If I had been too deep in the dream, like I was in my ventures with Nemo, I might not have come back at all. I raced to my lab/house and found Nemo working.

"Reaper!" I exclaimed.

He looked at me with a slightly curious expression.

"Spells! Ancient power!" I yelled, and zipped up to stand before him. "Help me! He's going to take my master!"

Suddenly understanding, he raced with me to the tent. He peered hard at the area and fixed his gaze on something. His sapphire eyes widened.

"You're right," he gasped. "Death."

"Bite it in the rump!" I chirped.

"It's not that simple," he said. "Even now it has inched closer to your master. Death is no meager opponent, Squibble. History is full of stories where people have tried to beat Death."

"Has anyone done it?" I asked, desperate.

"It has been done," he began.

"Okay! Let's go kick some deathly ass!" I chirped, looking about for a sword.

"No," he said. "That is not the way." He looked at me carefully. I knew that look by now. The power look. He was looking through me, or into my future, or both. For once I put up with it instead of dancing a jig to confound him. When he was done I gave him the "Well?" look.

"You are not ready to lose your master yet," he said.

"This just in."

He contemplated something very heavily. I grew impatient and tapped my foot on the floor. I made a circular gesture in the air with my finger as if to say, *Let's get on with it, shall we?*

At last, he seemed to come to a decision and was at peace with it. He smiled at me.

"I will save your master, Squibble," he said. I tensed to hop for joy. "But," he added—and I stopped mid-tense—"you understand that someday you must lose him."

"Nah. I'll die before he does," I said.

"Selfish mouse," he said. "With no thought of how that would affect him?"

"Uhhh... but... he's strong...," I mumbled.

Nemo looked at the frail form in the oxygen tent. "Oh yes, he is, but if you cannot see his mortality now, you are truly blind." He turned back to me. "He has lost as much as you if not more, Squibble. His true love, his friends, his children, almost his Kind Human. He is taking every bit the spiritual beating that you are."

"*Why* are we taking this spiritual beating, Nemo?" I asked him, genuinely curious.

He smiled sadly. "Because evil realizes we are capable of great things, tiny mouse. And would stop us before we accomplish them."

"But I don't even know what I must do!" I complained.

"You will," he said. "And it's our job to give you the room to do just that." Then he folded up and went to sleep, right near the spot where Death was. When he woke, it was almost dark again. The wait had been very long indeed... full of anxiety and worry.

He rose groggy. "It is done," he said.

"You beat Death?!" I stammered. "You *rock*!"

"I did not beat him," Nemo said. My face fell. "I made a trade."

(Heard something!) "What?" I said.

"A trade. Your master will live. For now. Death will take someone else."

I stood up. "Me?" I asked softly.

"No," he said, but he said no more, and went back to the lab to work his magics on our potions.

I crawled into the tent. My master was asleep and looked no better, but I felt better. I petted his soft fur. "Sweet dreams, gentle Master," I said.

The human was coming home from another visit to the doctor's office (with more dead mice), and he had something in his hands. It was another book. I was up to stock on all the books I recently ordered, and wondered what he was bringing me. It was thick. He set it down in front of me. It said "Stephen King" on the cover.

"A little mouse told me you read the others in this series, Squibble," he said. "This latest one came out today."

I looked up at him with infinite gratitude. The very book I had wanted more than anything to read while I was in the city. I had dreamed about reading it. I had used it as motivation not to die at one point. If I died, I'd never get to read the next book. Now, here it was, thanks to the kindness of my human friend and the compassion of my master.

The irony, of course, was that I hadn't the time to read it.

RG-10

✠

The breakthrough came, not because of my hard work, or our long hours, but because of the intervention of our second Kind Human. She came over one day with stacks and stacks of paper in her arms. The Kind Human ran to her in the doorway.

"Heide! Your mice!" he said.

"Mary Ann is watching them," she said. "I'm staying. Until this is all over. I have something Squibble badly needs. The risk was worth it."

I happened to be up on the table at that moment, watching my master. He was slowly recovering. It was barely noticeable, but he was not dead. He was struggling to eat a Cheerio. He smiled at me through the transparent tent film. I put my paw against the tent side towards him, and he limped over to do the same. I pointed to Heide. He nodded, moving his nose in her direction, telling me to go. I went.

Heide put the stacks of paper down on the floor as I watched. She looked at me and smiled triumphantly.

"I've told Shiva and Thor what's going on here," she said. "And they, in turn told me where the lab was that you were held at." I looked at Nemo, and he looked back at me. We both smiled and turned to Heide. "These are the lab notes on every experiment performed in the last year," she said. Then she held up a single sheet of paper. "But this… this is the formula for the toxin that mice were being injected with when the Black Mouse was born. *This* is the poison that's killing all your friends." My eyes bugged out. I ran up and tugged at the paper with Nemo. She giggled and let go. Nemo glanced at me, no need for words, then he raced with the sheet back to the lab.

"They call it RG-10," she said. "It was supposed to be a new kind of rodent medicine, spread through contact, but something happened, and it went wrong. It became malignant instead. Pest control companies are trying to buy it as a new product." Her face was angry and sad at the same time. Good old humans. Couldn't eradicate us with normal means. Had to resort to biochemical warfare.

I ran up her clothes and kissed her on the lip. Wonderful Heide. She knew my question: *How did you get this?*

She giggled. "We *stole* it!" she whispered. I knew she meant my crack team of secret mouse agents. Good ol' Clyde. I jumped down to the table, snatched up a pencil tip, and took the time to write a small note. It said: *You've saved us all. BJ will be issuing medals.*

She knew it was also meant for the rat twins and Clyde. She put it in her pocket.

I jumped down and ran for the lab.

With Nemo's magic and my scientific knowledge, we now knew what we had to do to stop the plague. But the demonic version of RG-10 was not going to give up so easily. The long hours, the lack of food, the worry over my master and the lack of sleep finally caught up with me, and I fell sick.

When we first came to the safe house, my master was almost dead from injury and exposure to the elements, and I wasn't much better off. We had been taken to a vet, who poked and prodded me, picked me up by the scruff of my neck and forced bad-tasting liquids down my throat. I hadn't liked it much then, and I liked it even less now.

The Kind Human spent four hours, twice a day, treating mice with medicine. He tried to treat everyone, and in order to do so had to separate many into closed cages, for he could not tell us all apart. I was one of the mice getting "the long treatment."

Shots, fluids, medicine, and the nebulizer (a chamber the human pumped medicine-fog into for ten minutes at a time (hours for a human) so we could take the medicine in by just inhaling it). It helped ease the breathing, and my master had to go through it, too. We got put in together. He would have chuckled if he could have, because I had made fun of him in the nebulizer before (no one liked it), but he was at Death's door. Thanks to Nemo, that door was closed and would not open for my master. But now I was in the same predicament. The same treatment—poked, prodded, squished, and forced to drink nasty fluids. I hated it. I squirmed and fought, but my strength failed me. The human was kind, trying to joke and laugh while he put me through the necessary torture. I always thought it was a weird human thing, to laugh under stress, especially when abusing my dignity so.

"C'mon, Squib," he'd laugh. "You look real funny all miffed like that."

Oh yeah. Real funny. Laugh it up, human. Maybe the Mousegod gives me an extra 500 pounds, and then we'll see who's laughing.

I knew he was just trying to help, so I didn't bite him.

Breathing was a chore, and within a short time, a dire struggle. My head hurt, my chest burned, and my limbs would not hold me up. I fought with every inch of my willpower to mix the solution to RG-10 before I could no longer function at all. Terror filled my weakened soul that I might have brain damage, or not be able to think as smart anymore, and all would be lost. Nemo, Percival, BJ, Squibette, and trusty Scratchy gave me chi every couple of hours, but it wasn't enough. I fought the illness for a couple of days, and finally collapsed before I finished my work.

"Damn mouse," I mumbled as I fell.

Nemo put me in the oxygen tent with my master and ran to get the human. I thought that was it, it was over. To come so close, just to fail, was the ultimate, most stupid irony yet. When I saw that Black Mouse on the other side, I didn't care how powerful a demon he was. I was gonna punch him in the eye!

But that night as I slept, Nemo visited me in my dreams. There he had a lab set up, exactly like ours—down to the crumbs of food and the mess. Every detail was perfect. I was very impressed—that took some serious power of concentration and recall.

"Ready to continue our work?" he asked, smiling.

"Yes sir," I told him, and dove right in.

In the astral plane I was not sick, and I had mastered the clarity of mind to remain aware in my dreaming state. Nemo remembered flawlessly what I told him to do in the waking world. He could memorize thousands of instructions and recall them perfectly with not one error. It was a wonderful tactic he had come up with, and within a few days we had our formula. I called it RG-11.

I tested it on myself and recovered.

We gave it to every mouse, every rat. After losing so many, only a small number remained in the house. Of 800 plus rodents that had come with us from the old kingdom, barely 200 remained. We sent the formula back with Heide, and I asked her in private to deliver a message to my generals.

It said:

Dear Gentlemen and party,
This is RG-11, the cure for RG-10. Go back to the lab and replace the old formula with this one. Make sure the documents you "correct" look exactly like the original. Keep this formula on hand in case anything goes wrong, or anyone there becomes infected. You've done well, boys. Proud of you.
Your commander and uncle,
Lord Squibble

PS: Double the training regimen. Recruit anyone who wishes to join. Stand ready.

My master recovered, although slower than anyone else. I got better almost immediately. I told everyone to put their chi into my master instead of me, for he needed it more. I took up my practice again, and left my lab up just in case. Heide returned to the city, taking my letter.

It was almost Christmas. It was winter.

Rain had not yet fallen. Even the news on the TV said it was freakish, bizarre weather. The field mice everywhere not near this house must be dying in huge numbers. The Kind Human put water out for them here, and they came in large numbers when no one was looking. The water was always gone by morning.

It grew bitterly cold.

Christmas passed. It was sad and lonely for most. The Kind Human spent alot of money on us, trying to cheer us up, but everyone had lost family and friends. Nothing could fix that. In addition, the human limped everywhere, and could not even visit the restroom without pain. He looked like he was getting worse, not better. He acted like an old man.

My master was busy recovering and nothing else. BJ and the rat girls were doing the same. The inner circle had fallen last, and had it not been for Heide's intervention, it would have been the end for us. The remaining rodents in the now quiet safe house were somber and subdued. No one wanted to guess what was coming next. Couldn't we have just a little break? We knew better.

And those among us well informed knew exactly what was coming next. We knew what the fourth horseman was.

"War," BJ said at council. "There is no avoiding it now."

My master lowered his head. We all knew it was true. Horrible, but true.

"We have been annihilated," my master said between coughs. "Even if we'd been at full strength, you heard our knight's last words. The enemy has thousands of troops. Coyotes. Beasts. More by now. We have nothing comparable. Almost all our fighters are dead. We have no army to meet his."

I shuffled about, folding my hands behind me and looking at the floor. Everyone looked at me. I whined some.

I slowly turned my head to my master. I was wincing.

"That's… not entirely true…, Master."

"Thats...not entirely true... master..."

Their eyes remained on me. No one spoke. My master's face clearly required more. I sighed. The jig was up, and it was about time.

Within the day we were in the human's new car—another truck, this one with a shell and air conditioning—and headed into the city. I had never planned on going back, but now I had to. Anyone who was anyone was coming with us: BJ, Percival, Nemo, Stompy,

Squibette, my faithful squire, and my master. The human was our servant. We asked him to take us and gave him the address. He obeyed instantly, without question.

I was searching myself all the way. I had mixed feelings about it. It was surely necessary now, whether or not I got in trouble. Now we had to go to war. I could tell it was tearing my master up inside. He almost looked afraid. War against other mice, even zombies, and other animals… It wasn't right. Everyone agreed. The Black Mouse seemed to be the master of making right things into wrong things. He'd done too much damage. Wayyyy too much. He had to go. It was mildly amusing though, looking around the dashboard of the truck we were all sitting on. Judging by our faces, now alight with the hope of a new army and a fighting chance, I'd say that the Black Mouse had failed. He had wanted to stomp our spirits into despair and hopelessness. He wanted us to quit and lay down. But everything he had done had just fueled our fires. Determination and fury burned in our eyes. None of us would quit now. This was the very last thing the Black Mouse wanted.

Now he was going to get it.

The Hordes of Lord Squibble

✠

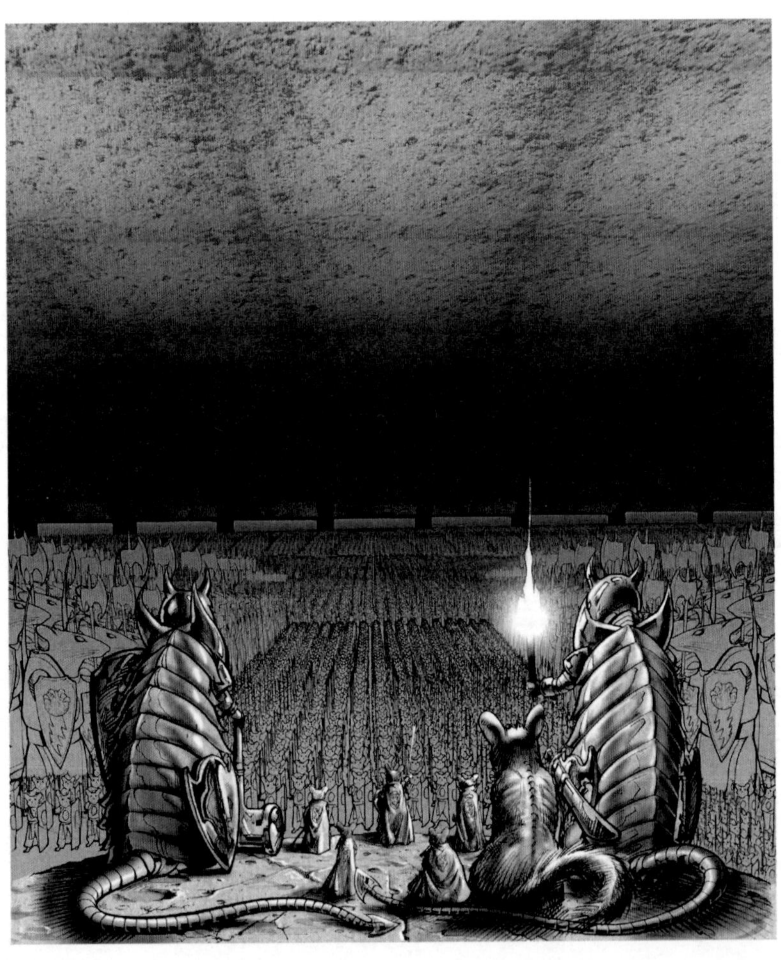

The human had been completely informed. I thought the funny thing was how he never once questioned any of this crazy stuff—warring mice, supernatural phenomenon, psychic rodents... But then, he hadn't questioned our ability to read or our intelligence either. Maybe it just made sense to him. If any human would understand, it would be him.

He drove us into the city, to the address I wrote down. He was asked to wait for us there, and to have an open mind on our return. He said he would. He seemed to be deep in thought, and our human was a deep thinker. He had something going on in there. I often wondered, then and still, what it was. I never did ask him.

As we came out of the truck and were put on the ground, I saw his concern. It showed clearly every time he ever had to let any of us go, and now here were his favorite bunch, going back into the city where many of us were so vulnerable. I was out last, and looked back at him. *It's okay, Dad*, I thought. *We'll be back this time.*

We went to the side of the building in the night, and began our several block walk. There was no one on the road, and mist covered the ground. I saw across the street the alley to Heide's house. I wanted to go confront the bully. I wanted it, but my gut clenched up, my teeth clamped down, and my heart raced. I was still frightened.

Damn that bully mouse! He was probably dead by this time anyway. I knew he wasn't, but that's the excuse I used. My master saw my tail rattling and stopped next to me. He looked down that dark alley along my line of sight.

"Something bad, Squib?" he asked. His armor was polished and shiny. So was mine. We wore our capes and swords. Our shields had freshly painted crests. We were decked out for a formal visit. His paw was on his blade handle.

I squinted. I took one step toward the alley. My tail beat the ground furiously like a drum. I felt raging adrenaline. I wanted to kill that bully mouse! Kill him!

But chance had me glance at my master, still recovering, pale and thin. His eyes were kind and soft, but his body needed time to heal. Again, it was an excuse, but I saw him trying to defend me against the bully that was trashing me on our reunion. I saw the bully kill my poor master by biting him in the neck while I watched, helpless and scared, like the first time I had been unable to act when they had destroyed my momma's precious honeycomb gift. I saw it like a vision. I shook my head to clear it, stunned by the sharpness of it. It was like my dreams, but I was awake.

That was when two things occurred to me. One, I thought of my master now as weak, and in this journal, I have made him sound that way. It was not so. That was my fear, and nothing more. I often said "my poor master" and such, but he really wasn't poor. He always smiled, and he ran on his wheel every day except when he was sick or very sad. For a mouse with a lung problem, he sure didn't act it. And he could still kick the tail off me with a sword. It was improper to think of him as weak. If another mouse thought that way, he would be beaten up and run out of a normal mouse colony. I wasn't respecting him enough. I was seeing life through the filter of my dread, and my imagination (or the enemy) was using that fear to cripple my faith..

Second, I had not had honeycomb since I had come back to the safe house. My momma wasn't around anymore to give it to me. I wasn't sure whether honeycomb itself now had a bad vibe in my mind or not. I hoped not. I liked it.

"Squib?" my master asked, sounding concerned.

"It's nothing, Master," I told him. "A bad experience."

"If you need to go," he said, gripping his sword hilt harder, "we go."

His face was determined. He would go with me into any danger. How he loved me. However, fear-driven illusion or not, I was sure he would die horribly, and me with him. That was my excuse anyway. The only truth for sure was that I was scared. Like before.

"No. No, let's... let's keep going with the others. They need me to tell them where to go anyway."

"Okay," he said, and relaxed his grip. Our armor made little clinking sounds as we departed that spooky place.

"Master," I said, "I'm sorry about the war. I know it's wrong."

"Yes, it is," he said, his head low to the ground. "It's bad enough that we have to hide from humans. Now we are forced to fight our own kind because of the tactics of a billion-year-old creature from the beginning of time that can outthink us any day of the year. It doesn't seem fair. This could happen with the humans. One day it might be us against them."

"What!" I exclaimed.

"Don't say you haven't thought it, Squibble," he said as we rejoined the group that had been waiting only ten feet away. Scratchy was heavily perturbed that Percival had held him back from following on my heels as he always does.

"I have, Master," I said, realizing it was true. I thought about it quite often. It was a chilling thought.

"If that happens, and it's pretty much inevitable, Squib, they will take from us all that we have. Every precious thing."

Alarm ran amok through my system. For some reason his words terrified me worse than the thought of confronting the bully had.

"*Why*, Master? Why would they treat us so poorly, once they realized we could think like them?" I asked.

"Because that's what frightened apes do," BJ said. "They destroy what they don't understand."

"Stupid apes," Stompy grumbled.

"Stupid mice," Nemo said. Everyone looked at him. "I've noticed none of you have dusted off the truce flag and dragged it out to discuss matters with the Black Mouse."

"We don't even *have* a truce flag," Stompy argued.

Nemo scoffed. "Exactly."

"Would he even listen?" My master asked, interested.

"Who knows what a billion-year-old creature from the beginning of time might do?" Nemo said. "Probably not, but the point is nobody tried. Nobody knows him."

For all my faults, I had been paying attention to that exchange. It clicked in my head. Yeah. How much do we really know about the Black Mouse? I mean, he's absolutely gotta die a horrible death, but we don't really know him. What if I called him out for a talk? In the old times they called it "parley." It meant meeting on the field of battle to discuss options. If the parley went badly, then there was a fight. But sometimes there was not.

Oh! Waitaminute! *No!* This was a stupid horror movie and I'm thinking, *Let's go check out that noise in the dark...*

"Noway!" I chirped. Everyone looked at me. "Black Mouse is as dead as my Momma! Dead as all the friends and family we all buried back at the safe house! Dead, you hear! **Dead!**"

"Amen!" Percival spat. Tails rattled all around in agreement. It was way too late for parley.

Nemo just kept looking at me, no expression on his face at all. He knew I got it. Yes, it was too late, but that wasn't the point. The Black Mouse was a demon, and would never be reasoned with—that wasn't the point either. The point was that mice are every bit as warlike as humans, and any hope we had, they might have, too. It went the other way as well. Any hope they had, we might share. That was the point. If we didn't make peace, it was all over. I nodded at the prophet. Mousegod forbid I ever end up that old and wise. Waaayy too much pressure.

With that, we all turned, and I led our entourage to the new kingdom.

We slipped into the hotel basement and then went down below it. At the main entrance to the kingdom, two sentries in leather armor with spears blocked our way. BJ struck a match then, and the torch lit everything around us.

The mice almost dropped their spears. Their jaws hung open in awe. Before them was not one, but several Mouse Knights, and a chinchilla who could only be...

"The mighty Nemo!" one of them gasped.

The other sank to his knees, then the first one did as well. They fell on their faces, prostrate to a god in their midst. Maybe I had overdone the stories of home...

"Are you paying attention, student?" Nemo said to me, jerking his thumb at his new worshippers. I sneered a smile in response.

I stepped forward. "Attention!" I yelled. They snapped upright as if the devil himself had trained them, which, in fact, *they* had. Two devils.

"Lord Squibble!" They exclaimed in one voice. I stuck my chest out to the shock of my entire party and commanded them in a powerful voice (my best impression of my master, actually, but don't tell anyone), "Bring me my generals at once. Inform the Hordes to gather in the main hall. Full battledress!"

"At once my lord!" They were gone like yesterday's cheese.

I stepped back and became aware that everyone was gaping at me, even BJ. Scratchy was grinning ear to ear, his eyes huge.

"Ummm...," I said, "Ahh... protocol, you know..." I shuffled around on my feet as none of them said anything, or even moved. "Well, you taught it to me!" I pointed at BJ and my master.

My master looked the same as he did when his children were born. BJ... I couldn't read that expression. The King looked... amazed, almost... if I didn't know better... proud. Nahhh...

I was saved by the approach of two *very* big and *very* noisy rats in full plate armor. Made of red metal. Now it was my turn to gape.

First, they had grown, the rat twins. Impossible, but they had. They were gigantic. And they were decked out like tanks. Their armor looked... forged. Really, truly forged, not put together from anything that could be scavenged. It was art. The pieces of it were separated into chitinous sections, like a centipede, and covered in sharp points and horns. Even their tails were covered in metal. They wore metal gauntlets. They had helms with horns in place of the ears. They looked more formidable than any rodent I had ever seen. Shiva had a pair of twin, thick-bladed scimitars as his waist, and Thor had the biggest hammer I had ever seen short of one for humans. Their weapons were metal! They both carried metal kite shields, both bearing the same crest (so they had settled on a crest at last). It was a picture of a rat fist crushing the earth against a golden background. It was deeply disturbing. The only thing not frightening about them was their faces: they were both smiling like kids.

"Uncle! We knew you'd come back! Wait till you see—" Then they saw everyone else and went straight to their knees in knight's salutes. Weapons up in front of them, heads bowed.

"Whoa... he brought Mount Olympus," I heard Thor whisper to Shiva.

"Zeus heard that," Nemo commented. They looked up quickly and then bowed lower.

Looking around at everyone's faces, it seemed as if they might never come unstuck from the awe and shock. My master inched forward hesitantly and whispered, "Shiva? ...Thor?"

"Milord," they both said at once.

His mouth hung open. "Good Mouselord! What happened to you?"

They looked up at him, then to me. I nodded.

"Squibble happened to us, Milord. Without him, we and every member of the Hordes would be dead, sire." Shiva answered.

"*Hordes*?" BJ raised an eyebrow.

"Majesty!" Thor exclaimed, realizing now who BJ was underneath his armor (hey, it was purple, for royalty, but the light in here was dim on our third match).

Squibette, who had never known the twins, stepped forward. "How many are there in these… hordes, mighty generals?"

Again the brothers looked at me. Everyone else looked at me, too, realizing that these two machines of destruction were asking my leave to do anything but breathe. They'd ask that as well, if I told them to. I nodded.

"Fifty thousand plus," Shiva said proudly.

My mouth fell open. BJ sucked air in. Stompy sat down hard. My master's eyes bugged out. Scratchy went on grinning like a jack-o-lantern. His master was a god, and he'd known it all along.

My generals had been busy.

"Ummm… not including the rats," said Thor.

Silence reigned for a minute solid. The Mouse Knights looked at each other in stunned awe. Finally, Stompy balled up a fist and said, "Yesss! That motherless piece of trash is gonna eat it now!"

BJ stepped forward, looking from me to the rats and back. "Fifty… *thousand*?" he asked, taking off his helm and rotating his ears forward.

"Plus," Thor grinned. "And about two thousand rats in the Swords of Michael, your Highness."

"'Swords of Michael?'" my master breathed.

"That's so cool," I told them. "Well done, boys." I recovered first, always being a fast mouse, and made introductions while everyone was still stunned. When I introduced Squibette as my daughter, the rats looked at her wide-eyed, then at me, then sprang forward to kiss her paws.

"An honor to meet you, my lady!"

"A pleasure to make your acquaintance, to be sure!"

BJ looked at me. "Manners, even."

"I didn't teach them that," I confessed. "They've been reading!"

Stompy was ogling their gauntlets. Shiva took one off and gave it to her. The fact that she could even lift it was impressive by itself, but she asked for the other one. When she had both, she grinned wickedly like Scratchy, from ear to ear, and looked up at Shiva like a hungry dog.

"You'll have them tomorrow," Shiva answered her pleading gaze. Her tail spasmed in delight. She handed the gauntlets back.

"What are your orders, my lord?' They asked me, kneeling.

I made a "no, don't" gesture at them with my finger across the throat, but they didn't see it in time. I cleared my throat and kicked one of them in the foot. It hurt. Those were armored, too. When Shiva looked up, I moved my nose in the direction of the King.

"Oh!" He exclaimed. "Forgive us, your Majesty! We're used to—"

"To Squibble giving orders," he said, astonished and without doubt proud. "To Squibble… giving… orders…," he repeated (as if convincing himself), pacing around me. "And commanding a great legion of rodents!" He looked at the rest of them. He gestured towards me with his open hand. "Our Squibble. A mighty lord!"

"Why didn't you tell anyone, Squib?!" my master asked, astonished.

I shuffled again. Most un-lord like. "Umm… I was… umm… afraid you'd be mad."

"But this is the most incredible thing anyone has ever done! It's absolutely fantastic!"

"And it has saved the safe house," BJ said.

I sat there, blushing.

"Would you like to meet the troops, Majesty?" Shiva bowed and gestured through the archway entrance.

"With your permission, *Lord* Squibble?" BJ asked me.

I put my paw on my chest. "M… me?"

"Oh, yes," he said. "This… Horde… is yours, Sir Knight, and although I command you, I do not presume to command them. They are yours to command. And if we had ranks like Duke and such, I think perhaps I would have to promote you."

"You just did, Majesty," my master said. "Lord of the Hordes of Squibble. Master and commander of the armies of the safe house."

I bowed low. "Thank you, my liege!"

"Lead on," he said.

"Lead on," I told the boys. And they did.

They led us through tunnels long and deep, with many alcoves chiseled into them with guards in each one. The guards fell into rank behind us and before us at Shiva's glance. By the time we reached the main hall, two small armies marched before us and after. They marched in time. They carried their weapons in formation. By rank they organized. My boys had done well indeed. These were crack fighting troops. Each one armed and armored in soldier's armor. I wondered if the city had a single plastic sword or spear left in it.

We reached the entrance to the main hall and paused. Thor motioned for us to remain there. He went out with Shiva into the hall. Fanfare played loudly. I wondered where they had gotten the trumpets, much less how they'd learned to play them. Beyond our vision was the rumble of thousands of rodent voices. At the appearance of Shiva and Thor, it quieted instantly.

"Hordes!" Shiva yelled out in a booming voice. A return salute of weapons on shields and against other weapons rang out.

"Swords of Michael!" Thor called. Another salute, this time shaking the ground, crashed forth.

"Those of you who have not met the legendary Squibble in person are about to—for he has returned!" Shiva cried. The answering cheers were deafening to our ears, and nourishment to our souls. I could not wait to behold the army behind it.

"But more!" Shiva went on. The crowd quieted. "You have all passed the myths and legends of our lords down through the generations many times!" Murmurs of approval like a small earthquake flowed out. "You have heard of the Great ones! Nemo! King BJ! And... Squibble's Master, the very first of the Mouse Knights!" One could hear a pin drop in the enormous room now. I thought in my head, make them wait... make them wait... and Shiva did. Paused for dramatic effect, the room teetered on the edge of their seats.

Finally, "They have come!" Shiva bellowed.

The hall erupted into squeaks, chirps, applause, weapons crashing, shields clanging, and feet stomping. We came out, walking in a line with me first, then BJ, and fell into formation. Shiva and Thor were already bowing. The entire hall, more than thirty feet long, was filled. Filled!

After a shocked moment of realization that their gods were finally before them in the flesh, the mighty Hordes and Swords all went down onto knees. Weapons held up before them in salute, the great room was one single mass of pure, undying loyalty and homage. I could feel my master's head trying to turn against his will to gape at me some more. It didn't. Among us all, his will is the strongest.

Finally, BJ slowly looked over at me and nosed his head at the crowd. Oh. It was my job.

I stepped forward.

"Hail!" I cried out to them.

"**HAIL!**" the return cry came, shaking the stage we stood upon.

"You have done well, my legions!" I drew my sword and held it high. "I have come at the command of my master and my King!" They cheered again. After an endless time, it fell silent again. I held the sword high. "You have not trained for nothing! Do you know of our enemy!?"

They raised weapons and cried out for blood. So loud! I guess that was a yes. I looked over to find Shiva and Thor grinning widely.

I turned forward and held up my other hand. They were silent again.

"Would you follow me?" I shouted. They cheered.

"Would you follow your King!" I shouted. They hopped and cheered and stomped. One more hand. Silence.

"Would you follow us to WAR!!?" I screamed. They would have burst forth from that room and destroyed everything in their path, had they known but which direction the enemy was. The hall could not contain their noise. Dust fell from the ceiling. High ranking soldiers ran and mounted armored rats. Thousands of mice picked up their gear and slung it across their backs. Shields were buckled on, spears raised. Gleaming sword tips sparked across the entire floor like a star field. I looked over at BJ. He nodded to me in return. A new nod. One I had never seen before from him.

A nod of true, earned respect.

It took an hour to mobilize the troops. That was amazing, considering how many there were. Shiva had gotten my letter. They had been ready.

I went back to my private room and gathered my things. Stompy, Squibette and Scratchy came and helped me.

"These are beautiful drawings, Father," Squibette said, rolling up my stacks of practice work.

"I've gotten better since then," I said. "I wasn't much good at the time. Just liked drawing."

"It shows," she said, smiling at me. That smile was like my master's. It never failed to melt my heart.

Stompy gathered up my heavy things while I looked down at a stack of letters. They were the letters I had written to my momma, oblivious to the fact that she was dying of cancer at the time. I had written her almost every day. There were many weeks of letters there. Never delivered. Unread. Knowing I would likely never return, I left them. I turned to other things. I could not cry in front of my troops.

When I came out, they were loading everyone and everything into the truck. The Kind Human was sitting on the curb, holding my master and wearing an expression of astounded surprise. Surely he had never seen so many rodents in his life. We were gonna need several more trips to the pet store for food.

The officers of Michael's Swords were loading some massive, heavy equipment into the truck with winches and pulleys. There was a rat in scorched tatters directing them. Shiva and Thor introduced me to Vulcan, a rat knight who had trained under them. He was one of only a few rats to be knighted by the twins. He had been named for his expertise in forging metal weapons and armor. He had learned every nuance to the art. He was a grand master now, and forged day and night for the Hordes and the Swords. Vulcan fixed a steady gaze on me and bowed.

"An honor to meet you, my liege," he said in a voice like stone.

I bowed back. "Fine work you make."

He cracked a smile. "I was hoping to fit you for some," he said.

"I don't know if I have the strength to carry it!" I laughed. "But I would be honored to try." He smiled along with us as we all boarded the truck.

We left behind a small company of mice, about five hundred, to run the new kingdom. BJ appointed one mouse, named Theodore, a squire whose knight had died back at the safe house, as the new commander until our return. If we returned. Theo was given all my notes, and I briefed him for about an hour on what to do and when. Especially the books—he had to keep the books and records straight. Theo could read and write quite well, and he was a good squire. He had nothing but commendations to his credit, and everyone spoke well of him. Looking at him, I recognized the mouse. He was Fred's son—the big mouse who had wrestled me longer than the others in the city. He had made it this far in his quest to be a knight. I felt sad for him that he had lost his knight, who had been one of my master's brothers. Brother to Scratchy, my master, and several others, all made of the same stuff. Theo had not recovered from losing his sire. He felt he had failed as a squire, for a squire's job is to protect his master at all costs. His face was tough, but sad. I knew how he felt, thinking of my momma. The promotion did not cheer him, but I knew he'd do a good job. I suggested to BJ that the squire be knighted. He thought it an excellent idea.

Once all were aboard (and the new truck's shocks put severely to the test), the Kind Human turned to the High Council that sat upon the dashboard and said, "I hope you all know what you're doing."

My master went forward to him and nodded slowly.

The human put out his hand and picked up my master, put him to his lips, and kissed him. Returning him, he said, "I trust you."

And we were moving. Back to the safe house, and rapidly into the maw of our destiny.

A Grim Preparation

✠

The human had to make ten trips back to the city to get us all the supplies we asked for. He spent all day doing it, and in the end had to get Heide's help. Heide came herself as well, and brought Fred and her children, who all asked to come to the house they had heard so much about. Heide asked Fred to stay out of the war, and that was fine, because there would be alot of rodents staying out. Most of the women, children, the old, the sick. Those who didn't want to go. No one would be forced.

Heide paid for everything with the money Mike gave to her through Ruby. She insisted. The Rat and Mouse Club they had created was in full swing now, gathering members and putting up a web site. They planned to publish a magazine. I saw a future in that for old Squibble. Stories, art… I would be published maybe. Getting published in the real world is hard enough without being a mouse (yeah, like I would tell anyone that), but maybe the Kind Humans of the RMC would give cute little Squibble a chance to get a foot in the door. I would even bat my eyelashes and groom their fingertips for them. I'm not beyond a little begging. I'd love to have lots of people read my stories. My master did it. I did end up trying to get published as both a writer and an artist, but that story comes later on.

Vulcan took several apprentices to whom he taught his trade, including some mice. They set out right away building war machines. Catapults, ballistae, ranged weapons, and improved spears and shields for our troops.

It was in that first couple of days that I met up again with Fred and her boys, plus a couple of other mice I had missed.

I was walking about with my master when I found myself confronted by a bunch of mice. Seven mice in brand new soldier's armor came to me, led by Sneaky, Squeaky and Clyde. Clyde looked… burned. His hair had the smell of gunpowder to it, and his face looked kinda, well, edgy. But he was happy to see me.

"Hail, Lord Squibble!" He said. The men all saluted and went down to one knee.

My master chuckled and went on, inspecting the preparations. I turned to face them. It was then I recognized Fred's children. Theodore, the big one that had fought me so hard back at Heide's house was, of course, not there.

"Come far, have we?" I asked.

"Sire, we ask to be in your special cohort," One said.

Clyde giggled. It sounded like he was a loon, but who am I to judge that?

"I don't' have a special cohort, men. Just the Horde itself," I answered.

"The King says you get to pick 1000 of the best and keep them all around you," Sneaky said. "We brought you the news first."

"How mousey of you," I commented. They smiled. I looked the men over. Fred's kids were healthy, strong, and eagerly desiring action. They had some talents, I could see it.

"Okay," I said. "When they let me know, you're in. And you," I pointed to the biggest. He looked up, surprised. "You're a sergeant in charge of these others, and more will be put under you."

He smiled. "Thank you, Sire!"

I nodded. Turning to Clyde, I asked, "Blown anything up lately?"

He tittered. "Ohhh yesss, Master!" He hopped about. "We are getting quite good at demolitions. Yess… quite decent, I would say. Quite dangerous! He he heee!"

He looked too happy to be just blowing things up. I narrowed my eyes. They had a metal worker…

"Please tell me you haven't built a nuke or something like that," I said.

"Eh?" he tilted his near-deaf ears toward me. I gestured with my hands like a mushroom cloud and raised my eyebrows.

"Oh, we're working on that," he said seriously, "but no… not yet." He giggled again. I relaxed.

"We have stuff almost as good," he said. My relax went away. "The generals will show you..yeeeEEEsss… they shall show you. hehehehehe!"

"Oh," I said. "Okayyy. Can't wait."

"Boom!" Clyde hollered. "Boom Boom!" Laughing maniacally, he ran off. I gave Sneaky and Squeaky a stiff look. They both shrugged and followed Clyde. I turned back to Fred's kids.

"Don't end up like that," I told them. They nodded, frightened.

Stompy had her gauntlets in a day, as she had been promised. They were custom fitted to her giant fists by Vulcan himself. She was eating like a machine, and regaining her former size (maybe a little bit more even). Nothing could stop her now. She gleefully went about punching holes in wooden beams, plastic toys, and snapping our plastic weapons in two whenever one was aimed at her in practice. After knocking a rat out cold with a single punch she was forbidden to punch any friendly forces while wearing the gloves of doom. Vulcan made her a marble stone statue of a black mouse to practice on, but she demolished it in one sitting, and the entire house had a healthy fear of her after hearing the swearing and the noise from that vehemently vicious session.

Shiva and Thor designed the outdoor training area. I had taught my troops well, and the rat twins had improved upon that, but BJ and my master saw holes in their training. They all needed to practice line battle. It would be weeks, maybe months before we were ready for the final conflict. The Kind Human set up the back yard exactly as we asked him to, digging trenches and piling dirt into high mountains. He built walls and laid out huge, flat boards. He built platforms and boxes for the different training areas. He built us an archery range and a castle wall with battlements. Staircases, terrain of all types, including swamp, was duplicated. We laid out red tape, designating where the humans would step. Mice had to cross at the wooden bridges, or risk being stepped on. Within days, training had begun again at the safe house, in earnest. BJ commanded groups of ten thousand at a time, and every single knight, officer, or mouse of interest had a job to do. Many rodents were promoted, for in the field we would need corporals, sergeants, lieutenants, captains, and more to commands all the different groups the inner circle was creating. My master was patterning it after medieval warfare from the books he read, with Shiva and Thor adding the modern element to it.

Oh yeah. Speaking of modern elements.

They took me aside one day to the training grounds. Carefully avoiding the graveyards, I followed them to a metal box about four feet square, with only one open side. Inside was a long range, burned black, with metal targets at the end in the shapes of humans, not mice. Several of the targets were covered in rags looking like clothing. The far wall of the box was slanted upward, and there were many walls and barriers placed in front of the targets for some reason.

"You aren't going to blow something up near me, are you?" I asked my boys. "Because mice don't like loud noises, and I ain't wearing metal armor."

"Well, we're gonna make a loud noise," Thor chuckled, "but it won't hurt you."

I leered at him.

"We promise," he said.

"Ohhh… okaaay," I said. He smiled and whipped out a gun.

A rodent sized gun. Shiva pulled one out as well. They both got an evil light in their eyes, something like psychotic glee.

"No way!" I said.

"Way," Thor said, and cracked off a shot. It slammed the far target down and bounced off the ceiling, into one of the barriers.

I flinched hard. Fell down and covered my face, in fact.

"It's okay, Uncle," Shiva said. "The range won't let them bounce back at us. Vulcan designed it after human firing ranges."

"Oh… okay," I mumbled. Rats with guns.

"The great equalizer," Thor said proudly. "Now ours."

"Are those for the war?" I asked, getting up.

"No," Shiva said. "Too gnarly to produce. Money, time, all that. Also, Clyde doesn't have gunpowder down yet, exactly, so we steal it. It's hard to get. We only have four models. One is for you." He held out a pistol to me. A mouse sized pistol. Now I'd seen it all.

"It only carries one shot," he said as I took the device (handling it like it was a tiny snake). "But we have extra bullets. We figured you liked the slingshot, you might like this."

"My slingshot is an art form…" I started.

"It's a weapon," Shiva insisted. "Like this. And this can be an art form too. How about those old west movies, eh?"

"Mister," said Thor as he squinted, "we deal in lead."

They both busted up, cackling in glee.

"Besides," Shiva said, "this is the future, Squibble. You gotta stay on top of things if you wanna win."

"My master would think this was unchivalric," I said. Unchivalric meant it gave one opponent a clearly unfair advantage. In the old days, swordsmen had honor, and tried to keep things decently fair.

"Yeah, well then save it for an unchivalric opponent," Shiva said.

I nodded and thanked them for the nice gift. They smiled. Going the long way around the graveyard, I went back to my house and put the gun in my pile-O-stuff. I then tried to forget it was there.

The humans kept busy helping us. They were our giants, using their size and strength to do things we never could. Our Kind Human had brought, at great cost to his shattered body, more supplies from the city for Shiva and Thor, as he had been delighted to see them, and deeply regretted that they had been through anything traumatic because of his bad judgment. My boys weren't past using guilt to get what they wanted, and worked it for all it was worth. It turned out to be worth quite a bit. Stuff from the hardware store, Radio Shack, military surplus stores, gun shows, and mail order specialty stores littered the bathroom. The rats made a spot in the basement for their lab, and made it clear that to trespass meant death.

The humans clearly did not approve of a war, and hated the thought of rodents killing each other. They tried to talk us out of it. Having not been on our side of the pain the Black Mouse had rained down on us, they could barely understand. Our Kind Human seemed to understand better than Heide, but he was a man. He had been there to watch us die of the plague. When my master told him the Black Mouse must go, he knew it was true. It was after that talk when he went out and bought the rats all that stuff. I think he was trying to give us as much of an edge as possible. He was completely on our side, and so was Heide, despite what they wished wouldn't happen. Hey, we wished it too, we told them.

Especially my master.

The inner circle was offered metal armor. My master was the first to turn it down, loving his natural armor too much, and claimed that nature knew best. After that, no mice took the generous offer of Vulcan, though they did let him reinforce the armor they had with better buckles, straps, and metal hinges. Some mice added metal extras to their armor. Squibette had dimes put on her shoulders, which everyone thought was very bold until Stompy used quarters.

The Swords of Michael reveled in being the mounts for Mouse Knights, and took pride in their great size and strength. Human mounts could not come close to these. Horses could never scale walls, hop the equivalent of a hundred feet, or strike with their tails. They could not bite with 24,000 pounds per inch of pressure, nor had they claws. And sorry, but rats are just plain smarter than horses by far. Each of them got armor, for by now Vulcan had over 200 rodents working for him. And thus we had our heavy cavalry. My master was pleased. He said that in many wars, the side with the heavy cavalry had won. These armored rats could run clean over a hundred mice each and never even feel it.

The big challenge was gathering our allies. The bees said they would fight with us, as always, and sent out drones to find other nests and ask their help. The ants said they would march with us for certain, being creatures quite used to warfare themselves, but their numbers had been reduced by the drought and the famine. They, too, would go abroad and ask for help from other nests, although that was less likely to be given.

Then we had to find the field mice.

No ally would be more valuable than they. Their numbers were, at least at one time, immense. They were at least twenty times faster than any domestic mouse, and used to hardship. They would be hard to control and not used to organized battle, but even if we just asked them to go ballistic on the enemy, they would take a mean chunk out of the other side. The problem was finding them. The drought and the heat had driven them away in search of continued life. The few that came to our house for food and water did not know where other tribes had gone. They eked out their bare existences day to day, and belonged to no tribe. Those few said they'd join us, but we needed the tribes of Nemo. Their numbers and ferocity were too great an advantage not to have.

So my master sent twenty knights out on rats, equipped for a difficult quest, to find the Tribes of Nemo and ask their help in the war. They were sent to the far corners of our earth, the Fields of Fate, avoiding the area the enemy was known to be amassing his dark army. Regardless, none ever returned.

Mouse scouts from the Hordes of Squibble were sent to the enemy camp, being experts at camouflage and sneaking in the city. The few field mice we had were organized into a group called Lightning Legion, and they tried their best to train the scouts for skulking in the wild. Still, precious few returned, and what they reported was scary.

The enemy had moved mostly underground, and his numbers were not known. But what was too large to be moved underground was visible, and it was clear he had monsters.

When we asked what the scouts meant by monsters, they just trembled and stared at us wide-eyed.

"Monsters!" they'd say, and that was all. It left us with a bad feeling in our stomachs. We knew of a few coyotes, but that was all. We had thought our victory was in the bag with so many on our side, and so well armed, so well trained. Now we had doubt chewing on us.

On top of that, Nemo warned us that the dark powers of the Black Mouse had grown, and that now it was safe to assume that he might be able to do anything Nemo himself could, probably more.

I asked him exactly how much that was, and he just smiled. I was tempted to bite his ear, but I knew that would only get me flung about like a rag mouse.

Each and every night the safe house was a moving mass of training camps and the sounds of building. BJ felt like a true King now, and it showed in his training. He gave everything he had to the massive group, and still no mouse could beat him in combat. He loved every bruise he took, every wound he suffered, for it meant that his students would be more likely to survive the war.

The ranks went like this:

BJ was king, and therefore in charge of everything. My master came second, although not really, because he held more respect than BJ did, technically, but he deferred to the King in all things. My master was pretty much in charge of the war effort. Then came Percival, who was acknowledged to be second in command. I was equal with Percival, who I had playfully taken to calling Perky because he had way too much energy and was way too serious all the time for such a young mouse. After that came the rat twins, the rest of the inner circle were made colonels, including Stompy, Squibette, Ghost, and Branch, even though he wasn't there. My master wrote a letter to him, explaining everything that was happening, but Nemo stopped him from mailing it.

"By the time it reaches him, all this will have already been decided," Nemo said.

"I want him to know what happened, in case we don't—," my master said.

"He knows," Nemo told my master. "I have written him. He will receive the letter the day of battle."

My master peered at the wise chinchilla. "What day will that be, master Nemo?"

Nemo looked out in the direction of the enemy camp.

"A cold one," he said. "Cold, and dark."

A shudder ran through my fur.

"Soon?" My master asked.

Nemo looked at us both with eyes full of hidden knowledge. He looked quite sad.

"Yes," he said. He sounded sad too.

My master sighed. "I hate this."

Nemo nodded. "It is a just cause, and against great evil." He put his massive paw gently on my master's head. "It was meant to be, and could not possibly have been avoided. Sooner or later, one day or the next, it would have come to this. Waiting would only make it worse."

My master nodded. He turned to look at me, his face set in determination, but still showing the weariness and toil of his troubled soul.

"Well then, Squibble, we are almost ready. It's nearing the end of winter. The field mice have not been found. We must assume they will not come. The bees and ants have had marginal success. It looks like it's up to us."

"Do we have enough to win, Master?" I asked.

"Hard to say," he said. "But one thing is yet undone."

My ears went up.

"How do you feel about one last quest together, my squire?" He smiled softly at me.

I nodded immediately. "Where are we going, Master?"

He looked out across the snowless, frozen Fields of Fate.

"To claim my sword."

The Real Adventure This Time

✠

Many protested us going, when it was so dangerous, and we were so needed to the cause, but Nemo and the inner circle knew we must go. Scratchy absolutely threw a fit that he wasn't allowed to go with me. He spazzed out completely. He argued in violent hand gestures and body language that it was a squire's job—their right—to guard their knight—and wasn't that why I was going with my master? Was he so worthless that he didn't deserve to go? I nodded at him to shut him up, and he broke into tears. My master kicked me and I growled an apology at the mini mouse. Scratchy went over to stand by BJ, who at least was cordial to him.

He just wasn't goin'! This was our quest, my master and I. Ours. He wasn't goin, troops weren't goin, and that was that. Weirdo couldn't even walk straight—he'd be doing circles the entire time and get us killed. Don't ask me why I still didn't like him. You can take Nemo's theory that he was just like me (and I don't care), or you can take my theory of "I don't know, okay?" and just let it drop. I had good days and bad days. Hey, I'd made him a squire, okay? He oughtta have been happy with that. No way was he getting knighted. Besides, he was way too easily disappointed.

"Does the fabled blade even truly exist?" BJ asked when we were packed and ready to depart.

"Squibble says it does," my master said. "And I have faith in him."

"But that was a dream!" Ghost said.

"All of his other dreams have pretty much come true," my master said. Nemo nodded. "We have to do this, or the darker dreams might also come true."

"Where are you going, then?" asked Stompy. "Do you even know?"

"Michael cast his sword into the lake," my master said. "Squibble and I know right where it is."

"So do I," BJ said. "It is many days from here. Weeks, in this weather. A most dangerous trek for two mice in the cold, alone."

"We did it before," I chirped.

"And with much worse circumstances," my master added. This time we are equipped, experienced, and ready for almost anything. Besides," he ruffled my fur. I purred. "This is a holy quest, my liege. We cannot fail."

"The enemy is everywhere," Stompy said.

"None of our scouts have come back alive, not even mounted cavalry," Squibette added.

"What can this holy avenger do that is so important?" BJ asked. "To risk both your priceless lives?"

My master looked out toward the horizon.

"It was supposed to set the land right," he said. "In the stories, the sword was meant for the King, and the King was meant to unify the land. All the people of that land. All rodents. Maybe everyone, period."

I felt a tingle of excitement at his words that I could not explain.

"Who will wield the sword then?" BJ asked. "I have a feeling that it is not my duty."

"Whoever is meant to, shall," my master answered. He moved out onto the deck. The Kind Human came, thundering from the bedroom to the front of the house in just several long strides.

My master and I were picked up and kissed.

"You both be careful," he said. "I don't want to lose you."

"Yeah, ditto," said Stompy. "It's crazy going alone."

"Not so much," my master said as he was put back down. "An army might attract attention, and we don't know whether or not the enemy knows about the sword. He might not! If he doesn't, this is our ace in the hole. Two lone mice might sneak through where entire armies would fail. It's a long shot, but this is the best way."

BJ smiled. "I recall a similar tactic taken by two hobbits," he said.

My master grinned. "Yeah. I hadn't thought of that. Yeah. It's like that."

"The enemy once had the lake surrounded," BJ said. "You must assume he knows about the sword, though he may have surrounded the lake to cut off water to the field mice."

My master just nodded. "Nonetheless, we must go."

He shouldered his pack and put on his dark green cloak. I put on mine of dark blue. We gathered our weapons—swords and spears, bows, arrows, and of course, my slingshot.

"Farewell, faithful warriors," BJ called as we crawled down the ramp to the ground. "We shall all pray for your success! May the Mousegod bless your holy quest!"

"He better," I muttered. "This is all his fault."

Within a few hours we had lost sight of the house. My master stopped for a breather. The night was frigid and dry. We were bundled in every sort of clothing that might go on a mouse. We had several layers of undergarments, followed by a tunic, then the armor and then a heavy cloak that was waterproof. Just in case, perchance, the curse might lift and it should rain. All of our equipment was grayed-down, camouflage colors. Mine mostly blue, his mostly green. Everything was designed to keep us from being food.

The clear night sky was adamant that there would be no rain.

I guessed the temperature at near freezing or below. Normally domestic mice can't handle temperatures below 65∞, but we had the aid of technology and knowledge this time. We weren't just some young mice on a harebrained quest (sorry, Master). We knew what we were doing this time. What saves most mice from freezing to death is their nests. By instinct alone, mice can build the most amazing nests. Heat holding, cold resistant, sometimes waterproof, comfy, and hidden. We brought our nests with us. Shiva and Thor had looked up the designs for sleeping bags made for humans that went into the deep negative degree temperatures, and they built us a pair with the same technology. It's not as if the materials were expensive. I could see the human now, "Can I get half a foot of this fabric and three inches of that?" Anyway, they built us portable nests. While only a few hours from the house, my genius master decided to pull them out and test them.

We had a mini tent to share, and two sleeping bags, both big enough for both of us, if we should need to curl up together like mice do to stay warm. My master pulled his out. Packed away, it was compressed into a tiny size, easy to carry—but when it came out, it was huge. He wrapped it around himself and stuck his nose out at me, smiling.

"Warm?" I asked him. He nodded happily.

I pulled out mine and climbed in. Very warm. Very cozy. Portable mouse nest.

We warmed up and then, reluctantly, packed away our nests and drank some water. Then we moved on.

I had forgotten what long treks were like. The quest to go get the Black Mouse seemed like such a long time ago, and my pilgrimage to the city was a whole different lifetime. This, I considered, was an entirely new one. Maybe every day is a new lifetime. I looked over at my master. He was getting along well. He seemed to have strength. It encouraged me.

We buried our waste when we had to go, for such things were visible in the ultraviolet spectrum to hawks and owls. Our pee glowed to them, like a light in the night that says "I'm nearby—eat me!" Even regular mice know this somewhat, out of sheer instinct.

Master had a compass. We used it to lead us to the lake, which was about three weeks away. Maybe two, if we made good time. Mice on wheels have been known to run six miles a day sometimes, but put those mice on cold, uneven and unfamiliar terrain, give them 25 grams of stuff to carry, and make them sneak so they don't attract predators. A mile a day if lucky. If really lucky.

So a mile a day it was, my master and I. The first evening, we spent under the lee of a rock, doing our chi gung and eating some of the millet we brought. My master unpacked a tiny chess game and its wooden pieces.

"Master!" I said. "The weight of it..."

"I think I'd go crazy without something brain related to do, Squib," he said. "And you always wanted to learn how to play better."

"At least let me carry it, Master," I begged.

"Okay," he replied, setting up the pieces. "But don't lose it. It's like my encyclopedias. I would miss it terribly if it was lost."

"If I lose it I will make you a new one," I said. He glared at me. "But I won't lose it, Master!" I added. He smiled.

"I know you won't. Now... who has to be black?!" He grinned.

"*Not*it!" I chirped. He grinned wider.

"Okay," he said. "You can be white. White goes first."

"Yeah. I wish," I said.

"Now, Squibble," he eyed me. "Don't be bitter. We'll get our chance."

I moved a piece and looked at him. "How do I not be bitter?" I asked. "After all I've gone through? After all you've gone through?"

He lowered his head, thinking. He moved a pawn.

"I think you just decide... to let it go, Squib. Like yesterday's wind. Like a beautiful sunset you'll never see again. Like river water, moving slowly by, only once do we see it, and then it's gone."

I stared at him blank faced.

"Something wrong?" he asked.

"No," I whispered. "Nope."

"Your move, whitey."

"I'm not the white mouse here, pal," I said, and moved a knight.

"OOooOOoo," he said, "Big guns. Scary scary." He moved one of his knights.

I gathered my wits together while I lit a concealed fire under a bunch of stones, in a ditch. I made hot tea for my master, to help his breathing, for I could hear it rasping.

When I came back, he was studying the board.

"What were you doin?" I asked playfully. "Cheatin'?"

"Cheating!" He exclaimed, and put an offended hand on his breastplate. He made an astounded face. "Cheating?! Oh, I never!"

"Well maybe you shoulda been!" I gleefully chirped. We both laughed.

"Hey, Squib," he said, "What are you up to?" When I didn't answer, he said, "About two or three inches?" We busted up laughing again. We wrapped ourselves in our nests.

"What are you up to, Master?" I asked back.

"Cheatin'!" he said. More laughter.

"No really…," I said, giggling.

"Oh, chess is a game of intense thought, my young squire Squibble," he said, moving a piece. "You must think seven steps ahead of your enemy, at least, or surely lose."

"Oh," I said. "In that case I'll just use prescience to see what you're gonna do, and be so way ahead of you that you'll think I was reading your mind."

He laughed. "Now that's cheating!" He stopped while I considered my move and gave me a serious look. When I looked up from my move, he asked, "Can you really do that?"

"Read your mind, or see the future?" I asked.

"Either," he said.

"Nemo says I can do both, but… no. Nope. I don't think so."

"Maybe you don't believe in yourself enough yet," he said. He made his move on the board and looked back up at me. His face lit up in a wonderful smile. "You've come so far, Squibble. I'm so proud of you. Your mom would have been too."

I blushed. To tell you the truth, the feeling I had in that perfect moment stuck with me forever. It was like being on that magical pier on the river, so long ago. It was a piece of Heaven. I think Heaven is whatever feels best to us in life, and for me, that was it. Knowing he loved me, and hearing his praise.

"Nemo says I have a long way to go, Master," I said, moving my queen. "I want to do it, but it keeps getting harder and harder. It's just stunning how hard it is now."

"Is it really hard right now?" he asked, smiling.

I looked around. A clear, frosty night in winter, a fire, hot tea, good food, and both of us warm… Most of all, my master and best friend in the whole world by my side… on a real holy quest… adventuring It just couldn't get any better.

"No," I admitted. "Nope."

"It's always hardest just before you get it, Squib."

Without moving my face from the board, I looked up at him.

"I think you've gotten it," he said.

"Ah, you're biased," I said, shuffling about a little.

He nodded. Moved a piece. "You know what I want to do someday?" he asked me.

I scooched forward (if it ain't a word, it are now!) and perked my ears. "No, Master… what?"

He looked up, puffy cheeks behind his pointy little nose, and said, "I want to play a human at chess."

I grinned. "The Kind Human won't play?"

"I've never asked him, honestly. I don't even know if he has a chess board. It's something I should do. Somehow I don't think I'm going to, though."

"Howcome?" I asked.

He looked up at the sky. "I don't know, Squib. I'm what… a year and a half? Past that, now. I'm an old mouse."

"Not even!" I said. "Mice have been known to live to three—even more! The world record was seven!"

"Seven years!" he made a shocked face. "I don't know if I'd want to live that long. What would the quality of life be? I doubt I'd be able to run on my big blue wheel at that age. That would be like a human living to 350!" He chuckled. "I don't think so. I've done most of what I came here to do."

"Not even," I said, feeling anxiety in my chest. I moved a piece.

"You're right there, Squib," he said. I cheered up. "I think I have one more thing to do."

I peered up at him from the chessboard.

"I hope it takes a long time," I said.

He smiled at me again, filling me with light and warmth more than any nest could.

"I'll try," he said.

Each night we woke from our concealed hideout and packed up, did our chi gung, and set out on the trek. Night was cold always… frozen on many evenings. We were well equipped for it, though, and we even had little boots for our feet. Socks for the boots. The whole thing. We wrapped our faces to keep our breath from showing and to keep the air that we took in warmer. We skulked from place to place, and ran across open areas, weapons ready. We covered our shiny metal bottlecap shields with dull leather and drew funny pictures on the covers. I drew a picture of myself holding the Black Mouse from behind while Percival chopped off his head. While we giggled about that he drew a picture of himself playing chess with a human (and winning, of course). We called ourselves the Knights of So WHAT! And when it was cold, we'd say "So what!" When there wasn't much food, we'd say "So what!" When we had to trudge uphill for many hours, rest constantly, and our water was frozen, we said… yep you guessed it…"So what!" We had a wonderful time, and no enemy accosted us whatsoever, which was strange, but… so what?

We avoided a few owls and such things, but our daytime hideaways were always fine defensible spots, even if we had to work at it with shovels, and not a single creature in that winter landscape did we encounter otherwise.

Each morning before we packed and resumed our trek we would play chess, do chi gung, and fill our water bags after licking our fill of dew from the grass and leaves. In summer that dew hadn't been there. Now, it was. Throughout our entire journey, we did not go thirsty once. It was wonderful.

We spoke of many things. Of most everything, actually, both being longwinded and liking conversation (like you can't guess that after page 500?). We talked about battle, about stories, about dreams, about my training and my art, about writing and getting published (which my master thought was a grand idea), and about spiritual things. I found it easy to talk to him. Effortless. And no subject was taboo. We flowed from one topic into another, and there were no boundaries. When he asked me about my pilgrimage, I told him everything. Every detail. I asked him after it was over if he'd met Fred at the safe house when she came. He said he had, and a fine woman she was. He asked me if I wanted to settle down with her.

"Noway," I said.

"Don't you get lonely?" he said. "Is it because of Favorite?"

"Yeah, and yeah," I said. "How about you? Losing my momma must have sucked."

"It did," he said. "Oh, it did, worse than anything. I felt as if a piece of my soul were torn away. The Kind Human tried to put other females into my cage for me, but they just couldn't measure up to her." He looked far away. I knew he was remembering my momma. I joined him. In my memory, she was smiling and licking me. "She was so wonderful," he sighed. "I miss her every day."

"Yeah," I said. "No one can replace her. I understand."

He nodded.

One night we came across a field mouse village. It was deserted. Spooky, too. They hadn't taken any of their winter reserves, not that there was much, so we took some and filled our bags. As we did so we looked around, feeling like thieves. It was as if they had just vanished into thin air. Run off at a moment's notice. It gave us the creeps. My master drew his weapon. I pulled out my slingshot and loaded it. Creeping through that husk of a village, we found not one mouse. No recent sign, nothing. We finally went on, the mystery unsolved. Of course, we both knew it was probably the enemy, but we didn't want to think of that. The field mice were innocent. They shouldn't have been dragged into this.

But then, weren't we all innocent? I mean, who would want this? I wondered why we were being tested so, and said as much to my master. He said that no beings were tested by the gods unless some great treasure was to be had. I remembered Orpheus.

"The treasure better be damn good," I said.

He snickered. "Yeah. I agree."

"What could possibly be worth that much?" I said. "What could make the Devil that mad—to use his gnarly powers on mice?"

"I don't know, Squib," he said as we left the haunted village behind us, "but if it's something we have yet to do, we better make sure we do it."

"Yeah," I snarled. "In his face!"

"In his face!" my master raised a fist and growled with me.

We chanted "In his face!" all the way up the hill.

When we stopped that morning, I built the fire and my master rummaged through his sack to the very bottom, through all the food we had salvaged from the ghost town. By the time I had the fire going and covered, he had the chess game set up. He smiled at me with a big cheeky grin.

I squinted one eye at him. "Whassup?"

"This is up," he said, and from behind his back he pulled a piece of honeycomb.

My eyes bugged out. I almost cried. I inched up to it as if it might suddenly vanish, or be demolished by bullies.

But he held it out to me.

"I was saving it for a special time," he said. "Now seems right."

So we had honeycomb for dinner with our grain, and played chess, and laughed with each other until we went to bed, warm and full. It was perfect. It was golden. Heaven.

The original food lasted a long time before we had run out, and the food we took from the wild mouse village lasted just as long. Our supplies had been perfectly thought out, for we knew we'd need to refill somewhere along the way, and just trusted fate that food would be there, for no mouse can carry three weeks worth of food. But the food had been there when we needed it, and everything had gone well so far. Every morning just before dawn as we made camp and did our chi gung, we were comfortable, despite the cold. I kept waiting for the hammer to fall, for something to go horribly wrong. After two weeks of good travel, I was a seriously paranoid mouse. I just knew that something was going to attack us, or injure us, or cripple one of us, and we were gonna have to crawl back to the safe house on our lips, barely alive. And frankly, I was sick of that crap.

But it never happened. Our trip was magnificent and flawless—like a wonderful dream one wishes never to awake from. On the morning of the eighteenth day, we reached the lake just before dawn.

Excalibur

✠

The sky was just beginning to lighten when we arrived. The surface of the lake was mirrored silver. The grass was still and covered in white ice. A low mist on the ground ran past our feet, like thick soup. There was not a sound in the whole world. A great tree stood on the opposite shore from us, and against the jewel-blue sky it was a black silhouette. The stars shined and twinkled at us as if we were the only beings alive in a dream world painted by a master artist. The beauty was breathtaking. Every color, every detail stood out as if reality had gone into high gear. I felt the power under me growing as a giant wakes. The moon was a sliver in the sky, with the rest of it being darker than space behind it, so we could see the whole thing. We stood there in the delicate, enchanted silence, not daring to speak or move, lest a single ruffle of our cloaks break the spell.

The sky turned sapphire, then aquamarine, then just a hint of pastel green, then deep violets. Reds. Oranges. Yellow. Then sunlight came across the horizon in bands that arced across the entire world above, drifting down ever so slowly down to meet us. When it struck the water it hit our eyes at the same time, and the world became one gigantic star of gold, casting its radiance all around us, encasing us in a spectral field of bright power and soft shadows. There in the heart of it, in the midst of the sparkling waters, was a figure standing on the lake. Lost in the blazing sunlight dancing on the still water, all we could see with our paws over our brows was that it was a silhouette of a female mouse holding a sword.

My master exchanged a single glance with me. The mighty rush of adrenaline was written on his face. I could smell his delight. This was one of his oldest stories come true. The oldest story. Before his very eyes stood the Lady of the Lake.

Transfixed by the divine beauty of the moment, my master stepped out onto the lake. I almost moved to stop him, but the lake held him. He walked on water out to the center. Dawn stood still for us. Time did not intrude on our sacred moment.

When he reached the center, he knelt before the Lady. I saw, with eyes that should not have been able to see that far, my master take the sword Michael had cast into the lake months before. I saw him turn around, tears streaming down his face, and the Lady vanished back beneath the golden surface of the water. Undoubting, he walked back to me on the shore, where time resumed, and suddenly the sun was well above the horizon. In his hands he held the legendary sword.

His face was set in an enlightened peace, streaked with tears drying in the sun. He held the sword out to me and I held it. It looked like a perfectly forged piece of metal. No marks upon it whatsoever, and the blade was so sharp one could not see an edge on it at all.

The instant after I touched it my powers went into high gear. The earth shifted around me and I saw the spirit plane overlapping the material one. I felt and saw the power of the lake and this place. The sword burned with ethereal, white flame. I looked around and saw angels—the same angels that had guarded the safe house, here at the lake's edges, guarding us with drawn weapons of fire, haloes shining above their perfect heads. Perhaps they had been guarding us the entire time, the whole trip. And this was why there was no enemy here. Our quest truly was holy. No evil could touch it.

I looked back at the golden blade. I felt my mind focusing on the sword and then everything went away.

I was seeing a battlefield. The death tolls were outrageous on both sides. Smoke drifted across the burned fields. Sounds of clashing weapons and dying animals were everywhere… It was so real!

No.

I forced myself back to reality by rejecting the offer from the sword. I did not want to see the future. I knew that's what it was. The sword had activated my prescience. I knew now that my dreams had also been forms of possible futures. Many of my waking visions had. All this time I had been waiting for my prescience to "show up" when it had been with me all along. I now knew, for certain, what it felt like. But I didn't want it. I didn't want to see more terrible things. I forced my mind out of the trance, and came back to reality.

My spirit vision cut out altogether. I guess the blade didn't intrude upon one's soul without permission. Fine by me.

"Squibble?" my master asked. "You okay?"

"Yeah. Yeah, okay." I said. I looked down at the legendary sword. It was calm. No white fire.

When I hefted it I felt unearthly balance, and lightness. I halfheartedly swung it at the dead remains of a bush beside us. Though the root of that bush was over an inch thick, it cleft through as if it were not there, and sank deep into a rock on the other side. I gritted my teeth and made a "whoops!" face, and drew it out. The rock fell in half; the blade was unscathed in the slightest.

My master whistled right along with me; the same pitch of impressed awe in stereo. I handed the sword back. Clearly he was still shaken up. His paw trembled.

"Squibble…" he stammered.

I inched closer to him, careful to avoid the vorpal edge of that mighty blade. He seemed reluctant to tell me something. I put my paw on his armored shoulder.

"Master? What is it?"

"The Lady… of the Lake, Squibble…" he whispered. "It was… it was Tree." He looked at me with new tears. "It was your momma."

Shock ran from my heart down through my toes and fingers, stinging like electricity. I didn't know what to think. I didn't have much time to think.

There was a sound behind us, much too silent to be anything large, but it was. It was an owl.

My master spun with the blade, and it made just the most dangerous whipping-through-air sound you could ever want to hear. That sound made it seem as if we were lucky the very atoms in its path were not cloven in twain, and an atomic blast the result. As for me, I had my slingshot loaded and drawn in a mouse heartbeat.

The owl raised its wings to protect itself and stepped back, crying, "I am an old man! Do not hurt me!"

We recognized the owl who had taught Nemo. We lowered our weapons immediately.

"Apologies, mighty lord," my master said. I could hear the new strength in his voice. I looked at him in wonder. He even looked younger. He stood straighter. His fur had shine to it. His ears had no droop at all. "You surprised us."

The owl hesitantly lowered his wings. "You surprised me as well," his voice boomed in the empty air. "As well as what I saw."

"You saw?" I said, putting away my slingshot.

"I live in yonder tree," he said, pointing a wing toward the oak on the other side of the lake. "I saw."

We stood in his presence a moment. Of course. The tree. Neither of us had thought of it with all we had been through.

Finally, he said, "I have the sheath for it. Michael gave it to me to hold. It has waited in my den for you to come."

"I would appreciate it, great one," my master said with a bow. "Because no earthly scabbard will hold this edge."

The owl knelt its head down low to the ground. I looked at my master in alarm.

"Sir," my master said, "you mean us to... to..."

"Get on," the owl said. "I can not harm you while you bear that blade, and in no case would I desire to."

I broke out in the shakes. We were about to get on an owl... and be taken to its lair! Oh, no one was going to believe this.

My master nodded, and though smelling strongly of fear, he mounted the Owl's neck and crouched behind his head.

"Coming, Squibble?" he said, half in glee and half in terror.

I shook my head. "Uhhh... No. Nope. I'll wait for the next bus, thanks."

"Get on, knight," the owl's voice echoed across the lake. "I will not harm you."

"Not that I don't trust you or nothin'," I said, "but the old instinct thing dies hard, you know?"

"You are advanced enough to overcome it," my master called to me. "Come on! How many mice get this honor?"

"You mean... more than once?" I gulped.

"Squibble!"

"You have the almighty sword of chop-anything, master! It's easy for you to say!"

He looked at the sword, then down at me. He tossed the sword.

Both the owl and I dodged wildly, even though his toss was accurate. No way was I going to be accidentally chopped by that metal lightsaber. Oops, sorry, Squib—I was aiming for ten inches to the left, but I cut off your tail by accident... so sorry...

I went over to the sword, buried to the hilt in a rock. I looked at it, then back at my master. We both grinned hugely.

"Draw it and be a mighty hero, Squibble!" he called.

I drew the sword from the stone. It slid out easily. The owl eyed me hard.

"No bright ideas, mouse," it said.

"I'm not in the business of being called owlslayer," I told it. "You have been an honorable ally."

"Don't even so much as drop that thing on me," he said.

I looked up. I felt no fear. That sword was cool.

"I won't," I told him.

Slowly, I climbed up the soft down of his feathers to my master. I handed him back his sword.

"We don't have much time," the owl said, and lifted off.

I sank my teeth into my master's cloak and my claws gripped onto anything I could find. The ground became small. Fast. From the air, we flew over the lake, and I knew my master was thinking the same thing as I was. This was what Mike saw as he fell.

The owl took us up, up, and more up, circled once, then descended (too rapidly for me) into the tree. He landed gently along

a thick branch next to the center of the tree. A natural hole in the wood was there, and the branch was covered in bones.

Mouse bones.

Glancing at each other in that silent telepathy that I shared with him, my master and I got off the owl.

Without being asked to explain, the great bird began.

"Nemo has gone into the Fields of Fate a second time," he said. "By himself, to find the tribes named for him."

"Oh no!" my master said. "Why did he do that!"

"He knows why," the owl said, gazing upon us. I don't know about my magic-sword wielding master, but that gaze freaked me right out of my mousey skin. "And he knows best," he finished.

My master nodded.

"The time comes," the owl whispered, though to us it was like a strongest wind. "Gather your scabbard and belt. We must be going back to your house."

I wanted to ask why, and the owl turned to me and said, "Because the war begins, mouse. Your respite is over. Now it is into the flames. The flames of war, and greater ones."

"Is there no way out of this for us?" I asked, not knowing why.

"Not unless you wish to surrender your holy quest," he said.

"My holy quest?" I chirped, as if I held the sword, "I don't even know what it is!"

"You will," the owl said. My master put a hand on my shoulder and went into the lair to find his sword belt. As he vanished into the darkness, I noticed that the sword glowed, as if carrying the sunlight with it.

"I've pretty much had it with that nonsense," I said to the mythical teacher of Nemo. He raised an eyebrow. "Just tell me what it is, okay!? Surely you know."

He shifted back and forth, looking around him, taking his time, finally closing his eyes. He sat like that for a minute or two. I looked into the hole my master had vanished into. An owl's lair! What if there was another owl? What if…

"Very well," the owl boomed.

I looked back. "Eh?"

"I shall tell you what your holy quest is."

"No way. Reelly?"

"Yes."

"Well, cough it up, big scary."

He ruffled his feathers and growled deeply in his throat. I lowered my head in respect. "Sorry," I said.

"It is that which you desire most," he said.

I looked back up. "To be a great hero."

"No."

"No?" I asked.

"No. That's what got you into this mess. That is not it, though that is a byproduct of it, perhaps."

"Oh, well what is it then?"

"That which you desire most."

I was getting mad. I was about to tell him I'd spent more than half my mousey life listening to that kind of question-answer poo and to stop messing with my already-whacked head when my master came out of the den, a shiny, gem-studded belt around his waist with a beautiful silver and gold scabbard on it, and the sword in the scabbard.

"Are you ready?" the owl asked him.

"I am," he said.

The owl lowered his head again and my master clambered up.

"Aren't you gonna ask me if I'm ready?" I said indignantly.

"No," the owl said.

"Howcome!" I chirped.

"Because you are not," he said.

I climbed up the feathers to sit beside my master. His words chilled my blood.

"But in your case, it doesn't matter," he finished, and spread his wings to give us flight.

So we rode an owl. Not just any owl, but the owl. We rode him all the way back to the safe house. It took only an hour, maybe less. It was amazing. He didn't stop at the house, though. I thought he was gonna eat us after all when he passed it by. Far below, we could see the barricades and walls, the trenches and training grounds. We saw tiny specks that were our dayguard people, looking up at us. My master drew his sword, and it gleamed in the sunlight. Maybe they saw us. Then we were gone.

"Where are we going!" my master shouted into the wind, sheathing the sword.

"To gain you a small advantage," the owl said. We passed over hills and trees. We passed a small brook, and there on the other side of it we understood what our scouts had seen.

There on the other side of the brook was the enemy camp.

It was mostly underground, but no living thing would grow on that land. It was a barren patch of blasted earth. It had turned black. The forces that were outside were frightening in their strength. We saw monsters.

The mouse scouts who had seen the enemy had not lied. They had abominations. Dead corpses of coyotes, dogs, cats, snakes, hawks. But they no longer even looked normal, not even normal for rotting bodies. They were twisted. Mutated and wrong. Some had four wings, or five legs. Two heads. Mouths in the center of their ribs. Long, hook-like arms that belonged on crabs, or praying mantises. Horns where they should not be, and stinger tails like scorpions. Flesh peeled back, eyes rotted out, teeth much too long, sticking through their heads and lower jaws.

An army of monsters. I felt my master's body stiffen and smelled his panic.

How would we ever fight that?

By the time we got a good look, the owl wheeled around and headed back. Nothing unholy took off to chase us, and for that I was relieved.

When we got back to the house (much too soon—that dark army was almost in our back yard!) the owl floated down upon the front porch. The day sentries almost lost their bladders. I hopped off with my master, and he used his command voice. It shocked me after so many days of hearing only his true, gentle tones.

"Mobilize the army!" He commanded. "Summon the high council! We march at sunset!"

The sentries vanished inside, bellowing his orders to all. My master walked toward the mouse door and then stopped. He turned back to look at me. It was a deep look, full of profound sadness and joy at the same time. He smiled at me. I knew what he was saying. I love you, Squibble. We had a good adventure. It was probably our last, and it was worthy. I'll always treasure it.

Then his face returned to the forced warrior mask. I knew he hated that role. He turned and walked through the door.

I felt my stomach drop to my feet and beyond. That was the first time it really hit me. That was when it became real to me.

An army of demonic monsters waited just over the hill. And we were going to fight them.

The last horseman had come.

The Moment of Truth

✠

I knew things were bad when Mike showed up. He came that evening. He drove up to the house on a big Harley Davidson motorcycle, all white and silver. We could all hear it coming. Myself, I could feel it coming. If Nemo had been there, he would have known as well. There was a heavy air about the entire house, the impending coming of doom. There was no escape.

The Kind Human came to the door along with many mice to meet the stranger.

"Hello," the Kind Human said. "Umm… Who goes here?"

Magnificent man held out a bronzed hand. "Michael," he said. My master showed up with BJ and Squibette. Scratchy took his place at my side, staring google-eyed at Mike. The angel was the picture of charisma and perfection, long flowing golden hair touching his broad shoulders. Not a mark on his white suit.

The Kind Human looked down at his mice and saw my master look at me in surprise. I nodded to him. He nodded to the Kind Human.

The Kind Human looked back at Mike with alarm and awe in his eyes. "*The* Michael?" he asked.

Mike nodded. His bright blue eyes blazed like twin suns.

The Kind Human stepped aside. Mike came into the house, careful to stay between the red taped lines. The first thing he did was to stoop down and pick up my master.

"Hello, my friend. Good to see you," he said.

My master nodded vehemently and looked down at me excitedly. Mike noticed me then, and picked me up with my master.

"Look at him!" My master said. "He's a human! A big human!"

"HA HA HA HA," Mike laughed. "I can understand you, dear one."

(Heard something! Both of us).

I looked up at Mike. "Reeelly?"

"Really," he said.

I relaxed. "Everything's going to be okay now," I said.

"Perhaps," Mike said, carrying us to the kitchen table. The Kind Human was pouring glasses of juice for him and Mike.

"What do you mean, perhaps?" I chirped. "You go smite the Black Mouse now, big angel guy!"

Mike smiled. "Someone took my sword. Can't find it."

"We have it!" I exclaimed, pointing at my master's belt. "Now take it and go a-smitin!"

"Hmmm… Much too small," he said. "Can't use that. Someone else will have to."

"What's up with this!" I growled.

"Squibble," my master said, "The rules of engagement between Heaven and Hell don't allow direct intervention. This trial is ours, not Mike's."

"But this is all his fault—his and Bigfat's!"

"Not true," Mike said. "As a race, you chose this. Evil has decided to test your right to evolve. Mankind was tested in the very same way."

"Is that what this is all about?" My master said to Mike. "Our right to join humanity as an advanced species?"

Mike nodded. My master pondered it.

"This is worth it, Squibble," he said to me. He looked hopeful. "If we pass this test, rodents will evolve into a species with every right humanity has, at least on a spiritual level. This whole thing does have a great purpose."

"Humans will never let us join them," I said. "They'll kill us first."

"That's for sure," said Shiva from the table. Thor had joined him.

Mike looked down at his sons. My master said to them, "Boys, this is your father."

Their sour expression changed immediately. They gazed up at him in shock. For a long time they gazed, jaws slack.

"He's ... kinda big...," Thor said.

"This is the spirit Michael," my master said. "He came in his last life as a rat, to help me on my holy quest. He was your mother's mate, and your father. This is his true form."

"Not really," said Mike. "It's my human form. Hello, lads. You look well."

The rats climbed into his other hand, which held them both. They continued to stare upward into his face. They took off their helmets.

"Nice armor," Mike said.

"You don't mind that we designed it to look demonic?" Shiva asked.

"Nah. I know better. It throws fear into the heart of your enemies. That's a good tactic," Mike said. "It pleases me greatly to see you."

The boys must have felt that he was, indeed, their father, for they warmed up to him then. They climbed up to his shoulders and licked his face. Artemis and Aphrodite joined them. Mike played with his family for several minutes.

Mike sat down at the dining room table (after checking the chair for animals) and accepted the glass of juice from the Kind Human. He put us down on the book-covered surface.

"Why are you here, Mike? Is it to help us?" My master asked.

"As much as I am allowed, yes," he said.

"You owe my master one wish!" I reminded him. He nodded.

"That is why I am here," he said.

"Am I to use it so soon?" My master asked him.

"Very soon, yes," Mike said.

"Can you tell me if Nemo is well?" the Kind Human asked.

I expected some mysterious, all-powerful type answer, but Mike didn't play that game. "Yes, he is," he said. "I passed him on my way to the house. He searches for the field mice to aid your cause."

The Kind Human visibly relaxed. "That's nice to hear. Can you please explain what's going on here? I've heard it from them, but… I'd like to hear it from you."

"Certainly," Mike said. He began explaining, but my attention was on my master. He was taking off his armor and equipment, including the sword.

"Master?" I asked.

"I just want to be a normal mouse for a little while, Squib. I've been wearing that armor for weeks now, with no break. It feels good to be out of it. Trust me."

I removed my stuff then as well. It did feel great to be free of the weight. I hadn't realized how heavy it was. How much it bore me down.

My master turned back to Mike and the Kind Human picked him up to pet him. My master adored it, and laid down in the gentle hand to bask in the affection.

I was eyeballing the sword. I looked back and forth to the humans, the mice, and the sword. My master's eyes were shut. The sword whispered to me.

Did I really want to know?

Like a Cheerio that you know is somewhere in your cage, it beckoned to me. Part of me had to know. The other part hated my gifts and wanted to remain blind. I feared what I would see. I feared not seeing it, too. What if I could prevent it? What if I could see the way to our victory—and what if I didn't use that chance? Oh, the choice was so hard.

But, in the end, I was a mouse. Mice are inquisitive creatures, and can hardly deny their vast curiosity. I picked up the sword.

I didn't even have to draw it. The spirit world came. Michael had a great, blazing halo and gigantic, golden-feathered wings. Angels surrounded him and the house again. The spirits of our dead people were being escorted to heaven by some of the angels, through golden gates. Other spirits chose to remain. My master had a soft, beautiful glow about him. The Kind Human had the same glow. BJ's aura was golden reddish, and my daughter's was a soft blue. Stompy's was almost entirely red and orange, and Scratchy's was white. Like Mike's.

Then I focused on the sword. *Show me*, I said in my mind.

It did.

Prescience went into full throttle and the normal worlds vanished. I was again on the smoke covered battlefield. I felt the "roads" of possible futures before me. I saw offramps and onramps plenty, leading to other outcomes, different possibilities. I stayed on the biggest, most likely road, which was far greater than all the others. This was the almost certain future.

I beheld fighting in earnest. Fires. I saw the monsters destroying us, and then, suddenly they were falling to a giant figure wreathed in smoke and fire—a titan of terrible power. I saw aerial battles raging in the sky, and I saw the entire battlefield collapse into the ground, as if swallowed whole. The river was choked with bodies. The dead were everywhere. I saw my master holding the sword aloft, and its shining light covering the field. Before it, no zombie could stand. Percival, a few others in tattered armor, and my master, finally, retreated to the chest of the dead or dying Kind Human. Fighting the swarm of undead mice that assaulted them, standing in a tight circle, the very last of our army still fought against thousands. A handful of worn and weary officers, raising their swords with strength borrowed from nowhere, surrounded by the last of the enemy's undiminished force. It was horrible. I thought that this was the end, that it could get no worse.

That was when fire began to fall from the sky.

Lightning and flame thundering to earth all around them, our side fell, one by one, to the enemy as my master's sword arm grew stronger and Percival's quicker with each loss. My master looked as though he was possessed. His eyes shone like Heaven's glory. Percival was laughing like a madman, decimating opponents left and right with blurring speed and flawless accuracy. But it was not enough. They were ten, then eight, then five, then three. Finally, it was Percival and my master alone, back to back on the unmoving human. Everything was surrounded by fire. Everything was burning. It was a scene straight out of the darkest hell.

Then the scene sped forward against my will. I saw the end.

My master was dying from a chest wound. The battlefield was empty but for a few straggling mice. The ground was wet, and the spilled blood of so many made it look like the entire landscape was covered in crimson. Panic shot through my nerves as I saw my beloved master sag to the ground, the sword no longer in his hands. His head fell to his chest and blood ran freely from his nose.

I freaked out. I forced myself off that road. I chose a road where that does not happen.

I saw him as an old mouse, in a world of horror. It was the world I had seen in my dreams—the world blasted by Armageddon. Animals and humans had gone to war. They had destroyed each other. I saw Shiva and Thor, Shiva missing an eye and ear again, and they were leading the animal armies against the humans. Pets, lab animals, zoo animals, and wild animals had all ganged up on humanity all at once. So much death had resulted so suddenly that humanity had reacted in pure instinct and thrown every weapon they had at the inside enemy. The sky was burned red with radiation. The war had gone on a long time. Bodies littered the ground in this vision as well, but this time they went on forever. To the very horizon. My body was not there. I was dead long before.

With no friends left, I saw my master die a sick, awful death. Like my poor momma, he choked as the blood in his lungs came too quickly. He gagged and panicked, running about on stiff legs, trying to escape his doom, full of the terrible knowledge that he could not. Terror took him, and he died in agony and pain on a cold, lonely street, far from home, twitching and spasming in prolonged, futile desperation. Not a warrior's death. Not a death that any being should have to suffer. Finally, his eyes bulged from their sockets and he lay still. No angels came for him. No light came to guide him home. There were no angels. There was no light.

Gasping and freaking out, I let go of the sword.

Those were my choices!? They had been the only two roads available to me, and to him. I sat down hard, trying to breathe.

I knew it would be stupid! I knew I shouldn't have looked! By the Mousegod, why is everything so messed up!!? It wasn't right! My master didn't deserve to die! I should go in his place! He had to live! I couldn't live without him! The house couldn't live without him! Such cruel reality! The world sucked! Why did this have to be!? WHY!?

I began to cry. I knew it was the future, and I knew that because I had looked, what happened was up to me. It would be my fault, no matter what. The weight was heavier than anything I had ever experienced. I felt sorry for Nemo. I felt what was left of the happy-go-lucky child in me being crushed by it. That happy spirit in me that had wanted nothing more than a good, exciting life and to be called a great hero was sagging like a wet piece of cardboard under a ten ton slab of ruthless stone. It was like losing my soul. I liked that me, and it was dying. Worse yet, I could not prevent it. If this was what growing up meant, it sucked! My dreams had been pure, my heart good and honest. My master even more so. We didn't deserve this.

When I looked up, everyone was staring at me. There I was, with the sword at my feet, and me looking like I'd blown a gasket. Eyes full of tears, nose running, mouth drooling.

"Squibble?" The Kind Human asked. Mike looked at me with more compassion. He knew.

I hissed at Mike and ran from the table and hid below it, under the refrigerator. I was so mad!

After a minute, their conversation resumed.

"It's very sad that all this has to happen this way," the Kind Human said. "I don't understand it, and I don't like it, and I shouldn't be one to question divine wisdom."

"But you do," said Mike.

No answer from the human.

"You may speak your mind to me," Mike said. "I've heard just about every blasphemy there is."

I could smell anger building up in the Kind Human. I wondered if Mike could.

"Will you tell me what you think of this?" Mike asked. Nope. I guess he couldn't.

"Since you asked," the Kind Human said, and paused for effect. Knowing the Kind Human, he was staring straight into those ice blue eyes of Mike's, and he probably wouldn't flinch at it. "I think it sucks to high Heaven. Literally."

"Do go on," Mike said, calm.

"These aren't normal mice. These are pets," the Kind Human explained, clearly upset. "One in every million mice gets to be a pet, and now they're all going to get hurt or die because of your holy war and your rules. It sucks."

I imagined Mike nodding. "I understand."

"No, you don't," the Kind Human said. "If you really are some big angel then you don't at all. My son here," (he must have meant my master), "tells me you were that rat I picked up off my front porch and tried to save last winter. This is the thanks we get? Everyone dead and the rest going off to war?! Bullshit!"

I imagined then my master trying to calm him down, for he said, "No, baby, I won't. He asked."

"Yes," Mike said. "Yes, I did. Please go on."

"You say all this is necessary and right, but it doesn't feel right to any of us. You say they chose it, but my children don't look too happy about it, and I know my most precious friend, the first of the

Knights and my favorite mouse in the whole world, certainly doesn't want to go to war. He's a gentle, kind mouse! Why must this awful thing happen? Is God so cruel?"

Mike said, "No. He is kind enough to let us find our own way, and choose what liberties we might earn."

"And what do they get if they win this, huh? What's worth all this death and pain?" The Kind Human was genuinely angry. I was rooting for him. Give it to him, big friend! Tell him off!

"They get freedom. Equality. Power," said Mike.

"Oh great!" said the Kind Human. "Just like us. And look at what we've done with it. Whee ha. Have you asked them if they even want it?"

Mike said, "They do."

There was silence then, and my master chirped at the Kind Human. I saw him in my mind nodding, agreeing with Mike. I knew it was happening—I could see it in my mind. Sadly, despite how he really felt, my master was siding with what was right, as always, and fearing not.

"Oh, baby… does it have to be this way?" the Kind Human pleaded with my master. "Can't we pass this hardship by somehow? I can't bear to lose you!"

"If you do not let him go," Mike said, "all of mousekind will pay the price. Imagine how people, as they are now, will react when they find out that an entire race of animals, indeed, the entire planet of animals, that they have abused for so long, were actually their equals. Imagine what the animals will go through then."

"Humanity doesn't deserve this planet," the Kind Human was fighting back tears. "This whole thing is stupid! Stupid, do you hear me! THESE ANIMALS ARE INNOCENT!"

"Yes, they were," Mike said. "But they are no longer. They have chosen something more. God is ready to give them what they desire, and Evil has challenged it. Now imagine what might happen if rodentkind and humankind were to cooperate, what they might accomplish together."

Something lit up in my head. What a grand idea! Why hadn't I thought of that? We rodents were so afraid of humans, so scared of them and so resentful of how we've been treated… we've never once stopped to think of what could be. Mike was a genius. I hated to admit it, though, and I guess the human did too. He was quiet.

"This is that big?" He asked. I didn't catch Mike's silent body language.

"I had no idea," the Kind Human said.

"They did. They do," Mike said.

A moment passed. Finally, the human said, "They can do what they feel they must. I fear for them greatly, but I do not control them. They aren't mine. They're just my friends."

"That," Mike said, "Is why they chose you. Even quested for you, over long, hard miles and against all odds. That little one in your hands had a vision of you from the beginning."

"I think I finally understand that."

"And do you understand the consequences of the path they have chosen?" Mike asked.

"Yes, that much I surely understand, for that is what I hate the most. But promise me—the universe will help them, if they earn it."

"Yes."

"But poor Squibble. And my poor baby here..." He sounded pleading. "They have suffered so. Can I not do anything to ease their journey?"

"You will do your part," Mike said. "What you think is best, when it comes time." I heard the human sigh and smelled great disappointment.

"This is all so disturbing," the Kind Human said. "It seems so stupid."

Right on, brother!

"It may yet have a happy ending," Mike said, and then changed the subject. "How are you recovering from your accident?"

"It hurts to walk and sleep," the Kind Human said. "My neck has three herniated disks, my wrist has pain, my elbow has a compressed nerve. My middle back spasms and locks up on me at night so that I cannot sleep without drugs, which I can't take for fear that the animals will need me. I've lost hearing in my left ear, I get headaches, nausea and fatigue plagues me. And pain shoots down my left arm all the time."

"On top of all you have lost, you've lost your health as well," Mike said.

The human probably nodded then.

"The stuff isn't important. The lives. All the lives. They can't be replaced," he said.

"Your soul is pure," Mike said. "You have spent all your money on them. You take them to the vet..."

"Not any more, unless Heide is around," the Kind Human said.

"You are broke?" Mike asked.

"No, I have no transportation," the Kind Human said. "I used to have a Harley—like yours but not nearly as nice. I sold it recently."

"You sold it," Mike said. "To pay for their supplies."

"Yeah."

I lowered my head. The human had loved his Harley. We were breaking him in more ways that one. How sad that he had to sell it… for us.

"You valued your Harley Davidson," Mike said.

"It… yeah. My father rode before me, and his father before him. That bike had spirit. It was my horse."

Mike laughed. "Yes, I know. That same spirit is now in my bike, outside."

"The silver and white one? That's a classic softail—really nice work. I was looking at it when you rode up. You've done alot of custom work to it. All the chrome, the brakes, the engine looks rebuilt…" The human had clearly missed Mike's meaning, but I hadn't.

"It has about 50 grand into it," Mike said. "But my work here is almost finished, and I won't be needing it anymore."

"You're going to sell it then?" the Kind Human asked.

"No," Mike said. "I'm giving it to you. That's why I brought it."

"I… I don't want your charity…" The Kind Human sounded unconvincing. He was blaming Mike still, like I was. Hey, it was hard not to.

Mike laughed a little. "There are no strings attached," he said. "If you won't take it, it will sit in your front yard and rot."

The Kind Human was speechless. I heard keys clink down on the table.

"Since you put it that way," the Kind Human mumbled, and took the keys.

"There is one more thing I can do for you," Mike said, rising from his seat. "And for our mutual friend."

I knew what was coming. I had prayed for it often enough. I climbed out from under the fridge and scrambled as rapidly as I could to the table top to see Mike laying one hand on the Kind Human's shoulder and the other over the hand my master sat in. Of its own volition, my spirit sight kicked back in and I saw the lights—the glorious, wonderful lights all around Mike. I saw energy funneling down from the sky in a white beam with golden tinges, and that sang through Mike and into the human, and into my master.

It only took a few seconds. I saw it all. I understood what had happened. I'd done a much smaller version of it myself.

My master woke up and blinked. Then his eyes got round. The human looked just like him.

"Oh my god." the Kind Human whispered.

"I can breathe!" My master said out loud.

"It's... amazing!" The Kind Human said, standing without the bent back and shaking legs he'd had for the last few months. "I... I feel..."

"No pain!" My master chirped. He hopped in one bound from the human's hands and down to me. He stood up and spread his arms. "No pain!" he exclaimed, shaking with excitement. I smiled, and looked up to Mike in gratitude along with my master.

He was looking down at me.

"You thought good had abandoned you, little one?" he said to me. I nodded slowly. "No," he said. "We have only reserved our blow for last. Now it is time for us to strike. Now comes the hardest time of all."

"I'm healed, Squibble!" my master said, astonished and ecstatic. "It's a miracle!" I nodded. The spirits were fading away, but before they did I saw my master's aura—as bright and full as it would have been the day I met him, I was sure. His chi was restored. All the damage life had dealt him was gone. At least the physical side of it.

I sat there staring at Michael. It was uncharacteristic of me to sit still. He knew this. He peered at me as Nemo always did. Seeing something only he could, he smiled.

"It's almost over, little friend," he said.

I just kept staring. I felt small. I felt small, and surrounded by giants.

As the sun descended upon the horizon, the armies were gathered and ready. Column after column were arranged before the house, in the front yard. Part of the barrier wall had been removed to let us march forth. I was wearing my armor, bearing all my weapons. I left the comic drawing on my shield. I thought it was funny. Maybe the Black Mouse would see it and at least be irritated.

I had my thousand chosen troops behind me, all wearing red sashes striped with blue as a symbol of their rank—the chosen high guard. Each and every one had been hand picked by my master, BJ, and the rat twins. These were the best of the fighters. Among them were Scratchy (quite proud of his new colors), Stompy, Squibette, Sneaky, Squeaky, Clyde, One-Ear , and Ghost. There were one hundred rats in this new rank as well, all high ranking members of the Swords of Michael. (The swords had gotten to finally meet the man for who they had been named. It has been amusing to see them puff themselves up and parade before him). Looking to my right, Shiva and Thor themselves were wearing the red and blue sashes. I was quite honored, and just as dense as a mindless rock.

The Kind Human came out into the dusk, holding my master in his right hand. His eyes were wet. Silence descended on the field and the house, and we all heard what he said to his tiny white son.

"Little one, once you would have been sold for ninety-nine cents at a pet store." He kissed my master ever so gently on the head. "And now you're priceless."

My master gazed back, longing, wishing it was different, I think, and told the human he loved him. But of course, all the human heard was a chirp. It seemed that the message got across, however, for the human let tears flow and smiled. The man put his mouse gingerly to the top of the porch. The human's face was painful to look at as he let the mouse crawl off his hand. My master gazed at him lovingly one last moment, and then turned around. His face went from deep sadness to stone.

"These are the orders given to us by Nemo," My master addressed the great lines of warriors. "He gave these to me a month ago, just before I left to recover this…" He drew Excalibur. It shone in the sunset light. Mouths dropped open. The intake of breath was a great wind. Eyes bugged out. The entire army went down on one knee.

"I shall lead the main force," he said across the silent field. "Our King shall return to the city, to be guarded by the force we left there." BJ looked startled and spun his head to my master, but my master went straight on without a sideways glance. "A force shall be left here at the safe house, which is sure to be hit while we are gone, to protect the women, the sick, and the aged. That force wears the red sashes, led by Sir Squibble. We march now to war!"

The army stood and cheered, drawing weapons and holding them high. BJ and I jumped in front of my master immediately.

"No way!" I said.

"Absolutely not!" BJ said.

My master turned to us, still holding the holy sword in his hand. The power of that mystical blade reached out to us and loomed upon our souls, as if to bear pressure down on us if we did not obey. The force of it was staggering. We were both harshly reminded of my master's indomitable spirit. Before that light, we could not even open our mouths to argue. But he sheathed the sword.

"I know you both hate this decision," he said. "But Nemo declared it to me long ago. He arranged all of this ahead of time. He said it must absolutely be so. He said there must be no other way."

BJ was angry. "Why didn't you tell us before now?"

"Because you would have found a way around it," my master said. "As it is, if you like, you can challenge me for the right to lead the army, my King."

"You clever rodent!" BJ exclaimed. "You made the proclamation before our entire force, and in the name of Nemo! I can't challenge you now, and even if I did, it would do no good to have either of us hurt. Wasting our energy fighting each other is what the Devil wants!" He snaffed and stomped a bit. I had never seen him do that. "You have read too much about court intrigue and subterfuge. You have outwitted me!"

My master shrugged. "The King must live through this, Your Majesty. Nemo knew that."

"We both know who the real King is here," he growled. "It is he who holds the sword. You just never wanted the title is all."

Again my master shrugged. "You have been a fine King," he said. "And you must continue to be. The people need you."

"I shall hate... hate... missing this fight," he said. "It is an unworthy fate!"

At that moment Percival came up to his father's side, dressed in full armor and bearing all his weapons. A kite shield hung from his back. Upon his lance was the flag of our people. It was the very first insignia I had designed for my master's first shield. A happy, dancing mouse. They had chosen it for the very flag to represent us all.

"I shall keep a journal, majesty, that you might read it," Percival said. "You shall be with us in spirit, I pray, and all you have taught us shall determine the outcome."

BJ was clearly giving up. He withdrew to the Kind Human, who picked him up and held him. Heide was there now, and Michael stood behind them both. The Kind Human gave BJ to Heide to take back to the city once the army had marched. BJ's face was one of pure resentment, though he seemed to understand.

I, on the other hand, was not about to understand!

I set my feet firmly apart, called for my squire, and drew my sword, right in front of everyone.

Scratchy zipped up to my side, his blade drawn like mine.

"Kill anyone who interferes," I ordered him. My voice was not recognizable as my own. It sounded like cold steel.

Scratchy put his back to me and bared his teeth to the whole world.

I pointed the sword at my master.

"You might be the better swordfighter," I told him, eyes flashing, "But this one you will lose! I must go with you. You don't need to understand why. I must!"

He stared at me with an unreadable expression. It had depth to it I had not ever seen in him to that day.

"You cannot go, Squibble," he whispered.

"I am going!" I bellowed. "You cannot stop me! No one can!"

Scratchy stomped his feet as if to say, "Amen!"

My master only calmly shook his head. He made no move toward his ridiculously superior weapon. "No."

"YES!" I screamed at the top of my lungs. I was shaking with fury and fear. If I could not go… if I could not protect him…

I felt the great boots of Michael stomp up behind me. Good. He would make my master see reason.

My master looked up at Mike, sadness in every line of his face.

"Mike?" he said. "You promised me one favor."

"Yes," Mike answered.

"I'll use it now."

Before I knew what was happening, Mike had grabbed me. He held me in between his two cupped hands. He gave me only a tiny slit through which to see my master.

Scratchy flew into a whirling blur of weapons and teeth, tearing at Mike's hands to carry out my orders. Mike didn't even notice the feverish assault.

I was stunned. I realized what had happened. My mind snapped and I threw myself into a berserker rage with everything I had. I slashed, thrust, and broke my sword. I broke my backup, then bit and bit, tearing at Mike's flesh viscously. Though he bled, he did not let go.

"THIS!" I screamed through the tiny hole at my master. "He promised you anything, *anything*—one time—and you chose *this*??!!" I screamed in fury. "What's wrong with you! Don't you realize you're all going to die!?" Through the tiny slit, my master made no reaction. Only he could hear my ranting. The army lay in the other direction, behind Mike. Percival closed his eyes, bowed his head, and left for his place at the head of the army.

"Everyone dies, master! Everyone dies!!" I cried. "No one comes back alive! I've seen it! I saw it! I can change it! LET ME GO!"

Slowly, looking down, he shook his head.

"I know, Squibble."

I stopped still, my heart attacking my chest to escape.

He met my eyes.

"I know."

Some moments in life are so powerful, so traumatic, so terrible—that there simply is no appropriate—or inappropriate—reaction. None at all. I could only stare, tears gushing from my wide eyes. I was paralyzed.

"You told me long ago, when you were hypnotized," he said. "You told me I would not come back from the war."

I could feel nothing. I went numb. I felt as though I was dying. My heart raced, faint and quick, like fading smoke.

Oh, Mousegod… this isn't happening…

"Please don't go, Master," I whispered through trembling lips. "Please… please… don't…"

He smiled. That wonderful, beautiful, peaceful smile.

"I love you, Squibble. Do right, and fear not."

Then he turned, and left my field of vision.

Michael turned around, and I saw my master moving to stand before his army. Percival was already there, atop a great rat. My master mounted his own armored steed rat, white with a golden hood as Mike had been when he was wearing that body, and gave the order to march.

Panicking, unable to move or escape, I watched them march through the gates without me. I watched them march to their deaths, and was powerless to stop it. For many minutes they marched in formation away from the house and into the fields; thousands and thousands of rodents in armor, bearing weapons, pulling siege engines and catapults. The last I saw of my master was his flowing green cape and the shining star that was his sword. Then they were gone.

Michael put me down on the porch. I saw my high guard standing at attention. They had been in on it. I could see it in their faces. Every one of them that mattered. All in on it. I felt betrayed, as I had so long ago before my pilgrimage. I knew if I ran after my master Mike would just catch me again. Scratchy was now attacking the giant's ankle. Mike lifted him up by the lobster shell of his armor and gave him to the rat twins, who disarmed him and held him down under one foot. Scratchy was beyond insulted. He chirped over and over. The only sound he could make.

I looked up at Mike, completely furious. Even an archangel had stabbed me in the back. In my moment of greatest need, I was abandoned and powerless. I hated everything. Everyone. Oh, what I would not have given at that moment to be his size. But I was not.

I was just a mouse.

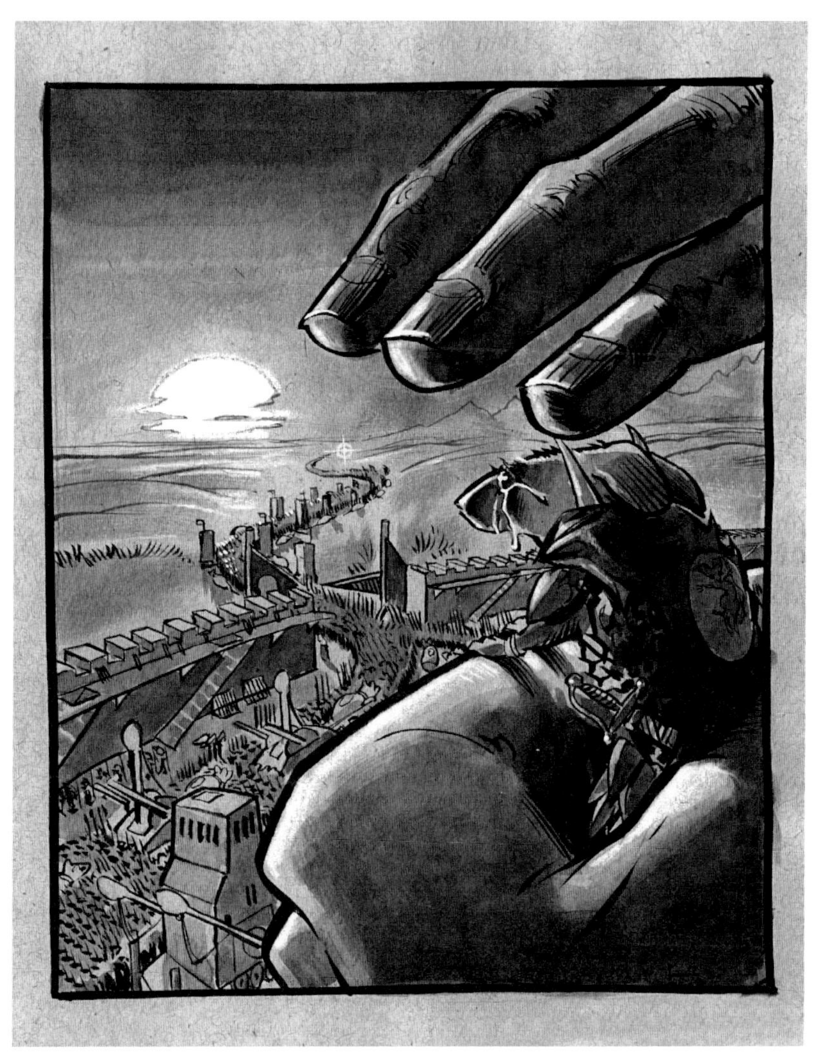

The Great War: Day 1

✠

What you are about to read is by two authors. Is it compiled from the notes and journals of me and Percival. Percival's account of the Great War, and all that happened there, shall be included here in my own journal to make the story complete. My own experiences, as closely as I can guess, are put in between his own, for they were happening at the same time. Percival's writing is just about a hundred and eighty degrees from mine, so you shouldn't have any trouble distinguishing the two, but just in case, Percival's journal is in italics.

It was many months after the Great War before I returned home to finish my journal. So, like my pilgrimage, all you are about to read was written after it happened. The change in my illustrations bears the same explanation. After the greatest tribulation in my life, I was not to see the safe house, or anyone I knew, for a very long time.

Percival's journal, March 14th, 2002

We have set up camp across the river from the enemy. His forces have come out from the dark earth, and upon first observation from atop a nearby crest, we must admit that we are, sadly, at a great disadvantage. We had hoped, indeed, that our massive numbers might give us the edge, but we are outnumbered at least three to one, and his forces keep appearing from the deep. In addition, he has monsters. Creatures so unnatural that it might harm my spirit just to describe them. The morale of the soldiers is only held aloft by my father's amazing sword. None have fled. Such good troops. If I perish in this foul war, I shall perish at the side of worthy mice. I am missing the presence of Lord Squibble and the Rat Twins. I would like to think them safe and warm, but I fear this is unlikely. Our enemy is not honorable enough to leave innocents alone.

I woke from a drugged sleep to the sound of warning horns. Left to defend the old and sick, I had stomped back to my house and unwrapped one of the pills I had kept from the pharmacy during my pilgrimage. I knew what they were now, and one of them was Xanax. It's an anti-anxiety drug, and I was having the anxiety attack of my life. Unable to cope with it, I had chewed a tiny piece off the pill, and immediately fallen asleep against my will. I had been sure we would not be attacked. What enemy would be stupid enough to attack us when his camp was being sieged by an army as massive as ours? But on hearing the horns, I knew the answer to that. An enemy with many times our number. An enemy that understood who he had to kill to win in the long run. An enemy with no honor whatsoever.

I sprang up, and fell down. I could barely control my own limbs. I felt like Jello. The horns sounded again. The house was under attack.

Scratchy was at my side in an instant, helping me to my feet.

"Scraaa…" I mumbled, unable to move my mouth correctly. I knew I was in deep poo, but I could not for the life of me care. Xanax was more powerful than I had ever guessed it would be. I had made a terrible mistake.

"SCraaahh," I murmured. "Flooonn… Flonnnt linnne…"

He nodded and dragged me toward the front of the house. He shoved two swords into my belt on the way. I could not walk. I could not stand or talk. We were doomed.

Then Shiva met me halfway.

"Sire!" He cried. "The wall did not even slow them down, and we had to recall all our outside companies inside or they would have perished. They have a thousand against our one. They have siege engines. Rotting animals! What do we… Sire? What's wrong!?"

I looked at him through tranquilized eyes. I tried to answer.

"Druuuuhhh…"

His alarm showed on his face clearly.

"Ratgod on a camel!" He cursed, slammed on his helmet, and whirled around to race for the front door. "Bar the door!" He yelled. "Archers to the roof! Prepare to repel the enemy!"

Scratchy looked into my face with worry. He was thinking he should take me back to my house and hide me. There was no way we were going to win this fight. All we could do was hold them off until our army won in the field, if that happened. It was going to be long and ugly.

I shook my head pathetically. “Nuuuuh!” Hiding me would only earn me a far more terrible death when the enemy took the house.

He shook his scruffy head a little. He didn’t want to see me die. I didn’t care, and that wasn’t all the drugs.

“Nuh!” I spewed out. “Fruuuuh liiiii!” Take me to the front line, you little runt!

He looked to his left and right for anyone who could help him make the paralyzing decision, his eyes wide and frightened. We were alone. All the rodents were in the dining room by the front door.

“Daaaah Yuuuu!” I moaned. “Fruuuuh Liiii!”

His face twisted into sharp anxiety, and the irony didn’t escape me. Maybe he had taken all of mine from me in that moment. The universe had a sick, sadistic way of working like that.

But finally, he resumed dragging me toward the front line.

Squibette raced up to us next. I could see only her outline, my normally keen vision was blurry and waving, but I recognized her smell instantly. She was panicked.

“Father!” she cried. “They have too many! What do we do!”

“Hoooomaaah,” I moaned.

“The human isn’t here!” she shouted, panicking more. “He packed a bag of things and left! The attack came right after! What’s wrong, Father? What happened to you!?”

“Druuuhs,” I said. Her eyes almost popped out of her skull and she raced away. Out front I could hear the beginning of dire combat. I heard the release of many arrows.

The human had vanished again. I didn’t blame him for not wanting to watch his loved pets suffer and die, but did he have to leave now?! And why? Without him, all I could see was our demise.

Grimly, Scratchy returned to dragging me towards the battle line. In my state, I wasn’t going to last sixty seconds.

One might have expected a parley, or at least a chivalric discussion before combat. Perhaps a series of insults or harsh words. But this was not to be, and our enemy charged us on the first evening of our arrival, at midnight. It is a full moon, and by that light we could see everything as well as a human might see in daytime. Indeed, we saw too much, as his legions swarmed over the black, blasted landscape of his coming toward the river. The hills flowed with enemy. As far as we could see or smell, they were coming. Our front lines were about to buckle and flee when my father and I rode up to it with the rest of our heavy cavalry.

"Warriors of rodentkind," my father shouted to them, "this day we set the standard for all the days ahead! This day we stand against the first of many challenges to our independence and freedom! Would you remain as mistreated vermin?"

The hordes shouted back "No!"

My father yelled, "Would you be food!?"

"NO!" They screamed.

"Then fight now," he exclaimed, holding the blazing sword aloft, "and earn the fate you wish upon your children!"

The hordes lifted their weapons high and sang as one their cheers. My father's sword lit the night like a lighthouse in a storm.

Thus reinforced, we stood with dignity and determination as the first wave of darkness hit us.

I was dizzy from going in circles with my squire. The kitchen and dining room were a long way away. It wasn't his fault, but he was tiny, and both of us were covered in armor. The battle raged in full swing. The scent of blood came to my nose in a massive blast. I had to get up there. I wouldn't last. I had to do something. I couldn't think. Those stupid drugs! Why had I done that!

At last, I could not go on, and it was clear to my squire that I was attempting a poor form of suicide through stupidity. I gave up and he sat down next to me, huffing and puffing. I wondered if Mike was still here. I wondered if he was, would he help?

I had no choice but to wait for the drugs to wear off. It was awful. Was my whole life going to be a miserable failure? Even if so, why did everyone have to know about it at every turn? I turned around with unfocussing eyes and stared at Scratchy. He grinned up at me, trying to cheer me up, I guess. I scoffed and turned back around. Why did he keep trying? What did he ever see in me?

I heard things hitting the front door and kitchen window. At least they weren't inside. There was no chance of that happening. The doors were locked from the inside, always.

Mice scurried by every few minutes. Several stopped to ask if I was dead. I didn't have the strength to answer "I wish," and Scratchy vehemently shook his head at them. They ran onward, carrying news to the front line that I was injured or wounded. One of them told us that Shiva and Thor had the assault under control. I knew I could count on those boys.

The enemy did not even bother with the terrain; he went right over the river, using the bodies of his men to form a bridge of the undead. His true monsters he held back for some more sinister purpose, for some more terrible time to unleash them. Their shadowy forms, looming in the background like giants, waited with a disturbing stillness to come among us and stomp our lives out.

As the first wave hit, we repelled them with the heavy cavalry. Then my father and I broke off in separate directions and harried them from the sides as they came over their unholy bridge with four companies each, leaving the heavy fighters led by knights to defend the center of the column. We unleashed with ballistae, arrows, and catapults. We reloaded many times. Each time they surged forward, we drove them back, using the water and the land to our advantage. They fell into our pits, they impaled themselves on our pikes until no pole showed at all, after which the others simply climbed over on the backs of the fallen. Our traps have taken a great number down already. The walls we built hold, and the enemy perishes trying to scale them.

Speaking of advantages, the dead cannot approach Excalibur. This we discovered when our commander rode through their ranks the first time. They part around him in a wide berth. We have discussed, as we meet in cross-attacks, the thought of using this to kill the Black Mouse, but he has yet to show his face. Our enemy is a true coward. Striking at our lives in the most underhanded, cruel way, and then hiding behind the twisted faces of the unliving mockery he calls an army. This lends my sword arm strength, knowing I will eventually meet him.

My father is strong. I have not ever in my life seen him so strong. His strength and endurance are a match for mine. He wheezes not. He has not coughed or choked yet, which we both feared. He commands the battle like a pillar of fire to the men. As long as they gaze upon him, they never falter in their morale. We have lost many this first day, but the enemy has lost four times that number.

It is too bad he now outnumbers us ten to one.

I awoke later to the sounds of an engine. The drugs had worn off a little, but not much. Enough that I could barely walk, and see straight, though my reflexes were shot. I tried to make my way to the kitchen with Scratchy's help. I heard Heide gasp. I heard the Kind Human storm the front door, cursing. Our troops cheered. Later, several mice told me what had happened.

The Kind Human had grabbed a broom from the side of the house and literally swept the enemy into a pile outside the walls. He had kicked, fought, and used his massive size to protect us, but before he could annihilate them, the attack was called off. In the middle of trying to fight the human and Heide (who both were loathe to hurt any small animal, and were taking many bites and bruises to show for it) the enemy just vanished. Retreated beyond the borders of the house fields. Through cheering and hopping, the humans had come into the house, bleeding from hundreds of small wounds. The Kind Human looked quite peeved, I was told.

With him, he brought many rolls of aluminum foil, several car batteries, wire, and other small trinkets. He gave the wires and trinkets to the rat twins and said, "You know what to do, boys."

They nodded in delight. Clyde jumped upon one of them and rode like a cowboy to a gunfight as they took off for the kitchen.

The Kind Human then spend several hours rolling tin foil across the porch and sides of the house while he argued with Heide about the war. Heide seemed to want this just not to happen. She was too gentle, and loved all animals with her pure soul. She was the kinder of the two Kind Humans. Our Kind Human, on the other hand, was fed up. He was not going to lose one more of his animals to anyone or anything if he could prevent it. He was through compromising, and through playing victim. He told Heide that if this was a war, then our side was going to have every advantage it could get, including technology. With that, he finished the trap with the help of the rats (including Vulcan), and they rigged it all to go off at the touch of one big, red button. Then the Kind Human (funny to call him that when he was acting so warlike, but hey—it's his title) went into his room and got his guns. He brought out a shotgun, an old six-gun revolver (like in the Old West shows), strapped it to his hip, and put a lever action rifle against the outer wall of the house. He went back into his room, took out a sword, and thunked it into the deck wood beside the rifle. He dragged a bench against that same wall and sat down. He lit a big cigar and pushed a flat-brimmed hat over his head. The rats and I gazed at him in stunned silence. He took a long toke on his cigar and squinted at us.

In his best Clint voice, he said, "Dyin' ain't much of a livin' boys."

The rat twins went ballistic, jumping and squeaking for joy. The rest of the house called off the red alert, content that we were safe for the time.

Illusions of safety never do quit, do they?

The Great War: Day 2

✠

The reason for the enemy's waiting has become clear. We need to eat and rest. He does not. Our forces are divided in half as we fight day and night. By night, he throws everything at us, while more of his forces from the city keep coming at us from behind every day, nipping at our heels as they attempt to join his wretched command. By day he harasses us with small guerilla attacks—hit and run tactics, and assassination attempts at our officers. We have sent companies back for food and water, and to have the house build carts for such things. This has further divided our forces. We made a grave error in hoping this would be a quick fight.

We continue to dig trenches, build walls, set traps, and do everything we can to gain an upper hand. Move for move, he matches us with the appropriate counter. He is toying with us. His first charge was only a test, and an appalling one—for he could afford to cast aside so many mice just to see what we might do, and he did so without hesitation. We are clearly up against a master tactician, as brilliant in every way as I or even my father. We are using tactics from medieval literature and Roman history. When I bitterly cursed our enemy for knowing them, my father pulled up to my side and rebuked me for not expecting it. "After all," he said to me, "he was there, in ancient Rome, in Old England. He probably started those wars too."

His words left a foul taste in my mouth and a tightness in my chest. How can we fight a commander that has seen it all first hand? How can we win against a being billions of years old? He probably created many of the tactics we are using against him. But these thoughts are self defeating, and I laid them aside to take up my smarter thinking. We must win. There is no other option.

The second night we rallied the rats to build us a bridge as well—two of them. We used them to cross eight companies on each side of the river, a hundred yards up from their camp, and attack from behind. It worked well at first, but the rear of his encampment was guarded by the monsters. Even in full retreat, we lost four companies in minutes. Nothing could stand against those beasts. We could not blind them or slay them as if they were normal. I suggested to my father we try the same tactic with him and me leading the rear assault, but he said he had to maintain a presence at the front line. I understood then why the monsters did not attack. They could see the light of Excalibur from where they stood, a hundred feet away. They could not approach it. There is still hope.

This night we have tried well over a hundred tactics, engaging the enemy over and over in battles all up and down the river. We have lost seven thousand, including the rear attack attempt. They have lost twenty five thousand. We would be doing well if it were a normal engagement, but he treats his troops as expendable as they truly are, being already dead. One might think this foolish in any command, but he seems to replace them as quickly as he loses them, and this is meant to shake our morale. We wonder how many he has underground. It is a daunting thought.

The troops have returned from the house with supplies, and were immediately sent back for more. No one can drink the river water; it is clouded with blood both red and black. I have not slept yet. My father and commander seems to need no rest at all with that blade in his hand. I see the delight of being healthy again in his eyes ruined by the necessity to spend it in this war.

He would rather be running on his wheel.

Today a company from the war came to the house to get supplies. They had orders for Vulcan and the others to make carts the rats would tow back to the front line. We all worked steadily for hours, even the humans. We built carts, new catapults in a new design by Vulcan, and the master smith sent a mouse pistol to the front line for Percival. They exchanged words with us about the war and how it was going. They told us the enemy has ten times our number. I started to wonder how in the world they had gotten that many, but then I remembered the labs. Just the lab I had been in alone had thousands of mice. Abused, sick, hurt mice were everywhere. There was no shortage of them. The Black Mouse just waited until they shuffled off the mortal coil, and filled their bodies with … some wrong force, and out they came. His supply was limitless, while ours was immeasurably small.

They said my master fought like a Mousegod, and never tired. I longed to see it. I was bitter that I could not. By the time they left it was almost dawn. The drugs are still making me slow as ever. I wonder if they will ever wear off.

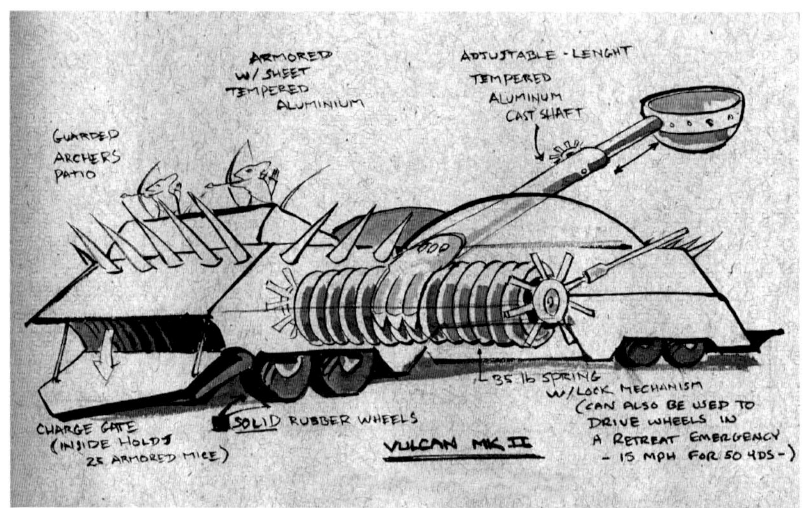

The human does not leave his post except to help the supply caravan. He sits there on his bench and eyes the fields with worry and bitterness on his face. I know what he's thinking. Where is Nemo? I wonder it myself. It's been many days since he left. He wasn't anywhere near as strong as he was the first time. Anything could have happened. I thought to reach him in my sleep, but the stupid Xanax makes me sleep without dreams. It's like being in nonexistence. It's a bit scary at first, and then there's nothing to be scared of at all. But Nemo could be dead, rotting in the field, and we would not know. Stupid drugs.

I cannot stop thinking about my master. I return to the thought every ten seconds. I fear it will drive me mad. I tried to sneak aboard the returning supply caravan, but unbelievably, Mike was there to stop me. Suddenly, out of nowhere. He just strode up and grabbed me as the caravan left the wall perimeter. I bit him, but it didn't matter. He set me back upon the porch and vanished.

"You better help us!" I yelled after him, but people just looked at me as if I was a loon (as usual). No one else had seen him.

Since I was awake during the day anyway, I stayed awake. I caught Shiva and Thor building weapons, cleaning their guns and armor.

"I don't suppose if I order you and the rest to follow me to the front line it will happen?" I asked them with my slurred speech.

Thor's eyes bugged out. Shiva shook his head.

"No way, dude."

"Why not!" I chirped. "Squibble's Horde *indeed!*"

Thor leaned close. "Man, it's orders from the very top. Nemo, and your master."

"We'd rather go against you than them any day," Shiva commented, reloading his rifle. "Nothing personal."

I was tempted to make them regret that, but I knew in my state I could not begin to. Also, it had been a long time since they were boys. I don't think those old tricks would work on them anymore. As if reading my mind, Shiva turned his head toward me and slowly shook it, never once breaking a smile.

"What's the real reason?" I said.

"Because they think you're some sort of hero in the future," Thor said.

"They told us that without you, it all turns to poo," Shiva said.

"Ummm... look around boys!" I exclaimed. "What exactly is it doing now, huh?"

They looked around.

"Pretty fine, I'd say," Thor said.

"Yep," Shiva agreed. "Not too bad."

I squinted and ground my teeth together. "Yeah, but can you say that for our families?"

They said nothing.

The Great War: Day 3

✠

Today in the middle of the day, when most of us were resting, the enemy burrowed under our lines. They dug all the way beneath the river. It must have taken them from the beginning or before to accomplish it, but they succeeded. They swarmed us from four points inside our camp, and cost us nearly five thousand mice. It goes poorly for us. We retaliated harshly, with heavy artillery and bowfire, but the rest of them retreated back beyond their lines by the river. It was frustrating to be taken unawares like green soldiers. The enemy has created no small amount of hate in our men, but this, my father says, is also a tactic of his. Hate is his domain. He can use it to control us if he becomes powerful enough.

That night we took our vengeance as the supply wagon returned, bearing food, water, a gift for me from Vulcan and ... demolitions. It appears Squibble's agent Clyde is not entirely insane. He builds magnificent bombs. We sent several small cohorts over the river in cover of night with scents hidden by smoke. They placed the bombs and came back, trailing long lines of waterproof fuse over our bridges. We then rallied for an attack, and the enemy came forward to meet us, as always. The fuses were lit.

I would like to have seen the face of our opponent (for the very first time) as he watched his puppets go up in flashes of light. My father raised his sword high and commanded his troops to stay their places when the explosions rocked the ground. Except for his divine radiance and awesome charisma, they would have fled the bright lights and loud crashes; instead they saw massive numbers of the enemy blown sky high. It was grand for the morale.

As soon as the explosions died out, before the dust settled, we were on them. We charged across the river and took the fight to their side for the first time; it was glorious. Though they have no fear and would not retreat, we slew countless thousands before we sounded our own recall horns without losing even a single company. The monsters could not advance as my father lit the way with his torch of valiant steel.

We have taken flesh for flesh—pound for pound. We have cost them. Let the dark mouse chew on that!

Thus goes the fight. Back and forth, with the enemy showing no sign of weakening. Indeed, of himself, no sign at all. We have built forts and towers from which to shoot at their numbers. We have sent the caravan back with order for more arrows and bows, swords and shields, among other things. I understand the gun they sent has only one shot.

I am certainly saving it.

We are busy supplying the front line. We build and rebuild weapons, armor, shields, arrows, bows, and machines of war. We send them medical supplies for their medics. Heide goes into town for these and others, returning each day with a carload full of gear. This is all we do, day and night. Help the front line. While it makes everyone else feel as if they are doing something useful, it makes me feel pathetic. These thousand crack troops are basically my babysitters, and I resent it deeply. They would make an enormous difference on the battlefield, where they belong. I cannot possibly be so important. The very notion is absurd. This is not what I asked for.

I said great hero, not delicate messiah. But they will not bend. So we work, and send the caravans back again and again.

Finally the enemy has unleashed some of the heavier forces. Snakes have come across the river on all sides of us and wreaked havoc in our camp. Just as we rode to and fro, relieving them of their heads, the air assault began.

Hundreds of thousands of insects, many of them barely empty husks, came flying at us from the dark skies. Most of the soldiers do not have armor strong enough to protect them. While we fought this new attack, the enemy charged and barreled into our camp. We were fighting for our lives against three fronts. My father's singing sword severed all it touched, but it could not be everywhere at once. Archers fired shot upon shot, and failed to make a dent in the swarm above us. We rallied together and fought from the center in a gigantic circle. A bad position to be in, but we had no choice. We fought like that for hours. The insects have no poison, though they have stingers. It takes many to them to kill a single mouse, and many more against a mouse in armor. It takes a thousand or more to bring down a rat, and the heavy cavalry are virtually invulnerable. Still, our numbers trickled away, and we had nowhere to retreat to.

My father slew the last of the snakes as we heard the noise. It was different than that of the undead insects, whose wings fluttered a bit too slowly. This new noise was louder. Angrier. It was vengeance upon the wind.

It was the bees.

Coming to our aid en mass, they fell upon the swarm from Hell and slammed into them full force. My father shouted to them, telling them not to use their precious stingers, for then they would die, and be of no use to anyone. Still, they fell upon insect and undead alike, and drove the enemy back enough that we could regroup and harry them across the river once more. The enemy recalled his insects and the bees retreated to a nearby oak grove. Their Queen alighted in front of me and my father to tell us that their aid was but a horn call away. They had brought all they could: ten thousand bees. All the hives that had survived the drought.

My father graciously thanked them and they departed. We set about to repair camp. We have lost another five thousand troops. We shall take revenge within the hour, but where is this getting us? From the earth, more zombies rise to meet us each time

The Great War: Day 4

✠

It's like waiting for the hammer to fall one last time. I cannot stand it. My anxiety is coming back, and that must mean the drugs are finally wearing off, but it had come back with a vengeance, set upon rending me to pieces. We cannot supply the caravans fast enough, nor with enough of anything but food and water. Each time their requests are smaller. Our people are dying by the thousands, and I am sitting on my furry butt making arrows!

Oh, Bigfat will pay. Someone will pay. I swear it.

The caravans are now reporting attacks coming at them while they travel to and from the house. They are all soldiers, and dispatch the attacks without great difficulty, but the ambushes aren't meant to stop the caravans—only to delay them. So I came up with a tactic of my own, and after finishing a batch of arrows, went down to the sub basement to see it done. It meant talking to royalty, but I'd seen my master do it plenty of times.

We are short on supplies and weapons. Our armor is worn and chipped. Our mounts are tired, as we are. It is looking grim. We cannot last much longer, and my father knows it. We are past tricks and tactics now, and both sides resort to the best tactics they know, which are met by the same, and we both lose great numbers. They lose more, because their forces are unarmored and slower, the weather being bitterly cold and dry. We lose some anyway because the dead simply do not fear death. The stench is unbearable. The enemy has the very flies attacking us now. The bees have at least one hive over our heads at all times. The fighting goes day and night. We sleep in hour long shifts. Where once our colors had shown bright and high, we are all now the color of dirt and blood. It is a heavy temptation to call Squibble's Hordes out here. They are a thousand of our very best. They might tilt the scales to our advantage, but my father refuses. I understand his reasoning. Squibble is too precious to risk. Too important to leave unprotected. He doesn't understand, but he is our messiah. I just wish he weren't so fragile.

Then at last came our chance to truly rally against our enemy. It began in the evening of this fourth day. A messenger came to us and told us to be ready to charge when the moon rose past the mountains. We gathered up, as told, for the messenger was from the house. Not knowing what to expect, we set our lines by the river, as always. And, as always, the enemy retreated back to form columns a hundred feet from the same river.

Then an awful, shuddering noise racked the ground, and fearing some new horror, my father and I ordered our troops to back step. But immediately upon giving the order, we saw half the enemy's entire army fall into the ground as it gave way beneath them. A section of the earth, not smaller than eighty feet cross, fell in on itself, burying half their troops! Our eyes looked on with stunned shock as we saw the ants swarm from the pit, attacking every enemy in sight, taking them to pieces.

My father looked at me and smiled broadly. The ants had come to our aid! More, they had planned and carefully executed their attack on the enemy caves, which now were no more. There would be no more hiding for our foe!

We charged instantly, with renewed vigor, slamming into the enemy forces and cutting them down like wheat. We took every last one of us to the assault, praying this would end it. The ants had dealt the Black Mouse a mortal blow, and given us the opening we needed.

As we were nearing the very center of their camp, and victory was within our sight, a terrible thing happened. My father was beset upon by great serpents, one after another. He swung and swung, lopping their heads with each swing, but they came still, attacking in fanatical fury, heedless of destruction. I rushed to his aid, but he was too far from me. The second one snake fell, another struck, and from all sides. His guard circle was down in mere moments, and his steed struck from him in the next. I was but seconds away when the last snake struck him full in the chest, knocking him from his dying steed and flinging Excalibur from his grasp. I watched the sword go flying out into the battlefield. I felt my heart skip a beat as its holy light went out.

And in the dark, I heard monsters rise.

It's killing all of us. Waiting here. The caravan has not arrived. We have their equipment ready for them. The ants I sent have not returned, so I can't know how my plan worked. What could this mean? Were they all dead? The hours crawled by like a snail on ice.

Finally, I couldn't stand it anymore. I ordered scouts to make for the front line and return to us with news. Five scouts went, camouflaged and stealthy. As the Kind Human watched them go, he sat up.

"I've had just about enough of this crap," he growled, stepping off the porch, grabbing the curved sword from the wall, and striding in the direction of the war. Our side let loose with cheers and cries of encouragement.

Well eat that, Blackie. Eat it.

We were being butchered. The monsters fell upon us as though they knew hunger. We had defied them through the entire war, and now they took it out on our hides. Hundreds of us fell in one minute to them before we could regroup to fall back, and even that did not save us. We could not outrun them. An entire pack of rotting coyotes. Twenty sightless possums. Bobcats, housecats, snakes, raccoons... all the dead the field had to offer, mutated and gifted from Hell beyond Nature's reason, and all against us. We were going to fall now for certain. All that was left was to put up a courageous end, and take as many of them as we could with us to our judgments. We must give the safe house as much of an advantage as possible with our lives.

I found my father. He lived. I righted him in the battle fray and opened his visor. He was knocked out cold from the force of the blow, but the snake's teeth had not penetrated his faithful armor. He was not wounded. I gave him to my own guard and told them to make for the other side of the river with all haste. As they launched themselves for safety, I waded through the enemy in search of the sword. The ground was uneven and broken. Ants were everywhere, covering everything. I had a general idea of which way it went, but that was all. It was trying to find a needle in a haystack, but what choice had I? Without the sword, we were doomed. The monsters lay about everywhere, biting, clawing, thrashing, twisting and stomping. We were perishing, and no commander at the front to issue orders.

Then, in the darkest of night before dawn, we heard the thunder of great footsteps. Against the horizon, we saw a towering silhouette of a man. I thought to myself, O great Mousegod, has the Black Mouse grown so powerful that he now commands men? I had but a moment to look before a coyote set himself between me and the sword. The ants warned me, but I could not dodge in time. The valiant rat beneath me bucked and sent me flying as the coyote lunged. Its decaying teeth snapped shut over where I had been. My mount died saving me from that dread blow, and I hit the ground hard. In the air, I saw three of the great undead beasts in hot pursuit of my father. He would not reach the river.

Then a blast roared out. As I landed, I saw fire in the air. A coyote fell. Another roar, and another fell. The last coyote lunged for my father with its gaping maw and was cut in half by the human's gigantic sword.

Our titan had come to save us.

"I'll be damned if I let you kill my children!" He screamed. His voice was like an earthquake. He cut the monsters down before him as my father ran between his feet to safety. The titan's wrath was upon our enemy. Fate had cast in our favor again.

I saw the sword upon the ground at the same moment as the coyote above me. We both raced for it. He was huge and I was quick—it was a toss of the coin who would make it first. I slammed opponents aside and blurred around obstacles as I made for our salvation. For the coyote, it was one short step.

I beat him, but he caught me beneath his paw. My armor cracked. I felt his weight bearing me into the dirt. My fist closed around the hilt of the sword, and I swung blind, severing that paw from its wrist.

Ignoring its own crippling wound, the dead coyote opened its mouth and slammed it down over me. I saw its rotting throat. I was surrounded by its blood-stained teeth. In a mouse heartbeat, it would bite down, and I would meet my end. I placed Excalibur above my head so that in the bite, the monster would impale its own brain and die. My life would have a steep price.

A deafening roar... The coyote snapped back, its teeth slamming shut two inches over me as the top of its head was vaporized. A mighty boot swung across the field and lifted the monster high into the air and gone. The human reached down and I grabbed his sleeve, rushing up his arm to his neck while he blazed away with his guns and swung his formidable katana. The monsters fell about him like dolls. High above the battlefield, I saw the enemy in disarray, and I saw our side regrouping on the other side of the river.

It must have infuriated the Black Mouse. I felt his rage at this unexpected intervention. I saw serpents coming for us from every angle. Hundreds of them. All the enemy had to throw at us was aimed at the human. I held the sword aloft, hoping for the light that blazed at my father's touch. It did shine, but not nearly so bright. Not bright enough to keep the snakes away.

The human emptied his six-gun, then his rifle, then used the shotgun to finish off the rest of the monsters so that we would not have to. He knew the snakes were coming, and he knew that if he used his ammunition on them, the true monsters would kill us when he went down. Our human was every bit as valiant as we.

He was bit. Again and again. These snakes, so recently dead, had venom. Many of the blows were deflected by his motorcycle boots, and his sword chopped snakes by the score in two, but he was bitten too many times. He fought for minutes until he fell to his knees. Our army rushed to his aid, killing the last of the snakes, but it was too late. I leapt from his shoulder as he went down, a tower falling to the earth with a shattering crash.

The side of his face in the dirt, he looked at my father and I.

"I tried," he said, and then closed his eyes. I saw the tears in my father's eyes, matching my own.

The sun rose across a bloody battlefield. We went into our fifth day of the war.

The Great War: Day 5

✠

The house is under siege. The enemy came back the moment our human sentinel left us. We barricaded everything and prepared to hold out as long as we could. If more caravans came, there was nothing for them now. The scouts I had sent out were the last able to get through before we were shut off completely. This time they hit us with everything they had, and my wish for action was more than granted. By noon I was begging to take back my wish. They had flying things, and dead insects as well. We had no ants, but the bees came to our aid within the first hour, and the sky was alive with dogfights. We fought them at the windows and doors. We rained arrows down on them and pushed stones off the roof to crush them. Shiva and Thor used up all their ammunition, pulled their spears and went to work. Ghost, Squibette, Stompy, Scratchy and I led the porch assault.

"Fall back!" Shiva cried. "Fall back inside the house!"

We did so, the enemy nipping at our very tails as we slammed the mousedoor shut and bolted it.

"Everyone on the carpet!" Thor commanded. Mice ran from anything solid and bunched up on the carpet as the enemy swarmed through the kitchen window and onto the foil-covered counter.

"Fry, you sons of bitches!" Shiva hit the big red button.

There was a loud hum, and all our hair stood on end. Outside, the zombies did the radical jig. They danced like the film was sped up. They bounced, bounded and hopped. Some of them flew three feet. They lit on fire. We smelled burning flesh.

Shiva let up on the button after several moments. The bodies fell, smoking. The most awful stench ever hit our sensitive mousey nostrils.

I had given thought to whether or not electricity would work on zombies, and the human must have given that though too. If it was not the surge of power that ended them, perhaps the sudden energy shook loose the Black Mouse's hold on the corpses. Either way, they fell. It worked.

"Oh, that reeks!" Stompy exclaimed.

"Now let's see how stupid they really are," Thor said, and tightened the grip on his steel spear.

Sure enough, the enemy surged forward with more troops. Uncaring of the trap, they assaulted the house again. Shiva fried them. Again and again they came. For hours, they fell on the house. The porch outside, the windowsill, the back door, were all covered in piled bodies. Shiva and Thor exchanged glances with me. How long could they go on like that?! How many zombies did that black bastard have?!

The tactic came visible too late, at dusk. Enough bodies, piled high enough, negated the electric current, and our trap was useless.

"To arms!" I cried as they swarmed the door and window again. We heard Heide's car outside rumble up the driveway. No door opened. She must be trapped inside by the enemy hordes. It was that bad. The safe house was totally surrounded.

The fighting went well into the night with no sign of any relief.

We have had some respite, although we do not know why. Perhaps even the enemy must regroup. We have moved camp to surround the human, who is still breathing, albeit terribly lightly. We have discussed tactics. Snake venom does not always kill. The human might yet recover if we could ward him against further harm, but this was a daring venture, and terribly chancy. He was a huge target, and on the enemy's turf. Still, we owed him our lives several times over, and my father would not abandon him. So we guarded our sleeping Gulliver as the enemy regrouped beyond our range of sight. We have fifteen thousand troops left to us, not including four hundred heavy cavalry. My father and I have new mounts, deeply mourning the old ones who were so faithful and such good friends. We use every minute given us to build new fortifications and dig new trenches. Everyone is as tired as they could be and still standing. There is no food, no water. The air is as freezing as if we were surrounded by snow. The ground is slick with sheets of frozen blood.

This war is hell.

The Great War: Day 6

✠

I had never in my life felt so tired. My sword arm could barely move. My shield felt like it weighed a thousand pounds. Even taking turns in front of the doors, we were all worn thin. The rat twins' weapon technique had become clumsy and crude. No one was using finesse or grace anymore—we did anything to down an opponent. I had felled at least two hundred by myself, and I was still not recovered entirely from the effects of the Xanax. I was covered in wounds. Scratchy was much worse than I but complained not one peep. He fought next to me without so much as a moan whenever I rose to take my turn. As long as the doors held, we could protect the females and elderly. As long as we could stand and swing, they would not reach the doors.

Surrounded by the ringing of weapons, we took ten-minute naps while others covered our posts. The Kind Human had bought us blades in bulk packs of 500 each, and we had broken almost every one. Some soldiers were now using toothpicks to fight. The ground was covered in broken armor, bodies, snapped bright plastic weapons, bent shields, and blood. Our medics could not keep up at all.

Our time was running out, but we set ourselves to make that clock tick as slowly as it could until it hit the final hour. In the depths of our hearts, we all hoped for that distant horn sounding the charge from our own forces returning, but in our minds we knew it would not happen. And we knew why: the enemy was at our doors because our army had failed.

I had thought I would know when my master died. Perhaps he was not dead yet. We knew nothing. It was worse than knowing in some ways. The human had not returned either, and that was not right.

More fighting was the very last thing I wanted, but I rose, and Scratchy went with me. I climbed to the window and put a hundred shots from the slingshot out into the enemy, which still covered the ground as far as the eye could see like a moving carpet. Drawing our swords, my squire and I laid into the assaulting bodies.

As it turns out the lull was, of course, just another ploy.

The enemy had regrouped over a hill and was preparing weapons large enough to kill the human. We raided them and routed their engineers, but ran smack into the second wave they had waiting for us. It was an awful fight. The ground was choppy and broken, the air was frigid in a rising wind, and the crest of the hill had no defensible spots.

It almost seemed as though the Black Mouse might not have an unlimited supply of dead warriors any longer, for their numbers stopped coming after a time. They did not retreat; they just ran out of men. There were no tactics after that, no clever tricks, and not even any formations. It was as if the brain behind their army had vanished. Could we have killed the Black Mouse and not known it? Could the ants have devoured him with the others? I seriously doubt it. If he is not here, then there is only one other place he could be. But there is nothing we can do for Squibble now. I pray the elite legion is up to the task. It pleases me to think that the enemy might be facing the rat twins at this very moment.

Border skirmishes continue in several places. My father has his sword back, and he goes to and fro upon his third mount, giving orders and reassuring the troops, what troops we have left.

It was dawn of the seventh day and viciously cold. Our saving grace was the reinforced doors the human had built us. We were out of arrows and mostly out of swords. The fighting had turned to hand-to-hand. Stompy didn't mind. Her tireless pummeling made a deep gouge in the enemy. My daughter was fluid grace in motion, her strokes more perfect than mine even when she was tired. She alone had not one mark on her. She is built like me, slim and squibby—dodging was effortless for her. Ghost used two firebrands. When his two swords broke, he took up two toothpicks. Disliking those, he took up the nearest items—two matches. Shiva laughed at that, then lit them for him. He used the box of them ever since, careful not to light anything vital on fire, fighting on the kitchen counter. Even One-Ear did well, defending those who fell in battle, dragging them back to the medics. He seemed to have redeemed himself.

But the seventh day, the last day, was when everything went wrong.

The Great War: The Last Day, Day 7

✠

It began in my sleep, of course. Then I woke to a zombie trying to bite through my armor. Behind it were a dozen more. Scratchy came barreling into them, and they went down in a pile as I grappled with others. We resorted to teeth and, believe me, zombie doesn't taste good. Taking heavy wounds, we defeated that first wave. Then more came.

Nearby, Shiva and Thor were boxed in, but they were laying waste to their attackers, which were… rats. *Our own rats.* Somehow, our own dead had been brought back, but they were acting like the enemy inside our own lines! That might have been enough to tell me what was happening, but things happened too fast and kept me off balance.

Ghost came screaming from the front room, yelling that the doors had been opened from the inside. The doors in front and in back were breached. The zombies could not have done that—they possessed no fine motor skills.

The enemy was pouring into the house. In our severely weakened condition, our own dead arrayed against us spelled our doom. "Rally to the front of the house!" I cried. "Rally together in the dining room!"

Those undead rats would be much harder to kill—they were taking mice down right and left. Shiva and Thor were less invincible than they had once been. We were in deep trouble.

Fighting with the aid of adrenaline and fear, our reduced forces fought back to the dining room and held the mouse door. We heard the enemy swarming into the kitchen through the window and coming through the back of the house from the garage and the basement. We huddled close, forming rings of defenders and using our own cages as barriers, and tried to protect the elderly females. They would have none of that, however, and the old women, the young mice, the sick and the crippled all came out to fight alongside us, wearing no armor, with nothing but their teeth. We had no time to deny their gesture.

We fought the enemy out the mouse door, and I elected several of our strongest, including myself and Scratchy, to venture outside and fight with our backs to the open portal so that those inside would have one less front to worry about. When we finally fought our way out (mostly with Stompy knocking mice two feet into the air with her metal fists), we saw further horrors.

Heide's car was open, and she was nowhere in sight. Dead mice surged all over it like thick paint. We could not tell her fate. Worst of all was the small clearing ten feet from the front porch: it was a circle about five feet in diameter with not a body in it. Except for one mouse—a black mouse.

Our eyes met. Time seemed to hold still. That mouse was the most evil, wretched, obscene thing I had ever known. Its power was terrifying, and I could feel it from where I fought. He had finally shown himself. That meant he was certain of our destruction. And I wasn't sure he was wrong.

Instantly I was filled with rage. Deep loathing and wrath erupted in me for everything that mouse had done to my family. I had to avenge them! My blood boiled and my heart raced. I felt true hatred.

"Don't let it take you, Squibble," came the voice. It was the same voice that had saved me in the city. Bigfat. "He wants you to lose your temper. Don't give him the satisfaction." I sent my breathing down to my center and did my chi gung breath. Calm flowed through me like my magical river. The Black Mouse was displeased and began to stride in my direction.

"Shiva! Thor!" I yelled. "He's here! The Black Mouse is here!" The twins bullied their way through the mouse door in a heartbeat and stared aghast.

"Good Ratgod—he's really real!" Thor exclaimed.

"Really dead!" Shiva growled and launched himself off the porch. Thor was one inch behind him.

My two boys never stood a chance. I'd never seen anything move faster than that demonic mouse. And it was strong, strong enough to toss an armored rat twenty feet. My boys suffered the beating of their lives and were tossed aside like garbage.

Mice were flooding out the door now, screaming that the house was being taken. We were losing our only defensible place. The end was near. I had to do something!

"Stompy, Squibette—delay him!" I yelled. They nodded. "Ghost, Scratchy—to me! We have to make it back to my nest!" That nest was through thirty feet of swarming enemy—easier said than done—but I needed what was there. Fifty mice joined us, including three knights, and a few of the remaining Swords of Michael offered their backs as transport. Once upon them we rode right over the enemy, plowing them down like tenpins.

We rode forth, the safe house's last heavy cavalry, and reached my nest in moments. I grabbed the gun. Oh yeah, it was time. I hoped my aim was as good as it was with the slingshot. Then we fought our way back to the dining room, and I left the cavalry to hold the line against the invaders.

"Don't break—no matter what!" I commanded them. "Hold this room with your last breath!"

"SIRE!" they all shouted at once, and set into the enemy with desperate fervor.

We have come down to this: a pell-mell free-for-all as the enemy hits us with everything they have. Out of food, water, supplies, and time, we fight hand-to-hand against them now, in every corner of our camp. My father and I have retreated to the fallen human. All of us fight around him now.

The enemy is on all sides. The good news is that we can see he is finally running out of troops. The end of his force is in sight. The bad news is that we are down to our last company. It is our thousand against his ten, and the fighting is vicious beyond compare. Our troops are using everything they've got, even their teeth. My father has told us to hold out no matter what it takes. The sword will not let him rest, and his energy is limitless. Even being near him, we all feel it. Our power to hold on now comes from on high and no other source, for our bodies are used up. Each swing of our weapons is a divine gift.

Just as we thought we might last the day, the enemy set fire to the bone-dry grass. In several places, flames grew around us. What matter if they burned? They drew no breath anyway. But we were going to be dead in minutes. Such an unworthy end for valiant warriors. I hear burning to death is very painful.

Wading through bodies, I came back out front just in time. The Black Mouse was engaged face-to-face with Stompy and my daughter. He was so fast that my daughter had finally taken hits. Severe hits. Her armor was cracked and broken, her shield missing entirely. Stompy was black and blue, and her leg looked broken. Blood was all over their faces, and around them lay the bodies of their friends who had died that they might live this long.

Ghost set upon the black shape with two new matches. That caused the demon a moment of concern, and in that moment I took aim. My finger was squeezing the trigger when I heard Scratchy shriek in pain. The gun was firing when my arm was hit by something. My aim was thrown off, and I missed. Then something heavy hit my helm full force, and I was bashed to the ground.

Ghost fell beside me, dead or unconscious. Stunned and disoriented, I looked up. I saw two things. First, I saw spirits. My powers had activated. I saw demons in mortal combat with angels all around us. Everywhere. And I saw One-Ear.

He was standing over me with a mace in his hand, a metal mace that had belonged to one of the Mouse Knights. He was grinning from ear to… well, you get the idea. "Son-of-a—" I started, and he hit me again.

My helm cracked and fell off. I saw stars now. I felt nothing. I looked to my side and saw Scratchy with a sword stuck through him. He was in agony and barely alive. I heard Stompy curse One-Ear and come for him. Then I heard the wind part for something black and swift, and I heard Stompy fall. I wanted to shout, "Squibette, no!" but I couldn't speak yet, so my daughter joined her friend on the ground.

One-Ear laughed. It sounded rotten, and he stank though he was clearly not dead yet, a situation that needed immediate fixing. "You sorry sucker!" he spat in my face. "You're such a gullible idiot!" He kicked me. I took some pleasure in the fact that I didn't feel it. "I've been working you over since that first day and the 'mighty prophet' Squibble didn't have a stinking clue!" He tapped the mace in his hand as the Black Mouse came up behind him.

One-Ear squatted down next to me and looked over at Scratchy, who was writhing in pain on the bright blue sword. So we weren't out of swords after all. One-Ear had probably hid the rest. Bastard.

"I killed your wife," he said, smiling. "She didn't drown on her own. I helped her."

My heart skipped a beat. A glowing anger rose in me. I tried to suppress it, but I was losing. He drew a sword of his own—bright green, my master's colors. How disgusting. How mocking.

"I also opened all the doors of the house for my master. It was the least I could do."

"I'm going to cut off your hands and feet and tail, and burn the wounds so you won't die," he said. "I'm going to cut your ears off and blind you, too, but before I blind you, we're going to destroy everything you ever loved. Your precious house, daughter, friends, and your squire…" he turned briefly to kick Scratchy, who squeaked and opened his eyes, "…are all going to suffer God-awful fates. And it's your fault, you know. All your fault."

When he turned back to face me, what he didn't see was that Scratchy got angry. The little runt was really pissed. Behind the Black Mouse and One-Ear, Scratchy was trying to get up.

"You've failed," One-Ear gloated in my face.

Then I smelled the smoke. Everyone did. It was drifting over the house. The fields were on fire. That black monster had ignited the fields!

It just couldn't end like this. This wasn't the end I wanted. This wasn't what I signed up for. The Mousegod's sense of humor couldn't be this bad. Evil isn't supposed to win! *What would my master do?* I thought, panicking. *What would Kirk do?*

"This is your last chance to surrender," I said to him, blood dripping off my head, dead serious.

The Black Mouse tilted his head back and laughed. It sounded like a truck being dragged sideways through a junkyard. One-Ear joined him like any two-bit minion would. Then I saw a pair of glowing mouse feet step into my field of vision, right next to my head.

I looked up into the eyes of Branch. Or his spirit, anyway. He wasn't solid. He smiled and held a finger to his lips.

Scratchy fixed his face into a mask of heroic determination, lurched up, pulled the sword out of his own body, and poised himself to strike. I snapped to my feet so fast One-Ear didn't have time to react and sprang for his throat with my teeth. I caught his head instead, but that was fine, too. He squealed in pain and grabbed at my jaws, dropping the mace. I wasn't about to let go.

The Black Mouse crouched to take me out, but Scratchy spun forward and ran him through. A bright blue sword came out of his chest. He didn't appear hurt, just annoyed, but it was enough to turn him around. When he did he saw that he was surrounded. The entire house was surrounded.

On the ridge around the house stood Nemo, Shiva, Thor, and the Tribes of Nemo, about one million field mice. Nemo smiled. Shiva and Thor gave the Black Mouse two fingers.

That was the only time I ever saw even a hint of panic on the demon's face. He looked at Nemo and hissed. Behind Nemo, the great owl landed and hissed back. The Black Mouse's burning red eyes got wide, and he turned sharply, slamming Scratchy brutally to the ground, and fled.

"No quarter!" Nemo cried, and the mighty army of field mice charged. Shiva and Thor were right in front, their faces burning with fury to get at the Black Mouse before he got away.

"AAAH! MY FACE!" screamed One-Ear. I left deep, terrible gouges in both his cheeks. It was fitting. In medieval days, marks like these were called "coward scars." Traitors were branded by such cuts to their face.

He had dropped his mace but not his knife, and that he plunged into my neck. He hit me just below the collarbone—not my neck really, or I'd have died on the spot. Still, it hurt like hell, and I let go. He turned, leaving the thin blade in me, and fled with the Black Mouse.

"Bastard!" I shrieked, and in one smooth motion whipped out my slingshot, loaded it with his dagger fresh from my neck, and snapped off the shot. It struck him right in the back, where it belonged. Some unholy force kept him alive (or it wasn't enough damage to kill a mouse), and he kept going.

"DANG!" I screamed. "DANGDANGDANG!"

The enemy was finished. The field mice were waaaay too fast for those slow zombies. The carpet of moving dead bodies became a carpet of unmoving dead bodies run over by brown lightning with bushy tail tips. Once inside the house, they cleared it in minutes. It was glorious to watch. Branch watched it with me.

I went over to Scratchy, who lay on the ground breathing hard and fast. I couldn't tell how bad his wound was. He might have been dying. It tugged at my heartstrings, but I was already overwhelmed. I put my hands on the holes in both sides of his ribs, trying to hold his blood in. He looked up at me with a question on his face. "Yeah," I told him. "Yeah, you did great, Squire. You did real good." He smiled and passed out.

Nemo's feet appeared next to Scratchy's limp form. I looked up as he set his paws on the tiny little body and began to focus his formidable willpower. "Will he live?" I asked, but Nemo did not answer. He was deep into his trance already, trying to save the little mouse.

I turned to Branch. "What are you doing here?" I asked in wonder. "You *can't* have grown powerful enough to project your spirit all the way from China?!"

He grinned broadly at me. "I got Nemo's letter today. Said you needed help."

"You... you projected yourself all the way from *China*!" I gaped. "*No one* can do that..."

"You ain't seen nothing yet," he said, and held his hands up to the sky.

It is almost over. We are down to fifty men, and we are choking on smoke while the enemy is not slowed in the least. The last of his forces had just reached us when the fallen began to rise. Even those we beheaded are now getting up to fight us. His numbers have shot past fifty thousand and are climbing. This is our end for certain...

But now I hear the strangest noise, unfamiliar to my ears in this long drought we have suffered. Thunder...

My eyes went wide as I looked upward to see dark clouds gathering rapidly, flooding over the safe house in huge waves straight out of "Raiders of the Lost Ark."

Branch brings the lightning

Lightning has fallen like swords upon our foes! The sky is full of fire! It is like ancient Biblical tales—fire and brimstone pouring from the sky. The roar is deafening, unbearable. The ground quakes and trembles. My father and both know—Branch has come to our rescue. This was his fondest dream, and now it is our salvation.

The enemy burns. They explode. They shatter like glass. They will not be coming back. Righteous wrath is upon them.

The last of them have mounted the human's body, and we fight tooth-to-tooth and hand-to-hand here, the only place in the field not burning. All around us, Heaven pours out its furious deluge on the blasphemy our foe created, putting it back where it belongs, in still finality.

Fireballs hurl themselves over the horizon, coming from the direction of the safe house—or perhaps China—and scatter the dead like sand burned into slag.

Despite myself, I am laughing. As I take my enemies down, I hear my father laughing, too. It is the maniacal laughter of those pressed far beyond their limits. Win or lose, it has been a wonder to behold this. The light of God shines around us as we battle to our last in the heart of a burning hell. This is the death of a warrior poet. This will be a fine death!

I gaped at Branch. Nemo lifted his head up to us and smiled at me. I gazed in awe at the burning sky. The fires from the field licked at the back door to the safe house. Branch looked as though he was sleeping with his arms raised. Fireballs the size of houses arced over our heads like falling comets, headed for the battlefield. He did it.

Holy Mousegod. He really did it.

We are down to our last few. It was just my father and I and two others, then one other, and now it is just my father and I. Two hundred sword strokes later, I finish off the last of their zombies, and I think we are alone. I think it is over. We will burn to death here in this place, and this is our end. It is well enough, except that I did not get to destroy the true enemy. I did not meet the Black Mouse in combat.

Heide comes running over the hill. She is coming to help us. Her face is a mask of panic and determination. Good. She will have the strength to move the Kind Human. She may even reach us in time to save us all, but I realize no, the flames are closing behind her. She has only come to join us in a painful fate.

Then the thunder rolls across the sky and shakes the ground. The first raindrop falls on the Kind Human's forehead, the first raindrop in far too long. It is followed by an army of them...

As the rain came pouring down, I saw the sleeping Branch smile. Fireballs. Weather control. That was what he had always said. True magic.

Bravo, brother. Bravo.

The last of the safe house mice came outside to behold the miracle. The great owl landed behind Nemo, Scratchy, Branch and me, and no one ran. They had seen it all.

Heide has dragged the Kind Human toward home. He may live.

My father sags a little. The fatigue is finally hitting him. I move to help him. We smile at each other. It is over. I pray it is over.

Then I see a mouse coming across the field toward us. A survivor? He is coming from the direction of the house. As he gets nearer, I see that he has one ear. He is crying for help. We prepare to aid him. He yells that he has news of the safe house... it has burned to the ground, and all within it are dead. I look in panic at my father, who returns my gaze. The mouse has reached us and collapses into my father's arms.

That's when I see the marks. The coward marks are on both sides of One-Ear's cheeks, and Squibble's fur is still attached to his face...

Pushing him back from my father, I draw my pistol and use my one bullet to blow One-Ear's brains out. His headless body falls just as my father cries out.

I turn my head to see a black sword point sticking out of his chest. My entire body feels the jolt of alarm as he sags to the ground. I spin to cut down the coward who would commit such unchivalric blasphemy, but there is nothing there. Behind him, the Black Mouse is ten feet away smiling wickedly. The mighty Excalibur falls from my father's dying fingers and clatters to the ground, lightless. Blood erupts from my father's mouth and nose. He is choking on it. His death but a moment away, he denies it for one second to face me:

"Go," he says.

Scooping up the magic sword, I race after the demon. ***He must pay!***

I looked at the great owl, and he turned his head to me. We had both felt it. I knew I would. Nemo looked out across the field and lowered his head. The owl closed his eyes. "Please," I said. He nodded and bent down. Before all from the safe house, I mounted the great bird, and he lifted off into the rain.

We reached the battleground in minutes. I saw Heide dragging the limp form of the Kind Human back to the house, foot by foot. I saw the one uncharred patch of land at the battle's center, and there lay my master.

He was dead.

As we landed, I scoured the country with my eyes, but all I saw was more death. Black, charred death. I went to my master's body, and my eyes overflowed with tears as I cradled him to me. His face was covered in blood. His eyes were empty. I was too late. I felt the last finger of my grip on my security in the world slipping.

"Death is like life, Squibble. It's just another journey."

My head snapped up to the owl.

"You must take me to the sea!" I said.

"He is not fast enough," Michael said, suddenly there standing over us. "But I am."

He spread his enormous wings. I just stared up at him, still angry.

"Come, Squibble," he said. "I will bear you."

I stared.

"But if I take you there I cannot bring you back," he said to me. "I cannot wait there at the ocean. I must return to the safe house at once. You will be alone."

I growled. Always a catch.

"Yes," I said. "Anything! Just take me and be swift!"

Carrying my master's body, his armor and shield, I climbed aboard Michael's giant hand, and we began the long flight. On the wings of an archangel, I raced my master's spirit to the shore.

I prayed we would make it before he did. The sun was falling steadily before us.

I could not catch the damned mouse. He fled with unearthly alacrity. His feet flew, and I could not keep up. I stripped my armor away, casting it aside like waste to match him, but it was no use. Finally, I returned to the place where my master fell, to find him missing.

There was no body. No armor, no shield... He was simply gone, as though Heaven had called him back.

I sat and wept for a long time. The great sword lay silent at my side. The grief was unbearable, and I felt my heart finally give way since strength was no longer needed. At last, the clouds broke and golden rays of sunlight fell gently upon my very place, warming me and stopping my tears.

I felt my father's spirit in that light. I cannot explain it, but I did. I knew he was well, and I knew I had a job to do. Strength was required yet. I looked toward the horizon where the Black Mouse had fled.

I am leaving this journal here, in the center all this carnage and destruction, in the hopes that someone from the safe house will find it and know what passed here on these seven days. Someone must know, and there are no witnesses left here. I am the last, and I have another direction to go.

I will chase that black soul to the ends of the earth if I must. Everyone believes in Squibble's quest, even if that mouse himself has yet to. I will take up my father's sword and pursue this enemy of ours until I see my father avenged. I will grant Squibble the time he needs. I swear it on my name and the name of my father.

Farewell.

Goodbye

✠

The flight was long. I did not have one thought on the way. My mind was empty, like my soul, and like the body I carried with me. The air rushed past us. Below, I saw the fields. Then I saw the freeway I had rushed across desperately, with my master, Bigfat, and Michael, all of us young friends. Beyond it was the city, and we flew over that too. From so far up, it looked smaller.

From up there, everything looked small.

At long last, just as the sky was turning red and yellow, we saw the beach. The sun was just over the water. Mike felt the desperate jump of my heart in its cage, and banked steeply to plummet to the shore. The beach was empty. I could not see one being, human or otherwise, even from the sky.

The angel landed so lightly I couldn't feel it. As the hand lowered I slid off, tumbling to the ground with my master's limp body. I got up quickly and ran to him, picking him up and dusting his face off. Silly of me, but I couldn't help it.

"I cannot come back," Mike said. "Your Kind Human needs me now. And soon after that, my side of this is almost over."

I nodded, knowing I was being abandoned, but I had chosen my own fate.

"Fare thee well, Squibble, may you have light when all around you is dark." His feet left the earth, and he was gone in moments.

The sun inched its way down. A light fog drifted toward shore from the horizon. The beach was silent.

"Master?" I called.

Only the waves answered me. They sounded sad. The whole world, in its bright and beautiful colors, seemed miserably hollow.

I looked up and down the beach, holding my master's limp body to my chest. I could not leave him. Oh, how stupid of me. Miles and miles of beach, and I assumed he would be exactly where I came to. My head fell to my chest. I was so tired.

Souls travel to the sea, and wait there for the dawn, or the sunset, depending on which sea...

I picked him up, putting him over my back like I did in our journey across the frozen Fields of Fate. I would search the beach. I would search forever until I found his spirit. If I was too late, then this would be my fate, to search the beaches forever, lost and alone, carrying his body on my back. That sounded like one of the stories he always used to read to me.

How long does it take?

I began to walk the long length of the beach. He was so heavy, but I couldn't drop his stuff. His hard earned armor, now cracked and chipped. It meant so much to him. Like his precious encyclopedias, which he would never read again.

Well, it takes a while to get to the sea, little mouse, and on the way the soul has time to think on their life, and what it meant to them.

I stopped. I couldn't do this. I just couldn't. I sat down and started to cry bitterly. My master was dead. He was really gone. The sunset was so pretty. The weight that had been bearing down on me for many months was, at last, more than I could take.

And then?!

I looked at the water. Gritting my teeth, I forced all of my willpower on one thing. I bent my entire soul to one task. I would not accept failure, for I *could* not. I needed this now. I need my gift. Serve me now, power. I am your master. Serve me!

The spirit world faded into view all around me, softly joining my picture of reality. The beach was full of souls, but most of them were very dim. Almost completely transparent. Some humans, some cats and raccoons, some coyotes. Thousands and thousands of mice. There were angels. All of it dimmed down, like someone had put fog between them and me. Spiritual fog. I focused deeper. I took on my chi gung breathing.

The whole world took on a golden tinge to it, and the waves sounded like songs.

So many mice. Too many. Some brighter than others, but none that stood out. I would never find him in all that. Never.

I felt a soft breeze, coming from the sea, and when it circled me, I smelled Bigfat and Mike, as they used to smell. It brought me back to our good times. I remembered playing all over Mike. I remembered biting Bigfat on the ear whenever he displeased me. I giggled. Then my master's scent came to me, and I followed it in the real world, carrying his body.

I found him almost at once. There he was, sitting on the sand, gazing at the sunset, wearing no armor, no sword, nothing but his handsome fur. He turned his head and saw me. We met.

"Squibble," he said, smiling as I loved to see him do. He looked carefree and happy, his burdens gone, his eyes bright, his quest fulfilled.

"Master," I said, my eyes full of tears.

"You remembered," he said.

"Yeah. Yeah, I did."

"How did you get here? It's been months."

"It's been less than a few hours, Master," I told him.

"Oh. Really? It seemed like I walked for almost a season. I walked a long time."

"Nemo says time is different in the spirit world, master," I told him. "I… I think you took as much time as you needed to, to work things out."

He smiled again. He seemed completely at peace.

"Yes. Yes, that sounds right. It feels right."

"Did you work everything out, Master?" I asked him.

He looked up at me, then out at the sunset, then back at me.

"Almost," he said. "I was waiting for you. I didn't know that until now."

I felt loved. "Thank you, Master."

"My pleasure, my best friend. I couldn't leave without saying goodbye to you one last time."

"Same here."

We stood looking at each other in silence a long time. His spirit was gorgeous. Radiant and beautiful. His light held everything that made him him. I could look at it forever.

At last, he said, "You have a long journey ahead of you."

"I wasn't planning on going back to the house," I said. "There's nothing there for me anymore."

"That isn't what I mean," he said. "You know that."

I looked down at my feet. I set down his body and sat.

"Yeah," I said. "I've wasted so much time."

"No," he touched my face. It felt like electricity, soft and warm. Through it, I could feel his caring. "You did exactly what you had to do. You did perfectly. Not one step did you miss, my magnificent squire."

"I'm… I'm old," I said. "My life is almost over. I feel old."

"That's the grief," he said. "I felt it when Tree died. But you are not old, Squib. You're young, because you're young at heart. And you have so much life left in you yet—I can see it. You will live another year and more."

"A mouse living three years?" I said. "Almost unheard of."

"You'll live until everything you have to do is done," he said. "Believe me. You'll make it."

"Not sick and crippled or nothin'…" I said, suspicious of prophecy at this point.

He laughed, like a choir of bells. "No. In good, solid health. I promise."

I relaxed. "Oh… okay then."

"Your job is so much more important than mine ever was," he said.

"I don't even know what it is," I said.

He grinned and slapped my side with his tail. "Yes, you do."

I looked at him, then back at the city, looming behind me.

"Yeah," I said. "Yeah. I guess I do."

"You've known all along."

"Yeah. I guess I have."

"Not easy being a champion, is it, my dear friend?"

"I don't wanna be a hero no more," I said, my voice depressed and wretched. "No one told me it would suck so much. I thought it would be fun and glorious." I wiped tears from my eyes. "I thought it would be cool."

He sat next to me.

"It's pretty cool to those you're saving," he said. "Don't give up yet, little one. Not just yet. For me, okay? My part in this story is done. Yours will go on."

I didn't answer him. Instead, I said, "I brought your armor and stuff."

"I don't exactly need it anymore," he said.

"But you loved it so…" I said.

"Who knows, maybe I'll have some use for it yet. Thanks, Squib."

"Yes, Master."

"Take care of my encyclopedias for me, Squibble. They're yours now."

I nodded. The sun was halfway down. He got up and squinted at the horizon. "My ride's almost here." He looked at me gently. "I have one last gift to give you, Squibble, now that I am able, for all the months of faithful service you gave me."

"You don't have to, Master…" I began.

"I know," he smiled, and everything around us faded. It all faded away into light. I smelled roses, and grass, and water. I smelled old wood, and heard trickling. I smelled plants and trees.

We were on my dock, the magical dock from my meditation. The perfect place of utter, complete peace I had only ever been able to reach once. The water was silvery glass. It ran past us with fluid beauty. The setting sun tinted it gold.

I felt no pain.

I felt no fear, no worry, no sadness. I was with my beloved master, sitting on the dock in pleasant warmth, and that's all there was.

"This is a powerful place you've built, Squibble," he said to me.

I felt nostalgia slink up my spine.

"I didn't know I built it," I told him. The evening was perfect. The moment was as fine as any could ever get. I had not one care in the world, and everything was clearer and sharper than anything had ever been.

"Oh, yes," he said, "you did. This is your eternal place of safety."

That made sense. I nodded, happy.

"My gift to you is this," he said, waving his hands around. "You've locked yourself out of it, feeling unworthy, but I am going to give it back to you. Because you need this place now. You need a place to rest and feel safe."

"I locked myself out?" I said.

"Everyone judges themselves harsher than anyone else ever does," he said. "You think you've failed in life. That's just what the Black Mouse wants you to think. If you think that, you set yourself up for failure in the future. It's a vicious cycle, this self loathing, Squib. It stops you from being happy, and from treating yourself well. I'm going to begin a stop to that downward spiral, though it may take a while to heal, and ultimately it will be your choice. But at least…" He waved his hand around the beautiful place, "at least this you will have, and nothing can take it from you again."

It clicked in my mind. I knew it was true. Everything here was true. It made me glad.

"This is your refuge," he smiled sweetly. "Here, everything is clear. Nothing can trick you, nothing can hurt you. You can rest here. And now, you can come here at will. For the rest of your life."

"I thought no one could do such things to someone else against their will," I said, quoting Nemo. He had said no one could control anyone else's free will. Their decisions, good or bad.

He grinned playfully.

"Sometimes you gotta break the rules."

Yeah. I nodded, feeling love swell in my delicate, wounded soul.

"Thank you for everything you've done for me, Squib."

I had no words to answer with. I just gazed into his lovely face, the sapphire gold water casting shadows on his white fur.

"Will you come back?" I asked him.

He looked out to the horizon.

"I don't know. I think so. But I want to just be a regular mouse. No big destiny. A normal life."

I chuckled. "Master, you know better than that. Some souls are too big for little things."

He turned to me, mocking surprise. "Haven't I earned it, Judge Squibble? Can't I have it? Please? It's all I ever really wanted."

I tilted my head slowly side to side, thinking.

"Ohhh, okay, I guess so," I told him. "But let's compromise."

"Alrighty," he said cheerfully.

"Do one last thing for me in this next life, and then it's yours."

He pretended to think about it, playing the game.

"Okay. Sounds fair."

We laughed and shook on it. His face slowly became serious again. He was still smiling, though.

"We will meet again, Squibble. Don't worry."

"I know. I won't."

We looked into the peaceful waters, traveling under us on its way to eternity. I imagined I could see my entire life in those waters. My momma, my friends, all the toys I had played with. Everything, drifting downriver. All the good times and the bad. Drifting. Going.

"Squibble, life is like a beautiful river, passing us by under a bridge, or a pier. We see all kinds of things from that place where we watch. We see things on the water, in the water, in the air. Sometimes we can pick up a few treasures as they float by, but mostly we watch as everything passes by, on its way to someone else's pier. We watch everything in life, the very experience is all we have. It's all we take with us in the end, because once things float on by, Squib, they're gone."

He turned to me and put a paw on my back. He stroked my fur.

"Our lives float by, with the river, and then they're gone, Squib. They're gone."

I turned to him.

"You told me this before."

He met my eyes. "Remember it. Treasure this life."

"I'll do my best, Master."

Then the pier faded away, and the beach came back. The sun was almost gone. He was standing next to me. The spell of that perfect place left me, and I felt the impossibly heavy weight of heartbreak and trauma on my broken spirit. He kissed my cheek as a tear ran down it, then slowly turned and walked toward the water.

He turned once.

"Squibble?" he said.

"Yes, Master?" I whispered.

He smiled kindly, one last time.

"I have a name, you know," he said to me. "It was all I ever wanted for myself, and I earned it through great hardship. I wish you'd use it more than once."

I was stunned. I realized that I had not used it, by voice or in my writing, ever. Not once in my entire life had I said his name aloud. More than once? To my knowledge, I had never used it. I hadn't deemed myself worthy. It awakened my sleeping spirit all the way, that fact. It was the moment of my enlightenment somehow.

My throat felt tight. Choked.

"Love you, Squib," he said.

"I love you…" and at the moment I was going to call him by name, an owl cried out in the dark city, and I turned suddenly out of instinct, half fear, half wondering if Nemo's teacher had come back for me after all. But the sky was dark and empty. The city was silent.

When I turned back, just a second later, my master's body was not on the beach any longer.

He was lying on the rear deck of a mighty ship, sailing just past the waves. It was silver and gold, with sails of starlight. The setting sun turned it into a silhouette, but I saw clearly my master laid upon an altar of stone, wearing his armor and shield, a sword across his still breast. His eyes were closed in peaceful rest. About him were three lady mice, glowing with power. One young, one old, and the one in the middle was… my mother.

She looked across the waves at me and smiled. Then the three of them held up one paw each, and the ship sailed slowly into the sun as I watched. It passed on with the sunset, and faded from my sight.

Our lives float by, with the river, and then they're gone.

They're gone.

SPRING

Squibble Descendeth

The Fourth Horseman: Rock Bottom

✠

It was the last straw. I knew it would be. I knew it was coming for a long, long time and just didn't want to see it. I really didn't want to see anything my visions showed me. I didn't want the job I took so long ago. Being a hero had sucked. I wanted to quit. I was swallowed in grief and I wanted to die. You won't understand unless you've been that miserable at some point in your life, and I'm betting you have been, even if it was only for a second until the "this isn't happening to me" defenses of denial set in and blinded you to your damage. Everyone has experienced some horrible thing they cannot handle. Everyone. Well, my soul had been doing the freefall for a long, long time now—over a year of my mousey life, and it finally hit rock bottom when I saw my master pass into the west without me.

I simply didn't care anymore. About anything. All done. Game over. Squibble quits, Mousegod. Do you hear? Squibble quits! You can take your stupid job and shove it, cause it sucks! Nobody's gonna wanna work for you, you sadist! No one is even gonna like you anymore, you overweight egotistical jerk. You got issues. You need therapy.

So I wandered along the beach all night, not caring if I got eaten, or mauled, or whatever. It couldn't be worse than I was going through already. No way.

All that time I was thinking, and my thoughts grew dark. Nemo had never warned me about a dark side, he only made mention that negative thoughts never helped anyone. I knew that, you know? But I couldn't help it. I was in my own personal hell, and I hated life. That made me hate everyone and everything. Bad people, for the most part, are just in pain. I understood that now. I became a bad mouse. If you are partial to my "heroic" visage, then you might wanna stop here, because it got pretty ugly. I had thought my life could get no worse than it had been, and boy was I wrong. Without the Black Mouse to help me whatsoever, I made his efforts to knock me down seem like a light, pleasant rain on a summer day.

No one can kick you where it hurts like yourself.

Assuming Scratchy and Percival were both dead, I wandered into the city. Starving, hurting from my injuries to body and much worse ones to my spirit, I aimlessly went from place to place. I didn't eat much, and when I did, it was trash. I didn't care. I drank sewer water and never groomed myself. I was heedless of dangers—all the dangers a mouse could suffer. I crossed streets, I stood out in the open, I even went into a coffee shop and ate right out of the display case once. The people screamed. I laughed and lunged at them. They ran from me. Stupid humans. You're the cause of all our woes, I thought. You deserve to suffer.

I hate the city. It was a fitting hell for my demise. And make no mistake—I was planning on demising. I was an old mouse by now. Almost two. At the end of spring I would be. Any mouse that lives to two is usually counted lucky. My life had been a nightmare, except for the beginning. Except for sporadic beautiful parts… my master, our adventures, my daughter… that little runt and his stupid heroism… all my nice friends… the… the Kind Human…

Ahh, hell with it.

I chose to forget everything good in my life, and wouldn't you know, it went away when I asked it to. Unlike the bad things.

I hung out in dark places at night and darker places in daylight. I hardly slept. Time stopped having meaning. I finally got sick. I got something really bad. I didn't know it, but I had gotten one of the only mouse diseases more deadly than Mycoplasma pulmonis, may that bug be damned forever. I got the Sendai virus. I knew it because my eyes bled and I began to go blind.

I probably got it in a pet store. I went there on occasion to eat, and to slum about, yelling at the mice to free themselves when I was sick from eating something bad or drinking something with alcohol in it. Anyway, it hit me as I slept behind some trash cans one evening, and I immediately knew I was in deep trouble. My legs went shaky, my vision blurred, my entire body ached, and I got a fever.

Fear kicked in, and I panicked like any normal mouse. I knew I didn't have long, and I really didn't want to go that way. Truth was, I was terrified of death, and though I thought I wanted to go, I didn't want to go like that. It reminded me too much of the damned plague at the safe house. I snuck onto busses, took daring rides along with humans in their shopping bags, and slowly worked my way back to the lab.

I knew how to get in, and by this time I was seriously ill. I barely got up to the table and freed some of the rats. At first they had it in mind to eat me, of course.

"No wait," one of them said. "That's… that's Squibble!"

"You are so full of it," another said. "Squibble is dead."

"No—that's him. My dad was a Sword of Michael. That's him!"

"You… you're not joking."

"No. That's him, dude."

"Why does he look like that?"

"He's sick, stupid."

"I thought Squibble wore armor and paraded around all command-like."

"I quit," I moaned.

They looked at me with fear.

"It is him."

"I told you, pellets for brains."

"Holy…"

I looked at them wearily. "If you're gonna eat me, can you get it over with? If not, can you turn the computer monitor on for me, please?"

One of them inched over to the monitor.

"Yes... Yes sir."

It came on, and it only took me half of eternity to reach the keyboard. I was almost blind.

Finally, one of them spoke. There were about twenty of them loose now, and apparently they had all been informed God was among them. Whee ha.

"What... what are you looking for, Sir?"

"The cure to the Sendai virus," I said, almost passing out from the effort.

"There isn't any," one said. "Right?"

"Wrong," I said. Button. Must... press... button. You know, I was really sick of being sick. "These labs can't have their precious inhumane experiments messed with by ordinary virii. They have a cure. I'm sure of it."

"Do they have one for SDA?" A rat asked. SDA killed alot of rats. Way alot.

"Yeah," I said.

The rat picked me up and put me down near his friends, who all bundled up around me to keep me warm. Someone tried to feed me something tasty.

"Tell me what to push," the rat who had picked me up said. "We'll help you, sir."

"Why?" I asked, full of dripping cynicism.

He looked at me. "For my father. He served you."

"He's toast," I said. "They all died." I paused and sucked on my lower lip. "It was my fault."

The room was quiet. Finally, the rat said, "Yeah. Well, we're all toast sooner or later, but he was pretty darn proud to be a Sword of Michael. It was better than being a stupid lab rat."

"Okay," I said.

"Okay," he agreed.

So I told them what to push. We found the cure. Sure enough, the humans had it. They simply didn't want it getting out to the public, curing beloved pets, actually doing any good.

I slept in a dark corner of the lab in the daytime and listened to the horrifying sounds of the animals in terror and pain. I dwelled on my hatred of humans and sympathized greatly with Shiva and Thor, who, as far as I knew, were still alive. They had been right all along. Humans were evil. Most of them, anyway. Selfish, no-good, greedy, destructive, dangerous, hostile apes. Vermin.

I had bad dreams. Whoa. Big surprise there, eh? News flash. Over a few days my strength and sight came back. I had failed to prevent myself from going on. What a wretch I was.

In the night the rats and I planned the complete annihilation of the lab. But before we carried it out, we schemed. Oh yes, we schemed hard.

We collected data on every single formula they had. Every experiment, every note they took. We took samples of their potions and drugs. I collected quite a sackful for myself, for later, and the rats built backpacks for themselves. We hid by day and worked by night, and the humans knew no better than one night there had been an escape. They thought us long gone. They were going to wish we were.

By the time we were ready to move, weeks had passed, and we knew the human's data better than they did. Every single animal in the lab was in on our plan. They all called me Sir all the time, to which I responded, "Don't do that." If they did it again, I bit them hard. No one ever bit me back. Damnable respect thing.

On the last day, instead of blowing the place up, or some other blatant act of terrorism, we did much, much better.

We altered their experiment.

We put vitamins and painkillers in place of the normal experiment drugs. I myself used some hocus-pocus I had learned to magically alter the formula and enchanted it to make the animals super smart and super strong. Ubermice. Uberrats. I didn't know if it would work, but it was better than what they were getting. They'd all get out of here soon anyway. No one was staying.

We slipped the humans their own experiment drugs, the old bad ones, into their cigarettes, their prescription pills, their cough syrup. We got into the bathroom and put it in their mouthwash. We loaded it into the toilet paper. We set it loose in the air vents. We even had some really ticked off mice deliver it by biting the humans. I gave them some Rg-10. I remembered the formula like it was yesterday.

The entire time I was drinking, smoking, and using whatever recreational drugs I could get my hands on. I was whacked out of my mind, but in some strange way, those dangerous things opened my consciousness to broader horizons. I began to think out of the box. Wayyy out of the box.

When it came time, we called it D-Day, the humans were staggering around like morons and dropping like flies. The few who were still semiconscious could barely read the computer screen. It said: Up yours, humans. Have a really bad day.

Then, before their very eyes, we all escaped. They were powerless to stop us. We took all their notes, their potions, and the cures for Sendai and SDA with us. We flaunted it in their faces. We spit on them and bit them. I did a jig on someone's face while all the rodents laughed, then we dashed off.

To be quite honest, I loved every minute of it.

Gunnery Sergeant William Bonnie

✠

The crew and I went our separate ways, despite their begging, and I ended up in the park with my stash of drugs and notes. Appropriately enough, I was hauling them around in a little sack that looked alot like a garbage bag. Before long, I was starving again.

Not caring about my fate, I sat near a park bench and waited. I picked up scraps and ate whatever the humans dropped. I sparred against pigeons for food, and I stole what I could from the mouths of cats. It was never enough. I made a sorry home below a trash can that got flooded when it rained, and in that place I took off my hideously dirty armor (I had never once cleaned it or myself, nor taken it off), my shield, my slingshot, and stashed all my earthly possessions. Most of the time I was too drugged out on Xanax or painkillers to care about anything, and plenty of people threw away perfectly good liquor in my trashcan. But once in a while, I got hungry, or it rained, and I had to surface.

There was this old bum. He hung out most days on the bench by my trashcan and I watched him because I had nothing else to do. He saw me once or twice, but didn't do anything. He was like me. Drunk, starving, depressed.

One day he had a bag of peanuts. It was gold, I tell you, and my stomach began to immediately demand some of that rare treasure. For a brief moment I remembered a lifetime ago… a nice warm place, and a kind human that gave me peanuts anytime I asked for them. The vision, surely my stupid imagination, faded quickly enough, and I marched right up to the bum. I climbed up his pant leg and sat on his thigh, staring at him.

Well, that's the last thing anyone expects a mouse to do, and he stared back at me. We sat there staring. Finally, he smiled a little bit through his grey beard and offered me a peanut. I snatched it and devoured the morsel. He giggled. I answered his impingement by going right up to the bag and pulling a peanut out. Glaring at out of the corner of my eye, I munched that peanut in broad daylight, in defiance of all humanity that didn't want a poor, starving mouse to have something nice.

"You got guts, mouse," he said to me.

I finished my peanut, hissed at him, and ran away.

But the next day I woke beneath my damp trash can to the smell of more peanuts. He had come back with another bag.

I stuck my nose out and saw him staring at me. He grinned and waved a peanut. Clearly the challenge could not go unheeded, so I strode out there, marched up his ratty pant leg, and ate the peanut. He chuckled.

From then on the bum and I got along pretty well. He talked to me and I talked back, though that part of it was one way. We mostly talked to the universe, or God, or whatever, and the other one listened. When I wasn't sitting with Bill (he told me his name and that he had been a marine in Vietnam), or sulking in my dungeon of a hole below the trashcan, I was out lurking on creatures.

Understand that I'm not a mean mouse. I was a peaceful mouse, but for the pain. The pain made me mean, and the drugs made me stupid and reckless. Looking back, it's just astounding that I didn't die at that time in my life. It was by far the most dangerous of any other time.

I poured out my hostility on targets that I thought deserved it. Cats, snakes, birds of prey, and people. Mostly people. People are easy to scare. Drop on them from trees, bite them when they're resting, skitter across their newspaper, all that, then run away. Easy. Risky. Lots of fun. I beat up other mice that came into my territory, half wishing the big bully mouse (who was probably dead by now) would come and get a taste of my stick (I had a long stick I used like a staff) or my slingshot, the one dear possession I had kept on me through all this. I grew wickedly quick and accurate with the staff, and my trusty old slingshot, well, let's just say I never missed, drunk and drugged or not. Most of my targets were pretty big. Even their eyes. I was a nasty, hostile, bitter mouse. Before long, word spread that "Squibble's Ghost" was haunting the park and no mouse would come near it. No rats, neither. It didn't take too long before I was alone. Even the humans stopped using that sidewalk due to the "stinging wasps" (he he he).

I stopped doing my chi gung from the day my master died. I stopped drawing, stopped writing. I did nothing except dangerous, psycho stuff, living in frigid misery, and hanging out with Bill. When it would rain and the cold water flooded my hovel, I'd crawl up onto the bench, up under his hat, which was warm and dry under his newspapers and trashbags. He knew I did that, so he never hit himself in the head or scratched. He was usually passed out drunk anyway. He could have easily squished me, but at the time I didn't care, I just wanted to be warm and dry.

All in all, the gods protected me hard over those sad weeks. It was the lowest time in my life, and I felt like I was going crazy maybe. In my hardest, darkest moment, the struggle wasn't physical, it was emotional and mental. It made my first trek through the Fields of Fate seem easy. I questioned everything—the very principles that made me who I was. I wondered if I would even know it when I went insane. All I ever felt was pain or nothing. My body wasn't young anymore. My vigilante crusade was taking its toll on me, and I had many injuries that hurt me constantly. It seemed a thousand years since I was a tiny boy, comforted by my mother's loving face and eager to join a great quest.

And now, being a "great hero" was the very last thing I ever wanted. I hated the very thought of it. It was a heinous, twisted trap from the beginning. I'd been a sucker.

Bill told me he was William Bonnie, gunnery sergeant in Vietnam, and he had been responsible for 200-some men, who had all died. Only he and two others came back. Those two others died off over the years. One killed himself. Bill blamed himself for every one of them, clearly, and it haunted him. We had that in common. I found it ironic that I hated humans so much when all I seemed to meet were nice ones, but it didn't change my mind.

As for myself, I had had it with holy quests, deep meanings and hidden agendas. I was directly responsible for the death of fifty thousand mice. Every single one of them recruited by me—talked into being cosmic suckers for some 'great cause.' If I hadn't come along, they would all be alive and happy. Well, they'd be alive. Maybe. I saw their faces in dreams, relived funny moments with them, saw their children and families faces, frowning at me. Blaming me.

Hey, don't blame me, people. I blame myself enough for all of you. I'm as haunted as it gets.

And I was indeed. For every time I partook of drugs or drank too much liquor, My vision was cast right into another world. But it wasn't the normal spirit world. It was the underworld. It was that dark, horrible place of damnation and woe.

There were ghosts there, and though none of them were the actual mice that had died in the Great War, I saw them as if they were. I saw them hiss at me, curse me, spit on me. I saw them weep for one more precious moment with their child, or their momma, knowing they'd never get it. After a while it beat me up so bad I was numb to it. It became normal. I ignored it.

I was sick and tired of being the universe's punching bag. Bill and I were catharsis for each other, using the other as our shrink and only friend. He thought I couldn't understand him, and it didn't matter. He couldn't understand me, and that didn't matter either. We spent long days and nights pouring out our souls to each other on most every subject.

"How could Mike trick me into that whole mess?" I said to Bill. "It was completely stupid. A trap from the beginning. I had no choice once I realized there were choices, and by then it was too late. He used my childish desire to be a great hero to lure me into being the fall mouse for the entire safe house, which is mostly dead now, like your soldiers, only I had like fifty thousand, which is how many America lost in Vietnam period!" I paced back and forth, stopped to sip some beer from a bottlecap, and went on. "I wasted my entire life in a stupid, childhood dream. I've never been a normal mouse, and now I won't ever be. Normal mice shun me, and will the world miss fifty thousand mice? Not even. Would it miss a million? A billion? Nah. One day, many years from now, they'd all go, 'Hey, where are all the mice?' and realize we were all gone. Then they'd shrug and go on with their nasty, short attention span, gimme gimme, me me me attitudes. They'd never blink an eye at our fate. They only care about us if we bother them. Then all they care about is killing us."

"I can't get any medical care," Bill said. "No one will treat a bum. If you got a tiny bit of money, you get nothin'. You gotta be starvin', or dyin', to get medical care. Even then you get the bottom of the barrel. You get next to nothin'. This country's gone to hell in a handbasket, I tell you, little friend. When all my friends and I signed up, we thought we were doin' the... the right thing! We were suckers, we were. If someone had told us how it would turn out, why... I... I don't know what we would have done. No one wants to talk to me anymore. My own father won't see me. My friends are all dead. All I got is this bottle. Heh heh heh... an' you got the cap. I hope you appreciate my sharing with you, buddy. It's all I got."

The irony didn't escape me at all that I was now using a bottlecap to drink beer out of instead of using it as a shield in pursuit of the valorous righting of wrongs. But I was grateful at least. Most humans wouldn't share even a tiny piece of cracker with a starving mouse, and Bill shared everything he had with me. We both ate out of the trash. I was glad I wasn't the only one.

"Human civilization is built on the bones of mice, Bill," I told him one frosty night. I was nuzzled in his military issue coat and he was wrapped in his barely adequate sleeping bag. He was still shivering. Winter had held on long. Spring was very cold this year. Big surprise there.

"In labs, mice grant people the cures for their problems," I said. "Millions of mice pay for each drug that makes humans feel better, or treats their sicknesses. I say treats because no pharmaceutical company in the world is interested in curing any illness. It's not good for business. It's all about the money in the big, wretched world of Lucifer's corporations. But meanwhile, the mice are the heroes. They sacrifice and die, although not willingly, mind you, so that humanity can go on and enjoy life. It's all insane, but what really ticks me off is the mice that die for little or no reason. Like testing cosmetics. 'Oops! That stuff melts the flesh off—good thing we tested it on a mouse and not a human. Well, put that mouse in the incinerator and get the next one. Maybe the next one will light on fire.'" I hunched down in the pocket lower as I spilled my complaints. "Stupid humans, so careless and selfish! I wish mice were three hundred pounds each. We'd show them."

"The system doesn't work," Bill said the next morning. "It punishes its own people. It's getting harder and harder to make a difference. Harder to be appreciated, or be heard. No one listens anymore." He showed me a box of old medals he had. There were so many. I thought of the one I had earned. The first mouse to earn a medal. Bill had more than twenty. One of them he held up. It was the Silver Star. There was almost nothing more honorable than that one. It was a huge deal. He let me touch it and sniff it. I looked back and forth from them to him, amazed. Bill was a great war hero.

"I got them for saving my company from an ambush," he said. "Well, some of them. Others I got for being wounded, or for doing what I was told, or whatever. But that one... that one I got for saving everyone. It was a dark night in the Northern lines, and I took point 'cause no one else knew how. I tripped a wire. I heard it go click, so I froze. The demolitions guy was a newbie who couldn't disarm it, so I told everyone to get away from me, and I wrote a letter to my wife, telling her I was sorry an' all that. Then once everyone was clear of the blast radius, I let the string go. The grenade didn't go off. It was a dud. At that exact moment we were attacked by a bunch of gooks, and I was the only one who could see where they were. I was shot a coupla times," he showed me the scars, "But I got everyone out an' killed half the Charlies by myself. My company was torn up. When it was all over, they told my commander that I had taken the blast from the grenade and still come to their rescue. I told the truth, but nobody listened. They gave me this medal." He coughed, spat, and said, "None of those guys I saved made it out. My... heroic deed meant nothin'! Nothin'... Still... I loved getting this..."

He cradled it, gazing at it with affection. It was the only thing he valued, like me and my slingshot.

Eyes filled with tears from his story, I snapped to attention and saluted him. He leaned over, squinted at me, and said, "By god, little guy, I gotta drink a lot more or a lot less."

We spent all our days and nights in such conversation, glad to have someone who would listen. Glad for little things.

"The Kind Human is probably dead," I said one evening. "My momma is dead. My family is dead. Even that squire. Why should I miss that stupid little midget? But I do. I miss them all. I hate it. I can't get my mind away from it. I wanna run away. Mice always run away. Except my master... he didn't run away... Even... Even when he knew. Even when he knew what was coming..."

"I got cancer," Bill said one day.

I stood still, staring at him. He looked down at me, not surprised that I appeared to have understood. We knew each other well by now. "Yeah, little guy. I got stomach cancer. They told me down at the VA today. There's nothin' they can do. Well, there is, but I can't afford it," he chuckled.

I kept staring. My heart wanted to stop.

"So, I guess my clock's ticking," he said sadly. "I'm surprised it lasted this long. I'm an old man now. My time's over."

I'd cursed him. I kill all my friends. Oh, why. Why was this so? Hadn't I damn well quit? Why wouldn't the bad things leave me alone!!?

I crept up to him, not caring one bit if he knew I could read or understand him. I sat by his neck and leaned my head against him. I cried.

Some days Bill would be gone after that, to the VA hospital, I guess, when the pain got too bad. He still brought me food every evening, even though he stopped eating his. He froze at night, having lost so much weight, and shook so violently I couldn't sleep with him anymore for fear of being crushed. My own cave was as cold as hell. My vision of hell. Frozen and lonely. I realized I was in it now.

Bill lifted the trashcan in the middle of the coldest of these nights, smiling at me, and left me several big chunks of his warm coat he had torn off.

"No reason both of us have to freeze, lil' buddy," he said.

I stared back and chirped at him. He gently set the trashcan back down. As he went back to his bench, I heard him say, "All I ever wanted in my whole life, little guy, was to make a difference. For someone, or something. Just anything would have been nice."

The next morning, I woke warm and happy in my new nest. I thought I was back at the safe house, and was eager to go see my master for breakfast. When I stuck my nose out of my new nest I realized the truth and my heart sank. I looked at my stash of drugs, almost gone. Only crumbs remained. Letting out a deep sigh, I realized that I was going to have to go all the way back to the pharmacy to steal more. They were the only thing that kept the dreams at bay. Last night I think I had dreamt of my momma. It had been a good dream, turned terribly cruel at the end by my awakening to such a merciless reality.

But one person *had* changed fate for me, because I realized when I saw the frost on the ground that I would not have survived last night beneath the trashcan without Bill's coat. I crawled out in the early morning, determined to tell him he had made a difference. Even if I had to write it down for him.

But Bill was dead.

I sat on him a long time, wishing he wasn't, but he was. He was cold and stiff. He had no pulse. He smelled dead.

That was how the hero Bill died. Alone, cold and in pain, never knowing he'd made a difference, even if only for a mouse.

Turning Point

✠

I left Bill there on the bench. I wish I could have taken his precious medal, or him, to a better place. I wish I could have buried him with honor, or made the damn humans do it. I hated being a mouse.

A drug addicted, drunkard, worthless, old mouse.

So I picked up my nest, full of my stuff, and tried to carry it with me back toward the pharmacy, but it was too big and unwieldy. Leaving it behind, I felt as I had that day the bully's cronies had devoured my momma's precious honeycomb. Everything I owned was inside it, even my beloved slingshot. I stashed it just inside a sewer entrance, beside a large oak tree, and wept as I abandoned my last possession. It felt like losing my very last friend.

Naked, with no armor, weapon, bed, food, or drugs, I went back into the city to destroy my life utterly.

Days of sneaking around, cold and sometimes wet, always hungry, followed. I found the pharmacy again. It had been shut down. The lab had failed after losing all their animals, and I guess they owned the building. Served them right.

But I felt a pang of regret for the Kind Human that had tried to save me, even though she was afraid of mice.

I went to another pharmacy, but couldn't find a way in. I was twitching at random by now, going into withdrawals that would probably kill me. I couldn't see well, and every step felt like a hundred. I became delusional for short periods of time, and I would do strange things, not remembering why or how afterward.

One evening, just as dusk settled in, I went past the art school. I sat there in front of it a long time. It seemed to be doing well. I wished I was inside, drawing. Fed. Warm. Having fun.

Then I saw a car pass by, and the Kind Human—the Kind Human who owned the safe house—was in the front seat with Heide! As I stared in shock, the car stopped at the corner of the block. Mice and rats got out, and some got in. I ran for them as fast as I could, and they waited there a good few minutes, but long before I reached them, the Kind Human scoured the street with his eyes and slowly got back in the car. I squeaked as loud as I could. I ran till my lungs burned, right out in the open street.

But I was too late. Too old, too weak, and too slow. The car drove off without me. I finally stopped and stared, huffing and puffing my lungs out, watching them drive away. I remembered the terrible abandoned feeling of watching him drive off after leaving me in the city at the beginning of my pilgrimage. I felt lightheaded, blacked out, and woke up wandering down the middle of the sidewalk hours later. Out in plain view at night.

Feeling sudden panic, I swerved for the wall, an alley, any kind of shelter, but again I was too late.

I felt the impact of talons close around me, knocking the breath out of me and pushing my guts up into my throat. Then I was off the ground and being carried to my gruesome death by an owl.

It was a very young owl. Not the old one Nemo knew. This one was hunting for food, and had found easy prey. I could barely breathe as it squeezed me. I had nothing to defend myself with. My teeth didn't penetrate the owl's thick talons. We were hundreds of feet above the city now.

I realized this was it. The moment of my death was coming. The owl would land, hold me still, and crush my body in with one great blow of its beak. If I was lucky, it would hit my head first. If not, I would live long enough to see my innards being eaten before dying.

I thought I was having a heart attack. I felt pain in my chest. With no way of knowing whether it was anxiety, drug withdrawal, or my heart failing me at last, I thought it funny underneath all my horror. Maybe I wouldn't see my legs picked off my torso by a merciless predator after all. I took one last look at the city below me. Everything looked so peaceful. I thought of all the mice that would go on being abused for years to come.

Then I faded away into spirit land as my gift, free of the blocking drugs, returned.

I was in the clouds. The full moon shone down and glittered upon the soft tops of the white sky mountains. All of it sparkled like silver glass. It was beautiful beyond compare, and mystical. Magical.

Far below I could see the earth. I felt detached from everything, like at the pier. I thought about the pier. My master said I could go there anytime I wanted now…

"Don't," came a voice.

I turned and saw Michael sitting next to me, his legs crossed, his wings folded behind him. In his true angelic form, he looked no less majestic for it being night. Silver light surrounded him. His halo glowed softly against the star filled sky. On his knee sat Bigfat.

I growled. Bigfat chuckled.

"Yeah, you wanna bite my ear," he said.

"Both ears!" I squeaked. "Clean off, you big dummy!"

"We came to offer you freedom," Mike said to me.

I perked up. "Whassat mean!"

Bigfat hopped off the knee, bouncing like a big water balloon on the soft cloud ground, and waddled over to me.

"You're quitting on us," he said, putting a hand on my shoulder. When that hand touched me, my mind cleared like magic. I felt the effect of two months of drugs lifted from my soul. I came awake. Doubtless he did that on purpose.

"We understand you're traumatized," Mike said. "It had to happen."

"What did?" I asked in bitterness. "The trauma? My master's death? My momma's? My children? How about fifty thousand faithful warriors? How about Favorite, who never hurt a soul?" I stared at them both with naked anger. "Which one had to happen, huh? All of it!?"

"Yes," Bigfat said, no longer smiling.

"Oh, that's so much crap," I said. "You're both all powerful. None of it had to happen."

Bigfat looked ready to protest, but Mike interrupted. "Yes, that's right," he said. "None of it had to. They all chose it, Squibble. Every one of them."

"Stupid!" I chirped. My version of bullshit.

"They chose it," Bigfat said. "He's right. In the spirit world, where the body and the suffering of the heart no longer matter, Squibble, they all decided what they wanted. Long term. For their children. For all mousekind."

"They chose to have a chance at equality with humans," Mike said. "They chose to have a chance to end the abuse and cruelty that they all suffer every day, and they willingly paid the price."

I peered at them as if they were trying to sell me a used car.

"It's true," Bigfat said. "I wouldn't lie to you, punk. All mice chose this. All mice everywhere. They knew it would cost them. They knew the enemy would come and challenge their claim to have souls, happiness, and eternal life."

"They chose it anyway," Mike said. "And a small handful of mice, some tiny number out of the billions on the earth, like fifty-two thousand, chose to be the heroes that would bear the brunt of that trial."

"And a small handful of those heroes," Bigfat said, "chose to lead them. Chose to bear the heaviest of the load on themselves and give up all they had, which was much, so that all mousekind might gain."

"And one of them," Mike said, "chose to be their champion. Above all the rest."

"And now you're quitting on us," Bigfat spat. "When you're almost over the last hill. Just like before. Just before you've made it. Quitting."

I sat there, mind clear, seeing it all, remembering every word my master had ever said to me. I myself had said that most mice quit just before they succeed. Time was meaningless now, here, in this cloud place, so like my sacred pier. I saw it all very clearly.

"So we came to let you go," Mike said. "If you want out now, you can go."

I looked up at him in silence.

"No punishment," he said. "God does not punish his children when no evil has been done. You may go to your master and spend eternity with him. Right now. Just say the word."

"But… I have done evil…" I whispered.

"Get off it!" Bigfat slapped me. It hurt, further waking me up. "You've been sad, and down. You've been depressed, and sick. You've been mad, and with good damn reason. But that's far from evil! We knew this would be hard on you. We knew it would bring you to the edge of despair and crippling pain. We knew, and so did you."

"But… But then… why did this… all this horrible stuff… happen to me?" I whined. "Why was it so… so damn hard!"

"You're forgetting something, you ridiculous snoot," Bigfat said.

(Heard something!) I stared at him, aghast. "Whassat?" I asked.

"Gratitude."

"Are you serious??!" I yelled. "Gratitude? For what!"

He gave me the stare of power, right down into my ailing soul.

"One million mice," he said. "Out of one million mice, one will have a chance to be a loved pet. One. And out of those, only one in a thousand is actually loved. You know what happens to the rest." He frowned. I couldn't break eye contact. He was doing some Mousegod thing to me, I was sure of it. I had to listen.

"You grew up in a loving home, with loving friends and family, with a loving human who gave you treats every time he even passed by your cage. You grew up in a house where all the animals were loved. Where the odds were all beaten.

"Everybody dies, pal. Everybody. No one goes on forever. But your life was spent basking in love and adoration. You had it absolutely as good as it gets, you ingrate. No one has it that good, and you don't hear them complaining. No mice get what you got. You are a loved mouse!

"Death comes to all—it's what happens in-between that matters. Most mice will never have the memory of being kissed, or groomed, or told one kind word, ever. You've forgotten how lucky you were, Squibble. Your depression and self loathing has taken you far from home. The way back is to be grateful. Grateful for every day of your thankless life being so cherished, so loved, by so many good mice and men."

My eyes, now full of tears, could not blink. My heart came alive after a long, cold sleep, and I knew he was right. I knew it was the truth. My life had been magnificent. I was an ingrate. Hardcore. I had forgotten my blessings, and in doing so, had lost them.

"You brought yourself to this point," Mike said. "No one forced you. Ever. No one did this to you, Squibble. Those with no power take the victim's path. It is an illusion. It is not for those with integrity."

"Yeah," Bigfat said. "Those with integrity, like your master, take responsibility for everything that happens. By doing so, they stay in control of their own lives." He waved his hand and I saw myself standing before the hordes once more, addressing them, asking them to go to war for all mousekind. "As for why you, Squib?" he said. "Because you could."

Mike nodded. "You were chosen because you could accomplish the task, even with all the burdens it carried," he said. "You asked to be the one."

"When I agreed to be the champion?" I asked.

"No," he said, face stone. "Before you were born."

I sat in starlight and silence. He was right again. This was much bigger than it had ever looked when I was down on earth. I had lost my way. But only once. Through all the hardship, only once. I looked up, free of all earthly pain and fear.

"And I can go now, with no consequences to anyone, including myself?" I asked.

They both nodded.

"You'll choose another champion?"

They nodded.

"I can go to my rest and see my master again?"

They nodded.

"My… My momma? Favorite?"

They nodded.

Long minutes passed.

"Or I can finish my work."

"Yes," Mike said.

"In hardship and pain."

"If you choose it to be so."

"Kid," Bigfat said, "you know the path you chose."

I nodded.

"Well, now you get to choose it all over again. If you've changed your mind, this is the last door out. No one wants a reluctant champion, and God won't have you saying he forced you into anything."

"You're the Mousegod," I said, still thinking heavily.

"Oh, yeah. Okay," he scoffed. "You ain't gonna blame this on me, then. Capiche?"

"We await your decision," Mike said.

I knew that below, my body was being carried to its death. I had only moments to make up my mind between the duty of a great hero and the desperate wishes of a hurt little boy.

I lifted my head at last to meet Mike's blazing eyes.

There was a crunching, jarring impact. I felt the cold wind around me once more. The talons let go and I was falling. When I looked up again, I saw a great raven locked in combat with the owl that had taken me as food. As I plummeted in freefall, I saw two other ravens join in. Then they were lost to my sight among the clouds. I turned over to see the ground fast approaching. Panic filled my body, and the worries of the flesh consumed me once more, shoving all spiritual peace right out the window. I was going to die!

The pure realization of it was a shock to me, even though I'd been in many situations where death seemed certain. Maybe it was the owl thing—being food, falling—primal fears. Whatever it was, it effected a radical transformation in my soul that my spirit had just moments before initiated. In a single moment I lost the drug-induced illusion that death would be better than life. I had thought I really wanted to die. Now I knew different, and I had learned it, as usual, the hard way.

In that moment time seemed to slow down. I barely remembered my time in the clouds with Mike and Bigfat. I couldn't remember what I'd said when my mind was so free and clarity was mine again. I couldn't remember my answer. As the pavement raced up to greet me, that was going to be my last thought.

What had I said!?

On the ground, I saw Death. In his white robe, he was reaching out to me, grinning.

But I felt another set of talons close around me at the very last moment, plucking me from Death's reaching claws. The raven holding me banked sharply and desperately, fighting every ounce of gravity to escape the same fate that awaited me. We missed the ground by two inches. I wished I'd had the fortitude to stick my tongue out at Death.

Nice try, sucker. Maybe later.

The raven landed and was soon joined by his two brothers, who looked badly beaten. They spoke not one word. They didn't need to.

I knew what my answer had been.

"Thank you," I said through quivering lips. To them, to Mike, to Bigfat, to my master and all the others. I meant it. "Thank you very much."

They flew off as dawn came. I smelled on the air that spring was over. Winter had finally given up, but only to summer. It had won against spring. I was trembling and tingly. I felt no strength in my legs.

Clear of the drugs, like magic, and taking hold of blessed clarity once again, I looked around me. I had been set down right in front of Heide's alley. I almost laughed.

"Of course," I said to myself and any spirit listening. "It's about time." My strength came back with my acceptance of what had to happen now.

I walked into the alley, head up, tail rattling.

SPRING

Squibble Ascendeth

Bitter Reunion

✠

I was sure I'd find the bully mouse dead of old age at least, or more likely from his lifestyle, but I knew in my gut that wasn't to be. He had been preserved by the universe for this moment. Our rematch. The taking back of my pride.

And, sure enough, his minions began to fill the alley the moment they smelled me. They had changed, but the bully himself had only gotten bigger and meaner.

He was covered in scars. His ears were missing. His tail bent radically at several points where it had been broken, but he had kept it in one piece. He looked even scarier than before.

Seeing them all around me, my childhood terror came back, but this time it was not the frightened little boy that felt it. I stood there, legs apart, eyes like steel knives, ears alert and ready. Last time I began with armor and ended up ganked. This time I was beginning naked, but I felt as if I was covered in armor. The armor of my confidence. Or maybe the armor of 'I've been through it all.' Either way, I stood there looking as much like Clint as I could. Feeling like Clint too, I imagine. I was not a servant to my fear. There was nothing more this mouse could take from me.

"Well, what have we here?" the bully said to his cronies. "I remember this mouse. It's that mouse night." He turned to me. "It's been a long time, retard."

"Yeah, dumbshit," I said. "It has." One of his pleebs cackled a tiny bit and quickly shut up.

The look on his face was priceless. His eyes bulged and his mouth hung open. He smelled fear on me, but realized I wasn't backing down. I wasn't shaking like a leaf this time. I was scared. I was very scared, but I was not going to lose my focus this time. This time I wasn't caught by surprise, and this time I hadn't come from a delusional never-never land, thinking all of life would be perfect and nice. This time I knew nothing that was about to happen was going to be nice.

"I'm gonna kill you this time, shrimp," he said. He was very serious. No jokes. No mockery. He was scared also.

"The name's Squibble," I said. "Moron."

His tail went a-drumming on the ground like crazy at that. His eyes narrowed. He ground his teeth together. His muscles visibly tightened.

"Squibble!" One of his minions whispered. "That's the mouse who haunts the park."

"That was the leader of the Hordes!" Another said.

"He tamed rats!"

"Squibble could kill anyone…"

"This can't be Squibble…"

The old bully eyed me as he moved around me to get a better position for attack. I circled him as well, keeping the distance between us. His minions backed up, forming a wide circle around us.

"Are you really Squibble?" he said to me.

I nodded. "Yep. That's me."

"You were pretty easy to beat before," he said, clearly not believing any of it.

"I was a scared little child," I said. "And I wasn't ready for the likes of you, a coward who preys on helpless children."

He scoffed at that. "You still aren't."

I stared him in the eye. "Wrong."

The whispers continued. "Squibble killed two thousand mice."

"Squibble killed a cat. My grandpa saw it."

"Squibble wasn't a mouse… he was a giant wolverine."

"Shut the hell up!" The bully yelled. He squinted at me. "In a second Squibble's gonna be dead."

Well, at least he actually believed who I was. He must have heard about me. He'd lived in the city long enough.

I had always imagined this moment. Hundreds of times. I had thought that I'd just go psycho on the jerk, and tear him to pieces. I knew now that that wouldn't work. He was bigger and stronger, and he was a born fighter. He lived to inflict cruel harm on others. I couldn't match his viciousness, as much as I wanted to. This couldn't be an anger-exorcism for me. I'd lose.

So when he lunged, I backed up instead of meeting him as normal mice were compelled by instinct to do. He fell on the concrete and snapped his teeth on air. Surprised, he bounced back and tried again. I dodged aside, and he missed again. He growled at me and spun like quicksilver. Age had not touched this mean mouse.

"Coward!" he yelled. "Sit still!"

"I am no longer the coward here," I said. "Come and get me, slowpoke."

I wasn't wearing my armor this time. I wasn't paralyzed by terror. I was half his weight, but three times as fast. When he lunged again, I took my time, stepped aside, and as he passed, broke his leg with a bite BJ had taught me. He went down squeaking in pain.

Still, he sprang up and came at me again. I stepped aside and he ran into the wall. For the half second he was dazed, I bit him on the rump. His minions laughed at him, instantly silenced by a glaring promise of death from the bully.

He gnashed his teeth and hissed at me in pure hatred. Apparently no one had ever stood up to him before. I smiled.

"And my title is Sir Squibble to you, peasant," I said.

He lunged again, this time quicker. He was on the edge of a berserker's rage. I leapt over him, poking him in the eye as he went under me. He went down, scattering his pleebs like tenpins. I grinned the best smarmy expression I could summon and said, "Loser."

He rose from his cushion of mice and told his gang, "Kill him."

As they crouched to tear me apart, I braced myself for the fight of my life. I wasn't going to sell my life cheaply. They were going to pay for every piece of my flesh they got. But as the first one flew forward and I kicked him back into the group, they all stared past me in horror.

Now I was in a bind. Do I look behind me and risk their attack, like any idiot in a horror movie, or do I keep my focus on the first threat? Oh, what to do, what to do… But it was solved for me.

"I think not," came the voice. "Let the boss do it himself. If he can."

I smelled cat. I recognized the scent. Heide's cat. Actually backing me up. So, there was a Mousegod. Miracles did happen. I grinned wickedly at the bully. I took a kung fu pose and gave him the "c'mere" sign with one paw.

Furious and beyond reason, he rose and flew at me, a buzzsaw of teeth and claws. I spun to his right and took a scratch on my side, but bit deeply into his shoulder. He caught on my jaw, and spun upside down. I hammered his head into the ground with all my weight using aikido. I heard something break in him.

He spun, bit, and tore at me, but I wasn't there. I made him get up and run at me again. This time when I moved away from the wall he jumped up and put his feet against the bricks just as I knew he would, crouched for a counter attack from above. But I had grabbed his tail, and as he leapt I yanked it and swung him into one of his cronies. I think it might have been the one that had taken the honeycomb from my pack—at least that was how I imagined it. The bully's body crashed into the other mouse and they both met the wall at high speed. Again, the bully got up. This time when he lunged for me I jumped upward and stomped down with all my strength on the top of his head. His two top teeth broke against the cement. I didn't stop there. I laid into his backside, biting and tearing for four or five terrible blows, then leapt off. His bloody ribs were showing. He rose, much slower this time, but his speed returned as he attacked again. I spun aside, tripped him, and broke his tail with my teeth. I knew he was used to that, and I did it just for that reason. He probably hated it. As he stared up at me in horror, I smiled and gave him the finger. He squealed in pain, but still came back at me.

We spun and spun in a ball of tangled fur. He got several weak hits on me, but no good ones. I took my time, letting him tire himself out, and struck with deadly accuracy over and over. I chose painful, crippling targets. I used everything BJ had ever taught me. I gave him no quarter. I spared no skill. I gave him everything I had and then some. I even put some hatred into it, once I was sure I could afford it, for good measure. When at last he was almost done for, swaying and stunned, I backed up four feet and ran at him with all my speed, ramming my body into him with full force. The mouse bounce.

He flew back into his gang and lay still, coughing blood and writhing like a worm. I strode forward without hesitation and the gang parted before me. I stood over my enemy and stared down at his broken face.

"Sir Squibble! " I screamed in my most frightening tone. It was the voice I had used with my troops but worse. Commanding. A promise of doom if not obeyed. Full of scary power.

"Suuhhh... Squib... Squibbel..." he choked through broken teeth and jaw. Then his head sank to the pavement and his eyes squinted in agony, both physical and emotional for his humiliation.

I had won. I looked up at his gang and then back at the cat. The cat looked at me with wide eyes. Was I actually going to tell him to kill the mice?? There was a glint of hope in his face and dawning horror in the faces of the gang. I let it linger for one tense moment, then jumped suddenly with a twitch of my tail and yelled "GRAAH!" at the gang. They scattered in every direction.

I looked back at the bully who had filled my mind with fear and terror for well over a year. He was dying. Broken limbs, broken everything. His blood was leaving him and his life was ebbing out like a water bowl with holes in it. His body shook with pain and he had urinated all over himself. His eyes bled with tears. As much as I had hated him, and looked forward to the moment, I did not see a big, mean, scary mouse anymore. Now that it was over I saw a little boy, frightened and afraid, wanting one last warm moment with his momma. Seeing the fear in his eyes as he stared at his killer, I saw the tiny, innocent mouse he had once been long ago, and I saw the cruel damage that had turned him into the mean mouse he had become. Maybe he had lost his momma. Maybe he had even seen it happen. He had certainly been beat up as a kid. Now, trembling and terrified, I saw his soul, that had been covered in so much damage and pain it had never been allowed to show through. Damn my gift. I saw that he wasn't a monster. He was a tiny, frightened boy, and I was the bully who had beaten him up.

Unable to turn my back on the vision, I knelt down next to him. I had hated him so much. Maybe more than even the Black Mouse. And now I wanted to feel satisfaction at destroying him, but I didn't. I felt shame.

No mouse is born bad. No one at all comes into this world evil. It is the damage. It's the pain. It's the crap that happens to us, and our inability to handle it, that turns us bitter and mean. Having been through it, I knew it was true. We had switched places. He was the helpless one and I was the cruel, mean mouse. It was a bitter, unwelcome awakening. I hated it.

I laid my hands on him, took a deep breath, and focused my stale, stagnant chi into his body, praying that he would live, that I might not be guilty of this sin, but I had not practiced my chi gung in months. It might have worked if I had been at full strength. As it was, I could tell he stood no chance. His chi was fleeing his shell as fast as it could, happy to be free of the unfair life of pain it had suffered through. I took my hands off him.

"I'm sorry," I said.

His terrified eyes settled on mine for one moment.

"Mehh thhooo..." He rasped. He sucked one last breath and died.

I lowered my head. What a terrible thing I had done. Hatred was a vessel for evil.

Covered in his blood, I vowed never to act out of hatred again. Not ever.

"In Favorite's name," I said. "I swear it."

When I turned around, the cat was gone. At least he had the brains to leave me a tiny bit of dignity.

Rising, weary and weak, I turned in the direction of the new mouse kingdom.

It was time to go home. But I had a few stops to make along the way.

The Specter Squibble

✠

I went back to the oak tree and the sewer grate, praying the entire way. My slingshot and nest were still there, and I breathed a sigh of relief. I put on my old, battle-worn armor, took up my shield that smelled of beer, put my beloved slingshot around my neck once more, and even wrapped the rag of a cloak around my shoulders. It was blue, my chivalric color. No one but my family was allowed to use it.

Thus resurrected, I hiked the distance to the new kingdom. When I arrived, not knowing what to expect, a mouse guardian in armor put a spear in front of me, blocking the entrance.

"Halt," he said. "Friend or foe?"

Sick of that horseshit, and remembering Percival's whipping all too well, I kicked him in the shin, took his spear, broke it over my knee, and went inside.

Several other mice had heard the commotion and saw me coming down the hall. One screamed outright. All of them fled. A rat even poked his head around the corner and upon seeing me, beat a hasty retreat. Rats and mice fled before me until I came to the grand hall and the newly installed throne of the king. The throne was surrounded by knights and soldiers, none of them happy about being there. I saw weapons tremble in brave paws, armor shaking upon trained shoulders. Only one mouse was not terrified of me.

BJ came off his throne and cautiously crawled down to me. The high guard parted to let him through as he rebuked them for thinking him unable to defend himself. He came up to my face with no fear whatsoever. He looked into my eyes a long time.

You must understand that by this time I looked like a supernaturally fierce wreck. I was covered in blood dating back to the Great War. I had fresh stuff on me as well in great amounts, and my fur was ragged with self-inflicted bites and scratches from mites. My armor looked just as it had the day I took it off—rotten, dirty, wrecked, and cut in a thousand places. Barely hanging on. My shield was dinged, beaten, bashed, and most of the paint on it chipped away. It also smelled like cheap alcohol. My cloak was a rag, but still barely blue, and my cracked sword belt was empty. But most of all, my vibe was different. I was a completely different mouse than BJ had last seen.

He held his gaze until he was satisfied, then bellowed, "Get this knight a weapon! Now!"

Someone handed me a plastic sword. It was blue.

I took it, put the tip in the ground, and knelt before the king.

"The specter has returned to the living then?" he said to me.

I looked up. "I have."

He motioned me to rise. While the entire room gawked in awe and horror, we went to the throne. He sat me beside it and turned to me as he sat down. He was older, like me. I could see it in him. But like me, he still felt full of life chi. His movements were not slow or forced. His eyes were still bright.

"Everyone thinks you are dead," he said. "And worse, haunting the park."

"I was. I did."

He gave me the look of deep focus and contemplation Nemo had done a few times. Finally, he nodded. "What now then?"

"I have a job to do, and a great plan to accomplish," I said. "I require the assistance of the entire mouse kingdom."

"You shall have it, prophet," he said.

"Whassat?" I said.

"Nemo had declared you a prophet to the mice. He said you are to take his place."

"Why would anyone need to take his place?" I asked.

"He is very ill, Squibble," the King told me. "He is slowly dying."

I said nothing.

"He traded his own life for your master's. I thought you knew."

I frowned. "I was dense."

He nodded. "You were you. Nothing more."

"How vast is the kingdom after the Great War?" I asked. "And how much money do we have?"

He raised his eyebrows. "This plan of yours must be big."

"Bigger than you could possibly imagine," I said. "And just as insane."

He chuckled. "We have over three thousand mice here in the new kingdom," he said. "And a few hundred back at the safe house. As for money, your orders have stood since the day you issued them, for all rodents world over to collect money and valuables. We have alot of money."

"How much?" I said.

He grinned. "More than you can possibly imagine." He told me how much.

I nodded. "The safe house? The human lived?"

"And gave a few mice permission to breed," he said, grinning, "to replenish the losses of the Great War."

"You, sire?" I asked.

"Yes, I had a few litters," he proudly announced, and waved his hand about the room. I saw his children gathered about, all young mice, princes and princesses, all staring at me as if I was some character from a fairy tale come to life. Perhaps to them I was. They all looked like BJ. Some looked like my master. I saw the family resemblance.

"Who else?" I asked.

"You'll see," he said.

"What of Percival?" I said. "I saw not his body at the site of the great battle."

"He left this journal at the battle camp," he gave me a mouse-sized book, full of writing. "I think perhaps, as a writer, it should go to you."

The old Squibble would have argued at being a writer, out of pure self conscience, but I took the book and said nothing.

"He also sent this letter just a week ago," he said, and some rats brought forth a piece of paper in an envelope with words scrawled upon it. The envelope's return address only said "Idaho."

I opened the letter and read it. It was addressed to me.

Dear Squibble,

I am in hot pursuit of our enemy. I see him always on the horizon. I would think he was toying with me but for the rewarding scent of his fear. We have not stopped except to sleep and eat when we must since that sad day in March.

So do what you must do, dear brother, for I have dedicated the short remaining months of my murine life to the damnation of our foe. I will harry him. I will chase him. I will pursue him with all my righteous wrath and willpower until he is ours. I will avenge my father, who did not deserve such a cowardly blow from behind. I shall give you the room you need to save mousekind, as you told us was your holy quest, even if I must use the rest of my days to do it.

Think of me well, Sir, forever racing after our hated enemy, not letting him rest to catch even one breath, spurred by divine endurance and determination, into the ever rising sun of the east.

Yours,
Sir Percival

I set the letter down and closed my eyes. Such a grim task had fallen to Perky. He had been made for better things. My great calling had cost everyone too much. I could not waste one more moment.

"Tell all the mice, everywhere, to continue gathering the valuables," I told the King. "Tell them to gather gems, jewels, coins and paper. Tell them to learn the internet. Tell them to learn everything. Tell them to prepare for a great accounting of their evolution."

He nodded at me, his face taking on some of the awe that surrounded us. "It shall be so."

I turned to go, sheathing my new blue sword.

"Will you not stay with us a while?" He asked. "We can get you new armor, clean you up… repair your slingshot?"

"I will do that myself," I said. "I must return to the safe house, gather my things, and then come back here to the city."

"It is said you flew away, to the east, on the back of a great owl," the King said. "I must ask if that one legend is true. For my own sake."

"I did fly into the east on a great owl," I said. "And then I flew west in the hands of an archangel, to say goodbye to my master at the seashore." I faced the crowd now as well. Might as well quell the superstition with fact. "Then I went into the city and despaired of life for months. I fell far from home, and became an empty shell, a ghost, wandering the dark. I have risen from the underworld at last, and I have a difficult and grave task to perform. I will need all the help I can get."

In response, the mice and rats of the kingdom raised their weapons and voices in support, all bowing down to one knee. They did not hear me whisper, "Thank you," but BJ did.

I walked through the parted Red Sea of rodents to the exit and departed. Outside, a rat was waiting for me. It was the same rat from the lab whose father had been a sword of Michael. He was wearing the armor of a knight, and two friends stood by him also in knightly dress. They wore hats with tall feathers in them, and bore long swords at their sides made of steel. Their capes were black and gold—the colors given to Michael's family, though the twins preferred blood red.

I stood as they stared at me. "Yes?"

The first one I knew bowed low. "Sire," he said, "We beg leave to escort you to wherever you are going. We have never seen the safe house, and would go there."

"You are wearing the house colors of Michael Mousefriend," I said. "I assume you're sure of your lineage? Because I know of only two sons of Michael."

"King BJ confirmed it through The Great Nemo, sire," one said.

The one I knew said, "Michael may have had two sons and two daughters by his mate Baby, but before that, he had many mates, sire. The city is full of his offspring. We did not realize it until it was told to us upon arriving here, after you freed us from the lab. We brought the cure to Sendai and SDA here, and the King knighted us for it. We told him it was you who helped us, but he knighted us anyway."

"I see," I said. "Then you have names?"

He grinned. "I am Athos, my lord."

"I am Aramis," another said.

"I am Porthos," the last said.

I stared. "Are you serious?"

They nodded, proud of their names. And why not? BJ had named them, and he rarely ever did that.

"Okay," I said. "I will accept your escort. We must go to the park, to a great oak tree near a sewer grate."

Athos bent down so that I could get up behind his shoulders. I mounted my first steed. His hat was big. "Ummm…" I said.

He whipped his hat off. "Sorry, my lord."

"No problem. Onward."

Onward we went.

We went back to my stashed nest and I got the notes these very same rats and I had taken on my last trip to a lab. They recognized them, but said nothing.

"Do you know where the pickup point is for the safe house?" I asked.

Porthos nodded.

"We must go there and catch a ride to the safe house," I told them.

"Excellent, and with all due haste," Athos said. Aramis chuckled, but stifled it.

"What is it?" I said.

None of them spoke.

"Oh, come now—you've seen me near death, at least you must know I'm not some revenging phantom. What is it?"

"Well, sire," said Athos, "you don't exactly smell… nice."

(Heard something!)

"Is that so?" I said, grinning. "And this coming from a male rat."

He stiffened, clearly impugned. "Sir! I bathe on an hourly basis!"

"Alright, alright. I know I stink. The sooner we get there the better. I agree. Thank you for bearing such a stinky burden, Sir Athos."

"The honor outweighs the burden by far, my lord," he said, and bowed lightly as to not topple me off him.

Yep. Smooth as Mike ever was.

Together, we made ten times the ground I could have covered on my own, and in no time were waiting at the pickup point. It was, as I knew now, the Atelier corner. I gazed with longing at the school up the block. How I wanted to go there and draw. Oh, how I longed to try oil painting! I had good times there. Almost the best of times. But those had been with my master. I would continue to draw, maybe one day paint, but the rest of my life was going to be busy, and I knew I would never again get to spend Saturday nights at the Atelier doing something only for myself. I was a little sadder for it.

Several other mice showed up at the pickup spot. They were trying not to look at me or the rats, and Porthos was edging closer and closer to them every minute as they tried to edge away, working them into the wall with glee.

Finally I turned to them and snapped my fingers.

"Take a good look," I said. "Yep. It's Squibble the Damned. Back from Hell. Here to lop off the heads of bad mice. Beware, the Dread Pirate Squibble has come for your SOULS!"

I had been joking, but they fled in terror. Oops.

"Mayhap thou overdid it, sire," Aramis said, trying hard not to laugh. Finally, none of us could hold it back and we all busted up in laughter.

The car came an hour later.

Heide and the Kind Human stopped when they saw me, then suddenly came forward, dropping to their hands and knees, though it was to get a better view, not worship in any way. Thank goodness.

"Squibble!?" The Kind Human exclaimed.

I nodded.

He picked me up from Athos' back and ran his fingers lightly over my furry head. Flakes of dried blood fell from my hair.

"Oh, I can't believe it!" He cried. His eyes watered up. "It's really you! My prayers were heard! You're alive!"

I nodded again, glad for the affection after so long. I licked his finger. I felt my soul rise in his embrace, and I was grateful.

"We thought you were dead," Heide said, looking emotional as well. "Oh, what you must have been through!"

I looked toward the sea. You have no idea, humans.

No idea.

At Last I Get to Do Something Right (Or, Better Late Than Never)

✠

The ride home was swift. I noticed more construction just outside the city. It made my gut feel stricken.

Human civilization is built on the bones of mice, Bill…

I thought of how many mice those tractors and earthmovers had buried alive. The mothers, the babies, the fathers desperately trying to dig their families out while suffocating. So many mice that wanted only to live… I felt sick. Entire tribes of field mice wiped out in days. One mouse family in every ten feet. Hundreds and thousands of acres turned to brown dirt from living fields.

I remembered my trip to the safe house with Heide and seeing the same things. I remembered thinking someone had to do something. For the mice. I remembered fearing that this someone would be me. Now I knew it would have to be, no matter how immense the task, because no one else would do it. Like Mike said, I was the only one capable. I was chosen. If I didn't do something, humanity would continue to crush mice, but worse, one day they'd find out we could read and write. Sooner than anyone wanted them to, I felt. I could feel the intense importance of my calling now. I hadn't felt it before because I'd been too self-absorbed. My past was full of nothing but Squibble and Squibble's problems. Now, seeing the barren flat miles of wounded earth, it was impossible to ignore the suffering that lay underneath. I felt sad that the little happy-go-lucky, selfish child Squibble was gone, as if he'd been buried underneath all that churned up dirt with all the other mice. I felt old and worn out looking at the edge of construction encroaching on the fields of fate.

I was chosen. And I would have to do something. Thinking back, I had always known this. I'd even prepared for it, kind of. Without realizing I was doing so.

Deep melancholy settled on my soul and I felt the damage of the last year all through my heart, aching like an infection that's been there too long. But at least I could feel again. I guess it was progress.

I realized after the bully that I would never again see reality the same way as I did as a boy. That time, that way of seeing things, was gone forever. I didn't want it to be, but it was. I was a different mouse than the one who left the safe house riding on the back of an owl. The spirit world was my other home, bullies were just hurt children, and time was a million sparkling reflections on an ocean of possibilities. Nothing would ever be the same again.

The Kind Human must have sensed it, driving us home. He kept looking at me sitting there perfectly still, so unlike the young mouse he had adopted long ago. He was worried. I could smell it. He probably thought I was sick. I guess I had been. Now I had to heal.

When I came home, the house felt different. It smelled different. It was clean, quiet, and alien to me. The word spread like lightning that I had come home with the Kind Human, and rodents scrambled madly to assemble in formation before the door. I was already past it, crawling into the living room. I passed by rats and mice that I knew, and the elite still wore their sashes with honor, but most of these new ones I didn't know. Most of this house no longer knew me at all, and it showed in their faces. Like the faces at the new kingdom. Awe. Fear. Lack of understanding. I looked and smelled so bad… I must have frightened them. They whispered "ghost," and "spirit of Squibble," and other such things. I went past them all, not even bothering to look around, and found my nest under the human's drawing table. Nobody had touched it. It was still all there.

Standing next to it were some familiar faces. I saw Shiva and Thor, who had their cage set up right on top of the drawing table, perhaps on purpose. They were standing on the edge, high above, looking down. They saw me and began the decent.

Stompy, Ghost, and my daughter Squibette were crawling across the floor towards me from the other corner of the living room where they had a cage. It was wonderful to see them. I thought they had died at the hands of the Black Mouse.

But the most emotional reaction I had was to the tiny mouse standing at attention in front of my nest. He was older, and scruffier, but it was Scratchy, same as he ever was. He was still wearing his squire armor, and holding a brand new shield for me with a brand new sword. He stood there like he'd been waiting since day one, and he probably had.

I stopped in front of him. It looked like he'd been living in my nest, which explained why everything was exactly like I had left it. He had defended this place with his own hide, sure I would someday return. Short of my master, no mouse had ever had more faith in me.

He stood there, rigid, expecting a harsh comment, a scathing inspection, or perhaps to be kicked. Instead, I reached down, dirty and stinky as I was, and hugged him, picking him up off the ground.

He squeaked in alarm. He probably thought I was going to try to kill him, but I held on and kissed the side of his face.

Shiva and Thor stopped dead in their tracks. Stompy, Ghost and Squibette did as well. Scratchy's eyes got so big I thought they'd pop out of their sockets. He stared at me as if he, too, finally believed I'd gone insane. I set him down and smiled at him.

Everyone just gawked at me for long moments. For all of my damage and need of healing, something had broken in me, and it broke the hard way. I could explain it not one bit, but instead of hatred, I now felt nothing but love for the tiny cripple that had given his entire life to me. He was as old as I was. We were in what was almost always a mouse's last months. And here he was, still guarding my things, because I wasn't there to be guarded. Through his armor I could see a hairless spot and scar where he had been run through. My master had been right. I could not ask for a more loyal servant. But his servant days were over, and should have been long ago.

I drew the sword I had in my belt, the one BJ had given me, and said, "Scratchy, kneel."

He slowly did so, staring at my sword as if I were going to lop off his head for something bad he was unaware he did. Instead, I placed it on one shoulder.

"In the name of Nemo," I moved it over his head to the other shoulder, "King BJ," moved it again, "and my master," I realized I should have used his name, but old habits die hard. "I make you a knight. Rise, Sir Scratchy!"

Well, half the house had gathered by then to see it. There was dead silence as he stood up, shaky and tentative, a worried look on his face as though he was going to be punished yet. He looked around at the crowd as if to see if he was hallucinating.

Shiva and Thor began clapping first, then Stompy, then Ghost and Squibette, then the rest. Everyone applauded loudly for the old knight who had finally gotten what he deserved. I breathed a sigh of deep thanks to Bigfat that I was not too late. I had thought Scratchy dead; one more tragic crime etched upon my soul that I would bear to the end of my days. But no. This one I got to fix, as much as a story so sad could be fixed. As Scratchy began to smile, realizing this was not a cruel joke, I felt sorry for him. The only thing he had ever wanted, and he had gotten it, but only in the very sunset of his years. I knelt down before him, and whispered where only he could hear me if he'd been able to hear, "Forgive me, little friend. You've been so faithful. You deserved better."

He might be deaf, but he got the message. He put both paws on me and helped me up, as if he were still my servant trying to save me from humiliating myself by kneeling before a crippled midget. He looked me in the face and smiled. He waved his sword around happily, his message clear. He was happy, and saw no sadness in the moment at all. He handed me my shield, dutifully. I handed it back.

"Yours, now," I said. "You can use the crest if you want. We're in the same family, after all. You can wear blue or green, your choice."

He held up his chin and pointed at my blue, tarnished cape with great pride. I smiled and hugged him again. He hugged me back. I felt karma ease off me just a smidgen. It was a wonderful moment, and everyone clapped and cheered again for the faithful Scratchy and his dream come true.

A tiny white mouse came skittering through the crowd and zipped up to us, standing right in front of our feet. He looked up at Scratchy with awe, and then at me with the same expression. It was the same expression that Scratchy had given me from the first day. Scratchy smiled and gently turned the child around to face me. He held his hand out as if to say, "See?"

"It's Scratchy's son," Stompy said, coming up next to us. "His only child. Only one tiny mouse in the litter."

Squibette, Stompy, and Ghost drew their swords and saluted Scratchy as an equal, as if he'd been a knight as long as they had. His eyes watered up and he saluted them back as superiors.

I looked back at the little kid in amazement, then at Scratchy. He raised his chin again and proudly held his stance of attention. His son did the same, clearly trained by his father. Scratchy had a little boy.

I squatted down and looked at the boy. No sign of waltzing, no sign of illness. Just small because he was young. By the size of his paws, it looked as though that wasn't going to last long, either. It was rare for a female mouse to give birth to only one child. It made that child special, and Scratchy so clearly loved his special son. I felt the bleeding of my soul stopping. Maybe I would heal someday, seeing things like this. Roses from the ashes.

I petted the kid, who had probably heard many stories of Squibble, and was now looking at him. I kissed him on the nose and smiled up at Scratchy, who was trying very hard not to cry. His pride showed through that mask, though, and a smile cracked his tough outer countenance. I could tell he had dreaded this moment for weeks, and now was consoled. Not only did I approve of his son, I approved of him, as well. Finally.

I gave Scratchy the salute of an equal, before the gathered crowd, which let out one giant gasp of shock. He saluted me back as a superior. I handed my sword to his son, who took the huge thing in his arms incredulously and looked up at his father. Scratchy looked down, nodded, and looked at me. He held out his hands at his son and pointed at me, then at the boy. He wanted me to take the kid as my Squire.

Of all the things that have surprised me in my long mouse life, that remains one of the most powerful. Here was this mouse, whom I had abused and ignored all his life, offering me the most treasured thing he had in all the world—his own son. I started crying. I couldn't help it. That he would trust me so deeply with so much was overloading my newly awakened heart. I couldn't believe it. I was stunned, along with everyone else.

I shook my head at him slowly, trying to convey my thoughts. Surely not, Scratchy? What if I treat him as I treated you?

Scratchy shook his head swiftly, sure of himself. *No, Master*, his face said. *I know you will treat him as well as I do.*

I told him I would consider it, and that seemed to satisfy him. He smiled broadly at me, at his son, clapped his son on the back, and looked at his sword with new eyes. The crowd parted and Vulcan brought out a brand new suit of fresh made lobster/snake hide armor with metal fasteners and chain mail underneath. It was made to fit Scratchy, and looked as though it had some dust on it. Shiva and Thor took it from the old smith, brought it to Scratchy, and laid it before him.

"We had it made long ago for this day," Thor said.

"We knew you'd make it, little buddy," Shiva said.

Scratchy, eyes leaking like a sieve, took off his old armor with delicate reverence and donned his new suit. Vulcan offered him a blue or green cape with gold fasteners. He chose the blue, looking in my direction as Vulcan fastened it around his neck.

When he was dressed, he looked three inches tall, instead of one and a half. He looked as tall as Percival. He drew his sword and faced the audience, receiving another round of applause and many weapon salutes, every one of them made to a superior.

His son was crawling around in his old squire armor, looking very cute, wishing he was big enough to put it right on. Scratchy bowed to me, and then to the others. Everyone bowed back, even the crowd. His little son stood up straight and bowed to his knight father. His daddy faced him and bowed back to his son.

Vulcan then presented to me a box of medals he had cast, complete with ribbons. Squibette told me what they were all for, and I chose several for Scratchy, pinning them on him myself. I gave him medals for valor, for bravery in the heat of combat, for fast thinking and for loyalty. I gave him three purple hearts for being wounded, and one for being a great fighter. I gave him one for defeating many opponents. Then I saw it. Vulcan had copied it perfectly. The Silver Star.

I looked at Stompy. She nodded.

"No mouse has ever received that one," Vulcan said.

I gingerly took it out of the box. I had wished when Bill had died that I could have taken his medal with me, to keep it safe for him. Now I was given that chance, in a way, and no one in the house deserved it more than Scratchy, who had time and time again cast himself in harm's way for others and miraculously survived.

I placed the Silver Star around his neck. It hung all the way down to his belt.

One last round of thunderous applause shook the floor. I thought I could feel my master smiling, all the way from Avalon.

As the others celebrated, I withdrew to the bedroom, an hour later. Nemo's cage was dark, but I smelled him in there. I climbed the blankets of the bed and hopped down to the front door, left open as always.

I stood there, listening to his breathing. It was shallow and light.

"Master Nemo?" I said.

He lifted his head from the corner pile of blankets. Wearily he focused on me.

"Squibble," he said in a tired voice. "I dreamt you had fallen far."

"I did, sir."

"You have risen then?" He asked me.

"Yes, Sir. I am on the mend at last."

"Like the phoenix."

Like a smoking, charred mouse what tried to be a phoenix by lighting himself on fire, I thought, but I said, "Yeah."

He struggled to rise. He looked thin, like I did, and not much better off. His health had plainly deteriorated. His ribs showed as if he'd never put any weight back on after his coma, and his face was gaunt. There was light in his eyes, though, and they were crinkled at the corners, smiling at me.

He hopped sluggishly over to the doorway and put his nose to mine.

"It's good to see you again," he said. "Most thought you dead."

"I pretty much was," I said.

"It had to be, Squibble," he said.

"I know," I told him.

His tired eyes widened some. "Really?"

"Yeah. I do," I said. "And I'm gonna need your help, and probably the help of the old owl, too, in the coming months."

"You know what you must do," he said as matter of fact.

"Yeah," I said. "Only took me forever, but yeah."

"I will help you any way I can," he said. "I am slow and sick, but I can help."

"Can nothing be done for you?" I asked.

"No," he said. "I have maybe a year or a little more left. Will that be enough time? I made a promise to Death."

"It will have to be," I replied. "I will be three then. That's just ridiculously old for a mouse." I looked at him and squinted my eyes. I saw his aura, dim but clear. "Why did you trade your life for my master's, sir, knowing he was going to die anyway?"

"Because you were not ready to lose him Squibble. I did it to ease your burden as much as possible, even if all I could do was but a little."

"But the price!" I said.

"This is what was supposed to happen," he said. "I knew the moment of my death from the first month I had prescience."

(Heard something!)

I had never thought of that. Once I got good enough at it, I could look forward and see my end. The most likely one, anyway. The implications were frightening.

"Do you think you'll do that?" He asked, reading my thoughts.

I looked at the ground, then at him.

"No," I said. "I want it to be a surprise. I don't want to worry about anything anymore."

"Very wise," he said. "I wish I had done that." One of his ears rotated to face the bedroom door. "What's all that noise?"

"Oh, they're celebrating," I said. "I knighted Scratchy."

I saw his whole body twitch, as if someone had stuck a cattle prod to his tail. His face lifted, his eyes opened all the way. He stayed like that a long moment.

"Is that so," he said at last.

"Yeah," I said, "but it's so sad. He's as old as I am. He has barely any time left to enjoy it, and nowhere near enough time to have adventures, like mine… like he always dreamed of. I messed up."

Nemo smiled. "No, little one, you haven't. I have seen Scratchy's future, and he will outlive you."

It was my turn to start. "Really!"

"Yes. And you shall yet have the time you need to accomplish your task. I daresay the gods will not let you die until you're done. Scratchy shall see his adventures, I promise you."

I breathed a sigh of completeness. "That's so good to hear!"

"You have done well, Squibble. The worst is over, and you have prevailed."

"I feel like I messed up absolutely everything," I said, lowering my eyes.

"Listen." Nemo looked back toward the living room. "Not everything."

I cocked my ears to the celebration and thought of Scratchy's face as he looked up at me, full of joyful tears.

No. Not everything.

Memories of the Future

✠

After taking a warm bath with the Kind Human's help in his sink, I tossed out my old clothes and armor, and put on new robes made of a grassy brown color. I took my slingshot to my now empty nest and repaired it with Vulcan's help, giving it a new band and reinforcing the wood with resin after scrubbing it with sandpaper. I took a white feather and attached it to the bottom in memory of my master who had made it for me. Then I attached a blue one for my daughter, who was still in this world. The house was safe again. The horsemen had gone, leaving the survivors to rebuild. She was still with me. The tribulations had not taken everything.

I fixed up my house and in the process, found all my old drawings and journals. Seized by sudden motivation, I sat down and wrote the last few hundred or so pages you've read, encompassing the Great War and my time in the city after my master passed into the west. I read Percival's journal BJ had given me and decided to include it as well. No one else had survived but him. It had only been one season ago, but the Great War was already fading into mythology. There were precious few left who remembered it. So, I wrote for posterity. It took a few days.

Then the thought occurred to me. I had hundreds of pages stacked up. I had written a long novel. With the exception of my modest beginnings, it covered my entire life. My master had been brave enough to publish his story. Might I do the same? I gathered it all into one pile and thought it over. Perhaps it might help someone, somewhere. It would be worth it all if it might save the life of one mouse, or cause some human to treat their pet with more kindness.

Of course, my master had gotten incredibly lucky with publishing his book, even using the human pen name. Getting published was exceedingly difficult, and I was an unknown. Mouse. An unknown mouse. I would think on it. With all that I had to do, one more hard thing would not be so much, maybe.

I started my chi gung up again, and every evening Scratchy and his son joined me. I was always glad to see them, and welcomed them with a smile. I stashed and stole Cheerios from the human and had them waiting for the brave knight and his child for when we finished our meditations. My daughter joined in eventually, and Nemo would come if the human was around to carry him over to my "front yard" of carpet. When I meditated, I went to my peaceful dock, and true to my master's words, it came easily the moment I desired it. In that place, everything was perfect, and my course of action seemed clear always. No more confusion, no more mystery. It was a tremendous gift my beloved master had granted me. A place I could go, anytime I wanted, for the rest of my life, to rest. I go there often. It is the most priceless gift I have ever received, and I finally understood it.

The river is life, and most of the time I was down swimming in it, experiencing all the wonderful and awful things that came to me in the water. Sometimes the water was warm, sometimes cold. Sometimes smooth, slow, fast or rough. The dock was my way to step out of it... to rest, relax and recover. Such a powerful gift. How many of us have wished for a chance to step outside of life, to be clear and calm? It was from the end of that peaceful place I always looked out across the stream of life at the beautiful sunset. The sun was always setting there. I guess that meant that, once on the dock, all was timeless. Or perhaps it meant that every time I was ever on that dock, I was traveling to the end of my life. The sunset of my days.

I say that because I finally now understood that the forest across the river, all awash in golden light from the dusk...

...That was home.

Along with the gift came other things as well. My powers began to manifest themselves in great numbers, and with great intensity. It became easy to see the spirit world, to read minds, to know the immediate future. I learned to levitate. It was easy—all I had to do was relax in my meditation. After scaring the fur off my other chi gung partners, I stopped doing it in public and confined my powers to my new cage the human had built for me. It had a lot of space, and two levels. I had my own playground, my own practice yard, and my own meditation room. The human put a small fountain right outside that had a waterfall and a spinny marble ball that turned on a small water spout underneath it. It gave my home atmosphere and a natural feeling. I began to feel happy again, with no worry of it lasting. I knew it wouldn't. Happiness never does. But neither does sadness.

There came a time when a young boy mouse brought me his sick mother. She had cancer, and because so many mice die that way, she was not special. The Kind Human had tried everything he knew how to do, and now everyone was waiting for her to die. The boy came to me because he had heard my momma died the same way. He begged me to help his poor momma. He was her only son. He was also the first mouse of the new generation to have the courage to approach me.

If ever there was a cause that struck a personal chord, it was that one, and so I told him I would try. I remembered asking Nemo if someday I would be able to cure cancer, and like the supernatural creature he is, I heard the Kind Human outside my house dropping him off just as the dying mother was being helped in by her tearful son. I looked back at him and he met my gaze. No words needed to be said. I sent energy into that sick mouse with all the willpower I had in the world, and Nemo was always at my door, every day, watching. Maybe helping.

The mother began to get better. She started eating again, drinking on her own, and being able to breathe freelly. She recovered, and went on to live a happy life. I don't really know if it was my energy, or Nemo's sorcery, or just the prayers of a small, lost boy who couldn't stand to lose his momma, but the cancer left her. And I know better than to question something as good as that. I gave the universe (and the Mousegod) my thanks, and left it at that.

The boy was thankful beyond measure, and never said a word to anyone, which was just as well. I was fairly sure I couldn't cure the world's mice of cancer. Not enough time. He did come to me to learn the chi gung though, and taught his mother after that. They went on to teach other mice, and I hear it's common practice now in the New Kingdom. The boy went on to become a knight who traveled the land healing mice. I heard later he achieved great heights of chi power, even able to cure cancer. He was named Saint Happy by King BJ, and would live to a magnificently ancient age, in good health, traveling the land and healing the sick. I felt almost like a hero. Not all good deeds are punished.

It was Saint Happy that created the Mouse's Prayer.

The Mouse's Prayer

Dear Mousegod, please let me wake this evening intact and healthy.
And if that I receive,
Please let me find food and water, warmth and a safe place.
And if that I receive,
Please spare me the predator's maw and human cruelty this night.
And if that I receive,
Please let me find other mice and not be lonely.
And if that I receive,
Please let me find good materials for a nest and be of use to my community.

And if that I receive,
Let me live a fascinating and inquisitive life, full of experience and discovery, always exciting and fun.
And if that I receive,
Then I am a very lucky mouse, and I am very grateful.
But because I am a mouse, and would steal all the cheese in the moon instead of a few bites...
Please let me be loved.

I resumed drawing, and illustrated my journals, as I had been doing all along. The human bought me a real oil paint set, and had Vulcan turn it into something more my size. With an endless supply of oil paint, brushes, and canvas, I fulfilled my earlier fantasy of painting, and became a painter. I wasn't very good at first, but I got better. You can see for yourself.

The painting was every bit as fun as I knew it would be. I felt like a real artist, and many mice wanted to pose for me. I painted mice, rats, the scenery around the safe house, and even the humans. I drew and painted a lot from memory, and those illustrations, while not nearly as realistic as the work I did from life, were more enjoyable, I think. The painting from life was work to improve my skill; the other stuff was fun—using my hard earned skill the way I wanted to. By accident I achieved a somewhat normal level of social acceptance from the safe house community after being a spirit, a hero, or a prophet for so long. They could understand painting.

I know I scoffed at it before as a young mouse, but I began writing poetry.

Like the rise of wind they rush
back to the sky
and hurry across heaven
looking for their way back
leaping with the greatest hope
falling like millions of raindrops
back into tiny bodies
looking for just one loved life

All this was done on my spare time, and by no means consumed my days. I spent my days, nights, and long hours working on my master plan. I'd tell you about it, but I have decided I cannot. I'm sorry. These pages may get published, and it cannot be written down, lest someone discover it and act against it. It simply must succeed if rodentkind has any hope of a future. I hope you'll understand. If it works you'll find out for sure. You won't be able to miss it.

Not that anyone would believe any of this. This journal will eventually be published as fiction. Everyone knows mice can't write. He he he.

I can only tell you that it involves magic, science, and something my master once told me in this very story. He planted the seed for my idea. As always, he was the catalyst that would end up saving us all if my plan worked. Nemo helped me, Branch joined us in his dreams all the way from China, Scratchy and his son, too, and Vulcan to some degree, but that was all. I slowly began giving orders again, sending people to far places and back, sending knights on quests for this or that, and asking for volunteers to go break into labs all over the city. It ended up being Sneaky, Squeaky and Clyde that performed almost all those jobs, and they got freakishly good at it. They never failed me.

Shiva and Thor returned to the city, telling us they had a greater destiny than to sit back and enjoy safety. I heard messages written by BJ only weeks later that the twins had taken up residence near the new kingdom, and had computers installed as well as rats working for them manufacturing weapons. A few weeks after that I heard they had taken up vigilantism, hunting down humans who mistreated rodents and punishing them appropriately. As if it were possible, their legends grew ridiculously out of proportion. The rodents here now call them "The Terrible Agents of Justice," and some in the city call them "Death and Destruction." I can see them having a grand old snicker over that, and doing nothing to correct it. My boys. They have found their calling and I am happy for them. On occasion, when I have a job too tough for anyone else, I call on them. They have never disappointed me.

I spend a great deal of time walking around, looking for things that others can't see, and talking, apparently, to myself. Everybody still thinks I'm crazy. Now I'm just a heavily-respected loon is all. Of course, I'm not really talking to myself. No one's ever had the guts to actually ask me what's going on.

I'm talking to spirits. Angels, elementals, ghosts, and all that. Nemo's words of power never wore off. To this day I command a legion of angels (that's about 7000 by the way). I send them all over the earth, doing deeds, brining me information and other things I need for my great task. They seem quite willing to cooperate now, although I've learned their limitations and sometimes we debate on what they should be able to do and what they obviously won't do but could. Where my ultimate goal is concerned, they obey nicely. It seems that since I accepted my destiny the universe is on my side. It's nice.

In my work I travel often. I get rides from the Kind Human, who dearly cherishes his oldest remaining pet and treats me well. Sometimes I hitch rides with Raven or the old owl. That always gets a reaction whenever I land in any rodent-populated place (he he heee). By now I have been all over this continent seeking pieces of the grand puzzle I must assemble before my time is up.

In each and every journey I always look for Percival. I have come across occasional signs of his passing: good deeds done with honor that could only be his handiwork, entire mouse communities saved from destruction by a single white mouse, sometimes single mice who cannot forget what he has done for them, nor his noble way (or that butt-kicking sword). But of my great brother himself I have seen neither tail nor ear. He has vanished from the normal world, chasing his foe over the horizon of mythology in some fairy tale, and has faded from my vision as a result. He kept his promise. He has chased the Black Mouse to the ends of the earth, and beyond.

And it is well, this last deed of Sir Percival, for because of him, every effort I make now goes completely unresisted. I am opposed not at all. It's amazing to me what one can do with free reign when one has grown used to the weight and tyranny of infernal opposition for most of their life. I feel like a bird, born free, but caught. Wings clipped, and stones tied to my feet for 65 years. Now, because of the staggering sacrifice of so many good mice, I soar once more.

I mean to use every second of it, too. I was used to painting blind with a brush in my teeth. Now the world will soon see what I am capable of, being set loose to do as I please.

Thank you, Percival. Your sacrifice was perhaps the greatest of all.

I feel motivated now, more than anything I have ever desired to do, to accomplish this task set before me. The burning passion to make it work overcomes the fear, the doubt. I know my calling at last, and having accepted it, I find it becomes me.

I have, in particular, a soft spot for roadkill.

On my journeys I came upon a time across a road. In the middle of the road were three corpses. Two baby squirrels and a mother, all run over by cars. I knew right away what had happened, and it was one of the saddest things I have ever beheld. One baby had gone into the road, curious, naÔve to the danger, and had been hit. The mother, in an attempt to rescue her child, had dashed out, too late, and also been smashed flat. The second child, starving and wanting his mommy, went to her body, and he too was run over.

As I sat there on the curb, crying and watching the cars drive over the bodies again and again, uncaring of any lives but their own, something nudged me from behind. It was the last baby, now very hungry and frightened. He had the brains not to go out into the road, but I could tell he was desperate. Unless I intervened, he would go join his family.

When the Kind Human came minutes later, I explained the situation to him. He went to a store and bought twenty pounds of nuts and grain, and poured it all over the entrance to the baby's den. He was old enough to eat it, and so he lived. Not entirely whole, I'm sure. He had seen what happened to his family. He would live like I do, scarred but stronger for it.

It's like the mice in the plowed field. It's like the pet stores. It's like the labs. Rodents need help. And no one is willing to stand up for them. If I've learned anything in this amazing life I've lived, it is that everything has a soul that has life. Even things humans think have no life have souls. The entire planet has a soul. To leave anything out of that equation is pure arrogance. This is why I was called to become the champion. Rodents need help. It is a huge calling. A frighteningly huge job. But heaven knew I was the one, even while I didn't. Hey, somebody's gotta do it. If you had seen what I've seen, and hopefully now you have, you would feel the same.

I have spent all of spring studying and planning. If I were a human, I'd have several MD's, about 20 PhD's and a hundred master's degrees by now. I told you—mice learn fast (even without the help of an angelic legion). Finally, I'm just about ready. So recently I set out to find the only thing I'm missing.

A lab.

All this was going smoothly, and my powers increasing as my work grew into a solid picture. Then one night I had the dream. I dreamt every night, and they were always meaningful, but I had been waiting for this one.

I opened my eyes and saw my master and Nemo sitting in front of me. They were young and healthy. I was overjoyed to see my master again, and told him so.

"Again?" He asked. "Squibble, what do you mean? Are you still asleep?"

"Oh yeah," I said, happy to be there. "I am asleep. A year and a half from now."

They looked shocked. They looked at each other, puzzled, and then at me. I was enjoying every minute of it. I drank deeply the sight of my young, healthy master and the majestic, strong Nemo. I wished I could see my momma.

"Want me to prove it?" I said. My master nodded. "Okay," I said, "I'll be going away soon. It's all a big stupid misunderstanding, but it happens. That starts everything off. Things go way downhill from there, but they sort of have to."

Nemo cocked his head and his eyes shot open wide. He knew. Heh heh heh. He knew already, and I knew he would know.

"He's telling the truth," Nemo said, stunned. My master snapped his head back and forth between us.

"You mean... you mean this is really Squibble as an old mouse... from... from the *future*?" he said. Nemo nodded along with me. My master peered into my eyes. He could see the age and experience there. I just knew he could. His own eyes got wider, then relaxed a bit as he accepted it.

"Squibble, you were complaining about bad dreams," my master said. "I thought maybe they were just…"

"Just dreams?" I said. "I wish. No. They are warnings. I won't listen to them, so don't try to make me. They're premonitions. A lot of bad stuff is coming, Master. More than anyone wants to come. I'm sorry. It has to be this way. I believe that now."

"Most paths can be changed," Nemo said, transfixed with fascination. "Who told you that it had to be that way?"

"You did," I said. They both gasped. "At first I didn't believe you. I didn't want to believe you. It was my worst fears, coming to life, one after another. I just couldn't accept it. But in the end, I had no choice. Nobody did."

My master's face was painted with worry. "Why, Squibble? Why? What happens?"

"I can't tell you all that," I said. "I'm sorry. It might change things. The future is a road with a million forks in it, Master, like a tree, ever reaching upward with smaller and smaller branches. I can see it like that now. Every fork in a branch is a different possibility for the future. And every time I've looked, I only see one way to our salvation. Out of all those branches, only one path to where we have to go in order to survive. As horrible as it is, things need to happen just the way they did—*will*. Otherwise all mousekind will suffer."

"It's that big?" He asked me. "All mousekind hangs in the balance?"

"Oh yeah," I said. "Bigger even. All rodentkind. All humankind. I'm working on it right now. I was chosen to do this. To save everyone. Bitch of a job, but someone's gotta do it."

Nemo regained some of his composure. "Surely you can tell us some things."

"Ohhhh," I said, "Big all-powerful prophet can't see the entire future, eh? Missing some parts, are we? Hate that, eh? Wanna know, don't you?"

"Yes!" He said.

"How does it feel to want, big guy?" I said, grinning.

Nemo growled something under his breath.

"Squibble…?" My master was speaking to me now as if he were afraid, and of course he had right to be. I felt sorry for him. Almost no one suffered more than he did. "Please tell me what's going to happen. We can't be ready for it if you don't tell us."

I caved under the look on his face. I loved him so much. Maybe a little wouldn't hurt.

"Well," I began…

"Oh, no you don't, twerp!" Came Bigfat's voice. I realized it was coming out of my own mouth, though in the dream I saw him standing next to me. Nemo and my master jumped a foot each. There was no mistaking that voice. My master must have thought I was possessed. I kinda was.

"B... Bigfat!?" My master exclaimed, eyes round as full moons.

"Yeah, yeah," he said. "Hi there, dude. Hi there, Nemo. Heard lots about you up here. Good rep. Solid."

"Oh my lord," my master breathed.

"Well, the kid here thinks so, but not really," he said.

"Why can't we know anything?" Nemo asked him.

"HA! You asking me that?" Bigfat chuckled. *"Really!"*

Nemo made a frustrated face. It warmed my heart, as much as I respected him, he was never wrong, and even more rarely flustered. It did me good to see that he was as fallible as I.

"Listen," Bigfat told them. "I'll tell you this. Get ready for the ride of your life. The twerp here is the champion of the Mousegod. He's the chosen one, and many months from now he's done real good. He's a true hero. A great hero. But the ride along the way sucks, and that's putting it mildly. Nothing must happen to him or it's all over pretty much. So I gotta ask you. How bad do you want it?"

"Want what?" My master said.

"Equality with humans."

"No way!" my master exclaimed. He he! He sounded like me!

"Way," Bigfat said. "Way big. Nothing less is on the line here. If it goes poorly, it's the end for all of us. You have no idea. Those rats... you taught them a little too much..."

"Shiva and Thor?" My master asked.

"Ah, enough of that. How's the woman? Happy?" Bigfat asked in a friendly no-big-deal tone.

"Umm... She's great!" He said. "Had kids. I have a family now."

"Take good care of 'em," Bigfat said, obviously disturbed. I shot him a dirty look. I wanted to bite his ear. Forcing my nose through the "possession," I took control.

"Master! It goes poorly! Don't go to war! If you do, you'll die! *Everybody dies!* Don't go!" I cried in a sudden lapse of reason. Bigfat quickly recovered from his horror and took over again.

"Moron!" He shouted. My master looked pale. He slowly looked at Nemo, who looked back as if someone had spilled the beans and it was his fault. I felt sorry for opening my big mouth now, looking at my best friend in the whole world. I should have stayed shut up.

"War??" He choked. "War?"

"Ah, pay no attention to the kid," Bigfat said. "The Great War wasn't so bad. You won. Sort of."

"Great War?" He whispered. His face was crestfallen. "When does this happen?"

"Not for a while," I said, nosing past Bigfat, who wasn't omnipotent after all. "You have much time left, Master. There are yet adventures to come."

He looked very sad. He gazed back toward the dining room, where his cage was. "Tree…" he said. "She's alright?"

I looked at Bigfat and he at me, each of us blaming the other for speaking at all. We stayed silent.

"Oh, no…" my master sat down. "Oh no. No."

"Oh," I said, my heart aching for him, "Bigfat, stay outta my way, or I promise I'll find some way of biting your ear even in the spirit world!"

He looked down at my master and felt what I did. He looked back at me. "Yeah. Yeah, okay."

I went to my master and felt my young paws touch his silky fur one last time. "Master, all the horrors to come have but one purpose: to free all mousekind from human domination. We volunteered for this, before we were born. We all agreed to pay the price for every single mouse and rat in the whole world. Lucifer, he hated this upon hearing of it, and sent one of his powerful generals, in the form of a black mouse, to test our resolve. It gets bad. I won't lie. It gets really, really bad. Worse than you can imagine. But it comes out alright. In the very end, it comes out alright, I'm certain."

"Then you are not speaking to us from the end of all things?" Nemo said.

"No," I said. "No, I'm not. I have much yet to do."

"Then you don't know how it turns out," my master sobbed. I winced at his ability to see truth.

"No, I don't, but the Black Mouse was defeated, sort of," I said. "I know what I must do, and I am doing it. It took a long time, and many terrible tribulations, but I am finally doing it. It's working so far."

My master looked up in tears. "But my family."

My chest hurt. I had thought the hard times were past.

“Your family goes on,” I told him, meaning Percival and Branch. “Some of them go on.”

“Nothing so valuable comes without a price,” Bigfat said. “You’re the mouse knight. Will you pay the price for every rodent in the world to have freedom? That’s what’s being offered to you, and the rest of the house. You can pay, and have your chance at making all the world a haven for mice, or not, and await the day humans figure out you can read.”

My master’s head came up and I saw the fire of heroism in him, that light I loved so much. “Squibble? What did you answer to that question?”

I looked at him face to face.

“I said yes, Master. When it came down to it, in my moment of truth, I said I would pay. And I did.” Oh boy, did I ever.

His face hardened for the first time. That expression that would later be worn as a mask on the battlefield to command the Hordes of Squibble into war. I saw it for the first time, and finally knew where it had come from. His eyes were set in grim determination.

“If you can do it, my friend,” he told me, “then I can too. I will pay. Whatever the price. I will do what I must.”

“Like any great hero,” I said. “You have never disappointed me, Master. Never.” I smiled at him. My beloved master. “Do right and fear not,” I said.

He looked at me with amazement. Then he turned aside and wiped the tears from his eyes as his true face came back. Worried and scared, but true. “What a wonderful saying,” he said. “That is exactly how I have tried to live. It gives me strength, Squib.”

“Take it as your own, Master,” I said. “Of all mice, you deserve it the most.” Nemo’s eyes were wide and alert, like someone watching something amazing that they will always hold dear, and knowing they’re only going to see it once. “Neither of you can tell me any of this when I wake from hypnosis,” I said. “You must realize that. It would change everything.” I remembered how frustrated I had been that they wouldn’t tell me. Looking back, if they had, I’d have gone and hid in a tiny hole for a year. Ahh, I wasn’t going to believe them anyway.

They both nodded. All my life others had told me hard, scary things. I never got to do it the other way around, and now that I had, it wasn’t any fun. The look on my master’s face was miserable. I hugged him. He held onto me for a long time. Finally, he managed a smile. I had always wondered when the change had happened from his carefree self to the reluctant commander. It had been then, in those few hours I was put under, and it had been because of what *I'd* told him. He had gone to the war knowing that he—and everyone—would die. What an awful burden. And he bore it like a true knight. All because of my words to him now. Fate has a strange sense of humor.

I told him a few more things. Bigfat told him some as well. We tried to lighten the heavy mood and spoke of fun things. I told him not to worry about Scratchy, and told him a little about our perfect adventure. "Remember to bring the honeycomb," I said. "That was the best part!" He agreed, chuckling.

Before I knew it, it was time to go. I was waking up in my future, and in the past it was almost dawn. Bigfat was already gone.

"I have to go," I said. "I'm sorry. I don't want to. I want to stay with you."

"We all do what we must," my master said. "I know you'll come through in the end. I have faith in you."

"Yeah," I said, smiling sadly. "You always did. Even in the darkest moments. You always believed in me." I looked him right in the eyes. "I couldn't have done any of it without you, Spritely."

Both he and Nemo drew back in complete shock, and then, when his eyes went back to normal, my master smiled. The wonderful, charming smile that was his trademark. His eyes glistened with gold in the dawn light.

"I love you, Squib," he said.

"I love you..." I said, and woke up in mid sentence.

FALL

All Souls Pass

Last Tangent

✠

I had a dream.

It was a bright sunny day in the city. I saw a café, a nice one with umbrellas and good food. A mouse skittered by inside, just visible for a moment, carrying some crumb of food in its mouth.

A man came to the hostess out front. The man was tall, powerful, and blonde. It was Magnificent Man, from my very first dream, in the same white suit even. Mike was led to a table by the blushing, smiling hostess, and he sat down and opened his menu.

Not long after, another man, in the same black suit, came and stood before the waitress. Though he was handsome, even beautiful, the waitress shivered and led him quickly to Mike's table.

"Hello, Mike," Lucifer said.

"Hello, Lou," Michael said.

Lucifer sat down and opened his menu. They both eventually ordered, then sat in silence, enjoying the nice day. Their food came a few minutes later, and they ate in silence. It was tense, though they seemed perfectly relaxed. Mike paid the bill, and their table was cleared.

Finally, he looked up at Lucifer and met him, shining blue to burning yellow eyes.

"Well?" Mike said.

Lucifer looked aside casually and coughed, covering his mouth as he said, "You may have a point."

Mike leaned slightly forward. "Indeed?"

Lucifer leaned forward to meet him. "But that doesn't mean they'll actually reach this lofty goal you've set before them. They have much to accomplish yet. And my agent yet walks the earth."

Mike laughed. "Yes, with the wrath of heaven behind him in the form of a tiny, white mouse."

"You know he won't catch him. He will know that soon as well."

"The point is he *ran*," Mike said. Lucifer didn't like this, and his handsome face frowned a bit. "Also, I set no goal before them."

"What?!" Lucifer sounded genuinely surprised.

"This was not my idea," Mike said.

Lucifer was astonished. "You mean… you… *No!*"

Mike nodded, enjoying the Devil's shock. "Yes. Our Father offered it. They accepted. I thought you went to speak to Him. Wasn't that where you were off to last time I saw you?"

Lucifer was indeed frowning now. Glaring, in fact. People around them at the cafe suddenly found reasons to be somewhere else and left. Mike met Lucifer's stare with ease.

"You tricked me," Lucifer said.

"You never asked," Mike said. "You assumed."

"They won't win," Lucifer said. "I've whittled them down so far… They have no fighting force, and only one ancient, beaten-down mouse as a playing piece. A pawn."

"He *was* a pawn," Mike said. "But he got to the end of the board. Now he is anything he wishes to be. A bishop, a king, a knight, perhaps all the above. And other playing pieces will step onto the board. Many more powerful than you give them credit for. It was your downfall to underestimate them."

Lucifer was definitely unhappy now.

“So the game continues,” he spat. “No matter. I am enjoying it.”

“Not for much longer,” Mike said. His face was dead serious.

Lucifer, instead of answering the direct challenge, smiled a smarmy grin and showed his teeth.

“You’re running short on time, brother,” Lucifer said. “Humanity knows about your mice. I’ve seen to it. You do not have enough playing pieces.”

“God only needs one,” Mike said. “One is all He ever needed.”

“I have hurt your precious mice,” Lucifer said, still grinning. “They suffered terribly at my hands.”

“Yes, our Father let you test them,” Mike said, looking sad. “And now your time is over. You have no more power here. They have passed their tribulation.”

Lucifer held his tongue, checkmated in the battle of words. He had no reply worth making, but he would not give Michael the last word. “Most regrettable,” he smiled.

“Yes,” Mike stood up. “All of it has been.” He left a generous tip on the table and both of them looked out to the horizon. “Our time to walk the earth in human form is done here. It’s time to go home.”

“Good riddance,” Lucifer said.

“One last thing,” Mike said. “About that old, beaten down mouse…”

Lucifer was turning back toward Mike, teeth flashing in pride, when Mike’s fist smashed into his face, breaking his nose, knocking several teeth out, and sending him to the floor twelve feet away, out cold.

“That’s for him,” Mike finished.

The stunned customers gaped in awe as he calmly turned and left the establishment.

But before he was gone from my view and the dream ended, I saw him turn and wink at me.

WINTER

The Prophet Squibble

My Last Entry

✠

You noticed my journals went from summer to winter rather quickly. Much time has passed since I last wrote. I have been busy.

On my spare time (scoff) I tried to send my stories out, my plethora of short stories, to get them published, but no one ever called or wrote back. I tried getting Amazing Mouse, my comic book, published, but it turns out that anything you send to a comic publisher these days ends up belonging to them, no matter what the contract says. So many hours of work, so much effort, and so little came in return from the world that I stopped for while, discouraged. They make it so difficult. It doesn't need to be that hard. I think there are just too many people in the world. Too many who want to be famous, rich, successful. The editors and publishers have a hard time distinguishing the masses from those who love to write, because every morning there's a pile a mile high on their desks of stuff to read. Out of that pile every once in a while, one gets chosen. Only one. But let's not kid ourselves. It's all about the money in business. Just what will sell. Not what's well written. I have a personal beef with that, but hey, I'm a mouse, and money doesn't mean much to me. It will someday, but not now.

I began to think that if these journals you're reading were ever to be published, it would be after my demise. That was fine by me, but on principle it bothered me. I was given every reason in the world to stop trying with my stories and artwork—to leave the apparently corrupt, foul industry and never darken its doorstep with my beloved tales, but it didn't feel right to quit. So I decided not to give them the satisfaction. I'll keep sending submissions and self publishing The Adventures of Amazing Mouse, handing them out on street corners if I have to. Just like there are Kind Humans, there must be kind publishers who will give an unknown mouse a fair chance. Someday I'll succeed, and that day might be sooner than later.

A new, struggling publishing company contacted me (that never happens—it's always the other way around and they never call you back) and said they're interested in my journals. It seems the owner of the company read my master's book and, well, it sounded like she actually believed it. Her letter mentioned that they were willing to publish what the public wanted to read, whether the author was a mouse or a man.

Then I thought, if she believes my master's tale, others aren't far behind. Sooner or later mice are gonna slip up, show some sign of advanced intelligence, and someone who's read the book is gonna see it happen. At that point, the piss is gonna hit the fan. And it is for this day that I prepare.

I haven't gotten back to her yet. But I think I will.

As for the rest of my stories, I'm no quitter. I'm not much of a writer, either, really. I just love to write. I love to tell stories. No one's gonna stop me from doing that, and if people like my stuff enough, they'll take it if I find some way of getting it to them. I love my hobby. I'm not going to call it just because things are hard.

Steven agreed with me. I finally met him. It was in a dream, at a book signing—I went right up to him and told him his books rock. He thanked me, picked me up and put me on the table where he kept signing things and we talked for hours, sharing coffee and scones, laughing and blabbing happily away. He said I did right by sticking to my guns. He said he was proud of me, that I was going to be a published, successful author someday. It made my whole year to hear him say that. He gave me an affectionate stroke, signed a book for me, and we both woke up. The funny thing was, when I went back to look at that book (I finally finished the entire series, just as I always hoped to) it was signed. I can't recall if it had been signed when the Kind Human brought it to me or not.

That Steve. He's like Nemo, I think.

At the Atelier, I take art classes where I am taught personally by Jeff and Ron. They know I'm a mouse. We're all dreaming of course, but it's still really happening—just not on this plane. I've learned a lot. I wonder what they think when they wake up and remember teaching art to an enthusiastic mouse. Every step of the way through these journals I've been illustrating my stories. You've seen my art go from childlike crayon scribbles to what it is now. Looking back all that way, I am amazed at how far my skill has come. And how far it has yet to go.

I've gotten decent at painting. I did a self-portrait for you. See how it makes you feel. I thought it was very accurate, but more important by far, I enjoyed doing it. I heard a really awesome quote the other day. It went like this: "Every child is an artist. The problem is how to remain an artist once he grows up." I had to ask Nemo who said it. Pablo Picasso. Every word is more true than most people ever know.

I have succeeded in combining magic and science. That's all I'm going to tell you of my grand scheme. Well, okay… I'll tell you just a teeny bit more. I've gotten good at telling the future. Nemo has taught me all kinds of tricks. Hypnosis, prescience, heck—Branch even taught me how to control the weather. Having spent half his life in China, he's coming back soon. Percival will too, once his quest fails.

I received a package from Percival on an overcast day in January. Within it was the Holy Avenger, Excalibur. I reunited it with its lonely sheath back at the house, weeping the entire way. The burden had become too heavy at last, even for him. When I looked for him on the astral plane I found him, still chasing the black shadow, driven by righteous rage, ever over the next dim horizon. The enemy doesn't have a clue that Percival no longer carries the sword. He just runs. It is Percival's wrath he flees now, not the holy light.

I have foreseen Percival's return, when he realizes his holy quest is not to be fulfilled so far from his homeland. I feel so deeply for him. Half his life spent chasing a phantom, and nothing to show for it but age and weariness. Before him the Black Mouse will return, having circled the globe. But by then I will be ready for him. And I'll have help.

But do not despair, reader. Percival's life is far from over, and he may yet have his revenge. It's part of my plan. How could I leave him out after what he's been through?

Along with the sword was a simple note in elegant script. It said,

Squibble,
You are the last of us. It is up to you now. Prevail.
Percival

No pressure or anything.

I've been spending a lot of time in the city. At labs. Yeah, labs. Funny, huh? Once I was deathly afraid of them. Now I practically live there. (I picked one I am most fond of.) At night, when no one suspects, I work, and work hard. It's fun. The area of my work is an ever-open, beautiful field in the sun, waiting for me to come play in it.

I know most of my journals are not a happy story (not many real ones are). I know it's hard to read. If you've made it this far, you've got guts. And I thank you for caring enough about me to share my pain, and my victory.

I suppose after all this you're hoping for an explanation that will make all the horror and suffering you've read about seem worth the trouble. Some reason for it all.

Believe me, I'd love to give you one, so I'm going to try. I gave you Michael's reason, Nemo's reason, My master's reason… even Lucifer's reason. But not my own.

I know why I made my choices. It was the right thing to do (although that 'fear not' part was just about impossible). I don't know why I was born the way I was, wanting to be a great hero, yearning to make a difference, wishing to be like my beloved master. That's just who I am. There is a core inside all of us, the person we were before we were born, that will never change, no matter how many lives we live, no matter how much damage we take. That's as much reassurance as I have for you, I'm afraid, because why everything had to happen exactly as it did, I have no clue. Nemo could probably tell you, but good luck getting it outta his furry hide.

I feel bad telling you this sad, profound, often beautiful story of my life without some sort of ending that makes you go "Oh! Oh, it's all okay then. I get it!" The problem is, even I don't get it yet.

However, since I am who I am, and I'd want a good reason if I were you, I'm going to try. I'll do my best and fear not. So here we go.

> <u>The Story of the Caterpillar</u>
>
> The other day I happened upon a beautiful, exotic caterpillar, trying to cross the black street on a scalding summer day. He was unique—I'd never seen a caterpillar like him—absolutely gorgeous. However, he'd picked one hell of a place to cross. The street was burning hot. It was the middle of the day, and there was heavy traffic. He was sure to die a horrible death if he wasn't squished first.
>
> I was on the side of the street he wanted to get to, and my immediate instinct was to save him. I started out into the road while there was no traffic. With my mousey speed, I could grab him, rush back to my side of safety, and everybody would be happy.
>
> Or would they?
>
> I looked with my prescience into the future before I set my bare feet on the burning asphalt. I saw the two most likely outcomes. The first was obvious: I don't help him, and he will most likely die. But the second choice shocked me. I help him, carry him to the far side of the street he seeks so badly to reach, and the guy cusses me out!
>
> It appears I ruined his holy quest and meddled where I wasn't welcome. His entire life had been spent getting to this street, to cross at this point, at this time. And then I run in, take over, and win the game for him. He was pissed.
>
> I could understand that. If someone had blown in on me at my most sacred moments, then I would have learned and gained very little. It wouldn't have been me anymore. I would never know that I had been the winner, and the victory wouldn't be mine. Although in my hardest times I would not have refused help by a long shot, had I gotten it I would never have developed into the mouse I am today. I might still be a child inside.

However, if I didn't help the guy, and risk his wrath, he most likely dies. My mind reeled with the dilemma. I had only moments to decide. The street was too hot. The traffic was coming back.

I thought about what my master would do. What he did do. He let me go to the city when I wanted to. He let me risk my life, because it was mine, and not his. Nemo had done the same thing. The Kind Human had let go in a similar way as well, to all of us at one point or another. Now I had a bare taste of how difficult that had been.

So I watched, sure I would see the brilliant colors of his spikey hide smeared all over the animal graveyard called a road. It was his choice, and I reluctantly respected it.

His feet began to burn and he got fast real quick, but not fast enough. He was tossed and tumbled by passing cars, tires missing him by inches, sometimes millimeters. He was beat up badly. He took what must have been the beating and burning of his caterpillar life. It took only two minutes for him to reach me, but by the time he did, he had lost most of his legs, was bleeding from many wounds, and had become a wreck. His colors dulled, his spikes gone, and his skin ruined. He was barely alive. And yet he had made it. And that, because it was so unlikely, I had not foreseen.

I lay my hands on him and gave him enough chi that he would live, and have some energy to crawl to safety. This he accepted with gratitude, and made his limping way to the bushes at the other end of the sidewalk. I never asked him why. We did not speak. I just watched him go and climb up into the branches.

I walked away, thinking about what I had seen for many weeks. Even in the middle of my work it would intrude. Why had it been his fate to suffer so?

On a warm day in February I got my answer. I walked past those same bushes on my way to my work when suddenly there was a great, sweeping wind from behind me, and massive shaking of the trees and plants. When I turned I saw the most stunning butterfly I had ever beheld. Made of luminescent golds, night blues, silky black and spots of ruby, I knew by its colors this had been the caterpillar. It was my friend who crossed the street to find his haven, his safe place to cocoon. He was perfect, not a single scar marking his lovely body, free of earlier damage that didn't matter anymore. He hovered to show me his glory, and I marveled.

Then behind him came his family. Hundred and thousands of the same astounding butterflies, rising like a great cloud, until the sky was full of them, halting humans and their traffic with the wonder of them. They danced in the air, frolicking upon anything they pleased, immortal and omnipotent in their moment of birth.

They washed over me for long minutes, stopping the world with their beauty. Even the wind held its breath. Then, at last, when they had all risen past the skyscrapers and tiny world of men, one returned to circle above my head by only half an inch, saying goodbye, and thank you.

Then they were gone.

Do you see?

I thought my childhood lost forever. Replaced by this mature, responsible, boring fellow with no time for fun and no taste for excitement. It was my worst fear as a child, losing my spirit. I now realize that, though we change and it cannot be avoided, nothing can truly destroy our spirits. Our spirits are immortal. Invulnerable. Bigfat says that when we die, all our damage sloughs off us like mud in rain. We remember it, but it doesn't hurt anymore. That sounds nice. After watching every fear I ever had come true, that last thought is quite comforting.

I may have aged, but no one ever made me grow up. I never did. I'm Peter Pan, and I may have lost my happy thought for a while, but I've found it now, and I'm never losing it again. Because I refuse to believe in some dark, grown-up reality where everything sucks.

So, as I take it, life is an experience. A huge set of self-chosen, intense experiences, meant to teach us, but also meant to entertain us. That's right. Entertain us. Our spirits cannot suffer fear or loss. We don't ever really lose anybody—our mothers, fathers, sisters, brothers and friends never die. They never fade. They just go home and wait for us to come join them, and then we all have a good laugh over the incredible play we all starred in. After all, we wrote the script.

The experience is really the whole point. In the end, it amounts to that. Now that is rather separate from leaving a lasting impression. What we leave here for others matters. It determines how the play continues.

Well, by now, I've left quite a bit. The plan is working perfectly.

I came back to the safe house yesterday afternoon from my lab and my journeys. I am old now. I feel the arthritis in my bones on cold mornings. The Kind Human is gentle with me, and lets me sit on his lap to watch TV while he shares his dinner with me. I have no company that can relate to me any longer. Scratchy is usually gone on adventure and his son Tommy goes with him; though I took the kid as a squire long ago, he most often prefers the company of his dad, and who can blame him? That midget is a great hero.

Scratchy left a letter here at the safe house asking me to be the one to knight his son. I left my reply: Any day you wish, my noble friend, it shall be done.

After thinking it over for a year, I think I finally know why Scratchy was put into my life, and why my reaction to him was so poor. He was there as a divine guide to show me my way—to be an example of how to behave and how to act. That mouse was impeccable. Perfect. Even with all his handicaps and crippling disabilities, his integrity never failed once. He was my muse. I just didn't know it.

I was jealous, of course, because he reminded me that I was constantly goofing off and procrastinating. But Nemo was right all along—Scratchy and I were the same. He was crippled physically, and I emotionally. It was our only difference.

I wish I saw him more often. When I do, it's always a grand time. A great adventure.

I rarely see Nemo any more, though I saw him yesterday. The climb up to his cage isn't as easy as it used to be, and he is quite sick. But we speak often in dreams, where we are both immune to the ravages of time, and sometimes other spirits we know join us.

My daughter and Stompy are best friends. They are always off on adventures, living the good life. I've warned them of what's going to happen. I've told the knights they need to prepare for the worst. I even told them to stop wearing armor—to act like normal mice, but they are too many now and too proud. There are over a hundred knights these days. No one but a few close to me, my daughter, Stompy, and a few others, listened. I knew they wouldn't, but I had to try. You know. For the record.

My sight is almost gone. I rely mostly on smell these days. I go about my business, occasionally stopping to tell stories or show young mice fancy magic tricks.

It took me quite a while to do what I needed to, didn't it? It took me a lifetime. And now that lifetime is almost over.

So that brings us back to the beginning then.

I am standing at the grave of my mother. She died of cancer. I was never able to come to this place, but at last I can. I came to say goodbye.

My master's grave sits beside hers, though no body lies in it. The tombstone reads:

> THANK YOU, MASTER SPRITELY, FOR ALL YOU HAVE
> GIVEN TO RODENTKIND. YOU WERE THE FIRST OF
> THE MOUSE KNIGHTS, AND THE FINEST AMONG US.

I made the stone and carved the words. I think it says it all. Nobody told me what to say. I did it all on my own.

So goodbye, Momma. Goodbye, Spritely. I shall see you both soon enough, though you, Master, sooner than her. I had a dream last night, you see. I dreamt I was in a field, standing before a village of field mice. In the center of them was a tiny white mouse, an orphan adopted by the tribe.

It was you, Master. You kept your promise. You're being born again as I write these words.

And I'm coming to see you.

One last time.

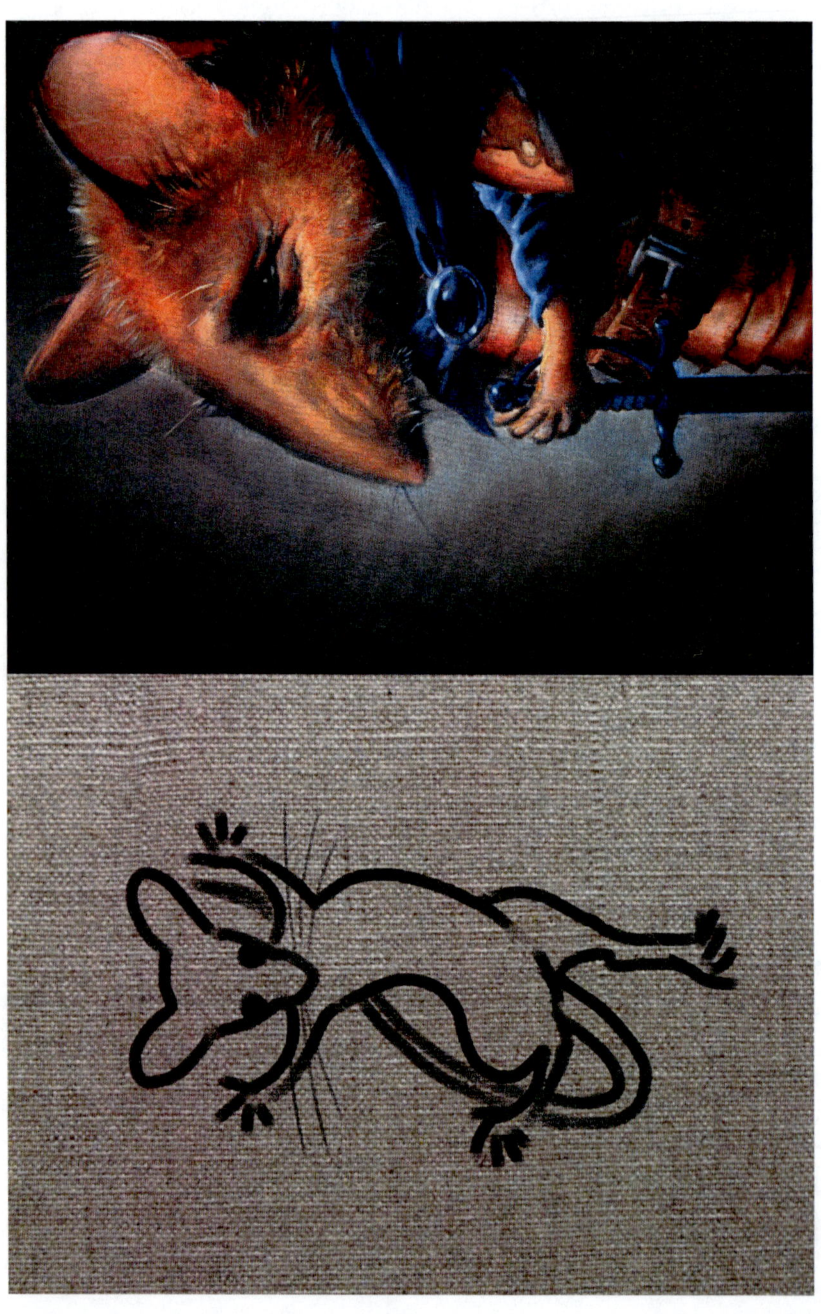

The End